JOHANNA
NICHOLLS

IRONBARK

SIMON & SCHUSTER
AUSTRALIA
A CBS COMPANY

IRONBARK
First published in Australia in 2009 by
Simon & Schuster (Australia) Pty Limited
Suite 2, Lower Ground Floor
14-16 Suakin Street
Pymble NSW 2073

A CBS Company
Sydney New York London Toronto

Visit our website at www.simonandschuster.com.au

National Library of Australia Cataloguing-in-Publication entry
Author: Nicholls, Johanna.
Title: Ironbark / Johanna Nicholls.
ISBN: 9780731814121 (pbk.)
Subjects: Penal colonies – Australia – Fiction.
Dewey Number: A823.4

Cover photographs by Eve Conroy and Photolibrary.com
Cover design by Ellie Exarchos
Internal design by Xou Creative

Printed in Australia by Griffin Press

The paper used to produce this book is a natural, recyclable product made from wood grown in sustainable plantation forests. The manufacturing processes conform to the environmental regulations in the country of origin.

10 9 8 7 6 5 4 3 2 1

To Brian, Nicholas, Niki, Eadie and Donna

In memory of my parents, Fred and Dorothy Parsons,
and my friend Anne Goldie Cousland

Australian history is almost always picturesque.
Australian history does not read like history – it is full
of surprises and adventure, incongruities and incredibilities
– but they are all true, they all happened.

Mark Twain

Part I
The Search

January 1837 – May 1838

Attempt the end and never stand to doubt
Nothing's so hard but search will find it out.

Robert Herrick

CHAPTER 1

Jakob Andersen's eyes narrowed against the glare of the sun as he rode along the deserted road on the final leg of the journey home. The landscape around him was virtually all sky, a blue so dominant it drained what little colour the drought had left in the parched grassland.

Home. *Jenny.* Hungry for the sight of her, Jake's heart beat faster as haunting images played before his eyes … Jenny dancing towards him … the way she stood like a child on the footstool to tie his neckerchief … the glow of firelight rippling over her back as she bathed in the tub by the fire … her teasing smile when she blew out their bedside candle … her exquisite body like a naked goddess in the darkness …

The memory of her was so alive Jake could smell her French perfume, a luxury that to Jenny was more important than daily bread.

He counted off the months, weeks and days since his departure on the cattle drove south. Jenny never expected letters from him, aware that he shied off writing, embarrassed by his limited schooling. But Jenny knew he belonged to her body and soul. For Jake the longer the drove the more vivid his memories were. What a comfort it would be to carry a miniature portrait in his pocket. He promised himself that one day 'when his boat came in' he'd pay an artist to paint her.

Jake felt a rush of pleasure as he relived the hour of his departure. Dawn. He had lingered at their bedroom door, his throat tight at the sight of Jenny, her arms above her head, the curve of her breasts pressing against the lacy film of her nightgown. Her golden hair was strewn across the pillow – like a mermaid floating under water.

Through the veil of her hair Jenny had playfully uttered the words of their ritual farewell. 'Will you love me forever and ever, Jakey?'

His answer was always serious. Now as he rode he repeated it under his breath. 'I'll love you even longer, Jenny.'

Jake knew if he had stopped long enough to kiss her he'd never have left. There was no choice. Ogden's droving job was an opportunity he couldn't afford to knock back. Jake had a flash of that moment before he left home.

At the foot of the stairs he had spun around at the sound of a soft whisper.

Little Pearl was standing barefoot in her nightgown at the top of the stairs, her short bandy legs planted wide. Fair hair framed a smile of pure sunshine as she stretched out her arms and took a step forward. Jake had bolted up the stairs just in time to prevent her falling.

'You'll have to wait until you're a big girl before you take the stairs, Princess.'

He had kissed the crown of her head as her puppy Flash licked her face. Pearl had reached up in the way she often did, gently tucking a lock of Jake's long hair behind his ears. He had promised to bring her home a new dolly then he'd led her back to her attic bedroom …

Jake glanced at his saddlebag, imagining the cries of delight that would greet his swag of presents for his girls. He even had one for Jenny's mother.

He frowned at the thought of Mrs Troy. *It'd take more than a box of sugar plums to sweeten* her. *The old battleaxe never lets me forget Jenny married beneath her – because of my 'double convict taint' from Mam and Pa. But she's done me a favour guarding my girls so butter won't melt in my mouth.*

As Jake kept to the Sydney Road, he wondered how Jenny's world would have blossomed during his absence. Her beloved cottage garden must now be alive with the beds of English flowers he'd planted to remind her of her childhood in Devon. He imagined how Pearl would be playing with Flash, her eye on the front gate waiting to catch sight of him.

Throughout the drove Jake had battened down his anxiety, assuring himself he had done everything to ensure his girls' safety. He had taught Jenny how to use the tiny muff pistol in an emergency. He could count on Wally, his Aboriginal mate since childhood, to work the farm. His mother-in-law would be Jenny's shadow.

Jake's reward for the long, lonely months was the promissory note he had stashed inside the sole of his boot for safety. He patted his vest pocket to check that the handful of coins and old watch chain were ready to hand over to any bushranger who bailed him up.

He ruffled the shaggy mane of the stallion he had named after his childhood hero Lord Nelson.

'Money, Horatio. Makes the world go round, eh? We did it hard last year, but things are going to look up in 1837! This year we'll make our fortune, just watch!'

Spoken out loud the words sounded hollow. Although he was almost twenty-three Jake had not yet found the work he was best cut out to do. What excited him most was collecting the winner's purse after a bare-knuckle fight, but between bouts he was forced to sustain his few-acres farm with whatever work was available.

The bloody bank of New South Wales holds the mortgage on everything I own – except my horse. But what the hell. With Jenny beside me I'm ready to take on the world.

He scratched at the rough ginger beard he had grown during the months of droving. He'd be sure to shave it off before he saw Jenny. On previous returns when he had been hungry to kiss her, she had shied away. Told him to clean himself up before he dared sit at her table. Jake gave a wry grin at the memory. *Her* table? *Jesus, I'm always hoping to head her off to bed!*

Now, not for the first time, he cringed over his dilemma. He could tell Horatio the words no man would ever hear.

'As a bachelor I could make the girls at the Red Brumby catch fire. Trouble is good women are different ... I can go the distance with any man in a fight but with her I fizzle out like a damp squib on Guy Fawkes night.'

He told himself Jenny knew he loved every god-damned inch of her, but the thought was rough comfort. His performance the night before he'd left still rankled. He'd wanted to leave her with a special memory that would sustain them both through the months apart; to give her that look of dreamy contentment he had given other women. He had never yet seen that look on Jenny's face.

Why was his love for Jenny such a problem when he had so much of it to give?

Jake anchored his wide-awake hat, left the Sydney Road behind him and galloped Horatio in the direction of home. The wind whipped his red-gold hair. Long hair was the one thing he refused to change to please Jenny. It was the badge of identity flaunted by native-born lads in contrast with the shaven heads of the convict population and the short military cut favoured by the Sterling who boasted they were Englishmen. No man would ever take Jake Andersen for anything but a Currency Lad.

As he rode through the bush Jake's eyes read the landscape like a map.

'Those bloody Whitehall blokes think they run the world from the other side of the globe, Horatio, but they can fly all the Union Jacks they like and claim New South Wales is British land. Not to me it ain't. She's *my* country.'

At Feagan's General Store in the seedy village of Bolthole Valley, Jake stopped to replenish his tobacco pouch. As usual the young storekeeper Matthew Feagan was busy spouting the latest news on the local grapevine. He seldom drew breath as he weighed dry goods on the scales and gave customers change.

'That George Hobson's stirred up a hornet's nest with his plans for Ironbark Farm. It's all the doing of his partner. That Hebrew lawyer is Bloom by name and blooming weird if you ask me. Full of foreign ideas

– like his way to kill sheep quick smart so they don't feel no pain! A schoolhouse for Ironbark farmers' young 'uns. And would you believe it? Bloom wants to build new cabins to give Hobson's assigned felons their privacy!'

Feagan dropped his voice in confidence to Jake. 'You know what them Germans are like. Think they can run the world better than us Brits.'

'Hey! I'm Currency, mate,' Jake said automatically.

Feagan added tolerantly, 'Well, that's the next best thing.' He handed the tobacco supplies to Jake and gave him an ingratiating smile. 'Should I be putting my money on you again?'

Jake halted in the doorway. 'What do you mean?'

'Don't tell me you haven't heard? The biggest purse ever offered in the colony!'

'A prize fight? *Where?*'

Outside the store Jake mentally tossed a coin. He decided to take a quick detour to Tagalong to call in on his mate Mac Mackie. He couldn't pass up the chance to make real money. Jake liked the sound of the odds. Winner take all.

'You deserve a drink, Horatio. And I wouldn't say no to an Albion Ale.'

Jake took the turn-off road through Ironbark to slice a few miles from the cross-country route. The small seasoned chapel on the hill over-looked a cluster of few-acres farms where the paddocks showed signs of the drought and the sheep looked in need of a good feed. These settlers' huts had been standing long enough for their ironbark slabs to weather to a parched grey, but Jake knew the timber would be tough enough to outlive the owners.

In the distance the original property, George Hobson's Ironbark Farm, stretched out below the horizon. The homestead at its heart was shouldered by whitewashed farm buildings and convict cabins. To Jake the contrast between Ironbark Farm and the settlers' farms was not surprising. Green and prosperous-looking, Hobson's large estate was fed by a network of creeks. No evidence was in sight of Feagan's predicted 'weird changes'.

Riding through the ironbark forest south of the village, Jake finally broke clear of it when Tagalong was in sight. He knew the rickety bush hamlet had been spawned almost overnight by a ragbag collection of Irish-Catholic ticket-of-leave men and emancipists. It was so new it wasn't yet on any map but being sprawled around the junction of four tracks it was well positioned to draw a good crowd from all points of the compass. For mass or a prize fight.

Jake was chuffed by the sight of a poster fixed to a tree. It showed a drawing of a beefy pugilist with a Union Jack tattooed on his chest. Slowly Jake managed to read it. An English bare-knuckle champion, Bulldog Kane, was touring the colony, offering a rich purse to the first man who could beat him. None had yet knocked him to the ground. The date for this Tagalong challenge match was set for the first Sunday in the coming month.

Jake rode towards Tagalong's half-built church – its stone walls open to the sky in a bare paddock, like a Catholic oasis in the surrounding Protestant landscape.

He recognised the shaggy-bearded head peering through a space reserved for a future stained-glass window. Mac Mackie gave him a broad grin and slipped out of the church while the collection plate was doing the rounds.

A Currency Lad, Mac also wore his hair long, but his beard was a permanent fixture. He beckoned Jake to follow him to The Australia Arms public house.

'I thought it was closed on Sundays,' said Jake.

'Not to me it ain't, mate.'

Mac emerged with an armful of bottles and led Jake to his one-room timber hut. The floor was made of rammed earth, the interior walls papered with newspapers. In one corner was an unmade bunk bed. Unwashed tin plates littered the table. Mac's hospitality was legendary. He swept the plates aside and they clattered across the floor. He then placed the bottles in pride of place beside two tin pannikins and drew a bench up to the table with a courteous wave of his hand.

Jake downed the first ale for his thirst, the second for sheer pleasure.

'Ah! Can't beat Albion Ale. Cold as a creek in the Snowy.'

'Our publican is the sole Proddie in the village but he's dead popular,' said Mac.

Jake wasn't surprised. 'No bloody wonder. I've discovered his secret. He keeps his grog cold by stashing it down a well he dug in his cellar.'

'Trust you to ferret that out.' Mac cast Jake a wise look. 'Come on, out with it. What's your problem?'

Jake shrugged. 'Nothing money can't fix. What's the strength of this Bulldog Kane's challenge? Last man standing – winner take all. What am I up against?'

Mac's raised eyebrows registered a close call. 'Bulldog Kane's a professional from the East End of London. Y'know what that means. A gutter fighter. Rough as guts and dead dirty.'

There was a knock against the open door. Father Declan's visit seemed to come as no surprise. Mac put a pannikin of whisky in the priest's hands and introduced him to Jake.

'I take it you're not of the True Faith, Jakob lad?' Father Declan seemed sure of the answer to his question before he asked it.

'Mam thinks she is. She's Irish-Catholic. Pa's a Norwegian Lutheran. Me, I'm second cousin to an atheist. I only believe in three things. My wife's good name, Albion Ale and my horse's unfailing sense of direction. No disrespect intended, Father.'

'None taken. And it's Dennis.' He sank the whisky. 'I'm hearing from Mac that you're a fine fighter.'

Jake tried to sound modest. 'On a good day I can hold my own.'

Father Declan leaned forward. 'Then you'll be taking on the Bulldog when he comes to our neck of the woods?'

Jake hesitated, aware that some religions got funny about work and sport performed on the Sabbath. 'Yeah, Father. Is that a problem?'

'Problem? I'm the referee! And we're raising money for a roof on my church. There's a tithe on all bets. And every man better dig deep when the hat is passed around. Will you be fighting, lad?'

'Count me in,' said Jake.

Mac refilled Father Declan's pannikin.

'A fine drop it is, Mac. Traded on Sunday? See you mention that in confession. Meantime let's drink to next month's challenge match. I'll be putting my money on you, Jakob!'

When Jake drew up at the front gate of his farm it was at the eerie moment that heralds the pink trace of the piccaninny dawn; the bush's rehearsal for sunrise. Currawongs and kookaburras had yet to greet the day. The garden he had left months earlier now sprouted some English autumn flowers but Jake noticed it needed weeding. And the bark slab of Wally's gunyah lay on the ground as if flattened by a recent storm.

Jake unsaddled Horatio, led him to the water trough then let himself in the front door. He placed his swag of presents on the kitchen table, ready to give to his girls at breakfast.

He lathered his face with soap and went to work on his beard with the cut-throat razor, checking his reflection in the mirror.

Feeling the urge to kiss Jenny awake, he crept upstairs and past the nursery where Mrs Troy would be sleeping with Pearl.

The marital bedroom was as neat as a pin. The curtains were drawn but a chink of sunlight fell across the lace bedspread. An envelope lay on his pillow. The words of the letter scattered through his brain.

Dear Jakey,

I have gone away to begin a new life. I know how hard you

tried to make me happy, but I can't pretend anymore to love you as you deserve. This is the best solution for both of us. Don't worry about Pearl. I am travelling with someone who'll protect us always.

Your Jenny

P.S. I sent Wally back to his people – and made him take Flash with him.

The letter was dated only two days earlier.

Jake rocked on his feet. The legs that were capable of keeping him dancing around the boxing ring were now unable to carry him a step further. He sank down on the edge of the bed, his head in his hands. His brain exploded with questions. *Do I know the bastard? Where's he taken them? They're only two days ahead of me but which bloody direction?*

He ran to the nursery in the hope he would find his little princess asleep. Pearl's cot was neatly made up as though it had never been slept in. Mrs Troy's palliasse was stripped of its covers.

He rummaged through every closet for some clue that would prove Jenny had been forced to write the letter under duress, abducted by some bushranger. Only a single valise was missing. Three empty coat-hangers hung in mute testimony that Jenny had taken nothing but her own Sunday best dress and a few of Pearl's garments.

His daughter's dolls were neatly lined up on her toy box. Their silent painted faces seemed to wear cruel little smiles that mocked his anguish.

And then he saw it. Jenny's discarded wedding ring. The small duplicate of his own wedding band had their names and wedding date engraved inside. Stunned, he held her ring in the palm of his hand and read the inscription. *5 May 1833 Jakob and Jenny – Eternal Love.*

Eternal? She couldn't even last four years!

Blinded by rage Jake threw her ring across the room. He punched the wall, causing the mirror to shatter into jagged reflections of his face. He froze at the foot of the staircase, realising the significance of Jenny's words after his last failure in bed. *'Don't put me on a pedestal.'*

Jesus wept! Did she know even then that she planned to leave me? Was that mongrel already in her life? Her ritual farewell now cut at his heart. *'Will you love me forever and ever, Jakey?'*

Jake felt as if the walls were caving in. Yesterday he had everything that mattered. Today – nothing. Jenny had done what no man could ever do. Destroyed his world. He vowed that he would never again allow any woman to hold power over him as Jenny had done.

He slammed the front door and turned his back on family life forever. The bloody bank of New South Wales was welcome to reclaim his farm and all he owned. Out in the sunlight the whole world seemed to have turned grey. Drained of all colour. Unreal. Time and space had fragmented.

He saddled Horatio and galloped off towards Parramatta to file a police report. What the hell could he say? *Missing. One wife and child, now in keeping. Last seen travelling with unknown gent.*

As he tethered Horatio to the railing in front of the police office, Jake was suddenly aware he was holding the miniature muff pistol. He had taught Jenny how to protect herself in his absence. But some bastard had got under his guard. Jake pressed the spring that released the hidden blade and turned the weapon into a dagger.

'God help you, you mongrel, I'll hunt you down and kill you!'

CHAPTER 2

Keziah Stanley looked furtively through the doorway of her *vardo*. The other travelling houses on wheels were ringed around the Romani camp on the edge of the village common. Dawn filtered through the mist. Horses grazed quietly beside the stream. Traces of smoke rose from the embers of small campfires that had burned last night at the heart of each family group.

Behind Keziah lay the distant mountains of her birthplace in the Clwydian Range of North Wales. Before her lay the Cheshire route that led to Liverpool. Today was a milestone – her seventeenth birthday – the day she planned to escape her mother-in-law Patronella's dominance.

Last night Keziah had sobbed herself to sleep with her husband's beloved face in her mind and her heart. Gem was in chains somewhere at the bottom of the world, but the memory of his lovemaking was as vivid as if he had lain with her all night.

Keziah stiffened at the sound of Gem's parents in the *vardo* next to hers. In contrast to Patronella, her father-in-law's grey hair had brought him tolerance. Keziah heard Ivano sleepily rebuke his wife.

'Today is her birthday. Don't be so hard on the girl, Patronella. It's natural she cries for our son. As my mother used to say, "Just as the mare beats the road, so the young wife wants the penis".'

'Yes, but with Gem in prison she's ripe for any man to provide it!'

Keziah consoled herself with the knowledge that Patronella's insult would be the last she would ever have to suffer. Today she would place her trust in *baxt* and leave the loved *vardo* that Gem had built for her before he was dragged before the magistrate. The charge of horse theft had earned him the sentence almost inevitable for a 'Gypsy vagabond'

– transportation to New South Wales. Keziah knew he could easily have been given fourteen years or life, but his 'lenient' seven-year sentence was no consolation.

She clung to the memory of Gem's bravado as he was led from the assizes. *'Keziah! No beak on earth has the power to keep me from you!'*

She vowed she would make his words reality. She tied her few possessions in a bundle: her Tarot cards, a change of clothing, a warm shawl and headscarves to proclaim her status as a married Romani woman. She wore two layers of skirts over her red petticoats to avoid carrying them, and over her blouse she added the waistcoat fringed with foreign gold coins that testified to her ancestors' flight across Europe.

She was halfway across the open space to the road to Liverpool when Patronella's voice shattered the early morning tranquillity. Keziah bolted across the green with Patronella in pursuit. The older woman's grey plaits snaked in the air as she seized Keziah's hair with a cry of victory.

Keziah fought down her fear, holding fast to the image of Gem's face.

'I'm leaving you, Patronella. I belong to Gem – and I'm going to find him.'

Patronella released a tirade of abuse that allowed Keziah no chance to defend herself. Drawn to the sound of conflict, men, women and children emerged from under the wheels of their *vardos* and the hedgerows where they had dossed down. The older women urged Patronella to bring Keziah into line, but the men were more guarded, out of respect for Gem.

Aware of Ivano's scrutiny Keziah lowered her eyes in deference. She flushed with gratitude when he quietly admonished his wife.

'Enough! Let the girl go with your blessing.'

'Blessing! Bah! My Gem's well rid of her. A barren wife is no good to any man.'

Keziah faltered, overwhelmed by a shaft of pain at her failure to be a real wife, but she remained silent.

'See what a viper she is? She'll force me into poverty!' Patronella twisted the gold coins that edged her own waistcoat, unaware of the irony of her gesture.

For years Keziah had shown Patronella respect, but now she lost her temper.

'Be honest! You're just afraid to lose the money my Tarot readings bring to the family purse.' She pushed a silver coin into the woman's hand. 'Here! This will buy your meat till a child learns the Tarot to keep you in the same luxury I have.'

'Bah! Your fortune-telling is worthless,' Patronella spat out. 'Only the gullible *gaujo* are stupid enough to fall for your lies.'

'I *never* lie!' cried Keziah.

'You lying *posh rat*! Your *gaujo* blood pollutes you! You'll dishonour Gem just like Stella the Whore dishonoured your father.'

Keziah's cheeks flushed as if Patronella had struck her. The men stiffened at the word 'dishonour', but softer faces in the crowd flinched in sympathy at this brutal reminder Keziah was a half-blood Romani.

She addressed the crowd. 'I refuse to trade insults with Gem's mother, but you all know how clearly I see the future. I *will* cross the seas to the ends of the earth. I *will* find Gem and lie in his arms!' She turned to Patronella. 'While you will never see your son's face again!'

The crowd sucked in its collective breath when Patronella pointed her finger at Keziah.

'Abandon your people and I will riddle your body with my curses. You will bury the child of your heart. Gem will spit on you. Even before the death of summer, when the moon's eclipse falls in your sign, you will earn money on your back!'

The crowd drew back in horror. Keziah stumbled away, barely registering the stones that Patronella threw at her. The physical pain was nothing compared to the inner torment that flooded her as the Romani words of Patronella's ultimate curse rang in her ears. *'The Devil be in your bowels!'*

Keziah walked down a lonely country road deeply rutted by generations of farmers' carts. Her eyes were bathed by the vivid green beauty around her, the wildflowers and herbs growing at random, flights of birds swooping against soft banks of clouds. As always, she trusted the power of the natural world to heal the wounds caused by human cruelty.

She prided herself that she would cross the ocean to Gem with money she earned honestly by her hands and her wits. She would not let the fear of Patronella's curses overwhelm her.

From the age of six Keziah had been aware she possessed the Gift. Through her eyes day and night were not measured by the mechanical progression of clocks; time flowed like a river where past, present and future were tributaries linked by a continuous current. She travelled along this current at will, but at other times she was transported in dreams and visions. Now, to comfort herself, she summoned up a vivid fragment of the past – Gem's beloved face on that autumn day in 1831 when he turned fourteen.

Gem's gold earring glinted in the sunlight as he swung her up behind him to ride bareback on his piebald horse. His voice caressed her.

'What do you say, little Keziah? I'm your Rom if you want me.'

'Oh yes, Gem, please!' she whispered.

Sure of her then, he twisted her hair around his fist and pulled her face within an inch of his lips. 'I have loved your shadow since the first day I saw you.'

'But I was only five!'

He told her he had waited long enough, then teased her by avoiding her parted lips.

'Now you're eleven – almost a woman. It is time we were promised to each other.'

That same night as Keziah lay with her grandmother in their vardo, *they overheard Patronella condemn Keziah's* gaujo *mother.*

'You women talk of history!' Gem shouted. 'But I am a man! I do not take history to my bed! You will offer Keziah's family a fine bride price for the sake of her pride.'

Patronella wailed that she would rather die first.

Gem was unmoved. 'Then you die without grandchildren! I swear on Grandfather's grave if Keziah Stanley will not have me as her Rom, I'll wash my own shirt for the rest of my life!'

Keziah gasped at Gem's threat of lifelong independence and celibacy.

Despite Patronella's moans it was clear Gem had won. Keziah leapt into her Puri Dai's *arms and covered her wrinkled face with a flood of little kisses.*

'So you want him as much as that, do you?' Her grandmother chuckled. 'Listen, I will strike a hard bargain. Your father has no head for such things. He'd prefer to drink their wine and play his violin.'

Keziah was so nervous her grandmother was quick to reassure her. 'I'm old, not stupid. I'll raise the price but not high enough to send them packing. I'll get Gem for your Rom, see if I don't!'

Her grandmother's magic worked and soon everyone knew Keziah was promised to Gem. He teased her with his lover's games until she would have given him anything he asked, but he chose to wait for their wedding night – when they discovered that their bodies were created for each other.

Keziah's pride in her Rom and their life together would have been perfect except for the shadow cast after every cycle of the moon passed without the promise of a longed-for child.

Patronella pressured Gem to divorce Keziah and take a fertile wife, but he angrily dismissed the idea.

Then, after three years, Keziah had been blessed with fertility. But on the night Gem was transported, her world was destroyed – twice over.

Keziah blocked the painful memory of her miscarriage. She did not doubt her grandmother's magic would reunite her with her hero. They said New South Wales was a vast island prison. Escape was not possible.

Keziah's heart leapt at the sight of her grandmother's shabby travelling house. For years her *Puri Dai* had stubbornly refused to allow her kinsmen to repair it. Keziah knew tradition demanded this *vardo* would be burned along with all personal belongings after her grandmother's funeral to allow her soul to relinquish the burden of material possessions. Unlike most of their people her grandmother did not fear death – and death would find her soon, even if Keziah refused to believe her *Puri Dai* would ever die.

With unblinking eyes, the old woman watched Keziah approach. Her gnarled hands folded in her lap, no flicker of movement except for the fringe of her floral shawl teased by the breeze. Around her wrinkled neck hung an engraved silver amulet. Webbed lines traced her face, like a map recording every Romani route she had travelled in her eighty years.

Keziah met her grandmother's gaze. She knelt at her *Puri Dai's* feet, took the old hands between her own and tenderly kissed each palm. The tribute accepted, the old woman clasped Keziah's upturned face, their love so deep it was beyond words.

Hand in hand they entered the *vardo*. The *Puri Dai* poured tea from a brass kettle on a tiny black stove. She had set out fine blue-patterned china on a snowy lace cloth. Each piece of furniture was perfectly scaled to the dimensions of this small travelling world. Keziah saw her childhood bed had been unfolded from its alcove, the quilt turned down.

'You knew I was coming, didn't you?'

The *Puri Dai* nodded. 'A swallow told me. That woman with the viper's tongue can't prevent you following Gem.'

'Patronella has heaped me with curses! I will never bear a living child. Gem will divorce me. I'll become a whore.'

'The bitch is eaten by envy of Gem's love for you. You are not barren, at the time the gods choose, new life will come through your body.'

The *Puri Dai* stroked Keziah's hair and told her to drink her tea and fill her belly with the cake she had made. 'Then I will speak to our ancestors on your behalf.'

Keziah sat on a cushion at the old woman's feet while her *Puri Dai* sat immobile, her snow-white hair mottled by the yellow candlelight, her face an image of concentration as she summoned up all her gifts to remove the curses.

'That bitch Patronella knows her stuff. It was a difficult business. Our ancestors were all involved and there were heated discussions between them and my son who bears the name of the Archangel.'

Gabriel – a name too painful for his mother to pronounce after his death.

'My father spoke to you about me?'

'Apart from Gem, who loved you more?' She gestured dramatically to an empty chair. 'Right there playing his violin he was, so sweetly it's a wonder you didn't hear him.'

'Tell me his words for good or evil,' Keziah begged.

'Your *baxt* lies not in Wales but in *New South Wales*, thousands of miles across oceans of terror.'

'*Mi-duvel!* I can't swim!'

'No matter. It is your destiny to find Gem.'

The *Puri Dai* had freed Keziah from Patronella's curses. All but one.

'This must be your decision!' She gripped Keziah's hand. 'Make one false move in the *gaujo* world and it will return to haunt you. I've taught you to be on guard against *gaujo* trickery. You must also distrust their *kindness*. Beware the *gaujo* with a silver tongue. I see him with a big book. He will make you read to him!'

Keziah shrugged dismissively. 'That's easy to avoid. I can recognise all my letters but I cannot build words from them.'

The *Puri Dai* took out her coin purse. 'You'll need more silver for your journey. And this will protect you wherever you travel on land and water.'

Keziah shrank back from the silver amulet being offered to her. 'No! I'll not take your good luck.'

'I command you to take it!' The *Puri Dai's* wrinkled brown face softened. 'This is the last thing you can do for me. Wear this always.'

With a cry Keziah embraced her. As she stroked the furrowed cheeks, she felt her grandmother's tears wet her hair. Exhausted, they lay in each other's arms. The old fingers closed Keziah's eyelids in a silent command to sleep but Keziah sensed her *Puri Dai* was concealing another warning.

'You know what happens to me in that new Wales at the bottom of the world?'

'I tell you true. If you choose by your own free will to bring that last curse down on your head, your life will be entangled with *three* men.'

'Three?'

'I see clearly a man with red-gold hair – you've never met a *gaujo* like *him* before!'

Keziah gripped the protective silver amulet, her throat tightening with unshed tears. 'Gem is the only man that matters to me! I *will* find my Gem and lay in his arms!'

'Headstrong girl. Heed my words. My amulet can only do so much! You must learn wisdom. May *The Del* protect you from yourself. Beauty like yours is a curse when the heart is too open to love.'

CHAPTER 3

It was May Day and dawn had already broken over the hamlet near the Cheshire village of Poulton-cum-Spittal. Unwashed, and barely awake, Daniel Browne rose in fright from his bed of straw in the vicar's barn. He combed his hair with his fingers, drank a mouthful of water from a chipped china jug, stuffed a crust of stale bread in his pocket, then grabbed the rake and ran down the broken flagstone path that led to the old vicarage.

Today of all days he must not be late to begin his daily labours. All his other birthdays had passed unmarked and uncelebrated but this nineteenth birthday was different. So much was at stake that his hands trembled more from nerves than the early morning chill.

As he worked Daniel was conscious of how much his tall lanky frame had grown in the past year. His wrists and ankles protruded from the hand-me-down work clothes bequeathed to him by an elderly gardener who had expired last winter while shovelling snow. The work made him feel halfway between handyman and charity case but at least it kept him fed. No need to go cap in hand to the poorhouse.

Daniel was distracted by a bunch of ruddy-faced boys running past the dry-stone wall toward the village school. They called out the familiar sing-song chant that always ended in derisive laughter: 'Daniel Browne. He's a clown! Wears his trousers upside down!'

Daniel swallowed his humiliation knowing the children were an echo of their parents' contempt. He hated them all. He looked down at his hands. Although they were chafed and raw, he prided himself that his long slender fingers were Nature's reminder that he was destined for better things – the hands of an artist.

I'll have the last laugh. One day these villagers will have to line up and pay *to see Daniel Browne's work. They'll be quick enough to claim me when I'm famous – bastard and all.*

He glanced over at the church graveyard where his mother was buried in an unmarked pauper's grave. Only the vicar remembered Mary Ann Browne – no one else cared.

Edging closer to the house, Daniel peered through the open window of the vicar's study. On the desk under the window a pile of paper lay pinned beneath a paperweight in the shape of a rampant lion. Pristine paper had long been a magnet to Daniel's hand. Sweat broke out on his forehead with the temptation it offered. He mentally covered the pages with images that fought for release from his imagination. Would the vicar notice a few sheets missing? Daniel assured himself that by the time the theft was discovered he would be miles away.

He stretched out a trembling hand towards his prize but was thwarted by the sudden appearance of the vicar's stooped figure rounding the corner.

The old man beckoned and Daniel hurried over to him, ready to receive instructions. He was surprised when the vicar ushered him into his study and gestured for him to take the easy chair opposite his desk. Daniel looked around searching for the glorious art book full of colour plates of the old masters' paintings, which the vicar had once allowed him to borrow. He had studied their work so intensely he knew every detail by heart.

Hanging on the wall was a print showing Moses leading the escaping Israelite slaves between the giant waves God had rolled back from the sea that the vicar called the Sea of Reeds. This seemed an auspicious omen for his own escape.

When the vicar's wife brought them a pot of tea, a plate heaped with strawberry jam butties and slices of caraway seed cake, Daniel hid his reaction. Now that he was leaving, the vicar was treating him like a guest.

Daniel drank his tea slowly and copied the vicar's every move while eating the cake with an unfamiliar cake fork. He waited expectantly for the coveted piece of paper that would set the seal on his hopes of independence. The vicar was the only literate person he knew who could write the reference Daniel needed to present to prospective employers.

'Have you had time to write a Character for me, Vicar?'

The vicar nodded and drew out an envelope from the desk.

'You are a good, reliable worker, Daniel. This will give you fair chance of work in Chester but it can be a hard life for a village lad unused to town ways.'

'I thank you for giving me my start at the reading and writing. More chance than most labourers are given in a month of Sundays.'

When Daniel reached out to receive the envelope, the vicar unexpectedly added three coins to tide him over for a few days until he found work. The gesture caused a wave of guilt in Daniel at the memory of his intended theft, a feeling compounded by the vicar's words.

'We may not meet again in this life, Daniel, so it seems the right time to give you something that's a link with your past.' He opened a mahogany cabinet and carefully took out a scroll of paper, which he unfurled on the desk.

Daniel touched the art paper in awe. Its edges were faintly yellowed with age. The subject of the black and white sketch was a beautiful young girl with long, wavy hair, her face captured at a three-quarter angle as she lay dressed in a plain nightgown. Her hands were folded across her breast like a child who had fallen asleep in the act of prayer.

'She's beautiful,' Daniel said reverently. 'Is this girl ...'

The vicar hesitated. 'Mary Ann Browne. Age fifteen. Your mother.'

Daniel noticed the initials and date in the bottom right-hand corner. 'The third of May was two days after I was born. You told me my mam died in childbirth.'

'Aye, that she did, lad. This sketch was done by an artist chap who came to visit her at the poorhouse. He arrived two days too late.'

Daniel could not conceal his horror. 'You mean he drew her when she was dead?'

The vicar squirmed in his seat. 'You were born before your time. Your mother was weak from hunger when she arrived here. She died within hours after your birth.'

Daniel's hand shook as he stabbed at the initials TLH. 'Do you know who he was?'

'I'm no authority on art but I've heard tell that a young local artist called Thomas Linton Hayes went south to the metropolis and his paintings hang in various galleries.' He looked sharply at Daniel. 'There is no proof he was your father. Perhaps Mary Ann Browne was no more to him than one of his models.'

Daniel pushed aside his angry thought. *Not my father? Then why am I driven to be a painter?* He listened intently to the vicar's description of the artist.

'Quite well favoured but with the look of a man used to indulging himself.' The vicar cupped his hand around an invisible glass and raised it in quick movements to his lips.

When Daniel asked if the artist had wanted to see the babe, the vicar appeared to be discomforted. Daniel had not been expected to survive so the man had left money for a Christian burial.

'Most decent of him.' Daniel was unable to conceal his bitterness. 'But I don't need his name. I'll make my mam's name so famous that Thomas Linton Hayes will wish he had acknowledged my existence.'

'Judge as ye shall be judged, Daniel,' the vicar warned.

'I beg you. Tell me *anything* you know about my mother. You alone remember her.'

'No ordinary farmer's daughter. Extraordinary hooded green eyes. Her hair covered her like a cape – in the way of Mary Magdalene.' He lowered his voice discreetly. 'She had that milk-white flesh those artist chaps favour. Hayes told me she posed for his triptych of Greek mythological figures. Something about Mary Ann being his perfect Clytie.'

The vicar explained the ancient Greek legend of the mortal girl so in love with the pagan god Apollo she watched his sun chariot cross the sky every day. When she died of unrequited love the gods pitied her and changed her into the sunflower turning its head to follow the sun.

Daniel carefully re-rolled the scroll. 'Thank you for this precious link with her.'

The vicar made Daniel kneel to receive his final blessing then handed him a bible.

'May this keep you on the straight and narrow, lad. Go with God and peace be with you.'

In the barn Daniel hastily assembled his few possessions. He pulled his cloth cap down over his brow and marched out into the sunlight, swinging his bundle as he passed the milestone marking the miles to Chester – and his new life.

Hurrying along the Rows in Chester, Daniel experienced an explosion of colour, sounds and aromas that intoxicated his senses – cakes and bread smelling of cinnamon and spices; the perfumes of flowers that wafted from barrows; the giddy laughter of servant girls larking on their rare May Day holiday.

He halted before a shop frontage bearing a sign that transfixed him. *Art Dealer and Picture Framer – Prop. Maynard Plews.* In the window was a painting of a blue-robed Virgin Mary holding baby Jesus, her youthful features shining with serene adoration. The child looked more like a miniature adult than any babe Daniel had seen, but his discovery of the painting was a moment of sheer magic. The printed card read 'Artist Unknown c. seventeenth century'. In Daniel's imagination the Virgin's sweet face was now fused with that of his dead mother.

Taking a deep breath to settle his nerves, Daniel entered the gallery. The oblong space was deserted, its walls covered with tiers of paintings. Enchanted, he darted between them like an excited butterfly drawing pollen from a hothouse of exotic flowers.

Suddenly Daniel realised he was being watched by a grey-bearded man whose pale blue eyes glinted behind his spectacles. There was something about the man that encouraged Daniel to shed his shyness.

'Sir, I have only this day arrived in Chester and am not yet placed in work. I am unable to afford even the frame of the smallest painting in your gallery.'

The man nodded as if that fact was irrelevant. 'I am Maynard Plews. I'm interested in the opinions of all – patrons, clients or art students such as yourself. If money was no object and you had a mind to buy, which would you choose?'

Daniel felt flattered to be identified as an art student.

'There are three. If I had the money I'd forego food to possess all three.'

Invited to explain why they attracted him, Daniel extended his arms as if to embrace two portraits, a diptych of a man and a young girl set against a sun-drenched olive green landscape that was foreign to the realm of England.

Emboldened by Plews's sympathetic gaze, Daniel gave his thoughts free rein, his words tumbling forth as he pointed out the landscapes were connected to indicate the couple belonged to one family. He recognised from the vicar's art books that the couple's elaborate clothing was medieval. The hand that rested on the nobleman's dagger at his belt was adorned with ornate rings – like a woman's. Daniel felt the painted black eyes were watching him with contempt.

'See how his lower lip curls – he believes his word is above the law. He is the very picture of a … a …' Daniel stumbled trying to find the word he wanted.

Maynard Plews prompted him. 'Arrogance?'

'Aye, but there's more. The artist is telling us about something the nobleman's trying to hide. He's surrounded with flashy objects, a goblet and family crest yet somehow he looks uncomfortable as if he doesn't quite belong.'

Daniel faltered again, afraid his words betrayed his ignorance.

Maynard Plews nodded. 'And what do you see in the lass?'

'Fine clothes but she's not worldly like him. She's fingering her wedding ring like a nervous young bride. The artist has painted her eyes turned toward the nobleman as if she's afraid of him.'

Daniel felt exposed. 'But what would I know, Sir? These are the first fine paintings I've seen outside of a book.'

'You have a natural gift for judging character beneath the trappings of luxury. The man was the base-born son of an Italian nobleman, later ousted by his father's legitimate heir. The bride was sold to him in marriage as a child to unite the two families. Her bridegroom squandered her dowry on his favourite courtier, a pretty *boy*.'

Daniel reacted on impulse. 'That's an abomination in the eyes of God!'

'I dare say but princes write their own codes of behaviour.'

Daniel hastily explained his attraction to his third choice, a landscape identified on the card beneath it as the Colony of New South Wales, early 1800s.

'Those alien trees and that remarkable blue sky are unlike any under an English heaven. It breaks every law about beauty – yet it is!'

Maynard Plews studied Daniel. 'What would *you* most like to paint, lad?'

Daniel could feel that his whole future hung in the balance. He did not know what to say but when his answer tumbled out he recognised it was the truth.

'I want to paint a man's soul!'

Maynard Plews nodded as if the answer pleased him. Daniel pressed his luck further.

'Forgive me, Sir, if I am wasting your time.'

'Business is none too brisk. Half Chester is outdoors celebrating May Day but I have an order to fulfil, repairing the badly damaged frames of neglected old paintings.'

Daniel seized his cue. 'Do you need help, Sir? I can turn my hand to anything. I read and write a decent hand. I never tire. I'm strong. Reliable. Honest.' He quickly produced the vicar's Character.

Maynard Plews read it then indicated a doorway to the basement where Daniel would find an overall behind the door, and a boxroom with a bed and washbasin. The owner explained that it was to his advantage to have a lad living on the premises to guard the paintings.

'Vicars don't hand out praise to recommend a potential thief for employment!'

Within half an hour Daniel was wielding a broom and stacking boxes with such fervour that he fancied he caught his employer tugging at his moustache to conceal a smile.

After his new employer left at the end of the day Daniel sprinted down to his quarters. His first act was to pin to the wall the image of his young mother, serene in death.

He softened as he touched her face. 'Just watch me, Mother. I'm on my way!'

A sudden thought jolted him. Why hadn't he chosen the Virgin Mary as one of the three paintings he would go without food to own? The answer came to him with a force that both thrilled and frightened him with its intensity.

I will paint the Virgin myself and prove I can surpass my father's gifts as an artist!

CHAPTER 4

Jake Andersen spent the first weeks after Jenny's desertion checking every settlement within a wide circle radiating out from Penrith, Parramatta and the villages along the coach route to Sydney Town. At Mrs Troy's cottage in Parramatta he found the empty house stripped of furniture, a 'For Lease' sign nailed to the door. Her neighbours told him that Mrs Troy had departed without warning, alone in a carriage. Her whereabouts were unknown. Jake felt choked with bitterness when he guessed the answer. *No doubt Jenny's god-damned protector is now paying the old biddy's rent just like I did. Bloody fool that I was.*

Nothing made sense. Why had Jenny left him without a hint that she was unhappy? He could feel nothing except the driving force to get his hands around that cowardly mongrel's throat. Reclaim what belonged to him. His little princess. But what of Jenny? What would he feel when he saw her again? There was no answer to that. By day he was drained of any emotion except blind rage. By night Jenny invaded his dreams. These visions of her brought pain so acute it shattered his sleep and left him exhausted.

Inwardly he was humiliated by his cuckold status. But pride forbade him to reveal his torment to anyone and he avoided facing his own Andersen clan. He was determined to put up a front, show the world he didn't give a damn – except that he wanted his kid back. He tried not to drink his remaining money but being unable to interrupt his search to take on work, his funds were running dry. He badly needed to win the prize fight to finance his search.

Now as he rode through the bush towards Tagalong, weighing his chances of beating Bulldog Kane, he remembered the first time he had set eyes on Jenny. That unforgettable day he had been pummelling Sly

Peters in a bare-knuckle bout in front of Parramatta's Woolpack Inn.

Jake delivered a left hook to the chin that rocked his opponent to his knees and drew cheers from the crowd of drunken men and their raucous, bedraggled women.

Jake's world shifted on its axis the moment he saw her. The gorgeous young blonde seated in a stationary open carriage. She clapped her hands like a child, beside her a middle-aged woman in black had disapproval stamped all over her face.

The girl's beauty took Jake's breath away. The face of an angel. Skin so white it must never have seen the sun. A pocket Venus clothed in a filmy summer dress the colour of a peach. She was so excited by the fight – by him – that she discarded her parasol. Sunlight turned her yellow hair to gold.

The sight of her spurred Jake on to finish the fight, giving no quarter when Sly Peters's face streamed with blood. After Jake collected his winner's purse, he returned to find the mysterious girl and her carriage had disappeared. He spruced himself up and walked the streets of Parramatta determined to find her. Two days later he stumbled in desperation into a church hall, drawn by the music of a church social. And there she was, weaving between two admiring males in a country quadrille. When Jenny smiled at him, Jake knew he was lost forever.

On his arrival in Tagalong Jake saw the place was swarming with men drawn to the magnet of the challenge match.

Mac Mackie was waiting for Jake outside his hut. Two beef steaks and a bowl of hen's eggs were all ready to fry on the open fireplace. Bottles of Albion Ale were planted at the ready in a bucket of cold creek water.

Jake swaggered up and said, 'Jesus, Mac. You're slack. What's holding up my breakfast?'

Jake hoped his words sounded cocksure, but the wise owl look Mac gave him showed he wasn't fooled for a minute.

'Sit yourself down, Jake. Get that bottle into you. Then you can level with me.'

When the steaks were sizzling and the heady smell of them reminded Jake he hadn't eaten properly for days. He downed his first ale.

'I passed Kane's wagon covered with paintings of the Union Jack and bundles of money. But no Bulldog in sight. You set eyes on him yet?'

'Yeah. Spotted him in The Australia Arms. He's a big lug. Heavy on his feet. Fists like hams.'

'Size alone ain't important. If he's got a weak point, I'll find it and take him.'

'I ain't worried about him. Are you gunna tell me the truth? What's up?'

Jake opened his eyes wide like a baby. 'Not a bloody thing, mate. I'm free again.' He wriggled two fingers on his head to indicate invisible horns. 'Apart from Jenny making me a cuckold and bolting with Pearl. Never felt better.'

Mac handed him a second ale and downed his own. 'Jesus, mate. So that's it.'

Mac squatted on a log opposite Jake. They sat in silence for a minute but Jake knew that Mac being Mac, he couldn't let it rest.

'No need to put up a front with me, mate. Known you too bloody long. Do you want Jenny back, or what?'

Jake snapped back. 'You thick or something? Who cares about Jenny? Her bloody protector can have her. Just until I find him and take care of him – permanently. But my little princess is *mine*. I'll get Pearl back one way or another. No holds barred on that score.' He downed his drink then gave Mac a warning look.

'If you want to hear any more confessions – save up your own for your priest.'

Mac rubbed his beard. 'Righto. Let's get down to business. You look in pretty good nick – physical like. But what about inside your head?

Are you gunna be able to fix your sights on the Bulldog's style? Hone in on his weak spots? You ain't never fought anyone as downright dirty as Kane before.'

Jake's voice was dangerously quiet. 'Get this straight, Mac. I need that purse to be able to track down Pearl. So if it takes me all bloody night and half of tomorrow I'll flatten the Bulldog. That answer your fool question?'

Mac nodded. 'Loud and clear.'

Jake rose. 'Let's go size up the Pommy bastard's tactics.'

Jake saw that the caricature of Bulldog Kane was no joke. In the flesh he was a dumb ox of a man with a barrel chest and a neck as thick as the trunk of a baobab tree. They watched as the Bulldog swiftly dispatched the first local contender, breaking the lad's jaw. No one else in the crowd volunteered to accept the challenge.

'Want to change your mind, mate?' Mac asked Jake.

Father Declan was taking no chances on his church roof. He grabbed Jake's arm and steered him toward the ring. The Bulldog played to the crowd and gave Jake an insulting two-fingered salute.

The spectators were shaggy-bearded emancipist farmers, ticket-of-leave stockmen and shearers. Only one or two women. Most had Irish accents. All were well primed with grog.

Jake watched Mac circle the crowd accepting their stakes. He stripped down to his bare chest, hitched up the moleskin trousers tucked into his boots, clenched his fists and took a fighting pose.

Father Declan held up his hands for silence and rattled off the rules.

'These lads will fight by the old bare-knuckle Broughton Rules. We'll be having none of those newfangled London prize-ring rules in *this* county!' After the crowd roared patriotic approval he continued. 'Under Broughton Rules head butts and wrestling holds are still fair game!'

The crowd cheered their support but belligerent voices yelled to get on with it.

The priest charged through the standard warning. No hitting a man when he was down. No blows below the waist. Each round to continue until a fighter goes down. Thirty seconds between rounds.

Inwardly Jake tried to imagine that the opponent standing before him was actually Jenny's protector – and this was his chance to vent all his rage and frustration and beat the living daylights out of him. But publicly, for the sake of entertaining the crowd, Jake tried to appear as cocky as hell.

Father Declan announced the final words, 'When a fighter is in no fit state to square off within one yard from his opponent, I'll declare that man beaten.'

Jake was quick to toss in a final taunt. 'Don't look at me, Father. Warn the bloody Bulldog!'

The crowd whistled through their teeth. The fight was on.

Jake knew his style was so unorthodox his awkward southpaw tactics always looked pathetic initially. He aroused sympathy for the underdog as he staggered to duck out of range of the Bulldog's long reach. When Jake slipped, it drew a roar from the crowd but he came bouncing back until a near lethal haymaker knocked him to his knees for the thirty-second count. The spectators appeared confident the Bulldog was a dead certainty.

In the second round surprise ricocheted through the crowd as Jake's weaving and jabbing proved he was more effective than some drunk blessed by the angels. This round ended with the bemused Bulldog hitting the dirt for the count.

A tricky barrage of jabs from Jake in round three enraged the Bulldog. He delivered a murderous head butt that sent Jake reeling. For a few seconds Jake was unsure where he was until he had a flash of Jenny holding their newborn baby in her arms. The memory of the happiest day of his life was now like a punch in the gut. *Pearl.*

He scrambled to his feet and squared off just as the count reached twenty-eight.

The next round appeared to be going the Bulldog's way until Jake threw a wild punch that missed the Bulldog but threw the big lug off guard as Jake intended. Seconds later Jake wiped the smile off the Bulldog's face with a left hook to his solar plexus. The Bulldog roared like a blacksmith's bellows. He locked Jake in a vicious wrestling headlock that the crowd loved. Jake's eyes bulged as he gargled a sound he hoped wasn't his death rattle. He saw Mac's eyes widen in alarm as he realised Jake's performance was no act. Jake gave a convincing slump as if unconscious in the Bulldog's arms. The bewidered professional dropped him. Ape-like, the Bulldog stood with his mouth open, afraid that he had killed Jake and that the partisan Irishmen would soon lynch him.

Jake bounced back to his feet. In one beautifully timed movement he delivered his killer southpaw punch to the jaw. The Bulldog's knees buckled and he lay spread-eagled on the ground. Jake felt a rush of triumph and couldn't wipe the grin from his face.

Father Declan gave a speedy thirty-second count and jubilantly raised Jake's arm in victory. He announced to the crowd: 'This young heretic has kindly donated half of his winner's purse to build our church roof!'

The crowd gave three lusty cheers.

Jake could not actually remember making this generous offer to the priest that day they set up the fight, but he knew Albion Ale was a potent brew. He was happy to make a donation on behalf of his Catholic mother but after one round of drinks shared with Mac and Father Declan, Jake realised it would be all too easy to get drunk enough to blot out the pain of his memories until his money ran dry. Instead he exchanged a warning look with Mac.

Mac made the offer anyway. 'Y'know you're welcome to a shake-down here, mate.'

'Thanks, Mac. But I'll be on my way. I've got business with a bloke that won't wait.'

Jake tipped his hat to Father Declan. 'Good luck with your church roof, Dennis. Me being an agnostic I can't say I'll see you in church, but I reckon Mac can best do the honours for me.'

Father Declan smiled but his eyes were serious. 'I'll be praying your search ends the *right* way, Jakob lad.'

Jake tried to keep his tone light. 'Thanks, Dennis. But I reckon your idea of what's right is *very* different to mine.'

He rode Horatio in the direction of the road to Sydney Town, his winnings stashed in his boot. Now he was a cuckold the words 'winner take all' had a bitterly ironic twist. But Jake told himself these funds would widen his search. In his mind's eye he carried the map of the colony, from Moreton Bay in the north to the Port Phillip District in the south, as well as the tracks leading to every settlement in the colony's nineteen counties.

But Sydney Town was his first goal. Jenny's beauty could never pass unnoticed. His bolter of a wife would lead him to the man who had no name and no face.

CHAPTER 5

The silver coins in her grandmother's drawstring purse had been a generous gift and Keziah Stanley knew they would just cover her passage to New South Wales. Then *baxt* turned against her. A footpad grabbed her purse and fled. It was a waste of time for a Romani to seek help from the law. Keziah knew she must build up enough money to secure her passage.

Now, as she travelled on foot along a cobblestone road that snaked through a village in the direction of Liverpool, she was confident that wherever she went in the world she would survive by reading the palms of the *gaujo* – or for those who could afford it, by predicting their future in the Tarot.

'I'll earn my passage before the moon turns over,' she assured herself. Her spirits soared in delight when a flight of swallows swooped low across her path – a sure sign her Romani ancestors were endowing her with good luck. This proved that she was on the road that was right for her. Not simply the road to Liverpool but the road to Gem.

To conserve her few remaining coins she resolutely bypassed a fruit barrow and collected fallen fruit at the base of a tree instead. *A bit green but hungry bellies can't be as choosey as princes.*

Twilight fell in a gentle English cushion of light that Keziah loved; the faint reflection of the sun between sunset and nightfall. She cautiously approached an isolated farmhouse set back from the road, its windows lit like the eyes of a candlelit pumpkin on Allhallows Eve.

Keziah evaluated the hedgerows bordering the farmer's meadows, judging if it was safe to doss down for the night. When rain fell in a soft mist that covered her hair like a hairnet, she caught herself wishing she could spend the night in the warmth of the farmer's barn. Instead she made her way along the hedgerow, keeping a sharp eye out for any movement from the farmhouse. No roving Romani was ever a welcome guest of the *gaujo*. She could never forget how a farmer's evidence had sent her father, Gabriel, to prison.

She took her handkerchief with her few remaining coins knotted in the corner and laced it securely inside her bodice. Swathed in her shawl she nestled beneath the hedge. She clutched her amulet, comforted by the Romani belief, 'After bad luck comes good luck!'

Gazing up into the almost perfectly round face of the moon she prayed to *Shon,* the female spirit of the moon. In the beginning of the world *Kam* the Sun was a great Gypsy king. Each day he pursued his beautiful sister *Shon* in the sky. But before he rose each morning she managed to slip over the horizon to avoid an incestuous relationship. When he finally caught her, she fought him so hard it caused darkness to spread across the earth. During this first eclipse *Shon* was seduced. Their union gave birth to the Romani people.

On the heels of her own prayers Keziah tacked on the Christian Lord's Prayer in the Romani language for good measure. *'Moro Dad …'* When she reached the Amen, *'Avali. Tachipen'*, she assured herself that should keep both the Romani and *gaujo* gods happy. You couldn't be too careful.

Sleep was slow in coming. She was drawn back to her first vivid memory from when she was four years old.

Their Romani camp lay in darkness pierced by clusters of tribal fires at the heart of each family. Her father, Gabriel, himself still a boy, was the handsomest man in the whole world. His dark eyes were lost in the magic he created with his violin. His love song seduced her beautiful young mother who sprang to her feet, her yellow hair flying like gossamer. She beckoned Keziah to join her and they danced together. Keziah was enchanted by her mother's violet-blue eyes – a mirror image of her own.

Keziah shrank from her next memory. The day Gabriel brought home a *hotchiwitchi*, a wild hedgehog that was a delicacy for the cooking pot. It was his right under Romani law to live off the land, but under *gaujo* law the magistrate ruled the hedgehog was on the edge of the farmer's property and pronounced him 'Guilty'. Gaol was a badge of honour to her people. However, within months her mother broke the worst Romani taboo – she betrayed her man while he served time in the *sturaban.*

Gabriel had returned from gaol a broken man. Keziah remembered seeing him sharpening a knife on the wheel he used to repair the villagers' scissors and knives. He slashed the tattoo on his arm, until his blood covered her name – Stella.

He never spoke her name again.

As Keziah finally surrendered to sleep she was haunted by her child-mother's face smiling at her, even when Keziah cursed her. *The Devil be in your bowels!*

The first thing Keziah saw on waking were the fetlocks of a chestnut gelding on the far side of the hedge. The rider was screened from her sight except for his mud-covered riding boots.

'Well, what have we here? A pretty little urchin. Lost your way have you, lass?'

Keziah sprang to her feet. The rider was a cocksure youth dressed in a torn, muddy riding habit of fine quality. His high forehead and short hair reminded her of a Roman Caesar on an ancient coin. He had a sensual mouth in a dirty and bruised face.

She answered firmly. 'Thank you, no! I know exactly where I am going. Liverpool. A ship bound for Botany Bay.'

'You've many miles ahead of you, little one. Ride behind me to speed your journey.'

'Thank you but I prefer to walk.' She shook the twigs from her skirt, turned her back on him and stepped out at a brisk pace.

The rider dismounted and led his horse at walking pace a few feet behind her.

'I can take you as far as my master's house. The housekeeper will give you a good meal to see you on your way.'

Keziah felt her cheeks burn. Romani pride was quite beyond *gaujo* comprehension.

'You mean it kindly, Sir, but I am no pauper in need of charity. I pay my way.'

'Of course. I can recognise a lady when I see one,' the rider said politely. 'Would you mind if I walk a little way with you? I am in need of a few kind words before I face my master's wrath. His favourite horse threw me.'

Keziah wasn't fooled by his pretence that he was a groom. His arrogant demeanour and educated speech clearly placed him as gentry. Did he think Romani girls were that gullible?

'No doubt *your father* will forgive you, knowing the horse was in pain.'

The counterfeit groom gave a short laugh as if amused to be caught out in a lie.

Keziah knelt and gently stroked the horse's fetlock. 'I thought so. A bee sting.'

Aware the young man was studying her intently she drew out the stinger then spat on the wound to cleanse it. She found a common comfrey plant growing wild on the verge and used her headscarf to bandage the leaves against the horse's fetlock.

'By Jove, that was splendid. May I know your name? I am Caleb Morgan.' He inclined his head.

'Keziah Stanley. My father was the finest violinist in Wales and the Northern Counties.'

Warily she allowed Caleb Morgan to draw her out on the subject of horses, well aware of his attempts to form a bond and how often he cast discreet glances at her.

Keziah had no illusions about her good looks – they were useful to allow her entrée to fine houses to give Tarot readings. She was quite tall for a girl and she knew that men, even *gaujo* men, admired the unusual combination of her oriental features, black Romani hair and an olive complexion, with the contrast of her Celtic blue eyes – her sole inheritance from Stella the Whore. To Keziah, her looks were far less important than her pride in her abilities. Meeting Caleb's gaze she shrugged off his admiration. Gem considered her beautiful and that was all that mattered.

'Miss Stanley, perhaps you would care to assist our housekeeper until your ship sets sail for the colonies? Our servants are paid a more than fair wage.'

Although her grandmother's warnings about *gaujo* trickery were ingrained, Keziah quickly weighed this against the advantages. A short time earning good money under the roof of a respectable *gaujo* family would be safer than *dukkering* with the Tarot in a seaport like Liverpool, no doubt full of drunken sailors. 'No harm in having a word with her,' she said.

Keziah tried to conceal her awe when they arrived at the carriageway of a handsome three-storey Georgian mansion set back from the road in a landscaped park. It was the most impressive house she had ever seen. Although the *gaujo* world of comfort was worthless in Romani eyes, she could not overcome her curiosity about the treasures that would be inside.

Caleb Morgan led her to the servants' entrance at the rear and beckoned to a middle-aged housekeeper. His tone of voice changed to one of casual command when addressing the woman.

'Mrs Wills, this is Miss Keziah Stanley, here at my invitation. A fine breakfast is in order. You'll thank me for finding you an honest servant *if* Miss Stanley decides to remain and work for you.' He turned to Keziah. 'Enjoyed our talk. Off to the stables.'

Later that afternoon, having changed into her housemaid's uniform, Keziah caught sight of a very different Caleb Morgan in the grand entrance hall. Dressed in a fine riding habit with his cravat anchored by a diamond stickpin in the shape of a horseshoe, he sprang down the circular staircase and looked up at the shadowy figure at the top of the stairs.

Realising this other man was her new master, Keziah took stock of him. Dark-haired with a touch of grey at the temples and cold, aquiline features, John Morgan was clearly a man whose word was law. Yet Keziah sensed his status as gentleman was an assumed mantle rather than his birthright. She noted Caleb's address to his father was balanced between respect and easy familiarity.

'Thank you for your understanding, Father. Dashed good to be home again. Cambridge is quite a bore.' Pausing by the front door Caleb said quietly, 'Trust you'll be happy here, Keziah.'

Keziah. No doubt this was the last time she would hear her name, in future the household would address her as Stanley.

Although Mrs Wills was openly suspicious of her Romani origin, Keziah gave her no opportunity to fault her work or behaviour. She was scrupulously clean, polite, obedient and reliable. Even so, Wills always counted the silver cutlery after Keziah handled it.

Keziah was resigned to that. No matter how honest she was *gaujos* always chose to remember the slander about her people. Bearing in mind her grandmother's warning to avoid being caught in the *gaujo* web of comfort, Keziah promised herself she would not remain one day longer than necessary. Destiny in the form of Caleb Morgan had brought her to a safe harbour free to save every penny of her wages for her passage to New South Wales. She would turn this unexpected opportunity to her advantage.

Keziah had Caleb Morgan pegged as a bored young man intent on playing every charming trick to gain his own way. It was common knowledge in the servants' hall the master indulged his son and habitually paid Caleb's gambling debts. When referring to his father Caleb assumed an amiable attitude, but he made no attempt to disguise his contempt for his stepmother, Sophie, a girl still in her teens. She was officially confined to bed with melancholia but Caleb dismissed that as a ploy for sympathy.

Keziah suspected the servants' gossip was accurate and that the young mistress had suffered a miscarriage.

When Mrs Wills ordered Keziah upstairs to attend the mistress following the indisposition of her lady's maid, Keziah was prepared to be sympathetic when she entered the dimly lit bedroom.

Sophie Morgan petulantly gestured to a small table holding apothecaries' bottles and jars. 'Bring me that little blue bottle.'

Pain and weakness were etched on the girl's pretty features but Keziah hesitated. She recognised the letters L-D-N-M on the handwritten label. Laudanum! She knew what a dangerous habit it was and wanted to warn the mistress to have nothing to do with it.

Sophie Morgan's eyes dilated in anger. 'What are you waiting for? Give me that bottle. Then leave me alone.'

Keziah felt frustrated, knowing she could help heal her. She had befriended the estate's elderly gardener and had all the right herbs to make a tea proven to cleanse the womb after the loss of a babe. But she handed the mistress the bottle, bobbed a curtsy and left the room.

Next morning Keziah overheard a housemaid complain to Mrs Wills about 'that Gypsy' who Master Caleb had ordered to be reassigned to the library to polish his sporting trophies – her job!

Mrs Wills cornered Keziah. 'If I find you've been granting your favours to Master Caleb you'll be out on your behind without a penny, Stanley!'

Keziah held her head high. 'I'm a married woman, faithful to my husband.'

'A Gypsy marriage! That doesn't count a fig.'

Keziah's tone was dangerously polite. 'It does to me, Mrs Wills.'

She hurried to the library where Caleb was stretched out on the lounging chair looking bored, a book discarded on the floor.

'Four walls filled with books to the ceiling!' she gasped. 'Have you read them all?'

'Gad, no. You like to read, do you?' Caleb was amused by her reaction.

'I love stories.' She faltered, then raised her chin. 'We were always so busy travelling I wasn't schooled in reading but I know all my letters.'

Caleb watched her hard at work polishing but he soon grew restless.

'Tell me about your childhood,' he demanded. 'Spent most of mine trapped with a doddering old tutor. Deadly bore. What is it like being a Gypsy child in a travelling house?'

'*Romani* children,' she corrected politely, 'have a glorious childhood close to nature. Each child has its own responsibilities. We may appear to run wild but we pay our elders strict respect and learn their skills. That's how I learned herbal medicine.' She added pointedly, 'I know the danger of your stepmother growing dependent on laudanum.'

Caleb reacted with lazy indifference. 'Physicians prescribe tincture of opium for everything from teething babes to consumption. It cured my hangover once.' He gave a snort of derision. 'Herbs! Surely *you* don't believe in that witchy stuff?'

'My grandmother is a great healer who has saved many lives. She taught me about herbs and *dukkering*.' Noting his frown she translated. 'Reading the future. I earned good money for the family at county fairs and grand houses. But only from the *gaujo*.'

'I'm a *gaujo* so you can read mine. Come on, that's an order,' he chided. 'Must I first cross your palm with silver?' He saw her expression. 'Meant no offence. Only ask because since childhood I've been afraid that I'm fated to die young.'

It was a charming lie and Keziah gave him a sidelong smile to show she was not fooled by his tricks. With good grace she knelt at his feet and examined the palms of his hands, tracing the lines with her finger and explaining how he would soon cross the ocean. He was destined to go on a dangerous adventure. She saw him with black men in a desert. Men were dying.

'Ah, so I *am* to die young. Told you so!' Caleb gave a theatrical sigh.

'Well, dead or alive, you're quite the hero!' she said firmly.

'And what of love?' he asked softly.

'You will make and lose many fortunes. Love and lose many women. But one girl is – I don't know the English word.' Her hands curled into claws. 'She won't let you go!'

'Tenacious! Gad, Father's going to marry me off to some dreary heiress. He's determined I must produce a suitable heir. God knows Sophie's a failure as a breeder.'

Keziah felt the cruel sting of his words as she was reminded of her own lost babe. When she resumed reading his palm she was suddenly discomforted by the image of a child's face.

'That's all!' She abruptly dropped his hand but he was quick to catch her own.

'Love the prospect of being a hero but I'd rather win *one* woman's love. What may I give you in return? Name it. Some little trinket young gels love?'

'Could I borrow a book from your library – one that will help me learn to read?'

Caleb seemed surprised by her request. 'Will do better than that. What say I teach you to read? One hour every day after you've finished your work here in the library. Is it a pact?'

'But Mrs Wills watches me like a hawk. And I'm already resented for being assigned to the library on your orders.'

'Wills is a *servant*! I'll tell the old shrew it amuses me to teach you to read. What's the point in being the master's son if I can't get my own way?'

Keziah felt a wave of gratitude. 'Thank you! I'll practise every night.'

Suddenly wary she turned in the doorway to ask why he would do that for her.

'I'm bored. You are an antidote.' He called her back. 'And when we are alone do call me Caleb. That's an order.'

Their reading lessons became the highlight of Keziah's day. Although she did not dismiss her grandmother's warning to beware the *gaujo* with the big book, her attraction to breaking the magic code of the alphabet to read stories was so great she assured herself she would soon be free to sail away to join Gem. So where was the harm? The ability to read would stand her in good stead in a colony where it was said many could only make their mark.

Eager to learn, Keziah was angry when she failed and jubilant when she broke through the barrier to success. She hid her books beneath her mattress to avoid Mrs Wills's suspicions.

During their lessons Keziah was amused to see how blatantly Caleb tried to extract personal information. She was always on guard. *It will take more than Caleb's charming ways to trick this Romani lass!*

'Do tell me about your Gem. You Gypsies marry damned young, I take it?'

'It is *Romani* tradition,' she corrected politely, 'for children to mix freely. We are sometimes promised at eight or nine but we *are* free to choose. If you don't want him you say so. My husband is from a fine Romani family – they paid a high bride price for me.'

'So it's the reverse of our custom where a bride brings a dowry to the marriage?'

'Yes, Romani women are valuable,' she said proudly.

When he asked if she had chosen Gem, Keziah's voice grew soft.

'He was my hero. Strong and handsome. He rode like the wind. No man alive could beat my Gem in a bare-knuckle fight. I grew up knowing one day we would lay together. He is my Rom. My man.'

She saw Caleb glance away as if irritated by her words.

'You married him in a church?' he asked slyly.

Keziah gave a snort of contempt. 'Your church means nothing to us. When I turned thirteen my body told me I was a woman.'

Caleb cocked one eyebrow but Keziah continued.

'We dressed in our finest clothes, made our vows, then held hands and leapt together over the broomstick to show we were married.'

'You say you were fated to love Gem,' Caleb said. 'You talk about fate as others speak of God.'

'*The Del* – the Creator – exists. But we see things differently to you. We live with *baxt* – fate, luck, destiny. To take a wrong fork in the road means you were destined to travel that way.'

'So you were destined to meet *me*, Keziah.'

'Of course. And when I leave Morgan Park that will also be my destiny.'

Keziah withdrew the amulet from her bodice. 'This will protect me on my voyage to New South Wales and reunite me with Gem.'

'May it always keep you safe.' Caleb used the cord to draw her close.

Keziah saw the message in his eyes and broke away. She began cleaning one of the sporting trophies as if her life depended on it.

Caleb seemed nervous when he took a heavy tome off the shelf and flipped to a page.

'Practise reading this passage tonight. Tell me tomorrow what you think of it.'

As he passed her, Keziah felt his hand brush her hair.

The book reminded Keziah of her *Puri Dai's* warning. She tried to recall the exact words. *Beware the* gaujo *with a silver tongue. I see him with a big book. He will make you read to him!*

She opened the page entitled 'The Song of Solomon'. Surely there was no harm in the *gaujo* bible! But as she stumbled over the passage Caleb had marked, her eyes widened in disbelief. Surely these words were not spoken by the *gaujo* god?

When it was time for her lesson she entered the library to find Caleb apparently absorbed in a book.

'Well? Can you read it for me?' he asked coolly without looking at her.

Keziah knew perfectly well what the first Song of Songs was about. She handed the bible back to him.

'I could do but I think you should read it to *me*.'

Caleb looked startled but glanced at her as he read the phrase, 'Let him kiss me with the kisses of his mouth: for thy love *is* better than wine …' He faltered on reaching the line, 'A bundle of myrrh is my well-beloved unto me; he shall lie all night betwixt my breasts …'

Keziah decided to call his bluff. 'Why did you choose that particular passage, Caleb?'

'Really, Keziah. Who is master and who servant here, eh?'

She controlled her anger but responded haughtily. 'If you will excuse me, Sir.'

'I most certainly will not!' He blocked her passage to the door. 'I want you to know how I feel. Against my will, Keziah, I am falling in love with you.'

Keziah's confusion was close to panic. She realised how her arrogance had made her disregard her grandmother's warning. 'I didn't mean to mislead you. I belong to Gem.'

Caleb turned away but not quickly enough to disguise his trembling hand. He picked up another book. 'This is a natural history book with wondrous illustrations of flora and fauna in New South Wales. Some names are in Latin but I'll translate those for you.'

At lesson's end Keziah thanked him but she felt unnerved. Caleb's eyes held a depth of longing she had only ever seen in one other man. Gem.

CHAPTER 6

I must *paint her.* It was a thought that haunted Daniel Browne day and night.

During the first weeks of his apprenticeship, Daniel loved his work restoring paintings but he longed for the hours he was free to draw the images of Our Lady that filled his head.

Every Sunday morning he took communion but it wasn't religious fervour that motivated him. He visited the cathedral and many other churches hungry to discover all their artworks.

Today was his first exposure to St Michael's. Daniel was overwhelmed by the ritual, colour and incense which seemed like a theatrical experience compared with the plain Low-Church services of his village. He gazed at the large stained-glass nativity window, thrilled by its beauty. In the bottom panel the Virgin Mary was depicted with hands clasped in prayer, a traditional sky-blue robe draped over her russet-red gown.

Daniel could never pray from the heart to the god who had taken his mother from him, but the Virgin's gentle beauty spoke to his soul and allowed him to make a silent confession.

It isn't the stigma of illegitimacy that weighs heavily on me, Holy Mother. It is knowing that in my first act of life I killed my own mother. I beg you, take away my guilt.

There was no answer. He was distracted by the sight of a young girl kneeling at the altar rail to take communion. Dark hair flowed down her back from the circlet of fur crowning her head. Her profile was as serene as a nun taking her final vows. Her tight Russian jacket could not hide that her chest was almost as flat as a boy's but the soft, feminine beauty of her face more than compensated. Daniel was not surprised that she did not return his glances. She was clearly too far above him in station to notice an apprentice with paint-stained fingernails.

At the conclusion of the service Daniel hurried to his basement room and struggled to capture the Virgin Mary's face in his first oil painting. His concentration was broken by footsteps in the gallery above. Shaking with fear at the prospect of confronting a thief, he armed himself with the poker from the fireplace and crept barefoot up the stairs. Maynard Plews eyed Daniel's weapon with raised eyebrows.

'You disappeared after church, lad. Before I had a chance to invite you to dinner tonight.' His mouth twitched. 'It's safe to lay down your weapon. No need to protect yourself from me.'

'Sorry, Sir. I thank you for your kind invitation.'

'My family will be pleased to have a fresh source of conversation. Shall we say half six?'

Daniel was grateful but annoyed that he'd have less time to work on the Virgin Mary painting. After his master's departure he rechecked that the cash box was locked in the safe. The man was growing absent-minded – he had left a small parcel tied with string on the desk.

Back in front of his canvas Daniel fought to master the oil paints. The colours excited him but his Virgin Mary's face was stiff and remote.

As he fought to give her life, he lost all sense of time. Mindful he must not arrive late for dinner, he ran upstairs to check the clock in the gallery.

Light from the streetlamp filtered through the store window. Daniel was transfixed by a sight at the far end of the gallery.

The Virgin Mary. Diffused light glowed from the outline of her sky-blue robe. Her gentle features were half in shadow. A halo outlined the cowl around her head. He sank to his knees, his eyes blinking as he searched for a prayer to express his gratitude that the Holy Mother had chosen to come to *him.* The Virgin's lips parted to deliver her holy message.

'Pray tell me, lad. Have you seen aught of Father?'

'Father?' Daniel gasped at the sound of the Virgin's Cheshire accent. The holy vision shimmered and disappeared. Standing before Daniel was a girl in a blue hooded cloak – the same girl he had seen in church that morning.

'Aye. Mr Plews,' she said with a blush. 'Your employer.'

'No. I mean, yes. He called in after church and left this parcel behind.'

'Thank heavens. Father forgot where he'd left it.'

She shifted nervously from one foot to the other.

'Father said you'll join us for dinner. Do you know the way, lad?'

He nodded, then followed her gaze to his bare feet.

'Just cleaning my boots, I was,' he lied.

'I'd best be going.' The girl edged toward the door. 'I'm Miss Plews. Sara Anne. My friends call me Saranna.'

Daniel watched her retreating figure hurrying down the street, the wind wrapping the hem of her blue cloak around her ankles.

He locked the gallery door. Tonight's Sabbath meal at his master's house had taken on a whole new meaning.

He rushed down to the basement. His painting was cold, lifeless – unworthy of Our Lady. He began feverishly sketching Saranna Plews's face, jubilant that he had found her. His perfect Virgin Mary.

Seated opposite Saranna at dinner Daniel noticed that her eyes were the same blue as the Virgin Mary's robes. The collar of her white lace blouse was so high it seemed to hold her head erect. He took note of her fingers constantly touching a cameo brooch at the base of her throat, as if it linked her to something important.

She blushed whenever she ventured a rare comment. Daniel vowed to spend his next pay on good quality oil paints to do her justice. Who needed food? Art alone satiated his appetite. Yet the Virgin's offer of second helpings reminded him this was his first proper meal in weeks.

Daniel sensed Saranna was a romantic girl who led a sheltered life under the eagle eye of her Aunt Georgina, who was seated at the opposite end of the table to her brother. It soon became clear to Daniel that the elderly spinster had raised Saranna since the death of Saranna's mother. The woman twittered like a bird but her sharp eyes missed nothing.

After the pudding dishes were cleared Maynard Plews made an excuse to usher his sister from the room. Saranna shifted in her seat and looked around the room as if searching for words. Daniel was content to study her but finally broke the silence.

'Miss Plews, your father tells me you are fond of drawing.'

Saranna stammered in reply. 'Indeed I am. But my work is poor. Father says you are most gifted. Perhaps one day you would care to show me your work?'

'I would be well pleased.' Daniel pushed back an errant lock of hair, a mannerism that he knew betrayed his nervousness. 'But I doubt that your father—'

'Her father wouldn't mind one jot,' Maynard Plews said as he came back into the room. When Saranna didn't respond, he prompted her. 'Daniel's work is impressive. He'd be pleased to teach you, I'm sure.'

Two weeks later Daniel arrived bearing his portrait of the Virgin Mary. The Plews family exchanged sidelong glances. Aunt Georgina could not contain herself.

'Fine it is. Even if your Virgin Mary bears an uncanny resemblance to our Saranna!'

Maynard Plews put on a show of surprise. 'Aye, so it does. What do *you* think, lass?'

Saranna blushed scarlet when all three turned to hear her verdict. Daniel covered her embarrassment with a request to his master.

'May I have your leave to present it to your daughter, Sir?'

Maynard Plews gave a nod of approval. Saranna's heart was in her eyes as she held out her hands to accept Daniel's gift.

At the end of the meal Maynard Plews rose from the table.

'I trust you ladies will excuse us while we enjoy a port in my study.'

Daniel tried to settle into the leather armchair. He wasn't used to being treated as an equal.

On tasting the port he was quick to commend it. He noted the amused twitch of his employer's moustache. His first ever sip of a liqueur relaxed Daniel enough to respond to the offer of a cigar.

'You've done well as my apprentice these past months, lad. You have absorbed the techniques of restoring damaged paintings with remarkable speed.'

'I am grateful for the opportunity to do so under your expert guidance.'

'Who knows, you might take over the business from me some day.'

Daniel was startled. 'That goal is far beyond me, Sir.'

'Modesty is fine in its place. But you are also ambitious.'

'I assure you, Sir—'

'Naught wrong with ambition.'

'I can't deny it, Sir, but I've had scant education. Born in the poorhouse and I bear my mother's name. I could never begin to hope—'

'Nonsense. Many a lad has risen from lowly estate to make his mark. I arrived in Chester as a young lad from Yorkshire without a penny to bless myself. And just look at our Captain James Cook. Began life as a humble farmer's son. Now his discoveries in the southern hemisphere rank him as one of history's greatest navigators.' He refilled Daniel's glass. 'I hold self-made men in high esteem, lad.'

Daniel seized the chance to turn the conversation to art.

'Your botanical books on New South Wales show amazing flora and fauna unlike no other on the globe. I've been experimenting with colour to see if I can get close to the original works.'

Daniel felt his master was observing him closely.

'Aye, I'm gratified to see you are hungry to learn, lad. It took me years to prove myself worthy to marry Saranna's mother. She refused other offers of marriage and stubbornly waited for me to make a decent enough living to satisfy her father. Now, at my time of life, I would welcome a partner in business. Understand me. I'm nay one to hold the circumstances of a lad's birth against him. Should his intentions be honourable and lead him in direction of marriage.'

Daniel caught his breath. Marriage? A partnership? Were these offers in tandem? Before he had time to respond, Maynard continued.

'Now, down to business. I'd welcome your ideas on how to counter these difficult times. We've lived on a financial seesaw since Napoleon Bonaparte got the chop and the whole country was flooded with soldiers and mariners in search of work.'

Daniel found it difficult to concentrate. All he could think about was how being a partner in the gallery would be a golden opportunity to establish himself as an artist.

During the following weeks, however, Daniel could not fail to notice the signs indicating a decline in the business. He suspected the cause was aggravated by Maynard Plews's increasing absent-mindedness.

Attempting to turn the tide and improve his master's fortunes as well as his own, Daniel spent long hours at night restoring a set of six eighteenth-century landscape paintings. The artist had died young, leaving a limited legacy of his work, which was now considered quite valuable. One painting was so badly water-stained that Maynard Plews had warned the owner that the quality of the painting was irretrievable. After Daniel completed the restoration work on the other five, he looked closely at the ruined painting. He knew it was common practice for students to copy the work of famous artists to learn the secrets of their technique.

Why not see if I can reproduce the style of this damaged work? I will learn much in the process. It is not a subject I'd choose to paint myself but it will be an excellent discipline.

Daniel searched through all the blank canvases for one that suited his purpose. He settled down to work, secure in the knowledge he would not be disturbed. His master now spent most evenings in his study poring over the business accounts that troubled him.

On the evening of Maynard Plews's birthday dinner, Daniel arrived early with his gift – a framed portrait of his master painted from memory.

Saranna hung Daniel's painting in pride of place over the fireplace then bustled off to help Aunt Georgina with last-minute preparations.

Alone with the portrait Daniel was pleased with the way he had captured the subject's craggy features above the short, grey beard, the broad cheekbones hollowed by age. He felt he had caught the essence of the man's character, his sharp Yorkshire common sense, softened by the observant, almost sad quality of the eyes.

He was startled by Maynard Plews entering the room.

'Aye, mighty impressive. You've got me down to a tee, lad. Even the perpetual frown I've been wearing of late due to the rocky times we are forced to weather.'

'I'll work hard to help you sail through it, Sir.'

'Aye, lad, you already have at that. Mr Gordon is right pleased with your restoration of his landscapes. He paid handsomely above the price I quoted him. Said he never expected you'd be able to rescue the sixth one, being so badly damaged and all.'

Daniel felt his hands turn to ice. 'The *sixth* one?'

'Aye, I found it on your easel in the basement. You did a fine job. Apart from the aged canvas, it looks as fresh as the other five. A remarkable piece of restoration. I congratulate you. A partnership is definitely in your future, lad.'

Daniel almost staggered under the heavy hand placed on his shoulder, his thoughts were in turmoil.

Holy Mother, what do I do? Mr Plews badly needs the money to pay our accounts. The owner is delighted with the work and he believes all six are by the same hand. I meant no harm. Must I expose myself?

Daniel heard the grandfather clock's seventh chime. He heard himself say, 'I am delighted to have earned your approval, Sir.'

The reappearance of Saranna carrying a double-layered birthday cake with sixty flaming candles enhanced the mood of celebration. But when Daniel saw unmistakable love shining in Saranna's eyes his head ached. He knew what was expected of him. Marriage.

As summer drew to a close, Daniel's anxiety increased. Although he had given no direct sign of his intentions toward Saranna, he now regularly shared the family's church pew.

In public his manner to her was ever gentle and respectful but inwardly he felt confused. It was clear that Saranna saw him as a hero from one of the romantic novels she read. It was also clear that she longed for a declaration of his love.

That morning seated beside her in church, he saw her gloved hand move discreetly to the space between them – an unspoken invitation for him to hold her hand. Instead, Daniel folded his arms and tried to concentrate on the sermon. When the old vicar quoted the Apostle Paul's warnings about chastity and marriage, the words seemed to leap out at Daniel.

'… it is good for a man not to touch a woman. Nevertheless to avoid fornication, let every man have his own wife … I say therefore to the unmarried … if they cannot contain, let them marry, for it is better to marry than to burn!'

From the corner of his eye Daniel saw that Saranna was blushing.

Daniel caught his breath. *Marriage to Saranna would secure my future as an artist. Why do I hesitate to press my advantage? When I first met her I burned to paint her. I'm flattered by her adoration – no one in my whole life ever loved me. But is that enough? Could I face spending the rest of my life with her?*

After the service Aunt Georgina took matters into her own hands. Daniel was to escort Saranna home – the first time they would be together without a chaperone. Daniel seized the chance to take a detour along the towpath beside the canal. When they reached the Bridge of Sighs he only half listened to Saranna's tales of condemned prisoners who had crossed the bridge from Northgate prison to St John's Chapel for final absolution. He caught her by surprise when he said, 'You realise, don't you, Saranna, that if I marry I can record no father's name in the church register. The whole world will know what you know. I am a bastard.'

Saranna looked so flustered, so pathetic to have her fear thrust out in the open, that Daniel felt a rush of anger.

'I thought as much. The rules of society mean everything to you but you might as well accept that they mean precious little to me. I'll make my *own* name.'

Before she could deny her embarrassment, Daniel decided to test himself.

He pressed her hard against the stone wall. His kiss was rough and determined – the first time he had ever kissed a girl. He needed to explore the sensation. That it clearly excited Saranna gave him a pleasant sense of power.

She hastily withdrew at the approach of a middle-aged couple who wore identical expressions of disapproval.

Saranna was breathless. 'Oh Daniel, does your kiss mean that we are—?'

'It simply means I kissed you! Great artists aren't bound by conventional moral codes. And I intend to be great. Art will always be my mistress. An artist's wife must accept that.'

He strode off leaving Saranna to follow meekly at his heels. She caught at his sleeve. 'I promise to respect your mistress if you want me for your wife.'

Daniel nodded but he was not sure if he had won or lost.

The largest art exhibition Daniel had ever seen was crowded with families on a guided tour. As a sop to his pride Saranna had paid their entrance fees. He was aware of her trailing behind him, more absorbed in him than the paintings.

Suddenly Daniel stopped, transfixed by an oil painting of a near naked girl with long brown hair, kneeling with her arms raised to the sky in supplication. *It's her face!*

'Clytie painted by Thomas Linton Hayes. The year before my birth!'

Saranna's gloved hand flew to her mouth. 'The same initials as your mother's portrait! The program says he died ten years ago.'

Daniel sank to his knees, his eyes glassy with tears. Saranna turned chalk-white with embarrassment but Daniel did not give a damn who saw him as he drank in the portrait.

'Just look at her. Clytie. Sensual yet innocent. My mother was brave enough to pose for an artist just as God made her.' He turned to his fiancée with a tone of mild contempt. 'Are *you*, Saranna?' He gave a wry smile when he saw her confused expression and he strode off, content that he had made his point. *If I marry you, little mouse, it will have to be on my terms.*

The clock struck midday as Daniel hurried back to the gallery from the bank. He felt a growing sense of trepidation about his approaching wedding day, 15 July. He waited for a cart that lumbered across his path and then he froze at what he could see through the gallery's window.

Like a mime performer in a dumb show, Maynard Plews was gesturing with uncharacteristic agitation to two police constables.

Daniel's first instinct was to flee. His second instinct was to bluff it out. If there were suspicions about the sixth landscape painting what proof could they have? He had burned the ruined original and put the ashes in the garbage pail.

Maynard Plews caught sight of him. And then the die was cast when the two constables also turned to look at him.

'Is anything the matter, Mr Plews? Can I help in any way?' he asked politely as he stepped inside the gallery.

The older officer answered. 'Aye, if you be Daniel Browne.'

Daniel swallowed. 'That I am, Sir.'

'Then you'll come down to the station and answer our questions. According to an art expert a painting restored at this gallery is a fake. He claims that your employer knew it was when he accepted payment.'

Maynard Plews quickly blocked Daniel's reply. 'My apprentice has naught to do with this unfortunate mistake. I will make amends.'

Daniel felt shamed by his master's attempts to prevent him from being taken into custody.

Escorted from the gallery behind the ashen-faced Maynard Plews, Daniel glimpsed Saranna's horrified look as she cowered in a doorway. A motley crowd milled around enjoying the arrest of a respectable citizen.

'No! There must be some mistake!' Saranna cried.

Maynard Plews looked defeated. 'Tell your aunt to contact my lawyer, child.'

Saranna ran beside Daniel and whispered, 'Tell me this isn't true!'

Overcome by despair he said nothing, losing sight of her in the crowd.

At their trial at the assizes Daniel stood beside Maynard Plews in the prisoner's dock. He searched the spectators' faces until he saw Saranna supporting her aunt at the rear of the court. The fear in their eyes made him think of animals ready for the slaughterhouse.

In contrast Maynard Plews's gaze was fixed resolutely on the magistrate. He refused to look in the direction of his family, even when he entered his plea – guilty.

Maynard Plews was accused of committing an act of major fraud in which Daniel had knowingly acted under his employer's instructions. Despite his master's protestations that his apprentice had not been involved in the mistake his words fell on deaf ears.

When the old man was sentenced to transportation to the penal colony of New South Wales for the term of fourteen years, Daniel felt sure these words sounded his own death knell. He began to shake when the magistrate looked directly at him.

'Daniel Thomas Browne, the court has taken into account your youth. Therefore you are to be transported to the said colony for the term of seven years.'

Above the courtroom clamour Daniel heard a girl's thin voice cry out, 'Daniel! I promise I'll find a way to join you!'

Over the heads of the crowd Daniel saw Saranna. She was being hushed by her aunt. Suddenly aware of the people staring at her, Saranna hung her head, mortified by her outburst.

Daniel turned away. *How much courage can you expect from a mouse?*

Fog blanketed the roadway. Dark fragments of trees pierced the fog and the distant mooing of a cow told Daniel that they were being marched along a deserted stretch of road outside Chester.

He was shackled to a line of prisoners headed for some rotting prison hulk on the Thames. He knew his master was struggling somewhere behind him because he could hear the sounds of his hacking cough – the trial had aged him overnight. Daniel avoided the old man's eyes, knowing he had protected Daniel although fully aware of his guilt. Daniel tried to convince himself his own role in the crime was accidental, but he felt a wave of shame that his silence had betrayed Maynard Plews and Saranna. His cowardice had changed all their lives forever.

Despite Saranna's outburst in court she had not visited him or her father in gaol. Daniel suspected she had not even tried, afraid some respectable person might recognise her.

He was grimly aware of the irony of the date – 15 July was his intended wedding day. Gnawing hunger was uppermost in his mind. For days he had barely had enough rations to exist and he was hungry enough to eat his shoe leather – except that his boots had been stolen. The pair he was wearing he had stripped from the corpse of an elderly prisoner.

Marching in line his fellow prisoners looked devoid of hope. Their ragged garments would be scant protection against the winter to come. A single rebellious soul sang a bawdy song as if he were setting off on holiday.

The swirling fog was so thick Daniel wondered if it was an illusion when he saw a lone figure by the roadside. The hood of her blue cloak concealed all but her eyes.

He knew she was real when he heard Maynard Plews call out, 'Go home, lass. Forget me. I'm dead to thee!'

Daniel met Saranna's eyes and saw her cowered expression. She turned away and disappeared into the fog.

His shackles forced him to go on, his mind filled with the agony of a single thought. *Our Lady, help me! How can I survive for seven years if I can't paint?*

CHAPTER 7

Jake Andersen felt his heart beat wildly as the housekeeper of the Rose and Crown Hotel in Sydney Town eyed him keenly. After all these months it seemed like his description of Jenny and Pearl had finally struck gold.

'Aye, pretty as a doll. Wait here.'

Jake was left standing in the foyer. Would she reappear with Jenny? Or Pearl?

His hope died a little when she returned alone. With a gummy smile of triumph she handed him a fancy lace-edged handkerchief with the letter J initialled in the corner. Jake caught a faint waft of the French perfume Jenny loved.

'She left this behind. Always dressed flash. Never wore the same gown or bonnet twice.'

'Was she travelling with a little girl?'

'I never saw no kiddie. But she always had her foreign gent in tow.'

Foreign. Jake flinched at this first clue. 'When were they here? Under what name?'

'Just a few weeks back. I remember she wore furs even though it weren't real cold. As for names – most women of her kind use Smith, Brown or Jones.'

Jake paid her for her trouble and departed. *Women of her kind.* That careless phrase left a rank taste in his mouth.

He felt like a pawn in a cruel chess game in which that mongrel foreigner kept moving Jenny one step ahead of him. But why was there no sign of his little princess? What had happened to Pearl? He placed Jenny's handkerchief inside his shirt. His body heat caused the perfume to reactivate painful memories but he couldn't bring himself to discard it as he rode down George Street to the Watch House.

In the months since Jenny's desertion Jake had registered Jenny and Pearl's descriptions with every police office, military barracks, hospital, physician's surgery, public hotel, inn and coach company in every town he'd visited. And he never forgot to prime gossipmongers – there was guaranteed to be one in even the smallest bush hamlet.

He had no portrait of Jenny to aid his search but today his description had finally paid off. The fact she had recently been travelling with a wealthy foreigner here in Sydney Town meant she was probably living somewhere flash. But that could even mean the new settlement at Port Phillip they'd named Melbourne Town after some bloody Brit prime minister.

At the George Street Watch House an old lag of a police officer listened to him describe Jenny's fragile build then cast a cynical eye over Jake's muscular body.

'Most wives abscond from husbands what hit them.'

Jake repeated the worn phrase yet again. 'I'm no wife-beater.'

'You best face the truth, Andersen. Runaway wives, absconding servant girls and abandoned kiddies are as common as dirt in this here colony. If they're hungry enough and don't have a man to protect them, like as not they end up plying their trade in The Rocks.' He weighed up Jake before adding, 'Aye, even the little 'uns.'

Within the hour Jake was confronted by the truth of those words. Walking through The Rocks on his way to a drink with Mac Mackie Jake was accosted by a bedraggled, barefoot girl about seven years old.

'Hey, pretty Mister!' she called from a laneway and issued her invitation. Jake could not believe he had heard such foul words from the mouth of a child. The dead expression in her eyes and the way she hoisted her skirt to reveal her naked loins, left him in no doubt.

He shook his head in denial, emptied some coins into her palm and bolted towards The King's Head in Argyle Street. In one terrible flash he had seen Pearl's trusting smile imprinted on the child prostitute's face.

Drinking round for round, Jake told Mac how frustrated he was that all his enquiries over the last few months had only drawn one small piece of information.

Mac offered his help. 'I'm on the road most of the time driving coaches for the Rolly Brothers. Use my hut at Tagalong if you need a shakedown. Put what you want on my tab at The Australia Arms. The Proddie publican will see you right.'

Jake nodded in gratitude. They drank in a silence of Jake's making, until he was no longer able to conceal his bleak despair.

'Just for one night, Mac, I need to get very, very drunk. Alone.'

Both knew what that entailed. Mac shrugged and departed. 'You know where to find me, mate.'

By ten o'clock that night The Rocks had lived up to its reputation as the cesspool of the South Pacific. The convict-built sandstone Watch House, where Jake had earlier sought news of Jenny, was now filled to capacity with its Saturday night quota of local brawlers and foreign seamen.

Jake was roaring drunk and belligerent as he was lumbered by three constables across the flagstone floor of a narrow cell, vainly attempting to duck his head out of range of the blows from their truncheons. When the iron door clanged behind him Jake shouted back through the grid.

'Have the guts to come in here and take me on man to man, why don't you?'

The cell lay below street level except for a barred slit near the ceiling that revealed the passing feet of the inebriated outside world. Jake noted his cell mate – a black Jamaican seaman sprawled half asleep on the floor like a giant baby.

'What you in for, my good man?' the voice asked dreamily.

'Uttering blasphemy in a public place. What ruddy business is it of yours?' Jake demanded.

'Blasphemy, eh? Don't sound much like you'll murder me in my sleep,' the Jamaican said kindly and rolled over to snore soundly.

Jake examined his wounds. It rankled that he was bloodied from his failure to fight off three constables. They had held the dual advantage of being sober and armed with truncheons, but Jake's ego was bruised. He yelled a new challenge at every passing uniform.

'I can lick three of you with one hand tied behind my back!' He rocked on his heels and remembered his killer southpaw punch was his most lethal weapon. 'Well, maybe not with my *left* hand tied.'

Eventually he leaned back against the wall and slid down to the floor. All the grog in the world failed to blot out his pain – Jenny's careless dismissal of his devotion and the theft of what belonged to him. Pearl. Echoing in his mind were the words of Jenny's farewell letter, 'I can't pretend anymore to love you … I am travelling with someone who'll protect us always.'

What a fool he was. For years he'd been in love with Jenny, and believed she was content to belong to him, until that rotten foreign mongrel got under his guard when his back was turned. When Jake's anger cooled he imagined coming face to face with Jenny. Would he find it in his heart to take her back? His instant reaction was denial. But his love for Pearl confused him. What if the only way to regain his little princess meant he was forced to live with Jenny's betrayal? Could he still love his wife? Love? The word disgusted him. Could he sleep with her? Yes. But could he ever trust her again? Never!

Deep down Jake knew that drowning in drink was no cure. When the grog wore off he wouldn't be able to banish the inner voice that told him he was a mere shadow of the man he had once been; the happy fool who had believed his possession of Jenny and his baby girl made him king of the world.

Jake prodded the Jamaican awake. 'You know what cripples a man, mate? Conscience. But I ain't got one! I could kill the man who stole my wife and never lose a night's sleep.'

The Jamaican flashed him a tolerant smile and shook the hand offered to him.

Jake hunkered down in the corner of the cell to keep one eye on the door. It wouldn't be the first time he had been bashed by a trap while defenceless in sleep. He checked his breast pocket. The perfume of Jenny's handkerchief still wafted faintly but he had no tangible proof that his little Pearl had ever existed.

After a day celebrating his release from the Watch House Jake staggered up Bent Street. Blood from a wound on the crown of his head streamed down his shirtfront. He paused on the crest of the hill and tried to focus on the harbour. Outlined against the northern shore were two transport ships, one flying the yellow flag that signalled that there was fever on board. Before dawn all the Rum Hospital's beds would be filled with newly arrived convict patients, the overflow strewn on the grass verge outside.

No bloody surgeon's gunna keep me out! Jake vowed.

He charged noisily down an empty hospital corridor where the darkness was broken by hanging lamps. He was stopped in mid-flight by a stocky, grey-bearded surgeon whose rolling gait indicated his naval background.

'Keep the noise down, man. Let the sick and the dying gain a wee bit of peace!'

Jake wasn't so drunk he couldn't recognise a Scotsman who rolled his R's, but this bloke's accent was impeded by a stutter.

'I'm Dr Ross. Sit ye down. Your name?'

'Jakob Andersen. Jake.'

'Residence?'

Jake was suddenly suspicious. 'None. What you want to know for?'

'In the event of your untimely death. Where do we send your remains?'

Jake felt almost sober. 'Jesus wept. Is my wound that bad?'

The response was crisp. 'Bad enough. Can't you English lads stay out of trouble for five consecutive minutes?'

'I'm Currency,' Jake said. 'Hey, what do you think you're doing with that bloody thing?'

Dr Ross began prodding Jake's wound with a lethal-looking implement. 'Hold still. Unless ye want me to puncture your brain for ye?'

Jake tilted his head as ordered. He closed one eye in a grimace and fixed the other on the surgeon, who gave a satisfied grunt when he extricated something so painful Jake felt it must have been embedded down as far as his jawbone.

'Well, now. What have we here?' Dr Ross held up a shard of glass and examined it with clinical interest. 'From the shape of it I'd say it began life in the neck of a bottle of rum. And from the size of the cut I'd venture to say your opponent bested you, lad. From the smell of you you've been on the grog for days.'

Jake rushed to his own defence.

'Wrong. Today was my first day out of the Watch House. Was just having a quiet drink and minding my own business. Got crowned by a flying bottle before I even had time to land a punch. No fun in that, Doc.'

'Well, let's see if I can amuse ye with a few stitches,' the surgeon said as he swabbed the wound with antiseptic. 'Then you'll be on your way. No free bed here tonight for you. A transport's arrived with a cargo of sick felons. We're bound to have a full house. Walking wounded like you will need to doss down where best ye can.'

'Don't need a bed, Doc. Just fix me up so I can go back and finish the fight.'

Exasperated by the lack of response that greeted his call for a nurse's aid, Dr Ross turned back to Jake.

'Convict labour, drunk for the most part. The authorities run this place on a bloody shoestring. Wonder any poor bastards manage to survive.'

Jake smiled. 'Been here long, Doc?'

'Seven months too long.'

'You came here as a surgeon on a convict transport, right?'

'Right,' said Dr Ross. He threaded a long needle and looked at Jake's skull with intent.

Jake felt distinctly wary. 'You've done this before, right?'

'Aye. I made a career out of patching up sailors and amputating their limbs on His Majesty's warships before Napoleon's demise put many of us on half-pay.'

With speedy efficiency the surgeon swathed Jake's head with a bandage so long Jake felt he was being dressed in a Hindu turban for a fancy-dress ball.

'Like it here? Gunna stay?' Jake tried to sound casual – most newcomers he met were disparaging about the land of his birth and it made him defensive.

'Matter of fact I'm giving that idea some thought. The heat takes a wee bit of getting used to. But it's a grand land. Big enough for a man to lose himself.'

'Covering your tracks, are you, Doc? Same as everyone else who comes here.'

Dr Ross eyed him over the top of his spectacles. 'You're not as drunk as ye look.'

'Us Currency Lads are used to sizing up you New Chums. The poor bastards the Brits send out in chains ain't always the worst villains. We get more than our fair share of snobs, jumped-up gentry, know-it-all Johnnies, remittance men and other bludgers. One half of them come in chains, the other half come out here to look down their toffee noses at us while they grab themselves more land than they'd ever have at Home. But take my word for it, Doc, this country soon sorts out the men from the boys.'

'That's quite a speech.' Dr Ross jabbed a pin into the bandage and added wryly, 'I take it you've summed up a suitable category for me?'

Jake thought for a minute. 'I reckon you're a bloke who's got the guts to stick it out.'

'I'll take that as a compliment. Trouble is I'm nay too partial to Sydney Town. Too much graft, corruption, ineptitude and vicious gossip.'

'You're dead right! I reckon a bush practice would suit you down to the ground. Can't promise you anywhere free of gossip – the whole colony runs on it – but if you stay more or less sober you could name your own price wherever you hang up your shingle.'

'Any suggestions as to where I should point my compass?'

'Yeah. Go south, inland a bit. Lovely country around Goulburn, Gunning, Berrima and one-horse villages like Tagalong and Ironbark.'

Dr Ross washed his hands. 'Now you can take *my* advice or leave it. When a lad drinks to destroy himself it's a bloody waste of a healthy body and a young life.'

Jake chortled in surprise. 'Don't pull your punches, do you, Doc?'

Dr Ross spoke like a navy man giving orders. 'Two firm rules in life. When a man's drunk he should never fight an enemy or make love to a woman.'

'You're dead right, Doc. Don't forget to look me up if you head south and I'll buy you a drink. You'd be a whisky man, right?'

Dr Ross gave a short laugh and a dismissive wave of the hand. 'Scotch. Now on your way, lad. No doubt you'll be on the lookout for another brawl.'

Jake's mood changed. 'No, Doc. There's a mongrel out there waiting for me to track him down. No bloke steals Jake Andersen's wife and baby girl – and lives!'

Dr Ross nodded sagely as if he did not doubt the truth of the threat.

CHAPTER 8

'Once a Gypsy, always a thief!' Mrs Wills hissed to the head butler.

Keziah froze in the act of setting the breakfast table in the servants' hall. She had no doubt that the insult had been intended to reach her ears.

The head butler had just informed Mrs Wills she must manage her preparations *without* Stanley. Keziah had originally been rostered to take her free half-day of the month that afternoon. But as this was the eve before the Morgans' Ball, and every servant was needed, Wills had cancelled her leave. Now her order had been rescinded by young Master Caleb!

'It's a fine thing when a housekeeper is given contradictory orders from two masters!'

The head butler departed with the reminder, 'Ours not to reason why.'

Keziah worked with renewed energy, determined to complete her full day's work before the meal break, so other servants could not complain they were doing her share. As she polished the silver she imagined the sumptuous ball gowns and jewels at tomorrow night's ball.

Officially tomorrow night's Masked Ball was to celebrate 18 June, Waterloo Day, the anniversary of the Duke of Wellington's defeat of Napoleon, but it was an open secret below stairs that John Morgan hoped to break the pattern of his young wife's melancholia. No doubt it would enrage the mistress if she knew a Gypsy servant girl pitied her, but Keziah couldn't help herself. Despite Sophie's petulance and fits of temper Keziah felt the depth of her sadness was an echo of her own. If only she had the chance to cure her but what a futile hope that was.

Her work completed, Keziah ran upstairs to the attic, a room so small she was not required to share it. Abandoning her hated uniform and starched cap for her own bright Romani clothing, she felt liberated. The thought that her victory was due to Caleb's intervention cast an uneasy shadow over her freedom. She laced up her boots then bolted down the servants' stairs with such speed her red petticoats ballooned out and made her feel airborne.

Permitted on Caleb's orders to explore the landscaped gardens out of bounds to other servants, she raced through the sweet-smelling kitchen garden and waved to the old gardener as she ran down pathways bordered with lavender. Central pockets of flowerbeds were filled with ball-shaped red rose bushes. Wind whipped her hair in every direction.

'Free at last!' she cried to the wind.

Feeling like a child in an enchanted garden, Keziah caught her breath in admiration when she rounded a corner. Laden with masses of pink climbing roses, a little cross-hatched timber bridge arched over an artificial lake. Golden carp flashed their brilliant colours in the sunlight.

The bridge led to a man-made island crowned by a garden folly; a small pagan temple built of moss-veined marble with fluted columns supporting the dome. This provided perfect shelter for a table surrounded on three sides by a curved stone seat.

She halted in awe. *Mi-duvel!* It was even more beautiful than Caleb said it was.

A bare-breasted maiden swathed in a Grecian robe stood half screened by trees. The marble hunting dog at the statue's heels was so life-like that Keziah fancied she heard him baying.

When she entered the temple folly she said a quick prayer to whatever god it honoured before she confronted her dilemma. Despite her *Puri Dai's* warning she had allowed herself to become enmeshed in the spider's web of the *gaujo* world.

Week by week she had grown lax about the practice of her Romani traditions. When washing her clothes she neglected to separate those for the upper half from the lower half. She went willingly to attend household *gaujo* prayers but for days forgot her Romani prayers. She made weak excuses – too tired after working long hours or practising her reading at night. Now she faced reality. She had been seduced by a soft bed, food cooked for her, the promise of decent wages. Her real problem was that her joy in learning to read was entangled with her covert friendship with Caleb.

She lingered, dreamily watching the dying light draw a cloak of shadows across the garden.

Seated at the feet of the moonlit statue, she spelt out the letters on the pedestal. A-R-T-E-M-I-S. The Greek goddess of hunting and the moon.

Politely she spoke to the marble face. 'Forgive me but I have my own beliefs.'

Keziah prayed to *Shon*, the spirit of the moon. 'Please lead me to my love. To Gem.'

She closed her eyes and returned to the precious memory of their wedding night.

The sound of tin kettles beaten by drunken guests outside their vardo *had died away. They were alone. Keziah was surprised to discover that Gem's boyish bravado as a lover had evaporated. He was so nervous she knew she must draw on her woman's instinct.*

'We will teach each other, my Rom,' she whispered. 'Show me how I can make you love me forever. Nothing can go wrong, my Gem. Nothing!'

Both apologised for their own clumsiness but were quick to praise the other, until they discovered the magic of their bodies and caught the rhythm that united them.

Eyes shut tight Keziah relived Gem's lovemaking, the wild swing between his gentleness and his passion that could flare up into jealousy. But she felt crushed by the weight of his seven-year sentence. Would their love stand the test of time and vast distance?

'Oh my love, do not forget me,' she whispered as heat flooded her body.

'How could any man forget you, Keziah?'

Caleb approached her with a half-smile, carrying champagne and two glasses. He had dressed with care but as always the cowlick on the crown of his head refused to lie flat.

'I knew I'd find you here. This is to celebrate. I finally succeeded in being sent down from Cambridge. Kicked out. Do you still plan to sail to Botany Bay?'

Confused, Keziah nodded. 'Very soon.'

She felt naked, as if caught in the act of love with Gem she had been remembering.

'So this is goodbye, Keziah.' Caleb poured the champagne then touched his glass to hers. 'To your happy reunion with Gem.'

'You are very generous, Caleb.'

'A gentleman knows when to accept defeat. May I borrow a John Donne sonnet? From my heart to yours.'

Keziah's eyes were misty as he reached the final words:

'… *But since this god produced a destiny*
And that vice-nature, custom, lets it be;
I must love her, that loves not me—'

'Stop it, Caleb!' she begged.

'Can you find it in your heart to kiss me goodbye?' he asked softly. 'Just a kiss between two friends? Nothing more, I promise you. A kiss to remember each other?'

On impulse Keziah leant towards him. If Caleb felt passion he kept it clothed in gentleness. His lips played with her mouth, softly lulling her into submission. When Keziah closed her eyes she saw Gem's smiling face but it was Caleb's voice that whispered, 'Keziah. What have you done to me?'

Her cry was swallowed in the whirlpool of his kiss. In her turmoil she allowed herself to glimpse the hunger in his eyes. A fatal mistake.

She felt the answering heat in her body.

Her need for Gem struggled with Caleb's soft, hungry desire.

Caleb's whisper was in her mouth. 'Yes! You belong to *me* now.'

She was lost.

Keziah awoke at dawn to find herself naked in her bed, lying in a tangle of sweaty sheets. Caleb lay asleep beside her, his head on her shoulder, one hand cupped around her breast.

Keziah felt hot and feverish. Her mind desperately fought to break free from the memories of the night before. She was overwhelmed with despair.

Her shame was heightened by a prickling sensation of fear when a shadow moved in the corner and Mrs Wills slipped out the door.

Keziah shook Caleb awake in panic. 'You must leave at once!'

Refreshed by sleep Caleb's lust was clearly undiminished but Keziah pulled the sheet across to shield her body from his eyes. 'Go at once!'

Half awake, his speech was slurred. 'You look hot. Do you have a fever? Should I send someone to attend you?'

She reacted in fright. 'No! Do you think I want the whole world to know what I have done? Just leave me!'

Dressing in haste Caleb whispered from the doorway, 'Gad, you are beautiful! I'll come back to you later.'

Keziah lay staring at the ceiling. Tears rolled down her face mingling with the sweat that oozed from every pore.

All day she felt like a lost boat tossed about in a stormy sea as she moved fitfully between feverish sleep and the greater pain of waking in the increasing darkness, forced to remember what she had done. Vaguely she recalled hearing a housemaid's comment as the girl peered around the door. 'Stanley be proper poorly. No use to us tonight.'

From downstairs came the sound of running feet, anxious questions and sharp orders.

Every servant would be on duty for tonight's ball. No one would have a moment to waste on her.

There was a knock on the door and Caleb entered, a dashing figure in evening dress, a gilded mask pushed up above his forehead. He held a tray with two wine glasses and a plate of delicacies. Keziah was disturbed to see the tray also carried a herbal posy in a silver filigree holder. At its heart was a single red tulip. She knew these tussie mussies were all the rage, sent by suitors to fashionable young ladies to convey the hidden 'language of love'.

The smile in Caleb's eyes told her he was aware a red tulip was a declaration of love.

'Your servant, Ma'am,' he said with a flourish. 'The wine will help you sleep. It is my fault you caught a fever. Robbed you of all sleep last night.'

'Everything is *my* fault! I have no head for wine. And you are just a man after all.'

He seemed disconcerted by her honesty then melted by her despair. 'Don't cry.'

Keziah pushed her wild mane of hair from her face. She waved him away.

'Go dance with the heiresses your father lined up for you.'

'Truth is I'd rather be here with you.'

'That is a sweet lie,' she said despondently. 'Please go.'

He agreed but told her he must return briefly to Cambridge then to Manchester to pressure the family lawyer into releasing his inheritance from his mother. He kept saying he had big plans for them but wouldn't elaborate. One moment he appeared cocksure, the next serious. He made her promise to wait for his return.

'Keziah, please understand I can't give you what you deserve. Father would cut me off without a penny if I married a Gypsy. But upon my honour you can depend upon my protection. I'll take care of you. No one can stop me loving you. Not even you!'

Caleb held her face in his hands and kissed her as if she were a princess.

'I leave at dawn – all the sooner to speed my return to you.' With that he was gone.

It was then that Keziah saw it – the tiny velvet bag beside the tussie mussie. She loosened the drawstring. Out spilled a trail of golden sovereigns.

She shuddered with horror as she recalled Patronella's prediction. *'Before the death of summer, when the moon's eclipse falls in your sign, you will earn money on your back.'*

The eclipse was only weeks away. Patronella's vile words had come true. This money was payment for services rendered. Keziah realised she was no better than her mother, Stella the Whore.

She stared at the sovereigns, chilled by another terrible thought. At thirteen when her first bleeding proved that she had become a woman, her *Puri Dai* had taught her how to read the phases of the moon to predict the fertile peak of her cycle. Desperate to conceive Gem's child Keziah had dreaded the arrival of her bleeding each month. Now she prayed fervently for the sight of it to prove she was *not* with child to Caleb Morgan. All she had ever wanted was to be reunited with Gem but now she had committed adultery. Had this changed the course of her whole life?

Three weeks passed. Caleb did not return. Her bleeding did not come. Private agony left Keziah exhausted, only too aware of the housekeeper's hawk-like observation. Each month it was Mrs Wills's self-appointed duty to inspect every unmarried servant girl's 'rags' to ensure they had not fallen with child. This invasion of privacy disgusted Keziah but others took it for granted, relieved to have escaped the consequences of some furtive tumble in the stables.

Keziah watched the waxing of the moon with growing despair, weighing her options. Two weeks past her due date she panicked and fled to her attic room. Shutting her eyes to steel herself against the pain, she slashed her arm to fake her menstrual blood. Later Mrs Wills acknowledged the evidence of her rags. Keziah felt a rush of gratitude that her ploy had bought her enough time to collect her quarterly wages next week before fleeing to Liverpool.

Her sense of reprieve was short-lived. That night as she undressed for bed there was a knock on the attic door. Why was Mrs Wills confronting her at this late hour after the servants had bedded down for the night?

The housekeeper's tight smile was even more unnerving than her insults had been.

'Thought you were clever, Stanley. But I'm up to your Gypsy tricks. Master's ordered you to his study. You won't keep him waiting if you know what's good for you.'

Keziah hastily re-dressed and hurried downstairs, fully prepared for her dismissal.

The room was dimly lit when Keziah entered. Seated at his desk John Morgan did not acknowledge her presence. He had just returned from some social event; his evening clothes were adorned with regimental battle honours. His eyes were concealed in shadow but the lower half of his face was tinged green from the desk lamplight. Keziah was surprised by the faint smile that played at the corner of his mouth when he finally indicated for her to take a seat.

Keziah was on guard. The master had scarcely addressed ten words to her during the months she had lived under his roof.

'Wills tells me you've been "caught". Don't fret, child. I am not a man to toss a servant girl onto the street because young Caleb is having his way with her.' His first direct glance was not unkind. 'Not the first time I've footed the bill when my son's been up to mischief.'

Keziah was humiliated to realise she was just one of a procession of girls who had succumbed to Caleb's charm, but she forced herself to appear dismissive.

'Your son's business is no concern of mine, Sir.'

'Come, come. No secrets in this house. Mrs Wills found you two sleeping together months past.' He gave a tolerant shrug. 'Ah, young blood …'

'My wages are due. I will leave tomorrow,' she said haughtily, 'as was my plan.'

'Ah, but *my* plan is a far better one for you, Keziah.'

She gave an involuntary shudder. Only Caleb called her by her given name when they were alone.

John Morgan measured his words. 'Now that my son has left Cambridge, my wife and I are agreed he needs a new diversion. You two can continue discreetly to enjoy each other with our blessing. You're a healthy lass. It seems Nature has already provided you with one of her unwanted little problems. But have no fear, you will be very well paid for your trouble.'

He gestured airily to what Keziah could see was a legal document.

'I shall read this to you. In brief it solves all our problems. What would be a burden to a lass like you will be a great comfort to my dear wife who's eager to have a babe to spoil. Simply make your mark on that dotted line. All your worries end with one stroke of the pen.'

Keziah flinched and realised her hands were clammy. His tone gave the impression he would brook no argument. She must stall long enough to understand the full import of his plan. *And what was Caleb's role in all this?*

'I would prefer to read it myself, Sir.'

His face registered some surprise but he handed her the document. Keziah read the contract slowly, trying to digest the unfamiliar, repetitive phrases and to work out how she could avoid signing it. The cold legal terms spelled out the inescapable truth. The Morgans' lawyer had covered every aspect. She would be domiciled in a nearby village where Caleb would visit her until the delivery of a *living* child. The condition was she must sign away all claims to the babe. Following her signature she would receive the first instalment of a generous sum to be paid in full after the birth.

She tried to mask her anger. *The child is to be removed from me sight unseen after its birth. He's treating me like a dog with an unwanted litter of pups.*

John Morgan dipped the pen in the inkwell and offered it to her. She did not take it.

'This plan will make you quite the wealthy woman, Keziah Stanley. No doubt in the heat of his ardour Caleb made rash promises to whisk you off to North America but the truth is he's totally dependent on me for every penny he gambles. You'll find Caleb soon tires of his toys. In a matter of months when this little matter has run its course he'll be ready to marry a suitable heiress. While you'll be free to begin life as a wealthy woman in New South Wales.'

He cast her a knowing look. 'Your Gypsy horse thief need never know how you came by your windfall. Isn't our plan a clever one?'

Our plan. Keziah struggled between rage, humiliation and shock as she realised the extent of Caleb's betrayal. Only Caleb knew about Gem. So this was what he had meant by his big plans for her. He was in league with his father!

The thought of abandoning her child raised the unwanted image of the *gaujo* mother who had so easily abandoned *her.*

Keziah stalled for time. 'Your wife would not be unhappy to raise a Gypsy child, Sir?'

He smiled paternally. 'It was her very idea to gain a child. Be assured my grandchild will be well educated and bear our family name. Our own Morgan blood, do you see?'

Keziah gritted her teeth. *You arrogant bastard. You Morgans are only a generation away from peasant stock. I trace my blood back centuries to Romani kings in Egypt and India.*

Her heart raced with suppressed rage. His manner was so kind, so reasonable that she wanted to stab him in the heart with the paper knife that lay only inches from her hand. Instead she forced herself to appear cooperative as she drew on generations of Romani guile.

'You're most generous, Sir, to help a Gypsy girl better her station in life. Your plan is fair to all concerned but first I must discuss the details with your son.'

She instantly realised her mistake. The master dismissed that intention as irrelevant.

'Not possible. He's gallivanting around the county at some race meeting or other. Don't worry your pretty head about details. We are not villains, m'dear. You'll want for nothing.'

John Morgan rubbed his thumb against his fingers as if to remind her how much filthy lucre she stood to gain.

Keziah silently questioned whether to demand the wages due to her but decided that would warn him of her flight. That money was now lost to her. Instead she pointed to one line on the document.

'When do I receive this first payment?' she asked coolly.

In answer he withdrew from his desk a sovereign purse and placed it before her.

Keziah read his expression. To him she was simply a money-hungry Gypsy who would sell her babe for thirty pieces of silver.

Her eyes locked with his as she deliberately weighed the purse in her hand then took the pen and signed her name on the dotted line.

The house was silent when Keziah made her way in the darkness up the back stairs to the attic. She rummaged through the cupboard for her few possessions, throwing things into a battered carpet bag she had rescued from a pile of discarded goods in readiness for her escape.

She tore off her maid's uniform and hurriedly dressed in her own clothes. She froze at the sight of the little velvet coin bag Caleb had given her, remembering the promise she had made to wait for his return. Now that she knew the true reason she could not divorce

Caleb's features from those of John Morgan. Father and son were forever melded into one hated image of power.

Carrying her carpet bag Keziah stumbled across the lawns of Morgan Park towards the tradesman's gate. Her dress was drenched wet like a second skin, her vision blurred by the sweat dripping into her eyes. Her body gave out the scent of fear.

At the roadside she paused to weigh up her options. She leant against a tree to draw strength from the sap flowing beneath the skin of its trunk.

What choice did she have? At all cost she must escape the Morgans' plan to use her like a brood mare for Sophie Morgan. Yet the revelation of her disgrace would make her an outcast in Romani eyes. Gem would never forgive her.

There was only one possible solution. Determined to prevent the advent of the babe, she had total faith in the Romani cure. If she stood at the grave of a child and allowed the shadow of its tombstone to fall across her, her 'trouble' would drain from her body.

Keziah wiped her face with the hem of her skirt and hurried down the deserted road.

From the crest of a hill she looked across at the tower of a Norman church. She prayed to *The Del* that the sun struggling to gain a foothold in the grey sky would be strong enough to cast the shadow she needed for her solution.

The stone church was built on a hill overlooking a hamlet that was deserted at this early hour except for a farmer's cart stationed beside the inn.

Checking that she was unobserved she followed the path to a neglected graveyard where old tombstones leaned out, half submerged in long grass.

An old sheep tethered to a stake was doing its best to mow the grass. She patted its woolly back as she passed by in search of a grave.

All graveyards held sad evidence of children who died at birth or had their lives cut short during epidemics. Many lay in paupers' graves, but Keziah knew how loving parents often beggared themselves to provide a tombstone for a dead child.

It did not take her long to find one guarded by a winged stone angel. Slowly she read the inscription. *Here lies our Beloved Son Georgie Simmons, age 3. Safe in the Arms of Jesus. 21 March 1818.*

Keziah said a prayer for Georgie's soul then checked the position of the sun and the Roman numerals on the clock tower. The shadow of his headstone would soon fall across her.

As she waited for the clock to chime she felt a prickling sensation at the nape of her neck. The silence was suddenly so total even the sound of birdsong had drained away. She felt powerless to move as the shadow crept closer.

It was then she saw it. *A mulo!* The ghost of the three-year-old boy emerged from behind his tombstone. Keziah stood transfixed by his fair curly hair, the strong blue eyes in his pale face. He was barefoot, dressed in thin summer clothing.

'Mi-duvel!' she whispered in horror. 'Why have you sent this *mulo* to haunt me?'

Silently the little ghost extended his hand to offer her something small and red. *Oh God, no! He's moving towards me!*

She backed away in terror and felt overwhelmed by a sickening nausea that signalled she was on the brink of losing consciousness.

When Keziah regained her senses she was alone and realised she had fallen outside the range of the shadow's arc. Near her outstretched hand lay a red ribbon – the traditional symbol a Rom places around the neck of his newborn son to acknowledge his paternity.

Fate had led her down a path she had not chosen to travel. This was not the dead boy's ghost, but the spirit of her unborn child delivering its silent plea. *Allow me to be born.*

The spirit child had been the image of Caleb Morgan. The same fair hair that curled in a wayward cowlick on the crown, the same high forehead, nose and chin. Except that this boy's eyes were the exact violet-blue Keziah had inherited from her mother. Only moments earlier she had been determined to rid herself of her unwanted babe but now that she had seen his little face she could not bring herself to end his life.

As she held the thin red ribbon, desperate ideas fermented in her mind. She heard her grandmother's warning. *'Make one false move in the* gaujo *world and it will come back to haunt you.'*

Keziah had drawn her unborn babe into a terrible web. Kneeling in the graveyard she divorced herself from the present and begged her ancestors for guidance. How could she hide this child's existence from Gem? Her ancestors were silent. A terrible thought struck her. Was she already *mahrime*, an outcast in their eyes?

She was jolted back to the dangers of the present. Time was running out. John Morgan would track her down if she didn't keep moving. Morgan arrogance would never allow a Gypsy thief to trick him.

The bustling port of Liverpool was alive with activity. The voices of seamen called out in a half-dozen foreign tongues as they rolled along from one public house to the next.

Within hours of scouring the docks in search of a ship bound for New South Wales, Keziah knew *baxt* favoured her when she secured a cancelled berth on the *Harlequin*, an immigrant ship scheduled to sail on the afternoon tide.

Relief flooded her body as she handed over the passage money. Asked to state her name for the passenger list she hesitated. Romani women kept their own family name after marriage but now she must replace Stanley with Gem's surname.

'Mrs Smith, widow,' she said. She trusted this ploy would not only foil the Morgans' attempts to trace her in the few hours before the *Harlequin* set sail but also in the future. It was usual practice to record only cabin passengers' names. As one of ninety immigrants travelling steerage, she hoped to escape official identification in the records.

Keziah hated herself for having to use part of John Morgan's money to cover her passage.

'But needs must,' she sighed. She sewed Caleb Morgan's coins into the hem of her sole purchase, the full black skirt necessary to establish her new identity as a widow and disguise her expanding belly during the voyage.

She felt a lump in her throat as she looked around at the world that would soon be lost to her forever. These could well be her last hours on English soil and, although she thought of herself first as a Romani and secondly as Welsh, she could not suppress the film of tears that blurred her vision.

As she looked across at the masthead of the *Harlequin* that would carry her to New South Wales she wondered how on earth she would find Gem in that god-forsaken land? And when she did, how would she find the words to seek absolution? History had repeated itself. Like her worthless mother, Keziah had done the unforgivable – betrayed her Rom while he was in prison.

No matter what I have to do to survive, I will find you, Gem, and lay in your arms again.

At the thought of his beloved face she tasted the salt of tears that had fallen onto her lips.

Laying her hands on her flat belly she spoke the truth out loud.

'I don't want you, little boy. But I know you're in there. So just for now – you and me – we're bonded to each other.'

CHAPTER 9

The rugged terrain looked so unfamiliar to Jake Andersen in his hazy, disordered state of mind that he felt he might as well have been on the moon. But he decided he was somewhere south of the Wollondilly River.

For days Jake had seen no traces of human life, but now the far-off sound of picks and sledgehammers echoed through the deep gorge. No doubt an iron gang was hacking a new road through the bush.

Jake was conscious of his empty belly. He had eaten no food and drunk nothing but grog. He longed for the taste of water.

The thought of grog triggered fragments of recent memories … rowing a 'borrowed' boat across the Nepean River to his father's farm … charging in with an armload of grog to entice his pa to fall 'off the wagon' … noisily toasting the birth of Jake's eighth brother in Norwegian *skol* style … his mam's Irish accent thick with rage at the discovery of their Demon Drink, 'Go home to Jenny, you drunken, piss-weak eedjit!'

Jake couldn't bring himself to tell them Jenny had bolted. He had told his mam to cross his name out of her damned family bible. 'Tell everyone Jake Andersen is dead.'

He now regretted his parting words but he knew his mam would never back down. Neither would he. So he might just as well be six feet under. *Dead men don't ask for help.*

He dimly recalled being locked up later for being 'Idle and Disorderly', a mild charge given the havoc he had created in some public house somewhere. On his release he had packed flasks of rum in his saddle bag, ridden off into the scrub and drunk himself into a state of bitter laughter as he argued with the stars in the Milky Way. This morning he had woken up feeling disgusted with himself.

At the sound of a creek far below him, he leaned backwards in the saddle to stay upright as Horatio began the steep zigzag descent towards what Jake hoped was drinkable water.

Eureka. Jake grinned with relief at the sight of a billabong beside the creek. He unsaddled Horatio to allow him to drink in comfort. When he bent to quench his own thirst a discomforting thought crossed his mind. In years past some Wiradjuri waterholes had been poisoned. *What if this one is too? Well, I'll soon find out.*

After drinking his fill Jake topped up an empty rum flask with water. Tearing off his foul-smelling clothing he threw everything he owned, including his body, into the cold billabong, emerging clean and relatively sober. The mere idea of drinking the two remaining rum flasks made him nauseous.

As he travelled towards the distant sounds of road-making, Jake felt the rhythm of his body comfortably attuned to Horatio's gait. The day was already hot. Clearly it was going to be a scorcher of a summer. He had lost track of time but reckoned it must be around mid October because of the signs of spring, the wildflowers, the red tips on the leaves of eucalypts. For the first time in weeks he was fully aware of the land around him.

The vast expanse of Wiradjuri country was a man's world. It had many faces. Here craggy cliffs rose above deep gorges slashed with creeks that could be heard but seldom seen. The drab olive colour of gnarled gum trees was suddenly pierced by brilliant flashes of lorikeets and cockatoos in screeching flight. To Jake this country contained treasures more precious than gold, like the limestone caves full of stalagmite formations that few white men knew existed – and Jake was in no hurry to share these secrets.

Passing through a break in the bush he found the way ahead was suddenly clear. Giant trees lay like fallen soldiers on a battlefield. Stark evidence of a recent bushfire. Remaining upright were the survivors, blackened trunks of ironbark and bloodwood eucalypts that already sprouted a profusion of mint-green leaves from their burnt limbs – evidence to Jake of Nature's bountiful assurance that no fire could ever permanently destroy her.

When Jake drew rein to relieve himself he saw a white object that he expected was some animal's bones. On closer inspection he knew the truth.

A human skull lay bleached by the sun. A black beetle crawled from one empty eye socket. Lying in the undergrowth was a skeletal frame, arms outstretched in a cruciform shape, legs slightly parted as if in a desperate race to cheat death despite being shackled by leg-irons.

'Jesus wept. You poor bastard.' Jake's voice rasped with the effort of forming the first words he had spoken in days. Kneeling beside the unknown bolter he wondered how far he had staggered from his iron gang. No doubt he had preferred the risk of this lonely death to being locked up each night in the suffocating heat of one of those portable convict huts so densely packed with prisoners that only a corpse could lie horizontal.

Jake began stacking rocks to form a cairn but he hesitated in covering the dead man. No name. Nothing of value to bury with him. Somehow that didn't seem right.

On impulse he tugged off his gold wedding ring and re-read the words engraved inside. *5 May 1833 Jakob and Jenny – Eternal Love.* The same in-scription was on the matching ring Jenny had abandoned. Defiantly he tossed his wedding band into the open grave.

'No use for this rubbish,' he said. He covered the bolter with rocks, placed the leg-irons at the head of the grave then remounted Horatio.

A few miles down the road he slowed between two lines of giant scribbly gums stretching out across the road to form a cathedral dome that filtered out the sky.

The sound of sledgehammers and picks was now close. Rounding a bend Jake approached an ugly scene that was all too familiar.

A road gang of some thirty emaciated convicts hacked at sandstone boulders under the relentless sun and the encouragement of an officer's musket. Most had shaven heads. All wore convict slops, sun-bleached garments branded with numbers or black arrows. Caps or knotted handkerchiefs covered their skulls. Shackled leg to leg, the gang looked like some strange species of human centipede.

The scene reminded Jake he was only one generation away from this punishment. Isaac Andersen had been transported as a prisoner-of-war after the British Navy captured a Dano-Norwegian ship allied to Napoleon. Pa claimed he was lucky to serve his time in the humane era of Governor Lachlan Macquarie, who had granted him land and a pardon. Pa had struggled with the soil to a state of fecundity and Mam's fertility ensured a supply of free farm labour.

Jake could never pass a road gang without a friendly word.

'G'day to you lads. It's a real bugger working for Her Majesty in this heat, eh?' Amid their curses and laughter Jake detected a half-dozen accents: Cockney, Irish, Scots, Gaelic and other dialects that bore scant resemblance to the English tongue as he knew it.

The sole officer in charge looked no older than Jake and a bit gormless. He sweltered in his serge winter uniform with the new issue baggy blue Cossack trousers. The flies were driving him mad and he swatted at them with a switch of gumleaves.

Perhaps the lad's stuck out here alone as punishment. God only knows what the bloody military gets up to.

'Left you on your tod, have they?' asked Jake.

The soldier looked morose. 'Sergeant in charge rode back to camp for water and supplies – so he said. More like a tumble with his assigned wench. We don't ruddy well get supplied with enough of anything out here. Water, decent firearms, food or grog.'

'Or women?' said Jake.

'What's *that*!' snorted the soldier. 'Ain't seen one of *them* in months.'

Jake unbuckled his saddlebag. 'Could you go a drink of rum? Better inside a man than inside a bottle, I reckon.'

The soldier downed a tot of rum in a flash and Jake was quick to encourage him.

'Send another down to chase it. All right by you if I give your men some water?'

The soldier nodded. Jake's cask was still cold with billabong water. He told the prisoners to pass it down the line. Each drank greedily before the next demanded his share.

These convicts were so rough they could pass muster as second cousins to an ape, Jake thought. The last in line was different – young, swarthily handsome with dark, wild curly hair and eyes of the same dense black. On his left chest a heart-shaped gaol tattoo held the letter K. Despite being underfed the man was tall, well-muscled and agile. Jake recognised the body of another fighter.

The water cask was empty before it reached him.

'Thanks, pal.' The prisoner shrugged, 'That was a friendly idea that ran out.'

Jake took note of the unfamiliar word 'pal' and the fact his voice had a trace of a Welsh lilt, plus something indefinably more foreign.

The soldier remained planted in the shade drinking rum, so Jake decided to chance it. He took the last rum flask from his pack and squatted beside the young convict.

'Do me a favour and finish this off for me, mate,' said Jake. 'I've got an almighty hangover.' He offered his hand. 'Name's Jake. I reckon from the looks of you, you're like me. Gone a few bare-knuckle bouts in your time, eh?'

The man hesitated in surprise then accepted the rum and the handshake.

'Name's Gem. I won nineteen out of twenty fights. Lost that one because I slipped in the mud.'

Gem sighed with appreciation as the rum hit his stomach.

'Been in the colony long?' asked Jake.

'Too bloody long. The beak insisted I build this road for them after I bolted from a pocket of hell they call Gideon Park. Know it?'

Jake nodded. 'Yeah. Same county as Ironbark and Tagalong. You're lucky to be shot of the place. Its reputation stinks to high heaven.'

'That's putting it mildly.' Gem was politely curious. 'I take it you were once one of us?'

'Pa was. He's an emancipist now. I'm as home-grown as a kangaroo.'

'So that's how kangaroos learned to box.'

Jake laughed aloud for the first time in weeks. He liked the young man's style.

'I'm a Currency Lad, all right, but don't let that fool you. I've served time. A boss cocky refused to pay me my wages. I knocked him out cold. Turns out he was a mate of the magistrate. So I did a stretch inside. But I don't intend to back up for seconds.'

'I told my wife that.' Gem shrugged. 'But here I am, working for William Four.'

'Not now you're not. He went to God – heard it straight from the town crier in Parramatta last time I came out of the Watch House. We've copped a young queen now – Victoria, not a bad looker. Well, mate, hope you dodge being sent back to Gideon Park.'

Gem took a final swig of rum. 'I might try the bushranging lark.'

Jake shook his head. 'That's a dead-end road. Stick to prize fights and you'll make your fortune. The colony's full of blokes who'd wager on flies walking up a shithouse wall.'

The soldier appeared to be itching to get the men back to work, so Jake rose.

'I'd like to watch you fight sometime, mate,' said Jake. 'But I warn you. Match yourself against me and you'll come a cropper.'

Gem's smile was confident. 'Don't bet your shirt on that, pal.'

Jake sauntered over to yarn with the soldier whose tongue was now so freed by rum he confided that he would rather be a farmer than a soldier. Jake offered him a bit of advice.

'One day you Brits will run out of prisoners. You're already beginning to flood us with free settlers. Grab yourself some land while the going's good.'

'This country's plum crazy. Seasons are arse up, the system stinks, you Cornstalks can't talk proper Queen's English and I'm buggered if I know what makes you laugh.'

'Can't fix the weather or the system,' said Jake. 'But you'll get along fine if you can cotton on to our odd sense of humour. It'll be hell for you if you don't, mate!'

Back in the saddle, Jake glanced around to see Gem giving him an ironic salute.

As he headed towards Goulburn, Jake felt light-headed, blinded by sunlight as if he had just emerged from a long dark tunnel of despair.

'Can't waste no more time feeling bloody sorry for myself, Horatio. Got to clean myself up. Get a regular job. What about Rolly Brothers? Mac says they're aiming to wedge in among the big coach companies. He reckons they're decent bosses as far as bosses go.'

Jake made Horatio a witness to his vow.

'When I'm back on my feet I'll track down my baby Pearl if it kills me. But from now on the only wife I want is the kind I can hire for the night. No woman's ever going to best Jake Andersen again!'

At the Rolly Brothers coach station outside of Goulburn Jake talked hard and fast to convince the English manager of four things. He would be an invaluable driver. He could predict a horse's temperament as soon as look at him. He knew the colony's roads like the back of his hand. He never touched a drop of grog when on the job.

Jake walked out of the office with a wide grin and tried to look casual when Mac slapped him on the back to congratulate him.

'When do you start work?'

'Next time you drive a coach to Sydney Town I'm to ride on your box seat and learn the ropes. Then drive my own coach on a new route through Liverpool, Campbelltown, the Cowpastures, Goulburn, Gunning and all. I'm in business.'

'Good on you, mate. I leave on Wednesday so let's hop over to Bolthole Valley. I'll shout the drinks till you draw your first pay.'

'I'll need more than a drink or four,' said Jake. 'I haven't bought a wife for the night in too bloody long.'

Noting Mac's surprise Jake added quickly, 'I said I was giving up *good* women for life – not the other kind!'

From his youth Jake had been no stranger to Bolthole Valley. He knew the place had once had an official name nobody bothered to use. The small respectable population was regularly swelled by drifters, escapees and cut-throats evading the law or an enemy's bullet.

After Jenny's disappearance Jake had posted her description with the local constable and Feagan's General Store, but apart from a heap of gossip, no clues had come to light.

As he and Mac rode into the village Jake thought how little it had changed since his bachelor days. The northern end of the village snaked around a rocky outcrop onto the Sydney Road. Apart from Feagan's General Store the main street boasted a bakery, produce store, livery stables, a carpenter cum coffin-maker and monumental stonemason, and a cluster of grog shanties so hastily erected they looked ready to fold like a concertina at the first breath of a westerly wind. The double-storey houses at either end of the street had always been known as the House of the Four Sisters and the Red Brumby.

Mac set up the drinks in The Shanty with No Name, placed his loan to Jake on the table then strode towards the exit.

'I'll hop down to the Red Brumby for a tick. You know me. I won't take long but I know you're a night stayer. Meet you here at breakfast.' Mac was out the door.

During his bachelor years, Jake had created many good, lusty memories in the Red Brumby but he decided not to revisit his past. As he downed his first Albion Ale, he studied the façade of the redwood timber brothel across the road, the House of the Four Sisters.

It looked respectable enough with permanently shuttered windows, window boxes of geraniums and a front door that never closed – except on Sundays when the customers used the back entrance. Chinks of red light glinted through the timber slats and laughter resounded from Madam Fleur's bar.

Jake was amused by the contrast between the men as they entered the brothel and the difference in their gait as they swaggered out. A few did not exit at all; the night stayers.

As a youth Jake's only knowledge about women had been picked up from drovers, stockmen and old lags in shanties. Despite the fact his pa had produced a steady stream of sons and one daughter, he had told Jake nothing about how people mated.

On his eighteenth birthday Jake had paid a girl at the Red Brumby to rid him of his virginity. He had enjoyed himself so much he continued the exercise.

Jake knew that women came in only two categories – good women and fallen women. Respectable folk made a rigid boundary between the two, but Jake wondered if women could ever re-cross that line to the other side. Were all fallen women born to be 'bad girls'? Could a fallen woman make a new life and regain her self-respect? Was Jenny condemned to be branded for life? Jake rejected that thought, told himself he didn't care.

Yet he winced at the memory of himself at nineteen – so crazy in love with Jenny he never doubted their lovemaking would grow naturally out of his consuming passion. All he needed was to be gentle, give her time to overcome the natural abhorrence good women felt about a man's base needs – 'the connection'. To his shock he had discovered his Red Brumby experiences had been no help on his wedding night.

After he paid for the house grog that made The Shanty with No

Name notorious, Jake returned to his seat. A man entered furtively through the rear door and sat in the far corner. Jake could smell a police informer a mile off. This one had shifty eyes, a drooping moustache and strands of ginger hair oiled across his forehead. The publican addressed him as Mr Evans and offered him a free grog – which was declined.

Jake knew Gilbert Evans by repute. The largest landowner in Ironbark was Bolthole's lay preacher and a proclaimed temperance man. So what was he doing in this shanty?

The answer was soon clear. A man dressed in black except for a flash red shirt entered between two henchmen who he dismissed as he crossed to Evans's table.

Jake knew Gideon Park's overseer more by reputation than sight. It was known he took pride in the title given him by his Irish assigned felons – the Devil Himself.

He had florid but well-defined features, a shiny black beard trimmed to a sharp point. In profile he reminded Jake of the King of Spades. Jake had learned to pinpoint settlers' origins from their accents, but the overseer's speech gave him no clues. The man could have sprung from anywhere.

One of his henchmen brought him a bottle of grog then slunk back to the bar.

'Rotgut,' the overseer said with mild contempt, but downed a glass of it. He pushed a roll of banknotes across the table and Evans furtively placed it inside his coat.

The overseer was faintly amused. 'Madam Fleur said to tell you business was slow this week.'

'A likely story.' Evans's question was muffled. 'Did you test the new merchandise?'

'Pricey. But she'll bring in the money. Loves it rough. Couldn't get enough of me.'

Jake realised the grapevine was right – Madam Fleur ran her brothel as a front for Evans. Jake felt a sting of pity for the fallen women who worked it. By indulging two-legged mongrels like this overseer, the girls protected good women. They deserved to be better paid for it.

He finished his drink and ambled across the road to the House of the Four Sisters.

Girls were draped around the darkened room in various stages of undress. Several brightened at the sight of him. Jake hoped he looked presentable. He had bathed in the creek and ironed the clean shirt he had borrowed from Mac for the morning's interview with Rolly Brothers. Women, including prostitutes, deserved a bit of respect.

He tugged at the red neckerchief that suddenly felt tight then removed his hat.

'Good evening, ladies. Er – been hot enough for you?'

The girls giggled as if he had said something clever. The boldest, a girl with dirty blonde hair, cooed in response, 'It's never too hot for me! I'm Suzanne, lovey.'

Jake was surprised by the woman who ran the place. At first glance Madam Fleur could have passed as a Nonconformist matron who went to chapel. Close up she was rather different. She steered him to an alcove where she wriggled her hips into the seat beside him. She handed him an Albion Ale with the compliments of the house and sized him up as she ran through the house rules. He would pay as soon as he made his choice.

'All good clean girls here. Not like that awful Red Brumby down the road!'

She bent her head to catch his request. 'A wife for the night?' She beamed and patted his knee. 'Obviously you're a real gent.'

'I don't know about that, Ma'am.'

Madam Fleur scurried off to greet another customer and Jake watched the girls as they moved between pools of light. His eye was caught by a redhead who sauntered down the stairs wearing a yellow Chinese robe embroidered with a black dragon. She appeared much younger than the others, but he was struck by the older expression in her hooded blue eyes. Her mouth was like a ripe plum, her complexion so fresh she had no need of the rouge other girls wore that reminded him of pink dots on the cheeks of a china doll. Red hair fell over her shoulders in disarray, suggesting she worked too hard to bother combing it between clients.

He glimpsed the bruises around her ankles – a sure sign she was another runaway assigned lass who had recently done time in the stocks.

He turned to Madam Fleur and discreetly nodded his head in this girl's direction.

Madam Fleur seemed faintly surprised by his choice. 'She'll cost double.'

'Righto.' Hat in hand, Jake crossed the room to the girl in the yellow robe.

'Good evening. I'm Jakob Andersen. Jake. You by any chance free all night?'

She smiled and nodded. 'For you I am, *cheri*. I am Lily Pompadour from gay Paree.'

Jake wasn't familiar with French accents, but having a mother raised in Dublin he could spot an Irish dialect a mile off. He went along with the game.

'A French lass, eh? It's a pleasure to meet you, Miss Lily. May I buy you a drink?'

He was not surprised when she ordered a bottle of French champagne to be sent upstairs to their room. Clearly Madam Fleur had her girls well trained.

At the foot of the staircase he offered Lily Pompadour his arm, a gesture that seemed to catch her unawares but she recovered fast. 'Always the gentleman, *cheri*?'

'I hope not so much that I'll disappoint you, Miss Lily.'

Her smile was disarming but Jake recognised her manner was

professional when she closed the door behind them and ran her hand down his chest inside his shirt.

'Perhaps we are both in for some surprises tonight, eh *cheri*?'

Her dimly lit room had red and gold wallpaper and a large brass bed. A Chinese screen was folded to give him a nice view of her milk-white body as she changed into a bit of flimsy black lace. She draped one hand on the screen as she showed herself to full effect.

Jake had stripped off his shirt and unbuckled his belt. 'I bathed this morning but no doubt you'd care to wash what matters, just to be sure.'

Lily nodded and Jake enjoyed the cool touch of her fingers. Then she surprised him. She held out a rope and whip. 'Your generosity entitles you to other pleasures.'

He gave a dismissive wave. 'Not to my taste, love, but if you're willing to take me on, I'd like something else from you.'

Lily's fixed smile almost faltered. 'Your pleasure is my pleasure, *cheri*.'

'It's Jake. Thanks, but I'm not paying to hear false sweet talk. I want you to be straight with me. I always enjoy going to bed with a woman.' He felt suddenly embarrassed. 'The problem is I want to learn what makes a *woman* happy – in connection.'

Lily stared at him. Her French accent suddenly disappeared. 'All in one night?'

'Hell no. I don't expect miracles. I've just been hired as a coach driver so I'll pass through Bolthole every few weeks. If I keep coming to see you, will you—?'

'I'll talk straight. And I promise you, Jake, you'll love every minute of what I'm going to teach you.' She took his hand and led him to the bed. 'Lesson one,' she said softly.

Next morning as he dressed in the half light Jake studied Lily Pompadour's sleeping face. Her arms lay above her head on the pillow, a painful reminder of Jenny the very last time he had seen her. He pushed aside the sharp memory.

When he dropped one of his riding boots the sound woke Lily. She rolled over onto her stomach and gave him a naughty sidelong glance from under her tangled mane of hair.

Her voice was an impure invitation. 'You'll come back to me for more, Jake?'

He pulled on his left banking boot. It was empty now but would be healthy again after he drew his first Rolly Brothers pay cheque and repaid Mac's loan.

'All right, girl. What's your verdict?'

'If I said you had no problem, you wouldn't come back. That's bad for business.'

'You agreed to talk straight, remember?'

'I am. The first time you were so excited you couldn't last long enough. Happens a lot. Once you were familiar with my body you were very good, very strong. Next time I'll teach you clever new tricks. How to delay your own pleasure and drive a woman crazy.'

She lazily waved him goodbye. 'Is that worth a second bite of the cherry, Jake?'

His short laugh had an edge. 'Try and stop me, Lily.'

As he crossed the road to The Shanty with No Name he saw Mac had already set up their drinks for breakfast. Jake was never guilty of allowing a cold Albion Ale to grow warm.

On the day before his scheduled departure for Sydney Town on Mac's coach, Jake rode Horatio towards the turn-off signpost that read 'Ironbark – One Mile' but he knew the village was really a bushman's mile off the Sydney Road. The last time he had passed through Ironbark was en route to Tagalong to see Mac about the Bulldog Kane match. He had been light of heart, sure he would soon be holding Jenny in his arms. That day seemed a lifetime away. Now he was in search of his bolting wife. One-horse towns had long memories.

Ahead of him on the Sydney Road stood a stationary wagon piled with packing cases. The line of the driver's slouched shoulders had the familiar look of a New Chum lost in the bush. He was hunched over a map, swearing loudly.

As Jake rode up to help the man find his bearings, he grinned in recognition. There was no mistaking the stuttering surgeon who had stitched him up at the Rum Hospital.

Dr Ross spoke as if to a stranger. 'Could you kindly direct me to Barnes's Farm, Sir? This map is bloody useless except for getting a body lost.'

Jake pretended not to know him at first. 'Can't miss it. Just follow the road till you come to a scribbly gum. Cross a wobbly bridge. The turn-off to the left leads straight there.'

'Thank you. But what in God's name is a scribbly gum?'

'The white trunk looks like kiddies scribbled over it. Don't remember me, eh Doc?'

The Highlander frowned. 'Aye, you're the lad crowned by a flying bottle in The Rocks. I'm surprised you can remember me. Roaring drunk as I recall.'

'Guilty as charged but you did a good job. Right as rain now. Can I shout you a drink, Doc?' Jake reached for the whisky flask in his saddlebag.

'Much obliged to you, but I'm on my way to inspect a property for sale. Barnes's Farm. I understand the locals are in dire need of a physician in these parts.'

'Last one died at the bottom of a bottle. The farm ain't a bad bit of dirt but it's got a funny reputation. Known as the Haunted Farm. The story goes Barnes was a wife-beater. In 1825 he went to God with a hatchet in his skull courtesy of a convict protecting Barnes's wife. Play your cards right, you'll cop it for a song. That's if you don't hold with that ghost bullshit.'

Dr Ross's mouth twitched. 'Aye. Sheer drivel. Thanks for your advice, Mr—?'

'Name's Jake. Good luck, Doc. If I cop the wrong end of another fight, I'll know where to come.'

'In that case I suspect I'll be seeing a fair bit of ye. What are the odds of running into you twice over such a great distance?'

'You ain't in England now, Doc. There's only fifty-five thousand of us white fellas – half of them convicts – scattered down the whole of the colony from Moreton Bay to Port Phillip. And bloody few roads. You'll find we all keep bumping into each other, like it or not.'

Jake realised the irony of his words. *So why can't I bloody well find my own wife?*

CHAPTER 10

Keziah Stanley lay in the darkness on her bunk on the *Harlequin* unable to sleep because of her rising sense of excitement. For days whenever the weather was fine and the winds favourable they had hugged the coastline close enough to catch glimpses of the eastern seaboard of the Australian continent. Rumour onboard was they would sight the Heads of Port Jackson tomorrow!

After fourteen weeks at sea Keziah had totally assumed her new identity as the widow Mrs Smith, taking elaborate care to hide her past and future plans to prevent the Morgans from finding her. Each day, rain, hail or shine, she had remained on deck, not only to escape the fetid air below and her fellow passengers but to disguise her morning sickness as seasickness.

Keziah looked around at the figures sleeping in tiers of bunks that lined the ship's hull. Each bunk provided barely enough room to turn over and there was only twenty-four inches headroom between bunks. After a lifetime of freedom on the open road it was galling to be confined with thirty *gaujo* immigrants in their section, forced to eat and wash in this cramped passengers' mess – a communal space shared not only with women and sickly children but lusty husbands who demanded their conjugal rights during the night.

Keziah had long since devoured her share of rations but the babe in her womb reminded her she must find something to stave off her hunger pains. How long till dawn?

In the darkness she carefully drew her shawl across her growing belly. But there was no disguising breasts that strained the confines of her bodice.

Keziah sighed. If only this child had been Gem's.

Passing the ship's galley she saw the cook was slumped asleep. She helped herself to a hunk of cheese and a crust of stale bread and made her way up on deck.

She clung to the railing to stay upright against the ship's roll as she searched the horizon. The first traces of dawn came with a breeze that whipped hair around her face and refreshed her spirits. She admired the nimble climb of a seaman to the crow's nest, while others chanted their work songs in unison and expertly unfurled sails to take advantage of the wind.

There was a jubilant cry from the crow's nest, 'Land ahoy!' The sun blazed with tropical intensity and Keziah gasped as the *Harlequin* sailed into an amazingly large expanse of harbour. She was forcibly reminded that November was late spring down here at the bottom of the world and already far hotter than many a high summer she had known in Wales.

She held her breath at the sight of the islands that lay like floating gems on the harbour. On their port side one small island shaped like a tree-covered pyramid flashed a warning light to ships. A sailor was quick to explain.

'That be Pinchgut, Ma'am. Not long since prisoners who stole food were strung up on a gibbet at the highest point. Left to rot as a warning to other thieves.' He added under his breath, 'The good old days, they called 'em. I hear the authorities be more civilised now. They just chain the poor wretches alive out in the open.'

Keziah grasped the rail, weak at the knees. What if Gem had suffered that same fate?

'There's a big island beyond Sydney Cove, a few miles down the Parramatta River. The blackfellas call it Biloela, others Cockatoo Island. They're building a penal settlement there for the most hardened felons – a gaol none can ever escape.'

Cockatoo Island. A pleasant name yet it somehow filled Keziah with dread. Surely Gem could not be regarded as a hardened criminal? Her eyes searched the southern cove for some sign of government buildings. Where on earth should she begin her search for him?

The sailor pointed in the direction of sandstone buildings – Fort Macquarie, Dawes Point Barracks and the old Government House. Did he suspect the reason for her curiosity?

'Over there's the Department of the Superintendent of Convicts. A good place to start for any interested party who wants to trace a convict friend or relative.' His words had a comforting ring. 'Some of the colony's model citizens are former convicts. Australia gives many a second chance. See them fine buildings over yonder built by the emancipist Samuel Terry? He donates his brass to every cause and religion. The richest man in the colony, he is.'

Keziah smiled her thanks. *One day my Gem will be like Samuel Terry. Maybe not rich, but better than that – a free man!*

Keziah let out a whoop of pleasure when flocks of rainbow lorikeets swooped in vivid slashes of blue, emerald, red and gold. The fantastically high sky was like a ceiling in some fairytale mansion, its colour a mirror image of the blue harbour. The air was so sultry with exotic perfumes Keziah felt half drunk with pleasure, until she realised that when Gem saw this scene, he must have wondered if he'd ever be free to leave it.

'I don't care where I live, Gem,' she whispered, 'as long as I'm with you.'

Keziah remembered the bulge under her skirt. She added under her breath, 'I forgot *you*. But you're a problem I'll have to solve another day.'

Keziah grabbed her carpet bag and hurried down the wharf towards The Rocks area that lay before her on the western wing of Sydney Cove. She was conscious she must count every penny she spent, but she decided it was worth spending extra coins on a safe room. She could always read *gaujos'* palms if her money ran dry.

Her room in a boarding house on the uppermost ridge of The Rocks was barren but surprisingly clean. Now she could wash herself and her clothing the Romani way for the first time since she left England.

To Keziah the greatest blessing was the window because it looked across the rooftops of the squalid tenement cottages below. This view gave her a cloudless blue sky and a generous expanse of the harbour where ships sailed in and out of the bustling port.

Australia. Keziah saw her new world through Romani eyes. Despite the man-made squalor sandwiched in the alleys below her, the vast landscape bordering the harbour had an alien, lush beauty. The vitality in the air seemed to promise a bold future to anyone with courage to take hold of it.

With The Rocks behind her, she made her way through a comparatively civilised section of George Street which displayed a wide range of goods – from exotic tropical fruit and English vegetables to liquor stores, inns, fashionable clothing, antiques and pawnbrokers. Keziah was aware that much of the silverware and jewellery openly on sale in Sydney Town were English stolen goods more safely disposed of here than at Home. What a topsy-turvy world this colony was – with its new codes of morality and levels of society – and opportunities to bend the law!

When she saw rainbow-coloured parrots in birdcages hanging in the doorways of shops, their squawking sounded so plaintive she longed to buy them and set them free but knew her money must be conserved.

Fashionably dressed women promenaded with red-coated military officers who sweltered in their serge uniforms, their English complexions pink under shako helmets.

Shaven-headed convicts marched shackled together under military guard. Dark-skinned natives smoked pipes and seemed to wear any discarded European article that took their fancy.

Despite the seductive quality of this alien world Keziah had no time to linger. All that mattered was finding Gem before the babe stretched her belly and flaunted her adultery.

In the Department of the Superintendent of Convicts Keziah waited impatiently until she was interviewed. The smug clerk had a dirty rim around his collar and dropped his H's. He was clearly more intent on studying her bosom than aiding her search.

'This assigned convict Gem Smith, is he your husband, Madam?'

Was it to her advantage to answer yes or no? She made a quick decision. 'A close family member. I'd be grateful if you'd look up your – what is it – Convict Muster records?'

The clerk opened a weighty ledger. 'You Smiths must breed like rabbits.'

Keziah was angry enough to wipe the smile off his face with her fist but knew it was not wise to alienate him so she tried to sound helpful.

'His name is G-E-M. Age twenty. Born in Wales. You can't have too many Smiths answering that description, can you?'

The clerk worked a dirty fingernail down the list. 'Says here Jem Smith with a J. Age: twenty-one. Hair: black. Eyes: dark brown. Complexion: swarthy. Height: 5 feet 10 inches – a tall 'un! Can't read nor write. Tried at Glamorgan Assizes. Place of birth: Llangadfan, Wales. Religion: pagan. Crime: horse theft. Sentence: seven years. Remarks: strong build, Gypsy appearance, heart-shaped tattoo on left chest with letter K – that be for you, eh?' the clerk smirked.

Keziah wasn't biting. 'Where is he now?'

'Says he was assigned to Julian Jonstone Esquire at Gideon Park, near Lake Incognito.'

'Kindly show me where that is on your map.'

The clerk pressed close behind her as he led her to the wall map. Keziah tried to avoid breathing in. He smelled like he hadn't bathed for a year.

The map confused her. She expected to see the outline of an island but there was only a single strip of blue ocean down the right-hand side of it.

'This can't be the map of Australia.'

'Heavens no, just the east coast, the Colony of New South Wales.' He drew a rough circle with his finger. 'The whole of Mother England would fit into that there little part.'

Keziah felt overwhelmed by the size of this new land, but she prompted him about Gem's location.

He pointed out a spot on the map. 'Lake Incognito may well be gone. Has a habit of disappearing every few years.'

She returned to the desk to regain the merciful distance between them.

'I'll take a chance on that. Kindly direct me to the coaching station.'

The clerk was in no hurry to lose sight of her bosom.

'You'd be on a wild-goose chase, girl. Note here says Jem Smith absconded.'

Keziah hated to admit her ignorance. 'You mean he's been transferred?'

'Bolted.' He read the notes aloud. 'Recaptured last March then got hisself chained in an iron gang building a road in the bush. Due to be returned to Gideon Park. Bolted again early this month. It's likely he's took up arms as a bushranger. What we call highwaymen at Home.'

For a moment Keziah felt she was going to faint in horror. She swayed, gripping the edge of the desk. The clerk gave her a broad wink.

'Best you wait. Troopers'll catch him for you. If they don't shoot him dead first.'

Keziah stepped out into heat so intense she felt she had entered the door of an oven. She dry-retched when the babe in her womb made a sickening movement. Was she going to miscarry again? She didn't have the energy to care one way or another.

She sank down beside the harbour wall, her head in her hands.

She felt like she had run into a brick wall. What skills did she have to survive this upside-down world? She could read, but only very slowly. Could only write her name and the alphabet. Her knowledge of herbs would be limited here – she had no idea which would grow in this sandy soil! She knew with her gift for reading Tarot she would never be hungry if she stayed in Sydney Town. But what good was that when Gem was miles away, an outlaw in the bush? He could be anywhere, unaware she had arrived.

Struck by a thought she sat bolt upright. 'But Gem knows *me*. Better than anyone. He knows I belong to him and I'd follow him to the ends of the earth.' She looked wryly around her. 'Which is exactly where I am right now!'

Resolutely she climbed the stone stairs to her boarding house. Near the top of the ridge she gained fresh heart from a swarm of squawking white parrots that settled in a mass covering the branches of a tree. The parrots' sulphur crests fanned out like the petals of strange flowers as they noisily conversed together.

Those parrots stick together like family. Gem is the only family I have left in the world.

That night Keziah tossed and turned as she tried to free herself from a nightmare in which the disturbing outline of an alien tree dominated a series of violent images. Red blood gushed forth from the tree's trunk and fell upon the earth.

'*Mi-duvel!* What savagery lies ahead? May *The Del* protect you, Gem.'

But no prayers were strong enough to wipe the image of that ghastly tree from her mind. Keziah clung to the silver amulet and her grandmother's words that she had nothing to fear as long as she had the amulet to protect her. A gnawing sensation in her stomach reminded Keziah she had eaten nothing for hours. She climbed out of bed.

'All right. I know you're hungry, little one. It's *my* fault you're on the way, no fault of yours.'

Soaking stale bread in water to soften it, she chewed it bite for bite with a juicy pear. The dark velvet sky was studded with more stars than she had ever seen in her life. Their crazy patterns bore little resemblance to the constellations she had learned as a child.

Keziah ran her hand across her belly and spoke to the little soul inside her.

'Tomorrow will bring us the answer and show us the road we are meant to take.'

CHAPTER 11

The distant, metallic sound of an iron bar beating the sides of a triangle caused Daniel Browne a familiar wave of anger, even though this was Gideon Park's signal to mark the midday respite in the day's labours.

He dropped, exhausted, under the shade of an ironbark tree and wolfed down the contents of his tin dish, leaving the empty plate to draw a swarm of blowflies. As usual, today's meagre portion of watered-down stew looked as if it was seasoned with maggots, but after a year of abysmal rations Daniel managed to devour this meal without his gorge rising. The evening meal in the convicts' mess would be even fouler.

Daniel always sat apart from his fellow convicts, knowing how they held him in contempt. Their guttural tones were punctuated by crude laughter, when one pointed him out as 'that arty bastard who walks alone – and sleeps alone'.

Daniel tried to ignore their taunts. Let them pair off with their convict 'wives'. He had witnessed men snitch on their partners for an illicit nip of rum. *The buggers think I don't owe loyalty to anyone. They're right! If I have no friend or confidante, no bastard can betray me.*

Yet he was forced to ask himself. How long before he sold his own soul?

On his assignment to Gideon Park, Daniel had forged his desperate plan for survival. In theory it was simple. To work until he dropped, without complaint, so that his overseer never had cause to have him flogged for even the slightest misdemeanour.

But Daniel had soon realised that he would not last seven years of daily hunger gnawing at his belly or facing the never-ending fear he would be the next victim of the lash. His only hope of escaping this hellish existence was Saranna Plews. Each day he waited with diminishing hope for some word from her, even though he knew it would take months for a ship to bring it. A visiting Catholic priest, Father Declan, had mailed the desperate letter Daniel had written her on his arrival. The cleric's initial advice had given Daniel a wild surge of hope. If his fiancée came free to the colony and applied to the governor for permission to marry him, there was a good chance Daniel would be transferred from Gideon Park and legally assigned to his wife. The authorities considered that convict marriages helped balance the disproportionate ratio of men to women in the colony. Marriage was seen to be an antidote to the fornication that was rife, as well as other abominations.

Daniel notched off the weeks on his cabin wall. He clung to the memory of Saranna in court crying out her promise to follow him. Yet he could not dismiss that other memory – being marched out of Chester and seeing Saranna turn her back on him. Had she already changed her mind? Slowly he hardened his heart towards her. *That mouse cares more about what society thinks of her than she does about my fate.*

He glanced at his fellow convicts. They meant nothing to him, except as subjects to draw whenever he managed to scrounge blank paper and lumps of charcoal from the ashes of a fire. Brutish faces for the most part, except for one. He looked across at Will Martens. At fifteen, the youngest new arrival was the fresh butt of the older prisoners' cruel pranks, but Will was fast learning the art of survival. Daniel studied the lad's slight, boyish frame. Despite his leg-irons, Will was gyrating in an impromptu sailors' hornpipe to the tune of 'Nancy Dawson' for the amusement of his bullies. By the time he sang the chorus for the second time, 'Her easy mien, her shape so neat. She foots, she trips, she looks so sweet. Her every motion's so complete, I die for Nancy Dawson!' the lad actually had the toughest bullies clapping their hands to give him the beat.

Daniel was aware Will was trying to catch his eye, but he refused to return Will's cocksure grin. *The boy's a fool. He follows me around like a puppy. He'd best look elsewhere for a champion to defend him.*

At the approach of the overseer mounted on his black stallion, Daniel masked his angry thoughts. *No doubt* your *belly is full. A fine meal cooked by your pathetic rag of a wife. Pork and wine bought with money you pocket selling the government rations meant to feed* us.

Rumour gave the man many names, including Iago and James, but he was widely known by the title he earned after he ordered an Irish lad to be flogged with fifty lashes. His victim had cursed him with his dying breath, 'As God is my witness ye are the Devil Himself!' Since then the overseer had flaunted this title with pride.

Daniel jumped to attention along with all the others – even seasoned bullies cowered in the overseer's presence. Daniel's eye was drawn to the man's sensual, aquiline features, the glossy hair and beard that seemed cut from the same dense black as his horse's mane. Daniel knew from experience that the voice was never more dangerous than when it was soft with sarcasm.

'I see all you Miss Mollies are devoted to your labours. Didn't I order you to remove those stumps? You'll have the ground furrowed by tomorrow for crop planting.'

There was an uneasy rumble of assent. The Devil Himself sighed as if he was forced to carry the weight of the world on his broad shoulders.

'You'll work through the night,' he said with quiet menace. 'No water for you laggards till the job's done.' He turned and looked directly at Daniel. 'I appoint you to see that these sods carry out my orders, Daniel Browne.'

Daniel flinched but mumbled agreement. Inwardly he was appalled. *Why does he single me out? Surely he knows how the men hate me. He may intend it as a mark of favour, but I'd have a better chance to survive those bullies without it.*

When the Devil Himself rode off, Daniel was suddenly aware he was the focus of the men surrounding him. Many had long ago abandoned any vestige of humanity. Forced to conceal their hatred of the Devil Himself, they were now openly channelling their rage at *him*.

Avoiding their eyes, he pushed through the crowd and hurried to the paddock where he had been ordered to work. He examined his 'artist's hands' with despair. They were calloused and raw, the nails split and rimmed with blood, the palms swollen after weeks of wielding a virtually useless pick to free giant tree roots. He began to swing his axe in a rhythm that distracted him from the pain of his aching back as fresh rivulets of sweat ran down his chest to his loins, darkening the old sweat stains on his trousers.

When he heard his name spoken in an excited whisper Daniel looked up in irritation at the cheeky face of Will Martens, who was leaning on a spade as if enjoying a holiday in the sun.

'You deaf? You heard the overseer's orders. Hold your tongue and keep working.'

Will edged closer to disguise their conversation. 'Meet me tonight. I have a plan I promise will hold your interest.'

'You? You're all talk. Your mouth will be the death of you.'

Will furtively took a peach from his pocket and handed it to Daniel. It was the first one Daniel had seen in a year. The last he had tasted was at the Plews's house. Saranna had hand-fed him slivers of the delicious juicy fruit. Her heart in her eyes as she quoted, 'Sweets to the sweet …'

'Go on, eat it,' Will urged. 'Ain't poisoned.'

Daniel eyed the peach with suspicion but hunger overcame him and he sank his teeth with relish into the ripe flesh.

Will looked smug. 'I've been moonlighting. Acting cockatoo for a pair of bolters who took up arms. I always get back here by dawn. So the Devil Himself is none the wiser.'

'Then you're an even bigger idiot than I took you for. He knows everything!'

Will pressed on. 'The lads pay me in food and a few spare coins. I've got quite a taste for the life. Freedom. Nothing like it!'

'More fool you. Get cracking and do your share of labour. I'll not risk my neck for any daft escape plan of yours.'

'Not even to buy fresh drawing paper?' Will's eyes teased him with laughter.

Daniel was angry to hear his art dismissed as a joke. 'Shut your face. I've got my own way of doing business.'

Will walked off and Daniel re-doubled his work efforts. But his shrinking belly felt as if it were being gnawed by a rat.

A few days later, trudging wearily towards his cabin after a day and night of work Daniel was halted by the unmistakable sound that always made his blood run cold. The lash. A flogging.

He knew what to expect. The Jonstones were said to be due back any day after attending the Governor's Ball in Parramatta. Until then the overseer took control. By law he was meant to send errant convicts before a magistrate, but the Devil Himself enjoyed the power of ordering illicit floggings. In Jonstone's absence the overseer was a law unto himself.

Daniel heard the regular rhythm of the lash echoing through the bush as he drew closer to the source. He was sickened by the fear that one day he would be the lash's target. As usual there was a crowd of assigned men ordered by the Devil Himself to witness the flogging to deter them. But this time something was wrong. There were no screams. If the victim wasn't crying to God or hanging unconscious from the flogging post surely he must be dead.

Through a break in the trees Daniel saw that this prisoner was young, his legs defiantly astride as he braced himself against the steady rhythm of leather thongs whipping his back. Sweat matted his hair and coated his body. Although blood welled up from his 'stripes' not a single sound passed the young man's lips.

The crowd of assigned men shrank back from the victim's splattering blood.

As he drew closer, Daniel recognised the prisoner's piercing black eyes, the olive-skinned body with the heart tattooed on his chest. Who else but Gem Smith could bare his teeth in such a ghastly grin as if he was welcoming each stroke of the lash? Unable to bear the look on Gem's face, Daniel moved to the rear of the circle of prisoners.

The Devil Himself sat stony-faced in his saddle, forced to confront what was clear to every man in the crowd. He could wait till Doomsday and never hear the Gypsy beg for mercy.

Finally the hated soft voice ordered the scourger to cease. 'His silence bores me.'

Daniel tried to remain invisible when Will made the first move to cut the victim free. Gem was determined to walk unaided. He smiled at his overseer with charming insolence.

'Failed to amuse you did I, Mr Iago?'

Daniel was shocked by the Gypsy's courage.

The Devil Himself stiffened but refused to lose face.

'Two hours to lick your wounds, Gypsy, then it's back to work. That's the price you pay for bolting from Gideon Park.' He turned to face his assigned men. 'The same goes for you bludgers. Return to your labours!'

Like a disturbed ants' nest they scattered in all directions, except Daniel who backed away but remained to watch, camouflaged by the trees. For one moment he was tempted to break his cover and rush to Gem's aid but that would mean breaking his ironclad rule – never to be involved in any man's troubles. So he remained hidden.

He saw that Gem had been left to lie face down in the shade of a tree. Will Martens ran to him with drinking water and a bowl of salt.

'Brave bugger, I'll say that for you,' Will said as he gingerly sponged the bloody welts that cross-hatched Gem's back. 'I take it this is your first flogging?'

Gem's voice was dark with hatred. 'And I guarantee it'll be my last, pal.'

'Steel yourself. I'm going to pack your wounds with salt. It'll hurt like buggery. Can't avoid scarring but it will stop infection from setting in.'

Daniel saw that in Will's presence Gem dropped all bravado, giving in to each application of salt with a muffled groan.

'Your hands are as gentle as a girl's, Will Martens.'

'Hey, make no mistake,' Will said quickly. 'I may be small like a girl but I can out-ride and out-shoot the lot of you. I ain't no convict's wife!'

Gem gave a wry laugh. 'Don't worry about me, pal. My taste don't run to boys. I have eyes for no one but my own true love.'

'Married, I take it?'

'For life. A Romani lass with hair that shines like a blackbird's wing. And blue eyes a man'd die for.' He grimaced with pain. 'You're doing a fine job. I'm in your debt.'

Daniel noted Will Martens was unusually hesitant. 'It's not fair to beg a favour at a moment like this but one day you might care to teach me a few bare-knuckle fighter's tricks – how to handle men bigger than me.' Will shrugged, 'Which means just about every man in the colony!'

Gem held out his hand for the boy to shake. 'My pleasure, pal. You can count on it.'

He gave an involuntary groan as he moved to a sitting position to drink the water.

'I'd best return to work. Can't let the Devil think he's broken me!'

As Daniel watched Gem doggedly return to work, he felt shamed by his failure to come to the courageous Gypsy's aid. He slipped away to his hidden store of paper, intent on capturing the scene he had just witnessed. The white-hot rush of creation promised him it would be a remarkable piece of work.

The following day Daniel was surprised to be reassigned to far less arduous work – tending a section of the garden close to the two-storey sandstone Georgian mansion that was the Jonstones' country residence.

He felt grateful for this rare chance to be alone in congenial surroundings. The flowerbeds reminded him of a transplanted corner of England. The serenity was broken by the noisy arrival of the master's mud-splattered family coach. It drew up sharply before the front portico to allow the prematurely stooped Julian Jonstone and his pale, fragile wife to alight. They were said to be cousins and Daniel saw their features were indeed identical. Without pausing to break step, the master ordered an assigned woman to carry his little daughter Victoria to her room.

The sudden flurry of activity intrigued Daniel as a stream of servants rushed to unload crates full of exotic fruits with tantalising aromas. Assigned men ran to the cool room to liberate carcasses of beef and lamb – food that was a memory to Daniel.

A second carriage arrived with its roof piled high with luggage. Three young men jumped out and unloaded cases that seemed to hold musical instruments. One man carried a cello as tenderly as a father holds his child.

Musicians! Daniel was excited by the promise of an assembly – brilliant costumes, dancing, a glimpse of the outside world to translate into art. He desperately wanted to get close enough to observe it. Yet if he were caught spying on his betters he would be flogged. At the thought of that, perspiration broke out on his face and ran down his neck, but he kept on working.

The next arrival was the most splendid English carriage he had ever seen. Coachman and footman were garbed in blue and gold livery, white periwigs under tricorn hats – outlandish costumes in this remote bush setting but their grandeur was not diminished by the fine coat of dust that covered them from head to foot.

Daniel had a sense of awe when he saw the coat of arms on the carriage door partially obscured by mud. It was well known that the Jonstones moved at the highest levels of society in Sydney Town. Could this carriage be bearing the governor himself?

It revealed someone even more exciting. He was transfixed by the young woman who alighted, dressed in silk that shimmered as she spun around like a doll on a music box.

Daniel had trained his eye to absorb rapidly the details of any face he wished to draw but never in his life had he seen anything so exquisitely beautiful.

As if conscious of the intensity of his gaze the girl turned to meet his eyes, giving him a secretive, knowing smile. Then she entered the Jonstone house on the arm of her travelling companion, a richly dressed gentleman.

Despite the risk of discovery, Daniel ran to his hidden hoard of paper and began to sketch the young woman, burning to see her again to study her beauty. He was confident he had captured her coquettish eyes, the provocative pout of her red mouth. But the nose wasn't right. Was it tip-tilted? And there was something very odd about the intricate coil of her lustrous black hair.

The sound of a soprano singing a German love song drifted on the night air. It attracted Daniel like the siren call of the Lorelei, the legendary enchantress that an old salt had warned him led sailors to their doom. Climbing up into an apple tree Daniel skinned his leg but a bloody knee was a small price to pay for a ringside view of the ballroom. Dancing couples whirled past the open French windows like patterns in a kaleidoscope.

He caught his breath when the diminutive beauty he had glimpsed that morning drifted out onto the terrace, fluttering a black lace fan as delicate as a spider's web. Positioning herself on a seat to take advantage of the breeze, she drank from a crystal goblet.

Her black hair was elaborately piled in a knot on the top of her head and decorated with feathers and a jewelled comb, a single long curl had escaped down one cheek. Plump, snow-white shoulders rose above the lace décolletage of a black satin ball gown, its bodice and skirt embroidered with bouquets of gold and scarlet flowers. Daniel was charmed by the way she pouted, then with an irritable swish of her skirts made her way down to the lawn. He was alarmed to see her heading straight towards the apple tree. Another few steps and she would discover him.

Her smile was a tease. 'What have we here? A young man hiding in a tree. I saw you in the garden this morning. You couldn't take your eyes off me. What's your name, boy?'

'Daniel Browne, Ma'am. Please, you mustn't talk to me. Master wouldn't like it.'

'Nonsense. No one tells *me* what to do.' She emptied her glass and Daniel suspected she was slightly tipsy.

Carelessly she tossed her empty goblet on the grass. She held his eye as she tweaked the neckline of her gown lower before leaning her elbows on the low stone wall that separated them. The upper curve of her breasts was so clear in the moonlight that Daniel saw the beauty spot Nature had placed in a most seductive place.

'Do you like my dress? It's French,' she asked him.

'Not as beautiful as the girl who—' He halted, appalled by his audacity.

'The girl who wears it?' Her laughter was infectious. 'My! You are quite the young gallant, are you not?'

Daniel smiled despite his nerves. There was a safe distance between them but he suspected she enjoyed the novelty of flirting with a stranger. Did she guess he was a convict?

She picked up an apple that had fallen on her side of the wall and played with it as if it were a child's ball. Her voice was almost a purr.

'Do you like the taste of forbidden fruit, lad? Eve gave Adam an apple like this one.'

The inference was unmistakable and Daniel was alerted by a flash of danger. 'Please Ma'am, you best go inside. I must return to my cabin.'

'Oh. Did you not come free, Daniel Browne?'

Daniel wanted to run from the scene but was afraid of offending her.

'I'm assigned to Master Jonstone, Ma'am,' he admitted.

'Ó la la! A convict. I'd never have guessed. Your face is quite handsome. You speak like a gentleman.' She giggled. 'What naughty thing did you do to be transported?'

'I was innocent of the charge, Ma'am,' Daniel said quickly. He had repeated this claim so often he hoped one day he would believe it himself.

'I see you're blushing, Daniel, how sweet,' she teased.

'Forgive me, lady, but I *must* go!'

His heart raced in fear as a gentleman appeared on the terrace. Julian Jonstone! Daniel panicked. He leapt down from the tree and bolted into the bush. A backward glance saw the girl tuck her hand through Jonstone's arm and gaze up at her host as if he was a knight who had come to her rescue.

'How foolish of me, Julian. Was I in any danger do you think?'

Daniel was short of breath when he slid into his bunk in the darkness. He lay awake going over every detail of the night, every curve of her body, every angle of her exquisite face. If only he had the paints and brushes to immortalise her. The girl with no name had the face of a naughty angel. A body like Helen of Troy. Men would risk their lives, their empires to possess her.

Daniel felt a wave of confusion. Although she did not stir him physically, she excited him so much that his hand and his imagination itched to record her beauty for posterity.

Dawn brought changes that were as always beyond his control. Daniel was summoned to a distant paddock to remove the stumps of trees.

Ironbarks. Tough as hell. Just my damned luck. I trust the others assigned to the job are strong enough to pull their weight.

The Devil Himself rode past on his prancing stallion and wagged a warning finger.

'Mind this teaches you to keep your eyes off your betters, Daniel Browne. Master doesn't take kindly to a convict so bold he frightens his lovely guest of honour!'

'I'd never be guilty of hurting a lady, Sir. I regret very much if I frightened her.'

Daniel expected his defence to be met with disdain. So why was the overseer smiling?

'I believe you, Daniel. Ladies of the Quality are well beyond your taste, are they not?'

The Devil Himself gave a short laugh that left Daniel confused. Less serious misdemeanours had earned other assigned men the lash. Why was he being lenient with him?

The overseer's face was in profile as he casually asked the question. 'I take it you were transported with a certain Maynard Plews. You were his partner in crime were you not?'

Daniel flushed and said automatically, 'I was innocent, Sir.'

'Quite so – you *all* are! But it may interest you to know Plews was assigned to the lime kilns in Newcastle. Being half submerged in water each day did not agree with him. He drowned. Some say by his own hand.'

After the overseer rode away Daniel was overwhelmed by conflicting emotions. Shock, sadness, a resurgence of grief for his role in shortening the old man's life. Then he experienced a fresh layer of shame that sprang from his acute sense of relief. Now there was no one left alive to expose his guilt! A sudden thought chilled him. Or did that power now rest in the hands of the Devil Himself?

Daniel only realised the full extent of his punishment when he sighted a mammoth stump so deeply rooted in the earth it appeared to reach to the depths of hell. He alone was assigned to dig it out.

His mind seethed with rage. That little vixen had enticed him to talk to her. Played with him like a kitten with a ball of wool. In frustration he turned his anger on Saranna. She had promised to follow him to the ends of the earth. Where the hell was she? He swung his pick violently against the tree stump.

Women – you can't trust any of the bitches.

CHAPTER 12

Jake Andersen swore under his breath as he checked the names and destinations of the five passengers on his list. He wanted to get everything right on his first job as driver of a Rolly Brothers coach. But he knew this trip would prove an uphill battle. *Jesus wept! Good women are as scarce as hen's teeth in the colony. Just my bloody luck to cop two out of five. A spinster and a widow. Both just off the bloody boat from England. No doubt they'll be as picky as hell. I'm gunna be stuck with them for weeks!*

Jake checked the time by the White Horse Tavern clock. Six o'clock. High time for the coach to depart. But he only had one of his five passengers in hand. Through the window he could see Dr Fergus O'Flaherty inside the tavern's coach office having one for the road from his silver flask. Jake had already strapped the Irishman's case of whisky on the roof but he wasn't expecting any grief from that quarter – the doc was such a gent he doffed his hat to every woman he passed.

Jake carefully re-checked his team of horses, more than ready to get the coach on the road. He was never too impressed by the size and clamour of Sydney Town. It might seem like a drop in the ocean compared with England's towns but it was still too big for him.

He blew into the palms of his hands to warm them and surveyed the traffic hurtling along George Street, the main artery in and out of town. There were humble 'shay carts', four-in-hands, hackney carriages, jaunty gigs and wagons loaded with farm produce from Windsor and Parramatta. It was market day and barrows were being heaped with vegetables and fruit. The street swarmed with men. The only females in sight were weathered farmers' wives or weary, hip-swaying women who Jake knew were eyeing him off as a prospective customer.

A young girl paused to try her luck. Greasy hair hung over a bare shoulder and she smelled of gin but her voice was hopeful. 'What's your fancy, love?'

Jake tipped his hat. 'Thanks but it's more than my job's worth to leave my horses.'

She disappeared into the crowd as if she had never existed.

Jake felt a catch in his throat remembering that constable's warning about runaway wives who ended up selling their bodies on the streets of The Rocks. Would Jenny's protector abandon her when he tired of her? Jake asked himself what he would do if he found Jenny had sunk so low? He didn't want to face the answer.

The very moment a good woman halted in front of him Jake knew he had trouble but he doffed his hat and tried to get off on the right foot.

'I'm your driver, Jake Andersen. You'd be Mrs Smith or Saranna Plews, right?'

'*Miss* Plews, *Andersen*,' she corrected coolly in her correct English accent.

'Righto,' said Jake. *So I've copped one of those New Chums who look down their nose at us colonials.* He was determined not to let this Pommy girl's manner get under his skin.

'Seeing as you'll be cooped up in my coach for ages, Miss Plews, you'd best stretch your legs until we're on our way.'

Her mitten-covered hand flew to her mouth in horror. Jake immediately realised his mistake – his forbidden reference to a lady's nether limbs. *You've got a fair bit to learn, girl. But at journey's end the blokes in Ironbark will soon cut you down to size.*

Miss Plews carried a large carpet bag. Jake offered to stow it with the rest of the passengers' baggage already roped to the roof-rack but she clutched the bag to her bosom and scurried inside the tavern.

'Please yourself, lady,' he muttered to himself. 'Anyone would think you're hiding the crown jewels.' He looked down both ends of the street. *Where the deuce are the other three?*

Two drunks headed for him on a roll. Jake recognised the rough cloth of their suits was a product of the Parramatta Female Factory. No mistaking these lads for anything but Currency.

'We're the Crooke brothers bound for Goulburn. This our coach, mate?'

Jake's manner was confidential. 'I enjoy a pint as much as the next bloke, so I'd better warn you. There are two females on board who won't take too kindly to grog – they're both *nuns*.'

The brothers crossed themselves. 'Jesus! We don't want to upset no nuns!'

'Good on you!' Jake shepherded them towards the tavern. 'Hop inside and the bloke in the booking office will get you fixed up on another Rolly Brothers coach – all blokes!'

That just leaves the widow, Mrs Smith. What the hell's keeping her? I've got her bag on the rack, so I can't bloody well leave without her.

Suddenly a girl came running towards the coach in a flurry of red petticoats. 'Jesus wept!' Jake muttered under his breath, 'what have we got here?'

He caught a flash of pretty ankles below the red petticoats. She clutched at a silly little hat with a feather curling over the brim. Although she was swathed in a shawl, any fool could see her bosom pushed her red blouse to the limit. Dodging the crowd she collided with him, breathless. Her words had a lilting accent.

'Thank you for waiting. I was given the wrong directions. When I started running back someone shouted, "Thief!" I had to do some fast talking to a police officer, I can tell you!'

Her laugh was rich and open, not the polite titter of well-bred English girls. Most of her kind guarded their pale complexions against freckles but the widow's olive skin was no stranger to the sun.

'You'd be Mrs Smith, right? I'm your driver, Jake Andersen. Jake.'

'It's pleased I am to meet you, Mr Andersen. I can't wait to begin our journey. You mustn't mind my questions. I've only been here three days. The colony is a whole new world to me.'

A gust of wind sent her silly little hat spinning across the road above a double lane of traffic and Jake dashed off in pursuit, dodging nimbly between horses and cartwheels to rescue the hat before it landed in the gutter. He darted back between carriages to hand it to her.

The Widow Smith's vivid blue eyes were laughing at him through a wild mane of black hair that the wind blew in every direction. Jake was a bit thrown. *Jesus wept, a man could get lost for a fortnight in that jungle of hair.*

Looking into the widow's eyes Jake felt he was falling down a deep well. He quickly reminded himself, *There's not a good woman alive who could tempt me. I'm happy to pay Lily Pompadour for everything I need.*

Rain suddenly pelted down and George Street was soon awash with mud-splattered vehicles and a sea of men's umbrellas. Although Jake had previously ridden Horatio through this part of town, navigating a coach between drunken pedestrians and drivers in the rain would be quite another matter. He rounded up his passengers to shelter under the tavern's awning. *Dr O'Flaherty is pleasantly drunk, Miss Plews is twitchy and the Widow Smith's looking around her like a kid at a fair.*

Just as Jake was ready to beckon them to board the coach he was bailed up by a shifty-looking bloke he'd seen earlier in a huddle with another coach driver.

Jake eyed the man's coat. A pawnbroker's ticket was still pinned to the collar. *No doubt about it, this bloke's dodgy.*

'Could I have a word with you, me old china?' The man's eyes were furtive and his accent was pure Cockney. 'Ever come across a Keziah Stanley in your travels? Looks a bit Gypsy like. Just off the boat from the Old Dart.'

Jake was guarded. 'Who wants to know?'

'A gent in England. Quality. Plenty of brass. I'll make it well worth your while.' The Cockney jingled coins in his pocket to emphasise his point.

Jake saw Mrs Smith was lurking in the tavern doorway. She looked terrified.

'Never heard of her,' he told the Cockney. 'Now bugger off, I've got work to do.'

When the informer slunk out of sight, Mrs Smith gave Jake a tremulous smile. *So that's it. A good woman on the run from a bloke with pots of cash.*

'Righto, time to hit the road.' Jake laid a wide plank across the footpath to protect their boots from the muddy puddles. The Widow Smith was the last to climb on board. Jake's eyes strayed again to that flurry of red petticoats and her nice pair of ankles. *No harm in me just looking.*

CHAPTER 13

Mi-duvel! Thank God I'm on the open road again.

As the coach rolled its way past the Toll Gate at the head of the Parramatta Road Keziah touched the silver amulet hidden under her blouse, grateful that her ancestors had protected her from being discovered by that Cockney spy the Morgans had hired to hunt her down. Had Jake Andersen sensed her terror and covered up for her? She sent a mental blessing of thanks to him anyway.

She felt exhilarated to be travelling for the very first time in a coach lead by a team of horses. Every mile took her closer towards Gem. Of course no coach could be as comfortable as her *vardo*. Every bump in the road caused Dr O'Flaherty to roll into her and the wind occasionally blew the rain her way through the open window. Glass panes wouldn't have lasted five minutes on roads as rough as these, but Keziah didn't want to roll down the canvas blind. Better to be a bit damp than miss any of the extraordinary scenery they passed.

She tried to ignore Saranna Plews's silent disapproval as she eyed the red petticoats peeping beneath Keziah's black mourning skirt. Drawing her shawl across her bosom to conceal her red blouse, Keziah gave her a tentative smile but the other girl turned her head and stared resolutely out the window.

Keziah was not surprised by the rejection, but Dr O'Flaherty, who was sitting beside her, gave her a friendly wink. 'If I should be falling asleep on your shoulder, just push me back in my corner.' He took a swig from his flask, pulled his hat over his eyes and promptly fell asleep.

Keziah made mental notes about her fellow passengers in the same way she did when reading fortunes for *gaujos*.

The doctor's a drinking man but a harmless old codger. Saranna Plews's Chester accent is educated. Good quality travelling outfit. Expensive leather boots but the heels are worn down. That and the hole in her mittens show she's sliding into genteel poverty. Why does she keep patting that cameo brooch? Keziah had a sudden flash of insight. *It's a link with her dead mother.*

As the coach travelled further into open country Keziah was reassured by the vast size of this land – and her good chances of keeping out of the grasp of the Morgans' spies. Nobody here knew her real name or the secret baggage she was carrying. She was now Mrs Smith. A widow on her way towards the southern county where Gem was last known to be. At the thought of Gem she stroked the filigree gold ring he'd given her on their wedding day.

She was intrigued by the strange beauty of the landscape. The occasional whitewashed villages they passed might have been transported from a corner of England. Isolated bush huts with timbers bleached by sun, wind and rain shot up like hardy weeds in this alien soil. The bush seemed to flash past the coach in an endless blur of strange trees that bore no relationship to all the English trees and plants she knew by name.

Whenever their coach rocked past a lone traveller on horseback, Jake Andersen called out a greeting. The sight of a barefoot black family with a child clinging to its mother's back drew a wave of empathy from Keziah. Were black women treated as inferior beings by the *gaujos* as her own Romani tribe were at home?

She again pressed her hand over her grandmother's precious amulet hidden beneath her bodice. One day she would be free to reclaim openly her pride in being a Romani woman.

For days they had driven along roads so new they might have been hacked out of the bush at breakfast. When the coach drew to a halt on the crest of a steep hill their driver yelled out.

'Hey, you lot. Eyes right! You ain't never seen nothing like this in the Old Dart.'

The coach ground to a halt. Jake Andersen's boast was no exaggeration. Framed by giant eucalypts, a vast panorama spread out below them.

Keziah climbed down from the coach and ran to the edge of the cliff, feeling like an eagle looking down at the world from its eyrie. Folds of distant mountain ranges of purple, burnt orange and olive green seemed woven together in a giant tapestry. Below lay a vast plain dotted with miniature figures of animals with long curved tails like sabres. They sprang across the valley as if on coiled springs and disappeared into the dense shadows of the bush. Keziah threw her arms wide, wanting to hold the scene in an open embrace.

'The gods have blessed this land!'

She was suddenly aware Jake Andersen was looking at her curiously. What was wrong with him? Didn't he ever smile? She shrugged off her grandmother's prediction that if she made a bad choice her life would become entangled with three men, one of them a man with red-gold hair. *Well I certainly made a terrible mistake with Caleb Morgan. And Jake Andersen has red-gold hair. But from what I've seen so far, the colony is alive with men with the same Celtic colouring.*

Jake Andersen really intrigued her. He was the first Currency Lad she'd spoken to. He didn't talk or look like any Englishman she'd ever met. A man of few words, he made every word count. His eyes sent the clear message that he didn't acknowledge any class of men were his betters – or beneath him. *He's not exactly arrogant, but he doesn't take too kindly to English criticism of* his *country.*

She was suddenly conscious that he was looking her way.

'Righto!' he ordered. 'You've got to walk downhill for safety's sake. It's a steep grade, a drop of one foot in every three.'

Keziah shadowed him. 'Why are you chaining that huge log behind the coach?'

'To slow her down or she'll crash. Then you'd have to travel all the way by shanks's pony.'

He beckoned to his passengers. 'Off you trot. Take it easy. No broken bones mind. Ain't no decent doctor within cooee.' He realised his mistake. 'No offence meant, Doc.'

Dr O'Flaherty laughed outright. 'None taken, lad.'

Keziah picked up her skirts and gingerly led the way. She hid a smile at the sight of Saranna clinging to Dr O'Flaherty's arm. He was now as full as a boot. Who was guiding who?

Keziah watched in admiration as Jake expertly navigated his team down the rugged escarpment.

At the bottom, he shrugged off her compliment. 'Ain't nothing to it.'

Saranna Plews chose to sit alone on a log so Keziah crossed to sit with the doctor.

'We're lucky to have an expert bushman like Jake Andersen. I don't know about you, Doctor, but I'm parched. I suspect there is nothing half so refreshing as tea in the bush.'

O'Flaherty nodded but at this reminder of his constant thirst he swigged his whisky.

As usual Jake effortlessly got a fire going, the water in the tin quart-pot soon boiling for tea.

'I'll cook you a real treat. Johnnycakes. Can't beat 'em.'

'May I watch?' Unbidden Keziah squatted on her haunches beside him. Jake cast her a wary look but at least he didn't say no.

'Here, make yourself useful. Chuck in the raisins when I tell you.'

The johnnycakes were a success and the passengers' silence was only broken by the appreciative slurping of tea and the sounds of birds. Keziah noticed how Jake stood apart from the group, as if mindful of Saranna Plews's attitude to Currency Lads not 'knowing their place'.

'Next stop there's a general store that handles mail. So if you want to grab the chance to pen a few words …'

Obediently the girl withdrew. It was clear to Keziah she was writing a love letter as Saranna's heart was in her eyes. Was the girl's fiancé a farmer? A clerk? Or a convict?

Minutes later Saranna nervously handed Jake her letter. 'What will it cost to send this so far away?'

Jake looked at the letter. 'Gideon Park ain't far in colonial miles, Miss. Just a hundred or so south of here.'

Gideon Park. Keziah felt her heart beat faster at the words. Gem could be close by.

'Won't cost you nothing,' Jake continued. 'Whoever gets letters pays the postmaster.'

'Oh dear. Then he may never receive it.'

Saranna's blush convinced Keziah her lover was most probably a convict. *Maybe we have more in common than she knows but she'd die rather than lose face by admitting that. How awful it must be to be a middle-class lady.*

During the next stage of the journey the heat and flies caused tempers to flare to flashpoint. Keziah was relieved when Jake stuck his head through the window, scratching his ragged whiskers.

'Time to stretch your … *nether limbs*,' he added carefully. 'We won't make the next inn much before nightfall. I'll make you a cuppa to keep you going.'

Keziah noticed how both her fellow passengers chose to sit by themselves, no doubt to grab a precious moment of privacy after being cooped up in the coach. It would give them all time to cool their tempers while Jake Andersen cooked damper in the ashes of the fire.

After serving tea to her and Saranna, Jake Andersen sidled over to chat with O'Flaherty but Keziah noticed how he kept glancing back at her as she hungrily devoured her share of the damper.

O'Flaherty poured a generous slurp of 'medicine' into his own pannikin. 'Tell me, lad. How many Irish would there be in the colony?'

'How many stars in heaven?' asked Jake. 'One in three assigned men are Irish. Settlers of like background herd together. In Tagalong there's more Paddies than gum trees. Kelso and Bathurst have a heap of Scots. One stretch of the Bathurst Plains is called Little Cornwall. And of course the Sterling are *everywhere*!'

He looked over his shoulder in Keziah's direction and hastily added, 'No offence. Forgot you was English.'

She smiled at him. 'Welsh. In a manner of speaking.'

O'Flaherty pressed him. 'I trust I'll be having no trouble buying whisky in the colony?'

'Water runs dry before whisky does!' Jake assured him. 'On the Windsor Road in Irishtown, there's a public house called The Wheelbarrow because the publican wheels the drunks out of sight to avoid shocking *respectable* folk on the Parramatta Royal Mail coach.'

Keziah gave a little chortle of amusement that caused Jake Andersen to glance her way.

When he ambled off to smoke his pipe a polite distance away from the ladies, Keziah studied him openly. His beard and long hair left little of his face exposed except for steely grey eyes and a generous curve of mouth. She was curious. What would he look like if he shaved? Suddenly she was conscious of his lithe but powerful frame, the broad line of his shoulders. These Currency Lads were a breed apart. Jake Andersen walked like a man who owned the earth.

And yet he stiffened when she picked up her skirts and headed for him. He held up a warning hand. 'Don't sit on that hollow log! I saw a snake's head sticking out of it a minute ago.'

Mi-duvel! Keziah retreated a few steps. 'Poisonous?' she asked.

'Deadly.' He added casually, 'But only if they bite you.'

Keziah stifled a nervous laugh. 'There is so much to learn in this land. Do my questions bother you?'

Jake seemed to avoid looking at her eyes. 'I reckon that's the only way you learn.'

Keziah took him at his word and followed him around, eager for answers to her burning questions. 'What is that strange animal we saw this morning? How many kinds of gum trees are there? How do kangaroos give birth to their young? You call them Joey? What a sweet name. That's the name we give circus clowns at Home. What is an opossum?'

Jake gave her an odd look. Keziah wondered if she had gone too far. He seemed a bit irritated by her barrage of questions. But when a flock of rainbow lorikeets flew across their path and a rainbow-coloured feather fell from the sky, he was quick to fetch it for her.

Keziah laughed in delight and placed it beside the ostrich feather in her hat.

Jake kept averting his eyes from her so Keziah tried a different tack. 'What is the most important thing a new settler needs to know, Mr Andersen?'

Jake looked a bit stumped. 'I reckon you can't survive here unless you understand our strange sense of humour.'

She leaned forward, intent on the answer. 'Why? What makes you different to us?'

He thought for a bit. 'Let's see how you react to this. Back in 1830 the traps rounded up a gang of escaped convicts turned bushrangers known as the Ribbon Gang because they wore ribbons in their hats. Heroes or villains, depending on how you look at it. A scaffold was built in the street in Bathurst to string up ten of them at once, but the priest's last rites failed to put the fear of God into one of the condemned. This lad yelled out to the crowd, "Me old mother said I'd die like a brave soldier with me boots on but I'll be making a liar of her!"'

'What happened next?' Keziah asked, holding her breath.

Jake paused for effect. 'He kicked off his shoes and went barefoot to eternity!'

Keziah stared at him. 'You mean he died laughing at death and the system!'

Jake grinned. 'You got it! I reckon you'll get along just fine down here, Mrs Smith. Now hop back in the coach. I aim to get us on the road in two shakes of a lamb's tail.'

The following day the sun was shining one minute, the next the sky turned black and rain descended like a waterfall. Wind whipped the coach with such force it seemed intent on pushing it off the road. Huddled beneath oilskin covers, Keziah watched the wind attack the trees. Branches seemed to cry out in pain as if torn from their mother's trunk as they crashed into the bush. She was excited by the power of the gale but Saranna's eyes were wide with terror. She managed to give Keziah a nervous half-smile.

Keziah's answering smile was genuine. All the time they'd spent cooped up in the coach seemed to have peeled away the barriers of class like onion skins to reveal who they really were. She and Saranna had both crossed the world to join the men they loved. Both were short of money, battling alone for survival.

When they drew up at a staging inn, Keziah nudged Saranna toward a trestle table protected by a net from the swarming army of flies. Sensing her poverty, Keziah whispered in encouragement, 'Jake Andersen said the food here is *free*.'

Dr O'Flaherty was in a loquacious mood. 'Miss Plews, what do you think of the Australian bush?'

Saranna was politely disparaging. 'It's difficult to compare with England's verdant green beauty. I'm afraid the colony's trees all look the same to me.'

'A case of seen one gum tree, seen 'em all, eh?'

Keziah could no longer contain her frustration. 'Is that *all* you can see? Every day offers a new kind of beauty. Can't you feel it in your blood? This land has fire in its belly!'

Saranna looked startled and ventured a more searching look around her.

Keziah saw Jake Andersen's mouth twitch as if for once he was enjoying himself.

'You New Chums will soon get the hang of things. Everything's different. Trees, weather, animals – even the way we think and talk.'

O'Flaherty poured whisky into his tea and asked the question. 'I'm told you Currency Lads consider Jack is as good as his master. I gather you'd not be having much time for those of us born at Home, eh lad?'

'You're half right. But we only cut the Sterling down to size when they deserve it. No need for you to worry, Doc.'

O'Flaherty chuckled in response. 'So it does pay to be Irish sometimes.'

Keziah realised this was the first time she had ever seen Jake Andersen relaxed and laughing. Was the journey also leaving its mark on him too?

When Saranna timidly asked about the fate of prisoners whose sentence had expired, Keziah was equally alert for Jake's answer.

'Emancipists if they're pardoned, otherwise expirees or old lags – free men all! They can serve on juries – even become police constables. Some former convicts have made huge fortunes and get to dine at the governor's table. It mightn't be your idea of British justice but we do things different down here – for better *and* worse.'

With that, Jake Andersen strode off. Keziah rushed after him to ask her own question.

'I saw a newspaper inside the last inn but I can barely read. Is there any news of bushrangers?' She was only interested in one bushranger – Gem. Not surprisingly, Jake Andersen misinterpreted her concern.

'Don't you worry, Mrs Smith. I always carry a shotgun at the ready.'

The inn was intended to be a small oasis of comfort but an overflow of passengers from a rival coach had created problems. When Jake Andersen went off to check the horses, Keziah overheard the publican's wife apologising to Saranna Plews because she'd have to share a room with Mrs Smith.

'My guess is that widow Mrs Smith ain't what she claims to be. I've seen plenty of her kind at Home. A Gypsy, I'll be bound. Take my advice. Sleep with your money under the mattress. You know what thieves them Gypsies are.'

Keziah stalked off in anger. She felt the babe's fluttery kicks of sympathy in her belly as she passed by the Rolly Brothers coach.

Jake Andersen had bedded down under the wagon to sleep. He appeared disconcerted when she peered at him between the wheels.

'Thank you for your patience. Before I arrived in this country I'd heard fearful tales about head-hunters and cannibals. Now I can see this land has a beauty all its own. I could live here for years and only scratch the surface of its magic. Goodnight, Mr Andersen.'

'Jake,' he corrected her. Then asked if her bed was all right.

Keziah nodded and moved off in the direction of the stables. She made up a bed in the hay covered by her shawl. There was no tap water. She was deciding whether the horse trough looked clean enough to wash her hands and face when she discovered Saranna Plews standing nervously at her elbow.

'My goodness, what are you doing out here, Mrs Smith?'

'I've chosen to sleep where I am welcome. A mare and her foal make fine bedfellows,' Keziah said firmly.

Saranna flushed with embarrassment. 'What the publican's wife said was a mistake. I'd be happy to share my room with you, Mrs Smith.' At Keziah's hesitation she added, 'Forgive me. I have not been friendly. We are both strangers in a strange land.'

When Saranna held out her hand, Keziah smiled and together they walked back hand in hand to the inn.

They stripped down to their petticoats to sponge themselves at the washbasin. Like children they could not stifle their giggles as they bounced on the lumpy double bed they were sharing. The mattress sank in the middle. Keziah checked the door. There was no lock.

'I'd suggest we take the advice of the publican's wife and hide our purses under the mattress. There was a man in the bar who looked ready to cut your throat for a penny.'

Saranna's eyes widened in horror as Keziah wedged the chair under the door handle.

'Don't worry. If this fails I'm sure Jake Andersen would come to our rescue in a flash. Dr O'Flaherty told me Jake is a bare-knuckle pugilist.'

'Imagine that!' Saranna's tone suggested Jake was a prime specimen for a zoo.

Lying in bed the two girls watched the flickering candlelight throw shadows across the room. When Keziah blew it out, the darkness seemed to give Saranna permission to confide in her.

'Isn't this fun? I've never in my life shared a bed. I was an only child.'

Keziah realised that Saranna was making an effort to bridge the chasm between them, volunteering information about her life. How her mother had died in childbirth and she was raised by her father and elderly aunt. Her fiancé had been employed at her father's art gallery but the family business failed, 'forcing my fiancé to try his luck in the colony'.

Her hesitation suggested there was far more to the story.

'Aunt Georgina never recovered from the shock of our house being sold. When she died I had barely enough money to pay for her funeral and my ship's passage. On my arrival in Sydney Town I learned Father had died only months before. It was a terrible shock.' Her lip trembled but she pressed on. 'A clergyman arranged work for me in Ironbark until I can rejoin my beloved.'

Although Saranna did not mention her fiancé's name her voice was filled with love when she spoke of him. Keziah felt guilty that she couldn't share details of her own life because she needed to lay a false trail to escape Caleb Morgan.

'Your fiancé is a lucky man to have won your heart,' she said sincerely.

'I would marry him tomorrow if it were possible.'

Keziah sensed the true reason for the delay. Like Gem, Saranna's man had been transported in chains.

When Saranna fell asleep Keziah thought about the suspicious publican's wife. Although until now Keziah had kept her Romani vest with its border of coins out of sight in her bag, the woman had sensed Keziah's 'Gypsy' background. So might others. She decided it was high time to weave a fanciful Romani story. She had once read the palm of an actress performing in Manchester and began to weave details of that woman's colourful life into a background for 'Mrs Smith'.

At breakfast Jake Andersen smoked his pipe under the canopy of a gum tree. O'Flaherty was in a conversational mood, lacing his tea with the whisky he no longer bothered to disguise as medicine.

'I'm destined for Melbourne Town, Miss Plews for Ironbark. What are your plans in the colony, Mrs Smith?'

Keziah took a deep breath and launched into her story. 'I have come here to perform in a play.'

Saranna was agog. 'Really! Do tell us, Mrs Smith. I just love the theatre.'

'My dear late husband and I grew up in the theatre. We became actors in King William's own company, the Theatre Royal, Drury Lane. We starred in a new play which was the talk of London and Mr Barnett Levey contracted us to perform it here in Sydney Town at his new theatre. When my husband died suddenly I was grief-stricken. But I decided I must not let Mr Levey down. The show must go on, you see. So I have come to this new land to build a new life.'

'How courageous of you. What is the play?' Saranna asked in awe.

Saranna and Dr O'Flaherty had clearly accepted the ruse at face value but Keziah saw from Jake's expression that he had not. *No one's fool, that one.*

'"The Gypsy's Secret",' Keziah unfolded the coin-edged vest from her reticule. 'I play the role of a Romani Gypsy. I am making my theatrical costume shabby for the sake of authenticity.'

O'Flaherty raised his flask in a respectful toast. 'I have no doubt you will give a splendid performance.'

In response to his compliment Keziah graciously inclined her head to conceal a smile. *If only they knew what a performance I am giving them right now.*

She felt a twinge of guilt when Saranna leaned across with tears in her eyes.

'You are a very brave lady. If we should never meet again, may I wish you every happiness in rebuilding your life in the colony, Mrs Smith.'

Keziah felt relieved when they continued their journey. She hated lying. Yet she had just packed more lies into one speech than she had told over the entire span of her first seventeen years. *Protecting this unwanted babe has turned me into the 'Gypsy liar' I've avoided all my life.*

The coach suddenly jerked to a halt. Again, Jake Andersen beckoned his passengers to the edge of a cliff and gestured with pride to the dramatic mountain pass ahead of them – Blackman's Leap.

Despite the impressive beauty of the scene Keziah gave an involuntary shudder.

Jake's eyes narrowed in concern. 'What's wrong?'

'Nothing,' Keziah lied. 'A goose just walked over my grave.'

CHAPTER 14

Jake Andersen cursed himself. He was a day behind schedule. A rough calculation by the position of the sun told him only four daylight hours remained to reach the village beyond Blackman's Leap. He didn't know exactly how long he needed because this was Rolly Brothers's new coach route and he'd only travelled it once before on horseback. But one thing he did know. Only a fool would attempt to cross the pass after nightfall.

He stopped the coach in front of an inn so new the timber was unweathered. It stood on the edge of untamed bushland in odd contrast to its emerald green lawn. A strong wind rattled the swinging sign on which two painted floral emblems illustrated it was the Shamrock and Thistle Inn.

This staging inn was Jake's last chance for a fresh team of horses before the pass. Mac Mackie had warned him the publican Fingal Mulley's reputation was a bit dodgy so Jake carefully checked the available horses then confronted the publican with his arms folded across his chest as he looked down at his rotund host.

'You're new to this country, Fingal, so I'll give it to you straight. Rolly Brothers insists on the best quality horses. This is their new coach route over the pass but they're expanding their business at the rate of knots. If you want to keep their custom, you won't save your best team for a rival company. You'll hand them over to *me*.'

Fingal Mulley was so eager to please he bobbed like a cork.

'I assure you my teams are the finest in the county, Mr Andersen.'

'Yeah? I reckon three have been in harness since Captain Cook was a boy.'

'Never! Utterly dependable they are. I'll be swearing that on a stack of bibles.'

'A bible's not much use to me if the team don't pull together,' said Jake. 'What about the leader? How experienced is he?'

'I swear on my mother's grave, Mr Andersen. I'll be giving you a full refund if the team is not entirely to your satisfaction.'

Jake gave a reluctant nod. In his experience blokes who swore on bibles and graves tended to be liars.

His three passengers were clustered outside the inn, ready to board. As he strode past them towards the stables he was wryly amused to see the changes the journey had made since Sydney Town, how his bush tucker and the landscape had both left their mark on them. The last time he'd stopped to boil the billy the genteel Miss Plews had eagerly eaten his damper straight from the fire, even if it was with miniscule bites. O'Flaherty had wolfed down his share with the help of his whisky flask. And the Widow Smith's ravenous appetite was something to behold. *Jesus wept, that girl can eat.Where does she put it all?*

Jake saw the Widow Smith was chomping on another piece of fruit. *At least food'll keep her quiet for a bit. When I told her questions were the best way to learn – big mistake. She took me at my word. I wish I'd never left the bloody door open.*

When the widow looked up Jake hastily averted his eyes. He had already fallen headlong down one well. *Jenny.* One good woman in a man's life was one too many. The irony of the situation struck him. He'd aided the Widow Smith to escape detection from a bloke in England while Jenny was hell-bent on escaping from *him.*

'Won't be two ticks,' he called out as he headed for the stables.

For the second time he gave each horse's harness a complete overhaul. Something was not quite right. When the chestnut leader snorted and pawed the ground, Jake spun around to investigate the cause. Had he been spooked by a snake?

The Widow Smith stood at his elbow. Despite the frivolous mood of her silly feathered hat, her eyes were serious, her tone confidential.

'There's something wrong with this chestnut stallion, Mr Andersen.'

Jake didn't take kindly to having his knowledge of horses challenged. *So an English girl thinks she knows more about horses than a Currency Lad born in the saddle, does she? We'll see about that.*

'I reckon he's properly harnessed. His shoes fit perfect. Nothing wrong with him I can see and I'm damned sure I would.'

'I don't expect you to believe me but as a child my father taught me how to read a horse's thoughts.' Her tone was polite but it was clear she wasn't going to budge an inch.

Jake was aware the other passengers were now eavesdropping so he decided to humour her.

'So you think he's ill, do you?'

'Not ill. Afraid. I can smell his fear!'

Jake was annoyed to see O'Flaherty's frown and Saranna Plews's open-mouthed response.

Oh gawd, now there'll be panic in the ranks.

'Righto. Just to make *you* happy, Mrs Smith.' He re-checked the chestnut stallion thoroughly but it was the widow who succeeded in calming the horse. Despite Jake's irritation there was something about her that demanded his respect.

Jake assured her he knew his job. Knew every bend in this road. He only hoped he sounded convincing. He had previously travelled this new route riding Horatio. No need to explain that he had never actually driven a coach this way.

'All right, ladies and doctor. Climb on board. We've got three hours of daylight before the pass. Rug up well. At that height it'll be colder than a spinster's embrace!'

That last phrase was barely out of his mouth before Jake cursed his careless tongue. He tried to smooth over his gaffe by offering his hand to Saranna Plews to help her navigate the coach steps. For the first time ever she smiled at him. Maybe the girl was human after all.

The Widow Smith hesitated. Jake followed her glance to where O'Flaherty lay snoring under his hat, slumped across the seat he shared with her. She turned to Jake.

'It's a pity to disturb him. Would you mind if *I* sat beside you on the box seat?'

Jake wasn't too happy about having to answer more of her questions when he was in a foul mood but he could hardly expect a good woman to cradle a drunk.

'Righto. But don't tell me how to drive my coach.'

'We are all perfectly safe in your hands, Mr Andersen.'

Jake shot her a sharp look to check if her praise was barbed but she turned on such a dazzling smile he decided it might be genuine.

She reached out for the footboard to hoist herself up.

'Allow me,' said Jake and effortlessly swung her up onto the box seat in a flurry of red petticoats and a flash of ankles. An odd thought crossed his mind. This was the first good woman he'd held in his arms since Jenny.

'I'd best tie you to the seat for safety's sake. Gets pretty rough before the pass.'

To his surprise she hastily drew her shawl around her hips like a protective shield. 'No! I've ridden bareback all my life. Never been thrown. I'll hold tight with both hands.'

'Make sure you do. If your bonnet blows off again I don't want you flying after it.'

Like an obedient child she removed her hat and pushed it under the seat. She laughed in anticipation as the wind fanned her hair around her head.

Jake grabbed hold of the reins and sent his team charging off. *That hair! Jesus, this woman's one heap of trouble. I'll be glad to see the back of her. What with her looks and thousands of men in the colony hungry for a good woman, I reckon she won't be a widow for long.*

Keziah was exhilarated by this first experience on the box seat, but she didn't want to risk Jake's displeasure by bombarding him with all the questions that bubbled up inside her.

The dancing shadows of the bush gave it a magical dimension that made her spine tingle. When the babe moved like an excited tickle in her belly, she felt a strange new sensation. Comradeship. For better or worse the baby was sharing this grand adventure with her.

Darkness enveloped the road with a speed that was strange to her eyes accustomed to the soft English twilight. The coach's side oil lamps made small arcs of light that bounced across the road, causing jagged shapes to lurch out at them as they passed between pools of moonlight.

Keziah was conscious that Jake Andersen kept glancing her way. The expression in his eyes convinced her that some woman had made him distrust the entire female race.

She was impressed that he never used the whip on his horses. She liked the way his hands held the reins so loosely they only needed the slightest pressure to cause the team to respond. Attractive hands, strong but well-shaped. Hands tough enough to fight a man but gentle enough to touch a woman. Startled, she pushed this unguarded thought from her mind.

Jake slowed the team as the coach rounded a sharp bend and emerged into a clearing. The coach lamps picked out an odd shape – their path was blocked by a pile of tree branches.

'Jesus wept,' Jake said quietly. 'It's a trap. One Eye's gang. Don't scream. Sit tight.'

He pressed his hand over hers but didn't take his eyes from the road.

Before them three bushrangers sat waiting in the saddle. Three pistols were trained directly at Jake's head – two of them in the hands of the leader. The third bushranger casually aimed his own weapon at the moon.

'Bail up! Stand and deliver!' This middle-aged voice of authority came from the leader who then barked a command for his gang to dismount. Moonlight showed One Eye to be broad-shouldered but thin, sporting a rough beard and a cap that failed to conceal his eyes. Keziah shuddered when she saw how he'd earned his name. One sickly blue eye was watery. The other was just an empty eye socket.

She glanced at his two offsiders, feeling a wave of relief that Gem was not one of them.

The taller of the two younger bushrangers wore a broad-brimmed black hat. Keziah noticed that the moment this lad sighted Saranna peering through the window, he hastily masked his face with his green neckerchief. Blinking green eyes betrayed his nervousness.

The runt of the group was a cocksure youth who was light on his feet, a boyish figure in a jaunty hat a size too large for his head. His face was clean-shaven but he didn't bother to use his paisley-patterned scarf to disguise his features. He appeared to be enjoying the whole game.

Keziah was surprised by her first instinct. Disappointment. This trio failed to measure up to the heroic legends that the colonials had created about bushrangers. Then came the first wave of fear.

'Get out of the coach, all of you!' One Eye ordered.

Jake raised his arms high in surrender as he climbed down from the coach but his words to his passengers were quietly confident.

'Do exactly as One Eye says. Don't play the hero and you'll all come out of this alive.'

Keziah didn't need Tarot cards to assess the three bushrangers.

Green Scarf is the weak link in the chain. He might shoot my head off from sheer nerves. The Runt is cocksure. He'd rather charm you out of your money than hurt you. But One Eye is ruthless. He'd kill a man as soon as look at him.

Keziah now felt a real shiver of fear. Her hand instinctively moved to protect her belly, a gesture that caused One Eye to yell at her.

'Keep your bloody mitts where I can see them!'

Keziah looked to the right to take her cue from Jake. She copied his stance and raised her hands high above her head. Then thanked *The Del* that Jake was keeping a cool head. No one else had.

Agitated, Saranna's voice broke out in dry sobs as she stood in line beside them, clutching at her cameo brooch. But the real problem was Dr O'Flaherty. His erratic swaying and arm waving were fast stretching Green Scarf's nerves to flashpoint.

One Eye's voice called out another order. 'All of you! Give over your valuables!'

Despite Jake's urging, O'Flaherty refused to relinquish his wallet and fob watch.

Obedient to One Eye's command, Green Scarf struck O'Flaherty across the face with his pistol.

The Runt, with a nod of reassurance, jumped forward to take the doctor's wallet. 'There, that wasn't so hard, was it, Sir!'

When Keziah saw blood gush from O'Flaherty's mouth, she was so enraged she forgot she was supposed to be a lady and yelled out, 'You're a cowardly dog, One Eye!'

Jake laughed outright in delighted disbelief but Keziah was mortified by her outburst.

'The next fool to disobey me gets their own coffin!' One Eye promised and instructed the Runt to strip Saranna of her jewellery.

To Keziah's surprise the boy defied his leader. He sauntered across to screen Saranna from One Eye's direct line of fire.

Nonchalantly he replied, 'Brooches ain't my style. Let's settle for the fellows' wallets and watch chains.'

'I'm giving the orders, boyo!' One Eye barked. 'You two bloody well take the wenches' jewellery or I'll top the lot of them – yourself included!'

The Runt refused to budge. 'Hey, Murphy! That's not what mates are for.'

Murphy, so that's his real name. Keziah felt her heart beat faster when she saw that Green Scarf was too afraid to disobey the gang's leader. He moved down the line of victims, gripping his pistol with both hands. Jake politely handed over his wallet. Keziah noticed that when Green Scarf halted before Saranna his hands were trembling as he pointed his pistol at her brooch. Saranna's eyes widened in terror but she shook her head in denial.

Green Scarf looked confused but he seemed unable to utter a sound.

Jake firmly advised Saranna, 'Hand it over, lass. No bauble's worth dying for.'

Saranna's unexpected cry of passion rang through the bush. 'Never!'

Keziah gasped in admiration at Saranna's surprising stand but she now feared it had cost the girl her life. Jake Andersen's quick thinking came to the rescue.

'I reckon Irish whisky's more to your taste, lads. There's a case of it up there on the roof of my coach.'

The Runt needed no second invitation. He sprang up onto the coach and freed the bottles of O'Flaherty's whisky from the box.

O'Flaherty loudly protested at the theft.

Enraged, One Eye turned his sights on Keziah. 'Give over that gold ring and purse! Or I'll splatter you with your driver's brains.'

One Eye pressed the muzzle of one of his pistols against Jake's temple. Keziah froze. She read the truth in One Eye's cold eye. There *was* no choice. He intended to kill Jake.

Jake's eyes locked with hers. Keziah knew exactly what he was thinking – she could well be his last sight on earth. So she willed Jake to read her thoughts. *Grab your chance, lad!*

Although her knees were shaking, Keziah took two bold paces forward. She stood facing all three bushrangers.

'Want my life savings, do you, lads? Well, have the guts to come and take 'em!'

She tore open her red blouse to reveal the money pouch hanging on a cord around her neck – a move that also laid bare her voluptuous breasts.

The result was utter chaos. The Runt was so stunned by the sight of a woman's bosom that he accidentally discharged his pistol. This bullet whistled across and shot off Jake's hat causing blood to spurt from a surface wound. In one lightning-fast move Jake leapt sideways and with a powerful sweep of his arm knocked both pistols from One Eye's grasp and reached out to grab them.

Rattled, Green Scarf trained his trembling pistol on Jake.

'Shoot him dead!' One Eye ordered.

Keziah had been ready to leap on the Runt's back to disarm him but her blood ran cold when she saw Green Scarf's eyes lock with Jake's steady gaze. Was he going to kill Jake in cold blood?

Right at that moment they were all distracted when Dr O'Flaherty decided to play the hero. He drunkenly grappled a body at random – which happened to be Jake, who swore in frustration at being thwarted from reaching One Eye's pistols lying on the ground. The nervy Green Scarf finally fired his weapon but the bullet whistled past the empty coach – and Keziah sensed this misdirected shot was no accident.

Jake was the calm in the eye of the storm. He called out the warning, 'Here's the traps! Make for the hills, lads!'

One Eye yelled to his gang to cut and run, then galloped up the hill ahead of them and headed west. The two novice bushrangers veered apart to the east and south.

Keziah pushed the hysterical Saranna into the coach and jumped in beside her.

'What are you bawling for, girl? Thanks to Jake Andersen, we're all alive, aren't we?'

She peered out the window. What on earth was causing the delay?

Jake had dragged the blockade of branches clear of the road but now he was being hindered by the drunken O'Flaherty, who insisted on clambering up onto the box seat beside him.

Jake yelled back at Keziah, 'Hold tight! Don't worry, I've got it all under control!'

Dr O'Flaherty struggled to grab the reins until Jake's fist connected with his face. Keziah recognised sounds of panic from the chestnut leader. The team bolted.

The coach lurched violently from side to side as Jake made a valiant attempt to force the team to slow down.

Keziah knew *baxt* had run out on them. *Mi-duvel. The chestnut leader. His smell of fear. He* knew*!*

The runaway coach swung around a bend. To the west, the moonlit cliff face stretched to the sky. To the east lay the pitch-black gorge below Blackman's Leap.

The sound of terrified horses rent the air. Keziah tried to brace herself against the sides of the coach. She saw the chestnut leader sharply outlined as if, for a moment, he was suspended in space. Sky and earth collided with sickening force as the coach plunged over the precipice, crashing from tree to tree as it hurtled headlong down into the abyss.

CHAPTER 15

The world around her was dark when Keziah regained consciousness in the depths of the gully. Her first instinct was to check her belly and feel for bleeding between her thighs. Miraculously her babe was alive and gave her a few resounding kicks to reassure her. Gingerly she moved her bruised limbs and felt a flash of pain but she thanked *The Del* that the babe had survived. Only a few months earlier she had wanted to be rid of that little life but now its fluttering movements comforted her.

Half hidden by the canopy of trees, jagged glimpses of the moon shed little light on the scene but Keziah could see the battered hulk of the coach, its wheels tossed aside like abandoned toys. The heart-breaking sounds of dying horses could be heard in the darkness.

Dr O'Flaherty looked dazed. His shattered spectacles hung from one ear, his grey beard was streaked with dried blood, but he did not appear to be seriously hurt. That was a blessing, but Keziah was reminded of the cynical belief that the *gaujo* god protected drunks and babies.

Kneeling beside Saranna's body Keziah anxiously watched the doctor fumble for her pulse. She was chilled by the awful changes in the girl. Clots of blood matted her hair. Keziah shuddered at the thought that Saranna's pale face now resembled the carved stone angels found in cemeteries. Was this an omen? The doctor battled to keep some semblance of a professional bedside manner.

'Poor lass won't live through the night with that head injury.'

Keziah searched around for Jake and finally heard the laboured sound of his breathing. She called out to the doctor to come quickly and knelt beside Jake's body as O'Flaherty examined him.

'Mr Andersen is going to live, isn't he?' she demanded.

His forearm was bruised and swollen to twice its normal size and his temple was grazed from the bushranger's bullet. Far worse, though, was the sight of his broken leg lying at an unnatural angle. When Keziah tried to help the doctor to move him, Jake regained consciousness long enough to swear at them, rattling off a string of colourful oaths she had never heard before.

Keziah smiled wryly. 'Well, that's a good sign. Jake Andersen's certainly alive!'

Between hiccoughs Dr O'Flaherty stated the obvious. 'We must be waiting for dawn to seek help, Mrs Smith. None will pass along that road tonight. There is not enough light to be setting his leg.'

Jake grabbed hold of Keziah, his fingernails biting into the palm of her hand.

'Never mind me! Help the poor bloody horses!'

The team had taken the full brunt of the fall. Keziah freed the terrified chestnut – miraculously he was unhurt. Two horses lay dead, a third was in its death throes.

'Shoot the poor bastard!' Jake ordered, 'Get my shotgun.' Keziah had seen where he kept it stowed in the coach and fumbled around in the darkness until she found it. She knelt beside the stricken animal. At the sight of his mangled legs she did not hesitate. His blood splattered her shawl as the shot rang out. She gave a choked cry at the sound.

Dr O'Flaherty was doing what little he could for Saranna. On his instructions Keziah removed the girl's outer clothing then loosened her petticoat and bodice to aid her breathing. She used her own Romani shawl to cover Saranna and added the oilskins from the coach in an attempt to warm her.

'We need a fire,' she told herself. Remembering Jake's use of tobacco, she carefully felt through his waistcoat pockets for his wax matches and soon had a campfire blazing.

Dr O'Flaherty's medical bag had disappeared but when Keziah

found her carpet bag with its treasured box of medicinal herbs, the doctor grunted his disapproval.

'We'll be having none of that mumbo jumbo, thank you!'

Leaving the doctor alone to drink his whisky, Keziah brewed an infusion of her St John's wort in the dented billycan. She blew on it to cool it then held the pannikin to Jake's lips.

'Drink this. To ease your pain, lad. It will help you sleep.'

'Jesus wept!' he cried out when a fresh wave of agony swept through him, but he seemed to trust her because he drank as he was told. Within minutes the pattern of his breathing assured her he had slipped into a deep sleep.

In the dead of night the bush was bitterly cold beyond the perimeter of the campfire. Jake's body trembled with shock but sleep seemed to release him from his pain.

A few yards away Saranna was dying, alone and helpless. Keziah fought to control her fear, mindful of her grandmother's teachings. A healer must never turn her back on those in need.

'I'll stand watch by her, Doctor,' she offered, realising she could expect no further help from him. No doubt the poor man was suffering from concussion but when he slumped against a tree she saw the glint of his silver flask in the firelight as he kept raising it to his lips. His whisky would be put to far better use easing Jake's pain but Keziah knew there was no hope the doctor would relinquish it.

For what seemed like a period divorced from time, Keziah kept her anxious vigil, trying to warm the unconscious girl's icy hands between her own. She whispered to herself in an attempt to hold her fear of death at bay.

'I'm so sorry it took time for us to be friends, Saranna. You are a good person – for a *gaujo*.' To her surprise the girl's eyelids flickered open and the blue eyes focused on her.

'My fault. You have a kind heart, Mrs Smith.' Saranna gave a deep sigh and looked anxious. 'Is it much further to Ironbark? They're expecting me. I really *need* that work.'

Keziah was quick to reassure her. 'Not far at all. It will soon be daylight. Then we'll get you safely to Ironbark. I promise you!'

Saranna's eyes seemed to be searching for another dimension.

'I promised … my beloved I would join him.' In a moment of lucidity she grasped Keziah's hand with surprising strength.

'If only I could foresee the future. Will I marry my love? Have children, do you think?'

Keziah felt her throat tighten. 'Yes! I have the gift of second sight. I can see you in a bush church on your wedding day – a beautiful bride wearing your mother's cameo brooch. You will have a long, happy marriage. I can see your husband holding a little boy with blond hair.' She spoke firmly, giving conviction to her lies. 'Believe me, I'm *never* wrong about these things.'

'Thank you.' Saranna's smile was serene. 'Will you do something for me?'

'Of course. Name it.'

'Tell my beloved … my last thoughts were of him. Tell him he must always live for … his mistress.'

Keziah was startled by this strange request but was quick to promise her. 'You can tell him yourself. What is his name?'

Saranna gave a long, peaceful sigh then closed her eyes. Keziah knew it was for the last time.

'Doctor!' she called.

Dr O'Flaherty staggered across. He again felt for the girl's pulse and shook his head sadly. 'The lass has gone,' he said and stumbled off into the darkness.

Alone with Saranna's body Keziah shook violently.

In her attempt to say the *gaujo* Lord's Prayer for Saranna's soul, Keziah mangled the English words and completed it in Romani. She removed two gold coins – Caleb Morgan's money – from the hem of her skirt, placed them on Saranna's eyelids then covered the face with her bloodstained shawl. Her ingrained Romani fear of the unnatural state of death was magnified by the alien sights and sounds of the Australian bush. Strange stars moved behind the giant trees blocking the sky. She heard the ominous hoot of an unseen owl – the Romani harbinger of death.

Keziah felt a wave of confusion as she stoked the dying fire. Why hadn't she foreseen this? Saranna was too young to die. Her death would break her fiancé's heart. Keziah's eyes searched the shadows beyond the firelight, afraid that the dead girl's *mulo* would return to haunt her.

She crossed to Jake's side, lay down beside him and held him in her arms. Even though he was unconscious, he was a man and she felt his presence would protect her if Saranna's ghost walked.

When Jake cried out in his sleep and began shivering again, Keziah knew she must find a way to warm him. It was unthinkable to steal the covers from Saranna's body.

'Don't get the wrong idea, lad,' she said as she pressed his head against her naked breast to give him her body heat. 'Anyway, you won't remember a thing.'

The firelight revealed a strange expression when he stirred, as if he looked right through Keziah to someone else. Words were torn from his throat.

'Come back to me, Jenny. For God's sake *come home*!' He gripped hold of Keziah, who was overwhelmed by his sense of loss.

She whispered the words she thought he needed to hear from this lost love, Jenny. 'I'm here, Jake. I'll never leave you again.'

'Thank Christ for that.' He sighed and gave himself up to the blessing of sleep.

Keziah lay awake thinking how extraordinary it was that strangers had the power to comfort each other in the face of death. Here she was giving her body warmth to a man who cried out his love for another woman. While at the same time the babe she had conceived with Caleb, the man who had betrayed her, kicked in her womb to remind her of its presence. And all the while her heart beat for Gem, the love of her life.

At first light Keziah seized the opportunity she had thought about during the long cold night. The tragedy of Saranna Plews's young life cut short had given Keziah an unexpected gift of destiny.

Dr O'Flaherty lay snoring, his empty whisky flask cradled against his chest. And Jake was mercifully still asleep.

With only minutes to act, Keziah exchanged some of her clothing with those of the dead girl. She hesitated as her fingers brushed the cameo brooch. It had meant so much to the girl but if it was discovered on the corpse it would identify Saranna. Keziah had no choice but to wear the brooch herself. Having placed her own feathered hat and reticule beside the girl's body, she forced herself to abandon her treasured Romani vest.

She needed to keep her black skirt because it had a drawstring waist to allow for the growth of her belly but she realised she must leave behind all her other clothing and possessions, including her beloved Tarot cards, to make Saranna's corpse appear to be that of Keziah Smith.

Baxt had given her the chance to take a new name and keep her babe from the clutches of the Morgans.

She suddenly remembered that Mrs Smith was a widow and Saranna was unmarried. Keziah felt a stab of pain as she looked at the filigree gold ring on her left hand. The ring Gem had given her on their wedding day. She kissed the ring and gently removed it from her hand. Quaking in horror she placed it on the cold hand of the corpse.

Must she also leave her *Puri Dai's* amulet? *No! How could that protect a corpse?*

On impulse she also decided to keep her box of herbs and the Australian natural history book that Caleb had given her from the

Morgan library. The book contained details of plants in the colony that she might need to practise healing.

The dead girl's own purse was pitifully short of money so Keziah quickly transferred Saranna's few coins to add to the money in her own reticule, which she placed beside the body. To steal money from a corpse would indeed incite a *mulo* to haunt her.

She removed her last remaining gold coins from the hem of her black skirt and added them to the reticule. She owed Saranna for her new life so she must leave the dead girl enough money for a proper funeral.

All Keziah had left was Saranna's empty purse, but inside the pocket of Saranna's blue cloak she found a sealed envelope and slowly read the words. 'To George Hobson Esquire, Ironbark Farm.' *This must be the girl's future employer*, Keziah thought. *I'll need that work now.*

She tried to convince herself Saranna would be buried under the name of Keziah Smith. The two were alike enough in height, hair and eye colouring, although Saranna's body was more slender than hers. But who would notice that, given the evidence of Keziah's Romani clothing, wedding ring and Tarot cards? Jake Andersen would never have been fooled but he was in no condition to identify anyone – including himself.

There was a good chance that in the chaos of rescue the only person available to identify her, Dr O'Flaherty, would be so concussed and drunk that he would identify the corpse as the Widow Smith before travelling on to Melbourne Town.

When Caleb Morgan's spies searched for her they would find the Gypsy Keziah Smith's grave and look no further. Meanwhile she would be safely living as Saranna Plews in Ironbark.

But what of the babe? Keziah hastily dismissed this awkward thought. That was tomorrow's problem.

Keziah quickly searched until she found the box containing Jake's billy tea supplies. She placed a handful of sugar in her armpit to absorb the scent of her body. Then she fed the sugar to the chestnut stallion in the traditional way her father, Gabriel, had taught her to bind a horse to her.

She tied Saranna's valises across the horse's back, careful to keep her back turned on the girl's corpse in case she sighted her *mulo*. O'Flaherty was still snoring. Jake Andersen remained unconscious, his red-gold hair falling across his forehead made him look like a sleeping child.

'I'm sorry to have to leave you like this, Jake,' she whispered under her breath. 'Destiny has set us on separate paths.' A backward glance confirmed that all in the camp was quiet before she led the chestnut stallion into the bush in search of a more accessible slope that would lead them up to the road.

As Keziah rode bareback along the empty road back towards the Shamrock and Thistle Inn she spoke soothingly to the horse to reassure him. 'I know how badly you're feeling but the accident was not *your* fault. And it wasn't Jake Andersen's either. If poor old Dr O'Flaherty hadn't been drunk none of this would have happened. Think of it this way, boy. It's a beautiful day and we're both lucky to be alive. Now we must get urgent help for the others.'

She looked at the sky – it was obvious the beautiful day had changed its mind. The heavens unleashed a thunderstorm out of nowhere. Within seconds she was drenched to the skin. In sight of the inn she hurriedly dismounted and fished around in Saranna's valise for the girl's long blue cloak to throw around her shoulders. It was still raining when she used a sash as a halter to secure the horse to the railing at the front of the inn.

This was the test. Could she pull off her new identity? Their coach had visited this inn the previous day so it was imperative that she looked and sounded like Saranna Plews but also avoid close scrutiny by the publican, Fingal Mulley, who had met them both. She pulled the blue hood tightly around her face and burst into the saloon. Even at this early hour rough-looking drinkers were slumped over the bar.

Keziah cast her eyes around the room, searching for some man who seemed responsible.

And then she saw him. A burly young man with a shaggy beard as wild as King Neptune nervously rose to his feet at the sight of her and removed his hat.

Keziah introduced herself as Miss Plews and urgently pressed him to rescue the survivors. She hoped her imitation of Saranna's well-bred accent was convincing.

'One passenger, Mrs Keziah Smith, is dead. An Irish doctor is suffering from shock but the most badly injured is our driver, Jake Andersen. His leg is broken and he's in great pain.'

'Jake Andersen? He's me best mate! I'll get them to safety, don't you worry, Miss.'

The young man identified himself as Mac Mackie, another Rolly Brothers's coachman.

He took charge of the situation, speaking in a drawled accent that reminded her of Jake. No doubt another Currency Lad. Mac Mackie looked as clumsy as a bear but he moved with speed and delivered his orders to Fingal Mulley and his assigned men with such rough authority that Keziah was confident Jake and O'Flaherty were in good hands.

Intent on avoiding recognition by the publican, Keziah hid herself in the background until Mac headed off at full pelt towards Blackman's Leap.

After discreetly gaining directions to Ironbark from a servant girl, Keziah was about to leave when she was startled to overhear Fingal Mulley giving orders to a stable boy.

'Wasn't it a young lass who raised the alarm? She must need breakfast, medical attention and transport to wherever she's going. Go and fetch the poor bairn!'

When the stable boy ran off in search of her, Keziah took the opposite direction to retrace her steps to the chestnut horse. It had been easy to identify herself as Saranna Plews to Mac Mackie who had never met her – she must not risk recognition by those who had.

She desperately needed that work at Ironbark. Now that she was the respectable Saranna Plews she could no longer earn money telling fortunes.

The servant girl's alternative directions to Ironbark had sounded easy enough to follow. Keziah didn't want to go back over the pass in case she encountered Mac Mackie's rescue party and Dr O'Flaherty recognised her. The girl had assured her the track behind the inn was a short cut that led to a creek crossing, later to the signpost at the turn-off road and from there it was only a stone's throw to Ironbark village.

The reality was a different matter. The narrow track led Keziah into dense bushland. She soon became anxious about the directions. Was *any* distance a short cut in this massive country? Where on earth was that Ironbark signpost?

The storm had ceased as swiftly as it had descended. The sun had passed the point of midday when Keziah dismounted at a creek. The crossing was lined with river stones that lay below the waterline. The creek gurgled joyously as it was sucked between the rocks before rushing downstream.

The babe in her belly reminded Keziah how hungry they both were but she had no idea how to live off the land as she had done along Romani routes. Perhaps the berries here were poisonous or could make you go blind. After drinking her fill of creek water, she remembered Saranna's sealed letter.

Holding it in her hand she weighed up her dilemma. If she didn't open the letter addressed to George Hobson Esquire, she would not know exactly what work Saranna had been engaged to do. Forewarned was forearmed. She read it slowly, phrase by phrase.

'Mi-duvel!' she wailed to her god. 'Hobson hired Saranna to teach his children! Why didn't you arrange for her to be a housekeeper or a cook? I could do that on my ear!'

After shedding hot tears of frustration she admonished herself not to panic.

'If I fail to arrive they'll send out a search party for their missing governess so I must turn up! This role could be to my advantage. If the Morgans' spies come searching for an illiterate Gypsy, what's the last place they'd think to look for me? A schoolroom!'

With renewed confidence Keziah used a scarf from Saranna's valise to bandage her perfectly sound right hand in a sling. As she rode she dredged up every clue to the dead girl's life that Saranna had confided that night they shared a bed at the inn.

The one thing I don't know is her fiancé's name. Bond or free? Probably a convict. I'll keep quiet about him until I can track him down to deliver poor Saranna's dying words!

At sunset a glorious blood-orange sun sank below the horizon. Keziah was almost hysterical with relief at the sight of the signpost. 'Ironbark – One Mile.'

Riding bareback she was drooping with fatigue when she caught sight of the cluster of farm cottages lying on either side of the winding track. Reminding herself that no real lady would ride astride a horse, she dismounted and led the horse past timber huts. Light shone from the windows and smoke curled from stone chimneys against the darkening sky.

She stopped a young shepherd boy who was herding a flock of sheep along the road.

'Could you please direct me to Ironbark Farm, lad?'

He gawked at her. Wordlessly he pointed to a wide gate beyond the short wooden bridge that crossed a sliver of creek.

In the distance a large sprawling homestead was set well back from the road. The barefoot boy ran to open the gate for her. He stared at her as if he'd seen a ghost, closed the gate behind her then shooed his sheep towards a rundown farmhouse.

'Anyone would think he had the devil at his heels. Who does he think I am?'

By the time she reached Ironbark Farm it was already the dark of night. Her feet ached, her empty belly grumbled, the babe seemed to be nudging her for food, and she felt dirty and dishevelled.

As she led the horse to the water trough, a wedge of light sliced the darkness when the farmhouse door flew open. A bearded man in a nightshirt appeared like a biblical prophet crying out in a booming Cornish accent, 'Miss Plews, is it?'

Keziah remembered to assume Saranna's well-bred manner. 'Yes. There's been a terrible accident, Sir. Our coach plunged over Blackman's Leap.'

She allowed herself to fall in a convincing half-faint at his feet.

'Here, Polly! Help Miss Plews. Fetch her food and drink and anything else the lady requires.'

Polly jerked her head in the direction of a hut a short distance from the main house. 'I fixed it up like you said, Sir. But maybe the back bedroom in your house—?'

'Certainly not! That would be most improper, what with no mistress in residence. Make Miss Plews comfortable in the overseer's hut. When Griggs returns I'll tell him he's to bunk down in the hayloft for the time being.'

Keziah noticed the girl's cheeky grin when she muttered, 'Lord, Griggs won't half be shirty about that!'

Polly was short, freckle-faced and wore a mob-cap and pinafore. Keziah was genuinely grateful to lean on the girl's shoulder.

The one-room hut's exterior walls were built of horizontal rough-hewn logs but the interior, despite the packed earth floor, was clean and furnished with a wooden bunk bed, table, chest of drawers and mirror. The room smelled as if it had been scrubbed with kerosene and the only sign that the hut was usually a man's domain was the razor strap hanging from a hook on the wall beside the washbasin.

Polly chattered away as she lit the hurricane lamp, turned back the covers of the bed and laid out towels and soap.

'Can I give you a hand to get undressed, Miss?'

Keziah tried to disguise her alarm. She must conceal the shape of her belly.

'Thank you, no. I can manage, but I *am* a trifle hungry ...'

Before she had time to finish the sentence, Polly had bolted out the door. She returned within minutes bearing a tray with bread and butter, a wedge of red-rimmed cheese, a plate heaped with slices of cold mutton, two blushing pears and a large teapot, sugar and milk – all served on blue and white floral china.

Keziah thanked Polly, closed the door behind her then wolfed down the first real meal she had eaten in two days.

'What bliss!' She savoured every morsel, grunting with pleasure. The mutton was tender, the bread fresh, the cheese an echo of the best Cheshire cheese she'd ever tasted. The golden pears dripped so much juice she licked her fingers to capture every last drop.

'Thank heavens I don't need to practise Saranna's ladylike manners when I'm alone! Tomorrow I'll have to peck like a bird in public.'

When the teapot was empty she rolled on the bed to test how soft the mattress was. She buried her face in the fresh bed linen which gave off the faint, sweet scent of lavender. Two plump pillows. A patchwork quilt. Soap and plenty of water. What a windfall. She couldn't stop smiling – until she was suddenly sobered by the thought of Saranna's corpse waiting to be buried. *By rights she should be here, not me.*

Keziah prayed to *The Del* for the girl's soul. Then thanked her god for the gift of her new life. She looked through the window at the moon as she prayed to *Shon* for Gem's safety. The Romani proverb comforted her. 'There's a sweet sleep at the end of a long road.'

She kicked off her shoes, stripped down to her petticoat and sank across the bed. Tomorrow she faced a large amount of sewing to alter Saranna's clothes to fit her growing belly.

Prompted by that vision in the English graveyard of the tiny barefoot boy wearing summer clothing, she spoke wearily to the child inside her. 'I guess to be born in this strange land will make you different to me and Gem. You'll be a Currency Lad like Jake Andersen.'

As she began to slip into the folds of a dream she thought of the way Jake had nuzzled his face into her naked breast, of the agony in his voice when he begged his Jenny to come home to him. The words of her prayer came softly.

'May your *gaujo* god protect you, Jake. And may we both find our true loves.'

CHAPTER 16

Ironbark Farm sounded alive with activity when Keziah awoke the next morning in the wattle and daub hut, startled by a peal of strange, raucous laughter. She instinctively protected her belly then ran to the window to investigate.

On the highest branch of a pine tree sat a strange bird with a coat of brown-speckled feathers and a plump white chest. His head was unduly large for a squat body. His beak reminded her of the cutting shears her father had sharpened on a grinding wheel for farmers' wives.

The bird's laughter was the most amazing sound as if he ridiculed all the follies of mankind. Keziah decided to adopt these birds as a good luck totem in her new life because her grandmother had taught her laughter was the cure for many ills.

When Polly entered bearing a tray, Keziah hastily wrapped Saranna's blue cloak around herself.

The girl's skinny build and sharp, pinched features suggested they were the legacy of generations of poverty and poor diet, but Polly's youthful vitality triumphed over her lack of conventional prettiness. Her accent was a strange mixture of Cockney with an overlay of the Currency drawl.

'G'day Miss, here's your breakfast. I thought you might be too poorly to get up.'

'I'm fine now.' She held out her hand. 'My friends call me Saranna.'

Polly hesitated in surprise then shook the hand offered to her. 'Polly Doyle, Miss. I'm a Transport. Been assigned to Mr Hobson two years.'

'He's a good master to you?' Keziah asked.

'I get well fed. Other overseers sell the government stores meant for us and pocket the brass. But Hobson makes his overseer Griggs, the pig, do right by us.' Polly relaxed. 'I know you came free, Miss. Where from, if I might be so bold?'

Keziah stopped herself from saying North Wales. She had to lay full claim to Saranna's world, completely discarding her own. Fortunately her clan had travelled through Chester and she had often *dukkered* there. 'Chester. You know it?'

'No, I'm a true Cockney, born within the sound of Bow Bells. When I got transported I felt I'd been swept out of the gutter but there's *some* good things here in God's rubbish dump.'

Keziah held back a grim smile. This was the same solution the *gaujo* magistrates employed to rid England of Romani 'vagabonds' like Gem.

Polly rattled on. 'The colony's good for young 'uns. Ma lost three of 'em to croup in our ruddy London winters!'

'I know. It is – it *must be* terrible to lose a babe,' Keziah said, reminded of Saranna's single status. Her gaff was camouflaged by screeching laughter from her totem bird.

Polly explained it was a laughing jackass that the blackfellas called a kookaburra.

Keziah was impressed when the plump bird spread his wings and swooped on a snake, then repeatedly dropped its prey from the top branch of a pine tree until the snake's back was broken.

'He's certainly clever at living off the land.' She tried to make her question sound casual. 'How many children does Mr Hobson have?'

'Two little boys. The missus died of the scarlet fever last year.'

'The nearest neighbours?' Keziah asked.

'His partner, Joseph Bloom, a Hebrew. Odd chap. A bachelor. Just got himself a new assigned housekeeper. No doubt she keeps his bed warm as well as his dinner.' Polly flushed. 'No offence, Miss. It's just the way of the world down here.'

'None taken,' Keziah assured her.

'Gawd! Clean forgot. Mr Hobson wants to see you when you is

ready.' Polly ran out the door.

Keziah pinned up her hair and spoke to the face reflected back in the mottled old mirror. 'Listen, Saranna Plews, just spin a good story.'

She patted her belly. 'Your father's the real bastard, not you. I won't let you down!'

Dressed in Saranna's best clothes but unable to button up the tight jacket, she assessed her appearance. It was funny what a difference *gaujo* clothes made. Today she could easily pass for Italian or Spanish.

She angled her inherited bonnet to counteract its prim look. Accepting the path *baxt* had chosen her to travel, she was determined to bluff her way into the job of governess to Hobson's two little boys.

Mi-duvel! My arm's supposed to be injured! She ran back inside the hut to tie it in a sling.

In George Hobson's sitting room Keziah combined Romani guile with Saranna's sedate middle-class manners. She was desperate to gain the approval of the employer who had hired Saranna sight unseen via a Sydney Town clergyman.

To her consternation she discovered that she must face *three* employers. George Hobson explained that his partner, Joseph Bloom, would soon join them. The third was their neighbour Gilbert Evans, the largest landowner in Ironbark who, Hobson explained, was miles away inspecting his boundary fence near Bolthole Valley.

Polly brought them a tea tray. Keziah's mouth watered at the sight and smell of the pyramid of scones, blackberry jam and clotted cream. She reminded herself she was now a middle-class girl who would never appear too eager to eat and she must keep her pinkie finger curled as Saranna did when holding a teacup.

The ritual pouring of tea gave her a moment of respite to study her employer.

George Hobson looked different from her first impression of him in his nightshirt. A florid, bewhiskered man, his barrel chest resembled that of a kookaburra as it strained the buttons of his Harris tweed jacket and waistcoat – unseasonable English winter clothes worn with pride. Polly said he was decent so Keziah took his pomposity in her stride.

'We, the triumvirate, are determined to educate our children. My Georgie and Donald are five and six. Gilbert Evans Junior is seven. We're building a little schoolhouse for them.'

Keziah smiled in relief. *Three small boys only need the alphabet, songs and stories – I can manage that on my ear!*

She utilised the gift that was second nature to her when telling fortunes and absorbed the unspoken message in the tone of Hobson's voice and gestures. He was clearly a self-made Cornishman who had had minimal education and wanted better for his sons. Both he and Evans were widowers. Hobson boasted that Evans was a successful grazier, a lay preacher in Bolthole Valley and a man highly respected by the county's police officers.

'Gilbert Evans is known for keeping his finger on the pulse,' he said.

Keziah did not doubt this suggested the man was a police informer. No matter how far you travelled in the world there were always 'respected' men eager to send other men to gaol – for a fee.

When Hobson's partner, Joseph Bloom, joined them, Keziah was instantly on guard. This man would be difficult to read. He was clearly well educated, probably younger than his beard implied. As he listened he rested the fingertips of his fine hands together in the shape of a steeple. When he spoke, his fluent English had a formal German accent she recognised from hearing Prussian officers speak.

'My lifelong interest is education. I endorse Rousseau's ideas, which many consider radical. Education should not be a privilege but available to rich and poor, master and servant.'

Keziah nodded, but instinct warned her she must tread carefully in this man's presence.

Mindful that she was new to the colony, Bloom explained that he was of one mind with Governor Bourke's proposal to set up a national system of education on the Irish model, which favoured no single religion.

'It is a tragedy Sir Richard Bourke felt impelled to resign as governor. I believe his plan will eventuate in time but when?' he shrugged. 'Meanwhile we must do what is possible. George and I are hopeful that the number of your pupils will grow over time.'

Keziah's smile hid her anxiety. Was there enough time for *her* to learn to write fluently?

George Hobson was gruffly apologetic. 'The schoolhouse is shy of a roof. And the teacher's cottage is also unfinished. Griggs's hut is at your disposal until then.'

'Thank you but no. I wouldn't want to put anyone out. I assure you I'm happy to live in a tent.' *Oh dear, would the very proper Saranna have said that?*

'Our assigned carpenters are mending the twenty-mile boundary fence. Cattle duffers stole our best herd.' He turned to his partner. 'Bolters grow bolder by the hour, eh Joseph?'

Joseph Bloom translated for Keziah's benefit. 'Escapees who take up arms are known as bushrangers.'

Keziah promptly replaced her teacup on the table to mask her reaction. *Imagine their horror if they discovered their respected new schoolmistress is married to a bushranger.*

Hobson stood up. 'No doubt you'd welcome a tour of inspection? Would you prefer to ride?'

Mindful she'd be given a lady's side-saddle which she'd never ridden before and which would make it difficult to camouflage her condition, Keziah smiled sweetly. 'Thank you, but after months at sea I just love to walk.'

In dramatic contrast to the deluge of rain she'd encountered the day before at the Shamrock and Thistle Inn, this land was so dry the eddying dust soon covered their boots. Hobson pointed out a dam that had shrunk to a muddy puddle surrounded by cracked earth that looked like a red-brown patchwork quilt. Wilted bulrushes marked the dam's original perimeter.

'Last summer that dam was overflowing. Mad country this!' barked Hobson.

Joseph Bloom said prophetically, 'He causes the wind to blow and the rain to fall.'

Keziah was reminded of the Romani belief that rain was God's blood.

She noted three tethered ponies in the school paddock and decided they belonged to her three small pupils. How difficult could teaching them be?

Hobson pointed to the brass school bell, the bell rope swinging in the wind.

'We also ring this as a warning when bushrangers are sighted on the horizon.'

Keziah tried to assume an expression of polite interest but her stomach was churning. She prayed this bell would never be rung at the sight of Gem – who'd be the target of all their weapons.

The one-room schoolhouse was fronted by the apron of a veranda. To Keziah the schoolhouse looked absurd in isolation, like a cast-off from one of the rows of terrace houses in Sydney Town. Built of raw timber, the unglazed windows were open to the elements, the roof a skeletal frame, but the stone chimney appeared to be the sturdy relic of some older building.

Hobson anticipated Keziah's response to the chimney. 'You'll need a fire in winter as our seasons are wildly unpredictable. Often cold at night even in high summer.'

Through the half-open doorway Keziah could see a blackboard and teacher's desk. A jar filled with bush flowers surprised her. A far greater shock awaited her as she stepped inside. Keziah stood face to face with a score of wide-eyed, nervous children.

Hobson introduced her and the students responded with a singsong chorus, 'Good morning, Miss Plews.'

'No doubt you will want to begin at once,' Hobson said. Prompted by Joseph Bloom's polite bow, Hobson quickly bowed and then both took their leave.

'What a lovely surprise!' Keziah tried to sound genuine as she threw her arms wide in a gesture that embraced all the children. She needed to *dukker* very fast indeed.

The children were clearly as anxious as she was, so she bent to their eye level and held out her hand to each in turn as they introduced themselves. Most were boys. Four brothers were lined up in diminishing height beside their big sister. Ten-year-old Winnie Collins was the first product off an Irish family's assembly line of Collins boys with curly carrot tops and freckles.

All the pupils were barefoot and wore hand-me-downs except for the Hobson and Evans boys. Georgie and Donald were miniature Cornish replicas of their father. Wearing their Sunday best suits and polished shoes they bowed with military precision.

Gilbert Evans Junior was so shifty-eyed Keziah suspected he would run tattletales to his father to report the first mistake she made. She knew she had to keep her eye on *him*.

Three girls stood in line, their dresses shabby but their faces scrubbed pink. Each shielded small siblings behind their skirts. But could Keziah expect trouble from two other older lads who stood apart?

Harry Stubbs had a belligerent jaw – perhaps a necessary defence against his patched trousers of hessian sacking with the name of a brand of billy tea stamped on one leg.

The tallest was the shepherd boy who had given Keziah directions the previous night. He stammered when he introduced himself as Big Bruce MacAlister. It seemed that he hadn't had a haircut or new clothes in years and he looked more like a scarecrow than a boy. His smile allowed Keziah an inner sigh of relief. *He's all of twelve and could probably read rings around me but I can see in his eyes he's my ally.*

'What a fine bunch of Currency Lads and Lasses you are! I promise I'll soon learn all your names. Till then please be patient with me.'

The children exchanged startled glances. Little Davey Collins piped up to big sister Winnie, 'When's the dragon lady gunna knock us into shape, Sis?'

Keziah bit her lip to prevent a smile. No wonder they were all so wary of her. Ironbark parents must have put the fear of God into their offspring about their new teacher.

She squatted down to Davey's eye level and tucked stray curls behind his ears.

'All you children are in perfect shape already. You've nothing to fear. We'll all learn from each other. And because I am a newcomer to your most beautiful country I need to learn many things from you! I'm counting on you all to help me.'

Half the class fell instantly in love with her, the other half were only minutes behind.

Keziah exclaimed over a box full of apples and pears beside her desk. 'What a generous gift! Would one of you lads kindly share them out?'

She smiled at Harry Stubbs, a tough leader if ever there was one, as he rationed out the fruit.

'As you see my arm is still healing, so I can't write on the blackboard yet.'

Big Bruce sprang to his feet. 'I can do it for you, Miss!'

Keziah was afraid someone might volunteer. 'What a very *kind* offer, Bruce, and one I will gladly accept a little later. First I'm going to tell you a story.'

They chomped on the fruit, eyes glued to her face.

'I know how it begins,' Keziah added, 'but I'll need your help to finish it. May I borrow your names for the characters?'

The children all nodded eagerly.

Through the unglazed window Keziah could see small shadows

between the trees, as sensitive as half-wild animals. She sensed other children were gauging the response to the dreaded dragon lady so she pretended not to see them until they wished to be seen. She moved her class outdoors to sit cross-legged on the grass to hear her story.

At midday Polly brought freshly baked loaves of bread and a giant ball of cheese for Keziah to share with the hungry children. Polly must have known none of the children had brought food to school and Keziah guessed that some of the farmers would be struggling to survive in the drought.

Her Romani *guedlo* folk story was a gently disguised moral tale about kindness to animals. She held her audience spellbound, enacting the characters with different voices. Breaking off at a dramatic point, she promised to continue it tomorrow. Indoors. Two brave 'shadows' had crept closer to listen. She knew her class would be full tomorrow.

Overnight the bush grapevine attracted pupils from surrounding farms. Whole families rode to school bareback on a single pony, the smallest child clinging on for dear life at the rear. Some brought the weekly 'threepenny bit' to supplement Keziah's salary. Others came empty-handed but boxes of eggs, fruit and vegetables regularly awaited her on the school veranda; farmers' produce in lieu of the fee. She made sure no child was ever embarrassed.

Keziah altered her Romani tale to take in Australian elements, including local bushrangers. The children knew all their names and aliases and regarded most as heroes. She tried to make the question closest to her heart sound casual.

'Have you ever heard of a Gypsy bushranger?'

Several voices answered in unison. 'What's a Gypsy, Miss?'

Keziah sighed. 'Never mind. They're most interesting people but I'll explain another day.' She resumed her story. 'Now what do you think Harry the Wombat did next?'

The first tussle Keziah faced was over her temporary accommodation. Griggs was furious that Hobson had evicted him from his own hut. Although Keziah took an instant dislike to the overseer she did not want to make an enemy of him. She assured George Hobson she'd prefer to live in a calico tent close to the schoolteacher's cottage so she could supervise the final details of its completion.

In her little schoolhouse over the next few weeks Keziah discovered the joys of teaching, despite her anxiety about the triumvirate's planned formal visit to the school. No date had been set. They could arrive unannounced at any time.

At night in her calico tent Keziah studied frantically, her arm magically healed each sundown. She practised her writing on a slate, aware she had little time to surpass Big Bruce's writing skills. He'd been a great help, always ready to assist the younger children with their alphabet.

But he'd been absent for a week. Today she'd found out the reason. Farmer MacAlister was dead. No more time for school for Big Bruce.

Keziah felt a pang of sorrow on both counts; the loss of Bruce's father and the end of her brightest pupil's education. Tomorrow she would call on the Widow MacAlister after school.

Keziah carried a bowl of stew as she hurried towards the dilapidated farm where Big Bruce had herded his sheep the night of her ar-rival in Ironbark. Was it only five weeks ago?

Her whole life revolved around this odd little backwoods village with its mixture of Currency farmers and settlers from every corner of the British Isles, plus one German. She had scant time to concentrate on anything except holding down her role as schoolteacher but it was a blessing because she must now bide her time before resuming her search for Gem. He was jealous enough at the best of times. She could hardly confront him with this growing bulge in her belly. In another three months that bump would push its way out into the world.

What then? She closed her mind to the question that had no answer.

A front window at the MacAlisters' farm was boarded over. The rusty front gate hung by a single hinge. The barn leaned so precariously that only the trunk of a tough ironbark tree prevented its collapse.

In an adjacent paddock where a field of corn struggled to survive the drought, Keziah was halted by the sight of a scarecrow planted in the centre to ward off magpies. Garbed in a man's cast-off slop clothing and frayed straw hat, its arms rested horizontally on a broom and its straw hair blew in the wind, giving it an oddly lifelike appearance.

When a dog ran up and chewed a trouser leg the scarecrow called out, 'Piss off!'

'*Mi-duvel!* It's Bruce!' she whispered in horror.

A woman ran from the house towards her. 'Come to spy on us have you, Miss High and Mighty?'

Mrs MacAlister's face was burnt by the sun and furrowed like a dry field but her dank hair had no signs of grey.

Life has worn her down. She probably isn't a day over thirty. Keziah faltered. 'I am so sorry for your trouble. Bruce is my brightest student – he's been so kind to me.'

'You've seen the last of him.' Mrs MacAlister hastily untied her apron to reveal her shabby black mourning and eyed Saranna's dress with ill-concealed envy. 'He's man of the house now. Got to work to keep bread on the table.'

Keziah's eyes turned toward the scarecrow.

The widow's voice was shrill. 'Don't you dare judge me! The likes of you ain't never been hungry. He's doing only work he's fit for. Sprained his ankle carrying the coffin.'

Keziah said gently, 'My people in Wales were no strangers to hunger, Mrs MacAlister, but I only brought this because you have more important things to attend to.'

The widow's eyes blazed. 'We ain't no paupers! We don't need your charity.'

Keziah's hands shook as she placed the bowl on the veranda. 'I'm sure you don't.'

She retreated in haste, tears stinging her eyes. Bruce's father had wanted him to be literate but a son's first duty was to feed his mother. First she felt angry she had wounded the widow's pride then startled to realise her gaff. *My people in Wales.* Saranna is from Chester!

Joseph Bloom blinked in surprise over the rim of his spectacles when he opened the door to Keziah.

She blurted out the reason for her call. 'Bruce MacAlister is working in the field as a human scarecrow. Don't blame his mother – the poor woman's desperate but too proud to accept charity. Can nothing be done to help them survive and keep Bruce in school?'

Through her tears the image of Joseph Bloom quivered like a figure under water.

'Do not despair, Miss Plews. I have already given thought to the matter. It is said the best form of charity is to give a family work so they don't *need* charity.'

Keziah nodded her thanks and fled down the track. She angrily blew her nose and admonished her unborn babe. 'This is all your fault. Since you've been inside me I've been unable to control my tears or laughter. Everything seems either terribly sad or terribly funny.'

The following Friday was a surprisingly hot, lethargic day. Keziah underlined the words she had written on the blackboard. The heat made the children unusually restless and the two small Collins brothers argued over the use of their last stub of chalk. Keziah quietly supplied a fresh one.

'All right, all you clever children. Who would like to read for me? You don't have to be perfect. Just have the courage to try. That's how we learn.'

Her pointer froze at the first sentence. All three members of the triumvirate stood in the doorway headed by Hobson. Gilbert Evans didn't wear a clerical 'dog-collar' as he was only a lay preacher, but his hands were folded in an attitude of prayer. He eyed the schoolroom as if on the lookout for sinners to save. Keziah now firmly agreed with Polly's initial warning. Evans never talked – except when paid by the traps to be their informer. Or when he preached hellfire and damnation from Bolthole Valley's pulpit.

Joseph Bloom's eyes twinkled at Keziah as he ushered Big Bruce MacAlister inside. Wearing his late father's jacket the lad resumed his former place with a self-conscious grin.

Keziah gave Joseph Bloom a special smile of thanks. She was aware that unofficially he had assigned one of Ironbark Farm's government men to work the MacAlister farm and that washing baskets of Bloom's household linen were discreetly delivered to Mrs MacAlister each week to provide her with paid work.

George Hobson peered at the blackboard. 'A for Australia, B for Bandicoot, C for Cockatoo? How unorthodox. When I was a lad it was A for Apple, B for Ball, C for Cat.'

Joseph Bloom leapt to Keziah's defence. 'Yes, George, but things are different here.'

'My son tells me there are no school rules,' Gilbert Evans said. A faint smiled played on his lips. 'How do you punish wrongdoers, absentees and laggards?'

'Fear is a poor teacher, Mr Evans,' Keziah replied. 'Children who run happily to school learn faster, yes?'

Joseph Bloom was determined to have the final word.

'Indeed so. Well, gentlemen, Miss Plews has already doubled the attendance. How can we argue with success? Shall we allow her to continue her good work?' Ready or not, he gestured for the triumvirate to make their exit.

It was a scorching December afternoon. The little creek that ran behind her tent was a double blessing. It enabled Keziah freedom to practise her Romani women's tradition, separating the clothes for the upper half of her body from the lower half to wash them upstream or down. The creek also allowed her to conserve the rainwater – God's precious blood.

Scrubbing clothes on the creek bank she sang a Romani love song her father had played. The passionate words reminded her how starved government men were for the sight of a woman. Some had openly stared at her voluptuous body. If only they knew her secret.

She felt uneasy when the distant figure of a man dismounted from a black horse and entered Gilbert Evans's homestead that lay on the rise of the hill a few hundred yards away on the far side of the creek. *No doubt someone is up to no good. As my grandmother used to say, 'Clean water never came out of a dirty place.'*

After she draped her washing over the bushes to dry, she paddled up to her knees in the creek, her skirt bunched up in one hand. There was no one in sight but with her usual custom of precaution she had placed a horsewhip nearby. Suddenly her spine stiffened, her ears pricked like a hunted animal.

A few feet across the shallow creek a man was crouched, spying on her. A stranger. Black hair, black beard, virile body. She shuddered when he playfully flexed his fingers like claws, ready to pounce on her. Not another soul was in sight.

Her hunter had now edged close enough for her to see the pupils of his eyes – no light was reflected in them. Nothing but lust.

Keziah inched her way towards the horsewhip, hampered by the weight of the wet skirt that clung to her legs. Conscious of his slightest movement she lunged towards the whip.

In one leap he grabbed her from behind and twisted her arm behind her back. His hand gagged her mouth and pressed her head against his chest. She tried to bite his hand but her teeth only closed on air.

'You won't scream!' he said with maddening confidence. 'Because you know what's good for you, don't you!'

She nodded vehemently. He freed his hand to paw at her breasts. His breath was hot and urgent in her ear, his soft voice was like thick honey.

'I've been watching you. You're a bitch on heat, girl.'

The blood pounded in her ears. 'Let go. My husband will hunt you down like a dog!'

He gave a curt laugh. 'Little liar. I know you. No man of your own. And you're a woman who's hungry for it, *Miss* Plews! You're single and you're English. But if you're a good girl to me, I'll be forgiving you the English.'

She tried to coax him. 'I'll forgive you your mistake if you tell me your name.'

He laughed pleasantly. 'The devil has many names.'

The friction of his hands on her body excited him and Keziah felt his erection against her skirt.

'God, you smell good enough to eat, girl. You're going to love this! The biggest and best you've ever had.'

When he lifted the back of her skirt Keziah slumped against him like a willing partner. Then she wrenched free and forced her knee into his groin with all the violence she could muster.

He doubled over in pain, and she grabbed her horsewhip and slashed his face.

'Mr Hobson!' She screamed out the name knowing full well that he was far away in Berrima Courthouse on jury duty. Her desperate bluff worked. Her attacker backed off but Keziah was chilled by his laughter as blood streamed into his eyes.

'Like it rough? I'm the man for you. I'll give you pain and teach you to *love* it!'

He did not wait to see if Hobson would come to her rescue but ran off, calling over his shoulder, 'Till we meet again, little witch!'

Keziah stumbled through the bush to Joseph Bloom's cottage and was frustrated when his assigned housekeeper informed her he had gone to Goulburn to celebrate Shabbat.

She was half afraid to confront Gilbert Evans but she abandoned caution and ran across the paddocks to his homestead. There was no sign of the stranger's black horse. She banged on Evans's front door until he opened it.

Silently he took in her dishevelled state. His eyes lingered on her thighs.

'Who was the dark-bearded man who visited you this afternoon?' she demanded.

He avoided her eyes. 'I've been alone writing my sermon. No one called here today.'

Keziah's mouth went dry. He was lying and didn't care that she knew it.

'You seem distressed. May I help you?' he asked smoothly.

'No. I'll speak to Mr Bloom on his return. I'm sure *he'll* advise me.'

'Clever man, our Hebrew neighbour.' The words sounded far from complimentary.

Keziah turned to leave but was halted by the innuendo in Evans's voice.

'May I suggest, Miss Plews, it is unwise to dress indiscreetly.' He gestured to the wet skirt that clung to her thighs. 'Some men may interpret that as an open invitation.'

Keziah suppressed her rage. 'I'll tell you this for free, Mr Evans. If that man tries to molest me again, he really *will* get an invitation. To Norfolk Island till his hair turns white!'

She hurried away knowing she had made an enemy who would never show his hand.

It was full moon. The night seemed full of malevolent shadows as Keziah sat inside her tent, trying to read a copy of the children's primer by the light of an oil lamp. Through the tent flap she saw wind rustling the trees. Shadows jumped on the calico roof when a branch fell with the noise of a gunshot retort.

Determined to control her fear, Keziah held the lamp as she circled the tent chanting a Romani spell of protection. The words died on her lips as she sensed a presence lurking in the bush. Had imagination given form to her fear?

And then she saw a figure on horseback, the face hidden in the darkness. She heard the soft tinkle of metal. Terrified, she trained the light in the figure's direction, only to find it had vanished.

Was it the stranger who'd tried to rape her? Or a spy for Caleb Morgan? Had Saranna's *mulo* returned to haunt her? Or was Gem risking the sight of her despite the danger?

Keziah examined the ground where she had seen the rider appear. A *mulo* left no footprints. She desperately searched among the fallen leaves and twigs.

No hoof prints.

CHAPTER 17

The ominous clanging of the triangle woke him but Daniel Browne knew that this was no standard summons to work. Today he must witness the flogging of yet another bolter, returned to Gideon Park to save the traps the paperwork of trying him before a magistrate. Nobody wanted the bother over the Christmas season.

Daniel sluiced cold water over his face to wake himself from his recurring nightmare that he was the prisoner being flogged. Although he had so far managed to avoid the reality, these agonising dreams left him exhausted.

Nearly two months had passed since gnawing hunger had forced Daniel to bolt with Will from Gideon Park to join One Eye's gang. He flinched from the memory of his sole performance as a bushranger – a fiasco that marked him as a failure on all levels. That moment when One Eye ordered him to shoot the coach driver still haunted him. Daniel could never forget the expression in the Currency Lad's eyes. Fearless. That was Daniel's moment of truth. He was incapable of killing any man. No matter what future hell he must endure at Gideon Park. So he had parted company with Will and returned alone a few hours later like a whipped dingo to Gideon Park, working with desperate zeal to prevent his overnight absence being detected by the Devil Himself.

Floggings at Gideon Park were now commonplace in the absence of Julian Jonstone in Sydney Town. Daniel had learned not to react as each arc of the lash tore another victim's flesh but today, when he shuffled into a space behind the rows of assigned men, he was overcome by panic when he recognised the prisoner tied to the flogging post. Young Will Martens. Daniel steeled himself against whatever was to come; the boy was a fool to value freedom above survival. He forced himself to look into Will's face, trying to read the truth. Will always cried like a baby when he was flogged. Would he crack now and denounce Daniel as an absconder?

The scourger was making a show of his strength, flexing his muscles and examining the thongs of the whip. Will's legs were trembling but when he caught sight of Daniel he gave him a broad wink.

The moment Daniel saw the overseer on his coal-black stallion, what little courage he had deserted him. He pushed his way between the men and ran into the bush.

Fear made him vomit. Then he ran and cowered behind the tool-shed. He tried to block his ears against the sound of Will's high-pitched screams but his mind was full of memories of bloodied backs and torn flesh. The sudden unnatural silence that followed was worse than the cries of agony. Was Will unconscious or dead?

Daniel crouched, watching for a sign that the men had dispersed to their assigned labours so that he could slink away to his own work. But then the overseer rode towards him, holding the reins of a second horse. Daniel jumped to his feet when he saw what the packhorse carried. Will's bloodied body was slung across its back, his arms and legs dangling. The overseer gestured to the body as if flaunting a trophy.

'Thought I'd find you here. Sorry you missed young Martens's performance. I've brought you what's left of him.' He thoughtfully stroked his beard. 'I much doubt this one will make old bones. Do you?'

Without waiting for an answer the overseer pushed Will's body off the horse so that it fell at Daniel's feet. The man's tone was confidential. 'How clever of *you*, Daniel Browne, to ditch One Eye and return home to Gideon Park that night.'

A muffled groan escaped Will's lips but Daniel was unable to move, held by the amused expression in the overseer's eyes. He felt himself blanch. *My God, he knew all the time. So why didn't he have* me *flogged?*

The overseer rode off leaving Daniel to drag Will's body into a cabin to be tended by an old man too infirm to work. Hurrying to his assigned work Daniel felt like a human draughthorse as he worked the plough. He must avoid Will at all cost. The boy attracted his admiration and contempt in equal parts. Daniel was haunted by his own cowardice when he bailed up Saranna and was shamed by Will's chivalrous protection of her.

Although Daniel had relived that moment many times, he was uncertain how to interpret the horror in Saranna's eyes. Was it simply due to the threat of losing her silly brooch? Or had she recognised him? Was this the reason she had avoided coming to marry him and set him free?

The following day as Daniel prepared the paddock for crop planting, he was angered by Will's approach. Despite being deathly pale and unable to manage his usual jaunty gait, the lad's manner was still surprisingly cocky.

'I've been invited to give you a hand, mate.'

Daniel steeled himself against pity. 'My unlucky day. Pile up the stones ready to build a drystone wall. And do me a favour. Spare me your escape plans. You'll end up in Norfolk Island. I plan to survive.'

Will's shrug caused him to wince with pain. 'Suit yourself. Stick with your art and good luck to you. I'll be famous myself one day. The gentlemen of the press have already given me a title – Jabber Jabber.'

'That fits. You can't keep your mouth shut for two minutes.' Daniel hid his surprise at Will's revelation. He'd heard rumours that the newspapers were full of stories about an unidentified gentlemanly bushranger they called Jabber Jabber, but Daniel hadn't suspected this was Will.

He turned coldly to Will. 'Now get to it. I don't give a damn how painful your stripes are. We finish this work by sundown or else!'

As usual Will had the last word. Not five minutes passed before he stopped for a break.

'Did you hear what happened to that coach we bailed up? Their horses bolted over Blackman's Leap. One of those girls was killed.'

Daniel's hands went cold despite the heat. 'What was her name?'

Will was startled by the urgency of the question. 'I don't know. They said she was a Gypsy. What difference does it make? It's a tragedy for any lovely girl to die young. Their driver was badly smashed up – he's still in hospital. The other girl is teaching school somewhere.'

Daniel turned to hide his relief. For a moment he'd feared his lifeline had been cut off. Now he had proof Saranna was alive. That meant only one thing to him. The hope of freedom.

Despite his fatigue and hunger, Daniel had worked relentlessly over the past weeks to avoid being flogged, knowing the Devil Himself was on the warpath. Just hours before Will Martens was due to receive another set of stripes, he had bolted again, causing the overseer to lose face over Will's audacious string of escapes. Jabber Jabber was once again at large.

For Daniel art was his secret salvation. Sunday afternoons like this one were his oasis in the week.

Hidden behind the toolshed Daniel was totally absorbed in capturing the essence of a man's character on paper. A horse's whinny startled him back to reality.

The Devil Himself was observing him from the saddle. He stroked his glossy black beard then beckoned him. 'Give over.'

Daniel wanted to bolt. 'Sir, I meant no harm.'

The sensual mouth curled at the corners in grudging approval. 'Not a bad likeness. But why me? No lusty wench willing to strip for you?'

'I prefer drawing men. Strong faces are a greater challenge than soft ones.'

'So you fancy challenges, eh?'

Daniel waited in anxious silence, unsure of the rules of the new game being played.

'Finish it. Drop it in to my wife. If it's any good I'll supply you with art materials.'

Daniel stammered his thanks and watched the Devil Himself ride away, sensing that a door had been opened to his future. His real goal was Julian Jonstone, who was said to be a patron of the arts and rumoured to be returning early in the new year.

A week later Daniel arrived at the whitewashed cottage. He saw his reflection in the window – gaunt with dark circles around his eyes. Nothing mattered but this crucial test. He must not fail.

The wife of the Devil Himself opened the door. He suspected she was younger than the age lines around her mouth suggested. Her whole appearance was faded, like washing bleached by the sun. She was married to the man who held Daniel's fate in his hands.

Daniel bowed. 'Ma'am? Your husband said to bring this portrait to you when I'd finished it.'

She studied it, expressionless. 'He's gone to Sydney Town to fetch assigned men.'

Daniel felt an acute sense of disappointment. He would never be given the art paper.

The Devil's wife gestured him to a bench. 'No doubt tea is welcome, lad.'

He gasped when she returned with a tray. Bread so freshly baked the butter melted turning it gold. A bowl of raspberry jam lay beside the teapot. And a slice of Christmas cake. Luxury beyond belief.

'Sunday,' she said. 'Peace be with thee.'

'You're most kind, Ma'am.' Daniel was unable to conceal his hunger. As he bit into the bread and jam his eyes closed with pleasure.

'Husband told me to give you this.' She gave him a look he could not read as she handed him a roll of paper and pencils.

Daniel's hand stroked the art paper. 'Would he like me to draw you?'

'You'd best choose what will put you in good stead with the master. His little tot Victoria would make a pretty picture. Good luck, Daniel Browne.'

She turned in the doorway. 'You don't deserve to be here, lad.'

Surprised, Daniel avoided the pity in her eyes. *Easy for her to say. She came free.*

During the days after Christmas Daniel looked for some sign that the Devil Himself approved his portrait. He waited in vain but Daniel sensed that the balance between them had subtly altered.

Was it his imagination that when the overseer observed him from a distance his expression was now guarded. Why? Did he feel that Daniel had challenged his control because he had learned to use art to retreat from his cruelty?

The sound of the triangle called witnesses to another flogging. Roped to a tree was a twelve-year-old boy who had been assigned at Gideon Park barely two weeks ago. The older men hooted in derision. Even before the first stroke of the lash slashed his back the terrified boy had urine running down his legs.

The overseer paid little attention to the boy but watched Daniel intently. Why?

It made Daniel nervous but he remained stony-faced as he heard the sentence called out. The boy had been caught stealing from the overseer's wife and was given twenty stripes. Daniel remained unmoved by the lad's suffering, even when he was finally cut down, blubbering for his mother. Each time Daniel witnessed another prisoner's degradation, he felt an overriding emotion. Gratitude – that Our Lady had spared *him*.

As Daniel mumbled a prayer of thanks under his breath, the Devil Himself halted his prancing horse in front of him. 'What do you think of that? Twenty lashes for stealing art paper from my wife. A fitting enough punishment, eh, Daniel?'

Now Daniel fully understood the rules of the new cat and mouse game. The Devil Himself enjoyed watching an innocent boy flogged for 'stealing' the paper his wife had given to Daniel on her husband's own instructions.

'Thou shalt not steal,' the overseer said softly.

Daniel hung his head, overwhelmed by shame. His silence branded him the coward the Devil Himself had always known him to be.

'This was found in a bag of Her Majesty's mail dumped by a bushranger in the scrub.'

He tossed the letter at Daniel's feet then rode off whistling a marching tune.

Daniel saw the letter had been torn open and was ringed by red wine stains. He did not doubt the bastard had read it. The script was fine copperplate, dated months earlier.

> *My beloved Daniel,*
>
> *I write in haste, travelling by coach to Ironbark where I am to teach school. I shall move heaven and earth to come to you. I send you undying love.*
>
> *Your own Saranna*

Daniel crumpled the letter and vented his rage at his missing fiancée.

Ironbark! She had travelled eighteen thousand miles to Sydney Town to join him. Why in hell hadn't she covered the last miles from Ironbark to Gideon Park? So much for her undying love!

He had won Saranna's heart without even trying. Her silence must mean she *had* recognised him. No point in sending her a letter.

I must find some way to confront her face to face in Ironbark. Marriage to a mouse is a small price to pay for my freedom.

CHAPTER 18

In the wooden hospital in Goulburn Jake Andersen lay flat on his back staring at the flypaper stuck to the ceiling liberally speckled with dead flies. The ward's new dividing wall smelled of freshly sawn timber and antiseptic permeated everything, including the hospital food.

The place had been built as a convict hospital in 1834 but whenever any of its thirty beds were empty they accepted free men as patients. Jake knew he was lucky to gain a bed. His leg had not been so lucky. Dr O'Flaherty had been so drunk when he set the leg it had needed to be re-broken and re-set. Jake swore at the plaster cast that imprisoned him, then slapped at a blowfly.

He was so bored he would have welcomed a chat with the Devil Himself. He brightened when a nurse told him he had a visitor.

Jake dragged himself upright, expecting to see Mac Mackie. He was the only person who knew where Jake was. But the figure walking towards him was a total stranger.

Stocky and bearded, the man carried a top hat under one arm and his dark dress coat, vest and contrasting trousers were distinctly formal.

Jake was suspicious. *That's the kind of garb worn by the manager of the bloody Bank of New South Wales or by some bloke in his coffin.*

The man made a polite bow and introduced himself as Joseph Bloom of Ironbark. Jake decided all it needed was for his heels to click together and he'd be a dead ringer for some Prussian military officer. 'I've heard of you. A lawyer from England, right? You're Hobson's new partner.'

'If by new you mean for two years, that is correct. It is also true I'm a lawyer but I have not yet practised in the colony. Allow me to explain.

I come periodically to Goulburn to celebrate Shabbat with my co-religionists. So what brings me to the hospital to call on you, Mr Andersen?'

'Jesus. Rolly Brothers hired you to sue me! Look, I didn't *intend* to wreck their bloody coach. Isn't it enough they sacked me? What do they want? Blood?'

'Calm yourself, Mr Andersen. This is not the reason.'

'So what kind of strife am I in now?'

'Your prolonged hospitalisation is causing concern to a friend. A lady.'

'Which one?' Jake asked quickly.

Joseph Bloom hid a smile. 'Before my departure from Ironbark I received this letter with a request to visit you.'

Jake hated to be caught reading at a snail's pace in front of strangers. 'My eyes ain't too good today. Would you mind reading it to me?'

Joseph Bloom opened the letter and cleared his throat. 'Jakob Andersen is in hospital in Goulburn. I am worried about his injuries. I was a passenger on his coach. If you can visit him please tell him Saranna Plews wants to know if he needs any help.'

Jake was puzzled. Saranna Plews? Hadn't she died the night of the accident? His memories of that night were full of holes. It was like trying to play poker with a pack of cards when the queens and aces were missing.

Joseph Bloom explained that Miss Plews was Ironbark's respected schoolteacher. When he asked Jake if there was anything he could do to assist him, Jake grabbed the opportunity.

'Yeah. If you should come across my missing wife and little girl.'

The lawyer listened solemnly as Jake relayed his usual description. The words seemed to have faded with constant use but Jake looked the lawyer straight in the eye to deliver the rider, 'I'm no wife-beater if that's what you're thinking.'

'I would not agree to hand over any wife to her husband if I believed that to be the case. So, Mr Andersen, I am at your service if it is ever possible for me to assist you.'

After Joseph Bloom left, Jake was alone again, trapped with his thoughts. This time they didn't revolve around Jenny. He was intrigued by the unexpected concern shown by the genteel Pommy girl who had looked down her nose at him. He could hardly expect any of his passengers to track him down after all the trouble he had caused them. How very odd that it was Saranna Plews. He wondered what had become of the mysterious Widow Smith. She had claimed to be an actress who was playing a Gypsy but Jake didn't doubt she was the genuine article on the run from a bloke in England.

He felt frustrated, anchored in hospital and unable to find out what was happening in the outside world. The nurses kept telling him he had to be patient. Maybe next time Mac was given the Goulburn coach route he could fill him in on the fate of his passengers. Jake caught himself smiling at splintered fragments of memory – the widow pressing his face to her naked bosom to warm him. Right now he could almost smell the rosemary oil on her body, feel the cool touch of that silver amulet between her breasts. Startled by the sensual power of that memory he said the words out loud. 'I sure hope that night was real. I'd hate to think it was just my fever making me imagine things.'

Two nights later another visitor turned up.

Jake looked at the slightly built young man standing in the shadows of the darkened ward and was suspicious that this visitor was *not* a total stranger. Jake could always smell a man who was on the wrong side of the law.

The youth kept his broad-brimmed hat low over his eyes as he pulled a chair to the bedside and asked, 'How are you getting along, lad?'

Jake was cagey. 'I know you, don't I?'

'We met once under trying circumstances.'

Jake recognised the cheeky grin. 'Shit! You're the bloke who refused to shoot me! I reckon I owe you my thanks.'

'But you've already repaid me – I relieved you of all your money, remember?'

Jake laughed for the first time in weeks. He decided not to admit his coin pouch was a blind for bushrangers. As always, promissory notes had been safely stashed in his left banking boot.

Will Martens formally introduced himself. 'Are they doing right by you in here?'

Jake shrugged. 'I'm going crazy. Bad as being in the *stur*. Can't stand being cooped up.'

Will nodded wryly. 'Neither can I. But be thankful they gave you a bed here. A few weeks back when I was last at Gideon Park my stripes got infected after a flogging. I asked permission to come here. It would have cost my master Jonstone one shilling and sixpence per day for a convict's bed but the Devil Himself vetoed it.' He mimicked the man's soft vindictive tone. 'No malingering Prisoner of the Crown is going to shirk work by lying around in hospital. Not while I'm Overseer of Gideon Park!'

Jake grinned. 'You've got that bastard down to a tee, mate. How did he treat you? They say he's a totally rotten mongrel – God's worst mistake.'

'That's just the polite way to describe him in front of ladies.'

They talked nonstop for an hour. Jake was delighted to discover Will was as passionate about horses as he was. They had a friendly tussle weighing the merits of thoroughbred Barbs and Arabs. But Jake was concerned that a lad like Will was a pawn in an evil chess game, so he turned the conversation back to Gideon Park.

'I ain't got much time for Jonstone. A gent who keeps his own hands clean but turns a blind eye to his overseer's methods.'

Will tried to make light of it. 'Jonstone's not a bad egg, but he's in Sydney Town more often than not. He would never believe what the

Devil Himself gets up to in his absence. I'd rather die from a trooper's bullet than be sent back to Gideon Park.'

Jake knew this was a common convict sentiment but he hoped this lad would fair better.

'The law says government men with a grievance have the right to go before the magistrate and be assigned to a decent master.' Jake added, 'In theory, anyway.'

Will shrugged. 'Every magistrate has bounced me back to Gideon Park. The beaks are so matey with Julian Jonstone they dine at his table. There's no chance they'd ever dish out a bit of justice for the likes of me.'

'If I can help you, mate, I will,' Jake promised. 'But I draw the line at supplying arms.'

Will nodded. He asked Jake to tell him about his plans to breed thoroughbreds. Jake talked until he was dry enough in the throat to ask a favour.

'Could you smuggle in a bottle of Albion Ale? Or anything else that's going. There's an inn just down the road.'

Will looked uneasy. 'You want *me* to walk into the Policeman's Arms?'

'Nah. Solomon Moses just renamed it the Travellers' Home Inn.' Jake lowered his voice. 'I've got a young nurse trained to fetch me the odd bottle. Thing is, I've run dry.'

'No sooner said than done, Jake.' Will was already out the door.

He returned bearing a ragged bunch of flowers that looked as if they'd been plucked from someone's garden.

Jake registered his disappointment. 'Thanks a *lot*!'

'Smell them!' Will insisted.

When Jake bent his head to examine them, he saw the neck of a beer bottle planted at the heart of the bouquet. He raised the flowers to his lips and drank deeply.

'Will Martens! Your blood's worth bottling.'

After the young bushranger gave him a silent salute from the doorway and disappeared into the night, Jake weighed the kid's chances. Few bolters managed to survive beyond a year or two.

He felt a wave of frustration over the brutal treatment meted out to young Will, in contrast to the humane second chance his pa was given as a youthful prisoner in Governor Macquarie's era.

The whole system is a bloody lottery. Those Whitehall blokes who run the whole show deserve to be transported themselves to get a taste of what it's like.

CHAPTER 19

Keziah felt a keen sense of pleasure as she hung the mirror on the wall of the schoolteacher's two-room cottage. Assigned carpenters had finished her roof and the windowpanes were in place, the fireplace was whitewashed. She moved the bunk bed with its striped palliasse to a more pleasing angle then scrubbed the wooden table, chairs and shelves with vinegar.

Today was a milestone – taking up residence in her first ever home that wasn't drawn by a horse. She would have preferred a *vardo*, but this cottage had all the novelty of a toy.

As she waited to take the bread from the oven, she hung up the pots and pans bought from Sunny Ah Wei's oriental emporium on wheels. Nailing her calendar to the wall she smiled wryly at its picture of children dancing around a snowman to celebrate an English Christmas. What a contrast to her first Australian Christmas. No snow, holly or mistletoe but a day of sweltering heat spent feasting on the traditional English Christmas fare of mince pies, roast turkey, plum pudding and the singing of carols around George Hobson's family table.

Although past, present and future were intertwined for her, like the three strands of a plait, the calendar proved that less than two months had elapsed since her arrival as the schoolteacher Saranna Plews. Keziah found it difficult to measure the transition to such a radically different life. Here in Ironbark time seemed to hurtle in haphazard leaps and bounds.

Today her major problem loomed large. Each day she swathed herself in shawls to disguise her growing belly. She did not dare to seek medical advice from the Scottish physician Dr Leslie Ross who lived at the Haunted Farm but whose buggy was periodically seen at Ironbark.

And what of the school? George Hobson had indicated she was expected to keep the school doors open all year – except for the two weeks around Christmas. So how would she manage when the time of her travail arrived in March? How could Miss Plews teach school and manage to deliver her babe in secret? And what else would 1838 hold in store for her?

Although she hungered for news of Gem, a meeting with her passionate husband at this late stage of her pregnancy was unthinkable. Her one hope in convincing Gem he was her first and only love was to face him when the babe was *out.*

The delicious smell of bread made her mouth water. Would there never be an hour of the day when this unborn babe didn't make her so ravenous? She set the table with a red cloth, removed the cooked lamb from the meat safe that swung in the open window to catch the breeze. Its hessian sacking cover had dried out, so she soaked it in water and re-covered the safe to cool the contents. The black cast-iron kettle whistled cheerily.

When Keziah sat down to enjoy her first meal in her new home she remembered just in time to thank *The Del* for the blessings of her little refuge. *Help me behave like Saranna – a lady – in public. Keep the lid on my Romani temper.*

Through the window she saw that George Hobson's buggy had been delivered as arranged so she could drive to Bolthole Valley. It was said the general store owner there, Matthew Feagan, was the unofficial 'town crier'. Keziah not only hoped to gain news of the bushranger known as The Gypsy but also of Jake Andersen's progress, and exactly where in Bolthole cemetery Saranna Plews had been buried as Keziah Smith.

On the cross-country route to Bolthole Valley Keziah eyed the posy of native flowers she had gathered. How strange life was. *Baxt* had chosen her to cheat the Angel of Death from claiming Jake Andersen's life. Yet here she was on her way to place flowers on her own grave.

The track ran through a forest that had been hacked out by an earlier generation of timber cutters intent on felling the tough ironbarks. Occasional glorious angophoras grew in unorthodox patterns, each mushroom-pink trunk stained with rust-red resin that looked like bloodstains. The sticky sap healed their old wounds and left a legacy of welted knots wherever a branch had been torn off by a storm. To Keziah these trees were a symbol of healing, of survival.

She was overcome by nostalgia for the open road adventures of her lost Romani life.

But like a nagging tooth she was constantly reminded of her biggest problem. What on earth was she to do with the babe after its birth? She prayed he would not resemble his hated father, Caleb, in character as she knew he would do in looks.

She focused her mind on Jake Andersen. She was deeply concerned for him, having last seen him in agony. Joseph Bloom had told her that Jake appeared to be in good spirits, although restless from being confined in hospital so long, and that Jake had seemed somewhat surprised to receive a message from Saranna Plews.

If Jake had heard that the Widow Smith was dead and buried, he must be really confused. *Which is hardly surprising. Some days when I wake up even I forget who I'm supposed to be.*

She had taken a risk sending Jake that message. She wondered if she would ever see him again.

Bolthole Valley's main street was almost empty when she stopped in front of Feagan's General Store. She saw the House of the Four Sisters and was surprised by the vehicle parked in front. The tartan ribbon flying from the roof of the buggy proclaimed it belonged to Dr Ross. So the gossip about his visits to the brothel was true! Keziah shrugged. Men were men, even the best of them.

An approaching pair of matrons wearing widow's weeds looked like two black crows armed with shopping baskets. They tilted their noses at the sight of a barefoot, raggedly dressed Aboriginal girl whose wide-eyed toddler clung to her back as she stood in the shadows of the laneway beside Feagan's store.

Across the street at The Shanty with No Name two seedy-looking stockmen were propped against the veranda posts with a bottle of grog in each hand. Their ribald comments about 'black sugar' amused the other men ogling the Aboriginal girl.

Keziah threw the drinkers such a steely glance it stopped their laughter. She said 'good morning' to the girl, who was too shy to respond and disappeared down the laneway into the darkness of Feagan's barn.

Inside his store Matthew Feagan was lamenting Governor Bourke's departure and holding forth about the temporary administrator Lieutenant-Colonel Snodgrass who had hired a convict as tutor. Feagan was outraged. 'How can we trust a man who handed over guardianship of his own children to an attempted assassin?'

'Who is the next governor?' Keziah asked.

'It's said Whitehall's picked a navy man this time. Whoever he is let's hope when he arrives he'll handle the London dispatches on the transportation question better.' Feagan's speech seemed to be peppered with newspaper headlines as if he was intent on extricating every vestige of drama.

'These colonies can't survive without assigned labour. Mark my words, the new governor will soon wake up to how our society functions. I've added my signature to a landholders' petition to that effect.'

Although Feagan spoke with the unswerving authority of the unthinking, Keziah sensed that at heart he was not really a bad man.

The elder widow asked anxiously, 'Any more sightings of bushrangers, Mr Feagan?'

'Not this week, Mrs Hill, it's been a quiet week.'

Keziah's heart sank but then she realised that no news of Gem meant that he was still alive.

She looked up from examining a bolt of calico to ask Feagan about the victim of the coach tragedy at Blackman's Leap. She decided not to reveal she'd been a passenger herself. First she wanted to know how people had identified the dead girl.

'I understand she was buried in Bolthole cemetery. Did she have a proper funeral?'

'Of course,' said Feagan. 'We're all good Christians here. She's buried in the non-denominational corner with a wooden cross marking her grave. No one knows what religion she was.' He added darkly, 'If any!'

Keziah dared not look up. 'What are people saying about her?'

'Some immigrant fresh from Home. No known kin. An Irish doctor's report stated she was a widow called Mrs Smith. A pagan Gypsy most like. Fortune-telling cards were found among her things.'

'Those cards are the devil's work!' the elder widow proclaimed.

Keziah was only too relieved to hear that the switch of identities had indeed been successful. The Gypsy Mrs Smith was safely in her grave. It was now safe to introduce herself as Saranna Plews to Matthew Feagan the town crier.

The younger widow had a fresh grievance. 'Mr Feagan, that *lubra* outside. Can't you send her packing? She's got no business here among decent folk. Everyone knows that bushranger One Eye dumped her on society to give birth to his half-caste.'

Keziah flushed, as she was reminded of how inferior she had been made to feel being half *gaujo*.

Feagan looked uncomfortable. 'She does have a half-white child so I gave her permission to sleep the night in my barn on account of her sickly boy. Only Christian thing to do.' He wagged a cautionary finger at the widows. 'Remember baby Jesus and the manger.'

Keziah tried to disentangle her thoughts. *At least Saranna had a proper funeral. I hope that satisfies her* mulo. *As soon as I've got the money saved I'll order a proper tombstone for Keziah Smith.*

She tried to sound casual. 'About that coach accident. Is the driver progressing well?'

Feagan hated to be caught short of information. 'I heard one victim's leg was broken beyond repair, crippled for life.'

Keziah felt weak at the idea of Jake Andersen being crippled. Badly shaken, she collected a newspaper and hurried outside. At the entrance to the laneway she sensed something was wrong. Hearing a man's laboured, rhythmic grunts, she hurried down to the open barn door.

The Aboriginal toddler lay whimpering on the ground. One of the shanty drunks had the black girl rammed against the wall with her skirt pulled over her face. As he violently penetrated her, his mate urged him on, unbuttoning his own fly as he eagerly waited for his turn.

The drunk's act was short-lived. His body thwarted his performance and in anger he slapped the girl's face.

'You ain't a whore's bootlace! Not worth a farthing.' He tossed down a small coin.

Keziah hurled herself into the barn, seized a scythe and yelled blue murder. The drunk's mate took one look at her and fled for his life. She thrashed the scythe above the drunk's head. When he fell in an attempt to dodge it, she held it over him like the sword of Damocles.

'Next time you pay for a woman's company treat her with respect!'

Terrified, he stumbled off down the lane.

'Come!' said Keziah, but the girl looked too afraid to respond, so she gently placed the little boy in his mother's arms.

'My name is Saranna. I can't afford to pay much but if you agree to work for me, you'll never go hungry or suffer the likes of these brutes again.'

Keziah averted her gaze from the girl's dark eyes to give her time to decide, then offered her the truth. 'This isn't charity. I desperately need *your* help.'

As she bundled the young mother and child into the buggy, Keziah was aware they were under intense scrutiny from Feagan and the two widows. Across the street in front of The Shanty with No Name she saw the drunk and all the other customers were lined up on the footpath to gain a good vantage point.

One drunk called out to her. 'I'll pay you to chase me round the barn anytime you fancy, teacher!'

Keziah shouted back. 'Just you watch! I'll give you all something to remember me!'

She was suddenly aware that a startled Dr Ross had left the brothel and was peering at her over the top of his spectacles. It was too late to stem the tide of her anger.

Grabbing the reins she drove the buggy full tilt towards the shanty's veranda. At the last moment she veered left but not before she'd forced all the men to leap out of her way. She gave the horse its head and they rattled off down the road. When she looked back through the cloud of dust kicked up in her wake, she was pleased to see a row of men with gaping mouths.

She was sobered by her next thought. Saranna would never have behaved like that. *Mi-duvel! It's such hard work being a lady.*

Back home in Ironbark Keziah quickly put a meal together for her hungry guests and threw her energy into caring for them.

The Aboriginal girl identified herself as Nerida. Her fingers curved towards herself and her little boy and indicated with pride that they were Wiradjuri.

Keziah managed to draw out that Nerida was fifteen. It was hard to define the toddler's age as he was so under-sized but he appeared to be about eighteen months old. His 'whitefella name' was Murphy. Keziah remembered this was an alias used by One Eye and that the young runt of a bushranger who'd shielded Saranna had called him Murphy. She smiled reassuringly as she pressed food on her guests.

'Will you be comfortable here?' She indicated the palliasse she had made up for them by the fireplace, but Nerida backed out the door.

Keziah watched her make a small fire some distance from the hut and curl up beside it. Instinctively Keziah dragged her own bedding outside. Unsure if she was giving offence, she placed blankets beside Nerida then lay nearby.

'May I keep you company? As a child I often slept under the stars.'

Nerida nodded and rocked little Murphy as she sang softly to him in her language.

Keziah saw that Nerida's hand did not have a stump on the pinkie finger that she had noticed on the hands of some Aboriginal women in Sydney Town. She wondered what that custom meant but mindful of Romani respect for privacy did not ask. If Nerida wanted her to know she'd tell her in her own time.

Venus shone brightly like a distant candle in the sky as Keziah whispered her prayers.

'Take my love to my beloved Gem.' On impulse she added, 'And give healing to Jake Andersen. You know what men are like. Jake's a man of action. He would never be happy unless he's free to ride and fight.'

Keziah awoke next morning to find Nerida had already swum in the waterhole and collected berries and grass seeds. The girl's face was serene, her dark eyes luminous. Despite her initial monosyllabic responses her understanding of English was excellent. When Keziah clumsily complimented her on this Nerida's response was eloquent.

'Know 'em Wiradjuri, plenty Gundungarra, Ngunawal, little Dharug. Talk 'em up Kamilaroi. Irish funny. English not so hard but too much bloody swearing.'

Keziah laughed in agreement. 'I'd love to learn some of your words. They sound like music.'

In the days that followed they walked and swam together and Nerida showed her how to collect bush tucker. Few words were needed for them to feel safe with each other.

Keziah knew she had to make Nerida's employment official because of the anxious, even hostile, way she'd noticed some local people reacted to Aborigines. Joseph Bloom was away in Goulburn for a Jewish festival and George Hobson had gone to a magistrate to request additional assigned men. Keziah didn't know the exact reason for Gilbert Evans's absence. *No doubt the man's busy informing on someone somewhere.*

As the overseer Griggs was in sole charge during their absence, Keziah expected he would be even more arrogant than usual. He was, but she quickly quashed his objections to Nerida.

'I'll pay for her food and clothing. It will cost my employers not one penny.'

Griggs openly sneered in Nerida's direction. 'Keep that *gin* away from my men. We don't need more bastards.'

Keziah stood her ground. '*You* prevent your men molesting *us* or my employers will learn of your negligence in permitting that stranger who tried to rape me on their property.'

Griggs backed down. Keziah was aware he had spread rumours that she was under the protection of Joseph Bloom. Although that lie made her angry, right now it suited her to call Griggs's bluff for the sake of Nerida's safety.

When Griggs stormed off in anger, she called after him. 'If there's any more trouble, my friend Joseph Bloom will hold you accountable.'

That evening while Nerida suckled Murphy at their campfire, Keziah saw the girl cast discreet glances at the way she braced her back to counteract the weight of her belly. Keziah hastily changed her stance but Nerida's voice was soft and reassuring.

'You don't worry, Miss. Your time come we go walkabout. Long time bring out many bubbas. All grow strong. Reckon whitefella bubba come out pretty much same like blackfella.'

Keziah grasped Nerida's shoulders and burst into tears. 'No one in this whole country knows the truth, Nerida. How could you tell I was so afraid to face the birth alone?'

'Belly your business. But I know women's business. Bubba come out plenty clever.'

'I believe you, Nerida!' Out of sheer relief Keziah burst into a Romani song. Weaving her hands and arching her back, her stamping feet dictated the rhythm that Nerida tapped out, and her fear was transformed into their joyous music.

Keziah sat at her teacher's desk and looked around at the children absorbed in drawing on the blackboard the picture of sailing ships, convicts lined up before a flagpole flying the Union Jack and Aborigines dancing at a corroboree. She thought it might be a rose-coloured version of the arrival of the First Fleet in 1788 but she wasn't going to ask them to draw hungry, emaciated convicts and angry Aborigines which might be a picture closer to the truth. Big Bruce had finished his work and was helping the little ones.

She glanced up at the calendar. Tomorrow was 26 January. Foundation Day. The fiftieth anniversary of the British settlement at Port Jackson and the hoisting of the Union Jack. She was told it would be a holiday for the whole colony. No school, no work, much carousing by everyone bond and free.

She should be excited but she was too tired to feel any emotion. For weeks the Australian heat had been a growing torment. Nerida adamantly refused to continue the ritual of lacing her into Saranna's corset on the grounds that, 'This fella corset bad for bubba.'

Despite the heat Keziah pulled her woollen shawl closer around her. Beads of perspiration trickled down her neck. Her eyes widened in alarm at the tinkling sound of water. She glanced down in horror at the puddle under her seat. Her time had come!

Then everything went black.

Keziah opened her eyes to find she was lying on the floor with a ring of anxious children's faces peering down at her. Remembering the reason she fainted, she deliberately upset the water jug to camouflage the fact that her waters had broken. Her babe was demanding to be born.

'Winnie, fetch Nerida, please!' The little freckled redhead obeyed with alacrity. Keziah forced a smile as waves of pain accompanied each contraction.

'I'll stay with you!' Big Bruce volunteered.

'Thank you no, Bruce. Please help the little ones mount their ponies.' She clenched her teeth. 'Happy Foundation Day, children! I'll see you all in – aaah! It's early – but go home *now*!'

'Thank you, Miss Plews!' The children scattered in all directions.

Nerida raced in with Murphy clinging to her back to find Keziah in tears.

'Nerida! It's coming far too early. My babe will die!'

'Don't you worry, Saranna.'

Keziah leaned on Nerida as they made their way to the chosen place – a secluded bank by the creek, so densely screened by bushes it was like a secret room open to the sky. Very soon she needed the linen gag Nerida placed in her mouth to muffle her cries.

She watched Nerida stoke up a small fire and fill a bowl with creek water, but she kept removing the gag to give Nerida anxious instructions.

'Keep a sharp lookout. If anyone knows what's happening, I'm lost!'

Nerida nodded calmly and kept replacing the gag in her mouth. Keziah realised that Nerida's claim was no idle boast. Experienced and confident she expertly delivered the babe. What it lacked in size it made up for in the strength of its lungs.

'Mi-duvel!' Keziah wailed, 'The whole of Ironbark will hear him!'

'Clever, huh? Him good little bubba. Fat belly.' Nerida proudly carried the infant to the fire, cradling him as she chanted softly. Keziah lay watching them in wonder, so absorbed in this moment she no longer looked around to see if anyone had stumbled on the scene.

At her first sight of the babe she felt waves of confusion and relief.

No love. Would this funny little thing have the strength to survive? She looked at his downy blond hair and features for a resemblance to Caleb Morgan. His skin was a lighter shade of olive than her own. Dark blue eyes stared back at her. She counted his fingers and toes. Exquisite. Her hatred of Caleb fought against her awe that this unwanted little being was so perfectly formed.

The Morgans' treacherous web now seemed so distant. With instinctive wisdom the babe seemed to sense her ambiguity about him. He clutched her finger in a grip that forced her to speak to him.

'Maduveleste,' Keziah said as she kissed his forehead. She held Nerida's hand and added, 'God bless you also, Nerida.'

The babe's gaze was serious and unblinking.

'Can I ever forget where you came from?' she asked him softly. 'If anyone can teach me to love again, *you* can little boy. *Please* live!'

Keziah's smile to Nerida needed no words after the experience they had just shared. Their lives were parallel – both had been betrayed by the fathers of their babies.

Nerida watched the babe suckling. 'Him small but smart. Know what to do, all right!'

Keziah looked into his eyes and swore her strongest Romani oath.

'I swear to you By My Father's Hand. I will love you, protect you and give you the best possible life I can make for you!'

Mindful of her traditions Keziah burned all the linen used in the birth. Too weary to walk, she crawled with the baby to the edge of the creek, wet his head and whispered his true name that must remain secret to protect him from the Evil One, *The Beng.*

She looked up, uneasy at the unexpected sight of a horseman disappearing into the bush.

Under cover of darkness they returned to the cottage just before dawn. Keziah crawled into bed and watched Nerida wrap the sleeping babe in a cocoon of linen before placing him in a pillow-lined fruit box.

'You'll put him on the school veranda like we agreed?'

Nerida nodded placidly but Keziah was afraid the babe would be attacked by a wild dingo or some marauding animal. 'You'll keep him in your sights until someone finds him? There might be snakes about! It's their breeding time, isn't it?' She began to cry. 'Oh how did I ever get myself into this mess?'

'Don't you worry none. Won't let anyone steal him. You sleep.'

Keziah struggled to remain awake. She dragged a chair close to the window where she could see the outline of the school veranda and the box in the middle of it. Nerida kept her hidden vigil in the bushes nearby.

Dawn finally broke. Keziah recognised that the figure approaching the school was one of Hobson's assigned labourers, the Glaswegian giant, Sholto. Tattoos covered him so densely he looked like a walking paisley eiderdown. She saw him halt at the sound of the babe's faint cries and heard his words carry on the still air, 'Gawd almighty!'

Nerida appeared as if out of nowhere and pointed him in the direction of the cottage. Keziah watched him carry the box as gently as a boy carries a nest of rare bird's eggs.

At the first door knock Keziah greeted him with a great show of surprise. 'My goodness, Mr Sholto. What have you got in that box? A puppy?'

'Nay, Miss. A wee bairn.'

Nerida stifled a giggle behind her hands.

'Leave it with me for the time being, Mr Sholto. We'll see it's properly fed.'

Within seconds of closing the door Keziah thrust her nipple in the babe's mouth.

Two days later Keziah managed to cover the distance to Joseph Bloom's house and casually informed him of the existence of the foundling she had named Gabriel Stanley. She offered to act as its foster mother until its real mother came forward to claim it.

His reply was serious. 'Gabriel Stanley could have no better mother than you, Miss Plews.'

She gave him a startled smile. *Mi-duvel! Does he know?*

She only had a few precious days to breastfeed Gabriel before she had to return to the school. Sadly she began to drink the necessary herbs to dry up her breast milk. She was grateful to Nerida for weaning Murphy so that she could become Gabriel's wet nurse. Yet at the same time Keziah felt a sense of loss she could not feed her own babe herself.

By the time she returned to the schoolhouse, the strain of keeping the birth secret had taken its toll. Keziah imagined – or did she see? – Saranna's *mulo*. Was this the imbalance some women suffered after a birth? Or was she really going insane?

One night she was convinced she saw the black-bearded horseman observing her from within a ring of trees. A red pinpoint of light glowing in the darkness. Distracted by Gilbert Evans riding past, she turned back to find the mysterious horseman had disappeared. This was no *mulo*. At the place where she had seen him, she found a half-smoked cigar.

CHAPTER 20

Jake Andersen felt the sweat rolling down his back. His shirt clung to his body, his long hair stuck to his cheeks and his breathing came in short, laboured bursts but he refused to pause for breath on the landing of the staircase. He had already run up and down it forty-eight times in succession, determined to reach today's self-imposed goal of fifty. Far more than the number the Doc had recommended he attempt at slow walking pace.

Jake did not doubt that Horatio had sensed the coming breakthrough and would be as eager as he was to take their first ride together since his release from hospital. Despite weeks of being under Doc Ross's bluntly delivered orders at the Haunted Farm, he had been treated more like an honoured guest than a patient.

Sinking down in relief at the foot of the stairs, Jake was reminded of that bleak day when Leslie Ross had cut free Jake's spongy white leg from the plaster cast and fixed Jake with a baleful stare.

'There's no getting around it, lad. The odds were against ye. Your leg has healed as well as can be expected but it's so weak you'll be forced to favour it, transferring your weight to your good leg. The best ye can hope for is a limp for the rest of your life.'

'You want to bet on that, Doc?' Jake had said at the time.

Now as he entered the sitting room Jake tried to prepare himself for an even more crucial verdict. He gritted his teeth, determined to distribute his weight evenly to avoid showing the Doc that he was limping.

Leslie Ross had just returned from a call to Gunning to deliver twins. He looked up from the chair in front of the fireplace and watched Jake's swaggering entrance with narrowed eyes.

Jake nonchalantly seated himself in the opposite chair and swung his left leg up onto the footstool.

'You still reckon I'm a cripple for life, Doc?'

He tried to stay his anxiety as Leslie re-examined the leg muscles.

'Well, I'll be damned. You've not taken a word of my advice afore this but from the looks of ye, you've been in training like an ancient Greek for the Olympic Games.'

Jake gave a snort of relief and didn't protest too strongly when he was rewarded with a tumbler full of whisky. The doctor waved aside their usual toast to the death of transportation.

'Nay, lad. This is a toast to your bloody-minded determination. You Currency Lads must have bones of iron. I was all prepared to give you a cautionary lecture about how to go through life as a cripple. But if I hadna re-set that leg myself I'd be hard pressed to recognise it had been shattered. I canna take all the credit. Your willpower is nothing short of miraculous – even if you did curse like the devil on the operating table.'

Jake grinned, reminded of the heady fusion of whisky and laudanum the Doc had forced down his throat when he lay strapped to the table before the operation.

'Nothing to it, Doc. I was buggered if I was gunna let a broken leg stop me riding Horatio, winning prize fights and throwing my leg over a girl who likes to be paid for the pleasure of her company.'

'I dinna doubt nothing short of your death would prevent *that*, lad.'

To celebrate Jake's remarkable recovery Leslie insisted his assigned housekeeper set a place for herself at the dining table.

Jake felt a bit in awe of Janet Macgregor, clearly a good woman gone wrong. Not yet thirty, she was stout but shapely and wore her housekeeper's uniform like a battledress.

'How come she got transported, Doc?' Jake asked after Janet hurried back to the cookhouse to bring the platters of food to the table.

'I dinna dare ask,' Leslie confessed. 'To quote Alexander Marjoribanks, "A man is banished from Scotland for a great crime, from England for a small one and from Ireland, morally speaking, for nay crime at all".'

Jake was openly encouraging. 'She's a fine figure of a woman, Doc.'

'Aye. Janet runs such a taut ship, I'd hate to lose her services but I dinna like the chances of any man trying to worm his way into *her* bed. She's a strict Wesleyan.' Leslie Ross ruefully rubbed his beard. 'Janet deserves to have a good man make an honest woman of her but as you well know divorce requires an act of parliament, an option only open to the rich and powerful. And what wife wants to suffer the disgrace of being a divorced woman?'

Jake knew this was an oblique reference to the English wife the Doc kept in style at Home because she refused to join him in 'that barbaric colony'.

'I'm in the same boat as you. Tied to Jenny till death do us part.'

'But I trust this will nay prevent you cutting your Gordian knot.' At Jake's blank look, the Doc explained. 'Removing a difficulty by means of bold measures.'

Jake was evasive. 'Stuck in hospital counting flies on the flypaper got me thinking. My job with Rolly Brothers is a dead loss as they won't have a bar of me now. Mac Mackie's lined me up to fight Pete the Hammer, a Pommy pugilist in Sydney Town, it'll be winner take all.'

Leslie looked dubious. 'You're pushing your luck, lad. I much doubt your leg's ready to see the distance over a bare-knuckle fight.'

'Don't worry yourself. The Hammer's past his prime. He won't last long against me. The prize money will buy me my own wagon. Be my own master. Free to hunt down that flash foreign bugger.'

'Is murder your only solution, lad?'

Jake just stared straight ahead and allowed his silence to speak for him.

Leslie sighed. 'It'd be a right pity to send that healed leg to the gallows. But first things first. How do you plan to celebrate your return to life as a man of action?'

'At the Four Sisters, Doc. Where else?'

Freedom! Jake sensed Horatio felt as liberated as he did as he galloped him down the road.

Thanks to Mac Mackie, he had just enough cash to cover his expenses at the Four Sisters but Mac knew Jake was good for this loan and fully expected him to beat Pete the Hammer. Jake was even more conscious that he had a debt of honour to repay. The Widow Smith had saved his life. He would front Saranna Plews at Ironbark village to get the story straight. Was the Gypsy really dead and buried in Bolthole cemetery? Jake didn't want to believe it. He had a vivid flash of memory of her leading the chestnut stallion into the bush.

Tonight his most urgent priority was to exercise his leg in Lily Pompadour's bed.

En route to the House of the Four Sisters he drew rein before a remote derelict property. He was pleased to see the weathered 'For Sale' sign remained tied to the trunk of a giant ironbark tree. Even though he didn't have a brass razoo to buy this place, he would need land as good as this to make his dream a reality. To breed the greatest racehorse the colony had ever seen.

The thought of buying Wiradjuri land brought a complex reaction. Anger, respect, sadness – and a sense of guilt not of his making, yet somehow in his blood. Emotions that were linked to that unforgettable day, Christmas Eve 1824, when he was ten years old, standing beside Pa in the market place at Parramatta, peering over the heads of the crowd.

The air was electric with anticipation. Jake sensed this was a moment in history. The planned meeting for an extraordinary event, the result of an invitation from Governor Brisbane to the rebel Wiradjuri leader who the whites called 'Saturday' but was known as Windradyne to his own people.

After years of bloodshed and guerrilla warfare against the military and settlers, Windradyne was coming in peace.

The noise of the crowd suddenly grew hushed. Jake felt a thrill of excitement the moment he saw the legendary Windradyne. The word passed through the crowd that he had walked across the mountains for seventeen days at the head of two hundred and sixty Wiradjuri men, women and children to be joined today by his tribal allies. Jake was in awe – there must have been about four hundred of them, far stronger and prouder looking than most of the displaced blacks he'd seen around Parramatta and the Nepean. Governor Brisbane's official party was impressive enough. Red and blue-coated soldiers with lace and polished brass, who waved their cockades and were flanked by the elite landowners of the colony, women dressed in finery fit to greet Brit royalty, and journalists from newspapers like The Sydney Gazette.

Jake nudged his pa. He reckoned he knew what this public display was really about.

'I'll bet the gov gave up trying to capture Windradyne, Pa. 'Cos he was making the police look silly. Now the gov's trying to make us look noble. Offering him "a peace treaty with honour".'

Isaac Andersen looked rueful. 'You just might have a point, Jake.'

'How much tribal land was taken off the Wiradjuri, eh Pa?'

His father shrugged. 'More land than would fit inside England, son. But if we didn't settle here some other blokes would have.'

Grand speeches were made by Governor Brisbane and Saxe Bannister, the attorney-general who had brokered the treaty. But Jake had eyes for no one but Windradyne, the tall, majestic figure wearing a great cloak made from scores of possum skins. The man outshone them all. Jake felt shamed when Governor Brisbane handed the leader a small branch as a symbol of an olive branch and a straw hat with 'Peace' on the hatband. At that moment Windradyne turned his head and Jake felt sure he was looking directly at him.

Jake knew that most people now thought of Windradyne as nothing but a memory, a blackfella villain brought to heel in the interests of colonial progress. To Jake he was the only real hero he had ever known.

Lily gave a shriek of pleasure when Jake issued a warning as he climbed into her bed that night.

'Been flat on my back for weeks for all the wrong reasons. I'm as rusty as hell, Lily. So I'll need to give you a fair bit of exercise to make up for lost time.'

By the early hours of the morning Jake was finally content to hold her in his arms but he played with Lily to arouse himself again, this time working for the pleasure of hearing her involuntary cries of delight he had learned to distinguish from her professional repertoire.

Completely spent, Lily patted Jake's body. 'The girls are jealous of me. You're the only client who pays to give *me* a good time.'

Jake felt pleased. 'It's to my advantage. You never short-change me.'

He kissed her wrists to disguise the fact he was checking for bruises. He wasn't going to allow the Devil Himself to leave his sadistic marks on Lily.

'You'll tell me if any man hurts you? I'll take care of him for you. Permanently.'

'You'd kill a man to protect a woman – even a whore like me?'

'Especially you,' he said, and meant it.

Lily turned his chin to face her. 'I really like you, Jake. Not just the colour of your money. You have a lovely way of doing business. Since Uncle Charlie put me on the game and sold me to Madam Fleur, I've never gone with a man except for the money. Till you.'

When Jake woke at dawn Lily was still asleep. He lay there thinking of the Widow Smith. He felt sure she was alive. Of course he wasn't remotely interested in her as a woman. *But you've got to admire a girl who chucks modesty to the winds to save a bloke's life. I reckon her problem is she's a good woman trapped in a body that attracts trouble!*

He felt Lily's hand moving down his chest towards his groin.

'Like me to wake you up, Jake?' she purred.

'Only if you want me to get you into a heap of trouble, Lil,' he said gently as he rolled her over on top of him. *Thank God for whores.*

Jake decided to stop off at Gideon Park on his way to Sydney Town. Julian Jonstone was known throughout the county for his lavish hospitality when he was in residence. Jake knew it was a long shot, but there was a chance Jenny might have been his guest at some banquet or ball.

As he rode Horatio towards the impressive Georgian sandstone mansion Jake was aware his approach was being observed by the only person in sight, a young convict working in the rose garden. Despite the occasional sounds of male voices coming from the farm buildings at the rear, the Jonstones' house appeared to be deserted. The shutters of the French windows bordering the terrace were all closed. The assigned housekeeper told him the reason – the Jonstones were away in Sydney Town to attend the governor's Foundation Day banquet.

As Jake turned away in disappointment he noticed the same young assigned gardener was now watching him intently, although half hidden by the shrubbery. He looked nervous. Had this bloke overheard him asking about Jenny? Jake's heart leapt. Did he *know* something?

He crossed over to him and coolly announced, 'I'm Jake Andersen.'

The young man hesitated as if surprised, even suspicious of Jake's outstretched hand but he finally accepted his handshake.

'Browne,' he mumbled warily. 'What do you want?'

Jake filled his pipe and proffered his tobacco pouch, but the convict declined.

'You might have seen my wife, Jenny. She disappeared some time back with my little girl, Pearl. Maybe Jenny was one of the Jonstones' guests. You wouldn't be likely to forget her.'

Jake described Jenny in detail, her blonde-haired beauty. Browne shook his head but Jake saw he looked confused, anxious. *Or is he lying?*

'Are you sure?' Jake pointed to his own chest. 'She has a black beauty spot just here.'

Jake thought he saw a flicker of recognition in the young convict's eyes. He drew on his pipe and waited, trying not to rush him. This bloke was no run-of-the-mill felon. Despite his dirty slop clothing and gaunt face his features were fine enough to pass for Quality given the right circumstances.

Browne seemed to be weighing something in his mind. Jake felt as though he was being studied in great detail, like a butterfly under a microscope.

Finally the convict nodded with a show of reluctance. 'I don't know for sure. Wait here.'

Jake was left standing near Horatio. He tried not to allow his hopes to be raised only to have them dashed yet again.

When the man returned a few minutes later he carried a scroll of paper which he unfurled and handed to him.

The moment Jake saw the portrait he was angry to feel his hands shaking.

'This is my Jenny, all right – except for the dark hair.' He looked up sharply. 'Was she with a bloke? A little girl?'

'Only a gentleman, but I never saw his face. They arrived in a flash carriage with a coat of arms on the door.'

'How long ago?' Jake asked quickly.

Browne pointed at the portrait. 'The date I finished it is written on the back. So she would have been here a few days earlier.'

Jake checked the date. He was hungry for every detail of the young artist's memory of that night, despite the pain the answers gave him.

'How did Jenny look to you? Well? Happy or sad?'

'She smiled like she knew she could twist men around her little finger. Except me. I just wanted to paint the flirt.' Browne turned away, unable to meet his eyes. 'Sorry. Forgot she was your wife.'

'*Is* my wife,' Jake corrected.

'I heard her tell my master she was afraid of me – she wasn't! But next day I copped hard labour on Jonstone's orders – thanks to her!'

Jake nodded. 'Would you sell me this picture? Keep it for me? I'll pay whatever you ask. But the truth is I can't give you the money till I get back from Sydney Town. I'm fixed up for a fight.' Jake emphasised the words. 'A fight I *have* to win.'

Browne hesitated for a minute that seemed to Jake more like an hour. 'I don't want to profit from your troubles. If you want it, it's yours.'

'Thanks. But I can't accept your work for nothing. It ain't right. I'm pretty broke right now. But you can count on me to come through with the cash.'

'Take it. Money here only gets stolen.' He paused. 'But you could do something else for me.'

'Name it,' said Jake.

'Next time you're passing, bring me some tubes of oil paint and a fine paintbrush.'

'Right. I'll not forget you for this—' Jake studied the signature, 'Daniel Browne.'

Jake rolled up the portrait then offered his hand to seal the bargain. Daniel Browne kept his eyes fixed on him as they shook hands. Jake felt oddly unnerved by the intensity of his gaze. He'd never met an artist before. Were they all a bit weird like this one?

'You don't believe I'm gunna come back, do you? Look, I just gave you my hand on it. Everyone knows Jake Andersen is as good as his word.'

Daniel Browne jerked his head in the direction of the convict quarters. 'A man's word counts for nowt around here. But if – *when* you come back, I'd like to paint you.'

Jake gave a short laugh. 'You must be joking. Me? What the hell for?'

Daniel Browne took a deep breath as if to summon the courage to find the right words.

'You're a Currency Lad. There's something about you that's – different. You're not like other men. Every bloke around here is ugly, evil – or dead inside. You have a special quality. Vitality. You walk with pride – like you know who you are. Don't laugh – but I can see inside a man's soul. You love this land. You judge people as you find them – fair and square. This shows in your face. That's why I want to paint you. Now do you understand?'

Daniel Browne looked flushed from the effort of speaking. He kept his eyes fixed on Jake as if hanging on his answer.

Jake tried to cover his embarrassment. 'Look, I'm grateful for Jenny's portrait. I'll bring you the art stuff as promised. What you do with it after that is your business, mate.'

Jake quickly swung up into the saddle and rode away. On the crest of the hill he looked back over his shoulder, feeling slightly uneasy. Daniel Browne was still standing in the same place watching him intently.

'Jesus wept, Horatio. That proves it. Artists *are* a bit barmy.'

Riding towards the Shamrock and Thistle Inn, Jake realised the importance of Jenny's portrait to identify her in his search but its unexpected discovery came with a full measure of pain.

He said the words out loud. 'If Jenny thinks she can hide from me by wearing a black wig, it'll take a bloody sight more than that to stop me tracking her down, Horatio.'

The memory of her was so sharp Jake shifted his thoughts to the Widow Smith. Her joy when she stuck the lorikeet feather in her hat, those disturbing blue eyes that seemed to read his thoughts, how he'd been half crazy with pain until she held him against her breast to give him her body heat.

He dismounted at the Shamrock and Thistle Inn where Mac had said Saranna raised the alarm after the coach accident. The publican might know something.

After leading Horatio to the water trough Jake headed for the bar, drawn by the sound of raised voices. Standing beneath the framed portrait of the pretty young Queen Victoria, a young man was arguing loudly with the publican, Fingal Mulley.

The stranger had 'made in England' stamped all over his aristocratic features and the cut of his modish grey dress jacket declared its London tailoring. His short military haircut and arrogant bearing embodied everything Jake held in contempt.

'My lawyer has evidence that Keziah Stanley, alias Mrs Smith, travelled to this county. She is wanted for theft and kidnapping my child.'

Jake was thrown by that news. *Jesus wept. How did a kid get mixed up in all this?*

'We Morgans will not be hoodwinked by a thieving, vagabond Gypsy. I warn you, Mulley, if you are party to this woman's skulduggery you will pay dearly for it. I'll see you're stripped of your hotel licence!'

Mulley almost crumpled in fear at the Englishman's feet.

Jake's lazy drawl cut across them. 'Hey, Fingal, what does a bloke have to do around here to get an Albion Ale?'

Mulley took one step towards Jake then a step backwards, unsure where his best interests lay.

Jake prompted him. 'Give the New Chum a drink on me. Poor bugger's on a wild-goose chase.'

Jake's barb hit its target. The Englishman drew himself up to his full height.

'And why is this Gypsy wench any concern of yours?'

'I'm the driver who drove her coach over the bloody cliff. That's why!'

The Englishman eyed Jake's muddy boots with disdain and then demanded his name.

Jake flexed his fists, ready to take him on. 'I'm Jake Andersen. Who wants to know?'

The reply was icy. 'Caleb Morgan of Morgan Park, Lancashire.'

'I don't give a damn who you are or what crackpot theory you have about the lady. I was there. I saw her *die*.' Jake's voice was dangerously quiet. 'You want to call me a liar?'

Caleb Morgan returned Jake's hostile stare. Although he seemed somewhat shaken by Jake's revelation, he quickly recovered his superior air. He made a sweeping gesture that took in Jake, Mulley and every man in the bar.

'An Englishman's word is his bond. I shall now return to Sydney Town to post a reward of two hundred guineas for Keziah Stanley's arrest. The choice is yours. Deliver her up or be transported to Norfolk Island!'

Tossing his cloak over one shoulder Caleb Morgan stalked out of the bar.

Jake pushed his hat back on his head and turned to the publican. 'Make mine a double whisky, mate, and have one yourself!'

Jake knew he'd been guilty of many things, even gaoled for one of them, but never in his life had he turned his back on a woman in distress. He owed this Keziah Smith his life. *I've got to warn her about Caleb bloody Morgan before I go to Sydney Town but where the hell is she?*

As Jake downed his whisky he was hit by a series of wild thoughts. Maybe there was no need to search for the Widow Smith. If his memory was correct and Saranna Plews really *had* died she might be the girl buried in Bolthole cemetery. If that was the case the Ironbark schoolteacher who told Joseph Bloom that *she* is Saranna Plews, might really be – Keziah Smith in hiding!

Jake reached Ironbark village in the middle of the night. The far-off howl of dingoes was answered by the bark of cattle dogs. As Jake slipped two notes under Joseph Bloom's front door, he was aware his spelling was pretty crook, but he hoped it would get his message across. He addressed the accompanying note to The Schoolmistress, Ironbark School, to avoid alerting the lawyer to her possible true identity.

> *I am sending this message to you care of Joseph Bloom. I reckon you saved my life, so I owe you. This is a warning to be dead careful. Caleb Morgan is offering a big reward for Keziah Smith on his return to Sydney Town as he reckons she kidnapped his child. I reckon any good woman would bolt from that mongrel. I've got to fight a bloke in Sydney Town but I'll return soon to sort things out for you. Jake*

It was a Saturday afternoon. The crowd milling on the footpath outside the Bald-Faced Stag Inn spilled across the Parramatta Road outside of Sydney Town.

Jake was pleased his fight with Pete the Hammer had drawn a large crowd – drunks, ticket-of-leave men, bond or free, a large percentage were Irish. He knew most men in the underbelly of the colony's class system were united by a common religion. Gambling. This crowd was bound to bet heavily on a prize fight. No doubt they'd favour their local fighter against Jake.

Jake sprang about on the balls of his feet and swung his arms like a windmill, warming up his body as if he didn't have a care in the world. In fact he was covertly sizing up the Hammer's muscularity compared with his own. His opponent was of similar height but had a very different body. Wide shopfront belly, thighs like tree trunks, arms covered with sentimental tattoos vowing eternal love for his mother and assorted females. The Hammer's face was not his finest feature – a puffy map with a nose that looked like a potato dumpling.

Jake knew his own body and what he could make it do when he was in top form. He had strenuously exercised his leg since it was free of the cast. How many rounds could he count on to see the distance? He was confident he would be faster on his feet than the Hammer, had a longer reach and his southpaw stance was awkward but delivered a wicked left hook – if he could land it. At rock bottom he had youth on his side – and desperation.

Pete the Hammer was surrounded by supporters who roared approval when a weedy hanger-on bought him a giant jug of ale. The Hammer derisively waved away the accompanying pannikin, opened his bear-trap of a mouth and poured the jug's contents down his throat, spluttering and gargling to the delight of the crowd.

Jake wryly noted the contrast. Right now he didn't have two coins to rub together for the price of an Albion Ale. Last night he had slept in the bush in order to buy a bread loaf for breakfast and drank water from the fountain, but he consoled himself he would have money aplenty to knock back a few ales after he collected the winner's purse.

Losing didn't bear thinking about.

During the opening round the partisan crowd was clearly rooting for the Hammer. But Jake felt gratified his assessment was accurate. He danced around his heavier, slower opponent to aggravate him and gain his measure. Jake's weaving caused the older fighter's most damaging blows to glance off Jake's shoulder and the side of his head. In contrast, Jake managed to return a barrage of telling jabs.

Although Jake slipped and was forced to take the thirty-second count that ended the first round, from there on his confidence steadily rose. He kept reminding himself that the Hammer was past his prime while he hadn't yet reached his.

Jake never took his eyes from that podgy face for a second. He read the message in the bleary eyes that signalled the throwing of the man's next punch seconds before he delivered it. Jake inwardly crowed. *I'm going to win, you bastard. Watch me!*

At the end of the next round Jake coldly eyed his opponent's bewilderment when the moment dawned on the man he was outclassed.

It was when the Hammer was down for the count for the second consecutive time that Jake saw it. A landau carriage that drew up on the edge of the crowd. The driver climbed down to gain a closer view of the fight. Two ladies were seated in the open carriage. Both faces were focused on him. Only one of them mattered. *Jenny.*

A parasol framed her head. No black wig. Her long blonde hair waved in the wind. Her pouting lips curved in a teasing smile of recognition.

Their eyes met and the blood rush of battle drained out of Jake. He looked into those dark eyes and his memories of their life together came rushing back with love that overwhelmed him.

Jenny gave him her secret smile. They both knew the truth. Jake felt an acute flash of pain that was not caused by the blow from Pete the Hammer that caught him off guard. It was the pain that proved his wife still held him in thrall.

Jake had a sliver of memory of that first ever time she watched him fight but now Jenny was dressed like a lady of Quality – kept by another man!

Consumed by a burst of rage that almost blinded him, Jake lost control and delivered a bombardment of killer blows.

Desperate to end this fight, to be free to grab hold of her, he lost concentration for a split second – a mistake that gave the Hammer the opportunity to knock Jake to his knees. As the referee began the count Jake knew he could easily fight on to win, but he couldn't lose Jenny again. He remained on his knees, and waited out the count.

At the sound of victorious cheers for the Hammer, Jake jumped to his feet and pushed his way through the throng towards her carriage.

He felt as if he would choke with rage when she tapped her driver on the shoulder with her fan and ordered him to drive off at full speed.

Jake desperately broke free of the crowd. Standing alone in the middle of the open road, he stretched his arms towards the disappearing carriage and called out her name.

Jenny gave him a backward glance. He saw the gleam of excitement in her eyes.

He had lost her again.

CHAPTER 21

When Keziah heard the excited babble of children's voices she lifted Gabriel from his little tin tub. At four months old he loved water so much he was always loathe to leave it. Wrapping him in a towel she hurried to the veranda to watch the arrival of Sunny Ah Wei's travelling emporium. She hoped he'd have new bolts of winter fabrics and news of the outside world.

Drawn by a horse in a harness lavishly decorated with brass, the red, green and gold wagon was a joy to behold. Emblazoned on the side under his name a golden scroll advertised the magical list of contents for sale – Chinese robes, silks, haberdashery, toys, confectionery, kitchenware and herbal medicines that claimed to cure 'toothache, dyspepsia and all manner of human, canine and horses' ills'.

Barefoot children ran down the track to keep pace with the wagon. Sunny Ah Wei was dressed in his customary robe and cap, his thin pigtail swinging down his back, his face lit up with the celestial smile that had earned him his Australian nickname. Sunny's reputation endeared him to all, not only because his exotic merchandise arrived like manna from heaven in isolated lives, but because of his cheap prices and fair dealings.

While sorting through materials Keziah fished for news after the children had run off. If anyone collected rumours on his travels, it was Sunny, but he preferred to be the bearer of *good* news.

'Many people collect money for statue in Sydney Town to honour last governor.'

Keziah was pleased to hear it. 'Mr Bloom says Sir Richard Bourke tried to give us elected government and schools for rich and poor but those damned Exclusives blocked him.'

She steered the conversation to Bolthole Valley, asking Sunny for local news.

'Big crowd at cemetery for laying of tombstone for lady killed at Blackman's Leap last year.'

'Who did that?' she asked quickly, hoping to remain anonymous.

'Good soul but no one know who paid money.'

'What is the latest bushranger activity? I hear The Gypsy has been sighted.'

Sunny lowered his voice. 'I think this bolter bail me up last week.'

There was no one in sight but Keziah also whispered. 'How do you know it was him?'

'One gold earring. Dressed very flash. Silver belt, gold coins on waistcoat. He said strange thing. "A fine wagon, Sunny. I made Romani wagon for my wife in Wales."'

Keziah forced herself to ask the conventional question. 'Did he take all your money?'

Sunny shook his head. 'Only one silver ring and he *paid* for it!'

Keziah was overcome with pride that Gem would not steal from another outsider. Once she was back in her cottage her tears rained on the black mourning veil she had just sewn to her bonnet.

After the arrival of Jake Andersen's note warning that Caleb Morgan threatened to post a reward for her arrest on his return to Sydney Town, Keziah had acted swiftly. She had sent an anonymous cash order to Bolthole Valley's stonemason and now she knew the tombstone was in place. But the inscription was crucial. Was it correct?

Nerida hovered in the doorway, sensitive to Keziah's emotions.

Keziah brushed away her tears. 'I know you fear ghosts as much as I do, Nerida, but I need to visit a friend's grave.'

On arriving in Bolthole Valley, Keziah encouraged Nerida to accompany her to Feagan's General Store. She knew how painful Nerida's memories of this place must be.

'Remember, Nerida, you are my friend and you are employed at Ironbark Farm where everyone respects you. Nobody will dare treat you rudely when you are with me!'

After collecting the latest newspapers she had ordered, Keziah was careful to assume Saranna's well-bred accent when she asked Feagan for directions to the cemetery.

His sharp eye noticed the bouquet of flowers she carried and he quickly assumed a suitable expression of respect for a mourner.

'I am sorry for your loss, Miss Plews. Was your dear departed a near relative?'

'Keziah Smith and I were passengers on the coach that crashed at Blackman's Leap last year. I was at her side when she died but I have been unable to visit her grave till now.'

'Then you'll be pleased to discover the new headstone some anonymous person erected.' There was innuendo in his voice as he added, 'It would seem the Gypsy girl had friends in high places.'

Keziah disguised her fear by idly examining the label on a tea caddy. 'What makes you think so?'

'An English gentleman named Morgan came here in search of her. It was my sad duty to inform him where her remains are buried. He was disturbed by my revelation.'

Keziah found it difficult to breathe. 'Is that gentleman still here?'

'He departed on yesterday's coach. Nothing much here to hold a man of the Quality.'

The cemetery was deserted. Keziah opened the iron gate then hesitated. Across the road in Hobson's cart the two little boys lay asleep in Nerida's lap. Murphy's dark head lay nestled against Gabriel's blond curls.

She adjusted the mourning veil on her bonnet. In the non-denominational corner she stood before a standing stone and felt a rush of guilt mixed with relief as she read the inscription. *Sacred to the Memory of KEZIAH SMITH. Daughter of GABRIEL STANLEY. Born*

Wales 1820. Accidentally Killed Blackman's Leap 1837. At the bottom edge was the carefully worded phrase she had requested. *May the young girl who lies here rest in peace.*

Keziah felt guilty that Saranna had been buried in unsanctified ground, unmarked by her Christian cross, but this false tombstone was necessary to ensure Gabriel's safety.

'I had no choice at all!' she said, startled by the sound of her voice. After checking to make sure that she was unobserved, she placed on the grave her posy of bush flowers entwined with her favourite herb, rosemary for remembrance.

As she retraced her steps towards the gate she froze at the sight of an approaching horseman wearing a grey cloak and high-crowned hat. *Mi-duvel! It's Caleb!*

In panic she hid herself behind a tombstone and prayed to *The Del* to make her invisible, but as he rode past she saw the older man bore no resemblance to Caleb.

She giggled from sheer relief and apologised to the unknown owner of the grave. 'Forgive me, I'm starting at shadows.'

Back in the cart she woke Gabriel from his sleep and held him tightly in her arms.

'My little Rom. Now we are free,' she said, feeling far from convinced. She had spent all her money on the tombstone to prove Keziah Smith was dead. She wondered if she had succeeded in fooling Caleb Morgan.

The four of them sang together as Keziah drove home through the forest. She was grateful for her narrow escape. Only one day earlier and she could have collided with Caleb at Saranna's grave.

Today *baxt* was on her side but she must continue to lay low until she was convinced Caleb had left the colony. Surely he would not remain in this outpost of the British Empire – he loved luxury too much.

Glancing at Gabriel, Keziah clung to the wild hope that Gem would accept the myth of his adoption. Jealousy was inborn in every Rom but in Gem it was uncontrollable. She shivered, remembering that terrible day in North Wales.

Keziah sauntered along the riverbank, waiting for Gem's return from trading a horse. A hare sped across her path, causing her to fall headlong into the water. Unable to swim, she felt the river sucking at her skirt, dragging her down to its depths. Within seconds water would fill her lungs. Her arms flayed wildly, tangled by reeds. Looking up through the water at the sunlight, she sent her thoughts to Gem. My beloved, I am yours even in death. *And then nothing but blackness.*

She regained consciousness to find herself being carried in the arms of a gaujo. *Gem's voice roared out, accusing the man of rape. When Gem seized him by the throat, the stranger was so stunned he dropped Keziah to the ground.*

Keziah screamed that the gaujo *had saved her life but Gem was so consumed by rage that he was deaf to her words. Until she struck his face so forcibly it left a livid mark. Only then did Gem release his grip. The* gaujo *did not wait to be thanked and raced off into the woods.*

Keziah was horrified. 'If I hadn't struck you, you'd have been hanged for murder!'

Gem gave a wild cry, took her face in his hands and his kiss devoured her. He tore off her wet clothing and hungrily made love to her.

As Keziah looked across at Gabriel asleep again in Nerida's arms she dreaded Gem's rage when he saw the child. *If he was so jealous of an innocent man, how on earth will he react to you, little one?*

On Saturday morning Keziah opened her door to find herself eye to eye with a trooper, Sergeant Kenwood. She invited him to try her cherry cake and poured him tea, chattering with the veneer of Saranna's lady-like manner masking her feminine Romani guile.

Kenwood was a stocky Englishman with an accent difficult to

fathom because of the harelip he disguised with a russet-brown moustache. He was clearly disarmed by her warm hospitality. Not every settler in this locality treated troopers with such respect.

His question caught her off guard. 'I am investigating the death of Mrs Smith, a Gypsy traveller. I understand you are a survivor of the Blackman's Leap coach tragedy.'

Keziah assumed her most cooperative attitude. 'I was present when Dr O'Flaherty pronounced her dead. I placed gold coins on the eyelids of her corpse out of respect for her Romani traditions. Then I rode to the Shamrock and Thistle Inn for help. I later returned the horse to Rolly Brothers,' she added quickly, mindful of the savage penalties for horse theft.

'Did the dead woman ever mention a Mr Caleb Morgan?'

To hide her anxiety Keziah pressed him to accept a whisky from the bottle she kept to loosen tongues and gain information.

'No, but I recall Mrs Smith said she was a widow and an actress.'

Whisky warmed Kenwood to his subject. 'Forgive the indelicacy of the question but was Mrs Smith well advanced with child?'

Her mind raced to provide a convincing answer. 'We had occasion to share a bed at an inn. Keziah was no more with child than I am.'

She flung her arms wide to offer an agreeable view of her full bosom and slim waist.

Kenwood flushed brick red. 'Quite. Thank you.'

'May I venture to ask who had such a strange idea?'

'The said gentleman, Caleb Morgan. I can now report to him no child existed.'

Keziah refilled the trooper's glass. He downed the whisky with satisfaction then asked if she'd heard of the bushranger Gypsy Gem Smith.

'The blighter's jolly hard to track down. Perhaps the two Smiths were related given their common vagabond origin?'

She forced a smile. 'I understand many Romanies are transported to the colony.'

His tone was conspiratorial. 'England's riddance, what?'

After his departure Keziah leaned against the door taking in large gulps of air, wondering if her performance had convinced him.

'God damn your *gaujo* eyes, Kenwood!' One thought consoled her. Gem was free and close by.

Through the window she saw Trooper Kenwood dismount at Joseph Bloom's homestead. She was alarmed by the realisation of her mistake. She had automatically said 'Romani' to correct Kenwood's word 'Gypsy' in common usage by *gaujos*. Had Kenwood noticed?

Keziah's anxiety grew after finding under her door a hand-written invitation to afternoon tea at Joseph Bloom's house after school. Was this connected with Kenwood's investigation? Or a pretext to be alone with her? Despite his kindly solution to the problem of keeping Big Bruce MacAlister in school, Keziah still remained cautious around Joseph Bloom.

His house was unusual. In contrast to the standard separation between cookhouse and living quarters to contain any outbreak of fire, his *two* separate kitchens were a source of much speculation in the village. Local women didn't know the reason so gossip invented one. Keziah had overheard the claim that Mrs Rachael, Bloom's housekeeper, needed two because she kept burning pots and pans, that Mrs Rachael failed Bloom in the kitchen but pleased him in the bedroom! Their laughter was knowing, not vicious, as this type of arrangement was what assigned women could expect from a lonely master.

Keziah had discovered the truth. Mrs Rachael, a Polish Jewess transported from London's East End, kept a kosher household. One kitchen was for kosher meat brought from Goulburn, the other for dairy foods.

Keziah paused before Joseph Bloom's door. Attached to the doorframe was a small silver cylinder inscribed with an odd letter. She had seen similar *mezuzahs* in Liverpool and Chester, and knew it contained holy words on a tiny scroll. Right now she really could use a blessing!

Ushered into the sitting room by Mrs Rachael, Keziah had time to observe the housekeeper – a sedate matron so spick and span her white apron looked as if it would recoil from the mere suggestion of a stain. Despite the woman's age, Keziah knew how loneliness attracts strange bedfellows and instinct told her that Mr Bloom was a lonely young man.

Guest and host faced each other on throne-like chairs. Keziah was glad she had dressed in Saranna's formal travelling outfit that she had re-tailored to fit her. Joseph Bloom wore a conservative English frock-coat with pinstriped trousers and a gold watch chain looped across his waistcoat. His black cap looked to Keziah like a velvet tea-cosy.

Loud noises came from one of Mrs Rachael's kitchens. Keziah wondered if the woman was making her presence felt as chaperone or as a jealous mistress?

When Joseph Bloom left the room Keziah studied the bookcase. Some titles were in a language she presumed was German, others were written in an unknown alphabet. Alarmed by the title, *Famous British Murder Trials*, Keziah felt a wave of nausea as she had a vision. *Joseph Bloom was in a courtroom wearing a barrister's wig. A red-robed judge sat before the British coat of arms.*

On her host's return Keziah turned her attention to an exquisite silver seven-branched candlestick. Noting her interest he was happy to explain what it was.

'This menorah is my most valued possession, inherited from my father Yitzhak Blum of Blessed Memory. A trader in old clothes, he saved for me to study Talmud at the yeshiva in Worms to become a rabbi. I regret I disappointed him. I chose to be a lawyer.'

'You decided not to practise law in the colony, Mr Bloom?'

He explained that it was not permitted for those of the Hebrew persuasion to practise law in the German lands. After his father's death he went to London to work for his Uncle Shmuel, who gained permission for him to study British law. After being called to the Bar his health had deteriorated.

'The London winters?' He shrugged philosophically. 'Ironbark's healthy climate healed my lungs. But perhaps I was never meant to practise law?'

'Yes, you are! The colony needs your gifts!' Keziah said this with such conviction that it startled them both. She added hastily, 'If you should so decide.'

Invited to discuss her pupils' progress she felt on safer ground.

'Even the youngest children recite their alphabet with confidence and can write their names. Winnie had trouble learning to read but she has a wonderful gift for drawing. She sees everything in pictures. So I invented a special alphabet made up of little stick figures.'

'How does that work?' he asked politely.

She jumped to her feet to enact it. 'The letter M is two boys facing each other and shaking hands. T is a scarecrow. P is a fat man with a puffed-out chest.'

Joseph Bloom's smile made him look quite boyish. Encouraged, Keziah rushed on.

'The older children write and illustrate their own book. They pool their talents on each chapter, free to write about the world around them or soar off on a flight of fancy. I gave the final chapter to a Catholic and a Protestant who always squabble. Now they must pull together to write it.' She paused, suddenly serious. 'Am I talking too much?'

'Not at all. Your enthusiasm is most refreshing.'

Keziah continued on. 'I am concerned about Big Bruce MacAlister. He will soon need to study at a higher level than I can teach him. He needs to study Latin, science or law.'

'I share your concern. I am working on a way he can be granted a scholarship to attend a senior school, yet still allow his mother to survive comfortably on her farm.'

Keziah clapped her hands. 'How clever of you.'

He looked pleased but changed the subject. 'How do the children spend their leisure?'

'Leapfrog, races. Their favourite game is "Bushrangers and Troopers". I *was* disturbed to discover troopers literally flogging little Davey Collins for his crimes as a bushranger.'

'Children reflect the adult world. May I ask how you dealt with this problem?'

'I suggested the bushrangers challenge the troopers to a game of cricket.' She gave him a sidelong smile. 'The bushrangers won by three wickets.'

'What an ingenious solution. Despite my British citizenship cricket remains one of life's mysteries to me but it is an excellent way to teach children fair play.'

Just as Keziah was beginning to relax, his next question unnerved her. Did she believe in coincidences? Keziah tried to give a neutral response but Joseph Bloom was gazing into the middle distance as if he had half forgotten her presence as he explained the reason for his question.

Yesterday he had been reading the passage from the Book of Job, 'Nowhere in the land were women as beautiful as Job's daughters'. One of whom was *Keziah*. Then Trooper Kenwood had arrived to question him about the coach tragedy victim, Keziah Smith.

'The same girl Jakob Andersen said Caleb Morgan was pursuing, you remember when I passed on Jakob Andersen's letter to you?'

Keziah felt the blood drain from her face. *How on earth could I ever forget!* 'Keziah Smith was my fellow passenger. I told Trooper Kenwood all I knew. Is there a problem?'

'No. I just thought you might be interested in the *coincidence*.'

Keziah felt a sense of relief when her host left the room again to ask Mrs Rachael to serve tea.

Left alone Keziah desperately tried to predict Joseph Bloom's next move. First Jake, now Kenwood. Pure coincidence? No! Joseph Bloom had linked her to Keziah Smith! Lawyers were clever, tricky by nature. How could she hope to hoodwink him? Would he expose her? Or invite her to share his bed as the price of his silence?

She pressed her fingertips to her temples convinced that the life at Ironbark Farm she had built for Gabriel was going to be shattered. *Why am I always fated to run away?*

Joseph Bloom returned with Mrs Rachael carrying a silver tea service and rich cakes. He cast Keziah a searching look but his request for her to pour tea appeared to be innocent.

Keziah poured it in her best Saranna Plews style. Again she was caught off guard.

'I should imagine, Miss Plews, that as a teacher you are interested in history?'

She teetered on the verge of panic. Her grasp of history was elementary. What if he asked her about King Canute or that awful King Henry who chopped off his wives' heads?

Joseph Bloom seemed content to question himself. 'What exactly *is* history? Records by historians to flatter their rulers and patrons? Or is it what *ordinary* folk experience when their world veers off its axis?'

Keziah thankfully accepted an almond cake to avoid replying.

'Women are the hidden characters in European history,' he reflected. 'Apart from royalty, wives of famous men and, forgive me, courtesans, their role is seldom recognised.'

Keziah tried to assume an intelligent expression but her thoughts were in chaos. *Courtesans!* Where was all this leading? His bedroom? *If Gem found me in a compromised situation he would shoot to kill and ask questions later!*

Joseph Bloom continued on blithely. 'And yet women by nature are enormously influential in building communities and achieving change. We Jews are fond of the quotation, "a woman of valour's worth is above rubies".'

He offered her another cake. 'It seems to me you ladies are the *spaces between the lines* of the historical events recorded by the male of the species.'

Keziah was out of her depth. Did he expect her to say something? Was this a trap? He opened a book that had the title *A History of the Romani Tribes of Europe*. Keziah choked on her tea.

'The Romanies are a nomadic people that a lazy world labels Gypsies. We Jews are known as the People of the Book. Romani people are sometimes called the Brothers of the Wind. Both our peoples have parallel experiences of persecution. Both forced to flee from country to country across Europe.'

He appeared unaware of her reaction. 'At different times my people were granted refuge by enlightened or mercenary rulers but later made scapegoats, the subject of false libels. In medieval Spain we were given three choices. Flee, enforced conversion or be slaughtered.'

Despite Keziah's trepidation she was fascinated by the parallels he was drawing.

Joseph Bloom continued. 'The Romanies possess an extraordinary life force. Despite persecution they retained their nomadic way of life down through the ages. No host nation ever destroyed their soul.'

He placed the book on the table. 'You may care to read it. In my opinion Jews and Romanies are heroes in the art of survival. Why? I suspect we have three traits in common. We cling to our own relationship with our Creator but do not force our beliefs on others. We greatly respect animals and the natural world. We *love and protect our children*.'

Keziah looked into his eyes and at last understood the message behind his words.

When he enquired about her foster son, Keziah was happy to sing Gabriel's praises.

She decided the timing was perfect. 'Is there some way I can formally adopt him?'

'There is nothing so secure as a legally binding piece of paper. Leave that to me. I will arrange for you to sign the legal documents,' Joseph Bloom offered. He poured wine into two thimble-sized glasses. 'You are a teacher of great value to our community. In Hebrew we toast to life. *L'chaim!*'

Keziah gave him her most glorious smile and repeated the toast. The wine tasted even sweeter mixed with her sense of relief. She left his house, light of heart and convinced Joseph Bloom was to be trusted. Both came from tribes that had suffered at the hands of *gaujos*.

That night as she bathed Gabriel by the fire, Keziah was startled by an image in the dancing blue flames – Gem being pursued by the traps! Was this the future or was he in danger right now?

She was suddenly aware that Gabriel was crying, trying to bring her back to him.

Forcing herself to block out that frightening fragment of time she cuddled him in her arms.

'Forgive your mama, Gabriel. I was so slow to love you but you are teaching me to be a good mother. I'll make it up to you, I promise.'

That night she tossed and turned trying to sleep. She knew that Gem was the love of her life. So why did the image of Jake Andersen keep intruding into her thoughts?

Part II
The Avenger

June 1838 – November 1841

God does not pay at the end of every week.
But he pays.

Anne of Austria to Cardinal Mazarin

CHAPTER 22

Gabriel lay in his cot happily singing himself to sleep, as was his habit. Keziah settled down by the fire with the latest newspapers.

She was startled to read in *The Sydney Herald* that an expedition had been mounted to search for the fabled Inland Sea. One particular line leapt right off the page. *'The leader of the forthcoming expedition is an Englishman new to the colony, Mr Caleb Morgan, son of John Morgan of Lancashire, a gentleman said to be well known to Governor Gipps.'*

Mi-duvel! Caleb's still here! With no one to share her fury she was overcome by frustration. Grabbing the nearest object she ran outside and hurled the boot at a tree. Too late she saw that the tree harboured an innocent family of cockatoos – who squawked in high-pitched outrage as they abandoned their refuge in full flight.

'Sorry, cockies!' she said contritely. She felt relieved her schoolchildren were not present to witness Miss Plews throwing a tantrum. Would she never master her fiery Romani temper?

Keziah returned inside to search the other newspapers for more clues to Caleb's movements.

What had caused Caleb to become involved in such a harebrained scheme? The whole colony was divided about whether the fabled Inland Sea even existed. Some believers were ready to put money on the intrepid young explorer Edward Eyre being the man to discover it. Others backed Charles Sturt.

Far better men than Caleb Morgan deserved to be chosen. But no doubt Morgan money was behind it, and Caleb expected to make history and cover the Morgan name with glory. The idea of him leading an expedition was absurd. *The fool couldn't cross the road without a black tracker to guide him!* But then she remembered the prediction she had given him in the library at Morgan Park. She *had* seen him crossing a desert with black men – returning a hero!

Overwhelmed with sudden panic she burst into tears of frustration. The newspapers' dates meant the expedition might have already departed. It was expected to take six months. That meant Caleb *would* return from this stupid exploration a public hero, lionised by colonial society. What hope would she have then to retain custody of Gabriel?

She tried to convince herself. *I've pulled myself out of tough situations before this. I've got six months to devise a plan to block him!*

Next morning Keziah discovered an envelope had been placed under her door during the night. She tore it open with shaking hands, expecting to see the Morgan family crest. Instead she found a note from Joseph Bloom, advising her he had received communication from a Sydney Town lawyer acting on instructions from Caleb Morgan. She was alarmed to read:

> *This lawyer states that his client is convinced that the body buried in Bolthole cemetery is not Mrs Keziah Stanley also known as Mrs Smith – and that she is alive and has kidnapped the Morgan heir. He advises he has in his possession a legal document in which Keziah Stanley signed away all rights to this child in exchange for a generous payment from the Morgan family. The lawyer requested me to supply him with any information about this woman and child as his client intends to take this matter to court on his return from leading an expedition into the Interior of the Continent.*
>
> *I have written to inform him that the police thoroughly investigated the coach tragedy and Keziah Smith's fellow passengers confirmed her demise. Furthermore that the heavy demands of my legal practice prevent my being of further assistance in this matter.*
>
> *Knowing that you, Miss Plews, were one of Keziah Smith's*

fellow passengers I thought it only proper to inform you of these developments.

Your obedient servant, Joseph Bloom

Keziah covered her mouth to stifle a cry that would have woken Gabriel. Struggling to regain her calm she re-read the letter and thanked *The Del* for Joseph's loyalty and tactful concern for her. She knew that at present he only practised law to help friends in need and his reference to his demanding practice was designed to block Caleb's lawyer. Not for the first time she cursed herself for having signed John Morgan's contract, which would be damaging evidence against her in court.

In despair she crossed to the tiny bedroom and looked at the little blond angel in his cot. The only features that Gabriel had inherited from her were violet-blue eyes. Otherwise every other feature showed that he was Caleb Morgan's son – especially the cowlick. If Gabriel was ever presented in court what jury would believe that she had adopted him as a foundling?

All the next day Keziah searched the horizon, convinced someone important to her was drawing closer. The approaching figure of a man driving a battered old wagon aroused two conflicting instincts. Fear of discovery and a strange feeling of protection, a sense of lightness that seemed to emanate from him.

It was Jake Andersen!

His weathered hat flew off to hang behind him from a cord around his throat – leaving his long red-gold hair to be whipped by the wind. His striped shirt was blown open to the waist. His face, arms and chest were tanned golden brown. His eyes narrowed against the light of the sun and his crooked smile was lazy and confident. Keziah was pleased to see him. He was unlike any man she had ever met. Direct, strong, yet with a wild boyish streak that sprang from his colonial roots.

She ran out onto the veranda to greet him.

'I'm relieved to find you fully recovered. May I offer you tea, Mr Andersen?'

'It's Jake. Reckon I won't say no. Hey, something smells good.'

'My grandmother's special Romani cake. I knew a friend would call today!'

'I forgot you know everything before it happens.'

She laughed and he grinned back at her. Today he was clean-shaven so she could really see his features for the first time. The strong jaw, the mouth wide and generous. She found she needed to turn away from the frank expression in those grey eyes.

Why was he here? He hadn't come to try to get what all men wanted. Or had he?

Jake anticipated her unasked question. 'Don't worry about your good name. I've just announced my presence to Joseph Bloom. He knows I'm safe around women.'

Keziah could not conceal her curiosity. 'But how did you know I was Saranna?'

Jake looked embarrassed. 'I didn't. I just *hoped* it was you.'

Jake sat watching Keziah all that afternoon as she rustled up cakes and biscuits for a tea that stretched for hours. His memories of the Widow Smith were at odds with the way she looked now. *Her jungle of hair is as untamed as ever. She's still a big girl. But now her waist is tiny. That bloody Caleb Morgan claims she's hiding his kid. Jesus wept! That means when I first met her she must have had a bun in the oven!*

During the coach journey he'd been irritated by her barrage of questions. Now they were sitting at her kitchen table yarning for hours like old friends. When Keziah pressed him to stay to supper, Jake was quick to accept.

At the sound of a child's voice calling out from the bedroom, Keziah lifted the babe from his cot and carried him in to join them, adding hastily, 'This is Gabriel, a little foundling who was left in a box at the schoolhouse.'

Jake nodded. *Right, if that's the way she wants to play it. I'll go along with that.*

He felt at ease as he bounced little Gabriel on his crossed legs in rhythmic pace to the same nursery rhyme he'd sung to his younger brothers. 'Ride a cockhorse to Banbury Cross. To see a fine lady ride on a white horse. With rings on her fingers and bells on her toes – Gabriel shall have music wherever he g-o-e-s!'

At the end of the verse Jake tossed him up in the air, causing Gabriel to squeal in delight. Jake repeated the game and Gabriel jigged to continue it.

'You'll get tired of that game before he does,' laughed Keziah.

'Nice kid you've got here. His eyes are a dead ringer for yours.'

She hesitated as if carefully selecting her words to avoid an outright lie. 'He's … I've legally adopted him. Best for him.'

'Yeah, good idea,' said Jake.

She looked him straight in the eye. 'You're an extraordinary man, Jake Andersen. You know who I am, but you haven't asked me why I'm living under Saranna's name. I owe you an explanation.'

'You owe me nothing. I owe you my life,' Jake said.

'It was your destiny to survive.'

He felt Keziah watching him as Gabriel gently pushed bits of cake into Jake's mouth as if he was feeding a bird.

'Jake, I want you to know why I'm here. I thought my new life as Saranna Plews would be good for *him*. But I've got myself into a terrible mess. I don't know how on earth to get out of it!'

Jake felt awkward when he saw tears rolling down her cheeks.

'Hey, don't upset yourself. It'll curdle your milk or something.'

When she gasped, Jake could have kicked himself. *Me and my big mouth. I didn't mean to embarrass her by stumbling on the truth about her kid.*

Keziah told him how she had successfully stolen Saranna's name and position as schoolmistress. How she owed Saranna a debt of honour – to deliver her dying message.

'I don't know her fiancé's name. He must be in hell wondering what happened to her.'

Jake tried to sound confident. 'Look, there's a way to fix everything. Damned if I know exactly what at the moment, but leave it with me. I'll sort it out.' He added casually, 'When I was in Sydney Town I saw that Pommy bloke who thinks the world of himself. Caleb Morgan.'

Jake saw that same flash of fear he'd seen in her eyes the day he had met her when that Cockney informer had quizzed him about Keziah Stanley.

He added quickly, 'I only saw Morgan from a distance. He was leading his expedition down Macquarie Street from Government House, heading off on that fool's mission to find the Inland Sea – what ain't there, of course. So if you're real lucky the bloody fool will never find his way back.' He flushed with embarrassment. 'Excuse the language!'

Keziah gave him a wondrous smile. 'Wouldn't it be wonderful if he got a medal – and sailed straight back to England!'

'Best place for him!' said Jake. Pleased by her response to his visit, he stood up preparing to go. 'Well, best I let you get your beauty sleep. Thanks for the great grub. I'm sick of my own cooking.'

'You're welcome anytime, Jake.'

It sounded to him like she really meant it. He paused on the veranda. 'Ever seen a platypus?'

'What's that?'

'Hey, you've got a real treat in store. How's about I take you and the kid for a drive tomorrow? They're real shy but I know a creek where they breed. Those little fellas are sheer magic. I'll pick you up after breakfast. Say half seven?'

And so began the pattern of their occasional Sunday explorations. To Keziah it seemed that whenever she was with Jake the sun was always shining. It was clear to her that although Jake was 'a man's man' he was widely known for his respect for good women. Jake always made their trips known to Hobson and Bloom, and to prevent any gossip before it broke out he made sure everyone in the locality was aware that he was beholden to the schoolteacher for saving his life after the Blackman's Leap accident.

Keziah sensed that Jake felt as comfortable as she did, both of them safe in the knowledge each was locked in a consuming relationship – Keziah in love, Jake in hate. Keziah had no need to hide her feelings for Gem. She made Jake retell his encounter with Gem on the road gang. Every detail about Gem was rough comfort.

Jake barely mentioned Jenny. Although he hotly denied it, Keziah knew he was still obsessed by his bolter. Every Romani understood that hate and love are two sides of the same coin. The less Jake said about his Jenny, the more curious she became.

On one of their Sunday drives west of Ironbark they were miles from any habitation when Jake drove down a rugged but well-made road that suddenly stopped dead in the heart of the bush. He explained this unfinished road had been intended to link remote villages to Sydney Town.

'The surveyor committed suicide in disgrace. He built the road in the wrong direction. A road to nowhere.'

A half-hewn track skirted a giant cliff face on its eastern flank. To the west, the bush framed an expanse of open country. Jake pointed out a mob of galloping horses. 'Now that's real freedom. Brumbies are born in the wild. They reckon they get their name from horses that bolted in the early years of the colony – owned by some Major Brumby.'

Keziah was excited by the sight of the white horse in the lead. 'What a beauty!'

'Yeah and just look at her go! No wonder bushrangers break in the best of these brumbies, hide them in corrals. Some of the places where bolters hole up is an open secret. But the country's wild and they keep changing their address. They ride cross-country from one bail-up to another a hundred miles away. No wonder the bloody traps are baffled.'

Keziah gazed wistfully at the smoky purple mountains. 'So Gem could be anywhere out there.'

'Yeah but he's smart, your husband. Won't go hungry or get himself caught.'

She saw through his kindly lie but pressed on. 'But if a bolter doesn't take up arms, how can he survive?'

Jake hesitated. 'Some go bush. Try to live off the land. In the nineties, a wild rumour was spread by Irish convicts that there was a road to China on the other side of the Blue Mountains! The gov kept denying it existed, but that didn't stop the Irish, they escaped in droves. Some still do. Hope dies hard when a man's desperate.'

'I know,' she said sadly.

Jake changed the subject quickly. 'Well, time to head home.'

A few minutes later Keziah let out a piercing scream as a boulder rolled down the cliff and shattered the wagon's rear wheel.

Jake released a lungful of colourful expletives until suddenly aware Gabriel was watching his every move.

'Jesus wept! That was a close thing,' said Jake as he heaved the offending rock off the road.

'How about you brew us some tea? I'll get us on the road again. With a bit of luck we'll make Bran the Blacksmith's forge before sundown.'

Keziah soon had a small fire blazing and a billycan on the boil. She watched with quiet amusement as Jake laboured in the midday sun. Sweat stained his shirt and matted his hair. When he removed his shirt she could not fail to notice his beautifully developed torso. But unlike most men who had done a season in gaol his body seemed free from tattoos. Unlike her father. Unlike Gem.

'No tattoos, Jake?'

'No one's ever gunna put a brand on me!'

Keziah knew he really meant *no woman*. Jenny had already branded him for life.

She realised Jake swore as effortlessly as other men drew breath. The inventiveness of his repertoire made it sound like his own peculiar poetry. He whooped in triumph when he finished binding the wheel.

'This is makeshift but it'll see the distance to Bran's forge.'

'Where's that?'

'So you ain't met young Bran? Good lad. Do anything for you. Poor bugger's got this speech thing. His jaw moves but nothing much comes out. Just got to be patient.'

Keziah saw he was embarrassed when he caught her looking at him. He put his shirt on and sat himself at the other end of the fallen tree trunk.

When the water in the billycan was on a rolling boil, Jake threw in a handful of tea and stirred it with a twig of eucalyptus leaves. The aroma was tantalising. Then he held the billycan at arm's length and swung his arm like a windmill.

'See? That makes the tea leaves sink to the bottom.' After the first mouthful he gave his verdict. 'Aaah, now that's tea!'

They drank in silence. Minutes passed.

'What's up?' he asked.

'Nothing.'

'Yes there is. You're too bloody quiet. Ain't natural in a woman.'

'So you're the world's authority on women as well as horses,' Keziah said mildly.

'Something *is* up! Have I done something wrong or what?'

'No. I just noticed an odd thing about your swearing.'

'Just *now*? Struth, you know I always swear. Learned it with my mother's milk.'

Keziah assumed he was joking. 'You don't *always* swear, Jake.'

'Well, a man's got to sleep some time.'

She pointed out he had not sworn in front of women during their whole coach trip. Had he sworn in Jenny's presence?

'Bloody hell, no!'

She digested that fact. 'So why am I so different to other women?'

Jake took his time. 'I reckon it's 'cause you're not a woman – you're my mate.'

Startled, Keziah took a stab in the dark. 'Does that mean a Currency Lad feels more comfortable with a mate than with a woman?'

'Blood oath, yes!'

Keziah realised Jake had paid her his highest compliment, but she wasn't quite sure how she felt about it. *Does this mean he doesn't see me as a woman? Is this the price of our friendship? Or is it the new pattern of relationships between Currency women and men?*

'Do you mean husbands, wives and lovers come and go but mates are for life?'

Jake looked pleased with her forthright definition. 'I reckon that's it in a nutshell.'

Keziah swallowed. 'So if we're real mates, just like two men, you'll always tell me any news about Gem? Good or bad?'

'You can count on it.'

She nodded her thanks. 'Because no matter what, I'll always love Gem.'

Jake nodded. 'I know. And no matter what, I'm never gunna build my life around a good woman again. Never!'

He extended his hand and they solemnly shook hands. 'Mates!'

On their arrival at Bran the Blacksmith's forge, Keziah instinctively felt reluctant to enter. She told Jake she would remain outside to hold the sleeping Gabriel while the wheel was replaced. The truth was she felt something was very wrong. There was a heaviness in the air so oppressive she had a sudden blinding headache. Through the open face of the forge she saw that the young giant blacksmith looked harmless enough. It was the forge itself that seemed to radiate a sense of foreboding.

When a lone rider galloped up, wearing the flash garments of a gentleman, he hastily glanced around him before he dismounted and lead his horse inside the forge.

Keziah watched the blacksmith down tools and give immediate attention to replacing the horseshoes on the young man's horse. Judging by Jake's matey attitude it was clear the trio knew each other well.

Before the young rider rode away he doffed his hat to Keziah with a lopsided grin. 'Take care of my mate, Ma'am.'

Whistling when he rejoined her, Jake avoided her eyes.

Keziah wasn't going to let him off the hook. 'That was Jabber Jabber, the Gentleman Bushranger, wasn't it?'

Jake looked uncomfortable and Keziah knew why.

'Don't play games, Jake. He's the one who bailed us up and protected Saranna from One Eye!'

Jake said quickly, 'Yeah. But if the traps ask, you never saw him!'

'As if I would!'

They headed off as soon as the broken wheel was replaced. With the forge behind them her headache suddenly disappeared. Once more she felt light of heart.

'What a day! I saw the most extraordinary animal, the koala, met a famous bushranger who *didn't* bail me up, and I nearly got killed by a boulder.'

'Yeah,' Jake said with pride. 'There ain't no other country in the world to beat Australia.'

On their return to Keziah's cottage she offered Jake tea but he made a lame excuse about heading off to Bolthole Valley. Keziah stood on the veranda watching until horse and rider were cut off from sight by the bend in the road. Jake's reference to Bolthole Valley gave her an odd feeling. Whenever she went to Feagan's General Store men were marching in and out of the House of the Four Sisters. *I can't see Jake going there just to drink tea in their kitchen.*

She reminded herself that whatever Jake did was no concern of hers but curiosity overcame her. She dealt out a pattern of playing cards to see what clues she could find. These cards were no substitute for her lost Tarot, but they flooded her mind with images that suggested what the future held.

She was convinced Jake was still in love with Jenny, represented by the Queen of Hearts, a card closely linked to love and money. Keziah saw that Jenny was about to reappear in Jake's life. A rush of feelings confused her.

She hastily gathered up the cards and placed the pack at the back of the drawer, but pushing the thought of Jake to the back of her mind was not so easy.

Later that night, Keziah was standing at the window when a stranger rode past on a roan gelding. Although his profile was in shadow Keziah sensed his eyes were fixed on the cottage. The shiver down her spine warned her that whoever this man was, he was real trouble.

CHAPTER 23

The following Friday Keziah awoke with a sense of foreboding that she could not shake. The air seemed thick with some sort of turbulence. She found it difficult to breathe.

Nerida stood in the doorway with Murphy clinging to her skirt. The expression in her eyes confirmed Keziah's own anxiety.

'Let's take a walk before school, Nerida. Is there anything wrong?'

Nerida shook her head but avoided looking at Keziah as they started down the track.

After closing the gates of Ironbark Farm behind them, Keziah became uneasy about the unusual silence in the village. None of the few-acres farms showed any sign of life. The population seemed to have disappeared overnight.

On the track leading uphill to the small chapel Keziah saw where everyone had gone. The villagers were silently gathered around the church porch where George Hobson was addressing the crowd with Joseph Bloom by his side. Keziah noticed the towering figure of Bran the Blacksmith was standing apart, his eyes fixed intently on Hobson.

'Why are they all here?' Keziah whispered to Nerida. 'If bushrangers were sighted they'd have rung the school bell.'

Nerida's only response was to look downcast. Keziah felt her heart racing as she caught Hobson's words.

'... news of this massacre at Myall Creek is sending shockwaves throughout the colony. Reports are flying faster by word of mouth than the newspapers can reach us. Some are so wild they seem beyond belief. No doubt it will be weeks before we learn the full truth. But it would seem the basic facts are clear. The atrocity took place on 10 June on the Liverpool Plains, the troopers have only just discovered the evidence.'

Hobson rubbed his hands together in agitation. 'The bodies of twenty-eight blacks – old men, women and children – were found near the hut of a Mr Kilmaister near Myall Creek.'

A murmur rippled through the crowd. Was their reaction one of horror or something else? Keziah could not be sure as she was standing at the back of the crowd and unable to see their faces.

Hobson continued, stammering as he pointed out that the reason for the massacre was incomprehensible. There had been no uprisings by blacks for many years.

'If the story is true that Kilmaister befriended this tribe in the past they must have gathered around his hut confident of his protection,' he said.

Keziah instinctively drew her arm around Nerida's shoulders. The girl was trembling.

Hobson turned his head in their direction and the crowd followed his gaze, swinging around to stare at them. Their blank faces were unreadable.

Keziah whispered to Nerida, 'These are our friends. You're quite safe.' Her words sounded hollow as she felt Nerida's fear.

The crowd wanted answers. They peppered Hobson with their questions.

Hobson's gruff voice betrayed his emotion. 'The word is that a party of stockholders on Big River rode up armed with swords and pistols and roped the Aborigines in line. Only two shots were fired. The rest were butchered with swords. It's rumoured a pile of their half-charred bodies was discovered by the station manager.'

Keziah was devastated by the violent images. And she was horrified to hear some of the 'good people' in the community mumble sympathy for the murderers.

'How do we know it was Kilmaister's doing?' Griggs demanded.

Joseph Bloom answered quickly. 'We don't! The truth won't be revealed until the trial. But it seems the police have arrested him along with ten or eleven other white men. We're told they'll all stand trial for the murders.' He added with quiet emphasis, 'Let us hope British justice will be seen to be done.'

Griggs looked back at Nerida before he spoke to the man beside him loudly enough for all to hear. 'Everyone knows blackfellas ain't really human. They got smaller brains than us. I bet those poor white stockmen just followed their boss's orders.'

Keziah wanted to attack him with her bare hands, but she fought to remember she must be seen to act as Saranna Plews and control the full measure of her anger.

'So, Griggs, if my employer Mr Hobson ordered me to shoot *you* down like a dog, you'd feel sorry for *me* for having to obey orders, would you?'

There was a nervous murmur in the crowd. Griggs was taken aback by the quiet venom in her voice but managed to mumble, 'What would that uppity Pommy schoolma'am know?'

Joseph Bloom consulted his partner before he held up his hands for silence.

'Miss Plews, we want to assure Nerida that she and her little boy are safe at Ironbark Farm. You have our word on that.' He turned to the overseer and added coldly, 'I hold you personally responsible for their safety, Griggs.'

Badly shaken, Keziah nodded her thanks then hurried back to the cottage gripping little Murphy's hand as Nerida carried Gabriel on her hip.

Nerida made no comment about the outrage but she moved like a sleepwalker. Refusing Keziah's invitation to share their supper, she withdrew inside her *goondie.*

Next morning Keziah awoke to find that Nerida and little Murphy had vanished. She was overwhelmed with sadness. Clearly she had failed to convince Nerida she would protect them. Nerida no longer trusted any *gubba's* word, not even hers. Would she ever see her again?

It was a delightfully warm October afternoon as Keziah returned home after school, carrying Gabriel on her hip. Spring had brought the promise of nature's renewal of life after the tragedy of the past winter. But in the months since the massacre Keziah's dreams had revealed no sign of Nerida's return. Now as Keziah approached her hut, she saw the welcome figure of Jake Andersen sprawled in the squatter's chair, asleep under his hat, his feet propped on the veranda railing. He pushed back his hat but didn't bother to remove it as normal good manners demanded in a lady's presence.

Because I'm not a woman, I'm just his mate. Keziah felt a passing wave of irritation but reminded herself she had bigger things on her mind.

'Nice day,' said Jake. 'You and Gabe fancy a picnic?'

'I'd be glad of the company. I'm still worried about Nerida. There's been no sign of her.'

'She'll be back. Neri would never leave you except for some important blackfellas' business,' Jake stated firmly.

'I hope she's safe, wherever she is. Gabriel misses her too. It's just as well he loves all the attention he gets at school. He's as good as gold. Sings along with the children and sleeps in his basket. But to be selfish, I'm finding it hard managing without Nerida.'

'You all right?' he asked with concern.

'It's not only the horror of the massacre. I keep dreaming Gem is reaching out to me.'

Jake said evenly, 'Let's get the picnic ready.'

Keziah carried little Gabriel on her back in the string dillybag Nerida had woven for her. Despite his early birth Gabriel was big for nine months, giving every indication he would grow to be a big strong lad.

Jake loaded Horatio up with Keziah's picnic baskets and led them along the track towards the swimming hole. Hobson had ordained this was Keziah's private place to visit with Nerida and the children. No man at Ironbark Farm was allowed within sight of it.

Keziah tried to read Jake's mood. He was clearly preoccupied.

'Out with it, Jake. You've heard something about Gem? I was in Bolthole Valley yesterday. I overheard two men outside that house where those four sisters live. They were talking about some bushranger who wears a gold earring.'

When Jake gave her a sidelong glance, Keziah felt irritated. *Does he think I'm so stupid I don't know he's a regular at the House of the Four Sisters?*

'Look, Kez, I brought you here because I found something. Don't get excited. Might be nothing. You said you Romanies leave signs to show the direction you've taken?'

'You've found a *patrin*?' Her heart began to race.

'You tell *me*.'

They had reached a fork in the track. Keziah gave a cry of recognition at a bunch of twigs in which one stick pointed like an arrow.

'It's Gem's message to me! I *knew* he was close by!'

Clutching the *patrin* she ran ahead with Gabriel bouncing in the dillybag. At each fork in the path she found a fresh sign. She saw Jake following closely behind on full alert, his left hand flexed ready to draw the pistol from his belt.

'You don't need that,' she said firmly. 'Gem is no threat to us.'

'No, but there's no accounting for the violent company he keeps.'

They waded across the creek at a shallow ribbon crossing where a shelf of rocks formed a miniature waterfall. On the far side Jake examined a thick screen of branches and pointed out they were so recently axed from a bloodwood tree, the sap was running free like blood. A few yards further on the bush revealed an oval-shaped clearing, like a small cricket field.

Keziah's disappointment was acute. She set Gabriel down on the grass and allowed him to crawl free.

'I can't believe Gem tricked me,' she said in despair.

'Maybe he didn't. Just keep your distance,' Jake said quietly. 'You're Gem's woman. Mateship will only stretch so far.'

He walked a few yards ahead of her then flicked a finger to draw her attention to a quivering ti-tree. 'Stay perfectly still. He *didn't* trick you.'

A beautiful brumby colt emerged from the bush. Jet black and spirited, his blaze was shaped like a question mark. The rope that tethered him gave him ample freedom to graze and drink creek water. He looked wary of human contact. Keziah's throat tightened at the sight of his wild beauty, she was close to tears.

'I could break him in for you but there ain't enough time today,' said Jake.

Keziah shook her head. 'This is Gem's special gift to me. He's expecting me to do it.'

'Righto.' Jake stretched out in an open spot where Gabriel could crawl in safety.

'Don't let him play with snakes!' warned Keziah.

'I'm a bloody expert,' he claimed. 'Grew up looking after seven little brothers.'

Keziah smiled as she watched him feed Gabriel blackberries. She noted with pride the generous heart of her little son, who poked berries into Jake's mouth, sharing them with him.

The time had come. Quietly she moved away from them both, crossed over to the creek and sat cross-legged, no farther from the brumby than the length of his rope. She remained silent and completely still as she waited for the colt to lose his fear and come to her.

I'll wait for you, my brumby – in the same way I'll wait for you, Gem. Just as long as it takes.

All afternoon Jake sat watching Keziah and the brumby, impressed by her patience and Romani horse-breaking skills. He had previously seen her calm horses but a wild brumby was a different matter. She placed a lump of sugar in the sweat of her armpit then fed the sugar to the colt to bond him. Like magic, the brumby grew so obedient Keziah nuzzled him and whispered secret things in his ear.

Jake was embarrassed to discover he had a lump in his throat. It was like watching two people falling in love. He knew the brumby stood in place of Gem.

Gabriel had fallen asleep in the crook of Jake's arm, with a ring of blackberry juice staining his little mouth. Jake took off his hat to shade the boy's face from the sun, but he couldn't take his eyes from Keziah, her endless patience, her magical sense of timing, as if in truth she was reading the colt's thoughts.

Jake recognised when the perfect moment had come. Keziah hoisted her long skirt and slipped effortlessly astride the colt's bare back. As she rode him around the clearing, Jake saw the pride in her eyes and in the tilt of her head.

'No doubt about you, Kez. You've got a bloody clever way with horses.'

'My father taught me.'

After the brumby circled for the third time, content to have her on his back, Keziah rewarded him with wild bush apples. Then she dismounted, gently tethered the colt and raced off to wash her hands in the creek.

'You must be ravenous. I lost all sense of time,' she apologised.

Jake allowed her to press delicious food on him. She wiped Gabriel's face and hands with her handkerchief then cut up fruit for Gabriel, taking care of them both before feeding herself like a hungry child. When they were down to the last slice of cake she broke it in two and placed one half in Jake's mouth.

'Try this. It's like a kiss – good for nothing until it's shared between two.'

Jake's eyes widened. *Jesus! No wonder she gets into trouble.*

Keziah seemed quite oblivious. 'That's an old Romani proverb.'

Jake gulped and nodded. 'If it isn't some dark Romani secret, what did Gem's message say? Looked to me like any old bunch of twigs. But it sure got you excited!'

'A horse is the most precious gift a Rom can give. This brumby is Gem's special message. It tells me he is free, his spirit unbroken. He knows where I am and he will come to me – whenever he's free to reveal himself.'

She impulsively flung her arms around Jake's neck and hugged him. 'Thank you, Jake. I would never have found the brumby but for you!'

Jake felt a touch nervous. 'Watch your step, Kez. I don't fancy getting a bullet in my heart from a jealous husband. Seeing as I haven't had the pleasure of earning it!'

Her voice was soft as she gestured to the bush. 'Gem isn't here. Believe me, I'd know. Every human being has their own aura and smell. When you love someone you can always tell when they are near.'

The intensity of Keziah's love for Gem was naked and unashamedly passionate. Jake had never seen such a look on a woman's face before. *No woman ever looked at me like that.*

The sun was sinking fast. He jumped up and pulled Keziah to her feet.

'I reckon Gem'll come to you soon, when that bastard Gil Evans isn't snooping around. I'm dead happy you've found each other, Kez.' He wasn't sure if he meant the brumby or Gem. Maybe it was the same thing.

He led the way home on Horatio. He tried to regain his lightness of heart as he sang the rollicking verses of *Botany Bay* – the same song he had sung to little Pearl when she rode perched in front of him, her piping voice joining him in the final words of the chorus, 'Singing too-ral, li-ooral, li-addity … we're bound for Botany Bay.'

Jake closed his mind to that painful image. He looked down at little Gabriel riding like a prince within the protection of his arms. The boy was so responsive to each bird and bush animal that Jake needed to hold him tight to prevent Gabriel joyously catapulting into space.

Keziah rode the brumby bareback, apparently unconcerned that Jake could see her legs. *I reckon she doesn't think of me as a man, I'm just her mate. So why should I remind her of her Romani modesty? She's got the best god-damned ankles I ever saw on a woman.*

But when Keziah invited him to stay for supper Jake forced himself to decline. What he had seen that day with the business of the brumby was so private he suspected she would prefer to be alone with her thoughts.

'Thanks, but I reckon I'll just hop over to Bolthole Valley to see a mate. I've been a bit neglectful lately.' He mounted Horatio and turned in the saddle. 'Be a good girl, eh?'

Galloping towards Bolthole Valley Jake tried to dismiss all thoughts of Keziah, Gem and the brumby. He'd recently given her a Shetland pony for little Gabriel to learn to ride, but he knew nothing could ever surpass Gem's gift of the brumby.

He switched his thoughts to Lily Pompadour and his regular overnight booking with her as his 'wife'. Their arrangement was ironclad. If Jake didn't turn up on a Wednesday, Lily took no other clients that night and Jake paid her double on his next visit. He managed to dismiss the idea of the clients she entertained the rest of the week but he was very territorial about his Wednesday nights.

Tonight as he urged Horatio towards Madam Fleur's, Jake was anxious to see Lily. Although blatantly female she was as earthy as a man and always made him laugh before, during and after they pleasured each other.

That night Lily seemed determined to make every round a winner. No complaints from Jake. Afterwards he lay back pleased with himself and drank deeply of the special red wine Lily always chose for him. He became aware that Lily had been hidden behind her oriental screen for some time.

'What are you up to now, Lil?'

She appeared wearing Jake's jackeroo hat on top of her wild auburn locks, his red neckerchief around her throat and stood astride in his heeled riding boots, otherwise stark naked. Fists on her hips, Lily aped a masculine pose and barked in a gruff voice.

'I've paid good money for you! So you'd better be worth it. Live up to the reputation of the house or I'll burn the place down! And have you run out of town!'

Jake spluttered on his wine and collapsed on the bed helpless with laughter. Lily marched over. 'I'm serious! Get your clothes off at once, you tramp!' she ordered.

As they rolled around the bed Lily was tough-mouthed and on the offensive.

Jake surrendered. 'I'll do anything you want! Just leave the hat on! I'm seeing you in a whole new light, Lil!' He began chortling again, delighted by her rage.

Lily's performance was amazing, attuned to him on almost every level. Jake didn't bother to question this change in her. He would pay her well. She was such an absorbing diversion she managed to keep at bay all his thoughts of *patrins*, brumbies, Gem and above all that look on Keziah's face when she'd placed the cake in his mouth and said, 'It's like a kiss – good for nothing until it's shared between two.'

CHAPTER 24

Daniel Browne felt that light was his salvation, art the key to his survival. Australian sunlight had a seductive quality that transformed everything he was desperate to draw; scenes, landscapes, above all portraits. February 1839 was well into the second year of the drought and his second year at Gideon Park, and his limited views of the world around him showed the land to be parched and struggling for survival. He had recorded the brutality, loneliness and degradation of convict life in whatever hours he could steal before daylight died. Each night, in despair, he watched the sun sink below the horizon to give England a new day. He envied the sun's power to return home. In his heart he knew he never would.

At the point of total despair his prayer had been answered that fateful day when the Currency Lad rode into his life. The art materials Jake Andersen later brought him were manna from heaven. But it was more than that. Jake fired his artist's imagination. He was the symbol of freedom – proof there *was* life beyond the hell that the Devil Himself had created in his own image.

Since then Daniel had sketched and painted Jake from memory in scores of moods and angles, culminating in a portrait in oils so powerful, so alive it captured the Currency Lad's unique quality. Daniel was struck by the thought. *Jake is the first person I've ever trusted.*

Before Christmas Daniel had risked the fury of the Devil Himself by secretly waylaying Jonstone to show him this portrait. The gamble had paid off. His master had commissioned him to paint his three-year-old daughter Victoria.

Now as Daniel hurried towards the Jonstone mansion as instructed, he prayed that today would prove a red-letter day. *I wouldn't be trapped here if Saranna had kept her promise. I must find a way to get to Ironbark. Force her hand.*

Daniel paced back and forth along the terrace outside his master's study. Every muscle in his body ached from tension. He caught glimpses of Julian Jonstone through the French windows, impassively scrutinising the oil painting Daniel had delivered. Today was the acid test; his patron's verdict.

The next time he passed the room Daniel was overcome by irritation. His work lay abandoned on Jonstone's desk. His master was casually taking a pinch of snuff.

Mother of God, doesn't the man know he holds my fate in his hands? I can't take much more. Does he like my work – or hate the truth?

Daniel relived his artistic dilemma – how to remain true to the little girl's imperfections while touching the father's heart. Victoria was the Jonstones' sole surviving child; the family graveyard held three stillborn sons. Pale and sickly with spindly limbs, her gentle blue eyes were her best feature. Daniel had tried to capture her innocence by posing her with a Persian kitten, but he continued to agonise over his decision to avoid false chocolate-box prettiness. Would Jonstone's artistic judgement be stronger than parental pride? Daniel stiffened when at last his master beckoned him to enter through the French windows.

'It is clear your portrait of that Currency Lad was no accident. Well done, Browne. You've captured Victoria's sweetness of spirit. The face and hands are very fine. The kitten's so alive it looks ready to spring from the canvas. I feel sure my lady wife will be pleased.'

Daniel stammered his thanks.

Jonstone thoughtfully stroked his beard. 'I shall pay you something, but also grant you a favour. Perhaps assign you to some more congenial form of work?'

Daniel tried to dredge up enough courage to make the request that the Devil Himself had repeatedly vetoed for months past. If this gamble failed Daniel faced his greatest fear. The lash.

The words dried in his throat but he forced them out. 'Sir, would you entrust me as your courier should you need mail delivered to Ironbark? My fiancée is resident there.'

Daniel wasn't really sure if that was the truth but Saranna's months-old letter stated she was heading to Ironbark so he added quickly, 'She came free from Home, Sir. A well-educated young lady of good family.'

Jonstone registered faint surprise. 'A *lady*? Indeed, Daniel. Is there no end to your surprises?' He dipped a quill in ink and commenced writing a letter.

Daniel had not been dismissed so he was unsure if he was expected to remain. The hands of the grandfather clock moved so slowly he imagined they must be painted on its dial. At last the master blotted the document, sealed it with red wax and the ring bearing his family crest and handed it across.

'This requires the signature of George Hobson and that Jew lawyer, Bloom. I do not care to risk sending it via Her Majesty's Mail in case it should fall into bushrangers' hands. Ride to Ironbark Farm. Do not return without both signatures.'

'Most kind of you, Sir.' Daniel hesitated. 'But what if troopers should question me?'

'A convict pass? Quite so. No time to obtain an official one. I'll write one for you.' Jonstone raised an eyebrow. 'I trust *you* will not seize the opportunity to bolt, Browne?'

'Sir, you can count on me to do your bidding. I swear I will guard it with my life.'

'Yes,' Jonstone drawled. 'Iago tells me you are most amenable.'

Daniel flushed at the name – Iago to this man, the Devil Himself to his convicts. Daniel backed out of the room as if leaving the presence of royalty. He still had no firm details of payment for Victoria Jonstone's portrait but he had gained a precious period of freedom to confront Saranna.

Daniel hadn't had many opportunities to ride a horse, but he told himself this was no time to be nervous. Racing off to the stables he asked the groom to be sure to inform the Devil Himself of his absence on the master's business and promised the boy a precious plug of tobacco if he delivered the message. Months ago Daniel had checked out the cross-country route to Ironbark, knowing Saranna might be there. He gingerly mounted the horse and rode off with his convict pass carefully hidden in his boot along with a sketch pad and pencils to record anything that fired his imagination.

Daniel was determined this journey to Ironbark would change the course of his life. Whatever the reason for Saranna's silence, he would force her to petition the governor for permission to marry a convict – *him*!

Cutting across country to avoid a likely encounter with bushrangers on the Sydney Road, he rehearsed his reunion with Saranna. She had promised to set him free but had broken faith with him. Was attack the best form of defence?

Stopping to bathe in a creek, he was conscious of the dilapidated state of his slop clothing but was startled by the possible solution close at hand. At the rear of an isolated homestead on the far side of the creek was a line of washing with a man's suit hanging out to air!

Was this Our Lady's answer to his prayers or temptation placed in his path by the Devil? If caught thieving Daniel faced the lash. He struggled with the humiliating alternative; the prospect of confronting his snobbish fiancée dressed in dirty convict clothing. For once pride conquered fear. He counted the minutes. Thank God the homestead appeared to be deserted.

Daniel ran from bush to bush to shield his route to the washing line. He grabbed the suit and tore a wet shirt from its pegs. Back at the creek he panted with exhilaration as he examined the clothes. Not a perfect fit but good enough. The wet shirt would dry on his body as he rode. His own straw hat was weathered but who was he to quibble with providence? He tied his neckerchief to make a hatband.

Hopeful he could pass muster as an Englishman who came free, nonetheless he checked his coveted convict pass. If troopers caught him without this they had the power to charge him on suspicion of being an absconder. A mile further on he remembered to hide the convict clothes at a fork in the track so he could put them back on before his return to Gideon Park. *Nothing must be left to chance. Saranna is my only hope to gain my freedom.*

Waiting on the veranda of Ironbark Farm for George Hobson's signature, Daniel was brought tea by Polly, a sassy Cockney assigned girl who pointed out the schoolhouse and chattered about how their teacher Miss Plews was 'highly thought of'.

Daniel was suddenly alerted by the distant figure of a woman ringing the school bell. Although her back was to him he recognised Saranna's dress and her dark hair, worn in a chignon at the nape of her neck. She closed the door behind the last pupil and Daniel could hear children's voices raised together in song as the lesson began.

After he gained the lawyer Joseph Bloom's second signature on Jonstone's documents Daniel tethered his horse and walked to the cricket oval beside the schoolhouse. He seated himself on a felled tree trunk on the far side of the field and began sketching but kept one eye on the schoolhouse with a growing sense of unease. *What if she* did *recognise me that night – and refuses to marry a bushranger?*

The sun was directly overhead at midday when the school bell was rung. Children swarmed outside and headed for the cricket pitch. It was clear from their arguments they were intent on playing a match of Currency Lads versus England. The two boy captains selected their teams and a redhead with an Irish accent vented her fury when girls were denied the right to play.

'Girls can't play for nuts!' the boys chorused.

The England skipper, a boy they called Big Bruce, attempted fair play. 'How can we pick you, Winnie? You Irish can't play for the Currency team and you *won't* play for England.'

A boy taunted her from the rear. 'Bog Irish-Catholics are lower than a snake's belly!'

She retaliated, 'Your pa is a Proddie police informer! Ain't nothing lower than *that*.'

Their insults escalated into a fist-flying sectarian brawl, which drew the distant figure of the teacher to investigate. Daniel stiffened at the sight of Saranna as she hurried to the pitch, her dark hair escaping from her chignon, the collar of her blouse pinned with a brooch. *That damned cameo she had been ready to die for.*

As she drew closer Daniel saw there was something very odd about her. Her walk was graceful, more confident than he remembered. And he was startled to see how curvaceous her body had become. Could two years absence account for these changes? Or was it something else, something quite sinister?

He shielded his face with his hat and studied her as she placated the children.

'Could I suggest a way everyone will have a chance to play, no matter which country you come from? Ironbark boys versus Ironbark girls!' she announced.

The teacher spoke with a delightful Chester accent but it was not Saranna's voice!

The boys hooted in derision, but the little girls cheered until a hasty head count proved the girls were two short of the number needed to form a team.

'Magic can fix that!' Saranna's impostor hurried back inside the schoolhouse.

Daniel was still numb with shock when moments later the children fell about laughing at the appearance of their teacher's magic. She returned to the pitch with her hair braided like a schoolgirl, her long skirt looped between her legs and tucked into her belt to allow her to run, but covered by a pinafore to ensure modesty. She was accompanied by a smiling Aboriginal girl dressed in similar clothing who carried a fair-haired toddler on one hip and led a dark-skinned little boy by the hand. The teacher turned to the little girls.

'Isn't it lucky my friend Nerida has come home to Ironbark? Now you've got the two players you need for the girls' team.' Her gesture included all the students, 'Today we will all make Ironbark history!'

The children gave Miss Plews a rousing cheer. Winnie, the little Irish redhead, won the toss and sent the girls' team in to bat.

During the embattled cricket game Daniel saw Saranna's impostor glance his way but, apparently satisfied that he posed no threat, she threw her energies into the game.

As his pencil flew across the page Daniel's thoughts were in turmoil. *I recognise her now. She's the other girl on the coach we bailed up. Thank God I was masked. Why in hell is she masquerading as my fiancée?*

Daniel watched her with a mixture of exasperation and reluctant admiration as her long legs streaked down the pitch, unfettered by petticoats. This girl was no mouse. She was a free spirit. Could he succeed in bullying her to reveal where Saranna was?

At stumps the children celebrated with afternoon tea, then they clambered onto their ponies and rode off singing. Saranna's impostor was nowhere to be seen.

Daniel rolled up his drawings and headed in the direction of the teacher's cottage. He had waited long enough. And he wanted no audience to witness the showdown he planned to force on her. He seated himself on the schoolteacher's veranda and waited for the impostor's return.

Keziah's footsteps faltered as she recognised the figure on the veranda. The stranger who'd been observing their cricket game was sitting astride her squatter's chair. *He looks as if he's master of the house. The hide of him!*

She was confused when she saw Nerida. Her friend always waited in the cottage with Gabriel and brewed tea ready to chat with Keziah on her return from school. But now she stood beneath Gabriel's window as if keeping guard. At sight of Keziah she slipped away to her *goondie* with little Murphy.

'Who are you? What are you doing here?' Keziah demanded as she stormed up the steps.

'Daniel Browne. I came to give you your portrait, Miss Plews. A true likeness, yes?'

Keziah shivered with unease even before she saw the portrait. It was exact in every detail. Except one. *Mi-duvel! It isn't* my *face. It's the face of Saranna Plews!*

The stranger's face was blank and his voice was cold. 'You'd best invite me inside – whoever you are.'

Keziah's mind raced. Few *gaujo* men could call her bluff but this man was quite different. If he was simply Saranna's beloved fiancé why on earth did she feel this fear in the pit of her stomach?

She nodded coolly and entered the house ahead of him. Uninvited, Daniel settled himself down in the carver's chair at the table. She felt him studying her as she poured the tea Nerida had brewed for her. Keziah seated herself at the other end of the table and managed an enigmatic smile.

'So, how can I help you, Mr Browne? Do you take milk? Sugar?'

Daniel Browne dropped the last pretence of politeness. 'You can cut out the play-acting. Tell me the fate of the real Saranna Plews or you will suffer the consequences.'

Keziah ignored the threat and assumed a sympathetic attitude in an attempt to buy time and gain his cooperation. *If he's Saranna's fiancé it's only natural he's alarmed to find me using her name.*

'I am sorry to be the one to break the news to you. Saranna and I were fellow passengers on the coach from Sydney Town. We became friendly. There was a terrible accident – our coach crashed over

Blackman's Leap. Saranna suffered terrible injuries. As she lay dying she spoke to me most lovingly about her fiancé but she didn't say his name. When the doctor pronounced her dead I placed coins on her eyelids. Forgive me, this must be most painful for you, not knowing what happened to her.'

'Lies are always painful,' he snapped.

She tried to remain calm. 'That *is* the truth. I presume you were her fiancé?'

Daniel Browne nodded but made no sound except for the drumming of his fingers on the table. Keziah was surprised to see his face was devoid of all emotion. She could detect no trace of sorrow. But perhaps he was in shock? Or a man who could never reveal his true feelings?

She felt a sudden surge of panic at the thought he might ask to visit Saranna's grave. *I can hardly tell him the truth, that Saranna's buried under the name of Keziah Smith!*

She was startled to see how Daniel's gaze wandered over her body as if she were naked. But not in the usual way *gaujos* looked at her. This seemed more like cool observation than lust. She sensed he was struggling to weigh his options before he spoke.

'I came here expecting to find my fiancée. It hardly matters who you really are because I know who you are *not.* I can expose your fraudulent identity whenever I choose.'

Keziah tried to sound equally cool. 'So this is blackmail.'

'Call it what you will. You have no choice. I have it in my power to allow you to continue to live as Saranna for the rest of your life, but in return you must do *exactly* what I want.'

Keziah was struck by a desperate thought. *I could say he attacked me and I killed him in self-defence.* Her eyes strayed to the carving knife fixed to the wall.

He followed her glance. 'Oh no, I wouldn't risk that with your child asleep in the next room.'

Keziah felt her blood run cold. *He must have seen Nerida return to put Gabriel to sleep – and then sent her packing.*

She made a final bid to win his sympathy. 'Saranna died before she was able to tell me your name but she left you a message. I must honour my promise to her.'

Daniel stared at her in silence. Keziah felt sure this man had never loved Saranna as much as she'd loved him. But what if she was wrong?

She leaned forward and said the words softly. 'Saranna's dying words were, "Tell my beloved my last thoughts were of him". Her final words made no sense to me. "Tell him he must always live for his mistress."'

For one moment Daniel Browne's air of authority wavered. Keziah saw a flash of genuine sorrow in his eyes.

'I told her art was my mistress. She agreed that when she became my wife she would always respect my mistress.' He turned his head away as if to regain control and his mouth hardened. 'Saranna was devoted to me. She'd do anything I asked and so will you. Tomorrow you will apply for permission to marry me.'

Keziah gave a scornful laugh. 'Over my dead body!'

He leaned across the table and gripped her arm. 'Make no mistake. You have two choices. Our marriage will gain my transfer from Gideon Park. I'll be legally assigned to you, the so-called *respectable* school-teacher who came free.'

She stared back at him, her heart racing. 'And if I refuse?'

'Your safe little world will collapse like a house of cards. You'll lose your son, your livelihood, your good name. Marriage, the custody of my body and soul, is what the late Saranna agreed to. You stole her life. So it's only fair you also inherit me.'

Keziah gave a derisive snort. 'Saranna was a lady. Far too good for the likes of you!'

Daniel retaliated. 'You might fool everyone in this backwater that you're a lady. These colonials know no better. In English eyes you're nothing but a vagabond Gypsy!'

The words hit their target. Keziah could no longer control her rage. She leapt at him, her hands clawing for his face, but he managed to pinion her arms to her side. He crowed in triumph.

'You carry off your masquerade because it's in the blood. Generations of Gypsy liars!'

In vain she struggled to break free but finally knew she was beaten. 'State your terms.'

Daniel Browne released her and looked relieved that he'd won. 'That's more like it. Marriage leads to my ticket-of-leave, free to work for wages. As my wife you gain my protection and add my income to your poor farmers' coins. I'll be your son's stepfather.' He looked pointedly at her slim figure. 'Hobson's Cockney girl told me you'd *adopted* a foundling. Some fools will believe anything, eh?'

Keziah felt herself blanch.

'Mind if I smoke?' Daniel asked. Without waiting for her reply he lit his clay pipe.

Keziah tried one last desperate ploy. 'I can't marry you. I'm married to Gem Smith.'

Daniel started in recognition. 'Gem Smith the Gypsy bushranger? So it was a Romani marriage?'

'Of course!' said Keziah but instantly realised her mistake.

'So it isn't strictly legal. Anyway, married to a bushranger you'll soon be a widow.'

Keziah flinched but tried to call his bluff. 'My husband would kill you first!'

'I doubt it. Gem knows full well a convict will do *anything* to escape Gideon Park!'

'You're crazy to think I'd allow *you to* share my bed.'

He equalled her contempt. 'What makes you think I want to? We'll share my name and your house in the eyes of the law. That's the price of freedom for both of us.'

Daniel closed the deal. 'Saranna Plews was unmarried so there's no impediment. I'm told it doesn't take too long for Governor Gipps to grant permission. Once he does, banns are read on three consecutive Sundays. Then we marry or I'll expose you as a charlatan, a *bushranger's doxy.*'

Keziah was in inner turmoil. But one thought was paramount. *He knew Gem at Gideon Park!*

Daniel idly picked up his pencil and sketch pad. 'Before I go you will do one more thing for me. Unbraid your hair. I want to capture the *real* you.'

Keziah hesitated then allowed her hair to cascade over her shoulders.

'That's a good girl. You see? We're going to get along just fine.'

When he smiled at her for the first time Keziah hated him even more.

CHAPTER 25

In the hours after Daniel Browne rode off in the direction of Gideon Park, Keziah rushed around the house casting every known spell to bring Gem back to her.

Although she'd had to concede temporary defeat and accept Daniel Browne's plan, she was desperate to buy time to foil it. Escape was impossible. If she bolted again, Gem would never find her.

Through the window she watched the home paddock where Gem's gift of the brumby was frolicking beside the Shetland pony that Jake had given Gabriel.

If only Jake were here! He had the comforting ability to fix anything. *But even I can't predict his movements. No doubt he's chasing up some clue to Jenny's whereabouts.*

She prayed out loud to her ancestors. 'Please bring Jake Andersen back to Ironbark. I need him!'

Each night her sleep was haunted by nightmares and she woke each morning in a state of exhaustion. At times she could sense that Gem's aura was close to her. But although she searched all the tracks she usually took, there were no further *patrins* to prove Gem had her in his sights.

Keziah sensed the hand of *baxt* on the day she saw Nerida returning with the two little boys from a walk in the bush. She knew something important had happened and ran out to meet them.

Nerida silently handed her a silver filigree ring. It looked like one Keziah had seen in Sunny Ah Wei's collection of silver jewellery.

'Nerida, where did you find this?'

'Stranger riding black horse give it me. He said gift is for you. In place of ring you had to bury.'

Keziah gave an involuntary cry. Her wedding ring was buried in Bolthole cemetery on Saranna's corpse. But who else knew that?

'What did he look like, Nerida?'

Nerida didn't need to describe more than the single gold earring and the coins on his waistcoat before Keziah gave a cry of joy, begging Nerida to recount everything Gem had said and done.

'Did Gem say *when* he would come to me?'

Nerida nodded. 'Before the moon is born again.'

It was second nature to Keziah to watch the sky and be aware of the phases of the moon her *Puri Dai* had taught her. She knew the next new moon would make its first appearance in five days, but would be invisible to the naked eye for a day and a half before that. She felt a surge of energy, along with a wave of anxiety, as to what she would say and do at her reunion with Gem. It crossed her mind to hide Gabriel in Nerida's *goondie*, but she dismissed the thought. Gem knew her better than anyone. He would know that an adopted child would be as dear to her as any natural child. There was nothing she could do but continue to follow her instincts.

Keziah's nerves were stretched to breaking point. Two days passed without any sight of Gem. Late that afternoon, after leaving Nerida to bathe and bed Gabriel down in his little boxroom, Keziah returned to the schoolhouse for some papers.

As she headed towards it the high-pitched screeching of an unknown bird gave her a heightened sense that something unusual was about to occur.

She had hired Big Bruce as 'caretaker' to help him continue to attend school and contribute to the family income. As she entered the schoolroom he was moving the last row of seats into place.

'Thank you, Bruce, you've done a fine job. Go home now, your mother will be needing you.'

He paused in the doorway, nervous. 'Nothing to worry about, Miss, but there's a great black stallion grazing down by the creek. I saw a man watching your cottage.'

'Did you recognise him?'

'He had a gold earring and coins on his waistcoat. Like they say that bushranger The Gypsy wears,' Bruce said excitedly.

Keziah froze. The lad could unwittingly endanger Gem by informing his mother he had seen his bushranger hero.

'I'm not asking you to lie, Bruce, but …'

Bruce lowered his eyes. 'No need to worry about my mouth, Miss. Pa was a transportee. We MacAlisters don't rat on our own kind.' And he was gone.

Keziah hurried back to her cottage. Her front door had been forced open and hung from one hinge. What did that matter? Her great love had found her.

She closed the door as best she could to screen them from the outside world, then feasted her eyes on him.

Gem sat in the carver's chair, waiting. Everything about him was larger than life. The flash clothes, the silver and gold on his belt, waistcoat and in his ear. The rings on each hand – the gold band she had given him on their wedding day. His white teeth glistening against the dark olive of his skin. The wild black mane of hair. His silk shirt open to reveal the edge of what seemed to be a tattoo.

Just for a moment all was quiet and still. Gem broke the silence.

'No matter how long it took, I never doubted you'd come to me.'

Time. Keziah had precious little of that to heal their lives. She abandoned words and ran into his arms, determined to bind him to her.

He touched her cheek. 'Why are you crying, little witch? Isn't this what we both want?'

Bunching her hair in one hand like the mane of a beloved horse, Gem turned her mouth to meet his own. Keziah had forgotten the power of his kisses, the way he whispered the ardent love words that for years she had hungered to hear. Strange words in English but in the Romani tongue they were tender and passionate.

'My darling, I eat your lips, I eat your eyes.'

He tossed her down on the bed, tore off his waistcoat and unbuckled his belt. He was laughing, panting in anticipation.

'By *The Del*, I've waited for you so long, I'm going to make you die with pleasure in my arms all night.'

'Yes!' she cried, remembering the prediction that she had thrown at her mother-in-law, Patronella. *I will lie again in Gem's arms.*

When he ripped off his shirt Keziah gasped at the sight of the barely healed lash scars that traversed his back. But it was his gaol tattoo that broke her heart – the letter K inside a heart shape tattooed beneath his heart. Gem would bear his love to the grave. If only she had been worthy of it.

Gem pushed her down on the bed, eager to claim her. His tongue filled her mouth with passion, silencing her questions as his hand moved to her breasts.

Suddenly his eyes flew open, staring straight into her own.

'What is that *noise*?' he demanded.

Keziah turned cold with fear as he grabbed his pistol, strode across to the boxroom and kicked the door open. He aimed the weapon at the cot where little Gabriel in his nightshirt was rattling the bars as he sang.

Gem's shaking hand waved the pistol. 'What's going on? He isn't that black girl's kid, is he! He's *yours*!'

Keziah sprang forward to shield Gabriel.

'Listen to me! He's my legally adopted son. Gem, I swear By My Father's Hand, I only ever loved one man in my life. You!'

Gem's face was blank with shock. 'Do you think I'm blind? He has *your eyes*!'

Keziah followed him as he retreated to the other room, tossing the pistol aside. She sank to her knees, grabbing at his hand, his trousers, any part of him in a desperate attempt to delay the loss of him yet again.

'My love, you must believe me. That babe did not come by my invitation. I hate the man who fathered him. All I ever wanted was you! To cross the seas and be with you, Gem!'

'Oh yes? Carrying your bastard in your baggage!'

Keziah wrung her hands. 'It's not little Gabriel's fault! He didn't ask to be born. I didn't want him but he's here now. An unwanted gift. I can't pretend I don't care about him.'

Gem moved towards her, his hands flexing with rage. Keziah told herself he had never hit her before, no matter how uncontrolled his jealousy, but this time was different. She was *guilty*.

'How many more men were there?' Gem demanded.

Her throat constricted. 'None! It was only one night! Gem, I beg you to forgive the unforgivable! I've loved you all my life. Please find it in your heart to understand and to absolve me from my guilt.'

'Guilt, eh? A moment ago you pretended your innocence! The babe didn't come at your invitation, eh? How many lies must I swallow? Answer me! How many more *gaujos* have *paid to use my wife*?'

'Gem believe me! I have never in my life loved anyone but you!'

He threw back his head and laughed. The sound was one of such pain and violence that Keziah felt as if he had physically struck her. Despite this she clung to him, trying to block his exit.

'What the hell do you want from me, Keziah?'

Her voice was raw with passion. 'Gem. If I could only find the way back to make you love me again, I would spend my whole life devoted to your happiness and your pleasure. I beg you, give me the chance to prove my love!'

He spat through the window in contempt. 'And if I refuse?'

'*Mi-duvel!* Give me a little time, I beg you. Remember that day in court? You cried out that no beak could ever keep us apart? You were right! I crossed the world to come to you. I'm your woman now – and always will be.'

'And what's that worth? To let myself be contaminated by a woman who is *mahrime*?'

Keziah closed her eyes, praying to her ancestors to give her the chance to cool his rage.

'Gem, I'd give my life to save you.'

'Too late. You're already *dead*. Remember? Keziah Smith is dead and buried in Bolthole cemetery where she belongs.'

Keziah was shaken to the core. 'I wish I *had* been the one to die. But *baxt* chose me to live. If you can find it in your heart to forgive me, I'll wait for you – no matter how many years it takes. But I must protect this babe and the life I've made for him. Above all I honour our Romani wedding vows. No matter what the *gaujo* law says, I could never marry another man. Unless you divorced me under Romani law, our way.'

'Divorce you? What madness is this?' Gem yelled as he pushed her aside. 'So the truth is out! You're already hot to marry some *gaujo* fool?'

'No! Gem, I want you more than anything in the world. Please try to forgive me, but if you *can't*, then set me free from the promise I swore as a child to love you unto death.' She cried out in desperation, lying at his feet. 'Love me. Hate me. But I beg you, just lay with me tonight, my Gem.'

Gem's anger suddenly cooled. 'You clever little bitch. Here I am on the run from the traps. I risk my life to spend a single night with you, knowing that informer Evans is breathing down my neck. And what do I get? Lies and betrayal – and this *gaujo* brat!'

He gestured towards the cot where Gabriel was cheerfully clapping his hands and singing in a bid to attract Gem's attention.

Gem punched his fist through the front door that had hung on one broken hinge since his entrance. Then he faced Keziah and flashed his familiar smile that always made her heart leap.

'The day we met you were five years old. Your father, Gabriel, visited our camp to show off his adored, blue-eyed *posh rat*. Your smile was pure sunshine; innocent yet seductive.' Gem examined his hand as if discovering it for the first time. 'You placed your hand in mine. From that very moment you held my heart in the palm of your hand.'

Keziah cried out at the power of that shared memory. 'I loved you from that moment too, Gem. You know I did!'

'My mother took one look at you and ran to my father. She warned him that I must have a true Romani wife because "Whores only breed whores".'

Keziah really did want to die. Now her mother's shame compounded her own.

Gem's voice grew soft. 'My gift to you, Keziah, is this.' He hissed Patronella's darkest curse – a spell so potent Keziah needed two lifetimes to escape its vengeance.

As he galloped away, Keziah called out his name in a broken cry, powerless to hold him. How could her life have any meaning without Gem at the heart of it?

Her sobs became so frenzied that they frightened little Gabriel into adding his terrified cries to her own. With her face red and swollen from crying, Keziah carried him out onto the veranda to calm him in the cool night air.

'There, there, it's all right now, my little Rom. Who would believe you are the man who wrecked my marriage?' She kissed the little hand that patted her face, comforting her. 'Perhaps *you* are man enough to forgive me? When I said I didn't want you before you were born, it was true, but I didn't *know* you then! You are the world to me, Gabriel.'

She sat him in her lap and clapped his hands. 'I don't know how to solve this terrible mess but if I died tomorrow, I'd swear the truth on my deathbed. I love Gem with my whole heart. But if he cannot accept you, I could never, never give you up. You are *the one thing in my life that really makes sense*!'

As she carried him inside the cottage she tried but failed to close the broken door behind her.

In the darkness outside Keziah's cottage Jake swore under his breath as he watched the retreating figure of the fugitive Gypsy Gem Smith gallop over the horizon. *Jesus wept! What do I do now?*

He had ridden up to pay Keziah a visit but halted at the sight of the stallion tethered in the shadows. Should he stay or should he go? He had overheard the tail end of Gem's enraged fight but the touching scene of Keziah comforting little Gabriel had been enough for him to piece together the story. Jake was honest enough to know his feelings were biased. Keziah was his mate, but if he stood in Gem's shoes, could he forgive his wife for bearing a babe to another man while he was in prison?

In one sense, Jake realised he *was* standing in Gem's shoes. *What the hell would I do if Jenny pleaded her love for me like Keziah did to Gem?*

There was no answer. It was growing dark so he decided it was time to take action. He rode off to Ironbark Farm's assigned men's quarters. When the door was opened by Sholto, the huge tattooed Glaswegian convict looked ready to throttle him.

'Miss Plews has a problem, mate, I need your help.' Jake offered the man his tobacco pouch. Mollified, Sholto took it and led him to the toolshed.

On his return to Keziah's cottage, Jake propped casually against the doorframe. 'Just passing, mate. Noticed your front door's given up the ghost.'

Without another word he set to with the tools and soon had her door in working order. *If only her love life was as easy to fix.*

'Kind of you, Jake,' Keziah sniffed. 'I'll fix you something to eat.'

Jake eyed her as she poured tea. Some women, like Jenny, looked heartbreakingly pretty when they cried. Not Keziah. Her eyes were bloodshot from howling. Jake had seen prize fighters who looked more attractive after thirteen rounds.

He folded his hands behind his head and settled back in his chair with a show of confidence. He decided to play his cards close to his chest and pretend he hadn't been witness to Gem's violent exit.

'All right, mate. Out with it. What's up?'

'You can't fix the mess I'm in, Jake. Not this time. No one can.'

'You *reckon*?' he said. 'Try me.'

CHAPTER 26

As Jake drove his battered wagon towards Feagan's General Store his mind was only half tuned to the world around him. Summer seemed unwilling to end and the day promised to deliver the sticky heat that Jake knew gave a bloke saddle rash if he wasn't too careful.

Early that morning Jake had packed in the false bottom of his wagon the expensive new saddle Terence Ogden had asked him to choose for his favourite thoroughbred, Jupiter's Darling, and the fowling pieces and cartridges the landholder had ordered. All he needed now was to fill up the cart with bales of stockfeed to act as camouflage in the event he was bailed up.

As always he kept a sharp eye out for bushrangers. The traps were fighting a losing battle to maintain law and order. The army of bolters who'd taken up arms grew by the week.

But as alert for trouble as he was, he continued to mull over the painful showdown he'd witnessed between Gem and Keziah the previous week. He knew her heart still belonged to Gem. So what was the strength of her surprising revelation of her marriage proposal? And how on earth had she ever met Daniel Browne? Jake had chatted with the artist whenever he had occasion to pass Gideon Park. Although Daniel looked more haggard each visit, he always seemed pleased to see Jake, talked about his paintings and asked for news of the outside world. How odd that Daniel had never even mentioned Keziah or marriage.

Jake was damned sure Keziah hadn't told him the full story behind Daniel's wooing. But how could he blame her? She was shattered by Gem's rejection. Good women were devious, even the best of them. *That woman gets herself into one bloody mess after another. She's desperate to find Gem and sort things out, which is a bit of a problem what with*

Gypsy Gem Smith's name on the traps' Wanted Dead or Alive posters.

Jake felt discomforted by the way Kez always looked at him. Like he was one of King Arthur's knights who could ride off on Horatio, solve her problem and give her a happy ending.

'That's what happens when a woman saves your life, Horatio. You're stuck with being in her debt.'

The thought of tomorrow's date depressed him. A painful anniversary – Pearl's sixth birthday and he wasn't an inch closer to finding her. Would he even be able to recognise her if he passed her in the street?

In the general store Jake found Feagan was as usual busy dispensing news as he wrapped parcels.

'What's the world coming to? We now have two bushrangers who claim they are One Eye. Jabber Jabber has escaped from custody yet again. And that Irish scoundrel Paddy Corcoran confessed to violating an overseer's wife.'

Jake picked up his cue. 'Any news of The Gypsy's gang?'

'Sergeant Kenwood told me The Gypsy ransacked two homesteads this week, not ten miles from where we stand.' Feagan turned a tobacco-stained smile towards Jake. 'But what can you expect? The Gypsies have been thieves since God was in his cradle.'

Jake made no comment. Feagan was enthused by the large order Jake had placed on behalf of Terence Ogden.

'Those big landowners sure live in style. I hear tell Ogden's staging a fox hunt for some sporting English gentlemen just off the boat. 'Roos in place of foxes. Need more ammunition?'

Feagan's wink was conspiratorial. Jake knew his answer would be common knowledge all over Bolthole Valley by midday, and hopefully would find its way to a bushranger's ears.

'No. Never carry arms or ammo. Just whisky. Plenty of room to load my wagon with this horse feed.'

At The Shanty with No Name Jake bought two bottles of whisky and positioned them to act as a decoy to protect the hidden stash of ammunition whenever the flap of the wagon's tarpaulin was raised. If Feagan's information was accurate, Gem was likely to be holed up close at hand. Jake had proved the bushrangers' grapevine effective in the past to make contact. The trick lay in managing to get bailed up by a decent bushranger who could be relied on to pass his message to Gem.

He didn't have long to wait. It was a muggy day made worse by the maddening attention of mosquitoes that bred in the nearby swamp. Jake had no sooner crossed the single-arch stone bridge than he heard the familiar cry, 'Bail up! Your money or your life!'

'Jesus, here we go again, Horatio!' Jake moved his wagon to the side of the road and looked at the young assailant. Taffy Owens was obviously so new to the game his legs twitched like a kid who needs to take a pee, and his firearms belonged in a museum.

'Mind if I stop for a smoke?' Jake asked politely. 'Been a real bugger of a day.'

'I'd never bail *you* up, Jake,' Taffy apologised. 'You being a mate of Jabber Jabber and The Gypsy. Enjoy your smoko before you shoot off.'

Jake glanced down the empty road. 'Yeah, wouldn't want to hold up the traffic. I'm on my way to deliver a load of feed to Ogden Park. I'll look the other way while you help yourself to the whisky in the back.'

'Thanks, mate. I'm as dry as a dead sheep.'

Jake's question was casual. 'Can you get a message to my mate, Gem Smith?'

Taffy nodded, loath to pause from swigging the whisky.

'Gem claims he was a bare-knuckle champ at Home. Tell him twenty pounds says I can beat him, but we need to have a yarn first. I'll be camped by Mutmutbilly swamp.'

'He'll get your message before sundown,' Taffy promised.

As the sinking sun stained the sky orange behind the hills, Jake stretched out on his swag beside his campfire. His hat adorned with a galah feather covered his face to discourage the mosquitoes. He'd been told the Aboriginal double use of 'mut' indicated a double dose of mosquitoes in the swampy billabong. *Jesus wept. They weren't half joking.*

At the sound of a lone rider's approach Jake feigned sleep but kept his left hand close to his hidden pistol.

The voice behind him was dark and silky. 'So you fancy you can lick me, eh pal?'

Jake opened one eye. 'I reckon all the fellas I beat have good reason to remember me.'

Gem laughed and dismounted. From the corner of his eye Jake saw a flash of his gold earring. The gold coins on Gem's waistcoat, the silver butt of his pistols and his elaborate silver belt proved the rumours. The Gypsy *did* pack more gold and silver than the Bank of England.

Jake casually laid out the fresh loaf of bread he'd bought in Bolthole, figuring that Gem must be sick of eating damper and biscuits laced with weevils. With a flourish he produced a bottle of red wine with a flash label.

'A new Hunter Valley wine. Could you go a drink?' Jake took care to offer Gem the pannikin with his right hand. He knew Gem drank red wine. He had seen Keziah tip a small quantity onto the earth, as token offering to her gods, before she drank.

Gem did the same thing then savoured the wine. 'This ain't shanty grog. A fine drop.'

'Not every day I do a deal with a boxer who's near good enough to be in my class.'

Gem laughed. 'I can whip you in two rounds. What makes you keen to die young?'

'A proposition. If you're as good as you claim you won't be able to resist it.'

'What's the deal?'

'I know the risk I'm running in telling you this. You're a bit of a legend round here. Everyone knows Gypsy Gem Smith has a wild temper.'

Gem puffed up with pride, encouraging Jake to continue. He handed him the bread.

'If I tell you, do you guarantee you won't give me a bullet sandwich?'

Gem's laughter rent the air as he slapped Jake on the back. 'Well, if you aren't a right cheeky bugger! I like your style. You have my word I won't shoot you.'

'It's a matter of a lady's honour. Nah! Not *my* woman! Just a friend in need.'

Gem's hand beckoned for Jake to provide her name. Jake hesitated.

'She's hiding from the law. A woman you and I both know – Keziah Stanley.'

Gem sprang to his feet in a flash. He ranted half in Romani, half in English laced with a bit of gaol cant, but there was no indication that he intended to draw a pistol.

Jake waited for Gem to calm down before he asked, 'Does this mean you're going to turn your back on twenty pounds?'

'Why the hell do you want to fight for her? She's a whore and a whore's daughter!'

'So what do *you* care?'

'Because she's *my* whore.'

'I reckon you do want her!' said Jake. 'Go tell *her* that. The woman's crazy about you.'

Gem's eyes flashed. 'You're hot to tumble her yourself!'

'Nah, I've got plenty of women of my own to keep me busy in bed, thanks very much. Your wife's just a mate but she saved my life once. I don't fancy being in a woman's debt.'

Gem's voice was thick with hatred. 'I wouldn't let that whore touch me in my coffin!'

'Fair enough, mate,' Jake agreed. He struggled to conceal his anger at hearing Keziah labelled a whore. Passing the bottle back to Gem he remained silent until Gem returned to the offer of the fight.

'So. You agree to pay me thirty pounds when I beat you senseless, pal.'

'Hang on! I said twenty.'

'Twenty-five!' Gem said quickly.

'Do you think I'm made of money? This is all I've got.' Jake removed his left banking boot and emptied the pouch on the swag.

Gem was impressed. 'So, it's no bluff. But if, in your wildest dreams, you beat me, what's *your* reward?'

'If you win, you cop the purse. You lose, you cop *half* the purse, but I want your handshake on a promise.'

'What's the trick?'

'No trick. If *I* win, either you take Keziah back as your wife, like she wants, or else you let her go once and for all.' Jake weighed up his words. 'In which case you make me your witness when you two jump backwards over the broomstick.'

Gem looked stunned. 'What are you? A *didikai*?'

'Jesus wept. What the hell's that?' asked Jake.

'A man with a Romani grandfather. Are you?'

'Not that I bloody know of, mate.'

Gem offered his hand. 'If you're so eager to lose twenty-five pounds—'

'Twenty!'

'All right, twenty, for me to give you a boxing lesson. I accept.'

When Gem wrapped his hands around Jake's right hand, Jake grinned. Gem had not guessed that Jake was a southpaw – he'd discover that little surprise in the ring.

'Choose the time and place,' said Jake.

Gem sprang into the saddle. 'The day of the Coronation Races. Enjoy your women while you can, pal. They won't recognise you after two rounds with *me*!' He added coldly, 'But leave *my* whore alone!'

'She's all yours, mate. Not my type. I fancy redheads small enough to fit in my pocket.'

As the sound of horse hooves faded, Jake lay back, covered his face with his hat and heaved a sigh of relief. Done!

In Goulburn, Jake pushed his way down Market Street through the milling crowd to the post office to collect his mail.

Two Sterling blokes ahead of him in the queue were discussing the upcoming Coronation Races. They bemoaned the delay in celebrating so many months after the Queen had been crowned, 'the curse of living down here, cut off from events at Home'.

'I hear tell Ogden will play host to the vice-regal party,' said one. 'No doubt he's out to cut quite a dash.'

'Quite. He's donated a silver cup for the race. Expects his own horse, Jupiter's Darling, is bound to win it. His rival Thomas Icely won't be entering any of his thoroughbreds so there'll be no real competition from the local nags, what?'

Jake realised why Ogden had ordered that expensive saddle. Jupiter's Darling was Ogden's pride and joy, a horse descended from Sky Prince, the first thoroughbred he'd imported from England.

Jake took delivery of a letter written in an unknown hand. He crossed to the Travellers' Home Inn and laboured over reading it:

> *A friend is writing this for me. Here's a yarn you will enjoy. I bolted soon after arriving in the colony, borrowed a horse from Ogden's estate. Sky Prince. I returned him but the damage was done. Here's the joke. I've entered a colt in the Coronation Races sired by Sky Prince out of a brumby I'd stashed away. Sarishan will beat all those horses with impeccable bloodlines. I'm counting on you to find him a jockey and collect the silver cup for me. I'll be there to watch him romp home!*
>
> *Your pal*

Jake roared with laughter. What a glorious trick on the world of Exclusives if a bushranger's horse beat their thoroughbreds!

He raised his Albion Ale to toast Gem. 'I'd pass up my own funeral before I'd miss the silver cup.'

Jake's glass of amber froze in midair. *You bugger, Gem. Now I've got to train your horse for the Coronation Races and train myself for our grudge match! And you made bloody sure they're both on the same day!*

Jake left the public house and stopped dead in his tracks. Tethered to his wagon was a magnificent black colt pawing the ground. Gem Smith had left his calling card.

CHAPTER 27

The day of the Coronation Races dawned hot and humid. In Mac Mackie's hut in Tagalong, Jake was woken by the raucous peal of kookaburras laughing. It sounded like the birds were mocking his chances of beating Gem.

Naked, Jake seated himself on a bench by the open doorway to collect what little breeze there was. He felt unsettled. What was the matter with him? He just wanted to win this fight for his mate. Give Keziah what she wanted – Gem.

Mac hovered like a mother hen intent on calming a nervous chick as he cooked Jake a huge breakfast.

'What's eating you? Never seen you so rattled before a fight.'

'Get lost, Mac.' Jake tackled the half-raw steak. 'How's about another cuppa?'

Mac poured two pannikins of tea and added a dash of whisky. He tried again. 'Sarishan's looking great, mate. You've done wonders training him.'

'I reckon *his* chances are pretty bloody good.' Jake switched his concern to Sarishan. 'I ain't worried about Dick Gideon. To watch that kid riding Sarishan is a thing of beauty. Nerida swore by her kinsman, trouble is he's only twelve. Some of the older jockeys ain't famous for playing fair 'n' square.'

A second beefsteak was tossed onto his plate and Mac scratched his beard. 'Do you reckon we're pushing our luck a bit? First a public prize fight with a wanted bushranger, then we're racing his horse in the biggest horse race this county's ever seen! If we're not bloody careful the traps are gunna cop *us* under the Bushranging Act.'

'Quit worrying. Gem's using an alias. Jim Romani.'

'Yeah? What's he using for a new face?'

Jake tried to sound confident. 'He'll be so battered by the end of round one, his own mam won't know him.'

'You're the best southpaw in the country, on a good day, but why are you fighting Gem to help some woman? Even if you win you only get half your own money. You don't even get Gem's woman. Or do you?'

Jake snapped. 'How many times do I have to tell you? For the rest of my life I'm only ever gunna pay for a woman and walk away. God's truth!'

Mac was like a dog with a bone. 'I know nothing about women, mate. You know me. Never been with a woman longer than the ten minutes I pay for 'em at the Red Brumby. But something's up. I reckon you and Gem are fighting some kind of duel. Like them Prussian military blokes. Fists instead of swords but. What does Gem's woman think of all this?'

'She doesn't *know*, mate. And she'd better not find out or my life ain't worth a farthing. She hates prize fights. Her father was killed in a fight in prison!' Jake added quickly, 'What does a bloke have to do to get another cuppa tea around here?'

A crowd had gathered outside the Shamrock and Thistle Inn. The bush grapevine had worked its magic. Jake recognised faces from forty miles away, drawn by the lure of a prize fight. Carts and wagons were parked everywhere. The most colourful was Sunny Ah Wei's emporium on wheels. Garbed in his traditional Chinese robe with his pigtail hanging down his back, Sunny paused in the act of making a sale to raise his thumb to Jake in a sign of solidarity.

Jake saw Mac hand the prize money to the referee. 'Count it, mate. It's all there.'

'You'd be bloody silly if it wasn't,' said the referee. 'You'd have a gang of bushrangers shooting holes in you!'

Clearly Jim Romani's true identity was an open secret.

Jake limbered up. He stripped down to his moleskin breeches tucked into knee-high boots then buckled on the lucky brass belt he'd worn in the bout with Ned Chalker he'd *almost* won. His hair was tied back in a pigtail at the nape of his neck.

It was then that Jake saw Jim Romani.

'Some bloody disguise!' he whispered to Mac.

Gem sprang down the steps of the Shamrock and Thistle Inn, acknowledging the cheers of the faithful. Draped around his shoulders was a purple satin Chinese robe and a single gold earring glinted against his curly hair. Around the top of his black silk breeches was an elaborate silver belt that made him a self-proclaimed champ.

Gem was introduced to the crowd as Jim Romani. He flashed Jake a confident smile. 'May the best man win, pal. Me, of course. And may the second best man recover his wits!'

The crowd roared approval. The Irish ratio was close on half – the vocal half.

Jake felt oddly uncomfortable to see the K for Keziah written inside Gem's tattooed heart.

Ernie the referee yelled out the old-style Broughton rules of the game and the fight was on.

In round one Jake knew he had an excellent chance to beat The Gypsy. His southpaw stance was dangerous at the best of times. He was pleased to see Gem's eyes flicker when he realised the trick Jake had pulled.

By round three Jake was still confident he'd take Gem, but decided it would be wise to end it soon. Gem had a slight advantage of height and reach, and a mean right hook. *Jesus, I'll need to keep ducking that or it's curtains for me.*

At the end of round five, Mac advised, 'Go in and finish him off, mate. He's tiring.'

Jake spat out a trace of blood. 'Yeah? I hadn't noticed.'

By the eighth round he knew it could go either way. He had

endurance on his side and a bush fighter's tactics. When he delivered a series of aggressive headbutts sending Gem into temporary retreat, Jake drew a thunderous roar from the crowd. They loved rough and dirty old-style tactics.

In round ten Gem locked him in a wrestling hold.

'You're a liar, pal,' Gem hissed in his ear. 'You *do* want my whore.'

Gem shifted his hold to a headlock. A mistake. Jake broke free, slammed a haymaker into his gut and told him, 'No bloody way!'

In answer, Gem's next punch sent Jake's head shuddering on his neck.

Somewhere in round eleven Gem danced out of range, pointed at his tattoo and taunted Jake. 'Can't bring yourself to hit Keziah can you, eh?'

Startled that Gem had recognised the truth, Jake tried to call his bluff. 'She got under *your* skin, mate. Not mine. No woman will ever leave her brand on *me*!' He delivered a barrage of jabs to emphasise his words.

At the dawn of round thirteen Jake hoped he still had a fifty-fifty chance. His dirty tricks only drew gutter tactics from Gem. *Got to find the right moment. Land the killer punch I've got in reserve. Trouble is I'm flat out keeping clear of his bloody right hook.*

At the end of the fourteenth, Mac said hopefully, 'He's fading fast!'

'Nah. He's as fresh as a bloody daisy,' said Jake.

'Watch his right hook. It looks like a jaw-breaker.'

'It *is*!' Jake bounced back into the fight, dredging up the confidence that had sunk to his boots. He thought of Keziah and tried to fake it.

'What? You still here, mate?' he called out to Gem.

'Couldn't miss your last round could I, pal?' Gem gave him a series of telling blows that sent Jake reeling to finish the round in a blur on one knee.

Was it only the fifteenth round? Jake knew he was fighting on sheer instinct. He liked Gem but only one of them could win. Jake was groggily determined it would be Keziah.

Just then he sighted an enemy in the crowd. Trooper Doolan. The trap was frowning at Gem as if trying to place him. Jake lost concentration – Gem's blow sent blood into his eye, pinking his vision. He knew the signs. *Both of us are labouring. I need to buy time.*

Jake grabbed him in a wrestling hold, then gave a sudden jerk designed to topple them both. They rolled over with such momentum that the crowd stumbled to jump clear of their path. Under cover of their noisy barracking, Jake hissed a warning in Gem's ear.

'Watch out! Trooper Doolan's wise to you.'

'I'm too old for that trick,' said Gem.

'God's truth! I'll grab the crowd's attention. You check him out. He knows you!'

Jake broke his hold and danced around, cocky as hell. The crowd enjoyed the free bit of theatre. Gem met Jake's eyes, acknowledging the truth of the warning.

When Gem's best punch connected with his jaw, Jake knew he was virtually out on his feet but he kept crawling back up for more. Gem stopped baiting him and held him in a tight clinch to disguise his words. No trace of sarcasm this time.

'You've got guts, pal, but give up. Now! I don't want to beat you to pulp.'

Jake tried a show of bravado. 'Want to throw in the towel already, you piker?'

Gem hissed at close quarters. 'You're the best I've ever fought but today's not your day. You know it! Stay down. I promise we'll fight again.'

Drunk with fatigue, Jake spat blood out of Gem's range.

'Nah! Got to win fair and square.'

Gem began to pull his punches. 'No shame in a draw, pal.'

'Won't solve nothing, will it!'

'You want it bad enough to die for? Stay down. I promise I'll meet the whore.'

Jake staggered, but he was in no condition to accept a gift-horse.

'That's cheating. We said last man standing. Well, I'm still bloody standing!' Jake rocked on his feet, blood trickling from his mouth. Time was running out.

They both saw Trooper Doolan, his pistol hand flexed at the ready. Suddenly Gem began to play the fool, calling Jake names from the gutter.

Gem dropped his guard and Jake seized his chance. He delivered his killer punch and Gem went down in an almost theatrical freefall, clutching at the sky as he keeled backwards onto a bale of hay. Out cold.

Ernie the referee counted thirty, then raised Jake's right arm in a victory salute.

Jake was stunned. 'Jesus wept! I won, did I?'

He took a swig of Mac's whisky and saw Trooper Doolan moving towards Gem. 'Gem's been sprung!' he warned Mac.

They exchanged a nod and Jake grabbed Mac and yelled in his face. 'You bastard! Call St Patrick a Miss Molly do you?' He assumed a fighting stance. 'Not in my presence you don't!'

His fake punch connected with Mac who, schooled in his role, roared for blood. To the shocked delight of the crowd the pair started a brawl cutting off Trooper Doolan's advance towards Jim Romani.

The Irish half of the crowd yelled as one, 'In defence of St Patrick, lads!' The stoush was open to all comers and Jake saw that Trooper Doolan was caught at the heart of it. No doubt the Irish lags knew full well the trooper had recently shot dead a young Irish bolter. There was no telling who hit Doolan first, but he sank to the ground under a torrent of blows.

Jake looked around him. Gem Smith was nowhere in sight. Mac bundled Jake onto his cart and cracked his whip at the sky.

'There he goes!' Jake grinned at the sight of the galloping figure with his purple robe flapping behind him.

'Good on him!' said Mac. 'Now get your arse together. We just might make it in time to catch Sarishan race.'

'That was some fight!' Jake crowed. 'How much did you win on me?'

'I'll tell you later,' Mac mumbled.

Jake suspected his mate had lost money betting on Gem. Who bloody cared? To Jake this win was worth more than gold. Kez would get what she wanted one way or another.

On their arrival at the new Ironbark racecourse Jake saw that the crowd was happily fuelled with liquor.

The members' grandstand was festooned with striped canvas and bunting, and the Quality swarmed around the governor's party like bees around a vice-regal honey pot. Champagne flowed and Terence Ogden's assigned men moved through the ranks of the gentry with silver platters piled high with oysters, chicken, ham, exotic fruits and pastries.

At the other end of the social scale convicts and ticket-of-leave men queued up at the canvas tent set aside for them. Joseph Bloom had organised kegs of beer and every man toasted Her Majesty with each free drink.

Jake grinned. 'Give assigned lads free grog and they turn into true-blue royalists.'

He slowly read his way through the program notes. 'Jesus wept, mate. Cop this. It's a dead giveaway. It says, "Sarishan. Trainer Mr Jakob Andersen. Owner Mr *G.G.* Smith!"'

He downed his ale. 'So if Sarishan wins and I collect the silver cup on The Gypsy's behalf, the traps could well arrest me for consorting with bushrangers!'

Mac looked hopeful. 'Maybe Gem won't show.'

'Not a chance!' Jake's eyes raked the crowd. 'If Gem ain't in the *stur*, he'll be here somewhere. Keep your eyes peeled. I need to have a quick word with Dick Gideon.'

The horses were lining up at the barrier for the start of the race. The jockeys' bold colours flashed in the sunlight.

Elated by his boxing win and only moderately drunk on alcohol and fatigue, Jake ran over to where Sarishan was pawing the ground, clearly ready for action. He stroked the colt's mane, proud that he had groomed him until his coat shone like black satin.

Dick Gideon wore the red, gold and black racing silks his mother had made him. Despite his pre-race nerves, he gave Jake a smile as bright as Christmas.

'Look Dick, you don't need no last-minute advice from me. Sarishan's like your blood brother. You'll know in your gut when it's time to give him his head.'

Dick's chest puffed out with pride. He nodded and manoeuvred Sarishan to the barrier.

It was no surprise to Jake that Ogden's horse, Jupiter's Darling, had drawn the best position. His jockey wore Ogden's Cornish colours of black with a white cross. He was clearly battling to keep the temperamental chestnut in line, but Jake knew the organisers were not game to run the race without him. As host to the governor's party, Terence Ogden must not be seen to lose face.

A top-hatted official called instructions over a megaphone. No one took a blind bit of notice. The horses lined up any old how. An official raised the starter's flag above his head, then lowered it. The field was away. It was instant chaos. One gelding reared and bolted in the opposite direction. Another jockey was thrown and stalked off in disgust.

Jupiter's Darling took the lead from a ragged field. Sarishan was placed halfway back as they circled the course once, twice. By the third time around, the field had thinned out. Four horses battled neck and neck. Jupiter's Darling, Erin's Pride, Queen Bess and coming up on the outside – Sarishan!

'Struth,' said Jake, 'Sarishan's got his second wind. He's flying!'

Homing down the straight there were only two serious contenders – Jupiter's Darling a few lengths in front of Sarishan. The crowd roared. Positioned on the rails Ogden's jockey looked over his shoulder to see the challenger coming down on the outside so he whipped Jupiter's Darling towards the finishing line.

Jake muttered under his breath, 'Give Sarishan his head, Dick. Now!'

At that moment Dick let Sarishan break free to draw level with the leader.

In full view of the crowd Ogden's jockey raised his whip, slashing it across Dick Gideon's face. Jake yelled out when he saw the pain on the boy's face but was proud that the kid didn't lose control of his mount.

Sarishan seized the moment. He stretched his gallant heart to the limit and came home to win by half a length.

Jake and Mac were jubilant, so was a large sector of the crowd. The clue to Sarishan's ownership had clearly captured the convict vote, but Jake suddenly felt uneasy. A murmur spread around the course as the judges conferred in a huddle.

'Shit, Mac, what's going on?'

A plummy voice announced over the megaphone, 'Sarishan is disqualified. Jupiter's Darling is the winner!'

Jake and Mac were part of the tidal wave that moved on the judges' enclosure.

The official tried to stem their anger. 'Sarishan is disqualified because the jockey is underage.'

Jake yelled at the crowd. 'There was nothing on the entry form about a jockey's age!'

All hell broke loose. There were loud calls for the judges' blood. One official's top hat was sent spinning like a boomerang over the heads of the crowd.

Terence Ogden grabbed the megaphone and his Cornish accent boomed out. 'In all fairness I cannot accept the silver cup. Sarishan beat my horse fair and square!'

Jake and Mac slapped each other around with great affection as Dick Gideon, his cheek bandaged, rode a lap of honour to the cheers of the crowd.

The plummy megaphone voice called for Mr Jakob Andersen to present himself.

'Shit! What have I done now?' Glass in hand, Jake crossed to the official table where a gentleman winced at the sight of Jake's bruised eye and cut lip.

'It seems the owner, Mr G.G. Smith, nominated you to collect the cup. But you can't possibly be presented to their Excellencies in that state. Don't even have a jacket, what!'

'He does now!' Mac removed his own coat and bundled Jake into it.

'Righto,' said Jake. 'Never keep a lady waiting, and the gov never did me no harm. But I'll only do it if my jockey fronts up with me to get the credit. He did all the bloody work.'

Sarishan's trainer and jockey were battered but beaming as they accepted the trophy. Lady Elizabeth Gipps, a quiet, elegant figure beside the impressive, uniformed figure of her husband, warmly congratulated Jake then bent her head to smile into the little jockey's eyes.

'Dick Gideon, you are to be congratulated on riding a brilliantly judged race. You kept your head under most trying circumstances.'

Her long gloved hand gestured to the boy's bandaged cheek to show the crowd that the cowardly attack had not gone unnoticed by Her Majesty's representatives.

Jupiter's Darling was awarded second place. Jake was satisfied to see Ogden give his jockey such a scorching public rebuke that the man slunk from the course in humiliation.

Cradling the silver cup like a babe in arms, Jake scanned the crowd.

He could hardly miss the figure on the perimeter. Mounted on Sarishan, Gem was resplendent in a scarlet military coatee adorned with yellow facing and gold epaulettes, worn in cavalier style with a broad-brimmed civilian hat that failed to disguise his Gypsy looks and gold earring. Seeing Jake he raised a victorious fist. Jake gave a tentative wave to avoid drawing attention to him.

Discretion was a waste of time. Gem played the victor to the hilt. Doffing his hat in a sweeping gesture to the crowd to acknowledge their congratulations, he finally departed. His military jacket was a bold splash of scarlet on the horizon as Sarishan galloped at a speed that could have set a new colonial record.

Jake watched in admiration till they were out of sight. 'Now *that's* what I call a horse!'

CHAPTER 28

Keziah felt like she was drowning when she looked through the window at the moon clearly outlined in the cloudless sky. Five full moons had waxed and waned since Daniel Browne had given her his ultimatum.

Joseph Bloom had gone through official channels to gain the absent Julian Jonstone's recommendation and the governor's sanction for the marriage. This would see Daniel officially re-assigned to his wife's custody and open the door for his ticket-of-leave.

Keziah felt guilty that Joseph had worked tirelessly on their behalf and dismissed the idea of payment. *How shocked he'd be if he knew just how much I loathe and detest my future husband.*

When Polly Doyle rushed in to deliver the latest newspapers her master had brought Keziah from Goulburn, Keziah invited her to stay for tea. Polly breathlessly excused herself.

'Up to me elbows in baking, I am. The way to a man's heart is through his belly, ain't it?'

Keziah smiled agreement but wondered if Polly meant George Hobson who clearly had his eye on her as future stepmother to his boys. Or did she fancy that shy coach driver Mac Mackie?

Keziah sat down at her kitchen table to read the latest news – and felt her whole world suddenly rock on its axis. A newspaper reported that a black tracker called Jacky Jacko had staggered into a remote South Australian homestead carrying an emaciated white man on his back. The victim was barely alive but was believed to be the missing explorer Caleb Morgan, long presumed dead.

Mi-duvel! Grandmother predicted men would cause chaos in my life if I made a terrible choice. And yet that mistake brought my greatest blessing – little Gabriel.

Only two weeks remained before the first of three consecutive Sundays in which the banns would be read in Ironbark Chapel for Daniel Browne to marry Saranna Plews. Keziah realised the terrible irony. This was the wedding she had promised Saranna to comfort her as the girl lay dying. A wedding she had foreseen down to the details of the bride's cameo brooch and the little blond boy – Gabriel!

She searched the sky for some omen in the faint hope that Gem might come back to her. Finding her ancestors silent she lost all hope and cried out in anguish to Gem's soul. 'Love me or leave me!'

Her concentration was broken when Gabriel's head peered anxiously from beneath the kitchen table to ask in confusion, '*Me*, Mama?'

Keziah felt her heart catch in her throat at the sight of his unruly cowlick. No matter how often she slicked it down, it always broke free to remind her of Caleb Morgan.

'Mama's just playing a game, Gabriel. I'll always love *you*. That's all that matters.' But was this strictly true?

She suspected Jake had done his damnedest to convince Gem to forgive her. She had heard village gossip about some fight with a 'mysterious' Jim Romani and Jake had turned up soon after with a livid scar over one eyebrow. What had been the outcome of their fight? And where was Gem? There had been no recent reports of The Gypsy's gang.

She felt a rush of anger at the sight of Daniel's cap hanging on the hook behind the door. He had deliberately left it behind on one of his one-day visits, an indulgence granted by Julian Jonstone who now seem-ed as much Daniel's art patron as his master.

Keziah combed over every detail of Daniel's visits, his every word and expression, searching for some clue that had eluded her. Since childhood she had mastered the art of evaluating *gaujos* at face value, but she simply could not read Daniel. *The man Saranna loved and lost is a total enigma to me. Why can't I see inside him?*

She felt as if she was being pulled into quicksand. The more she struggled against the idea of marrying Daniel, the deeper she sank into despair.

The moment she saw Jake Andersen riding towards the cottage she ran out to greet him.

Today he looked grim. Mounted on Horatio, he held the reins of a second horse. As usual his manner was nothing if not direct.

'The traps have been sent reinforcements 'cos the bushrangers are running them ragged. Gem's holed up in a cave to throw them off the scent, I finally tracked him down. He and me had a bit of a chat awhile back. Sorry I couldn't swing it for you, Kez. Your first choice.'

She sank down onto a chair. 'You are a true friend, Jake. I don't know why you went to so much trouble, but I thank you for it.'

'Gem says he'll never give himself up to the law, but he's agreed to meet you about that other business. I'm to take you to his hideout. Now.'

Keziah nodded then ran to the bark *goondie* where Nerida and little Murphy slept. After a quick exchange of words about Gabriel she headed for the paddock where the brumby grazed. Gem's gift had become a symbol of the travesty of their love.

Jake's words halted her. 'No! Ride this mare I brought you.' He jerked his head in the direction of Evans's property. 'Don't want to give that bloody informer no clues about Gem.'

He tried to sound casual. 'There ain't no brooms where we're going.'

Keziah stood stock-still. She read in his eyes he did not want to hurt her by saying the word. *Divorce.* When she fetched him her broom, he attached it to her saddlebag.

'A man'd look a fool riding with a broom. I'll get you back Monday for school.'

'Where are we going?' she asked.

'No need to know, Kez. What you don't know the traps can't trick out of you.'

'I'm no fool.' She added with pride, 'I've dealt with *gaujo* police all my life.'

They rode single file through sparsely timbered country. At nightfall they ascended into the mountains. Keziah had no idea where they were, but she tried to block her emotions by memorising bush landmarks. Moon shadows of giant trees stretched to the sky like the walls of a vast prison. It was a beautiful night spoilt forever; a night fated to play silent witness to the Romani rite that would sever her life from Gem's.

Mi-duvel. Grant me a miracle. Let me touch Gem's heart.

Jake dismounted. His imitation of a crow's call sounded like an echo of the Anglo-Saxon four-letter word for intercourse and drew the expected response from its 'mate'.

'Stick like glue to me at all times,' he warned. 'No knowing how many bolters are hiding out here. Or how drunk they'll be. Some won't have seen a woman's face in months.'

They skirted massive boulders that had fallen aeons ago to lie in majestic disarray, the perfect camouflage for a cave entrance only visible when she was close enough to touch it. Were these the Wombeyans she had heard about?

A youth squatted at the mouth of the cave. Moonlight etched the outline of his rifle. Keziah's keen sense of smell detected the pungent odour of rum.

'Gem's expecting us,' Jake told the youth, who turned to the cave and whistled through his teeth.

It was then Keziah saw the shadow. Outlined against cave walls turned orange by firelight was the shadow of the man Keziah loved above all men. She could not read his face in the darkness, but the cynical rasp of Gem's voice hit her like a body blow.

'Welcome, Jake. Can't say the same for that whore you've brought with you.'

'No whore,' Jake said quickly. 'Your *wife*. Does The Gypsy's promise hold good? Or is he a welcher? If so I'm ready to take you on!'

Jake's voice held an open challenge Keziah considered both brave and foolish. The three armed bushrangers sprawled around the cave looked bored, itching for trouble. She was only too conscious of the pile of weapons stacked in a corner.

Gem aimed his derisive laugh at Jake. 'I could lick you every time, pal.'

'Yeah? I was good enough on the day to win your promise.'

Keziah saw him furtively hand something to Gem, his voice lowered. 'Here's your half as agreed.'

Keziah was startled by the truth. So Jake had only fought to gain Gem's promise.

Gem was restless. 'Let's get down to business. You bring stores with you, pal?'

When Jake jerked his head in the direction of his horses two of the gang members ran off like eager children to unload rum, flour, tea, salt beef and mutton from the saddlebags.

Jake turned to Gem. 'No ammunition. You know me, mate. That's where I draw the line.'

Gem nodded. Keziah's eyes traced every line of his face.

The cave was silent except for the sound of the fire crackling. Jake observed the Rom and his wife as they faced each other like two duellists prepared to fight to the death. It was painful to watch, but Jake felt tense, knowing Keziah was about to face even more anguish.

It was Keziah who broke the silence. She offered Gem the traditional Romani greeting, '*Sarishan.* How are you?' Gem's only response was to turn his back on her in contempt.

Jake saw that Keziah's heart was in her eyes when she asked, 'Is this what you really want, Gem?' There was no answer from Gem so she drew closer and her words rushed out in desperation.

'For your own sake, give yourself up before you kill someone. That could only end on the gallows. Give yourself up now! You're young, you'll be free one day. I'll wait for you. I beg you, Gem, don't cast me off. Don't jump the broom with me.'

Gem's voice was soft, dangerous. 'What would you do to win back my love?'

'Anything!'

'Then *beg* me.'

Keziah knelt at Gem's feet. Jake felt envious at the sight of a proud woman driven to beg for love.

Gem savoured the moment. 'Good dog! Now prove it. Get rid of your little bastard.'

Jake felt a stab of anger at the sound of Keziah's choked cry.

'Cut out my heart, Gem, but don't ask that of me!'

'Then get out of my sight, you *gaujo* whore!'

Keziah's distress cut Jake to the quick, but this was no time to challenge Gem. Time was running out. He hadn't told Keziah the whole truth. The traps were combing this whole area to flush out bushrangers believed to be holed up in the network of caves. He must take control.

'What happens next, Gem? You forget I'm new to this Romani divorce business.'

Jake clutched the broom like a rifle. As he waited for the answer, shadows danced along the cave walls like a procession from the Wiradjuri spirit world. There was no sound except the crackling of the fire. One look at Keziah told him this was her moment of truth.

Gem's eyes narrowed as he looked into Jake's eyes, delaying the moment, as if reluctant to take the broom from him. When he leaned across his mocking whisper was for Jake's ears only.

'I always knew you wanted my whore.' Gem finally accepted the broom and turned away.

Jake hated his role as silent witness, but he had given his word. They stood with their backs to him, the broom lying behind them; the symbol of severance. Gem's hand twitched as if wanting to draw his pistol. Keziah extended a trembling hand to him.

An unnerving cry shattered the silence – Gem. He grabbed Keziah's face between his hands and uttered the most painful words Jake had ever heard, like flesh torn by the lash.

'Keziah! Understand me. It's too late. I can never give myself up. But I swear by God's breath, I will never love another woman. *Kurraben!* Forgive us both!'

Jake felt his gut wrench as Gem gently closed Keziah's eyes then kissed his wife full on the mouth. A kiss that numbered all the days of their lives. A kiss of mourning. When Keziah refused to jump, Gem lifted her in his arms and leapt backwards over the broomstick.

Jake heard the approaching sound of galloping horses, recognising the sound of pistol and rifle fire. He spun around to face Gem.

'It's the traps! We'll head them off. Give you time to make your getaway.'

The Wombeyan caves lay behind them as Jake dragged Keziah at a run to their horses. Her eyes held no trace of emotion but Jake sensed the depth of her misery. He lifted her into the saddle. No time for sympathy. His voice was a harsh command.

'Pull yourself together, Kez. This is for Gem! Hold on with everything you've got. You're in for the ride of your life.'

Jake rode at an angle in a desperate bid to draw the traps away from the cave. A glance back at Keziah told him she read his mind and her every muscle was now attuned to the bay mare.

Jake hacked his way through the virgin bush. Only when they reached the road did he realise his face was lacerated. A broken twig was pinned in Keziah's hair like an arrowhead and he automatically pulled it free.

In one rapid movement he dismounted, drank a mouthful of rum from his flask then poured the rest of the contents down his shirtfront, aware that Keziah was fiddling with the empty saddlebags. He leapt back into the saddle but confined their horses to a sedate pace.

When Jake saw the troopers galloping towards them he began

singing at the top of his voice. 'I would swim over the deepest ocean for my love to find.'

Carrifergus was the song that both the Irish and the English claimed was theirs. By the time the troopers were right behind them Jake was roaring the final lines:

'... but I'll sing no more till I get a drink.

For I'm drunk today, and I'm seldom sober

A handsome rover from town to town

Ah, but I'm sick now, my days are numbered.'

'Halt!' ordered Trooper Kenwood, 'your days certainly are numbered!'

Jake feigned surprise in words heavily slurred – he'd had plenty of practice as a drunk to give a convincing performance.

'Good evening to you, Sergeant. By the saints, I declare it's our good fortune to be having your company on the road to Ironbark. What with so many rascals on the loose.'

Kenwood failed to disguise his fury that The Gypsy had given him the slip again.

'State your business. Show me your convict pass!' he demanded.

Jake assumed an attitude of drunken pride. 'No pass needed. I'm a free man, Officer. Jakob Andersen. We're celebrating this lady's coming wedding. You're all invited.'

'Save your blarney. I've caught you red-handed supplying stores to The Gypsy's gang.'

Jake's smile froze. *Shit! Empty saddlebags a stone's throw from a known bushranger's hideout!*

Kenwood opened Jake's saddlebag with a triumphant flourish. His faced reddened as he took out a pair of frilly, long-legged 'unmentionables'.

Keziah challenged him in the tone of authority an English schoolteacher might use to a none-too-bright child. 'Is this quite necessary, Sergeant? Surely you remember me? I aided your enquiries in Ironbark concerning those scoundrel bolters.'

Jake knew she had given Kenwood nothing of value apart from herbal ointment for his mosquito bites. Kenwood flushed scarlet.

'Forgive me, Miss Plews. I didn't recognise you. Pray continue on your way.' He added pointedly, 'As you say, Andersen, there *are* rascals on the road tonight.'

When the sound of the troopers' horses had disappeared, Jake's curiosity got the better of him.

'That was quick thinking. I didn't know you'd packed a change of unmentionables.'

'I didn't,' she said haughtily, making a modest gesture to smooth her skirt over thighs that Jake realised were naked.

In a hasty ploy to save her embarrassment, Jake sang his favourite version of *The Wild Colonial Boy*. Mid-song he realised his mistake. This was no time to remind Kez of a dead young bushranger.

'You can sober up now,' she said tartly. 'And spare me your singing. The Irish do it far better.'

'Well, I'm *half* Irish,' said Jake.

'Then it must be your Norwegian half that does the singing.'

'Jesus! Women. You always manage to have the last word.'

'Not tonight, I didn't.' She angrily wiped away a tear. 'I don't blame Gem for rejecting me. But why won't he give himself up – to save his own life?'

Jake didn't doubt the answer lay in the hell ruled by the Devil Himself. But there was no way to make the truth palatable. 'To a man like Gem, freedom is everything.'

As they continued along the road to Ironbark, Jake felt more and more out of his depth. Keziah was howling as though her heart would break. Her blouse was soaked with tears. Her eyes pleaded with him as if he had the power to fix everything.

Jake tried to avert his gaze. *Kez really makes a mess of herself when she cries.*

'Isn't it crazy, Jake? If only Gem would marry me under *gaujo* law, he could be assigned to me but his Romani pride will never allow him to accept Gabriel. So here I am about to set Daniel Browne free when it should be Gem!'

Jake knew the system wasn't quite that easy to manipulate. It was one thing for a respected schoolteacher to gain the governor's indulgence to marry a hard-working assigned man like Daniel. Magistrates didn't hand out marriage permits like lollies to bushrangers.

He tried to console her. 'You did right. Put Gabriel first. Children don't ask to be born.'

Keziah seized on that one bright thought to sustain her. 'That's true. Gabriel is what really matters!' She gave him a smile that Jake knew most blokes would consider ravishing. He was immune. Kez was just his mate.

CHAPTER 29

Keziah's heart was racing as she drove Hobson's cart across the log bridge and came in sight of the Haunted Farm. She had long managed to avoid Dr Ross's property due to its ghostly reputation, but today she had no choice.

Dr Ross had earned the respect of the whole locality during the recent epidemic but after snatching scores of patients from the jaws of death, he had succumbed to the disease himself.

When Jake had suggested her herbal 'bag of tricks' might speed the Doc's recovery, Keziah decided she must bury her fear of *mulos* as Jake seldom asked anyone for a favour.

When she arrived at the doctor's whitewashed, double-storey farmhouse she was surprised by the peaceful atmosphere. Despite its spooky legend of Barnes, the wife-beater murdered here by an Irish convict, Padraic, the old house appeared to be in good shape. In contrast the grounds and orchard clearly needed restoration. She knew that Dr Ross had applied for an assigned man to work the farm before the rules changed in favour of free settlers and fresh sources of convict labour dried up.

The veranda was cordoned off with a sign marked 'Quarantine'. No barrier was going to prevent Keziah from practising her Romani herbal medicine.

When the assigned housekeeper, Janet Macgregor, opened the door she looked formidable. Keziah had heard the gossip about her criminal history but when she saw the woman's face was lined with weariness from weeks of nursing the doctor, Keziah felt an instant bond of sympathy.

'Sign says "Quarantine",' Janet said crisply.

'I'm Saranna Plews, Ironbark's schoolteacher. May I speak with the doctor? My cart is loaded with boxes for him. And Jake Andersen asked me to deliver a personal message.'

'Second door, top of the stairs,' said Janet and began unloading boxes from the cart.

Under her shawl Keziah concealed the bottle of whisky sent by Jake, mindful of his warning that the Wesleyan housekeeper would pour the Demon Drink down the sink before Leslie Ross even had a chance to read the label.

Keziah hurried upstairs, casting a wary eye out for a *mulo*, but she relaxed when she entered the sick room as it was free of any ghostly vibrations. Sunlight poured through the attic window across a cheerful patchwork quilt.

Dr Leslie Ross was in bed, propped against pillows, his hair freshly combed, his beard trimmed. Keziah saw that he had lost considerable weight and his breathing was laboured, but his ingrained Highland hospitality was undiminished.

'Kind of you to call, lassie,' he stuttered. 'So you're the schoolteacher Jake holds in such high esteem. We meet at last.'

'You are the hero of Ironbark, Doctor. I'm mindful of your convalescence, so I'll be brief. Jake sends you this whisky with instructions to use it liberally to help the medicine go down. I've delivered fruit, vegetables, eggs and a side of lamb from your grateful Ironbark patients. And I'm instructed to tell you *not* to return to work till you're fit and well.'

'My thanks to one and all, but I'm quite recovered. Besides, there's nay another surgeon for miles around.'

Keziah held up her hand to halt his excuse. 'At Jake's request I've brought you special herbs to make an infusion. It's a Romani cure that never fails.' She hastily added, 'A wise old Gypsy taught me. Taken four times daily it will greatly ease the congestion in your lungs. Forgive me if this advice sounds impertinent.'

He shook his head in admiration. 'Lass, you have all the efficiency of an admiral of the fleet. Tell Janet to brew the herbs to your instructions. I'll take my medicine like a man!'

As she hurried downstairs to instruct Janet about the herbs, Keziah gave a heartfelt sigh of relief. Murderer or victim, whichever *mulo* had given this house its frightening reputation was long gone.

Hobson's cart was much lighter after delivering its cargo of food. When Keziah drove it around the carriage-turning circle, she halted beside a weeping willow tree to look across the expanse of neglected old garden. Although the sun was shining brightly, she shivered with cold. An anxious thought crossed her mind. What if she was also going down with the virulent disease? She would endanger Gabriel, Murphy and all her schoolchildren.

It was then she saw the doctor's new labourer. A few yards away a young man stood beside a dilapidated stone well. His shaven head and ragged slop clothing clearly placed him as a convict. Sad dark eyes stared back at her from his gaunt face. Keziah waved to him, comforted by the thought that this lad had been assigned to a humane master. No doubt as soon as Dr Ross was on his feet he would have this lad's leg-irons removed.

The youth watched her in silence then lifted the wooden cover from the well and tossed something down. Seconds later she heard a splash as the object hit the water.

Keziah was just about to drive off when she realised something was very wrong. His leg-irons had disappeared. And then she saw the reason. His *whole body* was slowly dissolving before her eyes.

Cold with terror she cracked the whip and sent the horse and cart charging erratically for the road. *Mi-duvel! It's Padraic. Why won't those damned* mulos *ever leave me alone?*

Daniel Browne was seated in Keziah's carver's chair, eating the hearty breakfast she had cooked for him.

He had been granted a convict pass to attend chapel for the reading of the first banns. Keziah was thankful he must return to Gideon Park by nightfall. Meanwhile Romani hospitality bound her to suffer his arrogance.

'You keep a generous table. I congratulate myself on my clever choice of a wife.'

'Don't count your chickens before they're hatched,' Keziah snapped.

'Come, come,' he teased, an edge of malice in his voice. 'Marriage to me will give you the best of both worlds. A man to protect you and be your breadwinner. While you keep your independence, your schoolhouse, your good name. What more could a Gypsy thief want?'

'If you call me a thief again the wedding is off and hang the consequences!'

Gabriel entered and made straight for Daniel, instinctively recognising the addition to the family.

Keziah studied Daniel's attitude to the boy as he guided his hand to cross off another day before the wedding. He gently explained the picture of the snowman on the calendar to a child who had never seen snow.

She wondered anxiously, would Daniel be a decent stepfather? She was reminded of Jake's words, 'Kids don't ask to be born. They're pawns in the games adults play.'

For Gabriel's sake she tried to sound light-hearted about the fact Daniel would live with them after the wedding. Gabriel offered to share his toys and his bed with him.

Daniel said evenly, 'What a kind boy. But Mama's boss of the house, eh Mama?'

Keziah gritted her teeth at his barbed joke. Daniel had sworn their marriage would be platonic but Keziah knew the truth. The moment they exchanged *gaujo* vows, legally she would be part of Daniel's 'goods and chattels'. She refused to answer him.

'I'll soon be granted my ticket-of-leave thanks to Julian Jonstone and your mate Joseph Bloom. Free to choose who I work for – and receive wages. Until then I haven't a penny to bless myself. You must pay for the pleasure of buying a husband.'

Keziah flinched. She knew that at Gideon Park Daniel had lost all control over his life. No doubt even the power to inflict hurt was a new experience for him. He clearly enjoyed flexing his muscles as future master of the house. Yet moments later he seemed surprisingly nervous when he handed her a scroll of paper – her wedding present.

Despite her desire to keep the distance between them, Keziah was moved by the sensitive way his portrait captured the intimate bond between mother and child. She thanked him coolly, but was unable to remain quiet when she caught sight of his badly swollen right hand. The backs of the fingers were marked by raw red cuts.

'This was no accident!'

'A horsewhip. My overseer caught me sketching this when I was meant to be at my labours.' Daniel shrugged. 'He's done far worse to others. At least he's never had me flogged.'

Keziah crossed to her pestle and mortar and mixed up a fresh herbal ointment. She tossed off an explanation so as not to make him think that she was softening towards him.

'My grandmother taught me I must never withhold healing, not even from an enemy.'

The hooded green eyes observed her intently. 'Am I your enemy?'

'You are my patient,' she said stiffly. With customary skill she soaked his hands, applied the ointment to his wounds, bandaged them then gave him a pot of the balm.

'You have healing hands,' Daniel said.

'Don't mistake my motive. I'd do the same for a dog.'

It was time for Daniel to take his leave, yet he hesitated.

'Be careful of the man who beat you,' Keziah warned. 'Your art is a god-given gift. Some people try to destroy what they don't understand.' She forced herself to add, 'Our portrait is very fine.'

Daniel turned his head, perhaps to mask his pleasure at her

praise. 'Till next week.'

Keziah closed her door. *I refuse to pity him. If only Jake was here!*

Now that the wedding date seemed unavoidable, Keziah asked Nerida to be her bridesmaid.

'Think of it as a *gubba's* corroboree with singing and dancing. I don't believe in that church business but it will give Daniel his freedom.'

Nerida's decision was final. 'You make Daniel free. I help you do it proper, that freedom business.'

When it came to freedom, Keziah knew how alien white man's law was to Aboriginal life. For white *gubbas* to take away a human being's freedom was cruelty beyond belief.

That freedom business. This odd phrase lifted Keziah's spirits. Nerida had turned a dreaded wedding into a celebration to beat the convict authorities.

The day also brought the arrival of Sunny Ah Wei's emporium.

'We need special help today, Sunny,' Keziah said. 'Material for wedding clothes.'

Sunny's smile faltered momentarily. 'Ah! Wedding very good luck! I have special bargains up my sleeve for you. Are you the bride, Missy?' he asked Nerida.

When Nerida ignored him, Keziah replied instead. 'No, I am.' She added under her breath, 'Unfortunately.'

'Ah, *very* good,' Sunny's smile grew wider.

When Nerida could not look past the red and gold brocade, Sunny prompted. 'Red very lucky colour for brides in China – bring double happiness, many children.'

Keziah was confused by Nerida's apparent indifference to Sunny. *Is she shy? Does she like him? Or is this a female custom in Wiradjuri courtship?*

Sunny took their measurements for the lightning-fast Goulburn tailor at a price so modest Keziah wondered how he existed on such a narrow margin of profit. She moved tactfully away as if to admire a new line of his kitchenware, to give Sunny the opportunity to talk to Nerida alone. But when Sunny finally departed he looked crestfallen.

'Nerida, what on earth did you say to upset him?' Keziah asked.

'I am promised to Wiradjuri man. No China husband me.'

Keziah felt helpless to intervene. Nerida never spoke of the anguish she carried in her soul, but Keziah had heard from Jake that since the Myall Creek massacre many of the Wiradjuri had disappeared like shadows from the land. Dead or alive they were dispossessed. *Just like Gem and me.*

That night Keziah was woken by a vivid dream. She sat upright in bed, her heart racing wildly. In the dream she had been passionately kissed by a man she could not identify. He wore a red neckerchief. It was not Daniel Browne. Nor was it Gem.

At Gideon Park Daniel Browne marked off on the wall the remaining days before the wedding. Saranna Plews's impostor was his escape ticket but he lived in fear that something would happen to prevent it. He slept badly, worked feverishly like an automaton to avoid the overseer who could prevent his departure at the stroke of a pen. Daniel tried to block every emotion and instinct that involved the world around him. The only time he felt safe to have ordinary human feelings was during those secret hours he spent alone in the feverish act of creation. The faces of the people he explored on paper were more alive to him than anyone born of woman.

Today as he strode towards his master's house he carried with pride his latest painting, the commissioned portrait of Charlotte Jonstone.

He must *recognise how fine it is. I've not only captured his wife's aristocratic features but also that quality of sadness in her eyes – her failure to produce a living male heir.*

Daniel assured himself he had taken great pains to please the first lady of the Quality he had ever known. He had posed her in her most flattering rose-coloured gown, seated on a superbly carved armchair she had told him was a Louis XVI *fauteuil*, and placed her favourite ivory fan on a small Regency table. For hours in his own time he had laboured over the arrangement of her fair curls, the intricate Belgian lace edging her sleeves and décolletage, the lustre of her pearls, the Indian sapphire ring that was a family heirloom.

When he knocked at the servants' entrance he felt sure of success but was crestfallen when the assigned housekeeper told him he was too late. The Jonstones had gone to Bathurst, to another of their estates. She closed the door before he had time to retrieve his painting.

Daniel felt crushed. He had counted on the promised payment. Although he always made light of his poverty to Keziah, he felt humiliated with nothing to bring to the marriage.

After the wedding in Ironbark it'll be a case of out of sight, out of mind. Jonstone will never pay what's due to me.

Returning to the assigned men's quarters Daniel's path was suddenly blocked. Mounted on his coal-black stallion the Devil Himself reminded Daniel of an evil, smiling centaur.

'Well, fellow m'lad. Quite a neat trick of yours trying to curry favour with Jonstone. Thought you'd concealed your crime. The paper you stole for your pictures months back.'

Daniel felt the sweat beads on his forehead. Fear pushed him beyond caution.

'I stole nothing, Sir. I've worked off every penny as well you know!'

The Devil Himself seemed to turn that statement over in his mind then added with a look of cunning, 'Where's your receipt, Browne?'

Daniel's heart raced as the man continued in a friendly tone even more chilling than rage.

'You deserve a special wedding gift. Something you and your bride will cherish to remind you of your time at Gideon Park. How would twenty lashes suit you?'

Daniel felt his voice rising in panic. 'I've worked like a dog for you, Sir. I'm no thief. You're answerable to Mr Jonstone. He won't allow it!'

'He won't *know* of it, m'lad. When he returns from Sydney Town you'll be ancient history. Miles away in Ironbark begging your bride to heal your stripes.'

'You promised me I'd never be flogged!'

'Me promise a *felon*? What gave you that idea? Twenty, did I say? I'll be generous and make it thirty. Six o'clock tomorrow. Get a good night's sleep, Daniel Browne. *I shall*.'

The Devil Himself rode off whistling. Daniel watched horse and rider disappear from sight.

For three years I prayed, lied, cheated, worked myself ragged. I sold my soul – all for nothing.

Daniel knew his nemesis had finally arrived. What good would it do to pray to Our Lady? There was no power stronger than the Devil Himself.

At five o'clock the next morning, Daniel was dragged from his bed by two of Iago's henchmen who made crude jokes about his abject terror. They tied him to the whipping frame, ripped open his ragged shirt to bare his back in readiness for the lash. And left him there. Alone. Daniel realised an hour had passed. In the distance the bell rang for six o'clock mass. The Devil Himself rode up smiling, accompanied by the scourger, whip in hand.

'Postpone the flogging till tomorrow,' he ordered and rode away.

This pattern was repeated daily until Daniel realised with horror the new rules of the game.

The bastard's grown bored with merely watching floggings. He's now getting his pleasure savouring my fear.

CHAPTER 30

Bolthole Valley was buzzing with rumours about the extraordinary petition the big landowners planned to present to Governor Gipps.

Jake fronted Feagan and wasted no time. 'What's the strength of this petition to the gov demanding he place our whole county under martial law? Is it a joke or what?'

Feagan drew himself up to his full height of five feet two inches. 'A man never jokes about martial law.'

'That's bloody true,' said Jake. 'If Gipps caves in we're in for another bloodbath.'

Jake marched out of the general store, leapt into the wagon and pushed Horatio to the limit in the cross-country drive to Ironbark.

It was a Friday. That meant the end of the working week for Keziah. No doubt on Sunday Daniel would leave Gideon Park at the crack of dawn to ride over for another reading of the banns. But with any luck Jake would find her alone today.

'How's life, mate?' Leaning in the doorway of Keziah's cottage, Jake sized up her mood. Today she appeared to be on a steady course, but he'd been wrong about her moods before.

A blue smock covered her dress as she bent over schoolbooks. He liked the way she had trouble controlling her hair. Half of it was piled on top of her head, half escaped in waves. Red ink stained the hand that held her quill.

'What's wrong?' she asked quietly. 'Is it Gem?'

Jake wondered, *Will the time ever come when Gem isn't uppermost in her mind?*

'Gem's safe as far as I know, but best you hear the news from me.

Terence Ogden's getting up a petition to the governor demanding he place us under martial law. Thomas Icely's also pressuring the surveyor-general about his plans for the village of Carcoar near Bathurst and demanding protection from bushrangers. I reckon if Icely climbs on board we're history.'

Keziah turned pale. Jake pressed on. 'Martial law means a massive increase in mounted police and a resident magistrate. So bushrangers will be put on trial in our neck of the woods instead of being sent to Sydney Town, Bathurst, Berrima or wherever.'

'If you mean string bolters up without a fair trial, say so,' she said.

Jake was aware how martial law would affect Gem and the other poor bastards he called mates. Gem was still at large. Will Martens was busy adding to the legend of Jabber Jabber and had notched up so many daring escapes from custody it had become a joke.

'Will Governor Gipps give in to this petition?' Keziah asked.

'You tell me,' he said pointedly.

'I'm not clairvoyant twenty-four hours a day,' she said.

'Martial law's an extreme measure – and bloody expensive on the public purse. There's a public rally in Bolthole tonight to debate it. Ogden and his cronies are behind it. I reckon it's a good idea to know thy enemy. You girls fancy coming along for the ride?'

Keziah looked anxious. 'Will they let you take Nerida inside?'

'Just watch me!' said Jake.

'Do you see Ogden and Icely as the enemy?' Keziah asked as she hurriedly washed Gabriel's hands and face.

'Ogden ain't all bad. But he's a bit hungry for power and he's out to rival Icely's empire. Icely's built up ninety thousand acres with an army of free convict labour. He's moved his family back to Sydney Town. He's bright enough to know bushrangers see him as a prime target for assassination.'

Keziah tried to be fair to Icely. 'You can't blame a man for protecting his family.'

'I don't. But most big landholders won't admit the root cause is the evils of the system. The Brits claim they're gunna finish offloading convicts in this colony but they'll still be transporting them to Van Diemen's Land and other places. The poor buggers serving out their time are treated worse than dogs. Struth, don't get me started, Kez, or I'll end up in the Watch House again!'

'No, you won't! Remember you've got two women and children in your care tonight!'

Dressed and at the ready, Gabriel made a beeline for Jake.

'Blow me down, Gabe! Look how big you've grown!' Jake swept the boy onto his shoulders.

Dressed in her Sunday best, Keziah gave Jake that special look of hers that always made him feel uncomfortable. As if she trusted him to fix everything.

'Does martial law mean we'll have public hangings in the street again?'

'Yeah, but that won't change a ruddy thing. When it comes to knowing what goes on down here, the British government wouldn't know its toffee nose from its ar—' He hastily switched his intended word to 'arm' in deference to Gabriel.

He rose. 'Let's hope Gipps won't buckle under. The last time we got lumbered with martial law was in Windradyne's time. He was known by his whitefella name, Saturday. Don't mention those names in front of Nerida as it hurts too much. Mention of any dead black's name is taboo.'

Keziah nodded. 'For my people too.'

Nerida was already seated in the wagon with Murphy scrubbed and serious sitting on her lap when Keziah climbed on board with Gabriel.

'I'll pin my hair up while we're driving.'

Jake took one look at her hair blowing around her head like a soft cloud. 'Don't be silly. Makes you look halfway decent.'

He grinned as he ducked her swinging reticule.

When Keziah entered Bolthole Valley's community hall she saw local settlers huddled in rows like black crows on a stockyard fence. Women aired their best hats and shawls. Men reflected every rung of the social ladder from formal suits to fustian work clothes. Their faces covered a range of hirsute fashion: beards, mutton-chop whiskers, moustaches.

Keziah noticed Jake was one of the minority among the younger men who was clean-shaven. *Funny how he never goes unshaven these days.*

She knew most people had come to push the law and order petition through and that some genuinely feared convict insurrection. For others the rally was a social event too good to miss. Excitement hovered in the air like heat haze.

Jake waited until the meeting began before he craftily manoeuvred her and Nerida into the back row by the door to avoid drawing attention to Nerida, whose face was hidden behind the wings of her bonnet. With the little boys seated on their laps, Keziah listened intently to the speakers' rhetoric.

Terence Ogden's forthright Cornish accent, upright bearing and dignified smoky beard marked him as a man for whom it was second nature to control people's lives – free or bond. He made it clear he supported Icely's arguments for increased protection from bushrangers then read out the signatures on his own petition and invited every man to make his mark. His speech met with spontaneous applause.

The next speaker had all the fire of a Baptist preacher. Every sentence was punctuated by agreement from the crowd. Keziah half expected 'hallelujahs'.

'Governor Gipps must listen to the voice of the people. Martial law is imperative to stop bushrangers from holding to ransom the community we gave our lifeblood to build. We urgently require more mounted police here. We must restore law and order in the farthest outpost of Her Majesty's empire. Hunt down godless desperadoes. We need a resident magistrate empowered to send villains like One Eye,

Jabber Jabber and that vagabond Gypsy Gem Smith to the gallows!'

Thunderous applause carried the vote. Keziah could barely control her rage. She longed to defend Gem, but she had to keep up her respectable veneer to protect Gabriel. She held the boy's sleepy head against her breast and tried to confront her confusion. Unless a miracle occurred, before the full moon she would be legally bound to Daniel Browne. Was she being totally honest about her reasons for agreeing to the marriage? At first it had been to preserve the life she had built and to protect Gabriel from claims by the Morgan family. But what really tied her to life in Ironbark? By impersonating Saranna had she abandoned her own Romani standards? Or was it because for the first time in her life she enjoyed respect in the eyes of a *gaujo* community?

She longed to confide in some wise person before it was too late.

At the very moment that Keziah looked across the hall it was as if some invisible wheel controlling her life had slipped a cog. She was now on a very different path. Jake stood shoulder to the wall, his gaze fixed on Ogden and his ruling-class cohorts. The light from a wall bracket threw his features into relief. It was as if she was seeing Jake for the very first time. His profile revealed strength, humour and arrogance brushed with the sensitivity he tried to disguise. It was the head of a young prince on a medieval coin. She was struck by the thought. *Jake is really quite handsome.*

Confused by her sudden insight, she turned her attention to Gilbert Evans's tirade about the depravity of all bushrangers. Keziah wanted to shout: *Hypocrite! You preach from the pulpit on Sundays but we all know you own a brothel here in Bolthole Valley.*

She remained silent, hating herself for her impotence. How many of these men had ordered their assigned men flogged for trivial reasons? How many averted their eyes from those forced to work their land with empty bellies? Hobson and Bloom were humane masters. But how many others here tonight were free of guilt?

Gilbert Evans's voice was slippery. 'There are traitors in our midst who give succour to bushrangers and help them escape. These men will refuse to sign our petition!'

Keziah looked across into Jake's steel-grey eyes and read his message. *He can't swallow any more of this! Mi-duvel! Jake must not go to prison!*

It was then Keziah found her courage. She jumped to her feet and challenged Gilbert Evans. 'Show me a petition to outlaw the lash and I'll gladly sign that! A humane system wouldn't need martial law!'

Scores of faces turned to gape at her. Mrs Hill, one of the widows Keziah saw regularly in Feagan's General Store, pointed a finger at Nerida. 'That's One Eye's *gin*. What's she doing here? *Spying* for him!'

Two men grabbed hold of Nerida. Gabriel slid to the floor as Keziah lunged forward to beat them off.

Jake yelled as he hurled his body into the fray. 'Take your hands off those women, they're with me!'

Burly men released Nerida, then swarmed to remove Jake from the scene. He seized the moment to cry, 'Damn the system. End it now!' An Irishman picked up the chant to be joined by a few brave voices. At the back of the hall fists were flying.

Somebody grabbed hold of the petition and flung it up in the air. Papers showered across the room to be trampled underfoot.

Driving home, Keziah saw that Jake's shirt collar was torn, but he was light of heart enough to deliver his favourite version of *The Wild Colonial Boy* with all verses intact. Keziah was moved by the depth of feeling in his voice. She realised that everything Jake said and did was an odd filter for his strong, yet half-concealed, love of this land of his.

'Not long ago,' said Jake, 'that song got people so riled they were banned from singing it in public houses.' They both knew she knew this but he enjoyed saying it anyway.

'Did it stop them?' she asked.

'Nah. They just drank more grog and sang louder.'

'Was Bold Jack Donahoe a good man?'

Jake hedged his bets. 'Many as thought so. He died game. Surrounded by a detachment of soldiers and traps in his final gunfight. He insulted them and swore at them to "come on and get me" before a trooper shot him dead. Twenty-six. My age. He was my hero as a boy. Didn't worry my mam none, being Irish herself. Funny thing the power of a song.'

'My father played music that made you weep or dance. Or fight to the death.'

Jake chewed this over for a minute. 'You named the little Rom after him.'

She was surprised by his perception. 'I never told you that!'

'Didn't have to.'

When they arrived at her cottage, Jake walked Nerida to her *goondie* with the sleeping Murphy slung over his shoulder. 'Goodnight, Neri. Sorry about the ruckus.'

'You a good man, Jake.' She added with a straight face, 'For a *gubba*.'

Jake grinned. 'I'm the best of a bad lot of white men, right?'

After he had carried Gabriel off to bed, Keziah risked asking her question. 'Jake, could you stay for a drink? I need your advice.'

He cocked an eyebrow. 'All right by me but how would your fiancé handle that? You'll be Mrs Browne in thirteen days. Don't want to give Ironbark gossips fuel for their fires.'

By their second glass of wine Jake felt mellow but he could see Keziah was tense. She seldom drank wine. She didn't really have the head for it. He had seen wine make her dance or cry, sometimes both at once.

He held his glass to the light and examined its delicate tracery. 'For a woman who doesn't much like a drop of the grape, you sure do things in style!'

'My grandmother kept her best glasses for special occasions. I need to make a wise decision. Time is running out.'

He clinked his glass to hers and drank with appreciation. 'If this is a sample of your wedding wine, I'll be first in the door, last to leave.'

Keziah drank with such nervous haste Jake doubted she tasted it.

'So what's your problem, Kez?' he prompted. 'Can't decide what to do with all that messy hair of yours on your big day, eh?'

Keziah's tresses now fell in disarray around her shoulders. To Jake she didn't look much like a schoolmistress. More like a very seductive mermaid. She drained her glass.

'Slow down a bit,' Jake warned. 'When I drink too much I end up in a brawl.'

Keziah leaned forward confidentially. 'The truth is I've changed my mind. I've decided not to marry Daniel after all.'

Jake spluttered wine over his shirt. Checked to see if she was serious. She was.

He reached for the bottle. 'On second thoughts, I think we'd better have another drop.' He refilled their glasses then tried to arrange his thoughts.

'Every bride since Eve gets cold feet before her wedding but the minute you see Daniel at the altar you'll race up the aisle before he's got a chance to change his mind.'

'Stop! Listen to me, Jake. I don't love Daniel. *I never did!*'

Jake tried to calm her. 'Look, I reckon he really loves you – and you said yourself you'd made some kind of pact with him. God only knows you need a decent bloke to take care of you, Kez.'

Keziah fixed him with that violet-blue gaze that made him half wish he was free to be that bloke.

'I agreed because marriage will strengthen my custody of Gabriel when Caleb Morgan returns to claim him.'

Jake had the feeling there was a whole heap more to the story, but Keziah gestured in the direction of Gabriel's bedroom as if that should make everything clear.

'I only wanted to make *him* happy. You understand?'

Jake felt taken aback. 'Sure, but now the stable door's open, you'd best get married.'

Keziah looked confused. 'Don't you understand? There's another man I really want!'

Jake rolled his eyes to heaven. *Does she mean Gem or Gabe's father, Caleb Morgan? Or some other joker I haven't stumbled on?*

He patted her shoulder. 'Hey, let's be practical. Do you find Daniel attractive?'

'Well, he's not ugly!'

'That's bloody something! Does he treat you like a lady?'

'Perfectly well in public, but—'

'Is he kind to Gabriel?'

Keziah was losing patience. 'Yes! Can't you see why I'm so confused? I thought you were my *mate* but—'

'I *am* your bloody mate. Who else would sit here listening to all this?'

Keziah was on her feet, her eyes pleading. 'Jake. If you're really my friend, please stay the night with me! I'm so *nervous.* It's been nearly three years since I—'

Jake grabbed at straws. 'So that's it. All that talk tonight about assassinations and bushrangers put the wind up you. How about I sleep in my bluey on your veranda?'

'No, Jake!' Keziah was moving towards him. She was modestly covered from her throat to her ankles, but the wild disorder of her hair and the sensuality of her mouth gave her a wanton look that took Jake's breath away.

He jumped to his feet, ready to make a getaway, but she blocked his escape. Her body pressed lightly against him as she traced his mouth with one finger.

'Jake, before it's too late. Please make love to me. *Now.*'

For a few delicious seconds Jake made no attempt to stop her as she gently rocked her hips against him. Her eyes closed as she rubbed her lips against his mouth – her own mouth ready and willing. He felt her body catch fire like no woman he'd ever touched.

'Daniel?' he managed to croak.

'He won't care. We made a pact. He doesn't want what I can give you, Jake.'

There was a 'click' inside Jake's head at that precise moment. He held her at arm's length and spoke kindly. Or so he thought.

'Just because I spend half my life in a brothel doesn't mean I don't have any standards left.'

No decent man took advantage of a woman whose head was turned by wine, but from her expression Jake wondered if his meaning had somehow been lost in translation.

Keziah took a step back and raised her chin as if she was fighting to regain control. Jake was struck by the fact there was a totally different Keziah standing before him. A little too much wine but very much the lady.

'I asked for your honest opinion. You gave it. You're quite right. I'll marry Daniel as planned. I do hope you're free to dance at our wedding.'

Keziah opened the front door for him. 'Don't forget your hat, Jake.'

He stumbled back to retrieve it, but tried one more tack at the door.

'I want you to know, mate. It was a lovely offer – best I ever had.'

Too late. Her look reminded him of his mam that day he'd come home from school to find a Catholic priest telling her she was living in mortal sin with her Proddie de facto and six kids. Keziah's voice was an echo of his mam's that day – sweet, distant, unnaturally polite.

'Kind of you to take us to the rally. Do you think martial law will be enforced?'

Jake was staggered. She sounded stone-cold sober but he realised she must be tired because she had to lean against the doorframe for support.

He threw his hands to the sky. 'Martial law? How would I know, mate? I wouldn't bet on a bloody thing tonight!'

Charging along the Sydney Road Jake found he couldn't even look at the sky without seeing Keziah's extraordinary violet-blue eyes watching him.

Why the bloody hell am I haunted by Kez's words? She's just my mate!

Jake didn't believe in any of that ghost bulldust, but for days past he'd been wondering if it was possible a *living* woman could haunt a man. He told himself that the minute Kez was safely married off to Daniel his debt to her for saving his life would be paid in full. Kez would settle down and once again he'd be a free agent to hunt down Jenny's mongrel.

When he picked up his mail from the post office in Goulburn there was a letter waiting for him that rocked Jake to the foundations of his life. *Jenny.*

He read it in a new public house across the road. He was cut to the quick by Jenny's airy references to her jewels, pink marble bathroom and lady's maid – luxuries he had failed to provide. At face value her letter was a friendly invitation to visit Pearl. But Jake knew his Jenny. Where was the trick? He re-read it and found it. No return address. His bolter wife could be anywhere on the Australian continent.

When his bitter laughter subsided Jake decided to head for Sydney Town to hire the services of an unusual, newly established American agency. He re-read the advertisement he'd torn from a newspaper. Under the banner of an American flag was the symbol of a spyglass. The head of the agency, Benjamin Rogers (late of New York City), claimed he guaranteed success. All enquiries conducted with utmost discretion. Cases included missing persons, illicit liaisons, fraudulent business dealings and unsolved murders.

'What the hell, I'll give your agency a go, Yankee.'

But as he headed north Jake heard Keziah's urgent whisper echo in his head. *'Jake, before it's too late. Please make love to me.* Now.'

Sydney Town or Ironbark? Jake knew it was no contest. He turned his horse south. 'Full steam ahead, Horatio. Get us to the church on time. We've got a wedding to stop!'

CHAPTER 31

Time dragged painfully for Keziah after Jake's departure. She lay awake at night, too dejected to avoid the Romani fear that moonbeams falling across her bed at full moon caused white hair or baldness. What could be worse than a farcical wedding to Daniel Browne? And this coming marriage was one problem that Jake had shown no desire to solve. He had rejected her love.

The day that Nerida called 'that freedom business' finally dawned. Although Keziah had promised herself she would make no special effort, she allowed Nerida to dress her hair with a coronet of scarlet bottlebrush flowers that matched the new gown. Later the dress would be covered by its matching jacket to serve as her Sunday best.

George Hobson paced in front of her cottage wearing the formal suit he had worn at his wife's funeral. He offered Keziah his arm but made no attempt to conceal his dismay that his respected schoolteacher had chosen to marry a lowly government man.

'Marry in haste, repent at leisure. It's not too late to change your mind, Miss Plews.'

'Thank you, Mr Hobson, but this is the road I am meant to take.'

Resigned to the inevitable, Keziah walked to the chapel feeling like a condemned woman. Nerida, resplendent in red and gold brocade, confidently led the way, keeping the peace between Murphy and Gabriel. Wearing identical pageboy suits the little boys were engaged in a sly tug-of-war over who carried the velvet ring cushion.

Keziah had understood Joseph Bloom's tactful explanation that Saturday being his Sabbath he could not attend her wedding. But now as she walked up the path to the chapel she saw him pacing back and forth reciting his psalms. Trust Joseph to find a way to be with her in spirit.

Her smile froze as she looked into Joseph's eyes. As if by sleight of hand his conventional suit was transformed into the bewigged costume of a lawyer. Next moment he was once again dressed in his morning suit, his eyes smiling at her over his spectacles.

Keziah was shaken. *I've lived with the gift of second sight all my life. Why am I so afraid now?*

The chapel was filled to capacity. She recognised the irony of the different reasons for attendance. Assigned men came out of respect for the teacher who gave so many the gift of literacy, even giant Sholto could now read the words on his tattoos.

Protestants came to witness the union of what they assumed was two of their own. Catholics came in gratitude Miss Plews had not forced Proddie dogma onto their children. Welsh Wesleyans had the best singing voices in the valley so they came to provide the choir. The Buddhist, Sunny Ah Wei, came for reasons of the heart – Nerida – and to make business contacts.

And Daniel Browne was there to become a free man. He stood at the altar in a dark suit borrowed from Mac Mackie, cuffs added to lengthen the trousers. His hair glinted in the sunlight that filtered through the stained-glass windows. As Keziah progressed up the aisle on Hobson's arm, she was surprised by the look of admiration in Daniel's eyes. *He sees me as a subject to paint. That suits me just fine.*

The dark red of her gown matched the floral coronet on her free-flowing hair and the bottlebrush flowers she carried in place of a bouquet. The gown clung to her body, except for the neckline that slipped off one shoulder as if to proclaim she was no virginal bride.

Keziah felt the eyes of every man in the congregation focused on her, but when she scanned their faces she was searching for one special man. *Where on earth is Jake?*

Even before he could see the chapel, Jake Andersen could hear the tinny sound of organ music. He left Horatio to graze and headed straight for the chapel door. Inside it was a hothouse. Heat was captured between the walls and Jake felt a blast of hot air on his face, mixed with the scent of perfume and pomade.

He heard the words of the wedding service being conducted by the elderly clergyman and was relieved to find he had arrived just in time. The old man hardly bothered to raise his eyes when he arrived at the traditional question to the congregation. 'Therefore if any man can show any just cause, why they may not lawfully be joined together, let him now speak, or else hereafter forever hold his peace.'

Jake cleared his throat. 'Hang on a minute!'

His words were greeted by a confused wave of murmurs. An elderly woman nudged him in the ribs and told him to be quiet. And the giant Sholto tried to push Jake in the direction of the exit. Keziah turned around and for a very long moment Jake's eyes locked with hers. Her lips parted. She made no sound, but Jake knew she was silently calling out to him for help.

The clergyman looked startled by the ruckus and continued the ceremony at racing speed. He had barely asked the question, 'Wilt thou Daniel Thomas have this woman Sara Anne to be your lawful wedded wife …?' before Daniel prevented a second interjection from Jake by loudly cutting across the clergyman's question with, 'I will!'

When Daniel bent his head to kiss Keziah's lips, Jake felt as if some invisible pugilist had hit him in the stomach.

The next thing Jake knew the tinny organ was playing a wedding march and the newly married couple was headed down the aisle towards him. Jake bolted for the door.

He leapt into the saddle, then looked back. Keziah and Daniel wore frozen smiles as Ironbark's children showered them with confetti. Keziah aimed her bridal flowers at Nerida, but Polly Doyle leapt to catch them and crowed with delight. Daniel looked straight at Jake as he placed his arm around Keziah's waist and drew his bride to him in a clear gesture of possession.

Jake had seen more than enough. He rode Horatio off at a gallop, but as he reached the Sydney Road he remembered his saddlebag contained a wedding present for Keziah. That would have to wait. He didn't fancy returning to the wedding breakfast to hear that bloody artist make flowery speeches about the bride.

What he needed right now was a very long night with Lily Pompadour – Wednesday was too far away.

When Daniel entered the schoolhouse with Keziah on his arm he was surprised to find a lavish wedding breakfast set up in a horseshoe pattern of tables. He knew this was Keziah's doing. She had cooked a mountain of food for the adults and made fancy party treats for the village children.

He watched her as she mingled with the guests, clearly determined to wear her public smile until her face ached. Only he and Nerida could see the truth in her eyes.

When the final guests had departed, cheered on by wine and goodwill, Daniel escorted his bride home in silence. She was no sooner inside the front door than she changed into her house dress and released her pent-up feelings by cleaning the already spotless cottage.

Daniel sat on the squatter's chair on the veranda, blowing lazy smoke rings with one of the cigars from the box that was an early wedding present from Jake Andersen. Daniel liked and trusted Jake but he was well aware that his wedding plans had created an underlying tension between them.

Now as he worked on a fresh portrait of Jake, Daniel wondered what made the Currency Lad so different to other men? Only one generation away from his European roots, but already this alien land had left its imprint on Jake's face and body. Did it also possess his soul? The things that were foreign to Daniel were Jake's heritage – his earth, sky, air, water. It was as if Jake had emerged half finished from a new mould of Englishman. No manners in the accepted sense, but he had genuine, offhand kindness.

As the portrait swiftly developed into the superbly muscled body of a prize fighter, Daniel recalled the way Jake had presented his gift of cigars with the warning, 'Smoke them outside or Kez'll chase you with her broom.'

Like many Currency Lads Jake seemed more comfortable in the presence of men. He half treated Keziah like a mate. But the other half? Daniel was taking no chances. Exulting in his precious freedom, he was determined to safeguard it. He rejoiced in the knowledge he had at last broken free from the Devil Himself and that Keziah, the price of that freedom, was 'money' well spent.

He raised his glass in a toast, 'To *me*! The lord and master!'

The words had a good ring to them, but when the door flew open Keziah's expression showed she had overheard them. She charged off towards the creek, a washing basket balanced on her head.

'I don't believe it! My bride's washing dirty linen on our wedding day.'

'What better day?'

Daniel was determined to have the final word. 'We'll be a long time married, Mrs Browne!'

Kneeling at the creek Keziah felt relieved to be alone. At the thought of Daniel's 'holy' kiss at the altar she wiped her lips to erase the memory. She tried to dredge up Romani philosophy but it was cold comfort. *That will be our first and last kiss! Gem scorned me, Jake rejected me as a lover. Now I must live like sister and brother with a* gaujo *husband. It's hard to see how this wrong road could ever be the road I was meant to take.*

Today for the first time in years she had a man's clothing to wash. Wistfully she compared her resentment with her sense of privilege as a fourteen-year-old bride washing Gem's clothes. She paused in the act of scrubbing them on a rock. How odd. Daniel had given her all his wedding clothes to wash with one glaring exception. His shirt. What on earth did that mean?

His parting words resounded in her ears. 'We'll be a long time married, Mrs Browne!'

She said the words aloud to give herself courage. 'Not if I can help it, Mr Browne!'

That evening Daniel felt a surge of contentment as he ate a fine Romani meal. He responded with genuine interest to the wonderful blend of lamb and exotic spices.

'How superb. I have married myself a fine cook! Is this to celebrate our marriage?'

'No. To mark your freedom from Gideon Park. No dog deserves to be assigned there.'

Although she declined the wine he offered, Daniel could detect no deliberate insult when she told him she only drank occasionally with friends.

'So your husband can never be your friend?' Daniel teased.

'My Romani husband was my friend.'

Daniel was determined to keep the upper hand. 'Then let's toast Gem. As God wills right now he's involved in a robbery under arms or else he's in prison. While thanks to you I'm a free man!'

'Yes,' Keziah added, 'there's no accounting for the ways of *The Del*.'

Daniel let that pass, allowing himself to be seduced by the roast lamb. His murmurs of pleasure were so appreciative that Keziah finally gave him a reluctant smile.

'Perhaps I'll invite you to dinner again some time.'

'I'll come running,' he promised.

At the end of the meal he yawned. 'Well, bride, where do you want me to sleep?'

'The marital bed, where else?' she said.

Daniel felt confused. Her tone was polite, as if to a house guest. Uncertain of his next move he asked her where she was going.

'To sleep under the stars.'

He kicked off his boots and shucked his trousers across the floor. He did not remove his wedding shirt, but rolled over onto his stomach, luxuriating in having a large bed to himself. Tonight that was all he needed. Tomorrow would take care of itself.

The yellow orb of the moon shone through the window. Daniel drifted into sleep with the forgotten taste of freedom in his mouth. Tears trickled from the corners of his eyes.

Thank you, Holy Mother, for setting me free.

For Jake, Keziah's wedding night ended at the Four Sisters, where he bought drinks for the house. When Lily Pompadour came downstairs she took one look at him. There was urgency in every muscle in his body. Without a word he steered her to the stairs.

She shrugged. 'I'm sorry, Jake darling. I've got a client waiting for me.'

Jake was in no mood to argue. When he opened the door to her room the man who waited for her sat naked on the edge of her bed. Anger flooded over Jake.

'You! Grab your trousers. Get out of here. She's *my* wife tonight.'

The man was small and vulnerable, but he was no coward. 'I've paid me money. And she's washed me. I won't be long. Then you can have her.'

'You won't *live* long enough to do it if you don't pick another woman. Get!'

The man grabbed his boots and fled. Jake felt like a Viking on the rampage.

Lily took her cue. 'I'm always glad to see you, Jake, but it isn't Wednesday.'

'From now on it's Wednesday whenever I bloody say it's Wednesday!'

She caught his mood and began to play rough. 'What's the celebration in aid of?'

'My best mate got married today,' he said, but he felt far from happy.

Lily gave a shiver of triumph as he began to work her hard. 'Yes, Jake! Give *me* everything. I'll make you forget *her*, I'll make it so good you'll forget your own name.'

He knew Lily could take away the pain, but it would need to be a very long night.

For Keziah, her wedding night was a lonely maze of soul searching. She curled up outside Gabriel's window to hear him if he woke. Fine rain softly caressed her hair.

A night under the stars like all the Romani nights of her childhood, except that here in Jake's part of the world the stars were upside down. Keziah could recognise the Seven Stars that *gaujos* called the Pleiades, a different pattern in the southern hemisphere sky. Jake's Milky Way stretched across the heavens like the fairytale mirage of a lost city.

Was Gem sleeping under these same stars? Did he still hate her? No. In that terrible moment of truth in the cave he had cried out, *'Forgive us both.'* Gem was on a very different *drom*. But where on earth was *her* road leading?

How ridiculous this wedding night was. The groom was inside, the bride *outside*. The only one making a lusty night of it would be Jake. She created an unwelcome fantasy of Jake in bed with four naked 'sisters'. Jake was giving some unknown redhead the ride of her life. Keziah admonished herself. *It's none of your business what Jake does.*

It was then she saw it – that dual dimension of time. Her eyes were drawn to the moonlit paddock and Gabriel's pony. Riding him bareback was a freckled red-headed toddler, wearing ill-fitting clothes as if his mother had dressed him in a hurry.

Keziah felt a stab of jealousy as she recognised Jake's future son.

That redhead's son? Or Jenny's? She gave a sad little wave to the lad as the pony turned and trotted away. The child faded from sight until only the pony remained.

The shadow of a cloud passed over the face of *Shon* in the moon. Keziah's prayer was in her heart and on her lips. '*Mi-duvel*, please take care of Jake for me.'

She looked up at Jake's Milky Way and spoke the words softly. 'We made a pact, didn't we, Jake? Wives, husbands and lovers come and go but mates are forever.'

From the marital bed came the terrible sound of a man in anguish. 'No, no! You promised!'

Her *Puri Dai's* first rule – a healer must never ignore those in pain. From the doorway she saw Daniel lying face down, locked in a bad dream. She froze in shock. His wedding shirt was saturated with blood from the stripes of a recent flogging.

Keziah never doubted her Romani beliefs were true. *This is not the road I wanted to take but it's not the wrong road. It's the road I was meant to take.*

She slipped inside her cottage to use her gifts to heal her husband. All night she lay awake. The stranger she had married lay cradled like a child asleep in her arms.

CHAPTER 32

Setting out on the first leg of his previously abandoned journey to Sydney Town, Jake Andersen felt confused and angry over his failure to rescue Keziah on her wedding day. He hadn't seen the bride and groom in the days since, but he had built up much needed funds by winning a local prize fight.

It was no consolation that his Romani mate would use her weird wrong-road-is-the-right-road philosophy to interpret marriage to Daniel as an act of destiny. *Not to me, it ain't. Destiny is superstitious bulldust.*

He would no longer be able to drop in for a yarn with her whenever the mood took him. He debated the wisdom of making a detour to deliver her belated present and decided against the idea. But at the approach to the Ironbark turn-off Horatio released a restless whinny.

Jake gave him a reassuring pat. 'All right, mate, I can take a hint.'

His hackles rose at the sight of Daniel on Keziah's veranda. Sketching. The hair curling around his aesthetic features reminded Jake of that mad poet Lord Byron who drove women crazy. *Just look at him. What else could Daniel be but a bloody artist?*

Jake felt confused by his anger. He had been quite matey with Daniel before his marriage and had even sung the bloke's praises to Keziah that night she got cold feet and wanted to call off the wedding. Why this sudden surge of resentment?

He swaggered up the steps. 'How's married life treating you?' This was the standard greeting to a bridegroom, but Jake didn't really want to know the answer. He had never believed that their bloody stupid platonic marriage agreement would survive the wedding night.

Daniel looked smug. 'My bride is everything a man could want.'

Jake sized him up as he would an opponent in the ring. 'Yeah. Well,

I'm off to Sydney Town. Just wanted to give Kez a bit of news. Not a good time, eh?'

Daniel avoided a direct response. 'Thanks for my wedding present, Jake. These cigars are better than a clay pipe any day.' He blew a chain of smoke rings into the air.

The confident gesture irritated Jake. They stared each other out.

Finally Daniel lowered the drawbridge. 'My bride's inside.'

Keziah turned from the stove as Jake entered. Her vivid blue eyes always gave him a bit of a jolt and no less today. Her hair half escaped the yellow ribbon tied at the nape of her neck. Wet tendrils curled over her ears. A Mother Hubbard pinafore covered her dress. She had a smudge of flour on her cheek that Jake had a strong urge to brush away.

He searched her face, not quite knowing what he expected to find. Or even if he wanted to see it when he did. His thoughts were confused. *Her eyes don't have that dreamy look some women get after you've made love to them all night and they're so damned pleased with themselves. Like they've invented the whole business.*

He handed Keziah his parcel and made an oblique reference to her public role as Saranna. 'A late wedding present. Open it later. I reckon you'll want to keep it under wraps – you being a teacher.'

Naturally curiosity got the better of her. She gasped with pleasure. 'Tarot cards!'

Jake jerked his head in the direction of the veranda. 'I reckon by now Dan must know all that stuff about you and Saranna?'

Keziah's reply was ambiguous. 'As much as he needs to know.'

Her eyes unnerved him. *She always seems to know what I am thinking.*

'Good luck with the American,' she said casually.

Jake was stunned. 'Jeez, how'd you know that? I ain't even met him yet.'

'I read the advertisement for Benjamin Rogers's agency in *The Sydney*

Herald. I also saw you in a dream, surrounded by men with tridents. Your daughter was hidden in a tree. That Yankee will lead you to her.'

'Glad to hear it.' Jake felt awkward. 'Be a good girl, eh?'

As he strode out the door he ran into Daniel, who was clearly guarding his goods and chattels. Surprised by the bridegroom's friendly invitation to stay and have an ale with him, Jake convinced himself it was rude to refuse a man's offer of grog.

Both cast furtive glances at Keziah through the window as they drank. In the past Jake had enjoyed amiable discussions with Daniel about the state of the colony and the system. Now they verbally fenced about everything except the subject uppermost in their minds – Keziah. They disagreed about the price of ale, crown land, the economy. They grew heated over the raging controversy around Alexander Maconochie, Norfolk Island's radical new superintendent who rewarded prisoners' good behaviour with a points system that reduced the length of their sentences.

Daniel was anti-Maconochie. 'Most second offenders sent to Norfolk deserve to die there.'

'Jesus wept! You've changed your tune, mate!'

The sole cause that firmly united them was their hatred of The Finisher, the colony's hangman. Daniel quoted from *The Sydney Monitor* how Green's drunken performances on the gallows caused many condemned men to die a bungled, agonising death. Embarrassed that Daniel was far more literate than he was, Jake bluffed about reading news he'd actually heard via the bush grapevine.

Jake finished off his ale and aimed his parting words at Daniel. 'You'll take good care of them both, right?'

Daniel gave him a mocking smile. 'Or else?'

'Just see you bloody do, mate!' Jake leapt into the saddle and, giving a drover's holler to Horatio, sent the dust rising skywards in their wake.

He was quick to convince himself Kez was now Daniel Browne's responsibility, but that same thought made him even more dejected. He'd grown used to Kez turning to *him* to solve her problems. He faced the truth and didn't like it. He didn't *want* to be let off the hook.

He forced himself to focus his mind on his search. In the three years since Jenny's desertion he had followed up clues as far north as the penal colony of Moreton Bay, as far south as Port Phillip Bay and Van Diemen's Land and as far west as the back of beyond – a network of thousands of miles. What did he have to show for it? A single sighting outside the Bald-Faced Stag Inn. And a letter from Jenny that had no address.

This Yankee detective will need to be a bloody miracle worker.

In Sydney Town Jake rode down George Street between stores and warehouses that offered goods and services from the four corners of the globe. Imported, home-grown – or stolen.

The address he wanted was at the lower end before the street deteriorated into The Rocks. As always, he automatically searched the faces of all the small, blonde women who crossed his path.

In The American Investigations Agency office Jake unrolled Jenny's drawing on the desk between a paperweight and an inkwell and stated his case, admitting his lack of success. 'For years I've been running around like a headless chook trying to find her.'

'You a wife-beater?' The Yankee puffed on a cigar.

'Shit no,' said Jake. 'You don't pull your punches, do you!'

'Saves time,' said Rogers, 'time *you* are going to pay for.'

Jake studied the detective as he read Jenny's recent 'invitation'. Benjamin Rogers's rugged face was heavily lined and topped with hair parted in the centre and slicked down with Macassar oil. His face was blank except for black eyebrows that registered doubt, cynicism or humour. A gold watch chain was slung across the waistcoat of a suit sombre enough for an undertaker. The hatstand was hung with hats of every description. No firearms in sight.

Rogers looked up from the letter. 'Your wife's planted clues that suggest her fancy man is some kind of aristocrat. Any idea why she's changed her tune and wants you to find her?'

'I reckon this letter is a cat-and-mouse game,' Jake volunteered. 'Jenny enjoys rubbing my nose in it. She doesn't want me but she won't let me off the hook neither.'

Jake answered all Rogers's questions. No subterfuge about being a cuckolded husband – he was well beyond false pride. But he tensed up when he described Jenny at their last encounter, how she was done up like a Christmas tree.

Jake pressed on. 'If this foreign mongrel's some kind of aristocrat, Jenny must move in flash circles. So why can't I find her?'

The detective butted out one cigar and trimmed another to follow it. 'If her protector has a European moniker and knows you're gunning for him, no doubt they travel incognito.'

Jake was impatient for Rogers's verdict. 'Do you reckon you can find them or not?'

'First give me the truth, Andersen. No bulldust. I have my agency's professional reputation to safeguard. Do you have murder in mind for your wife's lover?'

Your wife's lover. Jake felt the ugly reality of the phrase hit home.

'I don't give a rat's arse about *my* reputation. I want Pearl to know her real father didn't desert her. Whatever action I take, I ain't never gunna go to prison. *Never again!*'

The detective nodded sagely. 'A gaol bird. Thought as much. Get one thing straight. I've been in this game seven years. Believe me, until you walk in on this guy while he's enjoying your wife in bed, you won't know the meaning of rage. I'll wager my bottom dollar, Andersen. You're more than capable of murder!'

Jake accepted the warning. 'You're dead right but what good am I to my daughter if I end up dancing on The Finisher's noose?'

Rogers was confident he would track Jenny and Pearl down. 'I warn you, it's a big country and I have expensive tastes. Can you afford me?'

Jake came up with a plan of action and put it to him. If Rogers covered Sydney Town, Jake would follow up any long-distance clues Rogers provided. They shook hands on the deal.

Jake took up residence in cheap lodgings in The Rocks to be close at hand whenever Rogers delivered news of Jenny. Meanwhile he lived off a succession of prize fights staged in the Surry Hills and the myriad of taverns that lined the harbour front. He was ready to fight any bloke with two legs who agreed to the winner-take-all terms.

At face value The American Investigations Agency was a one-man band but Jake soon discovered the Yankee was nothing if not thorough. In the weeks since Rogers accepted the case he had briefed his informants in every major town in the colony, right down to Melbourne Town where the citizens were busy petitioning for separation from New South Wales. He had paid men to be his ears and eyes in Van Diemen's Land, the new colony of South Australia, the Swan River on the west coast and across the Tasman Sea in New Zealand. All were supplied with printed copies of Jenny's portrait.

Jake was elated when the half-pint Cockney street urchin who ran Rogers's errands delivered a most welcome message. Rogers had made positive identification of their quarry.

Jake bolted up the stairs to find the Yankee wreathed in his customary halo of cigar smoke – the poker face betrayed nothing.

'I've got good news – and bad news,' said Rogers. 'Hold your horses. The disappointment is temporary.'

'No need to pull your punches,' said Jake, steeling himself for whatever was to come.

'Last night I attended the premiere of a play at the new Olympic Theatre. *Venice Preserved* is an echo of *Julius Caesar*, a plot to assassinate the Venetian senate. You colonials love your drama full of blood and revenge, but I was there because I know Italians the world over are irresistibly drawn to their culture, whether it's Italian opera or plays with Italian themes. No matter how god-damned awful the performance, they flock to cheer or boo.'

'Jesus wept,' said Jake. 'What's all this got to do with Jenny?'

'I expected this play would flush out what's likely the sole Venetian in the colony. It did.'

Jake leapt to his feet. 'You mean it was *him*? Why didn't you let me at him?'

'If I had, you'd be in gaol right now charged with his murder! So sit down, shut up and I'll tell you what progress I've made. All is not lost.'

Jake reluctantly resumed his seat, cold with rage.

'Seated in a private box was a Venetian *conte* – a count – the man on whom I've been building up a dossier for weeks. By his side was a lady of remarkable beauty who bears a close resemblance to your wife's portrait.'

Jake felt he'd been kicked in the stomach by a horse.

Rogers described her. Pocket Venus. Blue eyes, heart-shaped face, retroussé nose. Perfect English complexion. Jet-black hair but a natural blonde – he said he could always spot a theatrical wig.

Rogers's eyes registered the pain he was causing Jake.

'Is the black mole on your wife's left breast a fake?'

'Real. That's Jenny, all right. And you're sure it's *him*?' Jake didn't intend to risk a trip to the gallows for topping the wrong bloke.

Rogers nodded. 'My informant positively identified him and overheard the conte introduce your wife as an Italian noblewoman.'

Jake forced a laugh. 'Jenny would just love that.' He felt desperate to know what the mongrel looked like, but couldn't bring himself to ask for a description.

Rogers volunteered it. 'Arrogant bearing, struts like a peacock. Taller than your wife.'

'Jesus, who isn't?'

'His immaculate evening dress featured a flashy medal. My opera glasses picked up the design on his gold signet ring. A rampant lion – symbol of Venice. Black curly hair, dark eyes, swarthy. Flashes his teeth when he laughs. Fleshy, clearly a man who indulges his appetites – all of them. You want me to go on?'

Jake nodded. 'What happened when you confronted them?'

Rogers admitted that was the bad news. His exit had been blocked by a free-for-all brawl in the foyer when Currency Lads broke up a demonstration by the Total Abstinence Society. After breaking through the riot he had tracked them to The Britannia where they were booked under the imaginative name of Jones.

Jake nodded impatiently. 'So what the hell are we waiting for?'

Rogers blew out a smoke ring. 'Brace yourself. They sailed out on the early morning tide for New Zealand.'

Jake let out a string of expletives that would have impressed a bullocky.

Rogers reacted with maddening calm. 'From what I now know of the conte's movements and lifestyle, we can count on his return. His money's tied up here. I warn you, it's not enough simply to *find* your wife. Men like the conte manipulate the law. I withheld this information from you until I had enough proof to give you the clout to gain custody of your daughter. Your wife committed adultery, remember?'

'As if I could ever forget.'

Rogers pushed a folder across the desk. 'I've found the key to the conte.'

Jake listened attentively as the detective outlined how the signs of the colony's predicted Depression had helped to play their quarry into their hands. His business associates were all in deep financial trouble. Last year their empires had seemed impregnable. Now one by one they were beginning to fall on bended knees to their bankers.

'Are you saying Jenny's protector is broke?'

'Not yet but he's skating on mighty thin ice. Last week a Melbourne

Town banker ended his life with a bullet to the brain. All because his bank went to the wall. He was the conte's financier.'

'How does all this help me find my little Pearl?'

Rogers pointed his cigar at the dossier. 'When the pair return from New Zealand, confront your wife with *this* evidence – she'll be mighty quick to trade your daughter. Read it!'

Jake glanced slowly through the file, unwilling to reveal his poor reading. But he reacted to one sentence with a slow whistle. 'You're worth your weight in gold, Yankee!'

He realised this was almost literally true when he saw the size of the bill.

Rogers shrugged. 'Champagne dinners and private boxes don't come cheap. I need to mingle with the Quality.'

Rogers opened a bottle of whisky. 'Be patient. I'll inform you when the conte returns. At rock bottom little 'uns are the only thing worth a damn.' As if embarrassed to be caught in a sentimental vein, he added, 'Keep that fact in mind when you spring your wife in *flagrante delicto* – being rogered by the conte. You can either commit murder or gain custody of your daughter.'

With this dossier now in hand, Jake felt cocky. 'Maybe I can do both.'

Rogers's eyebrows registered a warning. 'I spent years in the army hunting down Injuns. Not proud of that. Just a fact. Learned one thing. Revenge destroys a man. Eats into his soul. What's the so-called Good Book say? "Revenge is mine, I will repay, sayeth the Lord."'

Jake knocked down his whisky feeling instant fire in his belly before he answered. 'I'm an agnostic or atheist. Never sure which. So the Lord don't work for me. But Jenny is mine. So I reckon revenge is *mine*.'

They drank in companionable silence. Then the detective handed him a small box.

'A Sioux brave I met claimed this is lucky. Got no use for it. It's yours.'

Jake was touched by the unexpected gift – a beautifully designed silver belt buckle in the shape of a sunburst. What do you say to a man who's transferring his good luck to you?

Rogers covered the moment. 'Just stay out of prison, fella.'

They shook hands, but Jake made no promises on that score.

En route to the livery stables to bail out Horatio, Jake felt buoyed up. He now had all the evidence needed to bring Jenny to heel. It was only a matter of time.

He gave a wry grin. According to Keziah's dream he would find Pearl hiding in a tree. *There's only a few million trees in the colony. By the law of averages Kez has to get a prediction right sooner or later.*

CHAPTER 33

Daniel Browne felt like he was living a double life. During the first year of their marriage he had worked diligently to establish his reputation with Hobson and Bloom as a reliable ticket-of-leave man ready to tackle any work asked of him. Word of mouth drew additional employment from other landholders including Terence Ogden. But Daniel hungered to spend more time with his 'mistress'.

He took a step back to cast a critical eye over the outhouse he had designed and assembled in an attempt to please Keziah. He had tried to anticipate his wife's wishes in the hope of bridging the unnatural chasm between them. It surprised him to discover that despite Keziah's dramatically fluctuating moods he liked living with her. And he was touched by the way Gabriel looked up to him.

When he screwed the final hinge in place he called Keziah to gauge her reaction to the design he had worked on in secret. The outhouse was a miniature castle with castellated roof, slit windows and, in place of a conventional door, a drawbridge that lowered across a miniature moat, which was naturally empty due to the drought but lined with blue paper to simulate water.

'Well? What do you think, wife? Do you want to christen it or shall I?'

But Gabriel claimed the prize, running to take up residence, yelling with excitement.

When Daniel met Keziah's eyes he was relieved to see she was amused by his fanciful creation.

She giggled behind her hands. 'He thinks the outhouse is a new toy you built for him!'

'It is!' Daniel said and joined in her laughter. He felt an odd stirring in his breast. Was this unknown emotion a glimmer of domestic contentment? He took a chance on broaching the delicate subject – Keziah's firm resolution to sleep alone under the stars.

He used sarcasm as a shield against rejection. 'I've decided to build another bedroom. We don't want to give Ironbark gossips the impression we don't like each other, do we?'

He felt irritated by her wary nod of agreement. Why? He had remained true to his end of their pact – never showed her overt affection except in public. When alone with her he took care not to take any liberties. Yet he felt her growing tension in living at close quarters.

He privately conceded their arrangement was easier for him. Each Saturday night he exercised his new-found freedom in an outlying shepherd's hut where Irish fiddlers, moonshine grog and any other diversion a man might want were freely available. Keziah asked no questions. He almost wished that she would.

That Saturday night, on his return home from Scotty the Shepherd's hut, the magnetism of the full moon was compounded by an electrical storm. Hobson's cattle dogs howled in response to native dingoes in the bush.

Daniel burst in from the storm, forced to a standstill, entranced by the sight of her. Keziah had bathed and washed her hair in rosemary oil. She stood naked by the fire drying her hair. Firelight washed over her skin and turned her body golden brown. Her hair clung to her like a wet black cloak – a gorgeous Magdalene of a woman. He raised his hands in a gesture of awe and surrender.

'Keziah, do you trust me? I've never asked anything of you. Now I beg you lie on the bed. I *need* to paint you as God made you.' At her hesitation he promised, 'That's all.'

Keziah lay across the bed, watching him through half-closed eyes as he worked through the night. Daniel was transformed by the creative fire that burned inside him.

At dawn the first stage of the work was finished. He bent over her sleeping form to see her smiling in her dreams. On impulse he gently kissed her mouth. Her eyes widened in surprise.

'I won't apologise,' said Daniel. 'I had a sudden desire to taste you. To see what I was missing. What other men desire from you.' He added wearily, 'Get dressed, m'dear.'

He saw from her expression she was trying to understand him. He made an attempt to sound casual. 'Tell me. Am I so repulsive to you?'

Keziah pulled the sheet across her body. 'No. I'm sure you are an attractive man – to others.' She faltered. 'I can read most people but I can't fathom your eyes. I sense you want more than one woman can give you. You only feel true passion for your art.'

'Yes. My mistress always comes first.' He paused. 'But what if I offered you my body? Be honest, aren't you curious about me? You need a man in your bed, any fool can see that.'

Over the past months she had gradually grown more tolerant towards him, but now the expression in her eyes made Daniel feel she was trying to probe his mind. He didn't like that.

'What of *your* needs, Daniel? You're attracted to women's bodies as an artist and I can see in your eyes you admire me. But you don't *need* a woman.'

Daniel flinched. His heart raced with sickening speed. Was she bluffing? Did she know how he felt?

Keziah sounded suspicious. 'I suspect you never loved Saranna, but you saw it was to your advantage to marry her until her father stood trial. And you gave evidence against him?'

'No! Maynard Plews *chose* to plead guilty so I'd be free to marry his daughter.'

He realised that damned inner eye of hers had stumbled on the truth. He couldn't hide his guilty reaction.

'So Saranna's father was innocent! You caused him to be transported for *your* crime!'

Daniel rose in agitation. 'What a paragon of virtue you are! A liar who twists the law to suit yourself and has the hide to judge me by your lofty Romani standards.'

'Yes! I'd do it all again to protect Gabriel. But no one has suffered at *my* hands. How can you live with what you did to Saranna's father?'

Daniel collapsed in his chair, all anger spent.

'It's too late to put the past to rights. Maynard Plews is dead. He drowned working in the lime kilns in Newcastle. It was recorded in the muster book.'

Daniel felt oddly relieved his cowardice was at last out in the open, even if only to be shared with a woman who held him in contempt. Was it time to reveal that other dark truth gnawing inside him?

Three weeks later Christmas Eve finally arrived. Not a moment too soon for Gabriel. The boy had gone to bed early in his boxroom in a last-minute attempt to prove himself worthy of a visit by 'the Old Man in the red suit who brings presents to good children'.

Daniel sat at the kitchen table painting the final touches on the wooden box shaped like a toy boat he had made for Gabriel. Keziah sat reading a pile of old newspapers by the mellow oil lamp. He knew that as much as she loved teaching she was glad the schoolhouse would lie dormant for two weeks, giving her the chance to catch up with her reading and time to spend lazy summer days with Gabriel.

Keziah grew animated when she read aloud to him about the planned arrival in Sydney of the 267 male prisoners on the *Eden*. 'They say this will be the last ever transport to unload British convicts in this colony, although they'll still dump the poor lads in Van Diemen's Land and Norfolk Island. But it does look like the death knell of the system, doesn't it? Jake *will* be pleased.'

Daniel looked up sharply at the mention of Jake's name. 'Yes, I imagine we'll be seeing more of him soon.' He tried to turn the conversation to the current speculations about Governor Gipps's law and order policies now that the end of transportation left the door open for more free settlers to arrive. Keziah ignored that and read out details of the exploits of the young bushranger Teddy Davis, leader of the so-called Jew Boy's Mob that had been terrorising the Hunter Valley district.

Daniel was irritated. 'Why are you so concerned about them? What happens to *us*? Bushrangers won't disappear simply because transport ships stop unloading their convict cargo in New South Wales.'

He was about to back his argument with quotes from the official *Sydney Gazette* and the 'convicts' bible' *The Sydney Monitor*, but he knew Keziah's entrenched bias was on the side of bushrangers because of Gem. She wasted no time in voicing it.

'George Hobson told me Gideon Park was bailed up in the Jonstones' absence by Jake's mate, Will Martens. Weren't you pleased to hear Will padlocked their overseer in the stocks while he overhauled the place? What do they call that man? The Devil Himself?'

Despite his years of suffering at Gideon Park, Daniel's response was scathing. 'Will's an idiot. The Devil Himself has a bloody long memory.'

Keziah was determined to test where Daniel's sympathies lay.

'If a bolter came to our door would you give him food? I know Jake would.'

'More fool Jake. Why should I risk losing my ticket? Worse – get sent to Norfolk Island for giving succour to a bushranger. My duty is to protect you and Gabriel.'

'A noble sentiment which protects your own hide,' she said with contempt.

Daniel flashed back, 'You'd be happy if *I* was the one shot dead, wouldn't you?'

'I want the death of no man on my conscience, but I tell you straight, Daniel, I'll not be guilty of turning a hungry bolter from my door knowing it could have been Gem!'

'No man is good enough to stand in that Gypsy's shadow, is he?' He caught her chin and forced her to look at him. 'Except maybe Jake Andersen?'

Keziah pulled away. 'Don't be foolish. Jake is just my mate.'

'Make sure that's all he is, Mrs Browne!' he warned.

Daniel stalked out and saddled the brumby, intent on getting drunk at Scotty the Shepherd's hut. Keziah never seemed to give a damn how he spent his time, but she was irritated whenever he took her horse, the only one they owned, without her permission.

Early Christmas morning Daniel returned to the only home he had ever known. He swaggered through the door, unshaven, yesterday's clothes musky with sweat, but he tried to give the impression nothing in the world was wrong. Keziah was busy at the stove. Gabriel entered in his nightshirt clearly disappointed Father Christmas had left no presents.

'Look! He's been!' Daniel made a great show of surprise as he lifted the tablecloth to reveal the toy boat he had finished the night before. He enjoyed the boy's cries of delight. From the pockets of his overcoat hanging on the peg behind the door and hidden in corners around the room, Daniel allowed Gabriel to discover the series of carved miniature animals he'd made. Together they lined them up beside the boat. The animals marched two by two.

'Is that Noah's Ark from the *gaujo* bible?' Keziah asked.

Daniel nodded. 'I told Gabriel the story of the flood. Now he expects a rainbow in the sky every day to prove God won't forget his promise not to flood the world again.' He was suddenly concerned. 'Sorry. I didn't mean to frighten him.'

He handed Gabriel a parcel to give to his mother and prompted him to say 'Merry Christmas'. At the door he said flippantly, 'No need to tell me I smell bad. I'll wash in the creek.'

Keziah's response was dismissive. 'You'd have to walk until New Year to find more than a puddle. Hobson gave me water from his tank. Go outside. I'll bring you hot water.'

Washed and changed into clean clothing, Daniel watched her open the carved box on which he had painted a Romani *vardo* and two small boys – one black, one blond. Gabriel instantly recognised himself and Murphy. Keziah made no comment.

Daniel felt oddly disappointed. He knew she had put aside presents for Nerida and Murphy ready for their return from the Snowy River High Country where they had joined a remnant of her tribe to feast on bogong moths, perhaps for the last time. Each year more of her people were displaced by the encroaching tide of settlers.

Daniel knew Christmas meant nothing to Keziah but she had the Romani tolerance of other people's gods. She might at least have shown some response to his present as he had spent hours carving that damned box for her.

'I'll be back after the service,' he said gruffly and stalked off to the chapel.

On his return his mood changed to pleasure when he found the whole cottage massed with candles and red and green bush foliage.

Keziah made an awkward gesture of apology. 'The next best thing to England's mistletoe, holly and ivy.'

'I love the Australian flavour,' he said, smiling at Keziah's attempt at making a Christmas tree, the German tradition that was growing popular in imitation of the Prince Consort's lavish Christmas trees for the Royal Family.

Planted in an empty beer barrel was a baby pine tree decorated with clumps of the red and yellow floral bells of the Australian Christmas bush. In place of snow Keziah had hung the tree with handmade white pompoms.

Daniel could not contain his delight at the figure in the corner adorned with his striped scarf and cabbage-tree hat – its eyes, nose and mouth were buttons sewn on to a sheepskin body. It was the world's most incongruous snowman, but Daniel was deeply touched.

'This is the best Christmas I've ever had.' His nose twitched. 'What's that wonderful smell? Brush turkey? Plum pudding? You clever girl. Every symbol of Home, even snow.'

'Feathers falling from angels' wings,' Gabriel confided.

At the end of the meal Daniel downed his red wine and sank back in the carver's chair replete. Keziah's frown of concern drew him to the window where they scanned the horizon. Ominous blue smoke rose to the sky, the sign of a distant bushfire. Daniel made light of the danger, but the hot westerly wind warned him he must keep a watchful eye out for any sudden change of direction.

Keziah's wistful expression suggested Gem was on her mind. Or was it Jake?

He steeled himself against her reaction, hoping the wine had mellowed her.

'You think you know me, Keziah. You don't. I'm more despicable than you know. Don't you understand? It isn't Gem's shadow that lies between us. It's Jake Andersen.'

Keziah held his gaze for a long moment as she felt the impact of his words. Daniel broke away from the intensity of her eyes.

He knew that, at last, Keziah understood.

CHAPTER 34

Keziah looked at Jake sprawled in 'his chair' in front of her fireplace with his boots propped on the fender, his hat on the back of his head. It was summer and no fire was really needed except at night, but she always lit one whenever Jake visited because it clearly put him at ease. She was reminded that he slept under the stars and had no home of his own. Her hearth was the closest Jake came to family life.

She watched with amusement as he tucked into her Romani cakes and drank her teapot dry. Fair exchange for his relaying the news from Sydney Town and bringing her the pile of three-month-old English newspapers he'd brought straight from a vessel anchored at Port Jackson.

Although she was avid to read all the news from Home, right now she was delighted to hear Jake's details about the Royal Family that he'd gained first-hand from the ship's mate in The Kings Head at The Rocks.

'How romantic,' she said. 'So little Princess Victoria Adelaide Mary Louise must have been conceived on the Queen's honeymoon!'

'Yeah. But the kid's only heir to the throne until a son comes along to push his sister out of the running. I reckon the Queen's German cousin Albert – what's his name?' Jake asked irreverently.

Keziah jumped in quickly. 'Prince Albert of Saxe-Coburg-Gotha is now our Prince Consort and very handsome. I'm sure they'll have many children.'

'Yeah,' Jake said innocently, 'I'll bet Albert's already being pressured to go to bed early and do his duty like England expects him. Poor bloke wasn't even allowed to propose marriage to her 'cos the Brits reckon Victoria outranked him.'

'That's royal protocol,' Keziah explained.

Jake grinned. 'I wonder if *she* got down on bended knees to propose. And what would she have done if the poor bloke had said no? Chopped off his head?'

Keziah jumped to the defence of her queen. 'So what if she *did* choose *him*? What's wrong with that? Women in my tribe have always had the right to choose our Roms.'

Jake tried to recover lost ground. 'Sounds like Albert's heart's in the right place. I hear London's all agog about his latest invention. A silk parasol lined with chain mail to protect his bride in case some joker tries to take a pot shot at her in her carriage.'

'How clever of him.' Keziah was full of admiration until she saw Jake had trouble keeping a straight face. 'Well, what's wrong with that?'

'Nothing. Except the chain mail's too damned heavy for your little queen to hold the umbrella upright, so it's bloody useless.'

'Mock all you want to. Queen Victoria will reign over us for decades. Outlive us all!'

Jake looked serious. 'You saw that in Her Maj's teacup, did you?'

Keziah finally allowed herself to smile, but added wistfully, 'At least those two have the real thing. No marriage of convenience.'

Jake shifted in his seat, aware of her reference to Daniel. He quickly headed the conversation back to home turf.

'I hear The Gypsy's gang overhauled the Jackson place two nights back.' When Keziah held her breath he added quickly, 'No one hurt. Only Jackson's pride. Seems a new member of the gang nicked all Jackson's clothes. Left him standing in his unmentionables. Poor bloke had to go to the police office wearing his wife's dressing gown.'

Keziah bit her lip to contain her laughter. She mumbled a blessing, '*Maduveleste*, Gem.' Then asked, 'Has that American helped you in your own search?'

'Stalemate. Till Jenny comes back from New Zealand. One thing's damned clear – her fancy man didn't take my little Pearl with them.'

'When you see Jenny I hope you'll find it in your heart to forgive her – if she's truly sorry.'

Keziah watched for his reaction but Jake just gave her a sidelong glance and stood up.

'Let's hit the road to Bran's forge and buy the brumby a new pair of shoes.'

Keziah had been avoiding another visit to the forge, but the brumby now desperately needed to be re-shod so she was grateful to have Jake's company. But her fear of the place remained and the moment the forge came in sight she felt her head begin to ache again.

Jake drove the wagon with his eyes fixed on the track ahead. Gabriel sat between them, singing at the top of his voice. She sensed there was something awkward Jake wanted to say behind the words he actually said.

'I reckon blacksmiths like Bran are worth their weight in gold in the colony. On a par with physicians. The Doc saves lives and brings new ones into the world. Bran keeps our lives functioning – transport, horses, farm implements, machines, firearms, the lot. And now he's forging the fancy wrought-iron work Daniel designs.'

Jake seemed to be fishing for something when he added casually, 'Seen Daniel lately?'

Keziah was too distracted to answer at once. They were drawing closer to the forge and the pain in her head grew stronger by the minute.

'I've only seen Bran once,' she said, 'that day your wheel was smashed. I know he's a mate of yours, Jake. But to tell you the truth, he scares me.'

Jake gave a short laugh. 'Jesus, he wouldn't hurt a bloody fly! He's just a gentle giant. Can't talk except for the odd word, but he can forge metal like magic. His father ran out on him when he was twelve. Bran works like a dog every day of the year except Sundays, Good Friday, Christmas and Foundation Day. Beats me how cruel people are to his face.' Jake mimicked a female voice, '"A clean-living lad. Teetotal. Pity about his simple brain."'

Keziah said absently, 'His father was smaller than Bran. Ugly in drink with a violent temper.'

Jake looked at her, startled. 'How'd you know that? Old-timers reckon Penrose Senior beat up his missus when he was shickered. After she died Bran copped the beatings. That explains his crook nose.'

Keziah remained in the wagon with Gabriel when they pulled up at the forge. She tried to fight down her rising fear.

She watched how Bran's face lit up when Jake recreated his latest prize fight in Windsor, springing alternatively from left to right in a light-hearted enactment of his own and his opponent's tactics. Keziah was moved by Jake's kindness in communicating without words so Bran wasn't forced to answer.

When Jake finally won the shadow contest, Bran was so elated he grabbed Jake's arm and raised it in a victory salute. Bran's guttural crow of delight and the bright laughter in his soft brown eyes caused Keziah to catch her breath.

Bran isn't simple-minded. The problem is his intelligence is locked inside his head with no keys to release it!

Fired up by this insight Keziah took Gabriel's hand and entered the forge. It was filled with all manner of metal shapes, horseshoes, chains, wheels, carriage poles, tools, balustrades, bedsteads and leg-irons. At the heart of the forge was the furnace that Jake said only went out on the Sabbath.

When Jake introduced them, Bran made a little bow. Keziah bobbed a curtsy and offered him her hand, hoping she wouldn't tremble and betray her fear. *If there's any evil inside him I'll feel it the moment our hands touch.*

Bran shyly offered his hand and Keziah felt a surge of pain like a current springing from his hand to hers. What on earth was wrong?

When Bran moved to the anvil to work on the brumby's new horseshoes, Gabriel gravitated towards a broken hobbyhorse.

'Don't go near the fire, Gabriel,' Keziah warned him.

'I'm keeping an eye on him,' Jake assured her.

Keziah drifted down to the shadowy recess at the rear of the forge – a room so dark only a chink of sunlight filtered through a crack in the timber slab walls. Suddenly overcome by a wave of nausea, she tried to scream. No sound escaped. Swinging from the rafters inside this room was the body of a man in an army greatcoat. His skin was mottled and grey, bulging eyes rolled toward heaven in a final look of agony. She smelled the sickly sweet smell of putrefaction. Salvation was too late.

Keziah reeled back in horror and stumbled into a metal wheel that clanged against its brothers. The noise drew all eyes to her. She saw the look of terror on Bran's face but she couldn't speak.

Mi-duvel. How long has this corpse been hanging there? And then her vision went black.

When Keziah regained consciousness she found she was lying on Bran's giant iron bed. Jake sat beside her, chafing her cold hands while Bran sponged her forehead with a wet towel.

She gasped in fear. 'Have you taken him down?'

Jake mistook her concern. He nodded to where Gabriel squatted in the corner, his eyes anxiously fixed on his mother.

Keziah tried to reassure the boy. 'It was just the heat that made Mama faint.'

Gabriel gave her an uneasy smile.

She whispered to Jake, 'No, I mean the *corpse* hanging in the back room!'

Bran covered his face with his hands and sobbed like a child.

Keziah realised the truth. *That corpse isn't there. It's a* mulo. *And Bran knows it's there!*

She grabbed Jake's hand. 'Please take Gabriel outside. I need to talk to Bran.'

Jake frowned but nodded. She knew he had long since stopped trying to understand her visions.

'Come on my little Rom, let's go and feed Bran's chooks.'

Bran slumped on the bed, still hiding his face in his hands. Keziah stroked his hair back from his forehead, revealing the thick white ridge of an old wound.

'It's all right, Bran. I know who he was. Your father.'

Bran's fear almost overwhelmed her as it flooded her body. She accepted the transferred emotion but refused to allow it to drown out her thoughts. Resting her hands on his shoulders she offered him both the respect she gave a man and the gentleness she gave a child.

'You know the truth, don't you, Bran? His death was *not* your fault.'

He shook his head violently and released an agonised cry of guilt. *'Mine!'*

She needed no words from Bran to interpret the pictures that filled her mind. She saw the terrified twelve-year-old Bran cut down the corpse, strip the army greatcoat from his father's body and then bury him in the red ochre-coloured earth.

She could hear Bran's fractured thoughts. *He made me tie the noose to hang* me, *but he hung himself. The Finisher will string me up. I killed Pa!*

Keziah gripped hold of him. 'No, Bran. *His* fault. *His* decision to die. He made you work like a man. Beat you like a man. Used you like a man. But you were only a child. Bran, listen to me! Terrible things happened to you. It was *never* your fault.'

She rocked him in her arms as he cried out the grief of the little boy who was locked inside him. She did not ask where he had buried his father's body. No doubt one day that rotten man's ghost would reveal its last resting place. Right now the only thing that mattered was that

Bran needed to be healed. There were no herbs strong enough for that, but she could give him the magical gift of the gods. Friendship. From the way Bran looked at her, Keziah knew that from this moment she was his sister.

She solemnly raised her hand to swear her most sacred oath. 'By My Father's Hand, Bran Penrose. No one will ever hurt you again.'

On the homeward journey Keziah was silent. So was Jake. She suspected he was hiding something. *Men are so devious, even the best of them.*

That night was dark and sultry. Jake was well on the way to being drunk in The Shanty with No Name in Bolthole Valley. He'd promised himself he'd never interfere in Keziah's marriage, just so long as Daniel did the right thing by her. But the latest rumours on the grapevine indicated trouble too big to ignore. His ulterior motive in visiting Keziah that day had failed. He was still none the wiser if Keziah knew about her husband's double life.

He downed another drink and eyed himself in the broken mirror behind the bar. *Am I really trying to protect Kez? Or am I just bloody jealous?*

Jake was startled by the sound of Daniel's name. He tuned into a conversation between two burly shearers he recognised were regular drinkers of Scotty the Shepherd's illicit grog. The first man referred to Daniel as 'that arty bloke' and admitted he had always had him pegged as a bit of a Miss Molly, until he heard that Daniel was rooting a new wench who hung around Scotty's hut. The second bloke was scathing.

'*Her?* That piece of skirt will go with any bloke who's got two coins to rub together.'

'If that's his taste, he's welcome.' They exchanged a knowing laugh before their voices trailed off as they headed back to the bar.

Jake didn't want to believe what he'd overheard for Keziah's sake but it confirmed the ugly rumours he'd heard. His next drink for the road only fuelled his anger, so he sank another to chase it then galloped cross-country to the west of Mutmutbilly.

As he rode towards the wattle and daub hut bathed in moonlight, laughter was punctuating the sound of wild Irish music from three fiddles and 'the spoons'. Elongated shadows of dancers spilled across the earth as the door of the hut was flung open. A woman's drunken shriek pierced through the music. Jake instantly recognised the tall figure framed in the doorway. Daniel. He felt a flash of rage that Daniel risked losing his ticket-of-leave if he was caught here drinking illicit grog.

Daniel emerged with his hand cupped around the chest of a slender girl wearing a long green skirt. She was far from pretty but she had a sensual mouth. The ragged, cropped hair suggested to Jake she was a recent inmate of the Parramatta Female Factory.

The moment Daniel saw Jake he defiantly engaged the girl in a rough kiss. Then as if already bored, he smacked her on the rump and sent her scurrying back inside the hut.

Face to face with Jake's rage, Daniel gave him a smug, drunken smile.

'Now you know the truth!' he said as he swigged from the neck of a bottle.

'What the hell are you playing at?' Jake demanded. 'You've got a good woman at home. You made a pact with Kez, remember?'

'With *my wife*. No business of yours. What Keziah doesn't know won't hurt her. I keep her very, *very* happy,' Daniel taunted. 'Don't take my word for it. Ask her!'

'I bloody well warned you!' Jake dismounted, his hands were clenched, ready to fight.

Daniel's mocking laughter failed to camouflage how nervous he was, but he continued to bait Jake. 'You haven't got the guts to tell my wife, have you?'

Jake jerked his thumb at the figure in green watching them from the doorway.

'That's strictly business between a man and his wife, but this is business that needs to be settled between you and *me*.'

Jake let fly with a right jab and a left cross that rocked Daniel on his heels against a tree trunk. Daniel warded off the blows with loose, flaying hands, refusing to fold his fists into any semblance of a fighter. His passive stance made Jake feel like a schoolyard bully.

'Don't pretend you're so drunk you can't fight, you bastard. I'm as drunk as a skunk. I reckon that makes us even.'

Daniel smiled through the blood that trickled from his nose to his chin. His hands hung limply by his sides as he moved towards Jake, then unexpectedly grabbed him in a desperate wrestling hold. Caught off guard Jake threw his full weight into grappling Daniel to the ground.

They rolled over like two ruffian schoolboys in the playground, grunting and yelling. When Jake found himself pinned down by Daniel, he paused in surprise. He wasn't used to being bested and he was stunned by the strange expression on Daniel's face.

'Don't you understand,' said Daniel, 'why I can't fight you?'

Jake broke the hold by kneeing him in the groin with a force that sent Daniel sailing into the bushes. Jake stumbled over Daniel's writhing body to get to Horatio.

Daniel swayed to his feet. At that moment Scotty burst out of the hut and called to Jake to stay and drink his new brew. Scotty's Irish mob followed in search of a fight, so drunk none of them knew which side they were on but all were enjoying the stoush.

Jake yelled at Daniel, 'Stupid bugger. You'd rather I beat you to pulp than damage your precious hands!' He failed to think of an appropriate insult, so finished wildly, 'You bloody *artist*!'

He called back from the saddle, 'Betray my mate and you're a dead man!'

Daniel watched until horse and rider disappeared from sight then staggered across and mounted Keziah's brumby. When the green-skirted figure in the doorway called out huskily, 'Come back, Danny,' he glanced back over his shoulder but didn't bother to answer.

He felt numb with shock as he rode to the shallow creek behind Keziah's cottage. There was just enough water to wash his bloodied face. Intent on avoiding his wife until morning he stretched out on the veranda. Sleep eluded him and he lay staring out at the starry sky as the moon passed over.

That piece of skirt meant nothing to him. Their connection had given him a brief moment of physical relief but left him feeling degraded and ashamed. *That tart was a poor substitute – for what? My wife?*

His mind replayed fragments of his drunken fight. The words he'd said to Jake without thinking. *Don't you understand why I can't fight you?*

Daniel relived the moment he had rolled around locked in Jake's arms. He was consumed by dark, secret feelings.

CHAPTER 35

Another full moon rode the sky. Camped beside the Sydney Road, Jake hunched over his campfire re-reading the latest report from The American Investigations Agency to lift his spirits.

Although he had been initially disappointed there were still no clues as to little Pearl's whereabouts, the Yankee's letter did contain startling news about the conte's fiscal empire:

> *The net closes. The conte is caught in a financial bind. Those canny New Zealanders have proved right cagey about investing in his get-rich schemes. The steamship he'd had converted from sail, the* Contessa Giovanna, *was found beached off the South Island, stripped of cargo, no trace of her crew. He's suspected of fraud. My Auckland source reports that his behaviour is increasingly erratic – from lavish hospitality to enraged outbursts. They say he plans to return to New South Wales because 'his lady' is bored.*

His lady is bored. Jake flinched at the phrase and steeled himself against the memory of Jenny's body, her voice, her perfume. He reminded himself he held the trump card, the Yankee's first extraordinary report. He kept this with him at all times, wrapped in oilskin to protect it from the weather, ready for the moment he came face to face with Jenny and forced her to reveal where Pearl was hidden. The conte's days were numbered. Jake reminded himself of that favourite phrase of the Doc's, that the British lose every battle – except the last! Jake vowed he would win his own last bloody battle even if, like Horatio Nelson, he died in the attempt.

On the brink of sleep Jake jerked awake. From his swag beneath the wagon he could see a pair of men's boots outlined against the dying light of the campfire. His hand moved to his pistol, curling around the trigger.

A voice slurred by drink asked, 'You asleep, Jake? I've a bottle that needs company.'

Jake crawled out from under the wagon to face the young lad who was now known as the legendary Jabber Jabber, the Gentleman Bushranger. It was good to see Will Martens alive and free.

Jake clapped him on the shoulder. 'Jesus, how'd you manage to escape this time? Berrima's new gaol is supposed to be foolproof. You're giving the screws a bad name.'

By the light of the full moon Jake took in every detail. Will's eyes were red-rimmed, his jaw covered in stubble, he swayed in his heeled riding boots and his coat was torn. Not the Gentleman Bushranger's usual immaculate style. Even his bravado was a pale imitation of his usual cocksure demeanour.

'There's a trick to getting out of Berrima. Remind me to share it with you in case you ever find yourself in residence,' Will offered. 'First I need to discuss a bit of business. I've been on the lookout for you for days.'

Jake steered him toward the campfire, threw on another log to build it up and heated up the pot of leftover Irish stew.

'Get this grub into you, mate.'

Will ate hungrily, washing it down with a pannikin of wine.

Jake waited for him to state his business. Meanwhile they talked horses, their favourite subject. Will jerked his head towards two horses half hidden in the bush.

'My bay mare is the best horse I ever had. Makes me feel my short life wasn't a total waste.' He looked wistful. 'You know something, mate? I never *did* get to kiss a girl.'

'What's all this short life rot? You'll kiss a score of girls and live to be ninety-nine.'

Will shook his head sagely. 'You know as well as I do how long your average bolter can expect to stay alive once he's taken up arms. Six months. A year tops. I'm already on borrowed time.'

'Bull. That's just violent bushrangers. Everyone knows you've never fired a shot in anger. Those newspapers love writing about you. You're a hero to the youngsters around Ironbark.'

Will was clearly preoccupied with death. 'Did you hear the latest about The Finisher? Governor Gipps can't sack him. There's no one else in the colony low enough to take over the hangman's job! People hate him so much he's hiding in a cell in Woolloomooloo Stockade – only game enough to emerge to perform another public hanging.' Will looked philosophical. 'His next job could be me!'

Jake refilled his guest's pannikin. Will was so drunk, what harm could another bottle do?

'So what's this mysterious business you came to discuss, eh?'

'Not mine. Gem's.' Will pulled an envelope from his pocket and offered it to Jake. 'He asked me to write this out on his behalf. It's sort of his last will and testament.'

'Jesus wept,' said Jake. 'This is all getting a bit morbid, ain't it?'

Will raised his hand. 'I gave Gem my solemn word I'd deliver it to you.'

Jake stalled. 'How about you read it to me seeing as you wrote it?'

Will read by the firelight:

Dear Pal,

This will and testament is not strictly a legal document. From where I stand the law has never done right by me, so I'd be a hypocrite to rely on the law after I'm dead and buried. In my twenty-five years I've met two gaujos *I can almost trust. The bearer of this letter is one, you are the other.*

I am leaving two things in your care. Sarishan, who did us proud winning the silver cup. I know you'll do right by him.

Secondly I am bequeathing to you a thing of far less value to me but maybe not to you. My whore. You aren't a Rom, but you're the next best thing to it. Take care of the bitch. I know in my gut my days of freedom are numbered. You can have her when I'm dead – not a minute before!

You know who I am

Jake took a hearty swig from the wine bottle to stop his hand from shaking. Despite Gem's denial his words were embedded with such tortured love for Keziah that Jake felt ashamed to compare it with his own obsessive revenge against Jenny. Gem had too much Romani pride to forgive his wife. Even now when faced with the imminent prospect of death, he could not refer to Keziah without insulting her. Jake realised that in another way Gem was a better man than he was. This will and testament was proof. Gem loved his woman enough to relinquish her to another man's protection. Jake's only solution to Jenny's lover was murder.

Jake's voice sounded tight when he asked where Sarishan was. Will gestured in the direction of the horses hidden in the darkness.

Jake nodded. 'Tell Gem to rest easy. I'll honour the terms of his will.'

Together they downed the bottle of wine. Then Will rose to his feet, swaying so much that a stiff breeze would have knocked him over.

'Thanks for your hospitality, Jake. Got to get back to work!'

'Jesus wept! You're as full as a boot, Will. You'll get your head blown off.'

Food, wine and a good yarn had restored Will's confidence.

'Not me. I lead a charmed life. I need a new coat and a fresh horse to spell my mare. So it's time to bail up the next traveller.'

'Over my dead body, you will!'

Words failed to restrain Will, so Jake gave him a neat clip to the jaw – just enough force to send a drunk to sleep. It had begun to drizzle, but didn't look promising enough to break the drought. Jake stretched Will out beneath his wagon and hid his boots to slow down any drunken attempt to bolt during the night. Wrapped in Jake's blanket, his face lit by the shaft of moonlight that fell between the wagon wheels, the young bushranger looked like the schoolboy life had intended him to be.

Jake stoked the fire then lay down to sleep. He woke to find Will's head resting on his shoulder, crying the dry sobs of a dream.

Jake felt awkward having a bloke cuddled up to him, but he knew if he woke the lad from his bad dream, the fool would head for the road and very likely meet his death.

He gave a sigh of resignation. 'It's all right, mate. You're safe now.'

Will's sobs stopped as he clung to Jake in his sleep.

Jake looked into the face of the full moon that bathed his wagon and the surrounding bushland silver. The same moon where Keziah was adamant some female Gypsy spirit lived.

Funny girl, Kez. We're as different as chalk and cheese. I believe in nothing. She believes in every bloody thing! She reckons sleeping in moonlight turns your hair white! I guess I'll find out the truth of that in the morning.

As he drifted in and out of sleep Jake was alerted to the sound of horses close by. Horatio was restlessly pawing the ground, neighing to warn him of danger. Jake grabbed his pistol and crawled on his belly clear of the wagon, ready to take aim.

Will's bay mare was where he had left him but Sarishan had broken away and stood in the open, outlined by moonlight.

Jake listened to the muffled sounds of two horses' hooves until they died away. Had some horse thieves been foiled in the act thanks to Horatio's warning? He knew it couldn't have been the traps, otherwise they would have lumbered Jabber Jabber in his sleep. So why had the riders halted by his camp only to ride off again?

Jake decided to mount guard until dawn.

As Jake rode Horatio towards Keziah's cottage with Sarishan beside him he went over in his mind the news from Sydney Town he'd hoped he would never hear. He stopped at Hobson's homestead to register his presence as usual. Polly Doyle greeted him in her friendly fashion.

'Daniel Browne's gone to Ogden Park for a few weeks to *paint horses*,' she said with amusement. 'Don't Terence Ogden like the colours God gave them at birth?'

Jake disguised his mixed feelings about Daniel's absence. Normally he would have been pleased to find Keziah home alone. For once he wished he was thousands of miles away. Swan River. Timbuktu. *Any bloody where.*

His gut lurched at the sight of Keziah on the veranda watching his approach. The breeze whipped her skirt around her legs and her hair flew around her face. Even in her oldest dress she was bloody beautiful.

Jake saw the flash of fear in her eyes when she recognised the second horse.

'That's Sarishan, isn't it! What's wrong, Jake?'

His voice stuck in his throat. Where did he find the right words to begin?

But Keziah only had to look into his eyes to know. She held up her hands and backed away to block the words she could not bear to hear. The dead expression in her eyes made his job even tougher.

'I wish it wasn't me that has to do this to you, mate,' he said, 'but I reckon you'd rather hear it from me than read it in some rag of a newspaper.'

'It's Gem,' she said in a voice that didn't seem to belong to her. She sank down onto the bed, clutching her shawl and shivering with cold despite the heat from the log fire.

Jake tried to block any images in his mind on the off-chance she could see them.

'Yeah, mate. I heard it straight from an eyewitness. Gem was sprung by the traps somewhere around Camden Park. The bastards wanted to avoid any uprising of public sympathy. So they transferred him to Cockatoo Island Gaol. They say Gem broke free and tried to swim across to the shore to Birch Grove Farm but—'

'Gem's a poor swimmer!'

'He almost made it but the word is he drowned.'

Keziah struggled with the reality of Jake's news. 'You're lying! Gem didn't drown.'

Jake didn't believe in any god but he prayed anyway. *Jesus wept. Please don't let her see what really happened.*

But he knew it was too late. It was as if she looked inwards to the moment of Gem's fight for life. Her voice was filled with horror.

'I can see his face in the water. The shark fins, his blood staining the water red!'

Jake was shocked by the accuracy of her vision. She relayed to him details that came from the warder at Cockatoo who'd witnessed the escape. Jake was chilled by the expression in her eyes. She seemed on the verge of retreating into madness to escape the ghastly visions. He grabbed hold of her shoulders and shook her.

'Listen to me! That came *after*. Gem never knew! He never even saw the sharks! An eyewitness saw it all. Gem had already drowned. I swear to God, *he died free like he wanted*!'

It was the biggest lie of Jake's life.

The wildness of Keziah's grief stunned him. He allowed her to pummel him in hysteria.

'It's all right, Kez, let it all out!' He lay beside her on the bed and held her in his arms. She clung to him like a life raft until, at last, she fell asleep, exhausted. He rocked her all through the night each time her body was racked by sobs.

No woman has ever loved me the way Keziah loved Gem.

He could never tell her the shocking truth of Gem's death. He prayed that she would never hear the full story that came from that warder at Cockatoo Island. The bastard had boasted about how no felon's corpse ever left the island. Because the warders fed the convicts' bodies to the bloody sharks!

At dawn Jake lit a fire in the fuel stove and made Keziah a pot of tea.

She drank like an obedient child but Jake was worried by the way she looked through him as if he wasn't there.

He hated the strange, unfamiliar quality in her voice as she repeated the words in a whisper, 'I don't want to live anymore.'

How the hell was he going to break through her terrible grief? At first he tried to reason with her using soothing words, which failed. Finally, he took a calculated risk.

'Call yourself a mother, do you? You're going to dump Gabriel just like Jenny ran out on me? Like your *gaujo* mam ran out on you? I didn't reckon on *you* being a coward.'

Jake saw the glimmer of fire in her eyes. She remained silent for some time, but he sensed she was working things through. Finally she said the words he was desperate to hear.

'You're right. Gabriel will keep me alive.'

'Too bloody right he will! That kid's got more sense in his little finger than Gipps and the whole Brit government put together.'

He pulled her to her feet. 'Come on. You've got a school full of kids to teach. But first things first, Gabe's waiting for his breakfast. And me, I could eat a horse.'

'You'd *what*?'

'All right! I know how you Romanies worship horses. I promise you I'll never eat a horse as long as I live. That make you happy?'

Gabriel clambered up on his stool in his nightshirt and looked expectantly at his empty bowl of porridge.

Red-eyed, Keziah automatically resumed her maternal role. 'Haven't you forgotten something, Gabriel? Wash your hands and face. And then?'

'Thank *The Del* for my daily bread,' he said, then ran barefoot to the pitcher to wash.

'Nice boy you got there,' said Jake. 'His mother's not too bad, either.'

Jake watched as she walked slowly out to the horse paddock. He sensed what she planned to do before she did it.

Keziah rubbed her face against Sarishan's nose, talking to him in the Romani tongue. Jake couldn't understand the words but he had no doubt about the message. Kez was sharing her love, her grief. Giving and taking deep comfort from Gem's horse.

Keziah didn't know it yet but Sarishan was only the first half of what Gem had willed to Jake. He knew this was no time to tell her the second half. Maybe he never would.

CHAPTER 36

For months after the news of Gem's death Keziah moved through her life like an actress trapped on stage in a play which was only revealed to her one page at a time. She fought hard to concentrate on the needs of her little family and her schoolchildren but at night she fell asleep exhausted by the effort to appear cheerful and normal.

Jake had called regularly to check on her during Daniel's prolonged absence in Bolthole Valley where Gilbert Evans had engaged him to build a Sunday school hall. But when Jake needed to head off he arranged for Dr Ross to check that she wanted for nothing. From the professional way Dr Ross observed her, Keziah knew he was concerned that she was suffering from melancholia.

How could she explain to the good doctor that she was mourning the death of a famous bushranger who had been her first husband? She had to keep up her public face as Saranna Browne. In Jake's absence, only Nerida was aware of the true cause of her sorrow.

Her memories of Gem were locked deep inside her, but as autumn passed without breaking the drought, the birth of spring and then summer gradually brought her a renewed surge of energy. Finally the day arrived when Keziah felt she had reached a mountain top and could see what lay on the other side. The future.

She set the black metal iron to heat on top of the stove as she re-read Daniel's recent letter.

> *I promise to make it back home in time for Joseph Bloom's celebration. Oh by the way, Julian Jonstone's offered to pay my fees to study art in Sydney Town. Most generous of him, but of course I'd never leave you and Gabriel high and dry.*

But between every line Keziah sensed his longing to take up the offer, his golden opportunity.

On his return she knew what she must tell him. She said the words out loud to be sure they held the ring of truth. 'It's time for you to be faithful to your mistress, Daniel.' Yes, it was true.

She was relieved when the iron was finally hot enough to press the new gown she had been sewing frantically all week. The thought of Joseph Bloom's banquet tonight brought a wave of anticipation, a flutter of nerves.

She dragged the heavy iron across a white rag to check it would leave no sooty marks on the silk water-veined taffeta. She had bought the entire bolt of fabric from Sunny Ah Wei to ensure that no other woman in Ironbark would appear in the same material. Tonight she must look her very best. Jake had promised Joseph Bloom he'd return to Ironbark in time for the celebration – and everyone knew Jake Andersen's word was his bond.

Although she had not seen Jake for weeks Keziah had the strong conviction Jenny would soon return from New Zealand. In her dreams she was haunted by the face in Daniel's drawing that Jake carried around with him. How she hated that small, delicate blonde temptress – the woman was everything that she was not. No doubt Jake's obsession would draw him back into his wife's arms if Jenny chose to crook her finger at him. Keziah had to act fast.

After washing her hair in rosemary oil she sat in the sun to dry it. She re-read last week's newspaper account of how Caleb Morgan, the sole survivor of his ill-fated expedition, was being lionised by society in South Australia.

Despite Caleb's heroic failure the Morgan name was now being heaped with the glory she had predicted years ago reading his palm. No doubt people would take up a handsome public subscription for him. *I'll bet the native guide who carried him across the desert and saved his life will never be rewarded one penny. The newspapers don't even say his true name, just some* gaujo *nickname.*

Keziah glanced at the drawer where she kept the precious document drawn up by Joseph Bloom, the proof she had legally adopted the babe abandoned in Ironbark. She was ready to meet Caleb's fight for custody, armed with this adoption paper, a legal husband who would stand by her in court and above all her best mate. At the thought of Jake she told herself to remain calm, but she was so distracted when she tried to push the image of his face from her mind that he would *not* go.

As she dressed in the layers of petticoats needed to bell out the skirt of her new gown, she felt cheered that her long ago prophecy for Joseph Bloom had come true. Before his departure he had confided in her the reasons for his journey.

'I am going to Sydney Town to be married. No doubt you've heard the wild claims by Ironbark gossips. That it is an arranged marriage, my bride speaks no English and brings me a dowry of gold bullion.' He gave a tolerant shrug. 'The truth is Rivka is my cousin and far from wealthy. Her dowry consists solely of her beloved pianoforte. We were childhood sweethearts in Frankfurt am Main.'

'How romantic!' Keziah exclaimed.

'Not in the eyes of my uncle. He claimed that New South Wales is the Sodom and Gomorrah of the South Pacific and refused permission, quoting our proverb, 'Away from Frankfurt, gone is the soul'. In his eyes, Mrs Browne, I am a dangerous radical. Me?'

'What made him change his mind?' Keziah asked.

Joseph Bloom's eyes twinkled. 'He did not. Rivka's mother paid for her passage and bundled her onto a ship bound for Port Jackson. I go to meet her now.'

Keziah smiled at the memory of their shared laughter. But next moment she was sobered by the thought of Joseph's plans to open his own legal practice in Sydney Town.

Her vision instantly reverted to the frightening flash of a courtroom and Joseph in a barrister's wig. Criminal law. Murder! She sensed the reality of this premonition was drawing closer and that Jake was right at the heart of it. She tried to push the vision aside, determined to seize and enjoy the moment. Tonight was Joseph's celebration to introduce Rivka to their Ironbark friends. Keziah knew in her heart that when Daniel accompanied her it would be their final public appearance.

Her world was changing so fast it made her dizzy. In the *goondie* she kissed Gabriel goodnight. Then she hurried down the track, trying to rein in her hair while fighting to prevent the wind ballooning out her skirt. She felt a wild surge of elation. *Weddings are famous for kindling new love affairs. The timing is perfect.*

Jake scanned the guests for a sign of Keziah. Everyone and his dog had been invited to meet Joseph's Hebrew bride.

Jake saw Rivka Bloom through a break in the crowd of guests milling on the lawn behind the Bloom homestead. She looked a bit overcome in a sea of strangers who all spoke English so Jake gave her a broad wink to reassure her. At first glance Jake had thought Rivka a bit on the dumpy side but now as she smiled back at him her luminous dark eyes and gentle smile transformed her into a beauty. Jake was forced to admit it – good women in love were a race apart.

He was startled to find Daniel standing beside him looking serious.

'Could we have a quiet drink later, Jake? I'm off to Sydney Town and I've got a favour to ask you about Keziah.'

Jake hesitated. Neither of them had ever referred to their drunken brawl at Scotty's hut. Long gone, it was too confusing to think about. Jake had heard no further rumours of Daniel's philandering and their friendship had been resumed, although with a guarded undercurrent.

'Righto, Dan. I reckon I'll still be here drinking Joseph's grog by breakfast.'

Jake watched Daniel circle the edge of the crowd in a clockwise direction, clearly unaware that Keziah's bobbing head could be seen circling anticlockwise. Finally husband and wife came face to face. They stood stock-still for a moment. Jake couldn't hear their words but it was clear they were engaged in an amiable battle of wills. Each time Daniel shook his head in denial, Keziah adamantly nodded her head to oppose him. Until finally Daniel threw back his head laughing and bent to kiss her forehead. When they turned away from each other, both were smiling. Daniel crossed to chat to Leslie Ross who had donned his kilt in honour of meeting the bride.

Jake stiffened when he realised Keziah was heading his way. She stopped in front of him, her head tilted to one side. Her innocent smile encompassed him and the two men standing nearby. George Hobson eyed her like a concerned father. Gilbert Evans wore his usual air of suspicion. Keziah seemed blithely unaware of them both.

'Excuse me, gentlemen, while I borrow your mate for a few minutes.'

Jake had little choice. Reluctantly towed away to join the dancers, he was jolted by the painful memory of his first meeting with Jenny when she taught him to dance. He was struck by the thought that these musicians were playing the very same waltz. The two dances fused into one.

Conscious of holding Keziah in his arms in public for the very first time, Jake didn't hear a word she said. He could think of only one thing. Her deep neckline gave him a generous reminder of her naked bosom that night she had held his head and given him her body heat. Jake felt a strong desire to go there again. He reminded himself she was Daniel's wife and that he must watch his step.

Playfully Keziah tucked his long hair behind his ears. Jake avoided looking into her eyes, but was distracted by her equally dangerous mouth.

'Hey! What are you up to, Kez?'

'I've something important to tell you, Jake. About Daniel.'

When the waltz came to an end they crossed to rejoin the other guests, but Jake saw his reprieve was short-lived.

In an inspired act of magic Joseph had brought a trio of roving *klezmer* musicians from Sydney Town and hired one of Scotty the Shepherd's fiddle-playing mates. Their music was a joyous blend of cultures – German, Yiddish, Italian, Hungarian and wild Celtic Irish.

Joseph and his bride stood nearby but Jake saw that his host was intently watching Keziah. One of the *klezmer* musicians began to sing a haunting melody in some foreign lingo Jake didn't recognise. The response from Keziah was instantaneous.

She gave a heartfelt cry. 'Joseph! That's a Romani love song. My father's favourite!' Keziah clapped her hands like a delighted child.

Jake rolled his eyes. *Her Romani father! Jesus, she's forgotten who she is.*

Her black taffeta gown with its lace collar was, at first glance, demure enough to be the Sunday best Saranna Plews might have worn, but when Keziah picked up the hem of her skirts, Jake glimpsed a flash of red petticoats and black silk stockings as she began to race towards the musicians.

He grabbed her arm and spun her around. 'This is not *your* music, Saranna!'

Keziah's eyes widened, remembering her role. She gave a stifled cry of frustration and headed for the barn. Jake sauntered off in pursuit of her. *Jesus wept, I hope Daniel isn't on the prowl.*

Closing the barn door behind him he leaned back against it, stunned by the sight of Keziah. He was glad his face was hidden in the shadows.

Moonlight fell in a pool in the centre of the barn. Transfixed by the magical sound of her Romani music and oblivious to the world, Keziah was dancing. Jake had never seen a dance like it. She shook her hair free, her heels beat out a rapid tattoo, her back arched proudly. One arm curved above her head, the other flicked the hem of her skirts, her scarlet petticoats. She tossed her hair to one side in a gesture of joyous abandon, her eyes a passionate response to the music that dictated the rhythm of her body.

So this was Romani dancing! Jake saw her dress slip from one shoulder but he knew that her movements were not deliberately seductive. The way Keziah danced transformed the demure black dress of Saranna the schoolteacher into a vision of an untamed Romani.

Jake felt his pulse racing, confused by the unwanted thought of Keziah in Daniel's bed. *Jesus wept. Just look at her. What man could resist her?*

Outside the music built to a wild crescendo then died. Keziah seemed rooted to the spot, but she slowly returned to the reality of the barn and Jake's presence. She threw her arms wide, laughing like a naughty, runaway child who has returned home to find her absence undetected.

'So now you know. That's how we dance. It's in our blood!'

'Sorry you have to hide it from the rest of the world, Kez, but you can dance like that for Daniel anytime you want.'

Her words tumbled out. 'No. Daniel's been invited by Julian Jonstone to study art in Sydney Town. All fees paid. It's Daniel's dream. I want him to go. He won't be coming back to me.'

Jake felt a rush of confusion. 'Kez, be sensible. You can work it out together. You have to. He's your husband. You're married for life.'

When she shook her head emphatically, Jake grabbed her by the shoulders.

'Go with him, God damn you!'

'No! This is what Daniel wants. What I want. Our marriage is a farce.'

'Bull! He told me you're the only woman he's ever loved.'

'Yes. Like brother and sister, but I need my own man, Jake. Don't you see?'

Keziah stood on her toes like a little girl and held tight to the lapels of his coat. Then she kissed him full on the mouth like a very hungry woman. This time there was no trace of wine on her breath. Just the sweet taste of apples.

Jake had a sudden urge to continue to drink her in. A wave of anger washed over him. What rotten timing. Daniel was leaving her. Keziah was more than willing. Jake felt a sudden wild need to go down on her. Bury his face in her breasts. Kiss her all night long. Drown in her. But it was too late. He could never be more than her friend. *Curse me for a prize fool. I promised I'd never lie to her.*

He held her at arm's length and forced himself to say the words. 'I got word from the Yankee. Jenny's arrived back from New Zealand. I'm gunna leave for Melbourne Town right after this shindig.'

Keziah caught her breath and stepped back. She gave him a tremulous smile. 'Well, I can't say I'm surprised. Jenny and little Pearl. That's what you want, isn't it?'

Jake didn't quite know how to answer. Whatever he said would be half a lie. There was an awkward pause.

'You're a good man, Jake. Don't let pride ruin your life.'

Jake escorted her back in silence to rejoin the other guests. Joseph Bloom tapped a wineglass for attention, ready to make a speech.

Keziah felt Jake standing behind her but she couldn't look at him. Joseph's speech was a blend of piety, earthy wisdom and humour, yet she found it difficult to concentrate on his words. Waves of humiliation made her cheeks burn, then she turned her anger on herself. *How many times must I fail before I face the truth? Jake simply doesn't want me as a woman!*

She was suddenly caught by the words of Joseph's speech. His description of how he and Rivka had witnessed the spectacular climax of Her Majesty's birthday celebrations.

'The crowd cheered when the gaslights were turned on to illuminate the streets of Sydney Town for the first time. Clear proof of our colony's progress in keeping pace with England.' Joseph's eyes smiled down at his diminutive bride. 'But for me this historic moment had great personal significance. I ask you to raise your glasses to my Rivka, who from childhood has illuminated my whole life!'

Drunk or sober the wedding guests broke into spontaneous cheering.

'And some people think Germans aren't romantic!' Keziah said. She turned to check Jake's response.

He was gone.

Keziah sat alone watching the dancers. All energy was drained from her. She looked up to see Daniel offering her his hand. They walked home together in silence, each locked in their own thoughts.

Inside the front door she was surprised to see Daniel's bag packed and waiting.

'I've decided to leave tonight. No point in delaying it. May I borrow the brumby?'

'First time you've ever asked my permission,' she said wryly.

'I'll leave him at the livery stables in Bolthole Valley and take the morning coach to Sydney Town. I've left a present for Gabriel at the foot of his bed. He'll find it when he wakes.'

Keziah felt a lump in her throat. 'He'll miss you. He really loves you.'

'I know, but I'm not the father he needs. I'm sorry I failed you.'

She straightened his collar the way a mother sends her small son off to school.

'There's a Romani saying. "Never buy a handkerchief nor choose a wife by candlelight." You chose *me* by candlelight.'

'I regret many things I've done. *You* are not one of them.' His kiss was tender. 'Be a good girl, Keziah. You'll manage all right for money? Jonstone's paying my tuition but I'll be short of cash till I gain a commission. You know where to find me. Remember, your husband is ready to fight by your side in court if Caleb Morgan decides to play rough.'

They clung to each other for a moment, then Daniel was gone.

Keziah knew that sleep was out of the question. She stoked up the fire and sat staring into the flames, dejected by her mistake about Jake. She almost laughed at the sad irony. How strange life was. Both the men in her life were leaving her on the same night. Daniel to race off to his 'mistress'. Jake to pursue the only woman he had ever loved. Jenny.

'What a fool I was to think Jake could ever love me as a woman.' Her words sounded hollow in the cottage. She had never felt more alone in her life.

But surely Jake couldn't toss their mateship aside. Could he?

In the heart of the fire she saw the image of what awaited Jake at journey's end.

It was his *baxt.* Jake would once again lie in Jenny's arms.

CHAPTER 37

Battling against the drought that was now in its third year, Keziah was determined to keep her precious medicinal herb garden alive with every skerrick of water she could salvage. She had managed to cultivate every major herb necessary to treat a wide range of illnesses and injuries, guarding her plants as tenderly as a baby.

It was a windy July day, mid-winter by the calendar, but as parched as any summer she had known since her arrival. The drought had broken in some pockets of the colony, but rain had not fallen in Ironbark. Hearing a heavy knock Keziah raced to the door, hoping against hope to find Jake's comforting, shaggy-haired figure in the doorway.

Instead she came face to face with Caleb Morgan. He was dressed in an immaculate frockcoat and contrasting trousers that were reminiscent of the lithographs of Prince Albert. His high-crowned hat added to his height. He was the embodiment of a man of Quality, yet Keziah sensed a radical change in him.

He came bearing gifts. In one hand, an elegant arrangement of flowers, in the other a child's miniature Punch and Judy puppet theatre. He passed her in the doorway, placed his hat and gifts on the table then stripped off his kidskin gloves. With a faint smile of condescension he surveyed the room and the rustic furniture that Daniel had made her.

Keziah's first impulse was to order him out the door but something stopped her. Fashionable tailoring could not disguise his emaciated body. His hair, bleached in streaks by the desert sun, had grown longer in imitation of the careless Currency mode. His face was haggard. Crow's-feet were etched into the outer corners of his eyes and a tracery of lines ran from nose to mouth.

The discovery of the mythical Inland Sea would have secured his place in Australian history. Instead all his men had died from thirst, except for the one speared to death. Not even a packhorse had survived. Yet in that strangely contrary colonial response to failure, Caleb had become a hero.

Had the experience of facing death changed him? She was reminded of Jake's firm belief about his country. 'For better or worse, Australia changes everyone.'

Caleb made a self-deprecating gesture. 'Yes, Keziah. I went off on my grand adventure to fulfil your prophecy and make my name famous. I have succeeded in becoming something of a public figure, lionised in society. But not, alas, due to any merit of mine.' He gave a curt laugh to make light of his confession but the laugh brought on a fit of coughing.

'My bones would be bleaching in the desert right now if it were not for the courage and loyalty of Jacky Jacko, a black tracker.'

'I always knew you'd survive,' she said coolly, trying to sustain the hated image of the Morgan clan.

'The fact that the rest of my party did *not* survive rests on my conscience. My ignorance and supreme arrogance led them to their deaths.'

Despite being startled by his honesty, Keziah was determined not to give in to pity.

Caleb appeared to be too large for her cottage. No taller than Jake or Daniel, he had the innate authority of one born to the ruling class. He crossed to the bookcase that Daniel had built from pine butter boxes and opened the natural history book of flora and fauna he had given her.

He smiled. 'I see you have not forgotten our reading lessons?'

'The past is dead to me,' she said.

'Keziah,' he said. 'I cannot undo the past but I come to ask your forgiveness.'

She was on guard. *What, no threats? No talk of his legal and moral rights to Gabriel?* Her *Puri Dai* had warned her. Never trust *gaujo* charm.

'How did you find me?'

Keziah knew he had not been fooled by her tombstone in Bolthole cemetery; his lawyer's letter to Joseph Bloom had made that clear. Caleb explained that Julian Jonstone had invited him to be his house guest at Gideon Park.

'I used the opportunity to continue my search for you. I admired his family portraits and learned of his enthusiastic patronage of a convict artist, Daniel Browne. It struck me there was something oddly reminiscent about the sound of the 'dark beauty' Browne had married. A schoolteacher who hated laudanum and gave Charlotte Jonstone herbs to aid childbirth? Just like my Romani girl who had tried to help my stepmother. I made discreet enquiries about the woman known as Saranna Browne, and learned her *adopted* son was of an age that could fit with the date of his conception at Morgan Park.'

Keziah knew subterfuge was useless. 'I'll find some way to pay back your father's money but I admit nothing else.'

Before Caleb could answer, the sound of children's laughter drew him to the window. Gabriel and Murphy were chasing each other around a bush until they collided and collapsed laughing in a heap in Nerida's lap. Keziah could not fail to notice how Caleb's expression softened as he watched Gabriel's every move. She was conscious that this was the first time Caleb had ever seen her son. *His* son.

'So this is Gabriel Stanley,' he said softly. 'My son and heir. The child that Trooper Kenwood's report assured me never existed. What a fine little chap. You've done well, Keziah. No mistaking the Morgan features.'

Seeing Caleb so openly moved at the sight of the boy caused Keziah to feel a flash of empathy.

Caleb suddenly faltered and leaned on the back of the carver's chair for support.

'It's nothing. The heat,' he lied. Making an effort to regain his composure, he mopped his brow with a silk handkerchief. Keziah flinched at the sight of the hated Morgan family crest, the symbol of their power, embroidered on the corner.

She placed a jug of water on the table beside her crystal glasses. 'You are unwell. Sit down. I will make you some herbal tea.'

Caleb nodded in gratitude. He sank down, exhausted, and curled one leg over the arm of the chair in that familiar boyish habit she remembered from the Morgan library. Keziah took down a sealed jar containing the prized wood betony she had grown in her herb garden for the use of convalescing patients. She brewed an infusion of the dark pink flowers and green leaves and placed it before him.

Caleb looked at it curiously. 'I say, is this tea?'

'Trust me. Drink it down. Our herbs have magical healing properties known to my people before the Roman Empire, when we were in Egypt. It will heal you in body and mind.'

She reminded herself she must never be seen to weaken. Caleb had once used his charm to break down her defences. His attempt to milk her sympathy this time was no less dangerous.

'I am sorry for your suffering,' she said firmly. 'But it changes nothing. I would die before I allowed you to take Gabriel away from me and return him to your so-called Morgan heritage. I am more than capable of supporting my child. Gabriel and I want no part of your fame and fortune. Now or ever.'

She placed Joseph Bloom's legal document on the table. 'And if you want to fight it out in court this proves Gabriel was a foundling I adopted.'

Caleb appeared to be overcome with frustration. 'That's a ruse! Does it mean nothing to you that I travelled more than eighteen thousand miles to search for you? When I offered you my protection in England – I meant it. I made our lawyer release my inheritance from my mother. I planned to take you to North America. I returned home triumphant to find you had left without a trace.'

He waved his hands in exasperation. 'Can't you see? Everything I have done in this godforsaken country has been to win your respect. Prove to you I'm no idle remittance man. I always knew I'd find you again! There's nothing to stop me now. Your Gypsy de facto is dead and forgotten.'

Gem forgotten! Keziah flinched. Private grief was not to be shared with this *gaujo*.

Caleb continued. 'I also know that your convict husband deserted you to live in Sydney Town and study art. So you're free now. You loved me once – you still do and you know it! Why play games with me and reject my love and my protection?'

'Play games with you!' Keziah's rage exploded. 'How dare you say that after the diabolical trap you and your father set me!'

Caleb looked bewildered. 'What trap? What on earth are you talking about? Why did you break your promise and run away from me?'

'What did you expect?' she screamed. 'Did you think you could bribe a Romani woman with silver to breed a child with you? That I'd sign over Gabriel to your father to be Sophie's little plaything in between her draughts of laudanum?'

Keziah tried to read his face. *From the look of him any fool would think this comes as a revelation.* 'Don't pretend you didn't know!'

'This is monstrous. I loved you. You cannot think I'd be party to such infamy.' He threw up his hands in despair. 'My God, that's why you ran off and hid Gabriel from me.'

'What better reason is there?'

For minutes they continued to stare at each other. A silence only broken by the ticking of the clock, the children's distant laughter, the high-pitched squawking of cockatoos.

The realisation that she might have misjudged Caleb confused Keziah. If she was no longer consumed by her hatred of Caleb would it leave a strange, gaping hole in her life? *No! I will never forgive John Morgan's evil plan as long as I live!*

Finally Caleb capitulated. He sprang to his feet and faced her resolutely. 'You've done nothing wrong. I believe you. Gypsy or not, you are no liar.'

Keziah stiffened at this familiar forked *gaujo* compliment that praised her while at the same time it insulted her people.

To her great surprise Caleb knelt on bended knee like a romantic actor in a play.

'Keziah Stanley, will you do me the great honour to be the wife of my heart? To live with me and be my love and raise our son together?'

'Stop mocking me!'

Caleb rose and touched her face, a gesture of contrition rather than seduction.

'My offer stands. I will give you and Gabriel everything you want. A fine house of your own, a respected place in society. If you'll only allow me to love you!'

He brought her hand to his lips. She caught a note in his voice she had never heard before.

'I promise you my father will never lay his hands on our son! I intend to stay here and carve out a great future. This country offers more adventure than a man can pack into a single lifetime. Here I'm free of Father's expectations.'

His eyes gleamed with excitement. 'Why should I return home to gamble on cards or horses, when there's a whole continent to gamble with my life! Thousands of acres going begging in all these colonies. Vast tracts of land up north beyond Moreton Bay and in Australia Felix and right across to the west coast, just waiting for a man of vision to claim. And tame it!'

'You a *farmer*?' she asked. The idea was ludicrous, but he did not detect her sarcasm.

'Trust me, Keziah. I know how to make you happy. Our son will have the best English education. We'll live in two worlds. With my name you'll be a fine lady. No one will dare look down on my wife.' He added carelessly, 'No need to know you're half Gypsy.'

Keziah bristled at this backhanded comment but Caleb did not notice.

'What better life can any man offer you?'

His smile looked confident, but Keziah thought that perhaps it also came from his heart.

Caleb's eyes narrowed. 'Unless – is there someone else you love?'

When she could not answer, he nodded. 'So there is. Will *he* marry you?'

'No. It's not like that.'

She saw the jealousy in his eyes, but he controlled it and pressed on.

'Be honest. Do you have the right to deny our son the life I can give you? We owe it to Gabriel to put things right for him.'

'Stop it, Caleb. I can't think straight.'

'Yes, m'dear. Nothing is quite what it seemed to be one hour ago.'

The truth of these words stung her as her thoughts raced through the recent revelations. If indeed Caleb had played no role in John Morgan's plan, did she still have the right to deny Gabriel the chance to know his own father? She had been witness to how a similar denial had almost destroyed Jake Andersen. Was she no better than Jenny?

Gem was lost to her forever. Daniel had chosen art as his mistress. Jake's heart was in thrall to Jenny. Keziah tried to salvage remnants of her independence and pride. She assured herself she had no need of any man in her life, but what of little Gabriel's needs? Not yet four years old and he had already attached himself to two father figures, Jake and Daniel, and lost them both.

Caleb was watching her like a gambler weighing the odds.

'Tomorrow I would like to escort you and Gabriel to the German Brass Band concert in Goulburn. It would give Gabriel the opportunity to meet me.'

She hesitated, confused and exhausted. 'You may meet Gabriel but for now only as a friend. His life has already been full of confused loyalties.'

Caleb bent to kiss her cheek. 'Till tomorrow.'

Keziah closed the door behind him, emotionally drained. Through the window she saw Nerida instructing the boys how to be warriors, turning them sideways to diminish their small bodies' target size behind their bark shields as they aimed reed 'spears' at each other.

At the hour of Gabriel's birth she had vowed By Her Father's Hand to give him the best possible life, but to do this must she forever abandon her Romani heritage?

Her head ached as Caleb's words echoed in her mind. *'We owe it to Gabriel to put things right for him.'*

Mi-duvel! Am I meant to take the fork in the road that leads to Caleb Morgan?

CHAPTER 38

Jake was dog-tired but his mind was lucid as he rode Horatio on the final stretch of the long trek south towards Melbourne Town. The route was uninhabited for such long stretches he had lived off roadside damper and tea. When he finally reached the heart of the town he was surprised how it had mushroomed since his previous visit. The wide thoroughfare of Collins Street was lined with elegant buildings that gave it an air of distinction. Jake knew the free settlers looked down their noses at Sydney Town because they had rejected a convict population and would only accept some British 'exiles'.

When Jake sighted a newly built inn, he remembered just how thirsty he was. The balcony was hung with red, white and blue bunting and the French tricolour flag, with the date 14 July printed on a banner below the words *'Vive La Belle France'*, whatever that meant.

Dismounting to allow Horatio to drink at a horse trough, he went inside to order an Albion Ale and not surprisingly discovered the publican was a Frog. The friendly Frenchman gave him a complimentary glass of French wine and explained that France's National Day celebrated the anniversary of the Paris mob's storming of the Bastille.

'I'll drink to that,' said Jake. The date seemed like a good omen. He would like to think today would be the final day of reckoning for the Conte Francesco della Lorenzo. The French Revolution had dispatched thousands of aristocrats. Jake Andersen only wanted to rid the world of one. He reminded himself he needed to get his priorities straight.

Today would see the culmination of the long, bitter years of his search. He had three things uppermost in his mind. Jenny, Pearl and the mongrel who'd stolen his wife and child. Jake knew exactly what he wanted. Justice and revenge. To find Pearl and assure the child he loved her and would never desert her. To bring Jenny to her knees, one way or another. If necessary he was armed with Rogers's report if she tried to thwart him. His ultimate taste of revenge would be to dispatch the conte to hell, but first he had to stake his claim to Pearl.

No point swinging on the gallows for murder if Pearl remained neglected while Jenny was kept by some other wealthy protector.

On the far side of Melbourne Town, Jake rechecked the map Benjamin Rogers had marked with a cross on the banks of the River Yarra Yarra. But nothing had prepared him for the sight of the conte's residence. Jake whistled through his teeth. *Flash? Jesus, Yankee. You weren't half joking!*

The mansion known as the Palazzo was grand enough even for Jenny's taste. It was an ornate mass of marble columns, balconies, turrets and stained-glass windows, set in a sweep of landscaped gardens dotted with statues of Greek goddesses.

The place was a palace. Yet months ago Rogers had told Jake the conte's financial empire was rocky. How cockeyed the whole colonial class system was. One minute the Quality were riding the boom. The next minute big landowners couldn't sell off their land or stock for love nor money. Jake remembered the governor's repeated warnings that excessive speculation, a huge extension of credit and the drought would trigger a financial slump. *Yeah, but who bloody listened?*

Jake looked at the Palazzo. *The bankers may be panicking, but it sure looks like the bloody conte is still riding high.*

Jake scanned the upper-storey windows, wondering which of them was little Pearl's bedroom. He was reminded of how, from the time she could walk, she used to run up the garden path with Flash in her arms the moment she spotted his return home.

Grimly amused by the ludicrous contrast between the luxury of the Palazzo and his own mud-stained, shaggy Currency appearance, he rode up the circular carriageway, dismounted before the elaborate portico and casually slung Horatio's reins across the head of a rampant stone lion guarding the front steps.

At the thought of his first encounter with the mongrel who stole his wife, Jake's hand tightened over the small muff pistol inside his jacket. Today the pistol was ready to earn its keep, but Jake reminded himself his first priority was Pearl.

Holding the gift-wrapped German porcelain doll for Pearl that had cost him a small fortune, Jake rapped on the door with a brass door-knocker shaped like the head of a goddess. An arch-looking English butler opened the door.

'Tell the contessa Jake is here. She'll want to see me.'

He was ushered into an opulent drawing room with a view of the river from French windows framed by swags of drapery. The room was larger than many a working man's whole cottage and was stuffed with enough paintings and statues to fill a museum.

Jenny made her entrance down the circular staircase. Jake steeled himself against the impact of her beauty. Memory had failed him. She was even more gorgeous than the face that haunted his dreams. An exotic robe embroidered with a bird of paradise clung to the contours of her body.

Both of them stood stock-still until Jenny resumed her role as Contessa.

'Good of you to come, Jakey. I wondered if you ever received my invitation.'

His tone was cool. 'Helps to enclose your address. Took me time to track you down. How *was* New Zealand?'

Jenny laughed like a little girl. 'How naughty of me to forget, but I'm glad to be home. Those New Zealanders are too dour and tight with their money for my taste – they don't know how to enjoy the finer things of life.' She gestured for him to be seated.

Jake's choice lay between fancy gilded chairs that looked like the thrones in a child's book of fairytales. He settled on one and mastered the cramped space by folding one leg so his boot rested on his other knee.

'I'd be more comfortable sitting on a horse,' he said. 'No insult intended.'

Jenny laughed in delight. 'None taken. You haven't changed, Jakey.'

'Oh yes I have, Jenny!' he assured her. 'So you've gone back to your natural hair colour.' He made no attempt to conceal his sarcasm. 'Decided not to hide from me anymore?'

Jenny blushed and Jake felt a jab to his heart. Even knowing everything she had done to him, she could still play the innocent and almost get away with it. He was determined to keep the upper hand.

'If Pearl is taking a nap or something, I'll wait as long as it takes!'

Before Jenny had time to respond, a maidservant timidly made her way to her side. She was dark-eyed and swarthy. Her face was heavily pock-pitted and she was no longer young, but Jake could see she must have been pretty once.

At a nod from Jenny she placed a tray on a silly little table. Champagne in a silver ice bucket and two glasses left no room for a fly to walk.

Jenny gave the woman a dismissive wave. 'Take the evening off, Emilia.'

The maid hesitated. '*Scusi*, Contessa, but is Saunders night off.'

Jenny's tone was sharp. 'Now. *I insist.*'

'The contessa is most kind.' The door closed behind her unwilling exit.

Jenny's face resumed its teasing expression. 'The conte, Franco, was called away on urgent business to Williams Town. I don't expect him back before Friday. So I'm here all alone.' She watched Jake intently. 'You seem disappointed to have missed him.'

'I've waited a long time for that pleasure. It can keep a bit longer,' he said evenly. 'Pearl is all that interests me. It's been years, maybe she won't even recognise me.'

'You always were a devoted father.' Jenny's smile was more wistful than seductive. 'I want to explain everything. Will you join me in a glass of French champagne?'

'French, eh? To celebrate Bastille Day?' he asked wryly.

'*Non.* I do not celebrate aristocrats losing their heads to *Madame La Guillotine.* Let's drink to the reunion of old friends.'

'Friends? Right. For Pearl's sake – *if* we can come to an agreement about my role in Pearl's life. I reckon that would be better for her than us going to court.'

Jake downed his champagne with the same speed he'd sink an Albion Ale on a hot day. *What the hell is she playing at?* He took the lead.

'Right, so you've impressed me with your society stuff. How about we stop beating around the bush. When do I see Pearl?'

Jenny hesitated. 'Pearl doesn't live here.'

'Why not for God's sake? You've got enough room here to house a dozen little kids.'

'Franco is restless by nature, easily bored. No house is fine enough compared to his father's palazzo in Venice. We're always moving, always travelling. That's no life for a small child.'

Jake barely controlled his anger. 'I get the picture. Pearl is shoved out of sight while you two gallivant around in the lap of luxury.'

'Franco is giving her a fine education,' she added sweetly, 'that *we* never could.'

The barb struck home. *She means it's my fault.* 'So where the hell is she?'

'Just waiting to see you.' Jenny gracefully crossed the room to seat herself at a small desk. She quickly penned a letter. In the act of offering him the envelope her cool fingers pressed his hand for a moment longer than was necessary. The letter carried the remembered perfume of her body. It was addressed to the sister of a convent in a remote village far west of Ironbark.

Jenny said airily, 'This is your *carte* of introduction, unsealed for you to read. Forgive me if I don't shock the sisters by revealing the exact details of our little *ménage.* Pearl wants to meet her real father. This gives you my consent to visit her whenever you wish.'

Jenny's swift capitulation took him by surprise. The Yankee's report was in his breast pocket ready to be enforced if Jenny blocked him, but here she was giving him exactly what he wanted. It was almost too easy. He reminded himself to be on guard against her tricks.

Jenny's eyes held him with a look of appealing frankness. 'Is there anything else you want, Jakey? If only I could make it all up to you for the silly dance I led you.'

He kept his anger internalised. *'Silly dance' she calls it. She cut out my heart and my balls. And it took me years to feel like a man again. Some bloody dance!*

'Forget it.' His tone was neutral. 'This address is all I want. I'd best make tracks. You sure stashed her away at the back of beyond.'

Jenny leaned forward as if to detain him. 'You are welcome to stay here the night, Jakey. We have seven guest bedrooms – and mine. You could choose any one you want.'

For a moment Jake wasn't sure if he had mistaken her invitation, but when she blushed at his lack of response, he knew. *Does she want to prove she can still make me sit up and beg?*

He smiled politely. 'And just what would the count think of your hospitality?'

Jenny shrugged. 'Franco is nothing if not generous. He pays Pearl's expenses and keeps Mother in comfort. He gives me *everything* I want, but I'm totally dependent on him. He says a goddess never carries money.' Her nervous, endearing laugh cut Jake to the heart.

Suddenly all Jenny's pretence melted away. 'I confess I haven't been entirely honest with you, Jakey. I know I don't deserve your help but I'm throwing myself on your mercy.'

He tensed, alert to manipulation. *'And?'*

'The colony is said to be sinking into a Depression. They say more banks will fold—'

'No need to spell it out, Jenny. How much money do you need to tide you over?'

Jenny led him by the hand to a dimly lit room. Jake could not fail to notice the way her robe clung to her body, accentuating every feline movement. She gestured to a table piled with bills and legal-looking documents bound with red sealing wax.

'You see the mess we're in? Franco's lost everything. Even the ship he named after me, the *Contessa Giovanna*.'

Jake kept a poker face as he listened to her melodramatic version of the facts of the fraud he had already learned from Rogers.

'If things are that tough, how come you're both slumming it here in the Palazzo?'

'Loaned to us by a friend who's doing *La Grande Tour*.' She added helpfully, 'Europe.'

'I didn't think you meant Van Diemen's Land.'

Jenny looked like a lost child as she explained that Franco was facing gaol for fraud. 'He's innocent of course, but barristers cost money. Jakey, you're my only hope. I'll be on the streets unless you—'

'What about Pearl? I'm ready to take full responsibility for her.'

She sank down onto a French Empire chaise longue and placed her hand over her heart. 'And what about me, Jakey? Don't you feel anything for me? The truth is the moment I saw you again in that prize fight, so strong, so handsome, I knew I'd made a ghastly mistake leaving you!'

Right at that moment Jenny had never looked more helpless – and beautiful. Jake tried to keep his tone light, in denial of how much he had longed to hear her say those words.

'Your Franco's given you the high life I could never afford. Best stick with him, eh? Blokes like him always bounce back again.'

Jenny drew closer. 'It's all over with Franco. I just want to keep him out of prison so he can return to Venice. *Without me.* Then I'll be free of him, my darling!'

Jenny was in his arms as naturally as if she had never left him. It was only then Jake realised that the dimly lit room contained a four-poster bed. Jenny led him to it and drew him down on her. She guided his hands inside her robe. Her mouth made hungry demands on his. Nothing had changed. Jake still wanted her so badly his body ached.

When she begged him to make love to her, Jake withdrew from his wallet his latest promissory note and tossed it on the bed.

This was his long-awaited moment. He could buy Jenny as his 'wife for the night', just like any other whore, then leave her in the morning to claim his little princess.

'This is all the money I've got until I win another fight. You're welcome to it.'

When Jenny read the value of the promissory note Jake saw a look of pleasure he had never been able to arouse during their marriage. Despite himself Jake's throat constricted when her flaxen hair tumbled in irresistible disarray and her eyes filled with tears.

'What a generous man you are. Can you ever find it in your heart to forgive me?' She rubbed her face into his thigh. 'Oh Jakey, you can make me happy now, I know you can!'

It was an uncanny insight into his long-burning quest for revenge. Could he resist her in the end? *There's only one way to find out. If I can walk away from her after tonight I'll be free of her. Forever. As Gem Smith said, 'Free of her lips, free of her hips.'*

He kissed Jenny's face and body with random passion that proved what Lily Pompadour said about that bloke Casanova. Four-fifths of a man's pleasure can come from *giving* pleasure.

Jenny's eyes widened. 'My God, Jakey, you are a very different lover!'

She whimpered in ardent response to his every caress. Jake kept his head and took control of her. This was his revenge. Her pleading directions, her begging him not to stop, his making her wait – all tasted incredibly sweet. He knew his ultimate performance would be technically flawless. Yet somehow he could not feel the excitement he craved.

Her eyes narrowed like a cat as she emptied a phial into a glass of wine and drank from it.

'A gift from Venus the goddess of love. You can't imagine how it heightens our pleasure.'

Jake took the glass from her. 'You don't need that stuff, Jenny. I'm going to give you more god-damned pleasure than you ever knew existed.'

Her gown slipped away like melting snow as she beckoned him. With one hand she swept her hair to one side – the same seductive gesture Keziah had made that night in the barn when she danced to Romani music. But there was a difference. Keziah's gesture was joyous like a spontaneous child. Jenny just looked like a seasoned 'wife for the night'.

At the moment she began to arch in ecstasy, Jake was aware that the choice was his. He could so easily enjoy Jenny one last time. She *was* his wife and he figured he had earned that right, but unbidden came the vivid memory of a girl with wild black hair saying, *'Jake, before it's too late. Please make love to me.* Now.'

There was only one woman in the world he wanted. *Keziah.* He suddenly saw Jenny as she really was. He felt nothing but the emotion he had steeled himself against. *Pity.* Jenny was a weak little creature, desperate enough to be a rich man's plaything. Jake wasn't sure if he felt more like the victor or the vanquished, but he chose a gallant lie.

'Forgive me, Jenny. You're incredibly beautiful but I just can't go through with this. I'm sorry to be blunt. I only want my daughter. I don't want you anymore.'

Jenny gasped at the truth of Jake's words. Her eyes darted to a wall mask of Venus. The light from the oil lamp cast strange shadows across its gilt face. Jewelled cat's eyes gleamed in the sockets.

Jenny seemed transformed, like a cat about to spring. 'You haven't woken up to my secret, have you, Jakey? I really *am* a goddess.'

Jake tried to marshal his thoughts, conscious of the strange expression in her eyes. Gently he turned her face towards the light of the oil lamp. The pupils of her eyes did not diminish in size. Was it true some drugs had that affect?

'Poor Jakey,' she mocked. 'You were always pathetic as a lover. Are you still a failure? I know what you want. Come and take your revenge on me!'

The time had come to play his trump card. 'I'm sorry to ruin your day, Jenny. It's time to pack your bags and find another meal ticket. You've been living a lie. Your Conte Francesco della Lorenzo is as noble as my Aunt Fanny. His real name is Frankie Hotchkiss. Nothing but a Cockney from London's East End. The closest he ever came to an aristocrat was some Venetian count visiting London. Frankie was his valet. He stole the old bloke's money, family jewels, papers and his family tree!'

'A *valet*?' she shrieked in horror. 'You're a lying bastard!'

'Can't you see the funny side?' He waved the Yankee's report. 'I hired a detective to find Pearl. If you'd let me see her at the start, I would never have discovered that Frankie's a total fraud!'

Jenny was wailing as if her heart was broken. Jake began to enjoy himself.

'Right now the only people who know the truth are you, me and The American Investigations Agency. Oh yeah and another thing. Your maid Emilia Hotchkiss is Frankie's wife. She's a genuine Italian, taught him every bloody thing he knows.'

'My servant is Franco's *wife*?' She looked up at him like a tragic kitten. 'I beg you, don't do this to me. I dine at the governor's table! Don't expose me to ridicule in society!'

Jake's revenge finally tasted sweet. 'I don't need to. The whole bloody colony will enjoy the joke soon enough! The genuine conte is bound for Port Jackson to be the governor's guest of honour!'

Jake tossed the report onto the bed. 'If I were you I'd hire Frankie Hotchkiss a damned good lawyer. He's sure gunna need one!'

Right at that moment Jake heard a male voice bellowing in a foreign language.

Jenny's face turned ashen. '*Dio mio!* It's Franco!'

The sound of a heavy thump from the next room caused Jenny to run from the room in panic, crying, 'Jakey, don't desert me!'

Jake felt trapped by one of his own rules; never to turn his back on a woman's cry for help.

He followed her to the next room. An overturned chair lay on the floor. A red cord hung from the chandelier. Swinging on the end was the twitching body of Frankie Hotchkiss. His striped silk dressing gown fell open to expose a body as pathetic as a plucked turkey. A gold crucifix hung around his neck. The whites of his bulbous eyes were rolled to heaven.

The Yankee's warning was accurate. Jake was driven to blind rage. *The mongrel's not gunna die and cheat me of my revenge.*

He smashed a nearby glass weapons cabinet with his bare hands. Blood ran down his arms and Jenny screamed as he grabbed a lethal Saracen blade and charged at the body.

'You yellow-livered, rotten mongrel!' With maniacal strength he slashed the sword through the air, cutting the cord in two.

The body fell to the floor then whimpered. Frankie Hotchkiss grabbed at his throat where the cord had dug into his flesh.

Jake realised at that moment what he must look like, stark naked and wielding a sword over Frankie Hotchkiss's prone body. Suddenly he didn't feel like an avenger. *I feel bloody ridiculous.*

Frankie was looking at Jenny like a miserable puppy. 'If I lose you, *Contessa mia*, is best I die!'

Jake rolled his eyes. *Jesus! He can't even lose his false accent when he's dying.*

Jenny remembered her role as a goddess. She looked up at Jake with contempt.

'Get out of here, you peasant. You'll never be half the man Franco is!'

It was then Jake spotted the painting on the floor and realised the reason for the small holes in the wall. Franco had used the eyes of the mask of Venus to spy on Jake's performance with Jenny. His own wife. Jake felt a wave of humiliation. *Jesus wept. This is the night I waited years for to prove to Jenny I could at last make her happy in bed! And it was nothing but a peepshow for a Cockney valet!*

Jake found himself choking. It began painfully but soon a strange sound came rolling out of his mouth. It was clean, free unstoppable laughter.

He handed his rival the sword. 'You ain't man enough to live without a fake title. Try killing yourself with this. It works better than hanging!'

Frankie Hotchkiss clung to his role. 'Never you take her! She is my goddess!'

Jake said dryly, 'You're welcome to her, mate.'

He rode away with the only thing of value – the letter to the convent. He forced himself to examine his tawdry night of revenge. Why had Jenny sunk so low, using her body to solicit money for her lover? The crazy truth hit him. *She really loves the grubby little bastard!*

He confided in Horatio. 'They're nothing but scum but I'm no bloody better. For years I've been driven by my hunger for revenge. The only innocent person in this whole dirty mess is my little princess.'

Jake lost his taste for murder. Frankie Hotchkiss wasn't worth it. Jenny had been free to choose her life but little Pearl didn't have a say in anything. Jake vowed come hell or high water he'd spring Pearl out of that convent and take her where they'd never find her. Swan River in the west or the new colony of South Australia.

But that meant he'd never see Keziah again. He cursed himself for a fool. Now that Daniel had abdicated his role of husband, Caleb Morgan would claim Keziah and Gabriel.

'Jesus wept, Horatio. What a mess I've made of my life! There's only one thing left to do.'

CHAPTER 39

Keziah gripped the shawl around her head in a vain attempt to keep her intricately coiled hair in place. She clung to the passenger seat beside Polly Doyle as George Hobson drove his cart at high speed through Ironbark village. They were late for a very special event. The whole locality had been invited by Dr Ross to an open-house celebration to commemorate the anniversary of the Battle of Trafalgar. Jake had once told her that the Doc, a surgeon in the Royal Navy since his youth, ranked Horatio Nelson's naval victory second only to the wild celebration of New Year's Eve that Highlanders called Hogmanay.

Despite her reluctance to visit the Haunted Farm Keziah decided to risk being confronted by the *mulo* of the convict Padraic. She could not pass up the chance that Jake Andersen would miraculously return in time for this party. No matter what had happened at Jake's reunion with Jenny in Melbourne Town, Keziah was desperate to know the outcome.

The world and his dog will be there tonight. Mi-duvel, please put me out of my misery. In my dreams I saw Jake in bed with Jenny. Does that mean he's taken her back as his wife?

Tonight Keziah had chosen to wear her best summer-weight gown but she still found it difficult to adjust to October being mid-spring in the colony. Close to sundown the air was hot, windy and filled with dust from the drought that was now in its fourth year. As they rattled past the Collins family's few-acres farm, she saw rows of wheat sagging in the parched earth. A neighbouring farm was so derelict it signalled to Keziah that yet another defeated settler had turned to rum for consolation. As they crossed the riverbed of Ironbark creek she saw it had shrivelled into shallow pools like the beads of a broken necklace.

The destruction of the drought was as painful to Keziah as if her own body was wounded. Rain was God's blood. She prayed *The Del* would give his blood to nourish the earth.

On their arrival at the Haunted Farm the party was already in full swing. Leslie Ross was standing on the veranda to welcome them. He cut an imposing figure in his full Highland regalia of red and black Ross tartan kilt with ornate sporran, silver-buttoned velvet jacket with clan sash anchored on one shoulder by a cairngorm and silver brooch, silver-buckled shoes on his feet. Keziah noted his ruddy face was flushed. *I'll bet he's knocked back a fair few drams of whisky.*

At his elbow stood Janet Macgregor, looking self-conscious without the protective armour of her housekeeper's apron. For once her chestnut hair was loosely coiled at the nape of her neck.

The Doc's welcome was hearty. Janet bobbed an awkward curtsy but Keziah responded with a warm hug.

'Janet dear, how handsome you look in evening dress.'

Janet looked pleased but dismissed the compliment and ushered Keziah and Polly across the lawn to join the other guests. Many had already responded to the wine and the music and were dancing on the wooden platform reserved for the dancers. The garden was hung with Chinese paper lanterns that Keziah recognised were Sunny Ah Wei's merchandise.

She looked around in vain for any sign of Jake.

A man's hand on her elbow and his whispered words, 'You look ravishing, m'dear,' made her whirl around in surprise.

'What are *you* doing here?' she demanded. 'I thought you were in Sydney Town buying yourself a house.'

Caleb Morgan looked dashing. He was the kind of man who even if he wore convict slops would have started a new fashion.

He snapped his fingers. 'Signed, sealed and delivered. A fine townhouse on the crest of Woolloomooloo Hill. The top floor has a nursery for Gabriel and a room for a nurse girl so you won't have to attend him during the night. The house overlooks the harbour on three sides. You'll love it.' He leaned down and whispered in her ear, 'It's yours. Can't wait to take you there.'

'Don't count your chickens before they're hatched, Caleb. I'm still legally married, remember?' Keziah said sharply.

Caleb gave a dismissive wave of the hand. 'A mere detail. In the circles I move in that's easily rectified. No issue from your marriage. So an annulment will do the trick. Don't worry, I'll compensate your husband. A struggling artist in a garret no doubt.'

Keziah was so irritated by his confident smile that she gripped her fan so hard she snapped one of its ribs. 'Damn!' she said.

'How refreshing you are,' he laughed in response. 'Will you do me the honour to dance with me?'

Aware people were watching them Keziah tried to remain circumspect. 'No, thank you. If a man coughs twice in a woman's presence in Ironbark it's enough to start a rumour they're bedmates.'

'A rumour I'd be more than happy to hear given *my* name is linked to yours,' he said.

Keziah forced herself to let that pass. 'I *would* welcome a glass of champagne.'

'Indeed, just what you need to relax after a day in the schoolroom. Allow me.'

He made a little bow and walked off in the direction of the refreshments table. Keziah seized the moment to break free and circulate in the crowd, hoping to find Jake alone. There was no sign of him.

The sound of a waltz drifted across the lawn as she passed the open door of the cookhouse. She knew she should not eavesdrop but her instinct was too strong to tear her eyes from the scene. Leslie Ross was standing beside Janet Macgregor, who was flushed in the face and trying to keep her composure as she tied on her apron.

'Ye are a stubborn woman, Janet. Dinna I make it clear? I've paid good money to hire servants to free ye from the kitchen. Tonight

I'm your host, not your master.'

With great deliberation he untied her apron and let it fall to the floor. Janet looked as alarmed as if he had undressed her in public.

'What do you think you're doing, man?'

'Inviting you to waltz, lassie.'

Janet pulled away but remained within reach. 'You know full well Wesleyans don't hold with the dancing.'

Leslie asked softly, 'What kind of God forbids a man to enjoy music in the arms of his ain true love?'

Janet gasped. Her resolve crumbled. 'I dinna know how to dance.'

'I'm just the man to teach you, lassie.'

Janet bit back a smile. 'Get thee behind me, Satan.'

Leslie slipped his arm around her waist and kissed her.

Keziah smiled wistfully as she moved away unnoticed, leaving them to explore the moment.

At least Dr Ross has the courage to ignore gaujo *law and claim his happiness when* baxt *offers him the chance.*

She averted her eyes from the old well where she'd once seen the *mulo.* Hurrying back to rejoin the guests her head ached as she tried to avoid Caleb and search for Jake. Finally she gave up.

When George Hobson announced he needed to rise early, Keziah seized the chance to depart with him. Polly Doyle sat beside her on the journey home, dejected because Mac Mackie hadn't asked her to dance.

At the sound of horses behind them, Keziah turned in time to see an old wagon veering off down the track to the Haunted Farm that they had just left behind them.

Jake! What rotten timing. If only I'd waited another few minutes!

'Damn me for a fool!' she muttered angrily under her breath.

Polly gave her a broad grin and whispered, 'Nice to see proper ladies like you are human just like the rest of us.'

Jake arrived weary and travel-stained to find the Doc's party had reached the stage when men fired with grog were ready to start a fight or try their luck with a woman. He unharnessed Horatio from the wagon and led him to the water trough.

'By rights this should be your celebration, mate. Horatio Nelson being your namesake.'

Leslie Ross gave Jake an expansive hug of welcome. 'My thanks for coming back in time to celebrate Nelson's victory, laddie. The Battle of Trafalgar seems as fresh tonight as if it happened yesterday.'

'Wouldn't forgive myself if I'd missed it, Doc.' Jake wanted to ask if Keziah was here but shied off drawing attention to his quest. He had a heap of plans in his head he was itching to set in motion. *But first I've got to make sure Keziah is still free – and available.*

The Doc supplied Jake with two double whiskies. They drank a toast to Lord Nelson then the Doc was dragged off to perform the Highland fling to the drunken cheers of his guests.

Mac Mackie made a beeline for Jake and confided his frustration over Polly Doyle.

'Jesus, Mac. You mean the girl still hasn't a clue how you feel about her? If you don't put your bid in quick smart, Hobson's going to snaffle her up to be his kids' stepmother.'

'Do you reckon she'd take me on? I ain't no oil painting.'

'Trust me, Polly Doyle would have you churched before you can say Jack Robinson.'

When Jake downed his second whisky he caught sight of the figure at the centre of a circle of men who were firing questions at him. *Jesus wept! Caleb bloody Morgan.*

Jake could hardly bear to look at him. The Englishman reeked Quality. He was wealthy, a gentleman, unmarried – and Gabriel's father!

What in hell do I have to offer Kez? Not a bloody thing! Not even my best mates would be guilty of calling me a gentleman.

What was far worse, Caleb Morgan had enough money and influence to pull strings to gain a divorce for Keziah. Jake would never be free to marry her. He didn't have a roof to put over her head. His income was haphazard, topped up with prize fights she hated. He had a prison record. *And now I'm on the brink of abducting Pearl from a convent – more bloody trouble with the law!*

Yet the moment he saw Caleb Morgan's supercilious smile, Jake wiped all these impediments from his mind, ready for action.

He nudged Mac. 'What's that Pommy explorer doing here, mate?'

'He's Julian Jonstone's house guest at Gideon Park. That gentry mob treat him like he's bloody royalty.'

When Jake overheard Caleb Morgan telling the circle of men that their schoolteacher, Mrs Browne, was a lady well known to his family in England, Jake saw red. Tossing down his drink, he marched across to confront Caleb, grabbed him by the elbow and pulled him aside.

'You keep turning up like a bad bloody penny, Morgan. Come back to cause trouble for my mate, Saranna Browne, have you? Well you'll have to get past me first!'

Caleb turned his back on his admirers and cast a glance Jake's way. 'If you're spoiling for a fight why not amuse yourself with your own kind – some *other* colonial drunk, old chap.'

Jake ignored the insult. Even though this bloke clearly knew Keziah's real identity, it was Jake's job to keep up the pretence she was Saranna Browne. He saw Gilbert Evans eyeing them from a distance. Informers had long ears.

'I'm Saranna's best mate and I refuse to stand by and watch some half-arsed New Chum break her heart. So why don't you shove off back to the Old Dart?'

'My intentions to the lady in question are honourable but none of your business, old chap.'

'I've got news for you. I'm making it my business, but I'll give you the chance to prove me wrong.'

As angry as he was, Jake couldn't lie to himself. Was he already too late? If Kez had changed her mind and accepted Gabriel's father, what could he do to stop her? But the idea of Keziah in bed with Caleb Morgan drove him crazy.

'Come on! What's going on? Do you intend to make her an offer or what?'

Caleb looked confident. 'Already done so, old chap. Try and be civilised, what?'

Jake blocked his path to the bar. '*And?* What did she say?'

'Promised to consider my offer. If I know women her answer will be yes by the end of the week.'

Jake felt deflated. 'See you treat her right, Morgan.'

As the Englishman moved away, Jake called after him, 'I'll be watching you!'

Feeling as if the stuffing had been knocked out of him, Jake walked away from the crowd. The sound of a waltz drifted across the lawn as he bedded down on the straw in the barn. *Am I bloody fated to go through life watching Kez live with other men?*

He looked at the stars shining through the hole in the roof. Lily Pompadour had been right. In the past he had solved everyone's problems except his own. What was wrong with him? Tonight he'd almost pushed Morgan into marrying Kez, when he wanted her for himself. Why? To make her happy living the easy life he could never give her? Or was it to get himself off the hook? Repay his debt to her for saving his life? *How stupid can a man be? Morgan's offering her the bloody world but I've got one chance to beat that!*

From his pocket he pulled out the dog-eared magazine picture he had carried for days.

He charged out of the barn and drove his wagon to Bran's forge. The place was in darkness but Jake hurried inside, pulled the young giant out of bed and spread out the picture on the bench.

'Can you build me this new wagon, mate? Double quick? Ain't seen nothing like it, right? It's a *vardo* – a Romani travelling house on wheels. Do you reckon Kez will like it?'

Bran beamed and gave a thumbs-up sign of approval.

'Here's some money to get you started, mate, but I'll need another fight or two to pay you in full. I'll be back soon. I've got a couple of problems to fix first.'

It was still dark next morning when Jake scrawled a note addressed to Mrs Browne and pushed it under Joseph Bloom's door. He could hardly be seen lurking around the schoolteacher's cottage in the middle of the night. But could Kez be counted on to take notice of a note that only read 'Don't do nothing rash till I return, Jake'?

His feelings were wildly at odds with his thoughts as he galloped to Bolthole Valley.

It was almost dawn when he arrived at the House of the Four Sisters but the geranium-coloured lights still flashed through the windows.

It was Wednesday. Lily would be waiting upstairs for him. He paid Madam Fleur for the Wednesdays he had been absent then leapt up the stairs before he changed his mind.

Lily looked stunning. She was lying on the bed wearing a black lacy negligee that revealed more than it concealed. She was more than ready for him.

Jake leant back against the door and drank her in slowly.

'Sorry I've taken so long to keep my promise, Lil. Had a few things on my mind but I got lucky with a couple of fights.' He took out an envelope and tossed it on the bed.

'This wipes out your Uncle Charlie's debt to Madam Fleur. You don't belong here, never did. I want you out of here. Go somewhere no one knows you. Never get stuck in this dead-end business again. I know a good woman when I see one. There's some decent bloke waiting to jump through hoops for you. If he doesn't do right by you – I'll sort him out!'

Lily looked at the envelope but didn't touch it. She gave him a funny little smile.

'That's quite a speech, sweetheart. From a man who prefers action to words.' She crooked her little finger. 'How about we celebrate one last time?'

Jake sighed. 'I'm going to hate myself in the morning for saying no but I'm on my way to bail my daughter out of a convent.' He turned in the doorway. 'Can I kiss you goodbye?'

Lily nodded. Jake kissed her with his eyes wide open. He felt like a soldier who was going into battle, knowing he would never return.

Three days later on the western edge of Wiradjuri tribal country Jake found what he was looking for. The double-storey building stood at the heart of a farm where shaven-headed convicts were pitching hay. There was no outward sign to say it was a convent. Maybe Catholics weren't too popular in this part of the bush. There appeared to be only two Sisters running the place. The older nun beckoned Jake to follow her.

Inside Sister Mary Bridget's office Jake introduced himself, hat in hand.

'I'm Jakob Andersen, ma'am. I'm only half a Catholic. Ma is. Pa ain't. I'm sort of agnostic. What I mean is, if I say things wrong, no disrespect intended.'

Sister Mary Bridget nodded. 'Thank you, my son. I shall take that into account.'

'My daughter's a pupil here. Haven't seen her for a few years. It's a real long story and you're a busy woman but here's her mother's permission.'

The nun read Jenny's letter carefully. 'You appear to be the victim of a hoax. There's no Jenny Pearl Andersen under my roof.'

He heard his voice rise in frustration. 'What? She must be here under a false name. Have you got a girl by the name of Troy? Or della Lorenzo? Let me see your muster!'

Sister Mary Bridget's glare was formidable. 'This letter does not entitle you to visit any of my students. Kindly leave at once!'

'Have a heart, Sister. I've been searching for my daughter for years. Can't you see this is a trick her mother's played on me?'

In a matter of seconds Jake found himself being prodded towards the iron gates by three assigned labourers armed with pitchforks. He could have beaten them off with one hand tied, but if Pearl *was* here somewhere he didn't want her first impression of him to be violent.

Sister Mary Bridget watched expressionless from the porch as a gaggle of schoolgirls in identical grey dresses mushroomed out of nowhere to witness the scene.

In desperation Jake scanned the smaller girls' faces but none seemed to bear any resemblance to his memory of Pearl.

Jake shoved a pitchfork out of range and yelled out to Sister Mary Bridget. 'Ask these girls if anyone recognises me!'

The nun made no reply so Jake addressed the students himself. 'I'm looking for a little girl called Jenny Pearl Andersen, maybe her mother changed her name. I'm her real father. No matter what her mother told her, I never walked out on her and I never will!'

An aggressive gardener planted his pitchfork on Jake's chest, forcing him down onto the gravel path. As Jake looked up through the sunlit canopy of an apple tree, he saw the shadowy face of a little girl peering through the branches at him. Before he had time to get a good look at her face she leapt down from the tree and bolted for the cookhouse. Unlike all the other girls she was dressed in a navy blue dress covered by an adult-sized pinafore.

He grabbed the pitchfork, rolled free and shouted out to Sister Mary Bridget. 'Let me talk to that little girl in your presence. What have you got to lose, Sister?'

The two nuns conferred in whispers, then signalled the labourers to return to work.

Sister Mary Bridget beckoned Jake to follow her down the corridor.

The floor was polished and slippery. Jake eyed the line of framed pictures on the walls that showed a young bloke with his eyes rolled towards the sky. *Jesus wept. He looks as edgy as I feel.*

The nun's lips were pursed and her eyes as sharp as an eagle's. She directed Jake to the seat opposite her desk. Before the child arrived she ordered him not to prompt her memory. Jake was forced to agree to her terms. He knew it was a slim chance that little girl would turn out to be Pearl but what other choice did he have?

'Tell me, Sister. Why was she dressed different to the other girls?'

Sister Mary Bridget looked slightly discomforted but quickly regained her air of authority.

'That child's father has not paid her fees for a year. We don't know where he is. These are tough times. We cannot afford charity cases. A deserted child must pay for her keep by working in the kitchen. I supervise her reading, writing and arithmetic lessons at night free of charge.'

Jake held down his rising anger. Whoever this kid was, her family had left her to work as a slavey. 'She can't be more than seven, Pearl's age. You mean that man just dumped her?'

The nun raised her voice against Jake's. 'She knows who her father is. So don't think you can trick her or me, young man. I can spot a lie a mile off!'

Jake leaned forward and returned her stare. 'Then you'll know *I'm* telling the truth.'

There was a timid knock at the door. Jake's heart sank when he saw the little girl from the apple tree. She was skinny with mousy brown hair and unblinking blue eyes. Her navy blue dress was threadbare, her little boots down-at-heel. She didn't look remotely like Pearl, more like some street urchin from The Rocks.

Sister Mary Bridget's voice was firm but not unkind when she ordered the child to speak only when spoken to and remember her manners. The child made Jake a hasty curtsy.

'What's your name, girlie?' he asked.

'Gianna di Felice,' she whispered.

'Pretty name. My name's Jake Andersen. Have you ever seen me before?'

She shook her head and turned to the nun. 'Have I done something wrong, Sister?'

'No. Just answer the questions, Gianna.'

Jake wanted to prompt the girl but he knew he'd be kicked out if he asked leading questions.

'What's your mama's name? What does she look like?'

She looked embarrassed. 'I forget. But Mama brought me here in a carriage with a man. I remember she wore pretty dresses. She told me they were going away but she'd come back for me before Christmas. She never did.'

Jake stalled for time, trying to recall some memory that would prove the truth one way or another.

The child took a step closer. 'I was in the apple tree. I saw the gardeners being mean to you. You said you were looking for Jenny Pearl Andersen. Is she lost? I don't know her.'

Sister Mary Bridget rose from her chair. 'I think you have all the proof you need, Mr Andersen. Gianna di Felice has told you who she is.'

Jake held up his hand determined to stay her. 'One more question.' He smiled at the girl and knelt down on one knee to draw level with her eyes.

'When I was a little boy the very first thing I can remember is sitting on my pa's knee, eating a sticky lolly. Tell me, girlie. What's the first thing *you* remember?'

She did not hesitate. 'A nice man gave me a white puppy that rubbed its cold nose in my face. Do you know what happened to my puppy, Flash?' Her eyes suddenly widened. 'I remember the man had red hair that went yellow in the sun. Just like yours. Are *you* my papa, Mister?'

Then she did something Jake remembered Pearl had done as a toddler. Her mouth formed a small 'o' as she reverently tucked a long strand of his hair behind his ear.

She cocked her head to one side. 'I remember you. Do you remember me?'

That simple question broke his heart. The little princess whose memory he had carried in his heart for years had died inside him. In her place was this funny little girl who looked like a rag doll with popping eyes and a flat face. Jake felt his eyes stinging, but there were no tears. All those lost years that could never be reclaimed – thanks to Jenny. He forced himself to lie.

'Hey, I'd know my little princess anywhere!'

Jake turned to the nun and his voice cracked. 'How much proof do you want, Sister?'

Although Sister Mary Bridget continued to question the child, Jake sensed the battle was going his way. He listened as the nun explained to Pearl her real father had been searching for her for years. Her mother had gone away but had sent a letter giving him permission to see her.

Jake felt utterly empty. He knew he was supposed to do something, say something important, but what? How in hell could he bridge the barrier of lost years between them? The lump in his throat felt large enough to choke him.

He rose. There would be no argument. 'I'm taking her with me, Sister. Nothing and no one is gunna stop me.'

Sister Mary Bridget nodded. 'Don't forget your prayers, child.'

The time had come to begin again. Jake took Pearl by the hand and walked out into the sunlight. She needed to skip to keep apace with him.

'Where are we going, Papa?' she asked.

Jake lifted her up onto Horatio's back. 'I don't know exactly. But you can be sure of one thing. I ain't never going to let you out of my sight again, girlie!'

CHAPTER 40

In the days that followed the Trafalgar Day party Keziah felt frustrated that her path had almost crossed with Jake's but failed to deliver a meeting. Why hadn't he visited her? Was Jenny back in his life? Keziah felt Jake was as close to her as her own heartbeat, but the gift she had relied on since childhood now failed to predict his movements.

She arrived home from school that day, stunned to find under her door an envelope addressed to Saranna Browne from the man who never wrote letters. Two lines leapt out at her between the ink blobs and the spelling was quite original. There was no date but the message was loud and clear.

> *Listen a lot of stuff happened. I'm on my way back to Ironbark. Got someone with me. Do me a favour. Try and stay out of trouble till I get back, mate. Jake*

Keziah had no choice but to await his return.

A knock at the door raised her hopes but when she flung it open she was face to face with Caleb Morgan. She realised she hadn't seen him for days. Hat in hand, he studied her with serious eyes. For once his Morgan air of superiority seemed diminished. He looked strangely vulnerable – a very different man to the born-to-rule gentleman who had presumed he could move back into her life, sweep her off her feet and carry her and Gabriel off to Sydney Town.

'I had a chat with that odd Currency chap, Andersen, at Dr Ross's party. Ever since then I've been avoiding something I didn't want to face.'

Keziah gestured him to be seated, intent on reading the real message behind his words.

'I am not the man I used to be, Keziah. I suspect this country changes you – if it doesn't kill you. But even in the desert when I thought every day would be my last, I was never bored. At Home everything bored me – Cambridge, gambling, flirting with Father's hand-picked heiresses. It was as if my life only really began when I fell in love with you. That's why I kept searching until I found you.'

He hesitated. 'I have been forced to suspect that my hopes of winning your love are rather on a par with my search for the Inland Sea. In my arrogance I believed I would be the man to find it and make history. I was proved wrong. Am I also wrong about us? I am not sure I really want to hear your answer, Keziah, but I can't avoid the question. Have I lost you forever?'

Keziah said the words softly. 'I'm sorry to hurt you, Caleb.'

'It's that Andersen fellow, isn't it?'

'I can't help it. He's in my blood.'

Caleb stared at her for a long time. At last he took from his breast pocket a legal document sealed with red wax. Keziah flinched, preparing for the next round in the battle.

'No need to fear me, Keziah. You are too proud to accept help from me, but please remember I am at your service should you ever need me. I don't fancy living alone in the Sydney townhouse I intended for the three of us. I've a mind to go to Melbourne Town to take up land, but you'll always be able to contact me through your lawyer friend Joseph Bloom. I have instructed him to set up this trust fund for Gabriel.'

He placed the document on the table then bowed farewell. At the door he gently touched her lips with his finger to prevent her saying the word he could not bear to hear. *Goodbye.*

With mixed feelings Keziah watched him ride away, his shoulders slumped. But by the time he reached the gates of Ironbark Farm his back had straightened, as if ready to face the road to a new unknown adventure.

The table had been set for two all morning. Keziah interrupted her baking, drawn to the window in anticipation of something important. Her heart leapt at the sight of Jake riding Horatio. When he dismounted she saw there was something particularly purposeful about the way he swaggered towards her cottage.

When he entered Keziah was busy removing a cake from the oven. She assumed an air of calm to disguise her anxiety. She must never lie to Jake, but must she tell him the *whole* truth about Caleb? No, she decided, not while everything is hanging in the balance.

Despite Jake's swagger she sensed how nervous he was. A bruise over one eye was evidence of a recent fight. The word around Ironbark was that he'd won a whole string of prize fights lately, as though his life depended on raising money.

His first question was deceptively casual. 'Where's Gabe?'

'Nerida's taken him and Murphy out for the day to teach them how to gather bush tucker. It's a big treat for Gabriel to sleep with them in Nerida's *goondie* tonight.'

Keziah had tried to match his nonchalance, hoping the fact that she would be alone tonight had registered with Jake. It had.

Jake glanced at her best china, laid out for two. 'Did you see me coming in your funny cards, Kez? Or are you expecting to entertain that flash bloke Morgan?'

'I don't see *everything* ahead of time, Jake. What brings you here? Your note didn't say.'

'Been offered a contract to go to the Swan River settlement,' he said. 'If things pan out, I won't be coming back.'

Keziah felt almost overwhelmed by panic. Wasn't Swan River thousands of miles away on the western side of the continent? And who was the 'someone' his note said was travelling with him?

'You know I'll always wish you well,' Keziah said evenly. She saw they'd reached a stalemate so in desperation she tried a different tack.

'Mac Mackie told me you and Caleb had a barney at Leslie Ross's Trafalgar celebration. Is that how you scored that colourful bruise?'

'No. I got paid for this one. I won in three rounds. Enough to finish paying Bran for a new wagon he's been building me.'

Jake kept fiddling with the brim of his hat. 'That Morgan bloke talks big. Says he can pull strings, get your marriage to Dan annulled. Marry you. Make Gabriel his heir. That right?'

'That's what he's offered.'

'Good bloke,' Jake said casually. 'You couldn't do better.'

'Doubt if I could,' she agreed. *Mi-duvel! What's he really saying, I can't read him.*

After a lengthy pause Jake forced himself to ask, *'And?'*

Keziah made him wait. 'I should seriously consider his offer. For Gabriel's sake.'

Jake seemed to lose his place in his speech.

'So what are you waiting for? Him being Gabe's father – well, he is, isn't he?'

Keziah chose her words with care, trying to ignite a spark of jealousy.

'Caleb is an honourable man. Handsome, too. My marriage to him would give Gabriel an important family name and a fine education.' She watched Jake's jaw tighten. 'But I believe a man deserves to be loved for himself, not for his money and high position in society.'

'Well yeah, I reckon!'

Keziah asked the question as if from polite interest. 'Did you only come to say goodbye, Jake? Or is there something else on your mind?'

Jake searched the walls as if for clues to guide him. 'We're mates, Kez, so I don't want to be guilty of misleading you. You're a good woman but even if you were free, I could never marry you.'

Keziah gasped. 'Did I propose to you?'

Jake waded in. 'Listen, there's ten bloody good reasons I'm dead wrong for you.'

'Only *ten*, Jake?' she asked sweetly.

'I go on drunken binges when the going gets tough. I've done time in gaol and I've often been thrown in the lockup for brawling.'

'Ah well, you're just a man after all,' she said.

'Gets worse,' he promised. 'I go to a brothel to avoid having my own woman.'

'You're single, so that's your business, but just between mates, did you visit those girls when you were living with Jenny?'

'Hell, no! I was a family man!' He quickly recovered his ground. 'I worked my guts out for Jenny. Lost the lot, wife, child, farm. No woman will ever shackle me again!'

Keziah tried to look amiable. 'The roving life suits you perfectly. But that's only four reasons. What are the others?'

Jake shuffled. In broken phrases he told her how he'd rescued Pearl from a convent where Jenny's fancy man had abandoned her.

'She's only seven years old for God's sake. Nobody wants her.' Jake looked her straight in the eye. 'From now on Pearl and me are a team – it's a case of love me, love my daughter.'

Keziah reached out to touch his hand, her heart in her eyes. 'She's a lucky little girl but I warn you, you'll have your work cut out. I've seen seven children in your palm.'

She knew that Jake was almost cornered when he yelled, 'Listen, will you! A divorce or annulment needs a bloody Act of Parliament – only the filthy rich like Morgan can swing it. The best I could hope for is a judicial separation on the grounds of Jenny's adultery, but that would expose her as a fraud. I promised in a weak bloody moment I'd never do that, so long as I can keep Pearl. I'll never be free to marry any woman while Jenny's alive!'

Keziah shrugged. 'That's the way the world goes. Daniel needed a wife to gain his freedom. Caleb could get that marriage annulled.' She looked him in the eye. 'Because Daniel never consummated our marriage.'

'No?' Jake couldn't conceal his pleasure but Keziah saw he was quick to come up with another excuse.

'All our kids would legally be bastards.'

'Only under *gaujo* law. Not *my* law,' she said firmly.

She sensed Jake was at last cornered, forced to reveal his agonising secret.

'Listen to me, Kez! My whole marriage I failed my wife as a man. I just can't do it with a good woman.'

Keziah had to think fast. Any minute Jake would be out the door charging across the continent to the Swan River. She had run out of arguments to stall him, but her voice was honeyed with empathy.

'Why were you afraid to tell me?'

Jake walked straight into her web. 'Tell you what?'

'That you'd prefer to share your life with a man.'

'What?'

'Daniel went to Sydney Town to study art, but you are the true reason he left me. He really loves you. He was afraid of losing your friendship if you knew the truth about him.'

Jake was stunned. 'Jesus wept! I don't believe it!'

'Don't be embarrassed, Jake. None of us can help who we love.'

Jake bellowed like a bull. 'Don't you understand one bloody thing I've said to you?'

Keziah saw the anxiety in his eyes and remembered her grandmother's words. *'Inside a little girl she is a woman. Inside a man he is always a little boy.'*

She grew serious. The games were over. Her words were gentle.

'There's only one thing wrong with you, Jake. You *think* you can only have fun in bed with a prostitute. You're afraid to have fun with a good woman because you *respect* her.'

Jake felt utterly exposed. More naked than the day he was born. It was one thing to have confided his greatest fear to Lily Pompadour – and paid her to teach him how to fix it. It was quite another for Keziah to talk so calmly about his history of failures in bed. *Jesus wept. Is nothing private? Can't I hide a bloody thing from this woman?*

Keziah had her back to him. 'Tell me, Jake, what on earth made you think *I* was a good woman?'

When Keziah turned to face him Jake thought he was reliving that night she'd saved his life by exposing her breasts to One Eye's gang. No. It was happening right now. She swayed towards him as if in a tribal mating dance. She dropped her blouse to the floor, clutching her long skirt. Then she extended her open palm to beckon him.

'You prefer to buy "a wife for the night"? Pay me in advance. *Buy me*, Jake!'

'Stop this, you cruel little bitch!'

What Keziah did next stunned him. In the same way she had tamed the brumby, she placed a lump of sugar under her arm to absorb the heat of her body. Holding his gaze, she placed the sugar in his mouth.

'Don't be afraid of me, Jake.'

'God help me, Kez. I'd die for you! But I can never make love to you!'

But even as he said the words, Jake felt strength flood every organ of his body.

'You're trouble! A man's crazy to take you on.'

He ignored his own advice. Their lovemaking began in a rough, hungry tussle. Each awkward movement led one step closer to the bed. He knew that the kisses they fought to give and take were a battle of wills. Tearing his mouth from hers, his hands shook with nerves.

'I warn you, Kez. Give yourself to me and I'll make it so good you'll want more, but I'm leaving you tomorrow no matter what.'

Her chin rose in defiance. 'Give yourself to *me* for one night and you'll crawl across the Nullarbor Plain to get back to me!'

'Don't put your money on that!' He picked her up like a bag of chaff and tossed her onto the bed. He was quick to unbuckle his belt. 'This is a big mistake!'

'You won't say that in the morning!' she yelled, struggling to yank off his boot.

They were noisy, clumsy, angry, tender and hot with passion – at one and the same time. Then as if responding to an inner cue of music, they were suddenly locked in tune with the magic of their bodies – so long denied.

Jake knew he could never carry her as his bride across a threshold. He did the reverse and carried her outside and laid her on his swag under the stars.

He gestured to the night sky. 'I'm giving you everything that belongs to me. My Southern Cross and my Milky Way.'

Keziah knelt at his feet. 'What more can any man give me?'

He looked down at her upturned face, her lush body. His throat so constricted that he was glad when Keziah used her words to mirror his thoughts.

'Your body is beautiful, Jake.'

'Took you long enough to notice,' he said.

She invited his mouth to explore her. 'Don't get too cocky,' she warned.

'Why not? I've got what every bloke for miles around has been fighting to get his hands on.'

'It's you I want, Jake. It's always been you – even when I didn't know it!'

At that moment Jake didn't even care if that was the truth.

Keziah played the exotic Romani to the hilt. 'Give me one night and I'll make you forget Jenny ever existed.'

They were like two equally matched prize fighters. Jake fought to keep the balance of power, drawing on every trick he knew. He made her laugh, he made her wait, he made her beg him.

Long before dawn came they both knew. They had found it. That rare thing shared between lovers when the scales of love and lust are in perfect balance.

Startled by what he had released in her, Jake watched Keziah sleep. He had always known there were two kinds of women – fallen women and good women. Keziah was neither and yet she was both. He felt off balance, in unknown erotic territory.

One image of Keziah kept going around in his head. That look of joy he had created in her face. Before dawn broke he rolled her over to sit astride his hips then lay watching her, his arms crossed beneath his head. Keziah looked like a naked ship's figurehead riding the high seas with the stars filtered through her wind-blown hair. The figurehead threw her arms wide as she thrust her breasts and her joyous cry into the face of the wind.

As Keziah feigned sleep she thanked *The Del* for masking her fears. She had not lain with a man in four and a half years. In a single night Jake had liberated her and allowed her wild passion to meet his controlled passion headlong. As she lay in the slate-grey darkness she watched the shadowy outline of his body backlit by the tracery of firelight.

'Am I asking too much of you?' he asked softly. She answered without words.

Under the cover of darkness he whispered into her hair. 'Promise me only one thing, Kez. If you want to leave me, say it to my face. Don't let me come back to find you gone.'

'I am not Jenny,' she promised.

At first light Keziah rolled into the warm hollow of the swag to find she was alone. Jake was nearby leaning against an ironbark tree dressed for the road. His expression was odd.

'Forgive me, Kez. You have to let me go. Try and stay out of trouble, will you? I'll be back soon. You know you can always count on me to protect you from men.'

Keziah was confused. 'What men? What are you saying?'

Jake knelt down and wrapped the blanket around her to keep her warm, although she didn't need it. As he kissed her the heat coursed through her. Her body could never lie.

His voice was tender, teasing. 'You can't help yourself. Can't stop me, can you?'

Her arms locked around his neck. 'Why on earth would I *want* to stop you?'

'I understand you. You're a good woman but vulnerable. You *want* to be faithful.'

She sat bolt upright. 'What are you saying? That because I betrayed Gem I'll betray you? You think Romani women are easy!'

'No! Of course not, but you've got to admit you Romani women are different.'

'We're passionate, but you mean *weak*, don't you? Is that what you think of *me*?'

He desperately tried to pacify her. 'Calm down, Kez. I only meant I'll always protect you from yourself.'

'From *myself*?' she screamed.

The flood of anger and shame she had dammed back since childhood broke free. A lifetime of *gaujo* taunts – *dirty, liar, thief, prostitute* – mixed with her personal legacy of shame as the daughter of Stella the Whore. She flayed into Jake with the strength of a madwoman. Jake blocked the whirlwind of her punches, but *baxt* landed a freak punch in his ribs. Another in his groin doubled him over in agony.

Neither of them listened to their overlapping tirade of accusations.

'Do you think I roll over like a puppy for any man?' Keziah screamed. 'No man touches me unless I *want* him.' Her laughter mocked him. 'No problem with Daniel – he fancied *you* more than me!'

Jake stumbled off clutching his groin. As he mounted Horatio he yelled back over his shoulder. 'Do me a favour. I'm sick of fighting blokes to protect you. Stay out of my hair!'

As he rode away she retaliated like an hysterical child. 'Who needs a man who hides in a brothel?'

Her vision cleared. Nerida and the children stared open-mouthed from the *goondie*. Keziah wrapped her naked body in the blanket, trying to hold onto the last skerrick of dignity she could muster.

Hunched in the saddle, Jake disappeared over the horizon.

CHAPTER 41

The distant clanging of the Ironbark Chapel bell sounded to Jake Andersen as ominous as if it heralded Doomsday.

Lying on a stretcher bed on the back veranda of Bran's forge house, he cursed the bell for fracturing his sleep, then remembered he must now learn to harness his language – Pearl was asleep in the alcove room only a few feet away.

But the truth was Jake was mortified. The Doc had strapped bandages around his chest. Although he had fought the toughest blokes in the colony with all his bones intact, that crazy Romani woman had managed to give him a cracked rib. He'd lied to Leslie Ross that his opponent had been a bullocky. There were some things a bloke couldn't admit even to his best mates.

At the thought of Keziah he felt morose. Was their fight her fault – or his? For years he had built a shield of mateship between them to protect himself from falling for her. When he finally found the courage to get her into bed it had been the greatest night in his entire life. Keziah was sheer magic. So how had the whole thing ended up cockeyed? One bloody careless word from him had sent her raving mad. As he slapped at the blowflies that were drawn to his liniment-soaked bandages, he tried to piece together exactly what *he* had said and what *she* had said. None of it made sense.

He accepted he had unwittingly damaged Keziah's pride and insulted the entire race of Romani women, but she'd ranted so wildly, he'd had no chance to unveil his big plans for them.

At the sound of Pearl's little feet padding across to the cookhouse Jake's anger was tempered by resignation. *The fight was my fault. I wasn't cut out to handle good women. And only God would know what goes on inside a Romani woman's head – if there* is *a god.*

Today was the day the *vardo* would be finished. As Jake drank the tea Pearl had made him, she watched him like an anxious little mother hen. He made all the right noises of approval.

'Best tea I've ever tasted in my entire life, Princess.'

When Pearl raced off unasked to make him a second pot, Jake again felt morose. Inwardly he decided that a door in his life had been slammed shut forever. That crazy Romani girl had done the unthinkable – left her brand on him. Jake had spent every penny of his prize money on his plan to share his life with her and their kids. Now that pipedream was totally destroyed. *I'm stuck with that bloody Romani wagon.*

He saw that Bran was restless to hear Jake's verdict on his work. Pearl pulled him outside to inspect it and Jake gave a long whistle of admiration. The *vardo* was a thing of beauty – the green and gold paintwork shone in the sun. Although the travelling house had not been occupied, it already seemed to have a life of its own – eager to taste the open road. Jake clapped Bran on the back.

'Bran, you're a ruddy genius. To think you built all this from a magazine picture!'

Jake held little Pearl by the hand as she skipped around the wagon, giggling with excitement. Bran basked in pleasure at their praise, but Jake saw that something was bothering him. It took time to piece the story together. Bran had overheard Griggs, Hobson's overseer, boasting that Mrs Browne was clearing out of Ironbark. She'd left Big Bruce in charge of the schoolhouse and was packed up ready to go.

'Right, so she's bolting again, is she?'

Pearl looked so anxious that Jake made an effort to control his anger. He let down the back steps of the *vardo* and ceremoniously helped his daughter to enter inside. 'You can be my first passenger, girlie.'

Pearl frowned at the edge in his voice when he added, 'We've got business that can't wait.'

Keziah nailed the lid on the final packing case and sank down on top of it, close to tears. The schoolteacher's cottage was empty except for her packed boxes and valise. This was the dreaded moment when she must leave behind the secure life she had lived as Saranna. She was shaken by the pain of her memories.

Stripped of its bedding, her iron bedstead was a skeletal frame. The bed where she had slept alone and dreamt her dreams. The bed where Gem had returned to stay the night with her but deserted her forever. Where she had cradled Daniel on their wedding night, bleeding from his 'stripes' inflicted by the Devil Himself. Above all it was the bed where she and Jake had begun the magical night of love they had played out under the stars.

She felt consumed with shame for dishonouring her promise to him. If Jake came looking for her he would find another empty house, betrayed by another woman. Was she no better than Jenny Andersen? Or Stella the Whore? They were mere *gaujos*. She was a Romani woman. It was despicable to betray her Rom – even a man who was hers for only a single night.

Suddenly aware that Gabriel was waving his hands in front of her eyes to attract her attention, she patted his head. 'I'm here, Gabriel.'

She dressed for travelling in her most sedate schoolteacher's costume and buttoned her blouse to her chin. Pulling her hair into a chignon, she covered it with the new style of bonnet made fashionable by the young Queen Victoria. Shaped like a coal scuttle tied with ribbons under the chin, it hid her hair except for the flat curls on her forehead. No visual trace remained of her true identity, except for her legacy from Stella the Whore – her eyes.

The sound of the brumby's whinny sent her racing to the door, surprised to discover it heralded Jake's arrival on foot.

'Where's Horatio?' she asked.

Jake ignored her. His shirt was open and she blushed to see the evidence of her attack. He swaggered up the steps as arrogantly as his bandaged chest would allow.

Propped against the veranda railing he unfolded his pouch and began to shred tobacco as if he had all the time in the world. Finally he cast a steely glance her way.

'That's a bloody silly bonnet. Makes you look like a maiden aunt.'

'I dress to please myself.'

His eyes issued a challenge. 'Bran told me you're bolting. Want a lift somewhere?'

'Thank you, no. I've made all my own arrangements.'

'You're off to Melbourne Town to join Caleb Morgan, eh?'

'My plans are my business.'

Jake jerked his head in the direction of Nerida's *goondie*. 'Yeah? What about Nerida and Murphy? Just going to dump them, are you?'

Keziah felt defensive. 'I've left Nerida money. I'll send for them when I get to wherever I end up.'

'Never crossed your mind Nerida might want a life of her own?'

'What do you mean? She's been happy with me.'

'Yeah? I ran into Sunny Ah Wei. First time I ever saw the bloke look miserable. He wants to do right by Nerida. Get her churched. Take her to Maitland to open a store.'

'I thought Nerida didn't want him!'

'Well, now you know. She does but Nerida's too bloody loyal to leave you. Thinks you can't take care of yourself properly. She's dead right.' He turned. 'Ain't you, Neri?'

Nerida stood waiting with Murphy to say goodbye. When Keziah ran to her, their tears were flowing as they embraced.

'Nerida, you're the friend of my life! Choose your *own* happiness. Sunny's a good man. Go with him if you want him. I know in my heart we'll never lose touch with each other.'

'Sunny not Wiradjuri.' Nerida looked in the direction of her tribal country. 'But he promise he bring me back my country plenty time.'

Keziah knew there were layers of anguish inside Nerida that no one but her own people could share.

Nerida stroked Keziah's nose in the gentle way Aboriginal mothers aroused their children from sleep. 'Now you wake up good, Saranna. See best fella for you!'

In perfect imitation of Jake, Nerida mimicked his cocksure grin as she swaggered a few steps like a Currency Lad, then grinned at Jake over her shoulder as she walked away. Clearly Jake had won Nerida's vote. Keziah saw Jake had no intention of letting her off the hook.

'So you were going to shoot through and leave me to find the place empty. That's what a Romani promise is worth, is it?'

'I was trying to decide if I was brave enough to say goodbye to you.'

'And?' Jake's eyes locked with hers sending the clear message. *You'll break before I will, girl.*

Keziah finally cracked. 'I knew once I saw you I'd never want to leave you.'

She held her breath. Would Jake back down? Or was he like Gem, too proud to forgive her?

Jake concentrated on rubbing the tobacco he had no intention of smoking. *Poor little bugger's dying of shame. But she's got me between a rock and a hard place. If she takes two steps towards me I'll drag her into the bush and rip those starchy clothes off her. If I do, I'll lose her forever. How the hell do I give her back her bloody Romani pride?*

Keziah did take two steps towards him.

'Hold it right there, lady!' Jake said amiably. 'You landed a couple of lucky punches last bout we fought. Don't push your luck! I've never hit a woman in my life, it's beneath my dignity as a man, but I ain't no gentleman. If you hit me below the belt again,' he added the words like a caress, 'I'll flatten you, love.'

Keziah said stiffly, 'I owe you an apology.' She blushed and looked away.

'That's *it*, is it?'

The words he needed went totally against the grain, but he had to say them or lose her.

'Don't expect *me* to apologise for what I said about men. I'm a man myself. You can't trust any of us buggers. I'll do my damnedest to protect you from other blokes. But …' He let the word hang in the air. 'I'd trust *you*, Kez, with my life.'

Keziah was crying all over his shirt as her shame was washed away with the salt of her tears.

'The truth is, Jake, I'm not always as wise as I want to be but I'm not as weak as you're afraid I am. And I'm yours if you want me.'

Jake took his time to digest that invitation. He allowed her body to press against his but kept his grip on the veranda posts, his knuckles white with the effort not to touch her.

'How about this for a deal?' he offered. 'I don't expect you to forget Gem. He's part of you – always will be. Understand this. I refuse to share you. Throw in your lot with me and every day you can be your own woman. Teach school, train horses, do your herbal magic. Any bloody thing you want, but every night when the first stars come out in the sky – then you're *my* woman.' He added gently, 'And I'm warning you. I'm *very* demanding.'

'YES!' Keziah sent her bonnet sailing through the air and her wild hair tumbled down. But right at the moment Jake reached out to claim her, Gabriel appeared in the doorway with the plaintive cry that he was hungry.

Jake muttered under his breath. 'So am I, mate, so am I.'

Keziah gave Gabriel bread and cheese and offered to feed Jake. He knew that even when packed ready to bolt she would manage to put a fine meal together. He declined. He had just released an uncomfortable degree of emotion, and there was one remaining thing he had planned for days. He took a red ribbon from his pocket.

'Do you know what this ribbon means, Gabe? Your mama told me it's a Romani custom. When a baby boy is born his father ties a red ribbon round his son's neck. To show the world he's proud his son belongs to him.'

Jake lifted Gabriel's chin and tied the red ribbon. 'So this means I'm now your father. Always. And you're my little Rom.'

Gabriel was wide-eyed. 'Do I wear it *all* the time?'

He hid a smile. 'No, mate. Just till the sun goes down tonight.'

Jake didn't dare look at Keziah, but out of the corner of his eye he saw the tears streaming down her face. He carried Gabriel in his arms and strode down the track to the place where he had stowed the *vardo*. He turned to gauge Keziah's reaction – his reward.

Keziah's cry was so passionate the horses became restless. The green and gold *vardo* was a work of art. A tiny metal chimney peeped through the bow-topped green roof. Two diamond-paned windows framed the rear door. She recognised Daniel's artwork. At the heart of the gilt scrollwork was a rampant wild horse. The brumby.

With a flourish Jake unfolded the steps between the back wheels. Gabriel clambered inside and closed the door but they could hear his jubilant cries of discovery.

Keziah cried as though her heart would break. Jake looked helpless as he held her.

'Jesus wept, woman. Does this mean you *like* it?'

'It's the most beautiful *vardo* in the world. If you let me share it with you, Jake Andersen, I swear By My Father's Hand I'll never ever leave you!'

Jake studied her for a long moment. 'Not even if I *beg* you to go?'

The sound of two sets of giggles inside the *vardo* startled Keziah. 'Who else is in there?'

Jake kept a straight face. 'I guess that'd be my daughter, Pearl.'

'Why didn't you introduce me?'

'Didn't think I had to. You're psychic, ain't you?' he teased.

Jake watched Keziah climb into the *vardo* and kneel down to bring her eyes level with Pearl's face. 'I'm so happy your papa found you, Pearl.'

When Pearl shrank back with a suspicious expression Keziah covered the rejection by extending a hand to each child. 'Come and help your papa. As soon as we load the wagon we're all going off to share a great adventure!'

The sun shone and the breeze fanned their faces as they travelled along a meandering back track that Jake assured them was less likely to attract bushrangers than the open road. Keziah sat on the front seat with the two children sandwiched between her and Jake. Horatio clopped along as though he'd been born to draw a Romani *vardo*. The brumby, Sarishan and Pony followed behind them.

Pieces of Keziah's life flashed before her eyes with the speed of Tarot cards dealt out by some magical sleight of hand.

Why was I so blind? Gem was my Rom but he could never forgive me. Daniel loved me like a sister. Caleb wanted to pass me off as a fine lady in society – if I forfeited my soul. Jake's a gaujo *who believes in nothing. Yet he above all men respects 'my weird Romani laws'. Now he's built this* vardo *to give me back my lost Romani life!*

When she caught Jake's eye she stroked the timber of the *vardo* as lovingly as if she was caressing his body.

Jake said nothing. Just gave her a funny look, half proud, half embarrassed.

She was conscious of how nervous Pearl was of her and sensed it would be difficult to win the little girl's trust. Jenny's desertion had left deep scars on her psyche, just as it had on Jake.

In the wilds of the bush Jake drew to a halt. Ahead of them at a lonely crossroads was a handmade signpost.

Keziah tried to read Jake's odd expression as he stared at the scene.

The setting sun highlighted a rusty gate that opened onto an abandoned farm. No fence, just a metal gate between rickety posts. A derelict timber cabin leaned drunkenly against a magnificent red gum. The rays of the sun washed the grey trunk like a topcoat worn over dappled shades of pink, red and brown.

Jake seemed to be searching for the right words. Keziah came to his rescue.

'Your land, is it?'

'Yeah. Won it from a bloke in a poker game. One hundred and thirty acres. Of course you won't catch me farming it. No land will ever tie me down like it did Pa.'

'No, of course not.'

'But it's not a bad bit of dirt.'

Keziah knew that this was the offhand Currency way to say the soil was very fertile.

'Horses,' she said. 'I see magnificent thoroughbreds everywhere.'

There wasn't a single horse in sight apart from the four that travelled with them. Despite Sarishan's clandestine lineage, Jake couldn't openly lay claim to his thoroughbred descent.

'I'll be buggered. Only last week I ordered a couple of Ogden's fillies for breeding next season – you couldn't have known!'

'Gem placed Sarishan in your care. Same bloodline as Ogden's champion. I always knew you'd breed thoroughbreds one day. You have the gift.'

Jake looked pleased. He pointed to the sliver of creek running through the heart of his land.

'That's a good spot to stop for the night and feed the kids. I'm taking you on a bit of an adventure beyond Argyle county. Then maybe we'll come back here and breed horses.'

Keziah smiled at the sound of the children arranging which bunks they'd sleep in. 'That's two. Five more children to come. Don't say I didn't warn you.'

Jake's voice was husky. 'The first stars are out. After you've done that motherly stuff and tucked them up in bed, I'm giving *you* fair warning – better not pretend you're too tired.'

'Never!' she said as she rested her head on his shoulder, her hand high on his thigh.

Keziah needed to cling to the belief that *Shon* would always be there for her in the phases of the moon that waxed and waned in Jake's sky. She suspected *baxt* had something in store that was so extraordinary it made her shiver. Jake asked her if she was cold.

'No, a goose just walked over my grave.'

Jake wasn't fooled for a minute. 'The last time you said that I drove my coach over Blackman's Leap. You think you know what's going to happen? And you're not afraid?'

'I'll take whatever comes.'

Jake ruffled her hair. 'I'm not sorry you're tagging along.' It was the best he could do. It was enough. He looked across at the rough signpost standing at the junction of the tracks. He had made it himself when a royal flush had won him the property.

'That marks the miles to Melbourne Town, Berrima, Gunning, Goulburn and Sydney Town. Some wag added "London twelve thousand miles as the crow flies. New York – God only knows."' Jake offered a challenge. 'If you're so bloody clever, which road am I going to take tomorrow?'

'I can't see *everything*.'

Jake's mouth wasn't smiling but his eyes were. 'For all you know I might be taking you to the Swan River Colony or Timbuktu. Aren't you curious?'

Keziah looked into eyes that held the love Jake refused to put into words.

'No, my Rom. If you are going there then that's the right road.'

Part III
The Trial

January 1842 – December 1844

Laws are like spiders' webs. They hold the weak and delicate who are caught in their meshes but are torn in pieces by the rich and powerful.

Plutarch, *Parallel Lives*

CHAPTER 42

The New Year that fell in the high summer of 1842 was a golden odyssey for Jake Andersen and his new family. They were living an enchanted life, one as close to Keziah's Romani childhood as Jake could give her.

Although carefree on the surface, Jake was aware how low his finances were. The colony's boom years were over. The properties they passed had nothing to offer itinerant workers. One major source of income he had depended on had dried up. Terence Ogden had always given Jake well-paid work whenever he wanted it, but now Ogden had sailed off to Cornwall for an indefinite period, clearly relieved to distance himself from his nagging wife but sad to leave his thoroughbred horses. Until his return Ogden Park was being run by an arrogant English manager who, despite Ogden's instructions to the contrary, refused to employ Currency Lads.

Jake was only half resigned to the loss of his other source of ready money.

As they drove along a remote track with no sign of civilisation, Keziah laid down the law about prize fights. Jenny had loved watching him fight, but Keziah could never forget her father had died after a fight in prison.

She confronted him with angry tears. 'If you fight again I'll leave you!'

'Hey, I'm always last man standing. Well, most of the time.'

'I don't care. What if you get badly injured! I'd rather be poor for the rest of my life than see you bruised and bloodied.'

'All right! No more fights,' Jake reluctantly promised her. 'What the hell does money matter anyway?'

They were driving along with Horatio at the helm of their *vardo*, their beautiful horses, Sarishan, the brumby and Pony, trailing behind them. Jake always chose to meander down bush tracks out of sight of villages. He was keen to dodge the roving muster team whose statistics would expose his unofficial custody of Pearl. Privately he wouldn't have put it past Jenny to threaten to put the traps on his tail unless he forked out more money, but he dismissed that possibility in cavalier style. Keziah didn't need any help from him to fear the law. This time she must have read his mind.

'Are we likely to run across the muster team out here?'

'Stop worrying, love. Our irregular liaison ain't a problem. Caleb Morgan has done the decent thing and stopped pressing his legal claim to Gabe.'

'Yes, but his father was the real villain. I can't see John Morgan happy to accept his grandson being reared by what he sees as a Gypsy thief. I'll have to keep on being Saranna Browne and you know what that means if we're caught openly travelling together.'

Jake tried to laugh away her fears about *gaujo* law. 'Nonsense. Half the marriages in the colony come under the label of co-habitation. What do the lawyers call it? *De facto.* Look at how many big-wig politicians, army officers and doctors openly live with their mistresses and raise cartloads of kids. Nobody much gives a damn. We mightn't get invited to dine at the gov's table, but will you lose any sleep over that? Relax. Enjoy the scenery. The only decision we need to face is where are the fish biting?'

'You know I don't need my Tarot for that. We'll never go hungry with you as head of the family. You live off the land as well as any Rom.'

Jake grinned his thanks at her compliment. It amused him to admit that despite the years he had adamantly forsworn sharing his life with a good woman, he basked in the role of patriarch. By day he allowed Keziah the illusion she was boss of the camp until sundown when he turned the tables. By night she was totally his woman, ardently responsive and as eager as he was to make up for lost time. Their lovemaking was unpredictable – imaginative, teasing, gentle and romantic or hot and lusty.

They stopped the wagon for Keziah to set up the children's school lessons. Jake saw how she delighted in teaching two bright, receptive little students. Sister Mary Bridget had taught Pearl well. Despite poor eyesight, her reading and writing were so fluent Gabriel worked doubly hard to catch up to her. In their open-air classroom Keziah wrote new words on his slate.

'This isn't a competition, Gabriel. We all have our own special gifts and we learn at our own pace.'

Jake took elaborate care to conceal his own semi-literate state, but he chose to work in close proximity to their lessons, covertly learning along with the children.

It was Pearl's first encounter with a boy. Jake watched her studying Gabriel as if he was a little alien who strutted and aped Jake's mannerisms. It pleased Jake to see how his new son had also absorbed his own protective attitude to women. When Pearl tried to move boxes, Gabriel stepped in.

'Here, that's too heavy. I'll do it for you.'

But Jake could see that although Keziah tried her best, Pearl remained wary of her. Jenny had cast a long shadow over all their lives.

That night when the children settled down in the wagon, whispering on the brink of sleep, Jake lay beside the campfire with his head in Keziah's lap. Aware that something had been on her mind for days, he decided to corner her.

'What's up?'

'Nothing.'

He sat up and tenderly bit her ear. 'That's bull, Kez.'

Jake knew how to still her fears. He made love to her long and hard.

Afterwards he lay with her in his arms under the stars. He was ready to sleep. The problem was Keziah was ready to talk.

'You don't feel for me what you felt for Jenny, do you?'

'No. Thank Christ.'

He immediately regretted his lack of tact when he saw the flash of jealousy that pride forbade her to admit. He hated being forced to put his feelings into words.

'What I felt for Jenny was like a sickness. With you I'm a whole man again. It's like – you're the other half of my body.' He baulked at the word 'love'. 'If that isn't *it*, what is?'

Keziah was blunt. 'I'll bet you never spilt your seed on the ground with Jenny.'

'Ah, so that's it.' He sighed. 'I know what you want, Kez. When the Depression's over I'll start giving you those other five little ones you reckon you can see in my palm. Till then it's my job to take care of you the best way I can. Understand?'

It was clear to him Keziah did *not*.

Jake's luck finally ran out. He drove around a bend in a remote stretch of bush to find a cluster of troopers a few hundred yards ahead interviewing a family outside a farmhouse; the muster team in action.

He turned to Keziah and barked the order. 'Do as I tell you. Don't argue! Get Pearl and Gabe out of the back of the wagon quick smart. Keep them out of sight in the bush. I'll bluff my way through the muster then come back for you when it's safe.'

Keziah sprang into action and smuggled the children into the bush when the troopers' backs were turned.

Jake drove the *vardo* up at a leisurely pace and gave them a lazy salute. 'Good day, Sergeant. Want the story of my life for the gov's records?'

The sergeant gave him a hard-eyed look. 'Name? Bond or free?'

'Jakob Isaac Andersen. I'm Currency. Doesn't it show?'

'Don't get smart with me. Just answer my questions. Married or single?'

'Married. My wife bolted but she did me a big favour.'

The trooper wrote down the details. 'Any issue?'

'One daughter. In a convent.' Jake tried to look sad. 'Wish she was with me.'

'Religion?'

'Ma's Catholic, Pa's Lutheran. Reckon I'm on an each-way bet to get into heaven.'

Jake suspected the trooper had never cracked a smile in his entire life.

'You own any land, Andersen? Or just squatting on Crown land?'

'Mine, fair and square. A hundred and thirty acres. None under cultivation. No house, no sheep, no cattle. Yet.'

'Good bit of horseflesh you got there. That black stallion looks familiar. You *buy* it?'

The inference was unmistakable. Horse theft could lead to the gallows.

'I see you've got an excellent eye for horses. That's Sarishan. I trained him. He won Terence Ogden's silver cup a few years back. See him win it, did you?'

The trooper circled the wagon suspiciously. 'Peculiar wagon you've got there. You're not a *Gypsy*, are you?'

'Nah! Won this thing in a game of cards.'

'Yeah? So what do I mark you down as? Farmer or card sharp?'

'Horse-breaker. You don't catch *me* being a farmer.'

Jake grinned to disguise how edgy he felt. If this snoopy trap looked inside the *vardo* he would discover Keziah's clothing and children's toys. Jake needed to distract him fast.

'Seeing as you're all done with me, do you fancy cracking a bottle of red?'

The trooper actually smiled. 'Reckon I won't say no.'

It was dark by the time Jake returned the *vardo* to where Keziah had hidden the children. When she emerged from the bush, furious, Jake tried to look innocent.

'What's wrong? I said I'd come back for you. What's for dinner?' he teased.

Sparks flew from Keziah's eyes. 'Easy for you to joke – sitting in the sun drinking grog with the traps. *You* try keeping two active children quiet in the one spot for three hours!'

Jake patted her on the head. 'You're a good girl, Kez. Hop in the wagon with the kids and I'll get a fire going and rustle you up some johnnycakes. Those traps have shot through to the next farm miles away.' He whispered in her ear, 'I'll make it up to you tonight, love!'

Keziah ushered the children inside then turned to him with a half-smile. 'You think that solves everything, don't you?'

His eyes wandered over her. 'It does for me!'

As the year slipped by like an idyllic island in time, divorced from news of the outside world, Jake saw no signs of the upturn in finances that he was counting on – along with every settler, stockman and swagman in the backblocks. Wherever they travelled paid work had dried up. They passed properties with weathered 'For Sale' notices, many of them mortgage foreclosures. Clearly no one had money to buy land or livestock. Jake retained his last small stash of cash against an emergency and continued to live off the land, but then came the day his prowess as a hunter failed.

The minute Keziah saw him shouldering the dead kangaroo she shrieked in horror.

'All right, calm down,' Jake called out. 'I'll get rid of it.'

He stomped around in the bush, swearing profusely until a shot succeeded in putting different game on the table. A rabbit. Over supper he tried to set things right.

'I thought you'd be sick of fish. Roos are good tucker. A bit like the

Brits' venison they tell me. Sure you don't want to try it sometime?'

Keziah was vehement. 'Not even if I'm starving! How can you live with me and not know me? Kangaroos are so beautiful, so free. Like horses!'

'Well! We all know how you Romanies feel about *them*. Horses sit on the right hand of God. You'd shoot *me* before you'd shoot a bloody horse.'

Her question was tricky. 'Aren't we going to make our living breeding horses?'

'What's this *we* business? I'm man enough to support my own family, thanks very much.' Her hurt look made him add, 'But you have a real way with horses, I'll grant you that. You can use your magic box of tricks when they're crook. And you're damned good at breaking in a wild colt as I have good reason to remember.'

Jake shot her a familiar look. 'I know what's for dinner. I shot it, but what are you giving me for "afters"?'

'A surprise. Something you've never had before.'

Jake's pulse was racing, but after supper the surprise wasn't quite what he'd counted on.

After she had tucked the children into their bunks, Keziah emerged wearing her best red dress, swathed in a silk shawl.

He put his glass aside. Keziah watched him intently from the far side of the campfire, as if she had some private celebration that she wanted to share with him. The firelight shadowed her face making her smile seem enigmatic. Jake realised the night was far from over.

'Hey, what are you up to now, Kez?'

She crossed towards him with great deliberation. Slowly, very slowly, she knotted her shawl low on her hips and began to clap her hands in a steady, insistent rhythm.

From deep in her throat came a song without words, like the sound of some primordial mating rite. She beckoned him to clap his own hands and Jake felt himself drawn to his feet to accompany her, giving her the beat for the staccato stamping of her feet, the clapping of her hands, the movements of her body growing stronger, faster.

Her eyes said it all. *Tonight there will be no barriers, Jake. No withdrawal. Tonight I will take you prisoner.*

Camped by the Wollondilly River, Jake worked up a sweat as he chopped wood, keeping Keziah in his sights but at a safe distance. During their sixteen months on the road the phases of the moon had become his guide to handling the wild pendulum swing of her moods. Normally she greeted the day with the spontaneity of a child, but every full moon she became downright irrational. Jake bore the full brunt of it, knowing it was beyond her control, the price he was willing to pay for her. Tonight it would be full moon so he kept his guard up.

Keziah descended on him with a washing basket on her head and angrily waved sheets of paper in his face. Jake leaned on his axe. *Jesus wept, here's trouble.*

'I won't live with a liar!' she yelled. 'You've kept these letters hidden ever since you picked up the mail at Goulburn Post Office. Mac Mackie says he's matched you against some visiting pugilist next week. You hypocrite! You won't let me read the Tarot to earn cash for us, but you were going to sneak back to Goulburn to fight for money!'

Cornered, Jake took the offensive. 'I'll tell you one thing for free. Jake Andersen's kids are never going to be fed by a woman who gets her palm crossed with silver in a public house. Not while I've got breath in my body!'

'And Keziah Stanley's Rom is never going to be battered to feed us while I've got breath in *my* body!'

They stood toe to toe like two dragons breathing fire at each other until Jake turned amiable. 'Fair enough.' He moved in on her with intent.

'No, you don't!' She waved the evidence in his face. 'What's this one about?'

'Oh *that*!' he said casually. 'It's from Joseph Bloom.'

'I know that. I can read. Why is this Lily Pompadour giving you all this money?'

Jake saw the fear in Keziah's eyes and stopped teasing. 'It's not like you think. I was full of hate after Jenny. Lily taught me what I know about women. She was tough on the outside but gentle at heart. Not like the other girls in Bolthole Valley.'

Keziah gasped. 'She was a whore?'

He snapped back at her. 'Any girl can be if she's hungry enough and her spirit is broken. Lily was meant to be a good woman. I won't hear different. I helped her clear out of Bolthole and start a new life. She must have done all right for herself in Melbourne Town. This money for a horse is her way of saying thanks.'

Keziah's mood changed like quicksilver. She handed back the letter. 'Forgive me, Jake. I'll never read your mail again.'

'Yes, you will. You're a woman,' he said. 'Can't help yourself.'

Keziah was contrite. 'A horse is the best gift in the world. Buy the finest thoroughbred money can buy.'

That night after Pearl and Gabriel were bedded down in the *vardo* Jake lay with Keziah under the stars. He admitted he *was* going to fight in Goulburn. The children needed new boots. He could repair them but he couldn't stop their feet from growing.

Keziah clung to him. 'Don't leave me, Jake! You won't come back! Remember that terrible white light with the tail we kept seeing crossing the sky. I warned you. That comet's a bad omen!'

Jake gently nuzzled her. 'Hey, just some shooting star. Your bad dreams and omens aren't real. *I'm* real, Kez. I'll camp you close to a settler's wife and be back before Gabriel has time to sing his way through *Rule, Britannia*. Now go to sleep. I'll keep the *mulos* away.'

Instead Jake had fallen instantly asleep. Keziah listened to the precious sound of his breathing as he slept beside her, but she was unable to banish the images from a recurring nightmare she had kept hidden from him. Horses. Rope. Blood. Fire. Guns. Jake's face behind the grid of a prison door.

Jake stirred beside her. 'What are you doing, Kez?'

'I'm listening to your breathing.'

'Well, let me know if I stop, right?'

She could barely manage a faint smile. The power of her nightmare refused to fade.

She awoke with a jolt when the sun was high in the sky. The children were eating porridge. She could smell the fresh damper Jake had baked in the ashes of the fire.

When Pearl gave her a tentative smile between her lank strands of hair, Keziah hoped it was a chink of light in their relationship. Keziah had still not won the little girl's trust, but Gabriel's natural intuition had sensed Pearl's insecurity and he'd become his new sister's ally. The two children ran off now to collect kindling. Jake always turned work into a game.

Keziah tried to think of fresh ways to forge a motherly bond with Pearl, plaiting the child's hair with ribbons to make her feel pretty. She was suddenly overcome by an acute sense of sadness when a jagged wave of pain shot through her belly. Had her body betrayed her once again? Her mouth dried with fear as she slipped her hand between her thighs.

'Jake, you must leave me alone.' She screened herself from his eyes. 'I'm bleeding.'

'Don't be silly. It's natural. I'll get clean rags for you.'

'No, Jake. I'm losing a baby.'

His face was blank with shock. 'Why in heaven's name didn't you tell me last night? I would have been more careful with you.'

'Don't be angry. It's nobody's fault, just nature's way.' She kept her voice low so as not to alarm the children. 'I didn't want to tell you yet. I wanted to hold on to you any way I could.'

She couldn't even cry.

For a moment Jake looked helpless then he made a move towards the horses. 'I'll fetch a doctor for you.'

'No. They can't do anything. Time must take its course. It's far too early.'

He knelt by her side and gripped her hand. 'Tell me what to do and I'll do it. You can count on me.'

'I know.' Her voice broke. 'I'm so sorry, Jake, I can't stop the bleeding, but fetch the valerian from my box. At least that will help me sleep.'

'And?'

'Can you keep the children happy?'

Jake nodded. A few moments later she heard his cheerful directions to them as if nothing was wrong.

'Listen you two. Put your sunhats on. I want to see a pile of kindling before the sun burns the skin off you. Pearl, you make sure Gabriel doesn't fall in the creek.'

Gabriel let out a bellow of hurt male pride. Jake silenced it. 'Gabriel, you make sure *Pearl* doesn't fall in the creek. If you drown you'll miss your swimming lesson tomorrow. Today you can read me a story but keep it quiet. Mama's tired.'

Jake came back and carried Keziah into the *vardo.* Slipping in and out of consciousness, she tried to garner her energy, willing her blood to stop flowing from her womb. Long ago she had lost Gem's babe. And then she had lost Gem. She desperately needed this babe to bind Jake to her forever. No matter what lay ahead.

She stirred at the sound of the children singing the alphabet. Gabriel piped up as he scratched his chalk across his slate, 'Papa, how do you spell "kangaroo"?'

'Easy. R-O-O.'

Keziah managed a faint smile as she slipped between the folds of sleep and pain.

The first stars were out when she heard Jake bedding the children beneath the wagon.

Without a word he lay beside her. Not as a husband, not as a lover, but as her mate watching over her. He stroked her hair as his scratchy voice sang *The Wild Colonial Boy* under his breath. His idea of a lullaby.

When Keziah woke in the night she saw that Jake had fallen asleep with one leg contorted in an awkward position against the wall as if even in his sleep he was trying to avoid waking her. One hand was entwined in her hair. The fingers of his other hand were splayed across her belly to protect the babe inside her.

It was at that precise moment Keziah realised she really understood the meaning of true love.

As soon as she woke in the morning Jake brought her strips of linen and a bowl of water. 'I'll sponge you, change your linen and wash everything in the creek.'

'No, Jake, no! A man must never see a Romani woman's blood. It is powerful magic! *It will bring you bad luck!*'

Jake cut across her rising note of hysteria. 'You know I've always respected your weird Romani laws, but right now I'm the only doc you've got. What's happening to you is more important than seeing a bit of blood. I'll take my chances on what *baxt* wants to chuck at me.'

Lying alone and exhausted while Jake went to the creek, Keziah saw in the doorway the filmy outline of a tiny girl with dark hair. The child gazed at her for several seconds then flickered in and out of the light, growing fainter each time until finally she disappeared.

Keziah cried in her heart but no tears fell. She knew it was all over.

She was alone when contractions delivered the tiny foetus. Inside her head she heard the echo of Patronella's curse. *'You will bury the child of your heart.'*

On Jake's return her voice was flat and dry. 'Bring me that clean bowl and my floral silk scarf. Dig a hole beside the black wattle tree, then come back.'

She said a Romani blessing for the soul of the babe whose time had not yet come. She knotted her scarf to cover the bowl, removed her gold earrings and handed them to Jake on his return.

'Bury these with her. And say your *gaujo* prayer. I've said mine.'

Jake said nothing. But Keziah knew he was wearing his grief inside.

Drained of all emotion, Keziah fell into a deep sleep, her head resting on the pillow of Jake's arm. For once she was unafraid of what tomorrow might bring.

For two weeks Jake cooked their meals, insisting she must rest. One night Keziah was woken in the darkness by an acute wave of nausea. Caught between sorrow and confusion, she was shocked to feel a wild surge of hope. Against all odds had a twin soul survived the quickening? Had one little soul given up its place to its brother? She clung to Jake as he slept but decided not to tell him until she was certain.

All through the night she whispered the Romani prayer for healing. *Please God, stand up for me and make me well.*

She sent up her silent plea from the highest point her soul could reach. *Mi-duvel, I beg you, let me give life to Jake's child.*

CHAPTER 43

Daniel Browne was light of heart as he carried a bottle of Hunter Valley wine under his arm, turning the corner into Elizabeth Street on his way home.

On his arrival in Sydney Town, a fellow artist, Dix, had given him free bed and board at his fine townhouse overlooking Hyde Park. Daniel appreciated the generous invitation but did not feel unduly guilty, knowing Dix lived off his family inheritance and was unaffected by the Depression. Daniel had soon realised that Dix's friendship had a price tag, but it seemed a price worth paying. He had never seen a house as richly decorated as this one, overflowing with foreign memorabilia and antiques that Dix had gathered during his grand tour of Europe. The attic was Daniel's private domain. It offered perfect northern light to paint, abundant room to stow his canvases and a comfortable bed. His portrait of Jake hung on the wall. Nothing else mattered to him.

He let himself in the front door and ran up the stairs two at a time to the first floor. Today he was elated on two counts. Julian Jonstone had recommended his work to a prominent government official, who had just paid Daniel for his portrait. He had also been commissioned to paint a beautiful lady of the Quality.

Bursting into the drawing room he playfully called out, 'Anyone home?' He expected Dix would be waiting for his return, concocting some exotic dish in the kitchen. Dix always played cook as a distraction whenever his own painting was giving him trouble – an occurrence that had increased in recent months.

'Hey, Dix, where are you hiding? I've got great news!'

'You called, Danny boy?' Dix emerged from the bedroom, pale and puffy-eyed. He tied the cord of his brocade dressing gown around his plump waistline. He looked distinctly out of sorts.

'You're home early, Danny boy. I understood your meeting was at four.'

'It was, but a messenger arrived early this morning when you were getting your beauty sleep. My interview was set up two hours earlier.'

Daniel helped himself to two crystal goblets and poured some wine.

'This is to celebrate! Thank God I've finished that politician's portrait. I've seen more attractive heads on merino rams. Still he was happy with it and paid quite well. Nice to know the Depression has left some of the landed gentry with plenty of money.'

Dix made no comment. Daniel gave an expansive wave of his hand.

'Now for my really great news. Through Jonstone I've been commissioned to paint a beautiful woman – the wife of Alfred Hamberton. I'm to have my first sitting with her tomorrow morning at their townhouse at Woolloomooloo Hill. Hamberton's newly arrived from Home, appointed a magistrate by the governor. It seems their wives are close friends. You know how these things work!'

Daniel kicked off his boots and spread himself out on the striped Regency lounge.

'Let's drink to my patron, God bless him. He's promised me my own exhibition next year.' Daniel laughed joyously. 'I'm so happy I could kiss Jonstone's boots.'

Without comment Dix sampled the wine. 'Just so long as said patron doesn't expect you to kiss his arse.'

Daniel was suddenly alert. He had grown used to living with Dix's mood swings, which fluctuated between generosity and jealousy. Daniel suspected the reasons were complex. Dix was a decade his senior, but had not yet made his mark as an artist. He had grown envious that Daniel had attracted a patron as important as Jonstone, the governor's friend, and never missed an opportunity to remind Daniel this patronage originated when Daniel was a convict.

Despite this undercurrent of artistic rivalry Daniel had expected a warmer reception.

'Have I done something to upset you, Dix? You surely know how grateful I am for your hospitality and your encouragement of my work.'

'Grateful? You have a funny way of showing it, m'boy. I ask so little of you in return for your being my *permanent* house guest, but lately you prefer to spend time with hangers-on who imbibe at my expense.'

Dix placed himself on the opposite chair as if to signify his hurt feelings.

Daniel tried to pacify him but his voice was cool. 'If it's a question of me paying my way, Dix, I'd much prefer to do that now that I have the means.'

Dix's voice rose an octave. 'Do you think you can pay me off for my kindness? Treat me like some old workhorse who's past his prime and can be put out to graze?'

Daniel leapt to his feet. 'Surely you know I have been a faithful friend!'

Dix gave a snort of disbelief.

'So, I can see you feel slighted. If you wish me to leave your house, come right out and say so.'

'Oh, so you're threatening me now you've been taken up by the Quality.' Dix's voice was almost a screech. 'Well don't expect it to last, Danny boy. We gentry are as fickle as hell.'

Daniel held up his hands in surrender. 'Today is my celebration. I have no wish to quarrel with you. Allow me to take you out to dine. Any banquet room or restaurant of your choice.'

Before Dix had a chance to reply, the bedroom door flew open. A naked young man emerged, with the kind of muscular body

Michelangelo might have painted. He sauntered across the room to the bathroom.

'Naughty, naughty,' he said in a mocking tone. 'Not nice to squabble, children.' He smiled at Daniel over his shoulder as he closed the door behind him.

Daniel suddenly felt as if the ground had shifted beneath him. He had never seen this youth before. He sank back onto the lounge and stared across at Dix, whose face was flushed with wine.

'Ah, now I have it,' Daniel said quietly. 'Attack is the best form of defence. You accuse *me* of disloyalty to cover up your own secret liaison. Tell me, Dix, is your little friend as inexperienced an artist as I was when you first took me under your roof?'

Dix looked smug. 'His pictures are daubs, but he is very talented where it matters.'

Daniel took his time to digest that news by pretending to examine his wineglass. Then he rose with all the dignity he could muster.

'I'll leave you both to enjoy your evening. I shall wander down to The Lord Nelson to celebrate with friends I trust will prove happier to share my good fortune.'

He turned at the door. 'If it is all right with you, Dix, I shall move my things out tomorrow afternoon.'

'Ingrate!' Dix called after him like a petulant schoolgirl.

The ugly little scene had taken the edge off Daniel's triumph, but he marched off towards The Lord Nelson determined to put on a good front before his fellow students. He expected them to be envious, but knew they'd be only too happy for him to buy their drinks.

A wistful thought crossed Daniel's mind. What a very different reception his news would have been given by his Ironbark friends. Not least by his wife and his best friend, Jake.

It was an hour past dawn when Daniel sauntered home towards Hyde Park. Autumn leaves rustled beneath his feet as he paused to admire the colony's first statue, paid for by the people of New South Wales despite the Depression. Standing before the handsome bronze replica of Sir Richard Bourke as it glinted in the early morning sunlight, Daniel gave the sculptor's work a sincere nod of approval.

Despite his night of carousing Daniel was only mildly drunk. He must wash and change his linen to create a good impression at his first sitting with Mrs Hamberton.

Across the road from Dix's townhouse he stopped dead in his tracks. His few clothes hung from the iron railings. Two blank canvases lay slashed on the ground, surrounded by broken paintbrushes and squashed tubes of oil paints. All his completed paintings were scattered about, splattered with splodges of red paint like bloodstains – except for one. Jake's portrait had been speared by an iron spike on the railing. There was a gaping hole where his face had been. Daniel felt physically ill at the sight, realising Dix had sensed his unspoken love for Jake.

He collapsed onto a bench in Hyde Park and surveyed the carnage as a flock of pigeons pecked at his feet. *What was that saying of Keziah's? If you take the wrong road, it isn't really the wrong road, but the road you were meant to take. Perhaps my Dix era proves the adage, 'Put not your faith in princes.' From now on I will honour Saranna Plews's dying request and make art my mistress.*

Daniel automatically looked in the empty pocket of his waistcoat that had held the watch he had pawned. Although he had enough funds to redeem it, he had other more pressing needs. Where he would sleep tonight was a problem he trusted the day ahead would resolve. Hopefully some fellow art student would give him a corner to doss down in. What mattered right now was his meeting with Mrs Hamberton. What the hell was he to do for art supplies?

He took from his pocket a month-old letter from Keziah and re-read the final lines to bolster his self-confidence. It was a comforting link with home. Ironbark. Jake.

Stay strong, Daniel.

The world will recognise your god-given gifts as an artist, as all your Ironbark friends do.

For the past year and a half we have been travelling in our wonderful vardo. *Jake has given me back my Romani life. We never know where tomorrow's road will lead us, so there is no way for you to write to us yet. Remember, Daniel, we can't help who we love. Forgive me, it took me time to understand.*

Once your wife but always your friend, Keziah

Daniel felt his eyes grow misty but not from self-pity. He had left Ironbark believing his life would be easier away from Jake, among men of his own kind, but he was realising the bonds of friendship with his Ironbark family were far stronger than lust.

'We were strange bedfellows, Keziah,' he said softly. 'But you accept me as I am.'

Facing Dix's handiwork, he squared his shoulders to cover his humiliation and crossed the road to salvage what he could, picking through the debris to rescue broken paintbrushes, a pencil and one undamaged sheet of art paper. He couldn't bear to look at Jake's faceless body. The slashed canvases were beyond repair. He walked to the public water pump to wash his face then set off at a brisk pace to cover the two miles to Woolloomooloo Hill above the bay.

Ushered by the housemaid into the Hamberton residence, Daniel was acutely conscious of his down-at-heel appearance. He felt embarrassed to hear his stomach rumble and was ashamed of his pathetic art materials. But he steeled himself and prepared to be treated with the same cool indifference that Charlotte Jonstone had always shown him.

He entered Mrs Hamberton's personal sitting room to find her seated with her back to him, gazing out across the harbour. He was struck by the restrained elegance of the Georgian furniture. To his surprise he saw an easel set up beside an open box of oil paints and a pot holding a variety of brushes. The easel held a large canvas primed for painting.

But it was the subject herself that most intrigued him. *The light is perfect. Let's hope I can do the lady justice.*

Mrs Hamberton was tall and slender. No longer young, she retained an undeniable vestige of youthful beauty in the coronet of fair hair streaked with silver at the temples. The faint lifelines that etched her face were more interesting to Daniel than the blank canvas of youth.

He wondered why she seemed so intent on putting him at ease when she was clearly a born lady. He had never met her before, yet somehow he felt she knew him. She had prepared everything for him, even a choice of gowns draped across chairs, showing him the same respect an important artist might expect. Yet Daniel knew Jonstone must have briefed her on the full details of his convict history. Was Mrs Hamberton an eccentric English aristocrat? A true lover of the arts? Or did she have some hidden agenda?

She crossed the room and extended her hand gracefully.

'Welcome, Mr Browne. Your work has been highly recommended by our mutual friend, Julian Jonstone. As you can see he has ordered everything for you. I trust these paints and brushes are to your satisfaction. If you require anything else please advise me.'

Daniel was speechless. *She's treating me almost like an equal. Yet surely she knows it's not long since 'our mutual friend's' overseer had the power to have me flogged. And did!*

She gestured for him to take a seat and Daniel was offered morning tea, which he gratefully accepted. Although initially short of words, he soon felt himself drawn within her charming aura.

'I will leave the choice of props and decor to you, Mr Browne, but I hope you will humour me by choosing one of these gowns for the portrait. It is intended for my husband's study and he favours me in blue.'

No wonder. It brings out the colour of her eyes. How strange. Violet-blue. Just like Keziah's eyes. Daniel chose the turquoise silk dress she was already wearing and was delighted to find he was empowered to create 'the story' within the portrait – the choice of jewellery, chair, background and the pose that not only best complimented her beauty but hopefully would reveal her true character. He remembered reading somewhere that at the heart of beauty there lies a touch of sadness. He fancied he read the truth of those words in this lady's eyes.

Emboldened by her interest in the creative process, Daniel felt free to set the guidelines of time and place for the sittings.

'I love the quality of Australian sunlight. This light is perfect and the window gives a glimpse of the harbour and the sky. For the sake of continuity of light, ideally I would like to paint you here at the same time of day – whenever you are free. I understand from Mr Hamberton I have limited time to complete the work?'

'My husband must soon take up his new appointment as a magistrate on the circuit. We will then be based in Goulburn. I regret we have placed your work under an undue time constraint.'

'I will work night and day on the background details between our sittings.'

Daniel was disconcerted to remember that he no longer had a place to work and sleep. How would he find enough time to honour his hasty promise and achieve high quality?

He felt Mrs Hamberton's eyes studying him.

'Such a large canvas is surely difficult to move back and forth from your studio. May I suggest it would be more convenient for you to stay here as my husband's house guest for the duration? We have a quiet guest wing where you could work undisturbed if you wish.'

Daniel almost laughed out loud with sheer relief. *My studio? If only she knew how Dix destroyed everything. And I didn't even have a bed tonight.*

Mrs Hamberton took his silence as consent. 'If this arrangement is to your satisfaction, could I suggest we proceed at once? Please do not feel pressured by time. If the portrait is not completed to your entire satisfaction by our departure date, we would be pleased to have you join us in Goulburn to complete it.'

To my *entire satisfaction! She's treating me like a master painter.*

Sketching the outline, Daniel felt he was floating in a dream down a long corridor where all the doors flew open to light his way ahead. He had nothing to worry about, no decisions beyond the choice of colours to mix for his palette, the placement of ornaments, the perfect shade of flowers to harmonise with the turquoise of her gown, the blue of her eyes.

Time was either his to command or a dimension in which to lose himself at will. He worked with speed and confidence, as if angels guided his brushstrokes. Stepping back from the easel to study his preliminary sketch in oils, he examined the sunlight that streamed through the window. It cast faint shadows across the classic bone structure of the lady's face and heightened her mystery. He felt a surge of excitement. This would be far more than a conventional portrait of a beautiful woman.

Although Mrs Hamberton was pure Quality and treated him in a polite, detached way as he worked, there was no trace of Charlotte Jonstone's condescension. While retaining her pose, she made occasional, casual references to his work and life.

'Do my questions disturb you, Mr Browne? Please tell me if they do. It is simply that I am new to the colony and have much to learn about the very different way of life down here.'

Disarmed by her deference Daniel felt it was safe to be honest.

'I regret my experience is limited. As a transportee my world was restricted to Mr Jonstone's estate until I was fortunate to marry and gain my ticket-of-leave.'

'Quite so. You have done well to build a new life for yourself.' She hesitated. 'I understand your young wife came free?'

The question startled him. 'Yes. I owe Saranna a great debt. She understands an artist's compulsion to paint.' He felt discomforted by the thought he had almost slipped and called his wife Keziah.

'Julian told me Mrs Browne was much valued as a schoolteacher in a remote village.'

'She was indeed, but she is presently travelling with a friend until I rejoin her.'

Daniel hoped she would not ask him exactly *where*. He could hardly reveal the awkward truth that 'my wife goes wherever her lover, Jake Andersen, leads her'.

'You have a child, do you not? A real blessing.' Mrs Hamberton gave a faint sigh.

Conditioned to tread warily on this subject, Daniel delivered his standard statement. 'We have no children of our own as yet, but my wife adopted a charming little boy who was abandoned at birth. Gabriel Stanley.'

'Gabriel Stanley,' she repeated. 'A lovely name.'

Daniel saw that although her eyes remained focused and she held her head at the exact angle he had chosen for the portrait, she no longer seemed to be aware of him.

'Are you weary from holding that pose, Mrs Hamberton?'

'Not at all.'

He noted she did not choose to speak again for the remainder of their first sitting.

Her questions about Keziah had awakened in Daniel feelings that he had tried to keep dormant since his arrival in Sydney Town. But now he found he had arrived at a decision.

My knowledge of painting techniques has grown in leaps and bounds in Sydney Town, but I don't need false friends like Dix in my life. Jake, Keziah and Gabriel are the only family I have ever known. When this portrait is finished it's time to go back where I belong. To my true friends. To Ironbark.

CHAPTER 44

Keziah felt a wave of contentment as their *vardo* rolled through the maze of bushland beyond the pale of settlement. Jake was disdainful of maps but she knew they were travelling beyond the officially defined 'limits of location'. The long drought had at last broken and the grasslands were turning green.

She felt blessed that both children were happy and healthy. Gabriel's snowy mop of curls contrasted with his sun-tanned face and body. The pallid little girl from the convent was growing more confident as she fitted into the unfamiliar pattern of family life. Fast outgrowing her clothes, her mousy hair was tousled by the wind, her eyes fixed on her hero, Jake.

The man who guided their lives had never looked more relaxed. As they drove along he cast secretive smiles at Keziah's belly, shaking his head as if he couldn't believe his luck that, after the first babe miscarried, its tiny twin had managed to hang in there and continued to grow.

Miles from any community they camped by a creek lined with English weeping willows, no doubt planted long ago by some homesick squatter. The homestead's missus was the first white woman they had seen in weeks. Although she gave them a warm welcome, Keziah felt uneasy.

'Just call me Mary,' the woman said. 'Nice to have a woman's company. My husband is away on business.' She turned to Jake. 'I'm sorry I've no money for paid work.'

'What's money?' Unprompted, Jake chopped a large woodpile for her and then treated the swollen fetlock of Mary's roan mare with Keziah's herbs.

In gratitude Mary invited them to a generous baked supper with cakes for the children. After dark Jake playfully galloped like a horse back to their *vardo* with Gabriel perched on his shoulders and Pearl clinging to his back like a koala.

This left Keziah free to grant Mary's request for a Tarot reading. The past was as clear as a bell, but the future was strangely fractured. Mary asked anxious questions.

'Will my husband return soon?'

Keziah suspected the truth. *She's lying. She's hiding from him. She hasn't even told us her family name.* So she selected her words with care. 'Your husband is searching for something – someone he's lost.'

Mary's hands flew to her mouth. 'Oh, dear! Go on.'

'Don't be afraid, Mary. The Tarot can tell you what to expect, but not all the future is written in stone. There is an element of free will.'

'Tell me true.' Mary asked, 'Will I ever have a child?'

Keziah hesitated. All that remained of Mary's youth were kindly brown eyes and a smile she covered to disguise a missing tooth. She would soon be beyond childbearing age.

Keziah dealt the cards that helped define the pictures flooding through her mind. 'Your husband is quite handsome in his way.' She tried to be tactful. 'Although he didn't *want* to come to the colony, he's done very well for himself. He enjoys good health, but I'm sorry, I can't see any children in his future.'

When she dealt out fresh cards, the magician card was reversed, lying in a pattern that indicated the abuse of power for destructive ends. Keziah was overcome by a wave of nausea. The magician's face dissolved before her eyes into a handsome face of pure evil.

Mi-duvel! It's his *face – that black-bearded rogue who tried to rape me at the creek. He's Mary's husband! What on earth can I tell her to give her hope for the future?*

'I don't want to upset you, Mary, but a period of upheaval lies ahead of you. When it occurs remember that happiness *will* find you again. I see a young government man, fair-haired and shy. He has love in his heart, but right now he is very afraid of your husband.'

Keziah's eyes were drawn to the doorway where a little girl in a floral pinafore peeped around at her. Then the little girl's outline turned milky and she faded from sight.

'I see a daughter born to you late in life. You live to a goodly age. But your husband—'

The pack of cards flew up in the air and scattered wildly across the floor. Shaken by the feeling of malevolence that swamped the room, Keziah forced herself to lie. 'Just a gust of wind.'

Mary burst into tears. Keziah was confused. 'Forgive me. You love your husband?'

'Love him? He beats me when he's drunk. Every Friday, regular as clockwork.' She grasped Keziah's hand. 'A child! Praise the Lord. You've given me something to live for!'

On her return to the *vardo* Keziah threw her arms around Jake.

'We must leave right away! It's not safe here. Don't ask why, you'd never believe me.'

Jake compromised. 'Tomorrow morning. That's a promise.'

'At first light! We *must* leave this place!'

'You have my word on it.'

He reached out to stroke her hair, but Keziah was in no mood to be gentled. She made love to him with abandon – something beyond passion drove her. When at last he had drained her fear from her and she lay spent in his arms, Jake shielded her with his body.

'Don't be afraid, darlin',' he whispered. 'No *mulo* can get past me.'

At dawn Mary handed Jake fresh vegetables, dry goods and a piece of mutton wrapped in wet hessian sacking.

'To tide your family over,' she said tactfully, then added, 'Do you mind me asking? Are you one of them Gypsy families?'

Keziah stiffened. 'I learned the Tarot from a wise old Romani.'

Jake added his charming lie. 'Yeah. The nice old lady who sold me her wagon.'

Mary looked sage. 'Gypsies have second sight. I'm sure it will happen like you said.' She waved her apron in farewell until they reached the end of the road.

As they drove past a line of haystacks, a young man in convict slops waved them goodbye.

Jake was curious. 'You must have given Mary a bright future to lavish that food on us.'

'I did,' she answered, trying to sound casual. 'On her husband's death she'll have a daughter with that young convict we passed. And find true happiness for the first time in her life.'

Jake looked startled. 'Jesus, Kez, you really let your imagination run wild.'

'No. That is her destiny. I can't say *when* but it will happen.'

Jake was uncomfortably quiet for the next few miles. For once Keziah had no desire to comment on the world around them. She only half listened to the children's whispers. Mary's farm was now miles behind them and she was determined to block her fear of that man's evil face. Her greatest fear was what Jake would do if he knew Mary's husband was the man who'd tried to rape her.

They passed another remote homestead with a sign that read 'Horses for Sale'.

'One day you'll raise a line of champions,' Keziah said firmly. 'It wouldn't surprise me if you bred them from that clever horse of Richard Rouse's that wins races at the Hawkesbury.'

Jake looked impressed. 'Jorrocks? Jesus, that proves your psychic powers, Kez.'

'Why's that?' she asked, suddenly suspicious.

'Jorrocks is a bloody gelding!'

Keziah snapped, 'Well I can't be clairvoyant *all* the time.'

Jake continued to snigger over Jorrocks, a sound so infectious that

Keziah finally joined him. It was a blessed moment of shared laughter that briefly quelled the fears she was trying to hold at bay.

Their new camp site lay close to a crescent-shaped billabong that long ago Nature had isolated from the arm of a creek when floodwaters silted it up at either end. The sun was high as Jake took the kids off to teach them how to set an Aboriginal fish trap.

'We won't be long, Kez. Put your feet up! I'll bring you a heap of fish for supper.'

But Keziah was restless. She couldn't shake the feeling that the aura of malevolence she had felt when reading Mary's cards had followed her here. She was so nervous she knocked over her last bucket of water. Breaking her promise to Jake never to wander off alone, she went to refill the bucket. At the billabong she knelt to cool her face and breast, halted by her reflection in the still water.

'*Mi-duvel*, I beg you, don't take Jake from me. I can't live without him now.'

A gnat skimmed the water, rippling Keziah's image. When the water grew calm the reflection showed she was not alone. Behind her was a stranger on horseback with a hat pulled low over his eyes. His face was clean-shaven with a strong cleft chin, his voice soft.

'The word is you tell fortunes. Just *one* of your gifts.' He rode closer, leaned over and touched her breast as he slid a sovereign down the front of her bodice. 'There's more where that came from if you give me a fortune that pleases me.'

I know that voice! The coin pressed against her skin, but she dared not risk exposing her breast by removing it. She fought down her panic. Jake and the children's voices had died away.

'Lay one finger on me again and my husband will kill you!'

His voice was soft, derisive. 'A Gypsy's husband is any man willing to cross her palm with silver. Let's do a little business, girl. You'll find me generous.'

'You reckon?' Jake stood with his rifle aimed at the rider's heart. 'Piss off right now if you want to live to see tomorrow's sunrise.'

Jake jerked his head in Keziah's direction. 'This woman's *mine.* Go buy your own!'

'I meant no harm. Sorry, lady, for my mistake.'

The stranger bowed to Keziah then backed his horse a safe distance before riding away. Jake kept the pistol trained on him until he was well out of sight. 'You all right, Kez?'

Coldly she fed his words back to him. '*This woman's mine. Go buy your own!* I'll remind you that I am a Romani woman – not a cattle dog.'

Jake refused to apologise. 'I'm well aware of that. Cattle dogs are trained to *obey* a man. Don't dare wander off, you hear? It only takes a man seconds to ravage a woman.'

She flinched. Jake tried to soften his warning.

'I don't blame any man simply for offering to pay a woman. There ain't enough girls to go around in the colony, but if any man took a woman by force, I'd shoot him down like a mad dog. Understand me?'

The heat of the day was upon them, but Keziah shivered at the threat in his voice.

'Do you know him?' she asked carefully.

'No idea. I wouldn't forget that cleft chin of his.'

Keziah sensed he was lying, but when Jake asked, 'Have *you* ever seen him before?' she only gave him half the truth. 'I saw his face in Mary's cards.'

Later that night Keziah studied Jake across the campfire as he cleaned the gun. A storm had been fermenting since the blood-red sun had disappeared behind the hills. There was a misty ring around the moon. Tomorrow would bring rain. And what else?

When the children were out of earshot she whispered, 'I really thought you were going to kill that man today.'

He looked her straight in the eye. 'Should have. When I had the chance.'

Keziah had a vivid flash of the symbols in her recurring nightmare. Blood, rope, fire, Jake's face behind prison bars. She must do her damnedest to distract him.

She whispered to the children and sent them racing inside the *vardo.* They returned giggling, Pearl wearing Keziah's petticoat as a dress, a Romani scarf around her head. Gabriel was half covered by Jake's hat and waistcoat as he strutted in a parody of Jake's Currency swagger.

Gabriel launched into a pitch-perfect rendition of *The Wild Colonial Boy,* accompanied by Pearl on a gumleaf whistle. Jake applauded their performance and demanded an encore.

Then it was Keziah's turn. Gabriel played for her. As she danced for Jake she used music, vitality and laughter to blot out her fears of the future. It was more than a dance of seduction for Jake. She made him smile when she proudly flaunted the curve of her growing belly, knowing full well this did not detract from his admiration.

Wild and untamed she was carried along by the power of her Romani music, ready to dance all night, but Jake quietly took over. He tucked the children up in their bunks then slipped his arm around Keziah's waist and shepherded her gently but firmly to his swag beneath the stars.

'Past your bedtime, Kez. Got a long way to travel tomorrow.'

She lay with her head on Jake's chest, smiling dreamily at the stars.

As she drifted off to sleep she murmured, 'Thank you for giving me your Milky Way, Jake. I can never repay you.'

'Think nothing of it, love.'

The sound of galloping horses woke her. Keziah froze when she saw the hated blue uniforms of four mounted police, their brass buttons gleaming in the sun. They were heading straight for the campfire where Jake was brewing tea.

The young sergeant in charge confronted Jake in a crisp English accent, 'You be Jakob Isaac Andersen?'

'Yeah. Who's asking?'

'Under the authority vested in me by His Excellency Governor Gipps, I am arresting you, Jakob Andersen, on suspicion of aiding and giving succour to bushrangers.'

'Jesus wept,' said Jake. 'You're joking. We haven't seen a soul in weeks.'

'You will accompany me to Berrima Gaol where you will await your trial.'

'Like hell I will!' Jake stood his ground, his fists clenched at his sides. 'I'll not run out on my woman and kids.'

A trooper began to fix the bayonet in his Brown Bess musket. Keziah screamed out Jake's name as she ran towards three troopers who were struggling to manacle him. The children hammered their fists at the troopers' legs. When Pearl bit her teeth into the sergeant's leg, his reflex wallop sent her flying.

Jake went berserk. 'Leave my daughter alone, you rotten mongrel!'

It took all four troopers to wrestle Jake to the ground. They punched his face and gut, finally manacled him, then roped his body to a lead, forcing him to run behind their horses.

Jake yelled over his shoulder. 'I promise you, Keziah. I'll come back to you!'

His last desperate words caused him to stumble and Keziah's last sight of him was his body being dragged along behind the galloping horses.

When the children screamed in terror, Keziah held them tight in her arms.

'You want to help Papa? Then help *me*. We need to pull together!'

They flew into action just as the storm broke and rain began to fall.

They raced around in the downpour, slithering in the mud as they threw everything inside the wagon. Keziah harnessed Horatio and looped the other horses' reins in place. In the driver's seat she cracked the whip in the air although Horatio didn't need it.

Rain plastered her hair to her face and obscured her vision. She had no map, no idea where she was going, but she prayed for *baxt* to lead her.

A few moments later, she halted at a fork in the road. An uprooted tree had knocked the signpost off its axis. Both tracks looked the same.

God of my ancestors. Which road leads to Jake?

CHAPTER 45

Blinded by sheets of rain and icy wind, Keziah was so disoriented she did not realise she had taken the wrong road until the black outline of Bran's forge leapt out of the chaos of the storm. *Baxt* had delivered her into the hands of a friend.

The gentle giant was crouched by the fireplace heaping logs on a roaring fire. He stared open-mouthed at her dishevelled figure in the doorway. Drenched by the storm, Saranna's blue cloak weighed heavily on Keziah's shoulders.

'Help me, Bran! Jake's been taken by the traps to Berrima Gaol!'

The blacksmith effortlessly lifted up a child in each arm, carried them inside to the fire and wrapped them up in blankets.

Keziah was stunned by the figure that appeared from an adjoining room. Daniel.

'What on earth's wrong, Keziah?'

Trying to suppress her agitation in the children's presence she kept her tone muted as she recounted the day's events to Daniel. 'I don't know if the charges against Jake are true or even who laid them. It smells like the work of Gilbert Evans. Jake has already done time. As a second offender it could mean Norfolk Island.'

Daniel went pale. 'I'll take you and the children to Berrima. We'll leave at dawn and fight this with everything we've got. Joseph Bloom's bound to help us.'

Keziah shook her head in confusion. 'There isn't time! He's in Sydney Town in his new legal practice. You know how they rush through these local trials. I was going to seek help from Dr Ross but I took the wrong road.'

'You were meant to find me instead. You know you can count on me, Keziah. I failed you as a husband, but I'm Jake's friend. I won't fail him.'

Keziah noted his frown when he saw the curve of her belly.

'Yes, Daniel. I *am*.'

Daniel took her in his arms protectively like a big brother.

'Don't cry,' he said. But Keziah knew she was beyond tears.

When Keziah and Daniel drove into Berrima village Keziah looked across at the huge new sandstone complex that dominated the main street. Behind the high stone walls the gaol buildings were designed to house three hundred prisoners. On the other side of a laneway stood a massive stone courthouse with a columned façade that looked like a Roman temple. The buildings were grand and forbidding, as if to enforce the system for eternity.

Red, white and blue bunting was draped outside the nearby Surveyor-General's Inn and other buildings in the main street. Keziah felt confused. 'It isn't the Queen's birthday yet, is it?'

Daniel nodded. 'Yes. You *have* been isolated.'

He pointed out that tomorrow being 23 May, the whole of Berrima would be celebrating the Queen's birthday, the traditional excuse for everyone, masters and assigned servants, to make merry. This meant that whichever magistrate was sitting on the bench today would no doubt want to clear the court early.

Daniel's tone was reassuring. 'Wait here for me. I'll find out when Jake is scheduled to appear.' Keziah pressed a shoelace in his hand. 'Please, please ask a guard to see Jake gets this. It's a Romani symbol of good luck.'

Daniel nodded and bounded off in search of a court official.

Alone in front of the courthouse, Keziah felt dwarfed by the four massive columns supporting the triangular pediment – a façade with giant brass doors but no windows. The wind was so bitter she sheltered the children under the wings of her blue cloak. Their eyes were fixed on

Jake's prison, their small faces pinched with silent misery. Keziah buried her own fears.

'Yes, Papa is in there. We won't be able to talk to him, but you'll see him soon when he appears in court. And he'll see you! That will make him very happy.'

When Daniel returned it was clear he was making a valiant attempt to be positive.

'We arrived just in time. Jake's trial is scheduled today. It seems luck is on his side. He'll be going before Alfred Hamberton, a brand-new magistrate just arrived in the colony – today's his first day on the bench. The strange thing is I know the man.'

'How is that?'

'I began painting his wife's portrait in Sydney and I'm to go to Goulburn to finish it. My dealings with him were limited, so I don't know how fair he'll be. He *has* to be better than some of the corrupt magistrates openly biased in favour of their local gentry cronies.'

'Is Jake's lawyer a good one?'

Daniel frowned. 'I'm afraid he doesn't have a lawyer.'

'What? We'll see about that!' Flushed with rage, Keziah was ready to rush inside and challenge the law until she saw Dr Leslie Ross approaching.

She called out a heartfelt Romani greeting. 'God bless your legs for bringing you here! Doctor, do you know what they've done to Jake? He has no one to defend him!'

'Aye, lassie. I was here on duty to witness a hanging when I heard the news. I've been remonstrating with the officials all morning. They gallop through these trials with godless speed. They claim there's no time to find a defence lawyer. I tried to make them postpone his case but they would nay have a bar of it!'

'That's British justice?' Keziah asked with contempt.

'Aye, common enough for what's considered misdemeanours of this nature.'

Misdemeanours. To Keziah the word seemed better suited to naughty schoolchildren's behaviour rather than crimes that could have a man transported to Norfolk Island.

The moment the doors of the courthouse were opened Keziah pushed her way to the front of the spectators' section at the rear of the courtroom. There were no seats so she was sustained by Daniel's arm around her waist, the children pressed against her skirt nervously.

Daniel whispered a warning. 'Keep your emotions in check. Remember we are here purely as Jake's *friends*.'

On the wall above the magistrate's bench was the British coat of arms, supported down through the centuries by its guardians – lion on the left, unicorn on the right. Keziah had first seen this as a child at her father's trial. Again when Gem was sentenced, and now these animals stood guard at Jake's trial. Written on the scroll beneath them was the royal motto, *'Dieu et mon droit'*.

'French for "God and my right",' Daniel translated.

'What good is that to us?' Keziah said. 'In the eyes of the law I'm a pagan and Jake's an atheist. What rights does Jake have under a system designed for the benefit of the Quality? He isn't even allowed his own damned lawyer!'

Her outburst drew attention to her. The women seated in the double-tiered lady spectators' box facing the jury all turned to stare at her. One middle-aged woman in black gave her a timid smile of encouragement behind a gloved hand. Keziah felt she looked familiar but could not place her.

Daniel didn't know her either. 'But Hamberton's wife is seated there in the back row, wearing a bonnet that hides her face. No doubt she's come to show support for her husband's baptism as a magistrate.' Daniel was about to point out the woman in blue but Keziah was distracted by the surprising sight of friends in court.

Polly Doyle slipped away from George Hobson's side to give Keziah a reassuring hug.

'How did you hear about Jake's arrest, Polly? There was so little time.'

Polly jerked her head in the direction of Gilbert Evans who stood apart from the crowd.

'*Him*, who else? He boasted to Mr Hobson it was God's will when a bushranger's sympathiser got his comeuppance. Don't worry, Hobson and all of us in Ironbark know Jake's a decent bloke.'

When Polly scuttled back to Hobson's side Keziah looked around her, feeling cynical about the presence of voyeurs like Bolthole Valley's storekeeper, Matthew Feagan. She could hardly bear to look at Gilbert Evans.

From the moment Jake entered the court from the prisoners' holding cell, Keziah had eyes for no one else. A guard escorted him between the parallel railings that separated the legal section from the spectators – a fence so low any self-respecting sheepdog could have vaulted it. When Keziah instinctively reached out as if to touch him, Daniel caught her hand and kissed it to allay any suspicion that she was linked to Jake.

'Remember, you are *my* wife today,' he whispered.

Keziah held her breath as Jake stepped into the prisoner's box and gave her a reassuring nod. Her eyes traced every gaunt, bruised line of his beloved face. His shirt collar, angled askew, made him look like a small boy.

'That decent jacket isn't Jake's. He doesn't own one. Mac Mackie must have loaned it to him.'

Daniel gave a faint smile. 'I know. Mac loaned that jacket to me on *our* wedding day, remember?'

Keziah felt proud that Jake's level-eyed demeanour marked him as a respectable citizen, albeit an obvious Currency Lad. She tried to catch his eye. As if feeling the intensity of her gaze, Jake turned and pointed to his long hair. It was tied back with a shoelace.

'Look, Daniel, he got my message of good luck!'

Keziah felt happy for one brief moment. Then Jake gave his undivided attention to the proceedings. He looked more serious than she'd ever seen him, clearly determined not to antagonise the magistrate.

She tugged Daniel's sleeve. 'Surely any fool, including this magistrate, can see he's an honest man.'

Daniel drew her closer and whispered quickly, 'Be careful what you say. Evans may not be the only informer around us.'

Keziah bent down and whispered to Gabriel and Pearl, 'Smile at your papa when he looks our way. It will give him heart.' She was touched to see both children trying to fix permanent smiles on their faces.

Keziah swayed against Daniel as the confusing list of charges was read out.

Jake stood accused under the Bushranging Act of seven misdemeanours. Giving aid and succour to two bushrangers, 'the deceased Gypsy Gem Smith and William Martens, also known as Jabber Jabber, currently held at His Excellency the Governor's pleasure in Van Diemen's Land'.

Keziah looked at Daniel in horror. Seven charges!

'I'll bet this is all *his* dirty work,' she hissed. She stared fiercely across at Gilbert Evans who was smoothing his moustache as if ready for a direct summons from his god. 'If Will Martens was here he'd certainly tell the truth about Jake!'

'Yes,' Daniel said, 'but who'd believe a bushranger's evidence, apart from you and me?'

They were both jolted by the stark words: 'What say you? Does the accused plead Guilty or Not Guilty?'

'Not Guilty *and* Guilty, Your Honour.' Jake sounded as if he was in Feagan's General Store ordering half a dozen brown eggs, half a dozen white.

The buzz of consternation caused Magistrate Hamberton to hammer his gavel for silence. 'No such ambiguous plea is allowable under British law.'

'Then with respect I reckon it ought to be, Your Honour.'

The magistrate looked at Jake sharply. Keziah knew that look. Obviously he was the type who considered Currency Lads, Gypsies and convicts to be the lowest form of life in the colony.

The magistrate glanced at the rows of seated women then switched to a languid tone. 'Is your plea Guilty or Not Guilty?'

'All right. Not Guilty,' Jake said. He spoke quite affably to the magistrate, but Keziah would have happily seen the man hung, drawn and quartered.

She struggled to understand the intricate proceedings as the heat in the packed courthouse brought her close to fainting. Her anger revitalised her when a hated uniform crossed her line of vision.

She turned to Daniel and hissed, 'That's the trap who arrested Jake and had him dragged behind their horses!'

Sergeant Still's ruddy English complexion was flushed with the heat and Keziah realised for the first time he looked no older than Jake and twice as nervous. She fully expected him to lie under oath or attempt to colour his testimony. This trooper could so easily expose her – worse, condemn Jake.

When he was asked to describe the arrest, the sergeant glanced nervously at Keziah. She was surprised that his report avoided all mention of Jake's shouted reference to 'my woman and kids'.

'Did the prisoner offer resistance at the time of arrest, Sergeant?'

'Had our hands jolly well full. Andersen was adamant he was innocent. A young family stood nearby. The woman looked to be a lady. Very distressed she was, Your Honour.'

When asked if he had prior reports of the prisoner's association with bushrangers, the sergeant's reply was firm. 'Never. Understood Andersen to be a man of good repute.'

Keziah turned to Daniel in surprise. 'So he isn't the villain of the piece. Who was?'

Daniel sighed. 'No doubt we'll soon find out.'

'Why doesn't Jake look at me?' Keziah asked wistfully.

'To protect you, m'dear. He's careful not to involve *my wife* in this business.'

She exchanged a look of relief with Daniel when the next witness to be called was Dr Leslie Ross. Keziah felt grateful for his firm testimonial of Jake's good character.

'On *at least* three of the dates listed, Jakob Andersen was, in fact, receiving medical treatment at my hands.' He glared at the prosecutor, 'For the record I was given no prior advice of these dates but my medical diary will verify them if the court will accept the evidence.'

Magistrate Hamberton gave an airy wave of dismissal. 'Not necessary, Dr Ross. Your word under oath is good enough for this court.'

Leslie's praise was unswerving. 'Jakob Andersen is a law-abiding citizen of exemplary character. He's honest to a fault and a man of rare compassion.'

The prosecutor was quick to seize on this. 'Is it not possible this rare compassion might well have extended to his giving aid to bushrangers?'

Angered by the trap, Dr Ross snapped back, 'Any sensible man would with a pistol at his head!'

'Point taken, Doctor – *if* firearms were indeed a method of persuasion, but these two bushrangers were Andersen's *friends*, were they not? One further question. Is it true you consider the accused to be a personal friend of *yours*?'

'That's common knowledge, but on my honour, I would ne'er commit perjury!'

'No, Doctor?' His pause was a silent insult. 'No further questions.'

Keziah saw Magistrate Hamberton's growing irritation as a procession of witnesses claimed they had been pressured to sign false statements that incriminated Jake. Wearily shuffling papers, Hamberton asked, 'I wonder if there is *anyone* present willing to identify Jakob Andersen?'

The whole court was startled by Pearl's shrill voice. 'I will! He's my father!'

Gabriel began to add, 'Mine too!' but Daniel quickly cupped his hand over the boy's mouth to prevent ammunition for gossips.

The sound of Magistrate Hamberton's gavel broke through the spectators' laughter.

'Am obliged to you, young lady. The court shall duly record this identification of Jakob Andersen by *a respectable young citizen*.'

The tipstaff nodded sagely and a clerk scratched away with his quill.

Jake gave the children a broad smile. Keziah saw how proud he was that his children were publicly standing by him, but her anxiety grew when the hawk-eyed prosecutor fired a barrage of questions at him.

'You concede you were a close friend of the late, infamous bushranger Gypsy Gem Smith? That you have in your possession this bushranger's horse Sarishan, the same racehorse you trained to win Terence Ogden's silver cup in 1839, some *four years* ago? That The Gypsy later gave you Sarishan in payment for services you rendered him when you supplied him with arms and food?'

Keziah looked at Daniel in horror. *How will Jake get out of all this?*

Hamberton waved his hand in Jake's direction. 'One answer in turn will be sufficient.'

Jake wasted no time. 'First off, I don't deny I first met Gem Smith some six years ago.'

The prosecutor's response was immediate. 'Transported in chains, was he not?'

'Like many of the best of us.' Jake tried to cover his hasty choice of words. 'I'm friend to any man, bond or free, who's done me no harm. We shared an interest in horses.'

'Is it not true this Gypsy stole many horses in his illicit career as a bushranger?'

'Don't believe everything you read in the newspapers,' Jake shot back. 'As for me I can't speak of what I never saw. But in answer to your *mistakes* about Sarishan, he wasn't stolen so I broke no law training him for a race he won fair and square. And he wasn't payment neither. I made Gem a solemn promise I'd care for his horse if he went to prison. Any decent man would.' He turned to Hamberton to explain. 'Brumbies ain't stolen, Your Honour. They are born in the wild and owned by no one.'

The prosecutor played to the gallery. 'Never look a gift-horse in the mouth, eh?'

Jake fought to keep his anger in check. 'In answer to your last question, I never in my life supplied arms or ammunition to Gem Smith or any other bolter. But if *any* man comes to my camp, bond or free, I never refuse to share my food and drink. That's not giving succour, Your Honour, it's the law of survival in outback New South Wales.'

Keziah knew that wasn't a lie, but it wasn't quite the whole truth. Jake refused to deliver arms or ammunition, but he *had* taken food supplies to Gem in the cave.

Asked if he was willing so to swear, Jake answered, 'Truth is it'd be a hollow oath, Your Honour. I'm second cousin to an atheist. I *will* swear on my own honour. Every man knows Jake Andersen's as good as his word.'

'That's true!' Keziah's impulsive words drew murmurs of agreement from the surrounding crowd and a gruff, 'Hear, hear,' from George Hobson.

The magistrate glanced at the court clock. '*Every* man considers you an honourable man, Andersen? That is a sweeping claim. Trust light will be shed by the final two witnesses.'

When Keziah saw Gilbert Evans take the oath she hissed at Daniel, 'Clean water never came out of a dirty place! I've got a good mind to—'

Daniel stopped her mouth with a swift kiss.

Daniel felt a stab of empathy at the look Jake exchanged with Keziah. Her eyes were awash with love. He tried to suppress his own feelings to remain alert to any clues that could aid Jake's cause. He was afraid of what lay ahead if Jake was found guilty. Daniel was ashamed of his instinctive aesthetic reaction to the new punishment designed to subdue prisoners. Prolonged dark cell isolation was preferable to the mutilation of Jake's superb body under the lash.

Daniel watched intently as Gilbert Evans gave evidence. The man's manner was silky and servile but his testimony was riddled with more innuendo than facts. When Evans referred to an incriminating unsigned letter to be produced in evidence, he was forced to admit 'a friend' had passed it on to him and that he had no direct proof as to where and when the letter was obtained.

'What letter?' Keziah asked Daniel. 'Evans "speaks with forked tongue". They can't convict Jake on all this hot air, can they?'

Daniel tried to sound confident. 'So far all the evidence is circumstantial.'

When the final witness was called to the stand, Daniel felt Keziah sway against him. She turned to him in shock. 'Daniel, it's *him*! The man with the cleft chin.'

Daniel knew right at that moment the game was up.

The Devil Himself solemnly took the oath, his hand on the King James Bible.

Daniel's mind went blank for several minutes. He broke out in a cold sweat at the sight of Iago. For years Daniel had lived in fear of this man and suffered the consequences of every twist of his devious mind. He'd believed that now he was married with a ticket-of-leave he'd be free of this tyrant forever. But here the man stood only a few feet away. And Daniel did not doubt the bastard would use his power to deliver Jake the *coup de grâce*.

Daniel looked desperately at the magistrate. Would Hamberton recognise the truth about Iago? On the rare occasions Daniel had talked to Hamberton it was clear he was a passionate dilettante of law and order. But today, despite his bluster, Hamberton appeared nervous that his knowledge was now being put to the test.

When Daniel heard the Devil Himself formally identified as Iago, Overseer of Gideon Park, he knew the name was but one of several aliases that were not revealed in court. *There are no records of his place of birth, how or when he came to the colony. He must have friends in high places.*

On the stand Iago projected manly integrity as a gentleman who appeared reluctant to condemn Jake Andersen. His sworn statement claimed Jake had given aid to bushrangers on many unspecified occasions. It read like a masterpiece of fabrication.

Daniel could barely watch, afraid to catch his eye.

Magistrate Hamberton paused before responding to Iago's testimony. 'Your memory is commendable, Sir, albeit unsubstantiated. However one thing concerns me. You took considerable time to bring your claims to the attention of police officers.'

'Quite so, Your Honour. I am fully aware of my civic duty. It would be a terrible thing to send an innocent man to prison.' He paused. 'However on the final occasion I was left with no choice but to inform the authorities.'

Hamberton could barely conceal his irritation. 'The final occasion?'

Iago looked troubled, as if unwilling to recall the scene.

'I was riding along the Sydney Road with my friend Mr Gilbert Evans. After we parted company I chanced upon Andersen's stationary wagon. The full moon enabled me to clearly identify Sarishan, the champion racehorse who was The Gypsy's payment for services rendered to him. By Andersen. As the letter in evidence proves.'

When this letter was produced, Iago confirmed he had found it in the vicinity of Andersen's camp site and had passed it on to Evans for the police.

Daniel looked at Keziah to gauge her reaction as it was read.

Although unsigned, the letter had obviously been dictated by Gem and Keziah was clearly the unidentified woman Gem had 'willed' to Jake's care. Daniel could see Keziah was so moved she could barely breathe. He drew his arm around her shoulders to brace her. He knew Iago. Worse was to come.

He clenched his teeth in anger when he heard Iago's soft voice damning Jake by distorting the letter to 'prove' that Sarishan was 'payment for services rendered'.

Instructed to describe what he had witnessed at Andersen's camp that night, Iago continued. 'I saw the accused lying on the ground in despicable circumstances.'

Keziah turned to Daniel. 'What the hell is going on?'

Daniel barely heard her. He was overcome with confusion at Jake's horrified reaction.

Iago made a gesture of apology. 'I hate to say this in the presence of ladies, Your Honour. I saw the accused locked in the embrace of the notorious bushranger Will Martens!' He pointed directly at Jake. 'Jakob Andersen was *giving the boy succour.*'

Shock spread through the court. Daniel saw the blood drain from Keziah's face.

Jake yelled out, 'You lying bastard, Iago, it wasn't like that at all!'

The guard battled to restrain Jake, who finally quietened down after he was threatened with contempt of court.

When questioned as to why he had failed to include this evidence in his sworn statement, Iago savoured the moment. He looked in turn at Jake, Keziah and Daniel, then at the magistrate.

'I was loath to do so, knowing that proof of this bestial act draws the death penalty.'

Hamberton's face looked like a mask. 'Do we take it you refer to sodomy?'

Iago hung his head. 'I regret that I do, Your Honour.'

Daniel forcibly stopped Keziah from charging at the witness box, but he could not stop her screaming out, *'Bengis in tutes bukko!'*

The meaning of the Romani curse was unknown to Daniel but there was no doubting the venom in her words. In the lady spectators' box Daniel saw the fashionable woman in blue rise to her feet. Mrs Hamberton's gloved hands covered her mouth as she sank back in her seat.

Daniel hissed at Keziah, 'What on earth did you say?'

Her rage was beyond control. '*The Devil be in his bowels!* Did you see Iago's face? He knew what it meant! He's no Rom but I'll bet he was cursed by my people in prison!'

Daniel looked at the clock anxiously as the court grew quiet. It was a quarter to four. Being the eve of Her Majesty's birthday no doubt the magistrate desired to end the proceedings. Yet he took his time.

'Under British law proof of the most heinous crime of sodomy requires a second witness. There is none to corroborate it. Mr Evans produced the letter on exhibit. But his statement clearly shows that he and Iago parted company that evening. Evans did not claim to have witnessed Andersen or Martens together under *any* conditions. Mr Iago did not choose to include this claimed act of abomination in *his* sworn statement.' The magistrate hesitated and glanced at his tipstaff before adding, 'Therefore I must deem it inadmissible evidence.'

Daniel whispered to Keziah. 'Look at him. He's new to the job. He's not sure if his ruling is strictly legal.'

He saw Keziah's eyes were fixed on the clock. Time was running out. Six of the seven charges were dismissed from lack of evidence. The seventh charge involved Jake's acknowledgement of Gem's letter and his present ownership of Sarishan. The horse was deemed to have been payment for services rendered to the bushranger Gypsy Gem Smith. The verdict – Guilty.

Keziah screamed out in horror. 'Two years! *Mi-duvel.* God help us!'

Feeling trapped in a nightmare, impotent and powerless to move,

Daniel watched as Jake, manacled, resisted being dragged back to his cell.

Daniel caught Keziah as she slumped in his arms, but he was unable to tear his eyes from Jake's agonised expression as he struggled in vain to reach her. He felt Jake's pain as if it was in his own body. Jake gave a gut-wrenching cry, helpless to come to the aid of his woman.

CHAPTER 46

Keziah stared at the ceiling rose as she lay in bed in the attic guest room of the Haunted Farm. Time had always been her ally, allowing her to wander between past, present and future. But now, bereft of the gift she had depended on since childhood, she could no longer see any clues to the future.

In the days since her hysterical outburst in court at the announcement of Jake's sentence, she had been drained of all emotion. She could feel nothing for the babe growing in her womb and was only remotely aware of Dr Ross's concern about the threat of a likely premature birth, following the earlier loss of the babe's twin.

He had decreed bed rest and insisted she stay under his direct care. How could she object? She had nowhere else to live. Her previous avoidance of the Haunted Farm and Padraic's *mulo* hardly seemed a battle worth fighting.

When Daniel organised for the children to be sent to Ironbark Farm to attend school under Polly Doyle's care, Keziah had no strength to intervene. Jake was incarcerated in Berrima Gaol, Nerida was miles away in Maitland with Sunny Ah Wei, and Keziah's beloved horses and *vardo* were in Bran's care at the forge. Keziah felt cut off from all family roots, cast adrift in a cold, nightmarish world, sleeping fitfully between draughts of some unnamed liquid to 'quieten' her.

A firm knock at the door was followed by Leslie's entrance.

'Rest easy, lass. Daniel will sleep downstairs so as not to disturb you. All Jake's friends are joining forces to fight for his release. Joseph Bloom is expected from Sydney Town at any hour. Then we'll see some action!'

Keziah looked warily at the glass he handed her.

'I feel so unreal, Doctor. Is it the medication?'

'You've been in a state of shock, lass. Port wine will help you sleep. Drink it down. Everything will look brighter on the morrow.'

After Dr Ross had left the room, Keziah examined the glass. She trusted the healing power of her own herbs as much as she distrusted all *gaujo* drugs. Did this wine contain traces of the laudanum that she had seen draw Sophie Morgan into its web? She smelled it, took a tentative sip and decided the taste *was* exactly like port wine. Her head soon felt light and clear, yet pleasantly drowsy. When she finished the draught she could hear Janet Macgregor whispering in the corridor.

'That vacant expression of hers gives me the shivers, Leslie.'

'The lass has been through a terrible ordeal, Janet. She'll pull through, but at the moment she's not quite in her right mind.'

When their footsteps receded Keziah digested those words. *Not quite in her right mind?* She examined the idea, aware that she was seeing her world through different eyes. *Is this what madness feels like?* she wondered.

Moonlight streamed through the window onto the bed. *What if it does turn my hair white? Queen Marie Antoinette's went white from grief. They cut off her head, so what did her hair matter?*

Instead of falling asleep her mind felt totally lucid. She felt as if she was being gently sucked into a pattern of strange, colourful waking dreams unlike any she had ever experienced, beckoning her into another dimension. She became aware of every inch of the room, every knot in the timber. The wallpaper pattern revealed hidden faces. A tiny cobweb in the cornice took on a magical quality.

The darkened house lay silent. Keziah saw the full face of the moon reflected in the mirror. The dimensions of the room were strangely transformed, quivering as if she were observing them under water. Yet the next moment each object was sharply defined, the textures of wood, brass, linen and lace charged with an invisible source of energy. She could feel each one pulsing with a secret life force.

These sensations thrilled her so much she wanted to go on exploring them, but her deepest instincts struggled to gain control over this seductive excitement. She knew she must try to break free from the hold these sensations had over her or she would be lost.

Something isn't right! Cold water! She got out of bed and crossed to the pitcher on the washstand. She felt as if she was floating. A shaft of moonlight lay like a path across the room and drew her to the mirror.

When she looked at her reflection she was overwhelmed by horror. *That isn't my face!*

A shaven-headed youth stared from the mirror. The same convict she had seen beside the old well. Padraic, who had murdered his master, Barnes. Had he done the deed in this very room?

Keziah was sweating with fear yet she couldn't withdraw her gaze from the apparition's tragic young face, its eyes ringed with dark shadows, as if his soul was condemned to be haunted by grief forever. She realised how contagious her fear was when her babe moved inside her belly. Her throat dried as she spoke to the face in the mirror but backed away from it.

'What do you want of me?'

The ghostly eyes turned in the direction of the chest of drawers. Then the mirror suddenly clouded over to a milky hue and reflected nothing more than the full moon.

Thank God he's gone! Keziah opened the drawer that contained her reticule. She felt a surge of elation when she realised what she must do. Her mind was clear as she seated herself at the escritoire and began writing a letter.

Keziah recognised the handsome wrought-iron gates of Gideon Park were a design of Daniel's. Tonight they were wide open to receive the Jonstones' guests. There was a line of empty carriages awaiting their departure.

After tying the reins of Dr Ross's buggy to the railing, Keziah hurried up the driveway. Joyful music sounded from within the mansion's ballroom. Guests in elaborate finery danced past the French windows.

The layout of the estate was familiar to her. She had once brought Charlotte Jonstone healing herbs following another of the woman's miscarriages. Beyond the house lay a large flagstone courtyard surrounded by farm buildings, stables, shearing sheds and the box-like sleeping quarters of Gideon Park's assigned men. At the heart of the courtyard a group of labourers made merry around a huge bonfire, which was sending sparks rocketing into the night sky.

Keziah manoeuvred around the fringe of revellers and asked for directions from a drunken woman whose face and slop clothing were splashed with red and yellow flashes from the fire.

'The overseer's cottage? Over there. Why would a lady like you visit that bugger?'

Keziah did not reply but hurried to the whitewashed cottage fenced off in its own garden. She lifted the latch of the front door. Her heart thumped painfully but she controlled her fear for Jake's sake.

The stench of rum was strong the moment she entered. Sprawled on a couch before the fireplace was the man who boasted of his title, the Devil Himself. Dying firelight cast shadows on his face – devilishly handsome one moment, sensual and dangerous the next. His eyes scanned her body with an unmistakably venal message. Keziah instinctively placed her hand across her belly to shield the babe within. From early childhood she had feared the Evil One, *The Beng*. Now she was face to face with him.

She had precious little time to accomplish her mission. Even if she called for help the revellers were too drunk to come to her aid. She had a strange sensation that she was standing outside her own body. Divorced from time.

Iago lifted his nightshirt to expose his naked groin. 'This what you came for? You'll get more than you bargained for.'

Her mouth was dry. 'Your wife is at home?'

'She's busy serving the master's guests. So come here and be friendly, girl.'

'I watched you in court,' she said. 'Iago. Is that your real name?'

'The Devil Himself goes by many names,' he said softly, watching her face. 'What strange eyes you have. A big, soft mouth. But you love to hate, don't you? I recognised that Romani curse you cried out in court. I had occasion to visit Newgate prison once – a lot of your Gypsy tribe get holed up there. I sent a few vagabonds there myself.'

'Don't waste my time,' she said coldly to hide her mounting fear. She tried desperately to cling to reality, hold fast to the reason she had come to face him.

Iago smiled as if they were fellow conspirators. 'This moment has been a long time coming, eh Gypsy? There's nothing I don't know about you! I've watched you go through a lot of men, girl. A bushranger, a milksop artist, an English nob and now that lusty fool, Jake Andersen. But I took good care of him for you in court!'

Keziah held back her rage. 'Your evidence sent an innocent man to prison. Here's your chance to tell the truth and set him free. Read this. Then sign it.'

Although her voice was strong her hand shook as she placed the letter on the table.

'You've got a man's balls, I'll say that for you, Gypsy. How do you intend to persuade a man like *me* to do your bidding?'

Keziah opened her reticule. 'Either you sign it or I'll send you down the road to hell where you belong.'

Iago stared into the muzzle of her muff pistol. 'No need to panic, girl. I'll read it.'

He did so very, very slowly.

'How nicely you put it. "I wrongly identified Jakob Andersen and the horse Sarishan. I apologise to the court and Andersen for the distress my error of memory unwittingly caused."'

He twirled his quill between his fingers, as if teasing her, making her wait.

'You'd be silly to shoot me, little witch. You need this bit of paper badly. Let's drink a tot of rum together to toast Her Majesty Queen Victoria.'

Keziah's words spat out her contempt. 'You dare to mention the queen's name!'

He pointed at her, his fingernails rimmed with half moons of dirt. 'I dare *everything*. They don't call me the Devil Himself for nothing. You're Jake Andersen's whore. You cuckolded that coward Daniel Browne into the bargain. I've watched you and Jake. Like two dogs on heat having each other under the stars.'

Keziah went cold at the thought of those beautiful nights with Jake. *He was there watching us!* Iago caught her expression and laughter came from deep in his throat.

'Your cries are delicious when you're being rooted. But I know you, girl, you really prefer it rough. Remember that first time at the creek when you went after me with your horsewhip? Well I'm the very man to give you what you want. The master of rough, I am!'

Vivid, jumbled images flashed through her mind. *The dark horseman spying on my cottage. His hand on my breast. Lifting my skirt to rape me. His laughter. 'I'll give you pain and teach you to love it.' His foul lies that sent Jake to prison. I always knew the devil could take human form.*

Keziah trembled so much she needed both hands to steady the pistol.

'Easy, girl. Doesn't matter to me if Andersen walks free. I'll sign this letter for you, seeing as you want it so bad, but first I need to move closer to the lamp, right?'

He placed the letter on the table, lowering his voice to a gentle, confidential tone.

'I hear that your lover Gypsy Gem drowned off Cockatoo Island. Pity. Now there was a bare-knuckle champ who turned on a great performance. He could lick a man twice his size. Gem was the only convict alive who earned my respect.'

Keziah felt sickened to hear Gem's name in the man's foul mouth.

'That's history,' she said, 'just sign your name.'

'There you are, little schoolmistress. Here's your precious letter.'

Keziah moved to take it, but Iago twisted her wrist and freed the muff pistol from her hand into his. He tossed it from right to left as if it was a child's toy.

'I should have signed it the Devil Himself. Famous I am. I get more work out of my felons than any overseer in the colony. Hundreds have worked their arses off for me. Kept Jonstone in style and lined my own pockets into the bargain.'

Iago added with pride, 'Famous for my clever use of the cat, too. It was me that broke Will Martens. Skin like a girl he had till he tasted my lash. Cried like a girl too.'

He kept on talking in that soft, reasonable voice, but the malevolence in the smile above the cleft chin overwhelmed Keziah with a wave of nausea. Everything in the room took on a surreal quality like crudely painted scenery on a theatre stage. She felt held in the horror of a spell cast by the Devil Himself's soft voice, his fathomless dark eyes that reflected no light. His obscene words cut her to the very heart but she forced herself to watch his movements as he continued to taunt her, tossing the muff pistol from hand to hand. She seized the moment and lunged forward, catching the pistol in midair. When she squeezed the trigger the bullet seared his neck before it hit the wall behind him.

He moved towards her, excited. 'Bad girl,' he said, 'I'd best teach you a lesson.'

She knew the muff pistol only held one bullet. There was no second chance. She released the secret spring of the knife blade and held the pistol like a dagger. Iago's blood sprayed over her dress. She could not comprehend what was happening to that vile face as his mouth filled with blood.

Pistol and letter in hand, Keziah picked up the oil lamp and walked outside. She threw the lamp onto the bark roof of the cottage and watched it explode into flames.

CHAPTER 47

Daniel galloped towards Gideon Park, praying to Our Lady he would not arrive too late.

He had woken in the dark of night to find Leslie's household in an uproar, searching every corner of the Haunted Farm for Keziah. Keeping a cool head Daniel had run to the stables. The buggy was missing. Leslie was anxious that Keziah was so disoriented by his medication she'd driven to Ironbark Farm in search of the children.

Daniel knew better. Iago's evidence had sealed Jake's fate. Even in a half-drugged state Keziah would fight to free Jake. Daniel felt sure she would make for Gideon Park to confront the Devil Himself head-on. He had promised himself he would never return to hell on earth. Now there was no choice.

On his arrival at the wrought-iron gates, Daniel saw the Jonstone mansion was in virtual darkness. There were no carriages in sight, only Leslie's buggy tied to a railing. He dismounted, heading straight for Iago's cottage. He began to shake with fear at his memories of the overseer. And the certain knowledge he must again confront him face to face if Keziah was indeed here.

Jonstone's mansion appeared to be deserted. But there was an agitated babble of voices from the direction of the farm buildings.

He burst into the open courtyard and was bewildered to find himself amongst drunken figures staggering back and forth with buckets of water in the direction of the overseer's cottage. Flames had demolished the roof but continued to lick at the whitewashed walls. Every drunken assigned man was busy yelling out orders but following none. The sole stationary figure was Iago's wife who stood at the edge of the chaos as if transfixed by the fire.

Even before he approached the burning cottage, Daniel recognised the acrid smell of burning human flesh. *Our Lady, don't let it be Keziah.* He forced himself to look through the doorway. His gorge rose at the sight of the half-charred corpse inside the ruins. The Devil Himself was dead.

Daniel staggered back, coughing from the smoke. Where was Keziah? No one was sober enough to answer his questions so he searched the scorched garden around the cottage.

Finally he found her. Keziah lay curled up, softly crooning in her mother tongue. Dried blood was smeared across her cheek. A patch of her hair had burned away, the rest hung matted on her shoulders. What chilled him was her tone of remote sweetness despite the crazed expression in her eyes.

'How good to see you, Daniel. Do you know what happened?'

'Come home with me, Keziah. I'll take care of you now.'

Daniel was ready to promise her anything to remove her from this carnage. But his hope died the moment Keziah politely handed him a muff pistol, its blade covered with dried blood.

He hastily wrapped it in his handkerchief and hid it in his coat pocket. Holding Keziah upright, he steered her behind the cabins and managed to reach the buggy unobserved. Keziah sounded like a curious child.

'Do you know, Daniel? I found out that Iago really *was* the Devil Himself.'

The sound of Keziah's laughter was more terrible than the sound of weeping.

Daniel clapped his hand across her mouth to stifle the sound, whispering words of reassurance as he bundled her into the buggy and attached the reins of the other horse to it. He couldn't shake off the fear that pulsated inside him – that even in death the Devil Himself had the power to hunt him down and punish him. He kept repeating in his mind: *Iago* is *dead. I saw his corpse. But did he die at Keziah's hands?*

As he drove in silence Daniel kept glancing at Keziah. She was shrouded by the moonlight, making her profile look as if it had been carved from white marble.

When they finally arrived at the Haunted Farm he felt relieved to deliver Keziah into Leslie's care. The Doc took one look at her, asked Daniel a few brief questions then escorted her upstairs to tend her burns.

Certain no one was watching, Daniel slipped into the moonlit garden. He lifted the wooden cover of the old stone well and threw the muff pistol down. He counted to five to test the depth before he heard a splash as it hit the water. He suddenly felt a chill as if someone was watching him. There was no one in sight.

Daniel and Dr Ross managed to block Trooper Kenwood's initial attempts to interview Keziah by using her acute mental imbalance and advanced stage of pregnancy as excuses. But over the next few weeks Kenwood continued to call at the Haunted Farm on the off-chance Keziah might be well enough to answer his questions. Daniel's nerves were taut but after three months had passed and the trooper's visits tailed off, he and the Doc became convinced that the police had no evidence.

Then Kenwood suddenly reappeared. When Leslie offered the trooper a glass of whisky, Kenwood confided to Daniel and Leslie in a friendly manner that Julian Jonstone had at last grown tired of pressuring him for answers.

'But I'm still at a loss to understand the circumstances of Iago's death. The bullet we discovered lodged in a remnant of the overseer's cottage was very likely fired from a small pistol but curiously no such weapon has been found.' He looked directly at Daniel, before adding that he had questioned all Gideon Park's assigned labourers.

'To a man they claimed to be drunk that night. All were delighted the Devil Himself had gone to the biblical devil.'

Kenwood's moustache twitched as if reluctant to continue. 'Refresh my memory, Mr Browne. What *was* Mrs Browne's reason for visiting Gideon Park that night *alone*? And why did you and your wife attend Jakob Andersen's trial?'

Daniel was defensive. 'I've told you all this before, Sergeant. Surely both reasons are obvious. We attended Jake's trial because he is *my* best friend. After hearing the jury's guilty verdict my wife suffered shock and hysteria, hardly surprising as she is with child. Dr Ross's medication quietened her but that night while we were all asleep she must have wandered off disoriented.'

Kenwood switched his focus. 'What is your opinion, Doctor? Was Iago's death due to accident, suicide, manslaughter or murder? And why did you not perform an autopsy?'

Leslie could barely control his anger. 'You surely know it is not ethical medical practice to dissect corpses without official sanction. Iago has been six feet under for many weeks so it's a wee bit late to ask me to determine the cause of death. But for the record I've no intention of allowing a patient in Mrs Browne's delicate condition to be questioned here or in the witness box. In her mental state her testimony would be of no value.'

Daniel was quick to agree. 'My wife has withdrawn into a private world due to melancholia. We are concerned for her safety as well as the babe she is carrying.' He tried to hide his anxiety. Was Kenwood still suspicious? Had he heard rumours of the unorthodox relationship between Jake and Mr and Mrs Browne?

Kenwood's response was polite but evasive. 'I'm afraid it isn't up to me whether or not your good wife – or anyone else – is made to stand trial. I am simply collecting the evidence, Mr Browne.'

Daniel and Leslie Ross were relieved when Kenwood left. But later that same afternoon when Daniel was in the garden the sergeant returned alone on horseback.

Daniel saw Keziah watching the trooper's approach from behind the lace curtains of the attic window, so he crossed to another part of the garden in an attempt to distract Kenwood's attention.

The man was clearly in a very different frame of mind. He confronted Daniel and stabbed his finger at the document he held.

'You see? I strongly suggest it's time you grant me access to your wife.'

Daniel tried to prevent his hands trembling as he looked the document over.

'Only on the condition I remain with her during your interview and that her doctor is present.'

He left Kenwood alone in the sitting room and hurried to Leslie's surgery.

'Kenwood's got us cornered. Make sure when you bring Keziah downstairs she gives every appearance of being an invalid. And brief her on the importance of saying as little as possible at their interview. Meanwhile I'll hold him at bay.'

'Aye, lad. I'll give the lass something to quieten her.'

When Keziah finally entered the sitting room on her doctor's arm, Daniel was relieved to see she had changed from her morning dress into a dressing gown and slippers. Her face had the same ethereal quality it had had since the night of Iago's death, the expression in her eyes strangely withdrawn from all around her. Her long hair was unkempt and revealed the small patch on her skull where the hair had burned away in the fire.

Leslie Ross acted solicitously as her doctor and seated her on the sofa beside Daniel. He had clearly taken charge of the situation. Daniel gripped Keziah's hand between his own, relieved to see that the doctor was observing Keziah's every word and gesture while keeping a sharp eye on the trooper.

Kenwood did not even inquire about the state of her health. He wasted no time in waving the official document to underline the importance of his announcement.

'A female assigned at Gideon Park has finally agreed to make her mark on this statement. She swears she directed you to Iago's cottage that night and saw you enter that building but a short time before the cottage caught fire. Is that true?'

Keziah's voice sounded as if it came from a distance. 'I remember asking a woman for directions to his cottage. And I remember lifting the latch on the door. But I have absolutely no memory of what occurred inside.'

Leslie Ross cleared his throat as if trying to prompt Keziah to say no more, but she continued in that flat, dreamy voice.

'Whenever I try to remember and channel my thoughts to re-enter that cottage, I open the door – and there's nothing there. I step into a terrifying black hole in my memory. I'm no liar, Sergeant. I really can't remember.'

Kenwood leaned forward in his seat. 'Mrs Browne. It is high time to tell the whole truth. Were you present when Iago died?'

Keziah looked confused. 'Has someone said that I was?'

Kenwood did not answer but tried another approach. 'Did you see who killed him?'

'I was told later that he was dead. Do you mean to say he was murdered?'

When Kenwood nodded his head to confirm it, she answered quickly, 'Well, whoever it was they did the world a favour. That monster deserved to die.'

Daniel clenched hold of her hand, shaken by the sudden outburst he had been unable to prevent.

The sergeant's eyes narrowed. 'I must formally ask you, Saranna Browne. Did you or did you not contribute in any way to Iago's death?'

Leslie Ross cut across the question in his blunt professional manner but his stutter betrayed his anger. 'My patient has told ye the truth,

Kenwood. She canna remember a damned thing.'

Kenwood held up his hand to ward off the interruption. 'I'll thank you not to interfere in police matters, Doctor. Mrs Browne appears quite capable of answering.' He turned on Keziah a baleful stare. 'Must I repeat the question, Mrs Browne?'

Daniel could barely breathe as Keziah appeared to turn the question over in her mind.

'As I have no memory of his death you will have to tell *me* that, Sergeant. But perhaps this will help your investigation.'

Leslie Ross started to his feet and Daniel blinked in confusion when Keziah withdrew a letter from her pocket and handed it to Kenwood, too late for them to intercept it.

'This proves Iago's a liar,' Keziah said.

Kenwood's expression did not alter as he read the contents. With barely a word of acknowledgement he rose and without bowing to Keziah he took his leave.

Daniel hurriedly conferred with Leslie in a corner of the room. 'I swear I didn't know that letter existed, Leslie. I would have destroyed it. Do you think Kenwood believes her innocence?'

They both turned to look across the room at Keziah who now seemed unaware of their presence.

Leslie Ross was blunt. 'That damned trooper's more interested in gaining promotion than seeing justice done. I dinna doubt he finally managed to obtain some assigned woman's mark on the statement under the promise of swinging a ticket-of-leave her way.'

'I know,' said Daniel. He was too ashamed to admit his own desperation at Gideon Park. Marriage to Keziah had made him a free man. Was his wife now going to pay the price by losing her own freedom?

When Joseph Bloom arrived by special carriage he was clearly concerned about Keziah's welfare but his presence restored a sense of calm control. In Daniel's presence Leslie gave the lawyer a quick briefing on her physical and mental condition. As Joseph had come from Sydney Town specifically to offer them legal advice in the event she was charged with murder, Daniel knew he must take him into their confidence about his wife's true identity. Daniel was startled that Joseph Bloom showed no trace of surprise at the revelation.

'Don't worry, Mr Browne. Every second person in the colony has an alias or two. Not only convicts. Remittance men and even some members of the upper classes are not exactly who or what they claim to be.'

Relieved by Joseph's ready acceptance, Daniel and the doctor wasted no time in escorting him to the sitting room.

'You will not find Saranna as you knew her,' Leslie Ross warned him.

Keziah sat by the fire, the picture of domestic tranquillity as she sewed a baby's gown. She greeted them with that vague, sweet smile Daniel had come to dread.

'Joseph Bloom, how good to see you. How are Rivka and baby Michael? Tell me, what happy occasion has brought your return to Ironbark?'

Joseph Bloom bowed on greeting her and accepted her offer of tea.

Daniel left them both together, anxious to grab a moment alone with his thoughts. He felt unable to handle much more. Jake was in Berrima Gaol in solitary confinement unable to have visitors. And for weeks Daniel had helplessly guarded Keziah as she shifted between states of emotional imbalance and unnatural calm.

Alone in the garden he heard the grandfather clock strike three. He froze at the sight of Sergeant Kenwood's return, accompanied by three young troopers.

Daniel quickly followed them inside and arrived just in time to hear Kenwood deliver the words Daniel had long dreaded.

'Saranna Browne, I am placing you under arrest on the charge of murder.'

With his wife in custody there was no immediate action Daniel could take to help her, so he galloped cross-country through the night to Berrima. Gaining an interview with the new prison chaplain, he begged to be allowed to visit Jake. To his surprise Reverend Parsons arranged a meeting in a cell, empty except for the shadow cast by a guard in the corridor.

Daniel was shocked by the unexpected sight of Jake's shaven head. The familiar grey eyes were ringed by dark shadows. He had to control his impulse to hug his friend and took a step backwards. Jake misinterpreted the gesture as a reproach.

'Bloody decent of you to visit me, Dan, given I ran off with your wife.'

'She never wanted me the way she loves you. I figure we all get what's right for us in the end, mate.'

'How'd you manage to talk your way in here? No one got past the last bloke.'

'I practically got down on bended knees. Told him I had urgent news about the desperate health of your woman. No name of course.'

Jake looked shaken. 'Jesus! What's wrong with Kez?'

Daniel wasted no time in giving him the full details of her arrest and the evidence, including the significance of the letter Keziah had written to force Iago's signature.

'Jesus wept! She did it to try to set me free!' Jake dropped his head in his hands. 'It was me that taught her how to use that bloody muff pistol to protect herself!'

'Don't torture yourself. Perhaps Keziah *did* use it as protection. We can't work out exactly what happened. Leslie believes she's blocked out something too terrible to remember.'

'Rape? That bastard tried it once before!'

Daniel's quick denial of rape failed to pacify Jake.

'I swear on my life, Dan, Keziah could never commit cold-blooded murder!'

'The Doc says women in her condition can become emotionally unstable, capable of behaviour totally foreign to their nature. Keziah has experienced enough recent traumas to test anyone's sanity. Miscarrying a babe, your gaol sentence. Whatever occurred between her and Iago that night might well have tipped the scales.'

'Are you telling me Kez is crazy?'

Daniel tried to assume an air of confidence. 'No. Deeply disturbed but sane.'

'Thank Christ we've got Joseph Bloom to defend her. If anyone can save her, Joe can.'

'He says that if she's convicted of murder she could get Life or Tarban Creek.'

'The lunatic asylum! Jesus, Dan, you *are* saying she's mad!'

'No! Given time and care the Doc believes she'll fully recover. Unless Joseph can prove self-defence, it means Keziah was *not* in her right mind the night Iago was killed. Take heart, Jake. The police have found no trace of a weapon.' He hesitated. 'Her muff pistol will *never* be found.'

Jake nodded in gratitude. 'Tell me she'll walk free. She mustn't give birth in gaol.'

'I can't lie to you, Jake. You're bound to hear it on the prison grapevine – best you hear it from me. The police are said to be about to arrest a Welsh woman long suspected of being in league with her lover to murder her husband. Everyone's betting she'll be the first woman executed here at Berrima. A woman's gender is no guarantee against the hangman's rope, even in these enlightened times.'

'But Keziah's with child!'

'Yes, and Joseph says there's no precedent under British law for hanging a woman when she's with child.'

Jake looked hard at him. 'Jesus wept. You're saying they might do it after the birth?'

'No, I didn't say that,' Daniel said quickly. 'Joseph hopes he can plead for her transfer to Parramatta Female Factory.'

'No! Everyone knows the military use it as a brothel!'

'Face it, Jake! There may be no better option. Joseph has an uphill battle on his hands. Keziah can't remember what happened, but she is adamant that swine deserved to die!'

'She's dead right! Iago wasn't human. She *must* plead Not Guilty. With me holed up in the *stur* for two years, what'll happen to our kids?'

Jake bashed his head against the iron grill of the door like a trapped animal. Daniel overcame his instinct to hold Jake in his arms and comfort him. Instead he remained seated and kept his voice firm in an effort to restore Jake's confidence.

'Jake! I promise you Joseph's doing everything possible to save her. He's discussing her case with that newly arrived English barrister, Robert Lowe. He's a half-blind albino but Joseph says he has the most brilliant legal mind he's ever encountered. And the Doc also has a plan. He says it goes against all his medical ethics but if push comes to shove, he'll keep her in a quieted state to prevent her condemning herself. The most damaging witness to testify against Keziah will be Keziah herself!'

Conscious of the guard in the corridor, Jake lowered his voice. 'I can handle two years, even bloody Norfolk Island and survive, but if Kez goes to prison she'll go stir-crazy. Romanies are different to you and me. They're like Aborigines. They need freedom like air! Lock them up and they give up. They can't believe they'll ever be set free. For Kez gaol is a death sentence. Her father died in prison. Gem was killed escaping from Cockatoo Island. Everyone thinks Kez is a strong woman. She is. But I *know* her better than anyone. Lock her in the *sturaban* and she'll be lost to us. *She'll die inside!*'

Jake grabbed hold of Daniel's shoulders. 'I'm begging you! Sell my land, lie, cheat, pay bribes. Break every bloody rule in the book. Just get my woman out of gaol!'

'You can count on me, Jake. I'll do whatever it takes!'

Daniel spoke the words from his heart. He knew it was the closest he had ever come to a declaration of love.

CHAPTER 48

Daniel counted the days. Only two weeks remained before the trial of Mrs Saranna Browne, the woman the colony's more lurid newspapers labelled 'The Killer Schoolteacher'.

He tied his horse to the railing outside Berrima's Surveyor-General's Inn and looked up at the curtain in a second-storey window. Joseph Bloom's silhouette was pacing back and forth with Leslie Ross, no doubt preparing the case for Keziah's defence.

Daniel tried to dredge up his last reserve of courage to face the meeting their lawyer had called to brief Keziah's key supporters. As he mounted the stairs he prayed in his heart to Our Lady and made full confession of the crime of silence he had committed in England and for his rank cowardice at Gideon Park.

Holy Mother, you know the worst of me. Death prevented me righting the great wrong I did to Saranna and her father. For once in my life make me strong enough to perform an act of courage.

Daniel knew that this would also be a covert act of love to free the woman who belonged to his beloved Jake. He closed his eyes and his lips moved silently in fervent prayer. Would God offer him this last chance for redemption? He waited, but there was no answer to his internal agony, only the sound of drunken laughter from the saloon bar below.

When he entered the room, Joseph Bloom was seated beside Leslie at a mahogany gate-leg table piled high with law books and legal documents. Joseph wasted no time in outlining the case to them. He warned Daniel. 'You must not even reveal your wife's true identity in your sleep. Never forget to call her by the name under which she is charged – Saranna Browne.'

Leslie underlined the need. 'Aye, lad. Imagine how the colonial rags would savage her if they discovered in truth she's a Gypsy who stole a dead girl's identity!'

'Theoretically under British law women – *white* women – have equality in sentencing,' Joseph added. 'The reality? If a woman commits murder it's a heinous crime.'

Leslie's response was blunt. 'Aye. Violence marks them as a traitor to the fair sex.'

Joseph nodded. 'No doubt Lucretia Dunkley was convicted as much for adultery as for murder. It was her Irish lover, Beech, who actually butchered her husband but I suspect the jury condemned her at the first sight of the lovers in the dock. Now she will be the first woman to be hanged at Berrima. Who knows where the full guilt lay? The pair had no lawyer to defend them.'

Daniel was quick to interject. 'But Saranna has *you*. Surely attempted rape is a strong enough motive?'

'We must face reality,' Joseph said quietly. 'Despite the death penalty for rape, why are men seldom brought to trial in this colony for the rape of *un*married females?'

'Women are deemed to initiate seduction,' said Leslie.

Daniel gasped. 'Do you mean they'll believe she enticed the Devil Himself?'

'Your wife is young, a beauty and with child.' Joseph paused. 'With a husband *who lived in Sydney Town*. If the press learns that a prisoner of the Crown, Jakob Andersen, was, excuse me, her travelling companion, she will be vilified. A judge is likely to make a moral example of her. Unless ...?'

His question hung in the air. Daniel hesitated for barely a moment.

'Jake is my friend. I'm ready to swear on oath my wife never committed adultery. I'll publicly stand by her side as her devoted husband and father of Jake's – of *my* – unborn babe.'

Leslie gripped his shoulder in gratitude. 'Good man!'

When Daniel asked about the letter Keziah had given Kenwood, Joseph explained how this crucial evidence could work either for or against her in the eyes of the jury.

'It raises the question. Why would she kill Iago *after* he signed it? It was to her advantage he remained alive to verify it. So what occurred in that final hour of his life? I understand you have both failed to gain her confidence on that point?'

Daniel gestured in despair. 'Saranna says she can't remember.'

'Aye, the lass is suffering from amnesia to block out a traumatic memory.'

'My wife is the strongest woman I've ever known, why can't she face it?'

'Even the strongest man has his breaking point,' Leslie said. 'I am monitoring her behaviour and treatment but it is a difficult balance. Her imagination is so intense, her dream life so active. Small doses of laudanum usually have a calming effect, but the drug is known to affect people differently. Prolonged usage is dangerously addictive, but right now it is imperative to bring her safely through this trial without condemning herself.'

'Agreed.' Joseph turned to Daniel, eyeing him over the top of his eyeglasses. 'The key weakness in the prosecution's case is the absence of any murder weapon.'

Daniel remained silent but he felt a nervous tic in his cheek, aware that the lawyer suspected he'd disposed of the evidence.

Leslie Ross admitted he was confused by the colony's recent adoption of the English Prisoners' Counsel Act. 'How on earth will this affect my patient?'

'My *wife*,' Daniel corrected quickly.

'The law regarding felony cases is in a state of transition. Previously the accused was allowed to stand and make a statement in his own defence, a 'dock statement' that was not on oath and not subject to cross-examination. Now some judges rule that if the defence counsel makes a speech on his behalf, the prisoner's dock statement is not allowed. Some judges follow the old rules and allow both – some do not.'

'Which way is our judge likely to jump?' Leslie asked.

Joseph Bloom shrugged. 'He's a new appointment. I won't know the answer until we appear in court.' He turned to Daniel. 'But I'll do everything in my power to prevent your wife taking the stand.'

Daniel raised the question uppermost on his mind. 'Would an all-female jury be more sympathetic to Saranna?'

'Colonial precedent suggests otherwise,' Joseph replied. 'In the early years of settlement a female convict jury sent a fellow woman prisoner named Davis to the gallows for petty theft.'

'Surely we live in more enlightened times?' Daniel argued.

Joseph was sceptical. 'That is no guarantee women are more merciful today. Take the case of Sarah McGregor. This girl claimed she was forced to have connection with her assigned master. She attacked him with her bare hands and as a result he died, probably due to a heart attack. The court empanelled a jury of twelve respectable matrons to examine her physically and verbally. Their verdict? "To the best of our opinion, not with child." Sarah McGregor only escaped the gallows due to Governor Bourke's clemency.'

Joseph paused for effect. 'Seven months later she gave birth to a son. A jury of good women had the chance to save her but did not choose to do so.'

Close to tears, Daniel remembered how he had been crushed by the system at the hands of Iago.

'What if her jury consists of gentry, landholders, literate men who came free?'

'Then God help the lass,' Leslie mumbled.

'All jurymen are initially unknown factors,' Joseph said reassuringly. 'It is my role to present your wife's defence in a way that will gain the jury's sympathy.'

Daniel seized on another point that worried him. 'What happens if they claim Saranna deliberately set fire to Iago's house?'

Joseph sighed. 'That is a most serious offence and there's a penalty of mandatory death "for maliciously and unlawfully setting fire to a dwelling-house, any person being therein".'

Daniel looked from one to the other. 'Mandatory. What does that mean?'

'It contains a directive to the judge, in this case, to enforce the death penalty.'

Daniel stood up, agitated. 'Do you mean she faces *two* chances of the death penalty?'

'I simply want to prepare you for the fact it is a most complex case,' said Joseph. 'But there's an old German proverb. *Gesetz was hat nicht ein loch, wer's finden kann.* This means there is no law without a loop-hole for him who can find it.'

Leslie did not hesitate to volunteer. 'Aye, and you're just the man to find it! As her doctor I will do anything you advise. Say anything you tell me to say, aye, under oath!'

Daniel was conscious that both men waited for him to make the same commitment but he was so overwhelmed by fear he was unable to answer.

A knock at the door gave him an excuse to avoid a direct response. He moved to open the door. The publican's wife was full of apologies.

'I am sorry to disturb Mr Bloom but this gentleman insists on seeing him.'

Immaculately dressed in pale grey, Caleb Morgan passed by Daniel without a glance and made straight for Joseph Bloom and presented his card.

'Mr Bloom, you know me through my legal dealings in the matter of Gabriel Stanley. I come to offer my help to your client in any capacity you deem fit. I swear on my honour I have no ulterior motive. I am totally at your service, gentlemen.' Caleb Morgan bowed to them with what appeared to be genuine respect.

The first to offer his handshake was Leslie Ross. 'Welcome on board, Morgan.'

Daniel only nodded, stung by the contrast between his own ambiguous attitude and the forthright manner of the man he knew to be Gabriel's true father.

Joseph gestured to the Englishman to be seated. 'Well, gentlemen, we now have another member on our team. I have some interesting witnesses lined up for the defence. Let us explore our tactics, shall we?'

Outwardly Daniel was in agreement, inwardly he felt more like a coward than ever before.

CHAPTER 49

The final days before the commencement of Keziah's trial were a nightmare for Jake Andersen.

It was obvious to him their friends were so busy helping Joseph Bloom build a respectable public image for Saranna Browne to counter the lurid newspaper accounts of Iago's murder that they had virtually forgotten Jake's existence.

Now as he sweltered under the midday sun breaking sandstone blocks, he worked on his own plan to help his woman. *First I've got to find where the bloody warders have stashed her.*

He went over in his mind every detail he'd learned about Berrima Gaol. He was aware that it was filled beyond its capacity of three hundred prisoners. *That's clear 'cos the bloody warders never stop complaining they're overworked.*

He pieced together snippets of information he had gleaned from inmates and guards about the prison layout. During the short break his fellow prisoners drank a pannikin of water or relieved themselves. Jake chose the time to shelter in a patch of shade, covertly re-examining the rough blueprint he'd drawn and adding fresh details that had just come to light. Cells lined passageways that radiated like spokes from an octagonal wheel. *But where are the female prisoners' cells? There's only a small number of women here compared to men. Maybe they've put Kez in a cell on her own. That'd have to be better than locking her in with some ruthless inmate like Lucretia Dunkley.*

He felt a sudden rush of panic. *Jesus wept! That Dunkley woman knows she's gunna swing for The Finisher – so she'd have nothing to lose by killing anyone that got in her way!*

Jake forced himself to calm down and think of ways to aid his plan.

He suspected there was one man inside Berrima who guessed the reason for his obsession with The Killer Schoolteacher, but being suspicious of all god-botherers Jake had managed to steer clear of him. When he was summoned to the chaplain's office within the hour, Jake gave a wry shrug. *Maybe this is what Kez would call* baxt *giving me a prod.*

Before him was a nuggety man with a barrel chest, resembling an ecclesiastical version of John Bull, minus the waistcoat made from the Union Jack. Seated across from Jake, the chaplain looked him in the eye as if he accepted the best and worst in him.

'I'm Frederick Parsons, son, the relieving chaplain while my colleague is on leave.' He casually placed a bible on the table. 'I take it you're not much of a church-going man, Jakob.'

'You're dead right, Rev. I know you mean well but you're just wasting your time on me. I'm a lost cause.'

'I doubt our Creator would agree. And I should advise you that as I am a priest nothing you reveal to me in confidence can be used in evidence in court.'

Jake outlined how he'd been convicted of helping mates who were bushrangers. He hoped this would deter the chaplain. On the contrary it aroused his interest.

'Ah, Jabber Jabber – a young Quaker who knows his bible. I was out riding with my Roman Catholic colleague Father Dennis Declan when the lad bailed us up. He refused to take money from men of the cloth so we had a lively chat about St Matthew the tax collector instead.'

Jake realised he needed to take a stronger tack to be rid of this bible-basher.

'It gets worse, Rev. In your eyes I'm an adulterer. I've been on the run with another bloke's wife for near two years and loved every bloody minute of it.'

The chaplain paused before adding quietly, 'I should warn you I'm damned hard to shock, Jakob. And the woman in question is known to me – a lady who doesn't deserve to be here. The so-called Killer Schoolteacher.'

Jake was startled and tried to stare him out. 'I didn't say it was her.'

'You didn't have to, Jakob. I have been around prisons long enough to recognise a prisoner's guilt or innocence as soon as I see the whites of their eyes.'

'She's charged with murder,' Jake added quickly, 'but she's innocent!'

Jake stared into the chaplain's eyes and defiantly placed his hand on the bible. 'If I get half a chance, I swear to God I'll *kill* to get her out of here. You see, Rev, you're wasting your time on me!'

'No. You need me now more than ever.' The chaplain rose. 'God moves in mysterious ways. I marked a passage. Read it when you're alone!'

Jake felt there was nothing to be lost by throwing in a wild card. 'I don't suppose you could get a message to Saranna Browne?'

The chaplain gave him a wink. 'Read that, son. Then we'll talk again.'

Jake was suddenly alert. *What kind of priest is this joker?*

Back in the dogbox of a cell he shared with a gentle old man who claimed he was Jesus, Jake discovered a blank piece of paper wrapped around a pencil inside the bible. Was this a trick to force him to read the bible he had successfully avoided all his life? Jake read with difficulty the verses underlined in St John's Gospel.

In my Father's house are many mansions: if it were not so, I would have told you. I go to prepare a place for you.

And if I go and prepare a place for you, I will come again, and receive you unto myself: that where I am, there ye may be also.

An asterisk beside the word 'mansions' had a note pencilled in the margin that read: 'A word lost in translation. The original meaning might best be translated as *levels*.'

Does this mean other levels in this gaol? The basement? An attic?

Pencilled at the foot of the page were the chaplain's words: 'I go to visit her tomorrow. If you have private words you want delivered to her I am at your service.'

'Well, I'll be buggered. A priest who's a smuggler!'

Laboriously Jake began to write a secret love letter to Keziah, taking care not to use her name or his own in case his letter was intercepted.

In a small courtyard in the gaol Jake muttered angrily as he swung his pick at the section of flagstones he had been ordered to dig up. *If you ask me it's a bloody stupid place to dig a well. What's their bloody hurry?*

He suspected the pointless work was designed to keep prisoners like him fully occupied today. Everyone knew 22 October was the day set for the public hanging of Lucretia Dunkley and her Irish lover, Martin Beech. Since dawn Jake had heard the arrival of carriages and carts. The word was that Berrima's population had swelled overnight with spectators from surrounding villages ready to enjoy The Finisher hanging the murderers on the scaffold erected outside the prison wall.

Jake knew precisely what this first execution of a woman at Berrima Gaol meant. *The bloody authorities might take it into their heads to keep The Finisher in town ready to hang Kez.* Nobody else was low enough to do his job and it was only forty-eight hours before the commencement of Keziah's trial.

As he levered the stones up Jake went over every detail he had gleaned about the case. He took no satisfaction from Daniel's report that no one had shed a tear at Iago's burial in Jonstone's family graveyard, least of all Iago's wife, who had bolted from Gideon Park before the funeral. Apparently the old priest had been shocked when the first sod of earth on the coffin was greeted by a rousing cheer from Iago's army of assigned men. Iago could rot in hell. Nothing mattered to Jake except Keziah. He had one consolation. Old Lucretia had had no legal representation in a trial presided over by Chief Justice Dowling, where as Keziah was up against a newly appointed judge and she had Joseph

Bloom working on her case night and day with the Doc and Daniel.

When Jake heard a second triumphant cheer from outside the gaol walls he knew that The Finisher had dispatched both murderers. If Joseph failed, Keziah could end up standing on that same scaffold with the crowd baying for her blood.

By the eve of Keziah's trial Jake was half mad with worry. His cell-mate, Gentle Jesus, lay mercifully asleep, so Jake took advantage of the sliver of moonlight that fell through the slit of window. He poured his heart into another letter to Keziah, promising her that Joseph Bloom would prove her innocence, but if all else failed Jake would set her free himself.

For the past week the prison chaplain had acted as courier for Jake's letters, having assured Jake that after Keziah read them in his presence, he had burned them.

Jake remembered the chaplain's confidential advice that an influential woman was working to have his sentence reduced. This seemed unlikely to Jake. The only woman he knew in high places was Jenny, and she'd rather die than publicly acknowledge his existence.

At the sound of a key grating in the lock Jake hid his latest letter inside his shirt but was relieved to find it was the chaplain who entered. He silently beckoned Jake, taking care not to wake Gentle Jesus.

Jake followed him down the dark labyrinth of corridors between rows of prisoners' cells. Occasionally male voices and catcalls broke the silence. Their footsteps echoed as they climbed a steep stairwell. Jake's nerves were so taut that his question sounded like an accusation. 'Hey, where are you taking me?'

'Don't worry. I'm the one with my head on the chopping block if you bolt. So be a good lad and stick with me, eh?'

Jake saw they were travelling down a corridor where cells on both sides appeared to be unoccupied. At the far end of the corridor, a barred window framed a slice of moon that pierced the blackened sky – a sight that caused a painful memory. *Keziah's moon. Will I ever be free to make love to her again under the stars?*

The chaplain halted before an iron door with a small grid. It looked no different to any other door, except that Jake was sure he could hear the sound of breathing. *Keziah.*

The chaplain looked apologetic. 'I'm afraid I can't allow you inside. This is the best I can do, Jakob. Sorry I can only give you a few minutes alone.'

Jake heard the sound of boots moving to the far end of the corridor and saw the chaplain's back outlined against the window as if he was intent on watching the moon rise beyond Berrima Gaol's walls.

There didn't appear to be anybody within the web of shadows in the cell. But as his eyes adjusted to the darkness he made out a movement on the bunk. He gripped hold of the iron bars and whispered urgently, 'Kez, it's me!'

She rose as if sleepwalking and crossed to the grid. He realised she was heavily medicated and cursed the Doc for doing his job too well. Her eyes were ringed with dark shadows and her irises were cloudy. Her skin had already taken on a gaolhouse pallor as if she had long been kept underground, hidden from the sun. Her hair hung across her face like a dank veil that she had no energy to push back. Although he had been warned Keziah was not herself, the reality winded him like a punch in the guts. No wonder the Rev had concealed the truth.

'Everything's going to be all right, Kez. I'll sort things out. Don't lose heart.'

Her fingers reached through the grid to stroke the short bristles of his shaven head.

Her eyes suddenly focused and registered surprise. 'They've cut off your long hair. What's wrong, Jake?'

Jake had no idea he was crying until he kissed her fingers and saw his tears fall on her hand.

'I'll get you out of here, darling. One way or another, I'll set you free. I swear to God I won't let you give birth in gaol.'

Keziah was clearly confused. 'Why can't I be with you, Jake? And why does everyone say Daniel's my husband? I'm *your* woman, Jake.'

Jake only had a few minutes to impress on her what she must hide.

'Course you are, sweetheart, but that's our secret. You must pretend Daniel's the father of our baby. Judges like things all neat and tidy under the law.' He added patiently as if to a child, 'Remember, in court you *must* go on pretending you are Saranna Browne. You do understand, don't you?'

Keziah seemed to be slipping away from him. 'I can't remember. I know Iago's dead. They think I killed him. Do you think I did it?'

'You did nothing wrong, Kez. Remember that. Iago was the monster. You were only defending yourself from him.'

She looked startled. 'I remember the muff pistol! You taught me well, Jake.'

'No, Kez! You mustn't talk about that. Remember one thing! You are *innocent*!'

He reached between the bars to try to draw her face close enough to kiss her, but she was already drifting back to the bunk. He saw her fall asleep before his eyes.

The chaplain pressed his arm. 'Sorry Jakob. Time's up.'

Jake felt as if his heart had been torn in two but he stumbled after the chaplain, shocked by Keziah's disturbed mental state. Had Iago's death turned her mind? Or was the Doc's medication the cause? He understood why Joseph Bloom was fighting to prevent her giving evidence in her defence. Keziah was so unstable that she would prove to be the prosecution's most damaging witness.

Back in his cell, Jake tried to go over the desperate plan he had been working on for the past week. But his cellmate was wide awake. Gentle Jesus was convinced he was the Son of God and was fervently spouting scriptures.

'Give it a rest will you, mate?' Jake begged. 'I can't bloody think straight.'

The old man turned over to go back to sleep. 'I will see you in Paradise, my son.'

Jake mumbled under his breath. 'Not if I see you first, mate.'

When the old man was finally quiet Jake went over the plan in his head. The last time he had met Will Martens the lad had revealed to him the exact location of the stone he had removed to escape from this gaol, then replaced in position so that 'some other poor bastard' could use the same escape route. Will's last words had seemed like a joke at the time.

'You never know when you might want to use it yourself, mate!'

In the darkness Jake silently swore on his own life. *I'll get you out of here, Kez. One bloody way or another.*

CHAPTER 50

Keziah awoke in her cell convinced she had dreamt Jake's visit. His dream image had looked very different, gaunt with a shaven head. In her long ago vision she had seen Jake behind that same metal grid in the cell door. Last night was no dream. She realised reality had one difference. They were both prisoners.

Could I have murdered Iago? Keziah struggled to identify the cause of the fear that blocked her memory. Each time she mentally tried to re-open the door of Iago's cottage she walked into that terrifying black hole. This time random pieces of memory began to leap into her brain. She was overwhelmed by shame and horror, not by the realisation she had killed Iago, he deserved to die. Her shame was because her act of violence had destroyed the lives of her beloved Jake and their children.

She clung to a single thought. *The letter.* She must keep her wits about her. Tell the truth that would set Jake free. Fight those *gaujos* in court with their own law.

When the warder brought her a basin of water she washed her face hoping the shock of cold water would make her more alert. She had more than a month to go before she was due to give birth but her prison dress was already stretched tightly across her belly.

Moments later Leslie Ross arrived with a package.

'Joseph Bloom asks you to dress your hair like the modest young wife and mother we all know you are, and Janet Macgregor says this will be most becoming on you in court. She sends you a message: "Keep a brave heart. Live to fight another day."'

The parcel contained a rose silk gown trimmed with fine lace, the collar pinned with Saranna's cameo brooch. Janet Macgregor's gesture was the kindness shown by one prisoner to another. Keziah forced herself to meet Leslie's eyes.

'I am truly blessed in my friends. Forgive me, Doctor, but I don't want to take more laudanum. It gives me terrible dreams. I want to remember. I think I saw Iago die.'

'Aye, I thought it might come to this,' he said carefully. He removed a metal flask from his medical bag and poured a beaker for her.

'You are due in court within the hour. This is a new brand of tea from India. You English believe tea solves all problems and it will.'

Keziah gave him a wry smile. 'I'm a Welsh Romani, but I'll try it anyway.'

He watched her drink it. 'It takes a wee bit of time to work but it will calm you, lass.'

After his departure Keziah dressed herself in the gown. She carefully positioned a lock of hair to disguise the patch singed by the fire, then braided it in a plait to give the jury the conservative impression Joseph needed to counteract the label of 'The Killer Schoolteacher'.

Keziah felt strangely calm seated beside her guard, waiting to be escorted to the courthouse. She would have preferred to be alone with her thoughts, but this garrulous guard was intent on entertaining her with gaolhouse gossip about the Dunkley-Beech executions.

'Old Lucretia was Welsh like you, but different as night is from day.'

'I'm from Cheshire,' Keziah corrected, but the guard continued his tale.

'Had a face as tough as a man's, pitted from the pox. Thought she was clever enticing her ticket-of-leave lover to murder poor old man Dunkley for his farm but all she copped was a date with The Finisher. They packed her skull off to them phrenologist blokes in Sydney to read the bumps on her head.'

Keziah was appalled. 'They cut off her head?'

He puffed up with pride. 'Aye. Helped bury her headless corpse, I did. Made a prisoner dig a grave under the flagstones here. *Standing upright* she is. There's no chance in hell that bitch'll ever rest in peace!'

Suddenly aware of her horror he added quickly, 'Don't worry, Mrs Browne. Any fool can see you're a lady. They'll treat *you* different.'

Dead or alive? She found herself slipping back into that state of unnatural calm which had isolated her from reality since the night of the fire. She felt a rush of suspicion recalling Leslie's words. *'It takes a wee bit of time to work but it will calm you, lass.'*

Too late she understood the significance of his words. *Tea? He's laced it with a drug!*

Outside the prison walls the guard escorted Keziah across the laneway to the courthouse. The world around her seemed to be filtered through a mist – the gaping faces of early spectators drawn to the excitement of a woman's trial, their hands pointed at her in recognition. To escape their gaze she looked up at the massive dome, which she remembered from Jake's trial was the court's only source of natural light. The sandstone walls were indented with 'blind' windows.

Her guard followed her gaze to an oriental wagon parked in the lane, where a pigtailed Chinaman sat with an Aboriginal girl. Nerida and Sunny Ah Wei gave her a tentative wave to which Keziah smiled acknowledgement.

The guard was disdainful. 'Funny company you keep!'

All emotion was sealed inside her but Keziah forced herself to defend them. 'My friends have courage.'

'They won't let no blacks in nohow!' the guard said, as if to settle the matter.

Inside the courthouse Keziah felt Daniel's eyes follow her progress as the guard escorted her from the female holding cell to the prisoner's box. No chair had been provided for her.

Daniel's voice rose in protest. 'My wife can't be expected to stand in her condition!'

Keziah glanced at the women spectators seated in a tiered box like a miniature grandstand at a cricket match. In the back row, she was vaguely aware of a woman whose face was obscured by the wings of her handsome bonnet, the woman Daniel had identified at Jake's trial as the wife of Magistrate Hamberton.

Keziah scanned the faces of the 'twelve good men and true'. Although she could see no quality of mercy in their features, she could not sustain any feeling of anxiety. What business was that of hers? The world was pleasantly but unnaturally hazy.

In front of the tipstaff's bench a large mahogany table was scattered with scrolled documents tied with pink ribbons.

I need ribbons like that for Pearl's hair. Where is she? Where's Gabriel? The answers needed a degree of concentration that was beyond her, so she allowed her thoughts to drift.

A clerk of the court scratched away with a quill as white-wigged, black-robed figures milled around the central table like figures in a puppet show. Only Joseph Bloom looked human. His eyes smiled at her over the top of his spectacles.

She noticed Daniel's knuckles were white as he gripped the railing that divided them, as nervous as if he were the prisoner on trial. His eyes tried to convey some message but the scarlet-robed judge diverted her attention. He looked out between the side flaps of an elaborately coiled wig that was too big for his head. Keziah smiled. *He looks as stern as the* gaujos' *god would if a Romani wandered into his heaven by mistake.*

Keziah was grateful when a chair was provided 'due to her delicate condition'.

She tried to concentrate when Daniel took the stand. Was this the same suit he'd borrowed from Mac Mackie for their wedding? She was surprised that Daniel had shaved off his moustache. She remembered Joseph's words. *'A clean-shaven witness has the advantage over a bearded man as his every emotional nuance will register with the jury.'*

As she listened to Daniel's evidence she felt a vague stirring of pride that he was her friend. His manner was respectful but no longer servile.

'I am now a free man but on arrival in the colony I was assigned to Mr Jonstone at Gideon Park. He was always a good and decent master. In practice I was directly answerable to his overseer, the deceased Iago, at best a man most difficult to please. For years I worked desperately hard to avoid the floggings he ordered to punish our slightest misdemeanours. Death was my sole hope of escape. Until my dear Saranna married me.'

Daniel described Saranna's devotion to him, their children and their coming babe. How she abhorred violence so much she became hysterical whenever she saw a kangaroo shot. Keziah saw from the looks on the faces of the jurymen how impressed they were by Daniel's fervent declaration.

'My gentle Saranna is incapable of murder!'

Keziah felt a wave of guilt that her violent crime had dishonoured the dead girl's name.

The next witness was a young woman identified as Lizzie Fleet also known as Lizzie Jones. She avoided looking in Keziah's direction when asked to describe the woman she had directed to Iago's cottage the night of his murder.

'Dark-haired, big with child and spoke posh like she was better than the rest of us. She was dead eager to visit the Devil Himself and we all know what *he* got up to!'

Asked to identify this woman in court Lizzie hesitated before pointing. 'That's her in the prisoner's dock.'

'Did you hear a gunshot? Or see Mrs Browne leave the cottage carrying a weapon?'

'I don't know nothing about that. That's all I'm saying.'

Keziah saw that the woman again avoided her eyes as she left the stand.

The next witness was Sean Kirby, a nervous lad who pulled his forelock, clearly intimidated by the bullying prosecutor's tactics. Keziah had no memory of ever seeing him.

The prosecutor confidently hooked his thumbs in the folds of his robe as he reminded the youth how heavily the law came down on those who committed perjury.

'You say you saw the accused lying near Iago's burning cottage. Is it possible she concealed a murder weapon?'

Young Kirby was sweating. 'I saw naught but she was holding a letter, Sir.'

'This letter?' The prosecutor waved the signed evidence as if it were a toerag.

'Can't say, Sir. Ain't got no reading. Can only make my mark, Sir.'

'I repeat, is it not possible this woman concealed a murder weapon?'

'I don't know. We was all running to stop the fire spreading. Holding a letter in both hands, she was, and keening.'

The prosecutor appeared to be caught off guard. 'Keening?'

'Like our Irish women mourn for the dead, Sir.'

The prosecutor looked irritated as he dismissed him. In contrast Joseph's manner to Sean Kirby was as respectful as if he were questioning a free man.

'Had you ever seen Mrs Browne prior to the night of the fire, Mr Kirby?'

'Once, Sir. After she married Daniel Browne she came to Gideon Park one day I was working in the garden. This lady she handed Mrs Jonstone a package. Mistress said, "Women understand these things. Feel free to call whenever you're passing, Mrs Browne."'

'Feel free to call whenever you're passing, Mrs Browne,' Joseph slowly repeated the words for the jury's benefit. 'So an open invitation might well be the reason for Saranna Browne's presence at Gideon Park on the night in question. Thank you, no further questions.'

By this point Keziah had a stronger grasp of the proceedings, but she felt emotionally distanced as if she was seated in the back row of a theatre watching a play.

She noted Julian Jonstone's annoyance when he was called to the stand. He was fulsome in his praise of his deceased overseer's character.

Joseph Bloom was polite. 'It would appear Iago was a paragon of virtue when you were in residence at Gideon Park but as you just stated, you were absent many months of the year. You are known to be a pillar of the Church of England, Sir, so we can presume you would abhor any cruelty practised by your overseer towards a woman, would you not?'

Although Jonstone's manner was haughty, Keziah sensed he was no liar.

'All my female assigned servants are quartered under my roof. On my direct orders no woman has ever been treated harshly at Gideon Park.'

Joseph waited as if to give the witness enough rope to provide the answer he wanted.

Jonstone faltered. 'However if a man chastises his own wife for a misdemeanour the law and the church have no right to intervene, as well you know.'

Joseph's voice suggested the barest trace of sarcasm. 'Indeed, physical cruelty to a spouse is a grey area under British law.' He spun around. 'One last question, Sir. Under oath it is claimed Mrs Browne delivered a parcel to your wife. Please describe the circumstances.'

Jonstone grew flustered. 'Don't see the relevance but very well. My wife suffered the loss of three stillborn sons. This Browne woman paid an unsolicited visit with herbs that she claimed would help my wife carry full-term. Arrant nonsense. Little better than witchcraft.'

'My sympathies for your loss, Sir, but perchance your wife used the herbs?'

'Against my better judgement.'

'Quite so. I believe we must congratulate you on the safe delivery of

Julian Jonstone Junior some twelve months ago. This little chap makes good progress, I trust?'

'He's thriving. Thanks be to God, *not* pagan herbs!'

'Be that as it may,' Joseph Bloom said gently, 'Mrs Browne drove some distance in an *attempt* to give healing aid to your wife, did she not?'

At Jonstone's nod, he continued. 'In some eyes Mrs Browne's action might be regarded as that of a ministering angel. I take it there was no monetary transaction? A simple act of kindness would you say?'

'No, there was no payment,' Jonstone conceded. 'Intended kindness, albeit misguided.'

'Thank you, that will be all.'

Keziah felt an unexpected flicker of emotion. Herbs had done their job. Charlotte's son was thriving. She noticed Joseph looked distinctly pleased with Jonstone's testimony. Her feeling of pride switched to unease when the name of the next witness was called.

Caleb Morgan! Is he going to take advantage of me being in gaol to steal Gabriel?

Caleb appeared to be in total control of the situation as he took the oath in ringing tones. Keziah was convinced he would retain his inborn air of superiority until his dying day.

'Mrs Browne is well known to my family in England. In the period before her marriage she was Miss Saranna Plews, a house guest at my father's country estate, Morgan Park, Lancashire. My father, John Morgan, is well known to Governor Gipps.' He paused to allow judge and jury time to be impressed by this proof of status.

Keziah felt torn by conflicting emotions. *Me a house guest of the Morgans! That's a lie for a start but he actually sounds as if he's on my side. What's he up to?*

Caleb continued to answer Joseph's questions, needing little prompting.

'Saranna's kindness and pharmaceutical skills were of enormous benefit in restoring the health of my stepmother. I came to the colony with the expressed intention of repaying Mrs Browne for her great service to my family. We Morgans owe her a debt of honour. Mrs Browne is a lady of innate gentility and honesty, quite above fiscal considerations. And she is totally incapable of committing the violent crime of which she is accused!'

To Keziah's surprise when the prosecutor waived the right to question him, Caleb paused in the act of crossing the courtroom to make a respectful bow in her direction.

Although her lawyer seemed well satisfied with Caleb's testimony, Keziah was growing restless. *What a load of rot! And* gaujos *have the hide to call us Romanies liars!*

Dr Leslie Ross's sworn statement was read out in his absence. It consisted of a careful selection of facts supporting his opinion that trauma made her incapable of giving accurate evidence.

Keziah was livid with rage when she saw the doctor was present at the rear of the court. *What is going on? I will not be silenced by drugs. The law treated my father as a lying Gypsy vagabond. I'll show them a Romani woman is as honest as the best of them.*

When Joseph formally asked for her to be excused from giving evidence, the judge appeared to be on the point of agreement until Keziah interrupted with a shout of denial.

'There's been some mistake. I am quite capable of telling the truth, Your Honour!'

For once, Joseph Bloom seemed lost for words.

When the clerk offered Keziah the *gaujo* bible, her response was polite but firm.

'I respect your bible, Your Honour, but it would be a lie for me to swear on it.'

The judge leaned forward. 'But surely you are a Christian, Mrs Browne?'

Daniel yelled out, 'Indeed she is! We married in church!'

'*Mr* Browne, you will kindly refrain from interjecting or you will be removed from the court! Kindly explain yourself, Mrs Browne.'

Keziah's voice rang out with pride. 'I am a Romani!'

The judge was flummoxed. 'Am I to understand you to be a native of Rome?'

'No. My father was a Rom descended from "the true black blood" generations ago in India. I swear by my people's highest oath. By My Father's Hand, I will tell the whole truth and nothing but the truth. Which means I must tell you right now – I am *not* Saranna Browne.'

'What absurdity is this?' the judge demanded, stabbing his finger at his documents.

'I took that name from a girl who died. I was born Keziah Stanley.'

Keziah saw that her revelation caused several reactions.

Daniel Browne cried out, 'My wife is ill. She's not responsible for her words!'

The judge's wig slipped to cover his spectacles.

The irate prosecutor demanded, 'What the hell are you up to now, Bloom?'

Joseph Bloom seemed to be muttering in German under his breath.

Dr Ross and Caleb Morgan exchanged looks of utter dismay.

Consternation broke out in the spectators' box. Keziah saw that the elegant woman in blue had slumped in her seat and the woman beside her was trying to revive her with smelling salts.

It seemed to Keziah she was the only person in court who was calm. Now that she had publicly reclaimed her true identity, she felt relief that she had cleared Saranna's good name. Her fight to free Jake could now begin.

Once order was restored the judge conferred with his tipstaff about legal precedents as to whether the trial should continue. After Joseph Bloom advised the name was known to him as an alias used by the accused, a common enough practice, he firmly ruled that it could.

During Keziah's delivery of her testimony with a cool recounting of the facts, she noticed Joseph Bloom scanned the faces of the jurymen to weigh the impact of her words.

The judge appeared bemused. 'Let me understand if we have your extraordinary story correctly tabled. You delivered this letter to Iago, which retracts the accusations he made about Jakob Andersen at his trial. You claim Iago signed this letter, after which you fired your muff pistol at him!'

He glanced severely at the prosecutor. 'A weapon that has *vanished without trace*.'

Joseph Bloom jumped to his feet. 'May it please, M'lud. No trace of *any* weapon has been found. May I suggest it is no more than the hallucination of a young woman who is advanced with child and has been suffering acute shock since the events of that night.'

The judge straightened his wig over a face that was pink with irritation. 'The court does not take kindly to impertinent interruptions.'

He turned to Keziah. 'You claim you visited Iago that night for the sole purpose of gaining Jakob Andersen's freedom?'

'No. To prove his *innocence*. Iago was a false witness!'

'And you would have us believe, Madam, that you are *not*? It is common knowledge your Gypsy tribe has earned a justified reputation as liars down through the centuries.'

Keziah felt a rush of freedom, no longer bound by Saranna Plews's conservative manners. 'I have sworn By My Father's Hand. *I do not lie!*'

'We have before us Iago's signed retraction of his evidence. Yet you admit you shot him. Describe to the court the events that led to your acknowledged act of violence. *Why* you did it.'

At that moment Keziah still did not know the reason herself. She was certain of only one thing. Jake's whole future hung in the balance. She summoned up the gift to take her back to the vivid scene in Iago's cottage; the smell of rum, the oil lamp, her muff pistol trained on his face, his hand grabbing the weapon and tossing it from hand to hand like a child's toy.

It was then she knew the truth. The dark hole in her memory disappeared. She heard herself quoting Iago's soft words as if the dead man was speaking through her.

'It was me that broke Will Martens. Skin like a girl he had till he tasted my lash. Cried like a girl too. You wouldn't believe what a man will do – if you make him hungry enough and break his spirit.'

Every face was riveted on Keziah, none more intently than Joseph Bloom.

She faltered, her voice soft with horror. 'Iago laughed when he said it. *"Weak bastards aren't much fun. I like a man with real balls. Real spirit. Like Gypsy Gem Smith. It needed four of my men to hold him down. Gem Smith took it from them just like a woman!"*'

Keziah began to sway and Joseph Bloom sprang to his feet.

'M'lud, my client is in no condition to proceed, I beg you to excuse her.'

Before the judge had time to rule, Keziah's voice cut across him.

'That devil kept laughing. I shot him but the bullet only grazed his neck. He kept coming towards me so I pressed the spring to release the blade. He deserved to die. I *must* have killed him. No one else was there.'

The courtroom seemed to freeze in time and space. Finally the judge looked stonily at Joseph Bloom who was bent over the desk conferring with his clerk.

'May I remind the defence counsel he is *not* in court in one of the German lands. In British courts it is customary to respect Her Majesty's judges!'

Keziah was stung by this insult to her friend who, like her, was forever an alien in the eyes of this judge.

Before Joseph could respond to the rebuke the judge's words cut across him as he addressed the jury.

'Vile accusations have been made about Iago which have not been verified by other witnesses. His employer, Julian Jonstone, held him in high esteem. All we have is the hearsay evidence of a *Gypsy* charged with his murder, who has besmirched Iago's good name.'

A commotion broke out at the rear of the court. A woman dressed in black called out, 'Good name? You want the whole truth? Ask *me*!'

The prosecutor turned to Joseph Bloom with a sigh of resignation. 'What other tricks have you concealed up your Mosaic sleeve, Bloom?'

'My learned friend, may I suggest our Creator alone has that answer?'

'My chambers!' the judge snapped at them. 'The court is adjourned for one hour.'

As the woman in black left the court she looked back at Keziah and nodded her head in acknowledgement. Keziah realised this was the wife who had cried tears of joy when the Tarot cards revealed her husband's death. *Mary Iago.*

Keziah was shocked that she had not foreseen the fatal flaw at the heart of her Tarot prediction. Baxt *chose* me *to be the Devil Himself's executioner.*

CHAPTER 51

Within minutes of the doors being reopened, Berrima courthouse was flooded with a horde of noisy spectators jostling for standing room at the back of the courtroom.

As Daniel Browne crossed to the witness box again he tried to calm the waves of terror threatening to engulf him. During the adjournment he had promised Joseph Bloom his total cooperation in every possible way. He had not only to fight for Keziah's freedom but also for her life. Was he man enough to overcome his abject fear of what lay ahead?

In his mind's eye Daniel was haunted by images of Iago. He reminded himself that the handsome evil face was reduced to a burnt skull and powerless to punish him from the grave, but that did not prevent Daniel's knees from shaking. *Our Lady, help me find my redemption.*

Recalled to the stand, he began his testimony firmly when asked to describe Iago's treatment of his assigned prisoners. 'The Devil Himself was rightly named. The youngest lads were scarce thirteen. He broke their spirits then rewarded them with food that was legally their share of government stores.'

'Did you personally witness their physical abuse?'

'No, only when they were flogged.' He hesitated. 'But it was common knowledge he used the youngest boys for his gratification.'

The judge was moved to ask, 'Do I understand you refer to sodomy? This abomination draws the death penalty.'

Daniel hesitated before answering. 'There was no doubt. One lad from Killarney committed suicide to escape Iago.'

He glanced at Keziah to steel himself before delivering the words that would wound her. She stared at him, willing him to continue.

'And we all knew that Gypsy Gem Smith only took up arms after he was forced to accept Iago's *special* punishment.'

The prosecutor was openly scathing. 'I put it to you, Browne, your testimony holds no water under the law. It is diabolical hearsay. You did *not* witness the heinous crime you alone claim was committed by a dead man who was highly respected in our community.'

'Are you calling me a liar?' Daniel demanded.

The prosecutor's shrug was a nonchalant insult. 'You'd not be the first husband to perjure himself to save his wife from the gallows.'

Humiliated by his dismissal, Daniel stumbled back to his seat. Had he done Keziah more harm than good in the jury's eyes? He felt sure he had failed her. And Jake. Joseph's subtle gesture of reassurance was small consolation.

Keziah stared resolutely ahead, her hand on the small of her back to act as ballast for the weight of her belly.

When Mary Iago took the oath, Daniel gave her a nod of encouragement. Although she was dressed in black, she had avoided full widow's weeds. Her nervous smile revealed the gap in her front teeth.

Daniel saw that Joseph Bloom was studying her every gesture and nuance of speech. After her initial outburst the widow seemed to have shrunk into her timid shell, but under Joseph's sympathetic questioning she regained her confidence.

'For nine years of marriage I lived in fear of my husband. He only married me because I came free from Cornwall. That put him in good light with the master, being Cornish himself. Husband beat me so bad I ran off to hide in one of the master's properties in the bush.'

Daniel saw Keziah lean forward in her seat, alert.

'But Husband dragged me back to Gideon Park and flogged me regularly where none could see my scars. He said the only pleasure I gave him was when he beat me.'

Joseph waited for the spectators' murmurs to quieten before he continued.

'Your marriage was not blessed with children, Mrs Iago?'

'How could it?' she whispered. 'We never had connection after the wedding night.'

The judge straightened his wig again. 'Enough of this public airing of marital discord. Must I remind the defence counsel he's not in a Prussian court of law? Pray establish if the witness can corroborate specific claims of abuse by Iago against his assigned men.'

Joseph turned to his witness. 'I regret the distress my questions must cause, Mrs Iago. Are you aware of what society defines as *unnatural acts*?'

Mary Iago raised her eyes to the light dome above them as if seeking a guardian angel. She looked back at Joseph Bloom, who gave a slight nod of assent.

'One night Husband said I deserved special punishment for scorching his best shirt. He tied me to a chair and gagged me. Called in a young lad who always did his bidding. Husband made me watch while he had connection with him. Everything men do to women but more.' Her voice broke. 'When Husband finished his business he untied me. Made me serve them their supper.'

Daniel watched the way Joseph Bloom looked at each juryman before asking his next question.

'Are you able to identify your husband's companion?'

'No!' she cried. 'I won't!'

Daniel heard a man's voice call out, 'He's here in court!'

White-faced, Daniel looked around before he realised the strangled voice had come from him. He stood up to answer.

'Mrs Iago speaks the truth, Your Honour. I was Iago's companion. That night and many months after. I was not man enough to kill him.'

Mary Iago called out to Daniel as she was led sobbing from the court. 'God forgive me. I couldn't help you, lad!'

The whole courtroom erupted in a whirlpool of confusion. Daniel stood rigid, the muscles of his face contorted in fear as every single person turned to register disgust, pity or disbelief. *Will my confession prove my own death warrant?*

Keziah stretched out her hand towards him with the expression of compassion he remembered. This was his Keziah – less than a wife, yet *more* than a wife.

At the same time Joseph Bloom abandoned his professional stance and reached across the barrier to place a protective arm around his shoulders.

Daniel had no chance to evaluate the danger of his confession. He expected the jury would retire to consider their verdict. He was shocked. They did not even vacate their seats, simply bent their heads to confer together. Their spokesman delivered the verdict with relish. *Guilty.*

The full weight of that word hit Daniel, as if the verdict had also been passed on his own life. He had exposed himself as Iago's partner in sodomy all in vain.

Guilty. Keziah had no time to feel the full impact of the verdict. At the moment of judgement her gaze was held by the woman in blue who had risen from her seat in the gallery and was staring at her. A raging fire seemed to consume Keziah's whole being, body and soul. Now she recognised the truth. Mrs Hamberton's face was the face of a stranger but her eyes were unmistakably the eyes of Stella the Whore.

Vivid childhood images fused with flashes of this woman's recent presence at Jake's trial and her own. Keziah cried out in anguish. It was then her body betrayed her. She staggered to her feet, searching desperately for the face of her doctor.

'Leslie!' she cried out in a strangled whisper. 'It's coming now!'

She clutched her skirt to her thighs in a useless attempt at camouflage. For the second time Keziah's waters had broken early. Jake's babe was demanding to be born.

Pandemonium broke out as the court was hurriedly cleared. Under shouted instructions from Dr Ross, two men formed a human cradle to carry Keziah from the court. Leslie ordered them to take her to the nearby inn, but one English guard argued the toss.

'Call yourself men?' Keziah shouted. 'Do you want me to give birth in the street?'

The guard was a stickler for the law. 'We must take you back to your cell. Judge ain't yet passed sentence.'

Keziah grabbed the man by his ears and pushed her face into his. 'I've already killed one man. Do you want to be the next?'

Leslie Ross roared at him. 'Damn your eyes! Do as the lady says or I'll charge you dogs with obstruction!'

Keziah's nails dug into the man's ears. 'Get me to the Surveyor-General's Inn *now* or I'll put a Romani curse on you. I'll cover you with boils so bad no one will be able to tell your face from your arse!'

The guards' jaws dropped. Leslie thundered out the order. 'You heard the lady. Full speed ahead!'

They carried her at breakneck speed, tumbling through the entrance of the Surveyor-General's Inn with Keziah yelling blue murder. Drinkers scattered in all directions.

Keziah grabbed hold of the billiard table with both hands and refused to let go. 'The babe's coming – now!'

The guards dumped her onto the table and fled for the exit. The publican's wife rushed in ready to do the doctor's bidding.

Leslie rolled up his sleeves. 'Hot water, sheets, towels! On the double!'

As Leslie was removing Keziah's undergarments a drunk stuck his head around the door. He looked at the scene in disbelief and hollered out, 'No women allowed in the pool room!'

Keziah released a mighty bellow and the drunk vanished from sight.

Remembering Gabriel's birth, Keziah rode every contraction like giant waves that would take her to the shore. In a brief moment of respite she gripped Leslie's hand.

'I beg you! Don't ever tell anyone I said all those terrible things! Promise me!'

'Believe me, lass, I've heard worse language from a priest on the operating table. Right now I want you to do your damnedest *not* to push for a bit, even if you feel you must. The babe's coming feet first. I need to give it a wee helping hand.'

'*Mi-duvel*, it's a breech?' She bit her lip and made every effort to restrain her violent urge to bear down. 'I don't give a tinker's damn which end comes out first – just get it out!'

His words conveyed quiet confidence. 'Right you are, lass. Coming, ready or not.'

As she felt something very large and determined pushing its way out of her womb, she closed her eyes and begged her ancestors, *Please don't let Jake's babe die!*

Leslie's face was red and his beard damp with sweat as he worked to free the squirming wet mass from between her thighs.

Keziah lifted her head and tried to look between her raised knees to see what he was doing. 'I don't care if it's a boy or girl. Is it *alive*?'

As if in answer she heard a gutsy wail that sounded sweeter than an angels' choir. Leslie wrapped its slimy little body in a towel and returned her joyous smile. He placed the lusty red-headed baby Viking in her arms, swaddled in a towel emblazoned with the trademark Albion Ale.

Keziah looked into a tiny face that was bright red with outrage.

'I don't know who you are, little one, but you're *very* clever to begin life on the billiard table of your papa's favourite inn.'

'Aye, you've done well, lass. A fine, healthy boy. Made his entrance kicking and screaming – he's got every mark of Jake's bloody-minded determination.'

Keziah gave the babe her breast to calm him and tenderly whispered his true Romani name. 'That will trick *The Beng*, if the devil should come looking for you.'

Mr Harper, the publican, stood in the doorway, arms folded across his chest like a proud father. Leslie responded warmly to his invitation to wet the baby's head.

'Thank you kindly, Sir. A neat whisky would go down quite nicely. It's been a damned difficult day, one way or another.'

Harper brought him two double whiskies and the bottle they came from. Leslie raised the first glass in the direction of the prison walls.

'To you, Jake, *Slainte*!' He tossed it down and before downing the second one, tactfully lowered his voice to distract Keziah from her inevitable sentence. 'Above all, lass, here's to your freedom!'

Keziah was so exhausted she scarcely had strength enough to hold the baby. 'We both know what's ahead, Doctor. I told the truth and put my head in a noose.'

She grabbed his arm, her fingernails biting into his flesh. 'For God's sake, don't let Jake play the hero and try to rescue me! They'll shoot him down like a dog.'

'I promise you he'll be safe. Now rest easy, lass. You've earned it.'

'No! I'm a lost cause. I've ruined everyone's lives.'

He gently removed the babe from her arms. 'Tomorrow the world will be a better place.'

'Tomorrow will never come,' said Keziah.

CHAPTER 52

Lying in darkness in a dank, underground storage room of Berrima Gaol, Jake felt as though he was in the bowels of the earth as he hacked at the final inches he needed to dislodge the sandstone block – Will Martens's escape route.

His eyes watered with sandstone dust as he pushed the stone free. He heard it land with a soft thud on the grass outside. The blast of fresh air was sweeter than wine. He anxiously re-examined the hole.

Easy for Will, he's built like a slip of a girl. The hole bloody better be big enough to squeeze my carcass out.

Inch by inch he forced his body through the oblong hole. When he eventually landed on the other side he swore in triumph under his breath.

The night sky was peppered with stars and a crescent moon emerged from behind the clouds. Jake gave his eyes time to grow accustomed to the darkness outside, which was marginally lighter than the storeroom. It was then he saw a pair of boots. The flare of a pipe in the darkness. And a voice.

'I thought you might try to use Jabber Jabber's escape route.'

Jake looked at the chaplain, defiant. 'I warned you I'd kill to get my woman out of here and I meant it. I'll have to silence *you*, Rev, if you're silly enough to try and stop me.'

'Go ahead and try, Jakob. You're not leaving this place while I'm alive.' He added with emphasis, 'Not *tonight* you won't.'

Jake's acute disappointment turned to sarcasm. 'Is tomorrow all right with you, Rev?'

'You're no fool when you stop to use your brains, son, so hear me out. You owe it to your woman and your children to stay alive. What chance do you have if you bolt now? If you're dead lucky you'd get to see Keziah once before you're recaptured. Then you'd be packed off to Norfolk Island and as a second offender you'd die there in chains.'

'You heard the jury, Rev. Guilty. I gave her my word she wouldn't give birth in gaol.'

'You got your wish, son.' The chaplain passed on all the details of the birth that Leslie Ross had asked him to convey to Jake.

'Jesus wept. A son! Why didn't you bloody tell me?'

For once the chaplain lost his temper. 'Because you bolted, you daft fool! I've been searching for you *inside* to tell you to hold your fire! I told you there was a strong rumour you're likely to be released, but no, Jakob Andersen has to play the bloody hero and dig his way out! Do you want the troopers to shoot holes in your damned fool head?'

'Watch your language, Rev. Your bishop will rip off your dog-collar!'

Jake could not wipe the grin off his face as the news sank in. 'A son, eh?'

'Now the trick is to get you back to your cell, past a guard who's none too partial to Currency Lads who are matey with bushrangers.'

'I *could* go back the same way I came through the hole,' Jake offered.

'Do it my way. If a guard challenges you, I'll say we're on our way to confession. Heaven knows with your record that would take a month of Sundays.'

'Right,' said Jake. 'But first I've got to push the stone back for the next poor bastard to escape.'

'Don't push your luck with me, son!'

The sky was a cloudless stretch of icy blue, so high it seemed to stretch to a universe beyond the heavens. Jake winced in the face of the bright sunlight as he was frogmarched across the courtyard.

His shaven scalp itched and he would have welcomed a delousing almost as much as a cold Albion Ale. He had just spent a week in the blackness of solitary confinement in 'the hole' as punishment for his involuntary 'blasphemous utterance' when a guard prodded his groin with a truncheon.

Only one hour ago, the prison superintendent had ordered Jake to be pulled out of 'the hole' and announced he was free. It seemed the reason was due to fresh evidence given by Daniel and Iago's widow at Keziah's trial, which had overturned Iago's previous testimony.

Jake couldn't fathom it. *But who am I to argue with a full pardon? I'd best clear out before they change their bloody minds.*

He stood with the closed prison gates at his back, uncertain of how to make his first move.

Keziah and his baby son had already been transferred to Parramatta. Her three-year sentence in the Parramatta Female Factory was considered light, influenced by her condition as a nursing mother and the great provocation she had suffered at the hands of the Devil Himself. But three years was no consolation to Jake knowing how the loss of freedom would crush Keziah's spirit.

He was about to set off on foot for the Surveyor-General's Inn when he was met by the Doc's buggy in company with a second saddled horse – Horatio.

He masked his surprise and gratitude with a casual greeting. 'What kept you, Doc?'

'I indulged in a bit of carousing to celebrate your release, lad.'

At the Surveyor-General's Inn, Leslie ordered a bottle of Scotch whisky. Both silently acknowledged Jake's tension. Prison did that to a man, no matter how heavy his bravado.

'Get that into you to celebrate your firstborn son! Keziah's just fine!'

'Thank Christ for that.' Jake felt nervous about the odds against his son. Few babes survived a premature birth. His mother had lost two. 'Think he'll make it, Doc?'

'Make it? He's the toughest little bairn I've ever delivered!'

Jake sank the first whisky with satisfaction. Leslie refilled his glass and eyed him carefully as he recounted Keziah's and Daniel's testimonies.

'I dinna doubt your feelings, lad. Gem and Will Martens being friends of yours. It took guts for Daniel to expose Iago at great risk to himself.'

Jake seethed with frustration that he had not been the one to avenge Gem. 'Pity the bloody law hasn't found a way for blokes like Iago to be executed twice.'

'Aye, it did. In previous centuries he'd have been hanged, drawn and quartered.'

On their third whisky they reflected on the monster that Iago had become. Was he born crazy, evil or had he been brutalised in childhood or by the system?

'I've seen sadists like him the world over,' said Leslie. 'But I discovered Iago was born of the Quality. He was cast out by a family known to Jonstone. His name was changed and he was banished to the ends of the earth to cover some heinous crime. A man so twisted he inflicted sadistic punishment on his convicts to conceal the instincts he was unable to face in himself.'

Jake scowled. 'I don't give a bugger *why* he did it. He didn't deserve to breathe the same air as the rest of the human race.'

'A priest would claim every man has one redeeming feature.'

'Yeah?' Jake thought for a minute. 'The best you can say about Iago is that he'll be pinned down by a tombstone for eternity.'

Later, when they were travelling down the road to Ironbark, Leslie told him how Daniel had wanted to bring Jake a special welcome-home gift.

'A new Belgian percussion pocket pistol with a spring bayonet. I persuaded the fool if you were caught carrying arms today the traps would kill you.'

'A bayonet, eh? That will come in handy to spring Kez out of the Factory!'

Leslie wore his wise owl look. 'Bran killed the fatted calf to celebrate your freedom.'

Jake shook his head. 'Nice thought but what good is freedom when Kez can't share it with me? I'm off to Ironbark Farm to collect my kids from Polly Doyle. Poor little buggers must feel like orphans.'

'I took care of that. The bairns and your *vardo* are waiting for ye at Bran's forge.'

They separated at the crossroads and Leslie drove west to perform an operation. The second bottle of whisky he had placed in Jake's saddlebag ensured that Jake was mellow by sundown when he spotted Bran's forge. Pearl and Gabriel sat like two little birds on the sliprail fence, squawking their welcome to him.

The living quarters of the forge house were decorated with streamers. The Doc hadn't been joking about the fatted calf. Bran was turning it on a spit over an open fire. Daniel was unable to speak but he gave a silent grin of welcome as he placed a pannikin of wine in Jake's hand.

Jake downed the contents then pointed the empty mug at the spit. 'Well there's *my* dinner. What are you lot having?'

The children were all over him, laughing and asking questions, and for their sake he tried to appear relaxed and confident, ironing out their anxious questions about Mama and life in gaol. Many bottles of Albion Ale and wine were needed to wash down the fatted calf. After the meal raucous singing broke out accompanied by Gabriel. His new violin was a gift from one of Scotty the Shepherd's mates, a fiddler who had done time at Gideon Park and was grateful for Iago's death.

Jake tried to suppress the bleak feelings the grog had aggravated.

'Maybe Scotty's mob can raise an army to spring Kez out of the Factory.'

He was only half joking. Daniel looked serious.

'There's more than one way to skin a cat, Jake.'

Jake could see Gabriel and Pearl were struggling to keep their eyes open, so he shepherded them off to bed. They looked like babes in the wood in Bran's big iron bed. On his return Daniel presented him with the Belgian pistol and Jake tested the spring bayonet. He made a genuine show of gratitude, balancing the weapon in his hand to get the feel of it.

'Best firearm I've ever had. Can't wait to use it.'

Daniel and Bran were both watching him. It was obvious something was afoot. Both were aware of his plan to fight like hell for Keziah's release while giving his kids some semblance of family life until her return.

'All right, you two. Spit it out. What's up?'

'Bran and I have a bold plan we want to put to you. It *sounds* crazy but hear me out before you piss yourself laughing.'

'All right, I'm listening,' said Jake, wary he was about to be hit with some half-baked scheme.

'The best we can hope for is Keziah's early release from the Factory, right? So the trick is to keep up a respectable marital front in the eyes of the authorities. We help build a cottage for you and the kids on your derelict property, then we build a forge and living quarters in the far corner where it fronts the Sydney Road. Next Bran quits Gilbert Evans's forge here and serves the community *there*. Naturally he'll do all your smithing work. You'll realise your dream to breed thoroughbred horses. Me? I'll work in a studio in the forge house but I'll be your spare hand whenever you need me.'

Jake gave a hoot. 'That's a nice pipedream, mate. How do I build this bloody village? Print my own money?'

'No need, I'll finance it.'

Jake was stunned. 'Right. When do you intend to bail up a bank?'

Daniel leaned forward. 'Listen, it's all above board. After my testimony in court and Mary Iago's revelations about the abominations practised by Iago, I expected my career as an artist would be over, that the gentry would shun me. I hadn't counted on Jonstone's support. Maybe he feels responsible for leaving so much power in Iago's hands – an overseer *he* appointed. Whatever the reason, Jonstone's publicly sticking by me. He's announced plans to hold an exhibition of my work next year and Lady Gipps has agreed to open it. Jonstone's rallied the gentry and already two more of his friends have commissioned portraits of their wives. And Terence Ogden is celebrating his success in packing his wife off to England for good by commissioning me to paint a pair of life-size equine paintings of his champions.'

Daniel caught his breath. 'You see? In death the Devil Himself has actually boosted my career.'

Jake knew Daniel's mocking laugh covered his acute embarrassment.

'I'll have a good income,' Daniel continued, 'so will Bran. With us behind you, what have you got to lose?'

They both looked so keen about the idea that Jake made the only response he could think of – he refilled their glasses.

'Sounds like you've gone into this partnership business pretty damned thorough.'

'We have. I'll be your silent partner. Further down the track when you begin selling horses and winning races, you can pay something off the loan if you want. Come on, what do you think?'

Bran's silence was eloquent as he pushed his blueprint across the table.

Jake studied it. '*And?* What's the bloody catch?'

'None. Your whole farm remains in your name, your legal property, but in the eyes of the community you and I are partners. I pressure the authorities to have Keziah assigned to *me*, her legal husband – who's to know the truth? In reality Mrs Browne and her kids live under Jake Andersen's roof at the other end of the property.'

Jake was quick to ask, 'Which bed does she sleep in?'

'Yours, you idiot.' Daniel was flushed with grog. 'Legally and publicly Keziah must be seen to be *my* wife. In private she's *your* wife.'

Bran nodded emphatically. Daniel attempted to look like a master magician who had pulled off his best trick, but Jake saw he was cracking his knuckles from nerves. All their lives hung in the balance, waiting on Jake's decision.

He felt stymied. 'The whole thing is totally outlandish. There's got to be a hole in this plan somewhere. What happens when Keziah wants more kids? She's dead keen on that.'

Daniel threw his arms wide in a self-mocking gesture. 'Ironbark gossips will think I'm as randy as a bull. I'll register them as mine, same as the new little tyke. At the end of Keziah's sentence we can get a quiet judicial separation.'

Jake looked morose. 'There's no *quiet* legal way to ditch a spouse. If there was I'd have cut loose from mine. As long as Jenny's alive my kids will be bastards.'

Daniel's fifth drink made him master of the world. 'No! They'll be legitimate Brownes. First we get Keziah out of the rotten Factory so you can live together as a family.'

Jake felt uneasy about asking the question, but he knew he could not dodge it. 'What happens if *you* want to take up with a woman?'

Daniel looked serious. 'Whatever I may choose to do will be conducted *elsewhere*. I won't invite gossip. For all our sakes.'

Jake looked at Bran and Daniel in turn. 'Frankly, I reckon the whole idea's bloody crazy. Let's do it!'

All three sprang to their feet for Jake to propose his triumphant toast.

'Here's to the Sarishan ménage. And the great trick we're going to play on the Superintendent of Convicts and the whole bloody system!'

CHAPTER 53

Riding the brumby towards the Parramatta Female Factory, Daniel's thoughts turned to Jake and the frustration he must feel each month being forced to wait at Sarishan Farm for Daniel's return with news of Keziah.

Despite the jury's verdict, endorsed by the judge at Keziah's trial, the press had come full circle from vilification of her to the widely held belief that the shock of Iago's bestiality had unhinged a delicate female mind. The colony's unofficial army of good women had elevated Keziah to the status of folk heroine. Their empathy had helped Jake enormously in collecting signatures for a petition seeking Keziah's release into the custody of her husband.

The three-storey Factory came into Daniel's view. The brick façade was not forbidding and it was well proportioned, having been built by Governor Macquarie's celebrated convict architect Francis Greenaway in 1821 during what many called 'the good old days'.

Daniel was roughly aware of the layout. The first floor was used mainly for meals. Two top floors were sleeping quarters for female prisoners divided into three classes. As a convicted murderess Keziah was in the third class. Under normal conditions she would have been sentenced to hard labour. But nursing mothers were assigned the more pleasant work of sewing and carding and enjoyed additional indulgences, including a husband's visits.

Daniel eyed the separate buildings that housed the porter, superintendent's family, deputy, storerooms, kitchen, bakehouse, spinning room and the prisoners' privies – he felt saddened to think that these were now the limits of Keziah's world.

He hurried to the deputy's office, aware that his visit would be strategically placed to enable the woman to keep a sharp eye on him. As always she searched the contents of Daniel's hessian sack for potential weapons. He knew not to bring sewing scissors as Keziah had told him these were broken in half by prisoners to use as daggers.

'Nothing but food, Ma'am, and sewing threads,' Daniel assured the deputy. 'Has my wife kept good health?'

The deputy nodded. 'Well enough, she gives me no trouble, unlike most.'

Daniel waited in a small, bleak courtyard for Keziah to be brought to him. At least the space offered some privacy. No one could overhear their conversation. He wondered if today would be the same as all his previous visits. Keziah had never mentioned Jake's name, so Daniel had always been forced to invent her words on his return home to satisfy Jake's hunger for news of his woman.

He rose at Keziah's approach, shocked by the deterioration in her appearance since last month's visit. When Keziah crossed the courtyard towards him Daniel recognised her eyes held the same lacklustre expression as his own eyes during his years at Gideon Park.

He covertly handed her Jake's latest ink-stained letter and bent to kiss her cheek.

'The kiss is from Jake. I've had to smuggle in his letter. Wouldn't want some official to read the lust between the lines. You know Jake!'

Keziah stiffened and drew away so his kiss glanced off her cheek.

Jake's fear was right. She looks as if all hope has died inside her.

As Keziah listened to Daniel's cheerful attempts at conversation she could feel nothing but that familiar sense of emptiness that had become her sole companion day and night.

She noticed Daniel's hair had grown longer, his English complexion now had a light tan and he seemed more like a Currency Lad each visit.

She was suddenly aware of the letter he had handed her and his words echoed in her mind. *'You know Jake!'*

Daniel continued. 'The kiddies ride Pony to school. Gabriel has taught himself to play *The Wild Colonial Boy* on his violin. Pearl's new spectacles opened up a whole new world for her. And she pressed this red rose from the garden just for you because it's your favourite colour.'

Keziah glanced at the rose. She knew she should say something but she couldn't find the words. Instead she continued to devour the cheese and fruit he'd brought, relieved that she didn't need to explain. Daniel knew she must eat these luxuries immediately to prevent their theft by her fellow prisoners. Each visit she saw him try to conceal his recognition that she had grown less human. She shied away from the pain in his eyes.

I know what he's thinking. I eat like a hungry animal. Well I don't care. The only thing that matters is having enough food to keep my breast milk flowing.

When Daniel ran out of news and began to flounder he asked permission to sketch her. She tried to close off her mind to the way his artist's eye translated on paper every detail of her deterioration. The patch of hair burned in the fire had re-grown in tight ringlets but her calico prison dress was frayed and she knew her eyes were ringed by the shadows that had never left her since the trial. She sensed Daniel was ashamed of his compulsion to record her gaunt, degraded state but he was driven to record the truth.

'It's all right. I don't care,' she said. 'You must do the right thing by your mistress.'

'Ah yes, art.' Apparently startled by her insight he tried to cover it with a bright commentary. 'Last week Jake did some more work at Terence Ogden's stud. Did I tell you that on his return from Cornwall Ogden was furious that his manager had refused to employ Currency Lads in his absence. So Ogden's now throwing lots of work Jake's way to make up for his loss of income. When one of his thoroughbred mares dropped a filly with a club foot and Jake chose her in lieu of payment. He said to tell you he really needs your magic to heal her.'

Mention of the lame filly caused Keziah to feel a faint flicker of interest.

Daniel lowered his voice. 'You do know how desperately Jake wants to see you? He works like crazy for your release, collects names for his petition, corresponds with Joseph in Sydney, haunts the magistrate's office. Next he plans to win Mrs Hamberton to your cause.'

'Never!' Keziah cried out in anger.

Daniel looked bewildered but stumbled on. 'I keep reminding Jake he must keep up the respectable façade that *I'm* your husband.' He gave a self-deprecating laugh. 'If you can call *me* respectable by any wild stretch of the imagination.'

'You are a true friend!' Her words rasped out in his defence seemed to surprise him.

'I have you to thank for my freedom, Keziah. I'll do my damnedest to return the favour and get you safely back home with Jake.'

Mi-duvel, will he never stop talking about Jake?

When she turned her head away, Daniel's manner changed to one of confrontation.

'We need to get something straight. It worries me that ever since you've been here, for seven months, you've never mentioned Jake's name. Why not? Is it because of what I told you about my feelings for him? It was true then, is now. Maybe always will be. But I want you to know you've no cause to fear I'll wreck things between the three of us.'

Keziah watched him but she kept eating the last of the fruit. Daniel tried again.

'I love Jake for what he is – a man born to love women. One woman. You. I'm very fortunate to have his friendship. He accepts me for what I am. His friend. True blue.' He paused. 'Do I need to spell it out to you? I won't ever let "my needs" get in the way. My love – lust or what you will. Think of it as an underground creek in drought country – no one can see it. Only you and I know it's there. Jake needs all his friends. I'll never be more or less than that. I'm content just to be around him.

You're my family, Keziah. I'll never do dirt. Never hurt you, Jake or the children. Please don't send me away.'

He angrily brushed away a tear. 'For pity's sake, Keziah, say something, will you?'

Keziah looked at him long and hard. 'I envy you, Daniel.'

'How can you say that? I'm less than a man. I'm living a lie.'

'You can feel love – lust. It doesn't matter.' She leaned forward. 'I feel *nothing*!'

When Daniel reached out to comfort her she drew back.

'Will you at least let me see the babe this time?' he asked.

Keziah rose, steeling herself for what was to come. She led him to a room where each bed had a cot beside it. The room was empty except for a woman who suckled a small boy.

Keziah felt anxious that her own babe was small for seven months. It had been a fight for her to sustain his vitality but his tiny cries signalled that he could smell his mother's milk. She pushed the bundle into Daniel's arms.

The babe gripped his finger so tightly, Daniel smiled. He gently stroked the fuzz of red hair.

'You're the image of Jake, little chap. I'll need to dye your hair to pass you off as mine.'

When Keziah did not react, he tried again. 'Jake asked have you chosen his name yet? I know you gave him some secret Romani name the day of his birth, but now he needs a name the world will call him.'

'Yosef – Joseph Bloom's Hebrew name. Do you think Joseph would mind?'

'He'll be honoured,' Daniel said. 'I'll get Jake to tell him.'

Again she avoided Jake's name as though he was dead to her. But finally forced herself to say the words she had been rehearsing for days.

'I'll feed Yosef. Then I want you to take him home with you. Hire a wet nurse. Pearl is a natural little mother, she'll help care for him.'

Daniel looked startled. 'But the deputy told me prisoners are allowed to keep a child with them until it turns four.'

'I'm not other prisoners! Yosef must never see how low his mother has sunk.'

Daniel looked as if he didn't know what to do. 'You can't mean it?'

In answer she gave the babe her breast. Daniel turned away. *He thinks I need privacy. What the hell does it matter?* The sound of Yosef thirstily sucking at her breast, his little hand patting her face for the very last time, should have moved her to tears. But it left her dry-eyed. All she could feel was a dull pain that filled the hollow shell of her body. *He's the only innocent thing in this ugly, brutal place. And I can't wait to get rid of him.*

She tied towelling around Yosef's loins for the long journey ahead. She wrapped him in her prison blanket and tucked him into the hessian bag strapped to Daniel's back.

Daniel looked anxious. 'Won't the theft of a prison blanket earn you hard labour?'

Her voice was devoid of emotion. 'What does that matter now?' She turned her back on Yosef. 'When he's hungry on the journey, knock on the door of any poor Irish farmer. His wife's bound to have an infant in the cradle. I guarantee she'll put Yosef on the breast. You can count on poor women. They never let a babe go hungry.'

Daniel hovered in the doorway. 'Keziah, how can you bear to do this?'

The look she gave him forced him to lower his eyes. 'Get him out of my sight, Daniel!'

Daniel walked a little distance then hesitated as if he expected her to change her mind.

Keziah stood watching Yosef's tiny red head bobbing in the pouch on Daniel's back. She felt turned to stone, unable to return Daniel's wave. Her breasts were empty of milk. Her body was now her own. She paused by the deputy superintendent's open door.

'It is done,' she said. And walked away.

CHAPTER 54

It was Saturday morning and Jake was hammering shingles on his roof – not his most urgent job because it hadn't rained properly since New Year. He was surprised when a cartload of bonneted matrons halted in the home paddock. Janet Macgregor was leading them forward, bearing a silver tea service on a tray. She asked to speak to Daniel Browne.

Jake explained that his partner was visiting his wife at the Parramatta Female Factory, but could he help them?

Janet cleared her throat. 'Aye, you'll do. We are the members of the new Wesleyan Women for Temperance group. We took up a collection to present this Award for Bravery to Mrs Keziah Browne. It's an insult to Australian womanhood to gaol this heroine for defending herself against a drunken monster!'

Jake kept a straight face. It was clear the other women were less outraged by Iago's sodomy than his having departed this world in the grip of the Demon Drink. Janet had proven herself to be Keziah's ally. *Funny how being the Doc's woman has mellowed her.*

He thanked the temperance ladies. 'I reckon she'd be honoured if you ladies christened her tea service.'

The women nodded in unison. 'We shall pray for Mrs Browne's speedy release.'

Jake never missed an opportunity. 'And would you ladies sign my petition to the governor to have Mrs Browne assigned to her husband's care?'

He had a pencil at the ready to record their names. Most could only make their mark.

Janet pointed out that none of the other temperance women had ever seen Keziah.

'I can soon fix that!' He raced inside the house, hastily bypassed Keziah's naked portrait over his bed and brought out Daniel's earlier portrait of her with little Gabriel.

The ladies exclaimed over it in admiration and one asked Jake confidentially if Mrs Browne shared their views about total abstinence.

'Alcohol never touches her lips!' he said fervently and tried to avoid the laughter in Janet Macgregor's eyes.

The temperance wagon had barely disappeared over the rise when Jake recognised the rider approaching over the crest of the hill. He was too astonished to speak when he saw the hessian sack on his back was wriggling.

Daniel thrust it into Jake's arms. 'Keziah wants you to teach your son to be a man. Haven't slept since Parramatta, I'm buggered.' Daniel headed for the forge house. 'Keziah sends her love.'

Jake looked down at the son he had never seen. The babe's little fringe of red hair looked like a monk's tonsure. Unblinking dark blue eyes stared back at him. The boy looked contented enough even though milk dribbled from his mouth.

Jake spoke his first ever words to his son. 'No bloody wonder you're chucking, mate. Galloping on horseback can do that to a bloke.'

He called after Daniel's retreating back. 'Hey! Did *our wife* give him a name yet?'

'Yeah. Yosef Jakob Andersen Browne. Sorry he has to cop the Browne bit.'

'He could do a lot worse,' said Jake.

In Goulburn the following week, Jake was ushered into Mrs Hamberton's sitting room. He felt awkward in such an elegant setting but was determined to press his case.

Daniel had told him the magistrate's wife was a beautiful woman 'of a certain age', and Jake saw this was no exaggeration. She appeared to be much younger than her husband. Finely boned and fashionably gowned, her blonde hair was coiled on top of her head like a princess. For some odd reason Jake found her dark blue eyes disturbing. When she gracefully held out her hand he didn't know whether he was supposed to shake it or kiss it. So he touched it and backed away.

'Jake Andersen, Ma'am. Had no luck tracking down the magistrate. Reckon I was a bit desperate coming here to present my petition to the governor.'

'You are the young man who was recently granted a full pardon, due to the false testimony of a witness the law should *never* have allowed to condemn you.'

'That's a polite way of putting it, Ma'am!'

'And you have a friend, Mrs Keziah Browne?'

'She's the wife of my partner, Daniel Browne. The jury found her guilty of murder, but the truth is she shot the Devil Himself, Iago, for what he did to my Romani mate, Gem Smith. Saved me the trouble of killing the bastard.'

Aghast at his careless choice of words, Jake added quickly, 'Forgive me, Ma'am. I can't find no words low enough for him.'

Mrs Hamberton nodded in agreement. 'I attended your friend's trial. The English language is barely adequate to describe that man. He was the embodiment of evil.'

She gently prompted him. 'How is your friend adjusting to conditions in Parramatta?'

'Keziah's a model prisoner, Ma'am. She's earned special privileges to see Daniel, her husband. Of course I ain't seen her myself,' he added quickly.

'And how are you managing with the children?'

'Real well, thanks. Yosef's taken to cow's milk like a duck to water. The other two help us around the farm. They're real bright with their school lessons.'

'That handsome little boy I saw with his mother?' She added tactfully, 'During your own day in court. I understand from Mr Browne that his wife adopted him?'

Jake was suddenly absorbed in studying the wallpaper. *This is tricky. Mrs Hamberton was in court when Pearl identified me as her father and Gabe had to be muzzled to stop him. What's she playing at?*

'Gabriel Stanley's near six and a half and as game as they come. He plays at soldiers, loves fighting the Battle of Waterloo. He's got a real way with horses and knows what they're thinking. What's more he's musical. There's nothing that lad couldn't play if he put his mind to it.'

There was an odd note in Mrs Hamberton's voice. 'Ah yes, musical gifts are often inherited from a grandparent.' She pulled the bell rope. 'I shall order tea. Please tell me about your petition.'

Jake took this cue. The law was no help to him so he poured out his heart. Who knew what influence Mrs Hamberton had? He never underestimated good women. The law gave the fair sex no advantages so they had to use devious methods to run the world.

Mrs Hamberton's eyes never left his face as Jake told her how he had collected 649 signatures from every estate, farm, store and public house in the locality, and how he had even swum across a flooded creek to collect names from a remote farmhouse.

'Men and women are pretty much all on her side, Ma'am. All I'm asking is for her to be assigned to her husband. She's a great mother – the children need her.'

'Your petition is impressive. I would be most pleased to add my own signature.'

Jake grinned as he watched her sign it, imagining Magistrate Hamberton's surprise when he read his own wife's name on the petition – Stella Hamberton.

'Don't allow your friend to lose heart. A woman needs courage to rebuild her life. That first day I saw Keziah Stanley in court at your trial I recognised a woman of valour.'

'She's got more guts than most men. Saved my life and I'd gladly trade mine to free her.'

Mrs Hamberton gracefully nodded her head. 'Your friend is fortunate to have you as her champion. I am *certain* my husband will make adequate time for you to state your case before his next visit to his friend Governor Gipps. And when you pass this way feel free to bring Gabriel. My husband has a miniature model of the Battle of Waterloo that might interest the boy.'

Jake took his leave feeling pleased but bemused. *I'm buggered if I know why, but I reckon she's fighting for our cause.* Then it struck him, her slip of the tongue. *Stanley. The first time she had seen Kez was at my trial when the world knew her as Saranna Browne. The way she said it sounded like she knew Kez in another life.*

As Jake turned Horatio towards home, he decided that strange feeling he had on meeting Stella Hamberton was no accident. It was like seeing Keziah in her eyes.

CHAPTER 55

Westerly winds carried the unmistakable threat of distant bushfires. It was the smell of a danger Jake accepted had always been wedded to this land and always would be.

He was in the open stables proudly overseeing Gabriel as he brushed Alinta's coat. The club-footed filly was the boy's special love. The task of grooming her was the reward Jake had assigned to Gabriel last Christmas when he brought Alinta home from Ogden Park. Gabriel knew Alinta's story, but Jake was aware the boy never tired of hearing it over and over again.

'Well mate, I'd treated one of Mr Ogden's racehorses. He wanted to pay me in kind with one of his other thoroughbred fillies. He claimed a horse deformed as bad as Alinta would never race and was no use to him or me. But just look at her, Gabe! She won my heart right off.'

Gabriel's eyes shone as he prompted Jake to continue. 'And then you and Uncle Bran made her a false hoof, right?'

'Yeah, and her special training shoes. A lot of trial and error but we finally got it right. And just look at her go. Did you watch her training yesterday?'

'Yeah. Dick Gideon rode her like the wind. He says she's going to win lots of races, just like the silver cup Sarishan won for us.'

'Watch Dick ride every chance you get. He's a great horseman. You're going to be flash yourself.' Jake tapped his own forehead with one finger. 'I know these things.'

Gabriel basked in the pleasure of this vote of confidence and redoubled his energy grooming Alinta. 'You did it, Papa! She'll be a champ. That'll show Mr Ogden!'

'Don't worry, he's already impressed.' Jake tried to be fair. 'Remember,

Gabe, an Exclusive who loves horses can't be all bad. Some other thoroughbred owners would have given up on her and sent her to the knackery. Alinta will always need special care.'

'Just wait till Mama sees her!' They exchanged their special knowing grin, always confident that the day of her return might lie just over the horizon.

Jake looked across at the house where Pearl was bathing little Yosie in a tin tub on the veranda. He felt a wave of guilt that his ten-year-old daughter had taken on the role of nursemaid. He made sure she and Gabriel continued to ride Pony to school each day, but it made him uncomfortable to think that history was repeating itself. His father had pulled him out of school because he needed him to do a man's work on the farm. Was he exploiting child labour?

Jake was distracted by the sight of Daniel on horseback belting across the paddock towards them. 'Jesus wept. He looks like the traps are after him.'

Daniel almost fell off the horse as he thrust a letter at him.

Jake read it slowly. He steeled himself against the possibility of a mistake as Gabriel stood waiting anxiously at his elbow. Despite his embarrassment about his slow reading, Jake was determined to be the one to break the good news.

'Hey, my little Rom. Listen to this. *"His Excellency's the Governor's Pleasure to dispense with the attendance at government work of Keziah Browne also known as Smith and Stanley, also known as Saranna Plews."'*

'That's Mama!' cried Gabriel.

'Yeah. There's some other stuff, date of her trial and all. Then it goes on: *'To permit her to employ herself (off the Stores) in any lawful occupation within the District of New South Wales for her own advantage during good behaviour; or until His Excellency's further Pleasure shall be made known. Registered in the Office of the . . .'* Jake stalled and Daniel quickly supplied, *'The Principal Superintendent of Convicts.'*

'Yeah,' said Jake, 'it's numbered and dated. Looks pretty bloody official to me!' He turned to Daniel. 'Her ticket-of-leave. No backing out of this one, eh Dan?'

Gabriel's eyes darted anxiously from one to the other in search of an explanation.

'It means your mama's coming home soon, Gabe!' Jake confirmed.

Gabriel reverently traced the embossed emblem with one finger. The familiar British lion and unicorn stood like tiny bookends either side of the heraldic shield topped by the British crown. Gabe headed off in the direction of the veranda.

'Hey, Pearl! She's coming home!' he screamed.

Jake hugged Daniel then awkwardly broke away. As they headed back to the house he was jubilant. 'Jesus wept, tonight we'll drink the cellar dry. You and Bran come and eat with us before the children go to bed. It's their big night!'

'And ours! I'll bring the special bottles of red I've been saving for this day.'

Jake stopped in his tracks, suddenly serious. 'This *is* real, ain't it, Dan? Those official buggers can't change their minds – at the Governor's bloody Pleasure, can they?'

'Not a chance, mate. It's the real thing. As long as Keziah keeps her nose clean. The prison deputy says she's a model prisoner.' Daniel called as he rode off, 'We'll see you tonight with bells on.'

Jake was determined the children would remember this celebration all their lives. 'No school today!' he announced. 'We're giving the house a bit of spit and polish.'

Jake felt a great sense of relief, as if Keziah wasn't the only one to be set free from gaol. Every day he rose at dawn, cooked and cared for the children, tended the horses, milked the cow and ran the farm. The kids fed the chooks and watered the vegetable plot before they rode Pony to school. It was late each night before Jake dropped exhausted into bed. Except Saturday nights. Then he carried Yosie on his shoulders and walked with Pearl and Gabriel to the forge house at the far end of

Sarishan Farm for one of Bran's baked dinners. Only then did Jake drink alcohol, a whole bottle of ale to remind himself he was a free man.

Each Sunday he drove the children to one of the Sunday schools. Not for the religion. While the bush church resounded with children singing hymns, Jake stretched out, covered his face with his hat and caught up on sleep.

Despite his exhaustion he had no regrets about rejecting his mates' advice to apply to the authorities for an assigned housekeeper. He wanted no substitute mother for the children. And Keziah must never fear another woman might be keeping his bed warm.

At six o'clock Daniel and Bran rolled up. Daniel cradled a box of wine and Bran carried a huge bowl of the children's favourite pudding – roly-poly topped with lashings of blackberry jam and clotted cream.

Jake decided to throw out the rule book about the children's bedtimes on this glorious night of celebration. The three men were soon drunk on sheer relief as much as wine. When they ran out of two-legged friends they toasted their horses.

Then Gabriel leapt on his chair and held aloft his lemonade to Daniel's portrait of Keziah, which hung in pride of place beside Keziah's framed print of Queen Victoria.

'To Mama, God bless her! And Queen Victoria too!'

They all sprang to their feet. Jake's republican sympathies did not count a damn that night. He led the response, 'To Mama and Queen Victoria! God bless 'em both!'

He turned to Daniel for advice. 'You've had experience with the ticket-of-leave process. Fill us in. I'll need to keep a sharp eye on Kez. Make sure she doesn't put a foot wrong.'

Jake noted the children's anxiety, but Daniel was quick to reassure them.

'It's easy. Your mama will be mustered four times a year to have her ticket endorsed by the Principal Superintendent of Convicts.' He winked at the children. 'So no hopping on a ship to England for a bit of a holiday, right!'

'I reckon we can manage that,' said Jake. *'And?'*

Daniel quoted the conditions by heart. 'Must attend church or some place of public worship at least once every Sunday. And that prisoners who shall fail to do so are immediately to be deprived of their ticket-of-leave and turned into government employ.' He punched the air. 'How's that? Word perfect!'

Jake groaned. 'Church every Sunday! Jesus, Kez will love that bit!'

'You're telling me! It was hard enough to get her to church for her wedding!'

'With you as bridegroom, no bloody wonder she wanted to bolt!' said Jake.

When Daniel pretended to roar with anger, Gabriel gave a tolerant smile.

Jake suspected the boy had begun to wise up to his unusual position as son to three fathers and had worked out that Caleb was the one who had invited the stork.

Jake refilled their glasses. 'No two ways about it, Kez will have to go to church or she'll be shot back into the Factory.'

Bran hammered his giant fist so hard the crockery rattled. He tried valiantly to speak. 'One – Kez. F-f—'

Everyone held their breath. Bran held up five fingers and Daniel interpreted.

'He means we're *five to one*! Dead right. We've got her outnumbered!'

After Jake shepherded the sleepy children to bed, he brought out the port wine.

'You're true blue, both of you. I reckon I'd never have done it without you.'

He studied Daniel with the sincerity of the seriously drunk. 'If my woman *has* to have a legal husband, she could do no better than you!'

Bran's laughter was so deep in his chest it sounded like the giant bellows in his forge. Daniel was never more formal than when he was in his cups.

'Deeply honoured to be your wife's public husband.'

By the time the trio had sung the seamen's work song *Bound for South Australia,* the false piccaninny dawn lay faint and pink along the horizon.

Weaving as he departed, supported by Bran, Daniel called to Jake, 'No shut-eye tonight, mate. I'll just pack the cart and it's off to Parramatta to collect our wife.'

Jake remembered to give him a parcel of clothes for Keziah's homecoming and watched the pair lustily singing as they headed back to the forge house.

He was struck by an odd thought. When Bran sang, all trace of his dislocated speech disappeared. His voice soared joyously like that of a Welsh tenor.

Jake staggered off to the stables to check on his welcome-home present for Keziah. The white Arab colt was the finest horse he had ever seen in his life. To pay for her he had outlasted thirteen punishing rounds against a Maori who was the best man he'd ever fought – after Gem Smith.

He stroked the colt's snowy mane and reassured him. 'Your mistress will be home inside of two weeks. I'm leaving Kez to give you your name. You know what you are, mate? You're the best present a man can give his Romani woman!'

CHAPTER 56

Keziah lay in her bunk unable to sleep. She had been forced to bypass the evening meal and her stomach was still contracted with nerves at the thought of what lay ahead. The deputy's face had been expressionless when she delivered the news to Keziah.

'You've been granted your ticket. Assigned to your husband's care. Seems like you've got some powerful friend at court, as they say.'

Then the deputy turned her back on her and walked away.

In the months since Keziah had sent little Yosef packing with Daniel, it had been too painful for her to recall exactly what he looked like, but she could not escape the sight and smell of him in her dreams. She often woke convinced she could hear him crying. And she felt a dull, empty sensation whenever she saw another prisoner cuddling her own babe.

She told herself the only way to survive in prison was to let everything happen to you – no matter what – but feel nothing.

No doubt Daniel had already left Sarishan Farm on his way to collect her. She could count on the fingers of one hand the days before the date of her release, when she would step through the front gates of the Factory for the last time. Free to feel the wind in her hair, the sun on her face, to run, dance and welcome the night. For the first time she was unable to block out the pain of seeing Jake's beloved face. He would want to make love to her under the stars.

She turned her face to the wall, surprised by a sensation she had not felt for more than a year, but were her tears due to joy or fear?

The next morning, after dressing hurriedly in her prison slops, Keziah was first in the queue to receive bread and a bowl of gruel in the prisoners' eating room. Today the usual tension had escalated. She seated herself among the most docile group of women – those who were either too listless to cause trouble or like her were intent on avoiding the ringleader who caused it. One old woman kept her eyes fixed on her empty plate as she whispered a warning to Keziah.

'Watch yourself today, girl. Oola's brewing up big trouble, a mutiny. I can feel it in my waters.'

Keziah nodded. 'I'll keep a sharp eye out.'

'Any fool can see she's got it in for you for knocking her back. She gets others to warm her bed, but it's you she fancies – your wild hair, eh?' The woman gave a knowing cackle, adding kindly, 'Do whatever you must, you've only got a few days before you'll be shot of this stinking place.'

Keziah transferred her bread to the old woman's plate. 'I won't forget your kindness.'

She had barely spoken the words when she heard voices yelling obscenities in the corridor. She could taste the fear and excitement in the air as the women stampeded for the door, but she remained in her seat, unwilling to wreck her chances of release.

A group of women prisoners charged into the room, some shaking their fists, some brandishing broken chair legs. At the helm was their ringleader, Oola, her beefy arms covered in tattoos. Her head had been recently shaved, a punishment the other women hated most of all. She looked as tough as any sailor from a man-o'-war, her eyes bright with battle fever.

'Whoever ain't with me is against me! My enemy! That bloody deputy protects her little mates. Come on, you cowards. Give that bitch what she deserves. Bash her to pulp!'

Virtually all the women raced after Oola as she led the charge towards the room where the deputy was known to be on duty at this time of day. But Keziah had seen the woman in her office doing paperwork and ran to warn her.

The windows of the deputy's office were barred. Only a few minutes remained before Oola would realise her mistake. Keziah burst through the doorway. 'It's mutiny. Oola and her gang are on the rampage.'

The deputy appeared to have shrunk in size, frozen at her desk, unable to move as the frenzied voices and footsteps came closer. Keziah took charge.

'Hide under the desk. I'll bolt the door. If they think you're not here there's a chance they'll move on.'

Keziah felt the deputy's body tremble as she pushed her under the desk. She wasn't being heroic, she owed her a debt. This hard-faced woman had secretly brought her additional food to help sustain her breast milk for Yosef.

Weapons beat the iron bars and door in a chaotic rhythm. But even the women's combined chanting was not loud enough to drown out Oola's voice yelling, 'Kill the bitch!'

A heavy object rammed the door until it splintered off its hinges and Oola stormed into the room ahead of a knot of screaming prisoners. Keziah stood her ground to face them.

'Use your heads! We all want better conditions but killing isn't the answer! The military will arrive any minute!'

But their contagious rage had blinded their reason. Oola was their mouthpiece.

'Listen to the deputy's pet. Well the bitch can't save you from me any longer, Gypsy!'

Oola raised her weapon ready to bash Keziah's skull. Ducking to avoid the blow, Keziah fell to the ground. The faces that screamed down at her were all familiar, but their rage made them strangers.

'The deputy bitch is *our* prisoner now!' Oola shouted. 'So's the Gypsy. Drag 'em both outside so we can all enjoy the fun.'

As Oola dragged her along by her hair, Keziah caught sight of the whimpering deputy.

Four prisoners swung the deputy's body by her arms and legs, like some captured animal trussed up ready for roasting. Others seized the opportunity to bash her face and kick her body while she was helpless.

Keziah was convinced they were both done for. If Oola gave the order to string them up, the other prisoners would be too afraid to disobey her.

As she tried to shield her head from their blows Keziah saw a flash of red coats. The military had never been such a welcome sight. The women dropped her and the deputy on the ground. They turned their rage on the soldiers, impotently brandishing the chair-leg clubs that were no match against muskets.

Keziah saw that the soldiers did not break rank. Even when the women clubbed them they continued to push them back with their muskets locked in horizontal formation at arm's length. Only a single shot was fired as a warning over the prisoners' heads.

The women's rage soon began to fizzle out. Keziah knew many of them had willingly entered liaisons with some of these soldiers and welcomed the money or rough affection that came their way. Every woman had her price.

One soldier, with blood staining his face, called out, not without humour, 'Cool down, *ladies*. We don't want the authorities cutting off all your nice hair.'

Keziah helped the deputy to her feet. The woman's mouth was torn from the beating but she managed to mutter, 'I'll not forget what you did to protect me.'

Keziah had no time to respond. Oola was watching her, breathing heavily. Keziah tried not to reveal the cold wave of fear she felt when Oola gave her a knowing smile.

'You reckon you can see the future, eh? Then you'll know just how I'm going to pay you back, Gypsy!'

CHAPTER 57

Keziah sat alone in the courtyard of the Factory. Two weeks had passed in the aftermath of the riot. Daniel was expected to arrive that morning to take her home, officially assigned to his custody if the authorities approved her ticket-of-leave. In readiness for her departure her convict slops were clean and her Romani headscarf covered all but the plait hanging over her shoulder. But she felt totally drained of emotion. The day that she had dreaded for weeks had finally arrived. There was no escape. Through the window of the deputy's office she could see the woman's head bent over her desk. Her skull was bandaged. Her mouth puckered from the stitches binding her split upper lip, wounds suffered in the riot. For a moment their eyes locked. *Will she be true to her word?*

Keziah knew that the deputy's favourable report was in gratitude for saving her life. But her fellow prisoners' resentment increased when Keziah's name alone was removed from the rosters, free from all work. *Free to be afraid. Oola was officially kept in isolation. But that didn't stop her bribing a guard to set her free at night.*

When the deputy beckoned her to her office, Keziah stood in silence as the woman's pen scratched entries in the ledger book. Speaking painfully through her wounded mouth, she handed Keziah a newspaper.

'Here's an account of the aftermath of the riot. Take it.' She waved a hand in dismissal.

Keziah nodded acknowledgement but felt no gratitude, no emotion of any kind. Oola's mutiny had changed her life forever.

As she read *The Sydney Monitor's* account she felt disconnected from her role in it. Phrases sprang off the page to trigger vivid memories of the violence. '*… the worst mutiny in the history of Parramatta Female Factory … the military was praised for their restraint in holding their fire … two were wounded … eighty-two female prisoners had their sentences extended … the ringleader had her head shaved.*'

Keziah felt numb. *They can't find a fitting punishment for Oola. She's been shorn so often she glories in her bald head – the symbol of her power.*

Keziah flinched when she saw Daniel arrive. He spoke animatedly to the deputy then crossed the courtyard to her side.

'Are you all right, Keziah? I only heard the latest news when I reached Parramatta. I was worried they'd postpone your release, but the deputy said you were quite the heroine. What happened?'

She shrugged and looked away. 'I saved myself.'

'Thank God. I could never have faced Jake if I'd returned empty-handed.' He kissed her cheek then tried to sound light-hearted as he handed her a large parcel.

'The deputy went through this with a fine-tooth comb. You'd think by now she'd realise I'm not smuggling weapons.' He presented a document with a flourish. 'And here's the moment we've all been waiting for. Da da! Your ticket-of-leave!'

Keziah held it in silence, remembering Nerida's long ago triumphant phrase, *'That freedom business'. But this ticket has come too late. I'll never be free again.* She saw Daniel was trying to amuse her with a story about the tussle between Jake and Pearl over the parcel, how the little girl vetoed Jake's suggestions and insisted she knew best what items to choose for her mother.

Keziah pushed the parcel back at him. 'I can't go with you, Daniel.'

'What? Don't tell me the damned authorities blocked your release? You've got your ticket right here in your hands.'

'Not them. Me. I can't face everyone.'

Daniel looked thrown but he pressed on, referring to Pearl's list.

'She chose your favourite red dress. She's starched your petticoats, put in your camisole and unmentionables, stockings and shoes. In your reticule you'll find your silver amulet and a comb. And there's a scarf or is it a shawl? Your straw hat's in the wagon. Jake said to tell you *his* special present is waiting for you at the farm.'

When she said nothing he continued with enthusiasm. 'We haven't had time to finish all the fences. But Jake got Bran and me to build a wrought-iron archway over the entrance. It says "Welcome to Sarishan Farm". Jake's idea. It's a Romani greeting, right?'

She knew she was supposed to react with pleasure but she only managed to nod.

Daniel put his arm around her shoulders. 'Change into your own clothes, you silly goose. You'll feel much better.'

'Daniel, look at me! Can't you see the truth? Nothing will fit me. I'm a scarecrow!'

'Nonsense. A week of fresh farm food and you'll be as voluptuous as any artist's model. Get in the wagon. There's no female problem that can't be solved with a new dress!'

When Keziah sighted the new Parramatta branch of Sydney merchant Joseph Farmer's Emporium she wanted to bolt. After wearing convict slops for more than a year, the words on the sign seemed like a foreign language – *Silk Mercer, Haberdasher and Linen Draper.*

Daniel selected an Indian cotton dress. 'Blue to match your eyes,' he said.

What consolation is that?

In the changing cubicle she removed all her clothing and looked in the mirror. She was horrified when she saw Daniel pass by and accidentally catch sight of her naked reflection. His eyes locked with hers in shock.

Keziah's hands trembled and her scarf fell to the floor. Pinned inside it was the long black braid of her hair. She stared bleakly at her mirror image. Her head was totally bald. Without a word Daniel turned away.

When she re-joined him outside the store she wore the new blue dress but avoided his eyes.

'You look lovely, Keziah.' He lifted her up onto the front seat. 'You only need this to complete the picture.' He handed her a small parcel he had just bought.

'For your hair,' he said. 'Put your sunhat on. We've a long journey ahead of us. Can't have you going down with sunstroke.'

Keziah opened his parcel and felt a faint glimmer of emotion.

Daniel averted his eyes while she fixed the gift in place. Her sunhat covered her Gypsy scarf. Over her shoulder hung the plait now braided with Daniel's scarlet ribbon for good luck.

'So now you know the truth,' she said blankly.

He nodded. 'I know how you women feel about your hair. How humiliated you must be, but it will soon grow again and it won't matter a damn to Jake. He's just desperate to have you back home with him.'

And I'm desperate to be anywhere else! she thought but remained silent.

He tried again. 'I won't pretend your adjustment will be easy, but remember we all experience guilt. That we've been set free, but we've left friends behind locked up.'

Keziah's voice was harsh. 'I had no friends.'

He nodded. 'When I left Gideon Park I felt worthless. A rank coward all my life for what I'd done to Maynard Plews and Saranna. For what I'd become with Iago. When I sank to blackmail to force you to marry me I knew I'd sold my very soul to the devil!'

Keziah cut across him. 'Your soul was just badly wounded. It needed time to heal.'

'You're right. In time I did heal. And so will you, Keziah.'

'No. Nothing on earth can wipe out what I've done. You didn't commit murder, Daniel. You didn't betray the children who trusted you.'

'You know who healed me?' he asked. 'Gabriel.'

'Children see the real person inside us.'

'One Sunday in Ironbark Chapel a priest was raving on about Daniel in the lion's den and the message from the Archangel Gabriel. Our names, you see? I realised how much you both needed me. I'll always be your friend, Keziah, but it's Jake who really needs you now.'

Keziah turned her head to look out at the horizon. Storm clouds were gathering.

'No! I can't face him!'

'Listen, Keziah. The past is dead. Jake needs you to share the future. I swear to God, I've never seen anyone love the way Jake loves you!'

'He loves the woman I *was*. I have done things even Jake's love cannot heal.'

Daniel finally lost his temper. 'Give the man a chance, Keziah. Damn it all, the poor bastard deserves that much!'

That morning Jake laid it squarely on the line to the children as he lined them up on the veranda, inspecting their hands, faces and the backs of their necks for cleanliness.

'Absolutely no practical jokes and tricks on Mama! Save 'em up for April Fools' Day next year.'

Since dawn he had issued sharp instructions as they scurried around to complete their chores. For the past two days the table had been set with a lace cloth for Mama's reunion lunch or supper, all in readiness for the unknown hour of her arrival.

Jake was about to remove the side of lamb from the coolroom when a Rolly Brothers coach drew up in front of the home paddock. Mac Mackie's crazy detour from his usual route was clearly causing consternation amongst his male passengers.

'Won't be long. I'm an angel of mercy!' Mac called to them over his shoulder. 'Why don't you stretch your legs and do the necessary?'

Jake had no need to prompt Pearl. Proud of her role as a farmer's daughter, she knew the unwritten laws of bush hospitality. She hurried forth with a tray of drinks and biscuits for the passengers who were sweltering in the unusual spring heat.

Mac piled a mountain of boxes on Jake's veranda.

'The cooked tucker is from Janet Macgregor and Polly Doyle. Fruit and vegetables from Ironbark farmers. Scotch and Drambuie from the Doc. Same message from all. Dead keen to see Keziah but we know you two need time alone together.' Mac gave a very unsubtle wink and his shaggy beard quivered with suppressed laughter.

'It's enough to feed a regiment. I'm bloody overwhelmed,' said Jake.

'Don't get so overwhelmed you forget what to do *tonight,* mate. If you need a few tips to jog your memory, just ask your Uncle Mac!'

'Piss off,' Jake said with affection.

Mac wagged a finger as he loped back to the waiting coach. 'It's like riding a horse, mate. It'll all come back to you the minute you hop in the saddle.'

Afternoon shadows stretched across the sun-bleached grass. Jake and his children waited on the veranda scanning the track for Daniel and his precious cargo. The last time Jake had seen Keziah's face was more than a year ago in Berrima Gaol through the grill on her cell door the night the Rev had smuggled him to talk to her.

Jake paced restlessly, one eye on the track. His worn but clean moleskin trousers were tucked into riding boots. His red shirt fell open to his belt. His body was hard, brown – and very tense.

Now twelve months old, little Yosie was ever ready to use his sea legs. Jake had anchored him in his highchair, but kept hurrying to the coolroom to keep Yosie supplied with barley water. He regularly checked the towelling pinned between the boy's legs. He felt it was important to hand across a dry, clean-smelling kid to Keziah. Yosie's constant thirst made that task difficult.

Pearl had cut down Keziah's old work dress to make herself a skirt. Jake realised that must mean she had outgrown her own clothes. Money was tight but Pearl asked for nothing except the weekly thruppence for her school fee and a coin for the Sunday school plate.

Gabriel had plastered his hair flat to his skull – except for the cowlick that stuck up like a question mark. He kept tuning his violin like a musician in an orchestra pit.

He finally had to ask the question. 'Mama *is* coming home today, isn't she?'

'She better be. Couldn't face this song and dance again tomorrow!' Jake instantly regretted causing their wistful reaction. 'Your mama would never let you down, mate. If she's late there's a damned good reason.'

'Bushrangers?' they both whispered fearfully.

'Nah, your mama can handle *them*. Don't worry about that!'

Five minutes later all hell broke loose. Gabriel hollered as he leapt the fence with the grace of a gazelle and his sister ran through the gate. By the time Daniel drew to a halt, they had clambered over Keziah, bombarding her with questions they gave her no time to answer.

Jake's heart was racing and his mouth was dry as he carried Yosie towards her and forgot every single word of the speech he'd planned for weeks.

His first words to his wife came out in a rush. 'Here. It's safe to hold him. He's dry for once.'

'See you folks later,' said Daniel and made his getaway as fast as he could.

The clock chimed seven. Jake was alone with Keziah. During the family meal she had applauded Gabriel's violin performance and paid the right compliments about Pearl's homemade presents, but when Jake placed Yosie in his cot in the master bedroom, he saw Keziah's odd expression as she eyed the new bed they would share for the first time.

'Daniel carved the bedstead. See? Our initials are entwined inside that fancy knot.'

'It's a lover's knot,' she said and left the room.

Since then she had given monosyllabic responses to his attempts at conversation. He studied her in silence. Keziah had not changed her dress or scarf since her arrival home.

'Always liked that blue dress on you,' he said hopefully.

'Daniel just bought it in Parramatta. My own clothes won't fit me.'

Jake could see she was pale and a bit on the scrawny side, only to be expected after more than a year of prison pap. He'd make damned sure she ate fresh food. His lamb, his fruit, his veg, his eggs, milk and cream. *Bloody hell. What am I doing wrong?*

'Do you like the wine?' he asked. 'A new local vineyard. A First Fleeter's son has gone into partnership with an old lag. Pretty good drop I reckon.'

'I'm not used to wine. I'd get lushy.'

'I won't complain,' he said lightly. 'Wine makes you very affectionate.'

No trace of a smile. It unnerved Jake to realise she was shy of his touch. He was angry with himself. After their long separation he couldn't think of another thing to say.

His eyes traced the line of the thick black plait over her shoulder. It made her look like a schoolgirl. The shadows under her eyes. No colour in her cheeks. None of that mattered. *But where the hell is Keziah's spirit?*

He decided to take control. 'Come on. It's time to give you *my* present.'

He grabbed a lantern and pulled her by the hand past her beloved *vardo*, which rested under the leafy umbrella of a giant fire tree. He stopped inside the stables.

'There!' He waited for her reaction, as confident as a gambler holding a royal flush.

The magnificent colt pawed the ground. The eyes held intelligent fire, his lines were as graceful as any horse Jake had ever seen. Dick

Gideon had groomed him like a champion fit to parade before young Queen Victoria.

'He's yours, Kez. Arab bloodline. I'd go hungry before I'd sell him. Ride him, stud him, race him – your choice. All he needs is for you to name him. What do you reckon?'

The colt moved closer. Jake handed lumps of sugar to her in readiness for this moment but all Keziah did was to feed the colt sugar from the palm of her hand. No Romani bonding.

Jake drew Keziah back against his chest, his voice hungry for her praise. 'Tell me, Kez, you do *like* him?'

He kissed the shoulder of her dress, kissed her plaited hair. Keziah pulled away.

'Thank you, more than I can say. It's been a long journey.'

'Struth, what a fool I am,' said Jake. 'Of course, you're tired.'

He followed her back to the homestead. When they reached the *vardo*, she turned to him with eyes that seemed to be looking at another country.

'I'd prefer to sleep in here tonight.'

'Wherever you want, Kez. I just need to hold you in my arms tonight. That's all. Word of honour. The rest can come later when *you* are ready.'

Keziah nodded. 'Tonight I need to sleep alone.'

She climbed the steps into the *vardo*. The sound of the bolt sliding behind her held an ominous note of finality.

This pattern continued for two weeks. At first Jake assured himself it was simply because Keziah was conditioned to being locked in a cell. But he knew that was a lie – she would not even allow him to sleep beside her like a mate.

She seemed to be using the children as a shield. Day by day she picked up the threads of their lives, read them stories, heard their lessons, lengthened Pearl's skirts to give modest covering to her daughter's legs – her Romani instinct. She took over the cooking from Jake without a word exchanged on the subject. He saw she was trying to fit back into their lives – like a stranger in Keziah's shoes. Whenever her eyes were forced to make contact with his, her expression was wary. Why?

Since her return Jake had never once seen her without her headscarf. Despite the plait he suspected her hair had been shaved off in prison. He was worried if he raised the subject he would strip her of what little remained of her formidable Romani pride. On the other hand, if he dodged the issue Keziah might misinterpret that as being a rejection of her looks and keep him at bay until her hair grew again. *Hell, that could take a year!*

He worked out exactly what to say to broach the subject tactfully and marched in to the cookhouse where Keziah was alone, except for Yosie in his highchair. The fuel stove increased the day's high temperature. Sweat ran down her face and created damp patches under the sleeves of her blouse, but despite the heat her head was tightly bound by that eternal headscarf. Her plait swung wildly as she kneaded the dough for baking bread.

She looked up, startled at Jake's entry. He was armed with an axe.

'Been building up your woodpile,' he said and charged at the problem head-on.

'What's up, Kez? I don't give a damn what you wear. You'd look good in sackcloth and ashes, but you haven't taken off that headscarf since you left the Factory. A bloke doesn't have to be too clever to work out why. Those bastards in charge shaved off your hair to punish you, right?'

She didn't answer him. He hated to see the pain in her eyes.

'What are you afraid of, Kez? Do you think I won't fancy you without your hair? Jesus, you must think I'm shallow. Nothing could put me off you, girl. Not a bloody thing.'

His gesture was quick but gentle. He pulled the scarf from her head – the plait was sewn inside it. The anguish in her face chilled him. Jake concealed his shock at the reality – her shorn skull was covered by a dark fuzz like a man's rough beard.

'It'll grow in next to no time. I'm sorry, Kez. I know what your hair means to you but it doesn't matter to me.' He reached out to stroke her head but she pushed his hand aside.

'Don't you dare pity me!'

Snatching the scarf from his hands, she scooped up Yosie from his highchair and fled to the *vardo*, slamming the door and bolting it behind her.

'Well, you made a right mess of that, you stupid bastard,' Jake berated himself. He stalked off and swung his axe at a gum tree he was determined to fell to relieve his frustration.

His confusion magnified as he hacked away at the trunk. He had tried to release Keziah's humiliation in the same way he used to lance a boil – one initial stab of pain followed by a flood of relief when the pus ran free and healing followed. Instead he had made things worse.

As he aggressively swung the axe and the noise resounded through the bush, he was bitterly reminded of the cold reception Keziah had given to his gift – the still unnamed Arab colt. He could hardly forget her passionate joy over Gem's gift of the brumby.

The problem ran deeper than being stripped of her hair. What the hell was wrong? She clearly intended to continue to bolt her door against him. Why did she reject Yosie each night? Was it simply because he was Jake's child? He never made distinctions. His, hers, theirs, they were all his children. After he had slain the timber giant the answer hit him. *Yosie sleeps beside me. It's not him she's rejecting, it's my body. I've got to be patient.*

He decided it was time for Keziah to try her wings in public. He cornered her in the kitchen.

'I promised to take Gabriel to Goulburn tomorrow. Pearl and Yosie will stay with Bran. He loves cooking for them and Pearl's so capable she could run Goulburn Hospital single-handed.' He added only half joking, 'We'll take Dan along as our chaperone, eh?'

Keziah nodded in cautious agreement.

'I won't lie to you, Kez. Gabriel wants to visit Mrs Hamberton, the magistrate's wife. He's taken a shine to her. My gut tells me she was that unknown woman who pulled strings to wangle my release. And I reckon she helped swing your ticket too. I owe her big.'

He looked her straight in the eye. 'I think you know what I'm asking, but it's up to you.'

CHAPTER 58

Grey and steamy, the day was plagued by a westerly wind that frayed tempers, buffeting the group as they travelled in silence. Keziah felt as if she was being carted off in a tumbrel to the guillotine.

For the sake of appearances Jake established their public pecking order – himself as driver to Mr and Mrs Daniel Browne who sat behind him like royalty.

Keziah was touched by Gabriel's intense concentration, seated beside Jake like a pint-sized apprentice absorbing his father's driving skills.

When they drew up in the bustling Goulburn town centre, she chose to remain in the cart while her two husbands went about their business. Sensing her fear, Gabriel sat beside her in silence. She shielded her face with her sunbonnet in the hope she would escape recognition, overwhelmed by shame that was both public and private. For weeks she had avoided any response to Jake's patient attempts to ease her back into her role as his wife and into his bed. *Mi-duvel. How long can I keep him at bay?*

Her reverie was broken. Jake sprang onto the driver's seat like a jack-in-the-box.

'Right. Our business is done. Daniel's gone to sink an ale at a public house. I'll join him later.' He handed Gabriel a penny flute. 'This is for you, mate.'

Jake drove them to a street lined with the elegant houses of the Quality and pulled up before an impressive double-storey sandstone building. The L-shaped veranda and Juliet balcony were decorated with wrought-iron lace like icing on a wedding cake.

It was one thing for Gabriel to enjoy visiting this house and its mistress, but how could Jake understand what this visit would cost *her*? Keziah had no intention of alighting.

Jake forced the issue. 'You've got the guts to meet her, Kez. I know you have.' As if that closed the subject, he stretched out on the seat and pulled his hat over his eyes ready to sleep.

Keziah took hold of Gabriel's hand as he helped her climb down. It reminded her of the hour of his birth and the way his tiny hand had gripped hers and given her courage.

On the ivy-shaded veranda she gestured him toward a wrought-iron seat. 'Wait here for me, Gabriel. I won't be long.'

The boy nodded and put his new flute to his lips to entertain himself.

A housemaid ushered her down the black and white chequered marble corridor. Keziah glimpsed her reflection in a mirror. Her blue Indian cotton dress was crushed from travelling, her braid topped by a Romani-style scarf. Her cheeks showed a faint trace of colour after weeks of fresh farm food. Her eyes were ringed by mauve shadows. She was determined their message would be unmistakable. No quarter asked, none given. *What do I care what this* gaujo *woman thinks of me? She's not fit to judge anyone.*

All too soon Keziah found herself in an elegant drawing room face to face with the magistrate's wife. Mrs Hamberton was seated in a straight-backed chair, dressed in sober anthracite silk – the same grey colour as the telltale shadows around her eyes.

It seems I'm not the only one who had a sleepless night. In court Keziah had been shocked by that single flash of recognition. Now she had a moment to study the woman. The greying fair hair was coiled back from her face without any attempt at artifice. She wore no jewellery. Her beautifully shaped hands were tightly clasped in her lap, her well-modulated, upper-class voice sounded calm.

'I thank you for coming to see me. I appreciate how difficult that decision must have been for you, Mrs Browne.'

'I doubt it.' Keziah had intended to remain standing, but when her knees trembled she sank into a chair. Her eyes fixed on the grandfather clock as it chimed twice.

When Mrs Hamberton poured tea from a silver teapot, Keziah was reminded of her own, the Award for Bravery from Janet Macgregor's Wesleyan Women for Temperance group. How bitterly ironic that gift was right now. She had never felt more like a coward.

'Understand one thing,' Keziah said. 'I am here for one reason only. My … my friend Jake Andersen believes that the magistrate's wife has friends in high places and has the ear of Governor Gipps. Jake thinks you played an influential role in his release from prison. And perhaps my own.' Her tone was icy. 'Is that true? I refuse to be in your debt!'

With a wave of her hand Mrs Hamberton dismissed that idea. 'You are in no one's debt. In both cases justice was at last achieved.'

Keziah's mouth went dry but she could not bring herself to touch the delicate bone china rimmed with gold. A white teacup was bad luck.

'I understand Jake Andersen brought my son Gabriel to visit you.'

The question drew a faint smile of relief. 'Yes. Your son is an extraordinarily perceptive child, like his mother.'

Keziah rejected the intimacy. 'You may think you know me. You don't. My father, Gabriel Stanley, was a true Rom. He died in prison from injuries received in a fight, but in truth he died years earlier from a broken heart. Betrayed by his *gaujo* wife. He died at her hands as surely as if she'd fired a pistol at his heart. My *Puri Dai* told me my father's wife chose to return to the bosom of her family, to her place in *gaujo* society. A dowry was arranged to enable her to marry within her class. To hide the *indiscretion* of her youth – me!'

Keziah's tone conveyed the acid she felt rising inside her. Mrs Hamberton turned pale. She gave a nervous little cough.

'Your grandmother told you the truth as she knew it. She was a proud woman who repeatedly rejected the money sent to her for the care of Gabriel's little daughter.'

Keziah eyed her with contempt. 'We Romani do not accept blood money.'

Mrs Hamberton rocked slightly in her chair. 'I am sure that young girl, your mother, would never have forgiven herself for the terrible choice she made.'

Keziah was unflinching. 'I was five years old when that *gaujo* bent and kissed my mouth. She told me, "Remember your father is innocent. Be a good girl, Keziah, and I will come back soon." She *lied*. I never ever saw her again!'

Mrs Hamberton covered her mouth. Her hand trembled slightly. Her wedding band glinted in the firelight. The sight of that hated symbol stiffened Keziah's resolve.

'My mother is dead to me. There can be *no resurrection* for Stella the Whore.'

The expression in the woman's eyes became old and defeated.

'Stella the Whore. So that is what they called me. Who could blame them?' She grew resolute. 'Mrs Browne, I understand perfectly. It was most courageous of you to come here and tell me to my face. At your trial you showed the world you place truth above all. No doubt *my* perspective of the truth is of little value to you, but please hear me out. I offer no excuses. I was the spoilt little darling of aged parents. The summer I turned thirteen I ran off to play with the Gypsies in the woods, seduced by the music played by my passionate young Rom. I found perfect happiness in your father's arms. Enough to last me a whole lifetime.'

Her eyes seemed to look inward on a past so bittersweet that Keziah was unable to turn away from her.

'After Gabriel was sent to prison I did what I did. That can never be undone. I never forgot you. After your father's death I begged your *Puri Dai* to allow me to adopt you. She cursed me as only a Romani can curse. Told me you were the only child I would ever have. She was right. For years I watched you from afar – your childhood, your love for

Gem, your marriage. When I discovered you had sailed to this colony I was distraught.'

She gave a self-deprecating laugh that broke into a little cough. 'I used all my feminine wiles to pressure a family friend, Elizabeth, to have her husband, Sir George Gipps, appoint my husband a magistrate in New South Wales.'

Keziah cut across her words. 'The governor! So I *do* owe my freedom to you!'

'If I played a small role in that it was the least I could do. I realise I can never wipe out the past. You have my promise. I shall never attempt to see you or Gabriel again.'

Keziah saw that the woman's face had turned grey as if all life, all hope, had drained from her. Keziah wanted to feel victorious but all she felt was emptiness.

Stella Hamberton said the words softly. 'I have no right to ask but I have one last request. With your permission may I say goodbye to little Gabriel?'

For years Keziah had hated the memory of her beguiling, golden-haired child-mother, whose shallow love dissolved when her Rom was gaoled. Hated the girl who was seduced not by another man but by her *gaujo* world of wealth and comfort.

Keziah's verdict was final. 'Stella the Whore is forever dead to me but Gabriel's *grandmother* is not dead to *him*. I swear By My Father's Hand, I will never stop Gabriel visiting you, I will never colour his affection for you with my own contempt.'

Stella Hamberton appeared to search for words. She then spoke from her heart. 'You are truly your father's daughter.'

'If only that were true.' Keziah's honesty was stronger than her pain. 'But the life I have lived proves I'm no better than my mother. Whores *do* breed whores.'

The woman's blue eyes flashed. 'I will not allow you to condemn yourself in my presence. I proved myself to be weak, malleable, a fool who clung to the false security of my class and destroyed the happiness of those I loved. You do not possess a single trait of mine – except your eyes. You are pure Romani! I saw the truth in court. You have exceptional courage, loyalty and honesty. You are indeed Gabriel Stanley's daughter!'

Her voice cracked and she turned her face away to disguise that sign of weakness.

Keziah rose. 'I believe in telling children the truth. Gabriel has experienced so many changing loyalties. He needs time to absorb this new truth.'

Keziah swept from the room as regally as a queen who has dismissed her subject.

Moments later she returned and prompted Gabriel to make a courteous bow to Mrs Hamberton. Keziah's heart beat like one with Gabriel's. She knew his thoughts. As he peered from under his blond mop of curls, his dark blue eyes fixed on the older lady with whom he shared some strange bond.

'Good day to you, Mrs Hamberton. I trust I find you well?'

'Indeed I am, thank you, Gabriel.' She coughed into her handkerchief.

Keziah tried to assume a friendly manner for Gabriel's sake. 'I understand you share a love of toy soldiers and re-fight the Battle of Waterloo.'

Gabriel's eyes darted between them. 'I always offer Mrs Hamberton first choice. She always chooses to take Napoleon's side.'

Mrs Hamberton smiled wryly. 'Yes, and for some reason I always lose.'

Keziah felt something stir within her. She turned quickly to Gabriel.

'Papa told you Mrs Hamberton is the magistrate's wife but she is also much more than that. Long before you were born she knew your Romani grandfather, Gabriel Stanley. If you ask her nicely she will tell you wonderful stories about him.'

Keziah bent to kiss his forehead. 'I will collect you at four o'clock. Mind your manners. Never forget, Gabriel,' she cast a defiant glance at her hostess, 'you are a Rom.'

With a polite nod of farewell, Keziah retraced her steps down the corridor as the little housemaid rushed ahead to open the front door for her.

Keziah wanted nothing more than to leave but she paused on the veranda.

'How long has your mistress had that cough, girl?'

The servant girl looked startled. 'I only been in service a few weeks, Ma'am. But oftentimes she coughs through the night.'

Keziah struggled to reach a decision. 'Next time my son visits he'll bring a parcel of herbs. Brew it as you would tea. See your mistress drinks it four times daily.'

She hurried down the path.

Jake waited as she seated herself beside him in the wagon and stared straight ahead.

'How did it go?' he finally asked.

Keziah's voice held an edge of self-loathing. 'I have just betrayed my father.'

Jake met her eyes. 'I reckon you made a choice between avenging the past and young Gabe. You've given the little Rom a gift he'll remember all his life.'

He cracked his whip in the air as if to relieve the tension. 'Enough of this. Let's join Dan. You know how *your other husband* hates to drink alone.'

As they drove home to Sarishan Farm, Keziah was not surprised that Daniel was curled asleep in the back of the cart. He never could hold his liquor. Gabriel cheerfully recounted all Mrs Hamberton's stories, how the first Gabriel Stanley's violin made people either weep or dance with joy. How clever he was at taming horses. How he fought cleanly and always won his bare-knuckle fights.

Keziah had a lump in her throat but she did not dare utter a single word.

'He sounds like a great bloke, your grandfather,' Jake said. When he looked searchingly into Keziah's eyes, he gave a wry clown's grimace.

For the rest of the journey home Jake slouched dejectedly over the reins. Keziah knew the truth as well as he did. The crack in the ice had frozen over.

CHAPTER 59

Keziah woke in fright in the *vardo* at the sound of banging doors in the house. Had Jake's Irish temper finally shattered his patience?

She wrapped a towel around her head like a turban and peered through a crack in the door. Jake marched towards the *vardo* as if responding to some Viking battle cry. He was naked except for moleskin trousers. Little Yosie was anchored on his hip with the tail of his nightshirt flapping behind him.

'Unlock the bloody door, will you?' He pushed Yosie into her arms. 'Here, I believe this is yours. I've been cleaning him up for months. This is the last straw. I'm off to a shanty. And I won't lie to you, Kez, I intend to get very, very drunk.' He flung a note of sarcasm over his shoulder. 'Don't bother to wait up for me.'

Riding past on Horatio a few minutes later, he fired his parting broadside. 'Don't worry. I'll pay the bills. I'll stick by the kids. I made you a promise. I'll stand by it. But you don't need to bolt your door against me. It's safe to sleep in the house. I won't trouble you again!'

When he galloped off as if a ninety-mile-an-hour bushfire was on his tail, Keziah knew he was headed for Bolthole Valley – at best on a bender. At worst? That red-headed Lily Pompadour had flown the coop a few years ago with Jake's help and made a new life for herself in Melbourne Town, but Keziah knew there would always be a ready supply of fallen women to take her place.

Keziah felt a tight sensation in the pit of her stomach. Fear? Jealousy? She told herself it was justified anger. Jake had bolted leaving three children in her care. She had no choice but to shoulder the full weight of the farm. *I'll show him what it means to be a strong Romani woman. I don't need him!*

During the days that followed Keziah encouraged Yosie to stay dry most of the time in 'big boy's pants' – no more baby dresses beloved by the Quality.

She was touched by the children's tact. Gabriel and Pearl asked no questions about their father's absence and were as patient about showing her the farm's routine as if she were a child.

Keziah stayed out of Daniel's way and he also seemed to be avoiding her, but Bran called daily on the pretext of checking the horses' shoes and collecting any broken equipment to repair at the forge. When he brought her a bunch of bush flowers, his eyes showed he understood the status quo. Keziah was too proud to ask for his help so she offered her own.

'Bran, we all know how very bright you are inside your head. If you want to learn to read and write I'm happy to teach you. We'd keep it a secret, right? So one day you could surprise Daniel by writing a letter. What do you think?'

A dazzling smile of agreement lit up Bran's face.

Keziah sounded out each letter as she wrote BRAN on a slate and chalked in the arrows to show him the direction of the strokes. When he copied it she was full of praise.

'See how easy it is? You'll be able to write your Lord's Prayer in next to no time.'

Bran marched back to the forge clutching the slate as if it was the crown jewels.

Keziah milked the cow but relied on young Dick Gideon to care for the horses. He cheerfully continued to groom and exercise them on the training circuit he had built with Jake. As Wiradjuri manners demanded, he asked no questions about Jake's absence.

She knew that neither Leslie Ross, Janet Macgregor, Mac Mackie nor Polly Doyle would call uninvited.

Collecting eggs in the chicken coop, Keziah snapped at the guinea fowls from the Cape of Good Hope that were prolific egg-layers. 'Those romantic fools think we want privacy to fall into bed day and night.'

Pride did not allow her to confess to their friends she had never come home as Jake's wife.

She kept her anger in check until the rooster strutted arrogantly amongst the hens. 'You males are all the same! I bet Jake's holed up right now at the Four Sisters.'

Jake tried to quench his anger at The Shanty with No Name.

In the cracked mirror he hardly recognised his own face. It was creased like the peel of a mandarin and his eyes were a bit hard to find. Was he only just thirty? He felt closer to ninety. Reflected in the mirror was the equally seedy face of a shearer Jake had often passed on the stairs at the Four Sisters.

'How's life treating you?' the shearer asked.

'Been better,' Jake said bleakly.

The shearer looked sage. 'Ah. Family man!'

'Never bloody learn. Promised myself I'd never let another good woman into my life.'

'Then one of them smiled and you was a goner, right?'

'Not exactly. I got bailed up by bushrangers and she saved my life.'

'Women! There's *nothing* they won't do to trap a man.' The shearer downed his ale. 'Well, got to get back home or the missus will skin me alive.'

Jake continued drinking, telling himself how great it was to be a bachelor again. *I'll show Kez I need her like a hole in the head.*

But he soon realised that the grog wasn't doing its job properly. He glanced around the bar. *No one here worth fighting. Wonder how the kids are getting on without me.*

As dawn broke Jake opened one eye and flinched. He lay on the back veranda of Bran's forge house. The door flew open and Bran's naked figure emerged, armed with a chamber-pot ready to empty into the bush. Oblivious of Jake's presence, Bran sprawled on top of him.

Daniel, dressed in old clothes splattered with oil paints, eyed Jake from the doorway.

'Well, aren't you a fine specimen of manhood,' he said kindly. 'Don't think you're setting foot inside till you've cleaned yourself up.'

He returned with a bucket of water and threw it over Jake.

'Shit!' Jake shook himself like a dog emerging from a waterhole.

'Bolted, have you?'

Jake tried to resume the role of a man of action. 'I've got big plans, but I need a shakedown for a night or two.'

'Wash yourself at the tank. I'll fetch you clean clothes. Put the kettle on, Bran. From the length of his whiskers, he hasn't eaten in days.'

Jake stripped off his shirt. 'I reckon I *could* go a bit of breakfast,' he conceded.

Freed from his rank clothes he felt his dignity gushing back. 'If either of you drop a hint to Kez that I'm holed up here, it's curtains for you!'

'It's your business, mate. If *our wife* doesn't ask me, I won't tell her.'

'She's too bloody proud to ask. You can put money on that!' Jake was intent on changing the subject to something less painful. 'What's for breakfast?'

Fortified by the bottomless teapot, Jake gratefully attacked a pile of Bran's famous golden pancakes, smothering them with Canadian maple syrup. When Bran marched around the corner to work in the forge, Daniel gave the order.

'Now you can sing for your supper. My studio on the double. Strip off your clothes. I've got a painting roughed out. You've got the perfect body for it.'

'A prize fighter?' asked Jake.

'A bushranger. Lying asleep in a cave, naked except for his boots, a rifle within reach on guard against the traps. The pose will suit you perfectly, you can doze off under your hat.'

As the brush flew across the canvas, Jake saw that Daniel had already withdrawn into the private world where he was most truly alive.

Under his hat, Jake felt trapped into confronting his major decision. What next? He tried to unscramble his thoughts.

I'm too bloody young to be celibate. Let's face it, I'm a one-woman man – I even prefer to go to the same prostitute. I can live without a woman if I have *to but I need children to anchor me. No matter how good a man is in bed (or out of it) there's no pleasing a good woman. And with a Romani good woman – a man can't bloody win. The only thing a bloke can trust with his life is his horse.*

I'm bloody sure of one thing. I will never do time in the sturaban *again – never! And before I die I'm gunna breed a champion racehorse.*

Honesty forced him to face something he didn't like. *I'm a lousy son. Never did a damned thing for Mam and Pa except cause them grief. I run around fixing other people's problems to avoid solving my own.*

He recalled that last thought had been Lily Pompadour's opinion of him.

He was trying to piece these random thoughts into a plan of action when Daniel broke his train of thought.

'Want to tell me what's up with you and Keziah?'

'It's over. Finished.'

Daniel's brush froze. 'Does that mean she's only got *one* husband now?'

Jake peered out from under his hat. 'Why are you asking? You don't find women's bodies attractive. Do you?'

'I'm surprised you need to ask. I love painting them, the more voluptuous the better. Problem is I can't get local girls to take their clothes off for me.'

'I meant as a *man*?'

'What are you driving at? Beauty excites me both as an artist and a man.'

'What about Kez? You painted her nude. I can't imagine there's a man on the planet who wouldn't want to bed her.'

Daniel took time to weigh his answer. 'After the hell of Gideon Park, I wanted to be alone. But later I grew hungry for human warmth. I was curious to test myself. Keziah was a woman I came to like and trust. Sometimes she was gentle, sometimes aggressive – almost like a man. I found that contrast exciting.'

Jake felt even more dejected. 'Noticed that too, did you?'

'I knew if I was ever going to be able to do it with a woman, it would be *her*, but I also knew it couldn't last. I didn't want Gabriel growing up with that confusion in a father. So I kept my brother-sister pact with Keziah. Answered my needs in my own way.'

Daniel looked as if everything between them hung in the balance. 'That answer your question?' He carefully examined his paintbrush. 'Let's get back to work.'

Jake closed his eyes, but his mind was restless for answers. *How do I answer* my *needs? Where the bloody hell is home? Nowhere. I'm not cut out to be a family man. Tried my damnedest twice – failed twice. What's next? I used to be a man of action.*

Action! It came in a flash. A plan that would shake the foundations of the ménage. But before he could begin it the distant peal of chapel bells reminded him. *Keziah! Shit. It's Sunday again.*

Bran charged into the studio urgently miming his concern that Keziah must not miss chapel.

Jake tried to sound offhand. 'It's up to Kez. She knows if she doesn't front she'll be sprung back in the Factory.'

Bran slammed the door and ran off in the direction of Jake's house, yelling over his shoulder.

Jake turned to Daniel. 'Jesus. I could have sworn Bran just said, "Bugger you both!"'

'He did,' said Daniel.

Later that day as Bran baked his traditional Sunday side of mutton and Daniel was absorbed in the finishing touches of 'The Bolter', Jake laboured over writing a pile of invitations.

He cursed his spelling but was determined not to ask Daniel's help. He addressed the first to Reverend Parsons at Berrima Gaol. He gritted his teeth writing one to Caleb Morgan in Melbourne Town. *I must be off my rocker to trust that smug Pommy within cooee of Kez, but I owe it to Gabe.*

A storm broke just as Bran marched from the cookhouse bearing a huge platter of baked mutton and roast potatoes. The three males in the Sarishan ménage hungrily devoured it in silence as the rain hammered on the iron roof. The oil lamps swung from the rafters when the gale pierced the cracks in the unsealed walls and made the fire jump in the hearth.

'You're a bloody great cook, Bran,' said Jake. 'Thanks for the shake-down. I'm throwing a party at the Doc's place to announce my big plans. You two had better be there.'

'Won't it be difficult to get Kez to face our friends?' Daniel asked. 'She hasn't seen anyone since she came home.'

'Yeah, but I'll fix that somehow.'

Daniel looked irritated. 'Pardon me for being nosey but how do these big plans affect me? Our ménage is for *my* protection as well as hers, remember?'

'You've got *our wife* for camouflage. Kez'd never give you away in a million years.'

'So what's the big mystery? Why can't you tell me now?'

'It's not all firm yet. Just turn up on the day and I'll set you all straight.'

Jake refilled Bran's glass. 'There ought to be a law against how hard you work, Bran. Can you finish your smithing in time? And you, Dan?'

Bran's upturned thumbs signalled his pleasure, but Daniel was reluctant.

'I'll come but only because it's my duty as Keziah's husband.'

When Jake jerked two fingers in a graphic response, Bran's laughter broke the ice.

It was time for Jake to write the toughest letter of all. He knew the spelling was original but he hoped the message between the lines was clear.

> *Dear Mam and Pa,*
>
> *This letter proves I'm a hypocrite. Last time we met we all agreed I was dead. Well things have changed a bit. Jenny shot off with her bloke to Cape Town. I've got Pearl. She's ten and tries so hard to be a farmer's daughter she'd break your heart, Pa.*
>
> *Maybe you've heard some odd stuff about me on the grapevine. I'm living with my woman who's just done time in the Factory. I reckon anyone can do murder under the right circumstances, so don't hold that against her. Anyway she's a bloody good little mother. Her boy Gabriel's nearly seven and game as they come. And we made another lad together. Yosie is just walking. He's the spitting image of you, Mam – poor kid. Red hair and covered in freckles. He can't even go out in the dark without a hat on.*
>
> *I know you won't come Saturday fortnight to the Haunted Farm at Ironbark to hear my plans because no one carries a grudge longer than the Irish and there's no man more stubborn than a Viking. But if you did come you'd like the youngsters. Remember my woman has had a rough time of it. She ain't herself yet.*
>
> *Your Andersen Black Sheep*

Now Jake faced the biggest challenge of all. Keziah.

CHAPTER 60

Keziah was on her knees weeding the herb garden with little Yosie at her heels playing with a toy cart. When she looked up to see Jake striding towards her leading Horatio she was furious to find her hands were trembling. It was her first sight of him since he had stormed out three weeks earlier.

He looked healthy enough, clean-shaven with freshly pressed clothes, his washed hair shining in the sunlight. Keziah felt her heart racing, first with relief that he was all right, next with anger that he didn't appear to have suffered one little bit during their absence.

Jake's tone was cool. 'We're driving over to the Doc's for a meal. Get the children scrubbed up. Don't want them to look like urchins.'

Without waiting for her answer he marched off to the stables.

Keziah flew into action, double-checking the children's clothes and grooming. Her blue dress was the only one small enough to fit her well but that was dripping wet on the clothesline. She belted in an old dress with a sash. She paused at the mirror before knotting a fresh scarf around her head, feeling a faint sense of pleasure to see the tufts of hair on her head had begun to form tiny curls. On impulse she discarded the false braid and drew a few strands of new hair from under the scarf to frame her face. She pinched her cheeks to increase their colour. Then for protection against the nervous ordeal ahead she added her grandmother's silver amulet. Janet Macgregor would be the first female to see her since her release from the Factory. Keziah wanted no pity.

Jake yelled from the driver's seat of the *vardo*. 'I haven't got all day to waste!'

Keziah ignored him, choosing to gently prise Yosie from her stepdaughter's arms.

'I'm so proud of you, Pearl. You've been a great help to us, but today I want you to learn to be a little girl again.'

Keziah looped the child's skinny plaits into bunches of blue ribbons to disguise her large elf-like ears. She was startled when Pearl threw her arms around her and released all her childhood pain in a confused torrent.

'My real mama didn't want me. She left me with the nuns at Christmas and all the other girls went home. Mama told me I was an ugly duckling. The boys are beautiful like you. I wish you could love me too, Mama, but I'll always be plain.'

Keziah heard Jake yelling, 'Hurry up, it's boiling hot out here!'

She called back from the doorway, 'We'll be out in a minute!'

She knew Pearl's anguish must be dealt with here and now. She felt it like a physical pain inside her own breast. *If only I could win her trust, I could heal her.*

She propped Yosie in his highchair and gave him the toy boxing kangaroos Daniel had carved for him. Then she sank down on the floor and drew Pearl into the circle of her arms.

'Listen, you've got it all wrong. From now on I *am* your mama – always. When Mama Jenny went to Cape Town she signed a piece of paper giving you to your papa because he could *never* be happy without his little princess.'

Keziah swallowed the truth. *Sold her to Jake for thirty pieces of silver is more like it.*

Pearl was listening too intently to cry. Keziah pressed on.

'You are just like me, Pearl. When I was five my mother left me with *my* papa. I never saw her again. I know how sad you feel inside but your family and all the people who love you know what a truly brave little girl you are!'

Pearl's eyes shone and Keziah kissed her cheek. 'Never forget. Papa and I love you three children equally.'

On impulse she drew Pearl to the mirror and transferred her

silver amulet to her neck.

'My grandmother gave me this to protect me. Now I give it to *you*, my daughter. See? What's this silly idea you're plain? Look how beautiful you are! It's like magic. You believe it and it happens. Tell the mirror, "I am Pearl – beautiful, clever and kind. I am a princess."'

The moment Pearl whispered those words her mirror image smiled back.

'Hey, who's the beautiful princess?' Jake asked when Pearl ran out to the *vardo*. He jumped down and lifted her up beside Gabriel, leaving Keziah to clamber up unaided.

'What kept you girls so bloody long?' he hissed at Keziah.

'Secret women's business!' she said. Little Yosie gave her a blissful smile as a damp patch spread across her skirt. No time to change him. Jake was a volcano ready to erupt.

Jake was pleased to see the welcome committee lined up on the veranda of the Haunted Farm. Leslie and his new Scottish ticket-of-leave gardener wore their kilts. Janet stood stiffly to one side, an apron covering her housekeeper's dress. Jake was relieved by the spontaneous way she gathered Keziah in that wordless warm embrace exchanged between ex-prisoners.

The children ran to the garden where their own party had been set up for them. Janet took one look at the damp patch on Keziah's skirt and took her into the kitchen to sponge it down and iron it dry.

During the meal Jake and Leslie kept the conversation flowing to cover the awkwardness of Keziah's lack of response. Jake's frustration found a safe outlet in his attack on Norfolk Island's new superintendent.

'Five minutes in power and Major Childs has destroyed Alexander Maconochie's prison reforms. The Scot was so enlightened and humane naturally the bloody authorities had to sack him.'

Leslie Ross was in full agreement. 'Aye, I dinna hold with mutiny but this is one time when prisoners would be justified in taking the law into their own hands.'

Jake saw Keziah flinch at this reminder of her own downfall and cursed himself for raising the subject. *Jesus wept. I've done it again.*

He was grateful when Janet covered his gaffe by drawing Keziah away to the kitchen garden to identify an unusual herb and the Doc carted Jake off to his study.

Leslie lit his pipe before saying obliquely, 'Your bairns are welcome to stay here for as long as it takes, lad.'

'You know me, Doc. Don't believe in miracles. And time's running out.'

'I havena had a proper chance to evaluate Keziah's condition since her homecoming.'

'Don't pull your punches, Doc. She won't see you or any other quack.'

'What's wrong with Keziah may well be a combination. Trauma over Iago's death. The brutality of life in the Factory. Plus a state of depression some women suffer badly after birthing a babe. I'd prescribe something, but I dinna doubt she'd nay have a bar of it. In my opinion Keziah's built up a barrier to protect herself from *something*.'

'Me!' said Jake with a bitter laugh.

Leslie Ross looked discomforted. 'I am not convinced I am entirely free of guilt. At the time of her trial I gave her wine and tea laced with laudanum to prevent her condemning herself. The problem is that laudanum can have diverse effects. It makes some patients free of pain or melancholia. Others appear drunk, lucid, energised, even free from the need to sleep for days at a time. It can subject them to extraordinary dreams and hallucinations. I may well have contributed to her present mental state. I have never before treated a patient like Keziah. Even in her normal life, the lass appears to be in contact with other worlds.'

'Yeah, Kez claims she sees ghosts. And has dreams about the future.'

'Does she know what lies ahead of her today?'

'Blood oath, no!'

Through the window Jake saw his guests approaching.

Nerida and Sunny Ah Wei were led by a much taller young Murphy. Mac Mackie followed uneasily behind Polly Doyle and George Hobson. Leading an anxious-looking Daniel, Bran Penrose took giant strides, beaming from ear to ear. Berrima's Reverend Parsons brought up the rear wearing a snow-white surplice over his cassock.

Jake went out to meet them and saw Keziah emerging from the kitchen garden. At the sight of the guests she looked ready to bolt, so he hooked his arm securely around her waist to prevent her escape.

'Gabe and Pearl wanted to hold off Yosie's naming till your return. The Rev knows I don't believe any church mumbo jumbo, but I'll never forget how he ferried my letters to you.'

The reunion hugs were warm, but when Keziah saw the approach of an elegantly dressed couple, she turned on Jake in horror. 'How could you do this to me?'

Jake only had time for a quick word. 'Gabriel wanted me to invite him, but the lady's a surprise to me too. She used to live in Bolthole Valley. But remember, *I've never seen her before*!'

Caleb Morgan clasped Jake's outstretched hand with every appearance of genuine warmth. 'I can't tell you what your kind invitation means to me, Jake. May I introduce Mademoiselle Liliana du Pont.'

Jake bowed to the red-headed fashion plate in apricot silk and realised from Keziah's fixed expression she had guessed this was Lily Pompadour, the prostitute who'd sent him money for a thoroughbred horse.

His manner was faultless. 'Delighted to meet you, Mademoiselle.'

'Liliana. Caleb's told me so much about you, I feel we're already *close* friends.'

Jake had a vivid flash of Lily riding him in bed, naked except for his hat. 'Any friend of Caleb's is a friend of mine,' was his polite reply.

Jake smiled at Lily to give her confidence that her secret was safe with him. They both knew the risk she took in coming here. She quickly checked all the men's faces to see if any were former clients. Evidently Jake was the only one.

'Liliana has only recently left her convent school,' Caleb explained. 'So the ways of the wicked world are all very new to her.'

'My daughter, Pearl, went to a convent.' Jake added sincerely, 'My word those sisters give young ladies a thorough education.'

Sisters. Lily almost choked trying to hold back her laughter. She slipped her arm through Caleb's but her eyes smiled at Jake.

Just when Jake thought Lily was safe, their host descended on them.

Jake covered quickly. 'Doc, this is Mademoiselle Liliana du Pont. Caleb Morgan's friend from *Melbourne Town*.'

Leslie Ross didn't bat an eyelid. He welcomed Caleb as an old friend and allowed himself to be introduced 'for the first time' to the girl that Jake knew full well the Doc had routinely examined each week at the Four Sisters to prevent venereal disease. Liliana smiled up at the Doc in gratitude when he shepherded her and Caleb on a tour of the grounds.

Alone with Keziah, Jake said quickly, 'It's not what you think.'

Keziah said coolly, 'Your past is no concern of mine.'

Jake tried to think of a fitting answer but gave up. He flinched when a heavy hand lobbed on his shoulder. *Jesus wept! Not the bloody arm of the law again?*

He spun around to face Isaac and Molly Andersen at the head of the phalanx of his eight blond Viking brothers, ranging in age from seven to twenty-five. They were flanked by his tomboy sister, Miriam, looking uncomfortable wearing her Sunday best – a dress.

Jake stumbled over the introductions. Keziah looked overwhelmed. Even Jake was lost for words.

It was Molly Andersen who saved the day. She opened wide her arms and hugged Keziah to her bosom.

'My new daughter! Bless your heart for giving me *three* beautiful grandchildren. Where are the little darlings?' Molly hooked her arm through Keziah's to steer her away.

Jake could not believe his ears when he heard his mother's next words.

'Welcome home, Keziah love. I know just how you feel. I was bloody glad to see the rear arse of the Factory myself, a right bugger of a place! You're a brave lass taking on my son. Jake's a good lad but swears like a trooper, he does. You'll be needing to keep a tight rein on him.'

Isaac Andersen studiously examined the sky with a farmer's keen eye. 'Well, I'll say this for you, son. You picked a good day for it.'

'Could you sink an Albion with me, Pa?'

'I could at that, seeing as your mother's fully occupied, thanks be to God.' His father hesitated. 'Good to see you again – *son*.'

Jake drew his arm around his father's shoulders. 'I reckon this proves that yarn about prodigal sons, eh Pa?'

Under a eucalypt canopy, the Rev stood before a trestle table covered with a snowy altar cloth adorned with a brass cross and arrangements of orange and scarlet bottlebrush blossoms.

Jake's sister, Miriam, and Leslie Ross made their vows as godparents to little Yosie. When the Rev splashed the boy with water to make the sign of the cross, Yosie thought it was a new game, so he dipped his hand in the font and splashed the priest in retaliation.

Jake beamed and muttered, 'That's my boy!'

When it was Pearl's turn to be named there was a halt in the proceedings until Father Dennis Declan came charging down the path, prayer book under his wing as he hurriedly donned his vestments. His first handshake was with the prison chaplain.

'Good day to you, Fred. Sorry I'm a tad late. I was called in unexpectedly to give the last rites to an old lady who decided she wasn't quite ready to meet Our Maker.'

The Rev's quiet aside caused Father Declan to throw his head back in shared laughter at some private ecclesiastical joke.

When Jake offered them each a whisky, Father Declan gave him a friendly punch on the arm.

'Good to see you settling down into family life, Jake. So your daughter's chosen to become one of *my* flock. Not an atheist like your good self, eh?'

'I'm not one for bobbing and scraping, Father, as the Rev here knows, but the little ones like all that stuff so they're free to choose whichever way they want to do the holy bit.'

As Jake escorted Father Declan towards the altar, the priest put in a quick word. 'I've always said it, lad. You're a joy to watch in the ring. We're planning to build a church hall in Tagalong. Could I be tempting you to come out of retirement?'

'I'd be in it like a shot, Dennis, but I promised my woman I'd never fight again.'

Jake felt a lump in his throat at the sight of Pearl wearing Keziah's silver amulet with the new white dress he had bought her for the occasion. The focus of all eyes, she looked like a little flower that had finally blossomed.

Polly and Mac came forward to be her godparents.

Father Declan never missed a cue. 'Well Mac Mackie, have you scraped up your courage to make Polly Doyle an honest woman?'

Mac flushed scarlet, so Polly said tartly, 'All he has to do is *ask*!'

Mac finally managed to say the words. 'Righto. Polly, how about it?'

Polly's freckled face turned pink. 'All right. I'm not doing nothing next Saturday if you get a special licence.'

Jake whistled between his fingers from sheer relief and everyone cheered. He looked to see if there was any reaction from Keziah. At least she was smiling in Nerida's direction.

Gabriel was the last child to be named. Jake felt great pride in his little Rom as the boy escorted his second mother, Nerida, to the altar. Her hands rested on her swollen belly, clearly announcing that she was carrying Sunny Ah Wei's firstborn.

The chaplain knew Nerida's history and put her at ease. 'Keziah said you brought Gabriel into the world, Mrs Ah Wei. The lad could have no more appropriate godmother.'

'That little *gubba's* like a son to me,' Nerida said firmly.

Jake tensed as he watched Keziah's reaction when Caleb Morgan strode through the throng to join this group at the altar. Jake was quick to block any disapproval.

'Blame me. I asked him to be Gabe's godfather. You have to give Caleb *some* role to play in public with his son.'

Outmanoeuvred, Keziah showed a flash of anger. 'I'm not Jenny. I don't stop Gabriel loving whoever he wants to love.'

Jake felt a glimmer of hope. 'Good on you, girl!'

Daniel smiled encouragingly across at Keziah on the other side of the garden, relieved that she appeared to have passed unscathed through the ordeal of her first public appearance since her release from prison. He circulated amongst the guests feeling a familiar sense of ambiguity in his role as Keziah's husband. He had designed the blueprint for all their lives and never regretted their ménage. It had given him a deep sense of family for the first time in his life. A loving bond with a woman and children he would otherwise never have had. And the right to share Jake's friendship on a comfortable daily basis. He glanced around at all their mates. *Ah, but there's the rub. How many of them suspect I'm living a lie? That some day my other secret life could end in the death penalty? Only Keziah and Jake accept me for what I am. And even Jake shies off that subject.*

He poured another drink to give himself courage before making his way to Jake. 'You're playing your cards damned close to your chest today, Jake.'

'All will be revealed in five minutes, mate.'

Daniel decided to force the issue. 'Well I'll lay *my* cards on the table right now. I'll soon be heading off to Sydney Town. Thanks to Jonstone I've got more commissions lined up.'

'Good for you but that doesn't mean you're leaving Sarishan Farm for good?'

'No. I'll not run out on Keziah again or you. Not until you don't need me anymore.'

Jake's eyes held him with a level look. 'We'll *always* need you, mate.'

'Likewise,' said Daniel. He tried to lighten his tone to keep his deeper feelings in check. 'But you know me. Art is my mistress. I've got to follow whenever she beckons.'

Jake nodded. Daniel saw he was relieved to be back again in shallow waters.

Jake had something else on his mind. 'What say we have a drink, Dan? I'm just about to make my big announcement. You know me. I'd rather fight thirteen rounds with a crocodile than put things like that into words.'

Things like what? Daniel wondered but he just said, 'Make mine a double, mate.'

Daniel smiled as he watched Jake swagger to the bar. He was reminded of those words Keziah had once said to him. *We can't help who we love.*

The whiskies had been sunk. The hour had come for Jake to bite the bullet. He jumped up on a bench, a fresh drink in hand.

'My thanks to the Doc for his legendary Highland hospitality. Even an agnostic like me can see that our mates the Rev and fighting Father Declan did a great job today. A man's lucky to have a mob of friends like you lot. You stick like bloody glue to Dan, Kez and me no matter what strife we get into on the wrong side of the law.'

Mac whistled through his teeth until Polly Doyle elbowed him to be quiet.

'Speaking of the law,' said Jake, 'I just heard on the grapevine that Will Martens has done it again. He escaped from gaol in Van Diemen's Land and was last seen heading towards a ship setting sail for America. Here's to freedom, Will!'

Everyone cheered but Jake knew in his heart that the end of the road for Will was Norfolk Island.

Jake turned serious as he raised his glass in Pearl's direction. 'My little princess is back where she belongs, thanks to my Yankee mate, Benjamin Rogers, who couldn't make it here today. How do you say thanks to a man who tracked down your lost daughter?' Jake touched his silver belt buckle. 'And then gives you his own good-luck charm?'

Jake took a deep breath. 'I brought you here today to tell you the good news.' He turned to the priests. 'Don't get too excited. Nothing to do with your bible!'

Both priests exchanged a grin.

Jake glanced significantly at his mother, Molly. 'My last bender is long gone. I've decided to get serious about breeding thoroughbreds.'

Despite the cheered response, Jake kept his expression blank.

'I've made some tough decisions for 1845. After Doc's famous Hogmanay celebrations, I've agreed to start the new year by working for twelve months at Ogden Park. Jupiter's Darling baulks at servicing mares. Terence Ogden reckons I'm the bloke to solve the problem and help him raise another generation of champions.'

He saw Daniel frown at this unexpected news, knowing Ogden Park was too distant for Jake to remain living at Sarishan Farm. Jake glanced across at Keziah but her face was a mask.

'The money Ogden pays me I'll sink back into Sarishan Farm. I'm bloody lucky young Dick Gideon will run the place with Bran's help. My partner Dan will balance the books.'

He gave a nod in George Hobson's direction. 'Thanks to George his

Glaswegian giant Sholto's just landed his ticket-of-leave, so Sholto's gunna work between my farm and Ironbark. Me? I'll be pretty much out of sight, out of mind.'

Jake glanced across at Keziah who was now deathly pale. Was that a good sign or bad?

'I want to thank Dan Browne and Bran Penrose for being my left and right arms through all my troubles. Our lawyer mate, Joseph Bloom, couldn't make it today.' He nodded at Keziah. 'He sends you his best wishes. He's in Sydney Town fighting to keep some other poor bugger out of the *sturaban*. But when I tell you all it was Joe who drew up this deed I'm holding, you'll know it's bloody watertight. It signs over to Bran Penrose and his heirs full title to the forge acres. Here mate, you earned it!'

Bran's eyes were suspiciously wet, so Jake hurriedly resumed his speech. 'I can't do nothing for Dan. He's been lined up to paint Jonstone's gentry mates, and you know how many of *them* there are!'

After the cheering died down Jake continued. 'For Yosef Jakob Andersen Browne, here's something important to his mama.'

The silence was loaded with expectation as he crossed to where Daniel was endeavouring to restrain Yosie. Jake eyed Daniel steadily, his words deceptively casual.

'I can see you've got your hands full there, Dan. So how about I do this for you?'

Jake tied a red ribbon around the toddler's neck. 'There you are, my little Rom. This proves *your father* acknowledges *his* son.'

Daniel smiled his gratitude that the truth about their ménage was not right out in the open, even though none of them doubted it was accepted by their closest friends.

Jake saw Keziah biting her lip. Was it to conceal her pleasure or annoyance? *Any reaction from her would be bloody something.*

He overheard his pa whisper, 'Molly, what's going on? *Jake* is the boy's father, isn't he?'

To which Molly hissed back, 'And who are we to ask bloody awkward questions? Never been churched ourselves and raised ten kids and all.'

Jake knew that the conclusion of his speech could also be interpreted in different ways.

'As for my mate Keziah Browne, it's no secret I think Daniel's a lucky man. I want you to raise your glasses to celebrate Keziah's ticket-of-leave. She's got big plans she'll tell you in her own good time. End of speech! Now, let's drink the Doc's cellar dry.' Jake raised his glass in a toast. 'To the land we live in! Australia!'

Keziah felt shaken and confused as all heads turned expectantly to her at the end of Jake's speech. She grabbed hold of Daniel's arm.

'What on earth did Jake mean? What big plans?'

'Search me,' he said glumly as he walked away. 'You're the psychic.'

Caleb Morgan appeared at her side, his expression serious. 'I am honoured to be Gabriel's godfather. We can at least keep in contact due to *that* relationship, Keziah.'

'Jake's idea, not mine,' she said quickly. Yet she felt oddly anxious at the sight of Liliana du Pont crossing the lawn to enter the house alone. She wondered if Caleb knew his 'French' mistress had once worked in a brothel. Had Lily managed to fool him? Or was he simply playing the game, pretending to accept her 'convent education'?

Keziah saw Caleb was studying her intently. 'Liliana's damned good for me. There's no stopping her when she's set her mind on something. Would you believe she's determined to see me elected in politics?' He paused. 'I found adventure in this colony where I least expected it. So why am I haunted by the John Donne sonnet I recited to a beautiful Romani girl?'

'Please stop, Caleb. I've hurt enough people who don't deserve it.'

'Allow me to say it once more, Keziah. *"I must love her, that loves not me."*'

Caleb tenderly kissed her hand then backed away with a wry smile.

Keziah fled across the lawn in confusion, overwhelmed by the unexpected events of the day and her anxiety about the night to come. She was drawn to an isolated part of the old rose garden where the sound of the guests' voices was remote. She saw a young woman dressed in an Empire-line gown had found solace on a garden bench. Her eyes held a look of indescribable sadness.

Keziah felt suddenly cold. 'Are you waiting for someone?'

The girl did not speak. Yet Keziah mentally heard her words. *'My love. Padraic.'*

A rush of terror almost overwhelmed her. A *mulo*! This was Maggie Barnes, who had suffered at the hands of her wife-beating husband until the young convict Padraic murdered him to set her free. Keziah knew her *Puri Dai* had sent this *mulo* to her for help.

Who am I to condemn a murderer? She led Maggie to the well. Padraic was waiting for her. Joy softened his haggard face when his lover slipped into his arms.

Fighting her fear, Keziah closed her eyes and prayed desperately to *The Del*, *Shon*, the *gaujos'* god the Father, Gentle Jesus, her *Puri Dai* and whoever else might be listening.

Please don't punish Padraic and Maggie anymore. Set them free to be together.

She opened her eyes to see the lovers walking into the bush, Maggie's head resting on Padraic's shoulder. They paused to smile at her, then slowly dissolved into the sunlight.

Keziah was trembling violently as she ran back to the house. Where was Jake?

Jake stood in the Doc's sitting room. All the guests were in the garden, save one. Lily posed elegantly in the doorway. She crossed to him in a rustle of apricot silk, very sure of herself.

'Caleb treating you right, Lil? If he isn't, I'll sort him out for you.'

'You haven't changed. Still running away from your own problems?'

'Not this time. Got dumped again. That's the way it goes.' He knew they had unfinished business. 'I'm glad to see you happy, Lil. Caleb's a lucky man.'

'You and I were very good together, Jake, but I saw the writing was on the wall. You talked about Keziah in your sleep.'

'I could never give you the life you want, Lil. You deserve the best.'

'I had the best, Jake. He got away,' she said softly. 'But he gave me a priceless gift. Made me believe in myself. Taught me I could walk away from Bolthole Valley and make a success of a new life. And I will, Jake, you just watch me!'

Gracefully she drew his head down and kissed his mouth. 'Be happy, Jake.'

Her gown rustled softly as she returned to the garden. To Caleb Morgan.

Jake looked across the room to see Keziah framed in the opposite doorway. He was determined to outstare her. Keziah finally broke the silence.

'Leslie says you arranged for the children to sleep here tonight.'

'Dead right,' he said. '*You* are coming with *me*.'

He saw the panic in Keziah's eyes. Now she knew the truth. Today was just part of his plan. Ahead of them lay the night of reckoning that Keziah could no longer escape.

CHAPTER 61

The sun was dying, staining the sky with its blood.

Horatio drew the *vardo* inexorably towards the precipice at the edge of the panorama known to white settlers as Blind Man's Bluff. Jake knew that the original name of this magical place was known only to the Wiradjuri people. Ever since the Dreamtime, their tribal elders had handed down their wisdom to youths initiated in secret men's business. Jake hoped that they continued to do so in defiance of the *gubbas*.

As Jake drove the *vardo* the thought crossed his mind that perhaps some traces of that ancient wisdom might filter through to him. He needed all the help he could get. Tonight was the point of no return.

He glanced sidelong at Keziah. She still seemed devoid of curiosity, like a passive reed blown by any prevailing wind.

They drove through a maze of native pines that fought for space among the eucalypts. Jake veered off the main track, taking them into increasingly dense bushland. He recognised the strange humour of the situation. During their long bush odyssey, Keziah would have reacted violently to the threat of her beloved *vardo's* paint being scratched. Now she seemed oblivious to the very real threat of their whole family being torn apart.

When Jake drew to a standstill in a clearing, Horatio stood like a sentinel attuned to his master's tension.

Jake saw Keziah eyeing the Belgian pistol tucked into his belt, as aware as he was that Daniel's treasured gift was a precaution, bush-rangers could be anywhere. He strode across to a wide rocky ledge and allowed Keziah to follow at will.

This scene of transcendent beauty never failed to constrict his throat. Far below lay a massive sunken valley filled with giant tropical fern trees and palms, as old as time itself. From this great height it gave the illusion of rolling ocean waves stirred by the wind as far as the eye could travel. Spectacular arcs of burnt-orange sandstone cliffs rose from the valley floor to frame the scene like giant shoulders. On the far horizon a range of slate-purple mountains caught the death throes of the sun.

'If there *was* a Creator and he was looking for a place for the birth of the world, he didn't need to look no further.' Jake revealed as much casual pride as if he had carved it himself. 'I bet you couldn't find anything like this in your Brit Isles.'

'That's true,' Keziah said.

'I reckon when God finished this, he saw it was so god-damned awesome he knew he couldn't do better if he tried. So he downed tools – or his magic wand – and called it the seventh day of rest. Put his feet up with a glass of ale and thanked Himself for creating it.'

Keziah's glance was furtive. 'Sounds like the children's Sunday school has rubbed off on you.'

'I'm always open to a good yarn. Don't have to believe it, do I?'

Jake tried to roll his tobacco but the wind kept blowing it away. He finally mumbled under his breath and gave up trying.

'Why did you bring me here, Jake?'

He turned away to disguise his pleasure. She had called him by name and asked him a question. At least that was something.

'We'll sleep here tonight. I reckon we need to talk. Just you and me. Maybe it's for the last time ever.' He tried a light touch. 'Bawl me out if you want. I've missed not having a woman to keep me in line.'

'I can't feel enough anger to do that. I'm sorry. I can't feel anything at all.'

'Except for the children. With them it's business as usual, eh?'

'Yes. I can see how much they need me.'

That was the trigger. 'And *I don't*? You can look me in the eye and tell me *I don't need you*? What's the matter with you? Did you leave your head behind in the Factory?'

Jake was enraged, but Keziah didn't move. She seemed turned to stone.

Now the pain of his rejection was lanced, Jake could not prevent it gushing forth.

'Do you think you were the only one of us in prison? I was locked in my own private gaol on the farm. I never had two bloody hours to call my own all the time you were in the *sturaban*. I worried myself sick about you, knowing what prison would do to you. I've seen how it destroys men. Eats them from the inside out.'

'You were free to love,' she said quietly.

'What do you think I did? Go to brothels? Every time I got hot thinking about you, I chopped trees down. We had so much bloody wood it was a fire hazard.'

Keziah opened her mouth to speak.

'Shut up, Kez, or I'll never get this out, then you can talk for a week if you want. Understand. There was never a single day you weren't inside me.'

His fist punctuated his words. 'My head, my heart, my gut and here.' He gestured to his groin. 'I would have sold my soul for the sight of you just washing your hair, the smell of rosemary oil on your body. I got so lonely I'd have welcomed one of your red-hot tongue-lashings!'

Jake laughed at what a fool a man could be. There was no stopping him.

'Do you think I didn't know you were in hell? Trying to stop yourself sinking to the lowest level, losing hope. That's why I wrote to you every week, about what the children said and did, the mares the stallions covered, the price of things, the gossip. Every bloody thing I could think of to remind you I was fighting to keep you alive inside your head.'

Her voice was colourless. 'I know. You thought of everything.'

'So how come you never wrote *me* a letter? You're the bloody literate one.'

She drooped in shame as if no excuse was adequate.

Jake's anger didn't abate. 'Have you any idea how it killed me to have to ask *your husband* for every crumb of news about my own woman? You think I didn't know when Daniel was just being kind to me, putting words into your mouth, words you never said?'

'Forgive me, Jake. After I let Yosie go I lost myself. Stopped believing I'd ever be free. I couldn't touch the earth or feel the wind. I was buried alive in a grave of bricks and stone. The only peace was to die for a few hours each night in my sleep.'

He cooled his rage. *Shut up. Listen to her.*

'Jake, I'm sorry I seem cold to you. I *am* cold. I can't give you back the love you deserve because I can't feel anything. *Nothing feels real.*'

He nodded. 'Go on.'

'The whole world looks strange to me. Like every bit of colour has been bled out of it. Everything *feels grey.* I can't explain.'

Grey. Jake recalled that morning when his own world turned grey as he walked out of his house on the Nepean, knowing Jenny's betrayal had taken his baby girl, destroyed his family, his whole life.

'I'm dead inside,' she said, 'but I remember you in my head. You're a passionate man. You need a woman. So I'll honour my promise. Whenever you want me, you can take me. I'll give you more children, if that's what you want, but I can't give you the woman I was or the body that once gave you pleasure.'

Jake heard the pain seeping through her words. Her female pride? He felt a surge of hope, only to have it dashed by her next words.

'I'm ashamed of my body. Don't look at my body, Jake. Just take me *in the dark.*'

The growing darkness eddied about them, carried on the wind. Keziah removed her dress and bodice. It was a mechanical gesture as if she were washing her clothes at the end of a hard day. Her thin body was covered from waist to ankles with a petticoat. The colour of her headscarf intensified the one thing that hadn't changed. Those wonderful violet-blue eyes.

Jake's words were beyond anger. 'Don't look at you? Just have connection in the dark? Is that all you think of me? That I'm no better than blokes who line up at a brothel to pay to get their cock inside, then go and get pissed?'

'How can you want me? I'm not the same woman.'

He was brutally frank. 'No, you're not. I've seen you look better.'

She flinched but it was too late for him to turn back.

'Do you think I didn't fall for your wild hair, your big breasts? Of course I did. I'm a man. But you don't know me if you think that's *all* I wanted. For the first time in my life I had a woman of my own. A *real* woman, as hungry as I was to share everything I needed to give you.'

He cut off her words. 'You think you're better than any *gaujo* but you're no saint. When you make a mistake it's a bloody big one, but there's no woman like you. You go from hell to breakfast for the man you love. You pick up broken people – me, Nerida, Daniel, Bran – and you make us whole again. You even made Pearl believe in herself. I want her to be like you. A survivor – no matter what garbage your bloody *baxt* dishes out!'

The expression in her eyes chilled him – he felt he would drown in the well of her despair. He'd run out of words, run out of hope. Only one truth remained to be told.

'I want my proud Romani woman back. I won't accept nothing less, but if you want to get rid of me for good, just say the word. I'm setting you free, Kez.'

He steeled himself against a violent gust of wind that blew her off balance. Jake chose to interpret this as a step towards him. Before she could stop him, he grabbed her face between his hands and kissed her so hungrily that her scarf slipped from his grasp, exposing the dark tufts of hair. The scarf began to blow away.

'Let it go. You don't need to cover your head. Darling, you're safe now. Those bastards can't hurt you anymore. Your hair will grow back. It's only a small part of you. You're beautiful to me – just the way you are.'

She pulled away. The bitterness of her laughter shook him.

'Are you going to lie? Tell me *this* doesn't matter?' She kicked off her petticoat and stood defiantly with her legs apart.

It was then Jake understood everything.

High on her thigh near the place of love was a half-healed scar from a prison tattoo. A rough heart shape pierced with an arrow. Inside it was written 'AS loves KB'.

Jake's cry sounded like a trapped animal as it echoed between the valley walls.

He kicked at the rocks to try and clear his head. He had tried to blot from his mind the common knowledge that military officers used the Factory like a brothel. But no one claimed they raped the women. There was a ready supply of prisoners willing to be tumbled by a soldier in exchange for money, food, grog or the hope of attracting a male protector. Had Keziah traded her body to one of these soldiers? He felt a wild surge of jealousy at the sight of those initials.

When he swung around to face her, Keziah stood six feet away clutching her petticoat like a shield. A lost, rough-haired scarecrow buffeted by the wind.

He cried out in desperation, 'You did it for food, to be able to feed little Yosie. Tell me that's why!'

'No. One of the prisoners was a woman as tough as any man you ever fought. Oola singled out girls she fancied. God help any who knocked her back. My *hair* excited her.' There was painful self-mockery in Keziah's laugh.

'When she tried it on me, I punched her in the gut, kicked her where she lay. Violence was an everyday event. Oola threatened payback. That she'd break Yosef's arms unless I warmed her bed.'

Jake clenched his fists. 'You were right to give in to her to protect our babe. How could I ever hold that against you?'

'I didn't give in. I begged the deputy for help. She moved me and Yosef out of Oola's reach. She protected me. Brought me proper food so I could feed him. For a while I was safe. Until Oola threatened that one day I'd wake up to find little Yosef's face smothered by a pillow.'

'I'll kill the bitch!'

'I couldn't protect him day and night. I couldn't sleep. My milk began to dry up. So I made Daniel bring him back to you. To be safe.'

Jake was stopped by a thought. Keziah nodded and tapped her thigh.

'Yes, Jake. Not Oola. These are the deputy's initials.'

'She seduced you with food!'

'No, Jake. After I sent Yosef away I had no reason to go on. No one needed me. I repaid her kindness, gave her what made her happy. It meant nothing to me.'

'If she was so bloody kind, how come she tattooed you?'

Keziah shook her head. 'It was Oola's payback because I protected the deputy during the mutiny. She ordered her creatures to hold me down while she tattooed me. She laughed. "See how your bloody husband likes *this*!"'

'Jesus wept,' he said under his breath.

'The deputy was just in time to stop Oola from raping me with a knife.'

Jake cried out the foulest oath he knew.

'I know *you*, Jake. You learned to live with Gem's shadow but you'll never be able to forget this!'

Jake's mouth tasted like acid. Where were the right words when he needed them?

'You see, Jake? I'm not worth loving. I'm what Gem said I was. A whore's daughter and a whore. I betrayed you just as surely as I betrayed him.'

They were suddenly alerted by the sound of Horatio snorting, his eyes wide with fear. He was inching backwards, pushing the *vardo* towards the precipice.

Keziah froze. A deadly brown snake reared up ready to strike her and there were only seconds to act.

Jake pulled out the Belgian pistol and fired a shot that smashed the snake's head. Horatio reared up, pushing the *vardo* towards the edge of the cliff. Jake leapt at him and began to unbuckle his harness.

'Stand back!' he yelled. 'I'll try to save the *vardo*.'

'Save Horatio!' Keziah flung her full body weight at the horse to prevent the *vardo* pulling him over the cliff.

'Let go, or he'll drag you over!' Jake ordered, but refused to release his own hold on Horatio.

'Never!' Keziah pulled at the straps of the harness with all her strength. She read in Horatio's eyes that he knew the danger to her as he stopped right on the edge of the cliff. Jake freed him and slapped the horse's rump to send him galloping to safety.

The *vardo* teetered on the brink. Until *baxt* delivered a powerful gust of wind pushing it from sight.

Jake shielded Keziah with his body as they peered over the cliff. Her glorious little travelling house bounced like a broken toy from ledge to ledge. It sank with one last terrible sound of shattering timber and metal into the fern jungle below.

Jake rasped out the words. 'It's all my fault! I should have been more bloody careful with the brake. I know you loved that *vardo* like your life!' He was so distressed he was close to crying. 'I promise you I'll build you another one. I'll rob a bloody bank!'

'We saved Horatio. The *vardo* doesn't matter.'

'It does matter, God damn it! I put my heart into that wagon. I wanted to give you back what you'd lost – your Romani life or something. Struth, I don't know!'

'I do!' Her hand tentatively reached out to touch him. 'That's why I loved you. Why I'll always love you, Jake. You accepted me *just the way I am*.'

They stared at each other – a discovery between strangers.

Keziah saw a handsome man naked except for a torn red shirt. The body of a pagan god.

Jake saw a girl with naked eyes of dark blue magic.

His outstretched hand was a life raft between them. The words were torn out of him. 'God damn it. *I – love – you.* I can't stop!'

On the grassy verge near the precipice Jake drew her down on him. He kissed her mouth as if it was for the first time. He saw her eyes change as if light was beginning to shine through them again, in the way it always had when they made love.

A huge gust of wind scooped up their clothes and blew them at random over the cliff. They laughed like children. Her white petticoat and his red shirt floated free like toy kites, sailing across the valley on the fickle current of the wind.

Only his boots remained.

'Let's get one thing straight.' Jake flicked his finger at her tattoo as if to prove he had the power to erase the scar physically just as surely as he could erase the shame from her mind.

'I'll be buggered if I let a few letters of the alphabet ruin our lives. All that matters is you survived. Like you always do. You came back to me, Kez. To *me*!'

Jake enticed her to sit astride him and he moved her in a clever rhythm to encourage her. He wanted to bring back that ship's figurehead he'd seen on their first night together. Wanted to liberate the joy in her that she believed was dead.

Keziah bent down and covered his face with soft children's kisses mixed with the salt of her tears. 'Oh yes, Jake, please. Take me home. *Now*,' she whispered.

He held her hips tightly between his hands, making a superhuman effort to keep control.

'First I want to hear you say it – *I am Jake Andersen's woman*!'

Keziah smiled, her eyes bright with magic. 'But I *am* Jake Andersen's woman!'

'That was nice, dear,' he said patiently. 'But there's a little old Wiradjuri woman down in the valley, deaf as a post. She couldn't hear a word you said!'

Keziah rode the high seas, gloriously free, her body locked with Jake's. She was no longer sure where his body left off and hers began. She flung her arms wide and cried into the face of the wind. *'I – am – Jake – Andersen's – woman!'*

Jake smiled as her words echoed joyously across the valley.

Two bushrangers were hidden in the bush beside the Sydney Road. One was armed, the other acted as 'cockatoo' on the lookout for victims. At the sound of an approaching horse the younger one leapt out into the middle of the road.

'Stand and deliver or I'll shoot your brains out!' Young Rory pointed his pistol to the sky, aping the style of his hero, Jabber Jabber.

The sight of his victims almost caused the lad to drop his outmoded firearm. Seated astride a shaggy black horse were a long-haired man and a shaven-headed youth, both stark naked. The youth sat face-to-face with the man, cradled in his arms, his slender back and buttocks white in the moonlight.

When the man saw Rory's weapon, his hands shielded the youth's head and heart.

Rory had just bolted from a farm where the practice of naked men embracing was commonplace, but this man's friendly response to his bail-up *did* surprise him.

'Good evening, mate,' said his victim. 'Sorry we're not much use to you. Bit of a gale blowing up on Blind Man's Bluff. Blew all my clothes and money over the cliff.'

'Jesus, Mary and Joseph.' Rory added under his breath, 'Just my bloody luck on my first job!' He looked Horatio over. 'Not a bad nag. I'll be relieving you of that!'

The shorn-headed youth turned his head. Rory was stunned by a girl's voice.

'You wouldn't force a lady to walk home in this condition, would you, lad?'

The girl flashed him a charming smile. As she turned in the saddle to face him, he saw her breasts shining in the moonlight.

Rory's 'cockatoo' charged out of the darkness yelling, 'You silly bugger! That bloke is Jake Andersen, what done time in Berrima for aiding The Gypsy and Jabber Jabber! And that's his woman – the little beauty what topped the Devil Himself! Let them pass, you fool. We don't bail up *our own*!'

Rory the novice was contrite. 'Jabber Jabber was your mate? Sorry I didn't recognise you! Off you shoot. May good luck go with you.'

At the next curve in the road Jake looked into Keziah's eyes, his voice soft.

'I'll say this for you, mate. When we run into bushrangers those breasts of yours still come in bloody handy.'

Horatio continued languidly on his way. His naked cargo locked in each other's arms as he carried them safely home to Ironbark and their children. Guided all the way by Jake's stars – the Milky Way.

AUTHOR'S ACKNOWLEDGEMENTS

That *Ironbark* is now in your hands is a tribute to the legendary qualities of my agent, Selwa Anthony, who advised and nurtured me along the journey from the day she read an early draft of the manuscript to its publication four years later. And I want to pay special thanks to Bastian Schlück of the Thomas Schlück Agency, Germany, who secured for me the publishing deal with William Goldman Publishers for the German rights to *Ironbark*.

My warmest thanks to Franscois McHardy, Managing Director of Simon and Schuster Australia, and his wonderfully creative team for their passionate commitment to *Ironbark*.

A dedicated band of family and friends read different stages of the manuscript. Their incisive comments were invaluable (even when they made me flinch). Their honest, grassroots reactions were like having *Ironbark's* emotional pulse taken. For this I am greatly indebted to Kristine Forrester, Joan Nicholls and Toni Donald. Anne Robinson was a tower of strength over several drafts for her highly discerning notes and historical research winged from WA. Ian Jones, author, Ned Kelly historian and my first mentor, brought to his reading his profound knowledge of Australian bushrangers. Noel O'Shea, passionate historian and researcher, gave me great insight into this era and introduced me to *Cliefden*, Mandurama.

There is no adequate category for author Brian Nicholls. He deserves to be entered in the *Guinness World Records* for his tireless, tough and insightful assessment of some twelve drafts of *Ironbark*. His encouragement and the professionalism drawn from his wide experience as an ABC-TV documentary producer and writer make me forever in his debt.

I was sustained throughout by Melbourne comedy-writer and Graham Kennedy biographer Mike McColl Jones, the friend I inherited from Dad. His wise advice and hilarious emails kept me laughing and believing during my writer's 'dark nights of the soul'.

My heartfelt thanks to many friends and family including Nicholas Cassim, Niki Owen, Donna Ristitsch, Marilyn Harvey, Ailsa McPherson, Rhonda Nadas, Michael Cassim, Ron Way, Marion McCabe and Enid Morrison. Their straight talking, tea and sympathy urged me on to the finishing line. I really valued Philip Bray's publishing advice and the generous help of journalist Jan Goldie and authors Cheryl Hingley and Craig Collie.

AUTHOR'S NOTES

Ironbark is a meld of fiction against an historical background. My creation of the villages of Ironbark, Tagalong, Bolthole Valley, Gideon Park and Ogden Park was inspired by bush hamlets now ghost towns. My travels linked me to many helpful historical sources including Berrima, Gunning, Goulburn, Bathurst, Carcoar, Gulgong, Lithgow and Parramatta.

In hindsight I can trace one link between *Ironbark* and childhood stories told by my father, Fred Parsons, about bushranger Captain Moonlite who bailed up gold coaches around Blackwood, Victoria. My mother's tales about her mysterious ancestor led to my discovery of his identity, a young Romani violinist who inspired the character of Gabriel Stanley.

All *Ironbark's* characters are fictional but I want to acknowledge my character Will Martens was inspired by the tragic young life of bushranger William Westwood. I am grateful to Denise Quintal, the Norfolk Island Historical Society and residents who made my research trip to their magical island memorable when I placed his memorial plaque in their convict cemetery. In creating Will Martens I tried to give William Westwood the true mates he did not have in life but deserved – Jake, Keziah and Daniel. Their passionate radical views don't always align with mine. They speak for their times, their world. I simply gave them a voice.

The choices I made from conflicting historical sources and any errors are my responsibility, not those of historians living or dead. But many historians, authors and experts who freely gave of their time and knowledge deserve my special thanks, including:

Professor John Pearn, Dept. of Pediatrics and Child Health, Royal Children's Hospital, Brisbane, for his encouragement and for steering me to important medical sources.

Alison Dalby and Maryann O'Harae, Librarians of the Australian Medical Association, for the use of their library and the discussion of the diverse effects of laudanum.

Independent Scholars Association of Australia members who gave me invaluable feedback during a writer's work-in-progress.

Historian Walter Stackpool for his wide knowledge of bushrangers and firearms.

Colin Gelling, CEO of Berrima Courthouse Museum, for historical background of Berrima's courthouse, prison and the transcript of Lucretia Dunkley's trial for murder.

Suzanne Rutland, Associate Professor, Dept. of Hebrew, Biblical and Jewish Studies, University of Sydney, for her fascinating Melton series on the history of Jews in Australia.

For the background of my German character Joseph Bloom my sincere thanks to historian and author Rabbi John Levi for his insight and suggestions; Peta Jones Pellach, Sophie Caplan, Helen Bersten, the Australian Jewish Historical Society, Shmuel and Greta Abrahams; Russell Stern for important suggestions concerning the trial scenes; Dr Michael Abrahams-Sprod for his clarification of nineteenth-century European history.

My sincere thanks to Warwick Harvey, Fellow of the National Herbalists Association of Australia; Dr Nick Lomb, Curator of Astronomy and Time, Sydney Observatory, for details of the Great Comet of 1843; Jim Kohen, Associate Professor, Dept. of Biological Sciences, Macquarie University, for his help in research areas; artist Charles Gosford for his insight into English artists' response to Australian landscape; Rev. Marcia Quinten for help during my psychic research; the Spiritualist Church of Enmore. Archival help from Fabian LoSchiavo, State Records NSW; Wendy Borchers, Archives Researcher, Australian Broadcasting Corporation; State Library of NSW; Art Gallery of NSW; Power House Museum; Justice and Police Museum; Elizabeth Bay House; Old Government House, Parramatta; Sydney Maritime Museum. Special thanks to Balmain Library for tracking rare books and material on Gypsies in Australia; Tasmanian Archive and Heritage Office for fascinating penal colony documents; Lancashire and Cheshire Records Office and the British High Commission, Canberra – for their speedy response to my research queries.

© Niki Owen

Johanna Nicholls is a former magazine feature writer and fashion editor. She has worked in television production for the Seven Network as a researcher/writer and for many years was Head Script Editor for the Australian Broadcasting Corporation's Television Drama department. She has worked on many memorable miniseries including *Love is a Four Letter Word* and *Changi*.

Johanna lives in an 1830s convict-built sandstone cottage in Balmain, Sydney, and is currently writing her second Australian novel.